French Tales of the
Red Planet
(Vol. 1)

FROM THE SAME PUBLISHER

Jean-Marc & Randy Lofficier. *The French Fantasy Treasury* (3 volumes)
Jean-Marc & Randy Lofficier. *French Tales of Alien Contacts*
Jean-Marc & Randy Lofficier. *French Tales of Cataclysms*
Jean-Marc & Randy Lofficier. *French Tales of Mad Scientists* (3 volumes)
Jean-Marc & Randy Lofficier. *French Tales of Vampires* (3 volumes)
Jean-Marc & Randy Lofficier. *Shadowmen: Heroes & Villains of French Pulp Fiction*
Jean-Marc & Randy Lofficier. *Shadowmen 2: Heroes & Villains of French Comics*
Brian Stableford. *Automata: The Imaginative Legacy of Jacques de Vaucanson*
Brian Stableford. *The Plurality of Imaginary Worlds: The Evolution of French* Roman Scientifique
Brian Stableford. *Tales of Enchantment and Disenchantment: A History of Faerie, with an Exemplary Anthology of Tales*
Brian Stableford. *Weird Fiction in France: A Showcase Anthology of its Origins and Development*

French Tales of the Red Planet (Vol. 1)

by
**H. Gayar, Georges Le Faure &
Henri de Graffigny, Guy de Maupassant,
Nicolas-Edmé Restif de la Bretonne,
Marie-Anne de Roumier-Robert
and X. B. Saintine.**

translated, annotated and introduced by
Brian Stableford

A Black Coat Press Book

English adaptations)
Marie-Anne de Roumier-Robert: *The Voyages of Lord Seaton to the Seven Planets* (1766)
Nicolas-Edmé Restif de la Bretonne: *Posthumous Correspondence* (1802)
X.B. Saintine: *Astronomical Journeys* (1864)
Guy de Maupassant: *Martian Mankind* (1887)
Georges Le Faure & Henri de Graffigny: *The Extraordinary Adventures of a Russian Scientist Across the Solar System* (1889)
H. Gayar: *The Marvelous Adventures of Serge Myrandhal on Mars* (1906)

ISBN 978-1-64932-393-4. First Printing: May 2025. Published by Black Coat Press, an imprint of Hollywood Comics.com, LLC, 18321 Ventura Blvd., Suite 915, Tarzana, CA 91356.

TABLE OF CONTENTS

Bibliothèque Métropolitaine

— H. GAYAR. —

Aventures Merveilleuses de
Serge Myrandhal

LES ROBINSONS
DE LA PLANETE MARS

L. LAUMONIER & Cᵉ, ÉDITEURS
44, Rue Notre-Dame-des-Champs - PARIS

Introduction

The French always have had an affinity for interplanetary fiction since Hercule Savinien Cyrano de Bergerac. In his *Histoire des Etats et Empires de la Lune* [History of the States and Empires of the Moon], published posthumously in 1657, and followed by *Histoire des Etats et Empires du Soleil* [History of the States and Empires of the Sun] (1662), both eventually collected as *L'Autre Monde* [Other Worlds], De Bergerac developed the concepts of rocket power, and not only of rockets, but of the use of second-stage rockets. His account is, in fact, the first description of a manned rocket flight in literature.

A remarkable feature of De Bergerac's work was his elaborate description of the alien societies that he encountered on his journeys, such as that of the Bird-Men who lived on the "dark side" of the Sun and hates men..

Charles Sorel, a contemporary of De Bergerac, wrote in his *Récit du Voyage de Brisevent* [Tale of Brisevent's Journey] (1642): "Some men have affirmed that there are many worlds, which some have placed in the planets, and others in the fixed stars; for my part, I believe there is a world on the moon." And he further predicted that a "Prince as ambitious as Alexander, who shall come to conquer this world," would do so using "great engines, to descend or ascend."

In 1686, Bernard Le Bovier de Fontenelle wrote his ground-breaking *Entretiens sur la Pluralité des Mondes* [Conversations on the Plurality of Worlds], a "documentary" treatise about life on other planets which speculated on what the inhabitants of each world might be like. (That was also the year when Isaac Newton published his *Principia*, in which the laws of motion and gravity were outlined.)

In 1761, Monsieur de Listonai (the pseudonym of Daniel Jost Villeneuve) penned *Le Voyageur Philosophe dans un Pays Inconnu aux Habitants de la Terre* (1761),[1] in which he described the journey of an Earthman to the hidden face of the Moon via a flying space galley. The novel was the most spectacular attempt to date to put a narrative flesh on the idea of progress as it was understood in the Enlightenment Era, and it remained the boldest and most wide-reaching work of its kind for at least half a century.

By the mid-to-late 18th century, journeys to Outer Space had become fairly frequent in French literature. Among these, we shall mention the Chevalier de Béthune's *Relation du Monde de Mercure* (1750),[2] depicting

---

[1] *The Philosophical Voyager*, Black Coat Press, ISBN 978-1-61227-367-9.
[2] *The World of Mercury*, Black Coat Press, ISBN 978-1-61227-410-2.

immortal winged beings inhabiting the eponymous planet; Voltaire's "ose encounter" with the alien Micromegas from Sirius (1752); Charles-François Tiphaigne de la Roche's meetings with Zamar the Selenite in *Amilec* (1754);[3] Marie-Anne de Roumier-Robert's *Voyage de Milord Céton dans les Sept Planètes* (1765),[4] an excerpt of which is included in this volume; and Guillaume de La Follie's *Le Philosophe sans Prétention* (1775)[5] in which Earth is visited by a crew of Mercurian scientists who come in an electric-powered starship.

As the 18th century ended, the French Revolution put an end to these fantasies, with the notable ex caption of Nicolas-Edmé Restif de la Bretonne, a man who produced over 180 books, many of them printed by his own hand, on almost every conceivable subject. He was mostly forgotten in France until being rediscovered by the Surrealists in the early 20th century. Restif gave free rein to his imagination in *Les Posthumes*, first written in 1787-89; augmented in 1796, and finally published in 1802.[6] In it, his super-powered protagonist, Duke Multipliandre, after visiting many exotic lands, boldly goes where no one has gone before, traveling to the Moon and Mars (the excerpt selected for inclusion in this volume), then to the other known planets of the solar system and numerous other worlds then unknown to science, including trans-Uranian planets, a comet and three planets within the orbit of Mercury, and interacts with their peculiar inhabitants. After that, Multipliandre sets off to visit several other solar systems, including those of Sirius and Vega, and several nebulae, before concluding his journey in the "astral center," into which the entire universe will one day be dissolved.

The first, but historically least important, tale of interplanetary travel in the 19th century was Achille Eyraud's *Voyage à Vénus* (1865)[7] published the same year as Jules Verne's classic *From the Earth to the Moon* and Henri de Parville's far more interesting *Un Habitant de la Planète Mars*.[8] In the former, a French spaceship propelled by a "reaction engine" manages to reach Venus, the seat of peaceful society, in which the sexes are equal and solar-powered robots toil in the fields. In the latter, a meteorite dug up by a Colorado oil prospector turns out to contain the mummified body of a Martian.

The preeminent French astronomer Camille Flammarion then popular-ized astronomy and cosmology, and discussed the physiological properties of extra-terrestrial life in *La Pluralité des Mondes Habités* [The Plurality of In-

---

[3] *Amilec*, Black Coat Press, ISBN 978-1-61227-033-3.

[4] *The Voyages of Lord Seaton...*, Black Coat Press, ISBN 978-1-61227-446-1.

[5] *The Unpretentious Philosopher*, Black Coat Press, ISBN 978-1-61227-136-1.

[6] *Posthumous Correspondence*, Black Coat Press, three volumes, ISBNs 978-1-61227-513-0, 978-1-61227-514-7 & 978-1-61227-515-4.

[7] *Voyage to Venus*, Black Coat Press, ISBN 978-1-61227-005-0.

[8] *An Inhabitant of the Planet Mars*, Black Coat Press, ISBN 978-1-934543-45-0.

habited Worlds] (1862), *Les Habitants de l'Autre Monde* [The Inhabitants of Other Worlds] (1862), *Les Mondes Imaginaires et les Mondes Réels* [Imaginary and Real Worlds] (1864), and *Les Terres du Ciel* [Lands in the Sky] (1884), in which a man and woman who die at the top of a mountain find themselves reincarnated on Mars.

In 1865, Baron Alfred d'Espiard de Colonge in *La Chute du Ciel ou Les Antiques Météores Planétaires* [The Fall From The Sky or The Ancient Planetary Meteors] first hypothesized that life on Earth had, in fact, originated on another world, and may have started on our planet as the result of deliberate seeding by another race. And in 1877, Italian astronomer Giovanni Schiaparelli called the peculiar markings he observed on Mars *canali*, leading to widespread speculation over whether these "canals" were constructed by intelligent beings.

In 1877, Jules Verne in his novel *Off on a comet* had chronicled the adventures of a band of valiant Frenchmen, led by Hector Servadac, who used a passing comet to hitch a ride and conduct a rudimentary first survey of the Solar System.

In 1887 engineer Henri de Graffigny wrote his own account of a pioneering space journey in *De La Terre aux Etoiles* [From the Earth to the Stars], in which a small group of Earthmen travel to the Moon, then to Venus, and then aboard a comet throughout the Solar System. This was markedly improved after de Graffigny teamed up with Georges Le Faure to pen the far more ambitious *Les Aventures Extraordinaires d'un Savant Russe* (1888-96),[9] prefaced by Camille Flammarion, an excerpt of which is included in this volume..

In it, a Franco-Russian space expedition uses a nickel-magnesium alloy spaceship, the Ossipoff, launched from a cannon built inside the Cotopaxi volcano, to travel to the Moon. Then, the explorers used a jet-propelled craft to take them to Venus. They then travel to Mercury using the pressure of solar winds on a hollow sphere. They continue their journey to Mars, using a fragment of Mercury torn away by a comet, using a balloon to go down to the red planet, wearing pressure suits. After having established contact with the Martians, the explorers fly to Jupiter in a barrel-shaped, reaction-powered starship.

As the 19th century neared its end, in 1896, Pierre de Sélènes reported in *Un Monde Inconnu*[10] that the original Gun-Club cannon from Jules Verne's novel had been sold to an Englishman and that another space launch had dispatched another crew of explorers to the Moon. This time, they suc-

[9] *The Amazing Adventures of a Russian Scientist*, Black Coat Press, two volumes, ISBNs 978-1-934543-81-8 & 978-1-934543-82-5.
[10] *An Unknown World*, Black Coat Press, ISBN 978-1-61227-302-0.

cessfully land on our satellite and meet the advanced, utopian civilization of the Meolicenes who live inside our satellite.

The last novel included in this first volume is part of a series of novels dedicated to Martian exploration, which will be collected in our second volume. In H. Gayar's *Les Aventures Merveilleuses de Serge Myrandhal sur la Planète Mars"* (1908),[11] the eponymous hero reaches Mars via a psychic-powered ship named *Velox*. The planet is inhabited by the Houas, small, red-furred anthropoids who live underground, and by the Zoas, beautiful winged humanoids, also referred to as Elohim. In a later version, published in 1927 as *Les Robinsons de la Planète Mars* [The Robinsons of Planet Mars] under the pseudonym of "Cyrius", Gayar got rid of the psychic energy and instead used the planetary force of attraction; he also added German villains to the plot and prophetically rechristened the rocketships V1 and V2.

Jean-Marc & Randy Lofficier

---

[11] *The Marvelous Adventures of Serge Myrandhal on Mars*, Black Coat Press, ISBN 978-1-61227-265-8.

Marie-Anne de Roumier-Robert. *The Voyages of Lord Seaton to the Seven Planets*
(excerpt)

Voyages de Milord Céton dans les sept planettes *[sic]*, ou Le Nouveau Mentor, *was first published in four volumes in The Hague in 1765-66, with the by-line* "traduits par Madame de R.R.*" It was subsequently reprinted in volumes 17 and 18 of Charles Garnier's collection of* Voyages Imaginaires, songes, visions et romans cabalistiques *[Imaginary Voyages, Dreams, Visions and Cabalistic Fictions] in 1787, with the spelling of the title adjusted to render the seventh word as* "planètes,*" although* "planettes*" is retained within the body of the text.*

"Madame de R.R."—who was the author rather than the translator of the work—was Marie-Anne de Roumier-Robert (1705-1771). She was born into an aristocratic family that had already come down in the world considerably by the time she was born; her paternal grandfather was a provincial prosecutor but her father was obliged to go into commerce to make a living; her mother, whose maiden name was Bourée, was the daughter of an advocate. Her father was acquainted with Bernard Le Bovier de Fontenelle (1657-1757), author of Entretiens sur la pluralité des mondes *(1686; tr. in 1687 as* Conversations on the Plurality of Worlds*), the enormously influential popularization of the Copernican theory of the solar system. She met Fontenelle on more than one occasion when he came to dine in their home, and retained a sufficiently elevated idea of his importance to grant him a place of honor on the world of the Sun featured in her own work, where all the great minds of Earth and other worlds go after death to live in the City of Philosophers, but if she ever read his masterpiece she does not seem to have taken its lessons aboard, as her own account of the solar system is extremely confused.*

Marie-Anne's parents died while she was still young, and the debts her father left caused a posthumous bankruptcy that left her devoid of any inheritance; the relative who became her guardian put her into a convent, from which she only emerged to be married off to an advocate named Robert. The only brief biographical memoir written by someone who apparently knew her, Joseph de Laporte, contained in volume five of Histoire littéraire des femmes françaises, ou Lettres historiques *(1769), has nothing to say about Monsieur Robert except that he was highly esteemed in his profession, and does not make any mention of his death, but the preface of* Voyages de Milord Céton *finds her alone and* "without support*" in struggling with her tribulations, and strongly suggests that she was a widow by then. Laporte also reports that her health was apparently poor and she was often ill.*

Whether she was a widow or not, it was not until relatively late in life that Madame Robert decided to try her hand at writing. She might have taken some inspiration from the examples set by Madeleine de Scudery and Madame de La Fayette a century earlier, in the days when the de Roumier family was peripherally associated with Louis XIV's court, and from the slightly more recent success of Francoise de Graffigny, but she was undoubtedly also aware of some of the contemporaries featured alongside her in Laporte's volume on the works of living writers, where she takes second place behind the former actress Marie-Jeanne Riccoboni (1714-1792) and ahead of Madeleine de Puisieux (1720-1798), an occasional collaborator with Denis Diderot. Madame Robert's works follow a pattern not dissimilar to theirs, including both naturalistic "sensibility novels"—the ancestors of stereotyped modern love stories—and fantastic "moral tales" borrowing motifs eclectically from Antoine Galland's pastiches of Arabic folktales, Madame d'Aulnoy's Contes des fées.

Madame Robert published two sensibility novels prior to venturing into new literary territory in Voyages de Milord Céton, *the first of which,* La Paysanne philosophe, ou Les Aventures de Madame la Comtesse de *** [The Philosophical Peasant Woman] (1761-62), *detailed the complex but relentlessly moral love life of an orphan peasant girl adopted and brought up by an aristocratic woman. That novel was reprinted three times, and thus appears to have been considerably more successful than* La Voix de la nature, ou Les Aventures de Madame la Marquise de *** [The Voice of Nature] (1764), *another tale of an orphan in quest of true love; the plaintive preface to* Voyages de Milord Céton, *as well as certain comments in the account of life on the Moon, suggests that the relative failure of the second novel might well have impelled her to attempt something more eye-catchingly unusual. The text of* Voyages de Milord Céton *contains some passages suggesting, somewhat disingenuously, a strong disapproval of the public's liking for such fantastic works, but if Madame Robert felt some resentment at the fact that she was pandering to that appetite, it certainly did not prevent her doing so wholeheartedly, and at great length.*

Voyages de Milord Céton *belongs to the tradition of lunar satires spectacularly launched in France by the posthumous publication of Cyrano de Bergerac's* L'Autre monde, ou Les États et empires de la lune *(1657; tr. as* Comical History of the States and Empires of the Moon*) and more recently carried forward by Charles-François Tiphaigne de Le Roche in "Zamar" (1754)[12] and* Le Voyageur philosophe dans un pais inconnu aux habitans de la Terre *(1761) signed "Monsieur de Listonai."[13] Madame Robert had definitely read the latter work, as she borrowed a passage from it, rather clumsily, to shore up a description of laboratory apparatus in which she was clearly out of her depth, and she almost certainly read Tiphaigne's novel too; both works carried forward, in*

---

[12] Black Coat Press, ISBN 978-1-61227-033-3.
[13] Black Coat Press, ISBN 978-1-61227-367-9.

their own idiosyncratic fashion, the traditional notion of the Moon as an abode of folly, which is reproduced, with an equally idiosyncratic twist, in Madame Robert's satirical depiction of that particular "heaven."

It seems probable, too, that Madame Robert was familiar with the Chevalier de Béthune's Relation du monde de Mercure *(1750)[14]; although her account of Mercury is very different from Béthune's, the patchwork narrative strategy she employs, including both allegorical and anecdotal inclusions, is similar, as is the stratagem of an introductory account with a salamander. Her novel's subtitle, however, indicates that its principal literary model is not an interplanetary fantasy at all but François Fénelon's* Les Aventures de Télémaque *(1699), in which the protagonist is taken on a educational tour by his tutor Mentor, who gives him extensive lectures on the kind of government that he ought to adopt when he succeeds his father Ulysses as King of Ithaca. Madame Robert's account of the more far-ranging educational tour to which Zachiel subjects Céton and Monime is to a large extent an homage, and certainly echoes many of the criticisms that Fénelon made of the court culture of Louis XIV's reign (which resulted in his expulsion therefrom) but also rebukes the earlier Mentor to some extent for the implication of lèse-majesté contained in his more radical ideas about parliamentary government.*

After publishing Voyages de Milord Céton, *Madame Robert went on to publish a third naturalistic novel,* Nicole de Beauvais, ou L'Amour vaincu par reconnaissance *[Love Vanquished by Gratitude] (1768) in the same year as the fantasy novella,* Les Ondins, *three years prior to her death.*

Like many writers of philosophical extravaganzas, however, Madame Robert appears to have been using the writing of her novel as a means of clarifying her own ideas about various matters, and attempting to fix her own moral compass by working on some difficult issues. That is undoubtedly the explanation of some of the story's inconsistencies, and also its incessant repetition of the conclusions it attains. Not all the issues in question were resolved, and it is arguable that the remaining ambiguities and ambivalences are more revealing of her own state of mind and the confusions of her historical moment than the firm commitments she makes. Her attitude to war is one interesting instance, as her occasional polemics against it—and famous warriors receive remarkably short shrift in her allegorical account of the Temple Of Glory on Mars—are counterbalanced by her account of Céton's preparation for a military career and by the striking intervention of Monime in the battle fought in the climax of the plot.

`B.S.

Chapter I

---

[14] Black Coat Press, ISBN 978-1-61227-410-2

We arrived on the planet Mars at nightfall. Dusk had already dressed the landscape in somber livery; silence marched in its wake; the animals and the birds had taken refuge in their places of retreat, the only one that remained was the nightingale, which, accustomed to amorous wakefulness, spends entire nights singing. Hesperus, the conductor of starry bands, was shining at their head; the firmament was sparkling with bright sapphires. The Moon was rising with a nebulous majesty, unveiling her tender light with the bearing of a Queen, extending her silvery mantle over the obscurity. The genius, continuing his rapid flight, took us down into a sandy and arid plain.

Monime, gripped by fear and scarcely able to breathe, begged the genius insistently not to stop on that planet.

"I implore you, in the name of the amity that you have avowed for us, to take us to another world. The name of Mars alone frightens me; I imagine that it is filled by barbaric and ferocious citizens, that everything only breathes for combat, blood and carnage. What do you expect me to do on such a world? Is a woman made to confront its hazards?

"Rid yourself, dear Monime," the genius said, "of these puerile and frivolous fears; my design is not to expose you to the fury of combats. But my dear daughter, do you not want anything done in favor of Seaton? It is only here that he can make his apprenticeship in the métier of war; you're not unaware that a Lord like him cannot be occupied with any other employment, nor achieve any other than military rank. If you love him, you can never give him greater evidence of amity than by stimulating him yourself not to neglect any of the means that present themselves to make the most of his courage."

"Which means that today," said Monime, with a kind of chagrin and impatience, "you would like me to resemble those women who only find pleasure in the choice they make of a soldier for a husband, and of seeing him leave for the army without being obliged to go with him. Content to be distanced from him, they enjoy the satisfaction, or at least the hope, of believing him to be more than a hundred leagues away for a long time. If they were deprived of that time of liberty, of which they doubtless take advantage, a warrior, or anyone else, would then become indifferent to them.

"In any case," Monime added, sardonically, "the strongest Hercules can never hold firm before an Omphale; one of our gazes is sufficient to change their club into a distaff. Let us therefore allow them to ornament themselves occasionally with the name of hero; we render them effeminate often enough. Finally, my dear Zachiel, if you are absolutely insistent on forcing me to make a long sojourn on this planet, I want to disguise myself; I declare to you that I shall don the uniform, the sword, the plume, the high collar, and the spontoon; I shall buy a regiment and become a colonel at a stroke. Perhaps you will tell me that in that accoutrement, which will rejuvenate me even more, I shall appear to be no more than a child—fine reasoning; I'm sure that I shall see more than one in this world who, having reached a superior rank, doubtless thinks himself important and believes himself more skillful than the most experienced, although less expert and more infantile than me."

Monime persisted for longer in attempting to make the genius take another decision, but it was a waste of time; her representations were futile, and it was necessary to set forth. After Zachiel had dissipated some of her fears with stories that were as amusing as they were singular, the charming young woman saw that she was constrained to vanquish her repugnance, no longer daring to oppose the will of the genius openly.

Our voyage was very pleasant; the roads were full of post-chaises, carriages, heavy wagons and mule trains, but especially of people, who seemed to be the most content in the world.

One said: "This is a campaign that will advance me to the head of the regiment; and if I'm rendered justice, I'll have every reason to hope for a good pension and a government post at the end of the war."

"The country is rich," said another. "We'll be able to obtain fine booty there."

Several of them wanted to wager that the war would be concluded by that single campaign. "It isn't possible," they said, "that the enemy can hold out even for two months."

In sum, all of them were marching with great confidence; they only talked about places taken, victories won. To hear them, one might have thought that the cities would advance to meet them that that the armies would take flight merely at the news of their approach.

Obliged to quit that road to take another, we encountered a few battalions returning to the army. They did not seem nearly as content as the first; as much as the others seemed enthusiastic, these appeared discouraged and weary. Monime mistook them at first for poor cripples, who were begging for alms on the highways. Officers soldiers, servants and horses were all equally fearful and pitiable. Their speech corresponded to their faces.

"We were led to butchery," they said.

The general had lost his head; the cavalry had advanced ineptly; the infantry, poorly commanded, had not done its duty.

"Why, said one of them, "before exposing us, did they not sent scouts to reconnoiter the position? If the enemy had been closely watched, their maneuvers would not have been hidden. Our spies are poorly paid; that's why they neglected to inform us."

In sum, each of those military men was only content with himself, and all had a desire to utter a thousand maledictions against a state of affairs with which they seemed extremely disgusted.

That sad spectacle was not calculated to renew Monime's courage; her fear and dread increased. "Let's leave this vile Mars, she said to Zachiel. "Let's take another route; I feel myself oppressed by the air, which is assuredly too keen for the delicacy of my temperament; the vapors are already overwhelming me and my heart is palpitating as we advance further on the planet."

Deaf to Monime's complaints, the genius continued his route without deigning to respond. We soon discovered the most eminent and celebrated place on the entire planet, the famous Temple of Glory to which all the citizens of the world flock.

"The grave and serious expression you adopt will never deter me, my dear Zachiel," Monime continued. "I even dare ask you for a favor, before you go on into this frightful country. Begin, I beg you, by taking us to that magnificent temple. A noble presentiment informs me that a sojourn in that admirable place might calm my senses, reanimate my courage and reconcile me at the same time to the rest of the planet. Gods, what do I see? You're frowning! You're going to refuse me again; I shudder; don't pronounce sentence on me."

"What you're asking isn't reasonable," Zachiel said. "It's not by way of the Temple of Glory that one succeeds in the empire of Mars; on the contrary, one has to pass through the most difficult ordeals and along the thorniest roads to arrive at that temple. I can't change such a just law in your favor; Renown, to whom the guard of the temple is confided, would be bold enough to refuse us entry; she only opens up to those she knows, and whose name has already been transmitted throughout the world."

"Do you think, my dear Zachiel," said Monime, looking at him with an enchanting smile, "that there are not devious routes here, as there are everywhere, by which one can introduce oneself through some false door? Personally, I think that one can make heroes, like doctors, by the fireside. The Renown of whom you speak does not have a very sound reputation for accuracy, and if she doesn't look any more closely in order to open the door than to blow her trumpet, it must be admitted that people often get in with more facility than you imply."

The slightest things sometimes determine victory; that reflection gave all the advantage to Monime. Zachiel gave in, and the carriage that as carrying us became the chariot of triumph on which our amiable conqueress led us like captives to the Temple of Glory.

That admirable edifice is situated on the summit of the highest and steepest rock there ever was. Once, it was enclosed by high walls, very difficult to approach, but several roads have been flattened; nowadays more accessible, one can arrive there easily from several directions, on roads that appear newly traced.

The temple gains considerably from being seen from afar; its beauties are developed successively; the further they are from the center, the more brilliantly they shine; their gleam is proportional to that distance.

Scarcely had we arrived at the foot of the rock than it confronted us everywhere with nothing but frightful precipices, Zachiel having maliciously guided us to the least accessible place. No well-beaten road presented itself to make the ascent. It was then that our courage failed. I had initially joined in with the genius to combat Monime's fears, but I began to tremble like her; shame prevented me from adopting her language, but in the depths of my heart I shared her sentiments.

Another sight, even more forbidding than the rock, inspired further repugnance in us. It was a pile of horribly disfigured cadavers covering the floor of the valley. Gripped by astonishment and horror, Monime and I looked at Zachiel without having the strength to speak to him, but it was easy for him to read in our eyes what was passing in our soul.

Looking at us with a serene expression, he said: "Those corpses that you see do no merit your attention or your pity; they are here in ignominy and forgetfulness, because they were never more than failed heroes, and falsely brave; several of them came to break themselves against the spur of rock you see to your left, which is known as the False Point of Honor; they are people who, in order to avenge an imaginary insult, have dishonored themselves by a shameful death, who have perished, not in battle, which ought to be the bed of honor of the truly brave, but in duels that are only appropriate to vile gladiators. There are hired assassins who put all their honor into taking men's lives; people who make honor, virtue, vice, infamy, truth and lies depend on the outcome of a combat, who have no other rectitude, no other justice and no other reason than murder, as well as the strongest and most skillful, who believe themselves the most worthy of immortality, all their virtue being measured at swords point.

"Some of those you see on the other side had received the most fortunate dispositions from nature to become great men one day, but, by virtue of the abuse they made of them, they were only pernicious men and great scoundrels. Such, in particular, is the one you see near here suspended by the feet, head down, covered in blood that seems recently shed and whose stain will never be effaced. Do you know him, my dear Seaton? It's the author of all the misfortunes of your fatherland, as well as those of your family in particular: Cromwell. You shudder at that name; you're right, my dear; England would have been happy if it had not given birth to that monster, who ought to have been its glory but will forever be its opprobrium. He began by soiling it with the blackest of assaults against its king, and after having engaged it to condemn him to death of a scaffold, he ended up usurping the crown and becoming its tyrant.

"Look a little further on and you will see Totila, King of the Goths, who rendered himself frightful under the emperor Justinian I. That Prince fought numerous battles, as many at sea as on land, where he always had the advantage, and in spite of the resistance of Belisarius, whom the emperor sent against him, he besieged and took Rome, destroyed it almost entirely, burned the Capitol and toppled half the walls, ordered the citizens to abandon the city under pain of death, and treated those who did not profess his religion cruelly.

"That big pug-faced fellow you see over there is Attila, King of the Huns, the scythe of nations; he had a subtle intelligence, was ambitious, full of cunning, finesse and treasons, cruel, arrogant, rascally and reckless. The seat of his empire was in Sicambria, on the Danube. He was called to the aid of Genseric, King of the Vandals, against the Goths, and same with an army of five hundred thousand men, ravaged all the provinces of the Roman Empire and put all the places through which he passed in Germany and Italy to fire and the sword; but the run of his victories was finally stopped in Gaul by Aetius, the chief of the Romans and Merovech, the King of the Franks, who destroyed more than a third of his army in a single day and constrained him to flee to Hungary. The Prince, after having crushed a number of provinces, demolishing all their cities, attacked Aquileia, sacked Milan and Pavia, and finally died of a flux of blood that suffocated him, occasioned by his execrable debauches.

"There is Nicocles, tyrant of Sicyon in the Peloponnese, who was expelled from his states and died of hunger and cold. To the right you can see Hermias, son of Artane Donien,[15] who fought a bloody war against Memnon—who, after having vanquished him, had him sown up in the skin of an ox to serve as a plaything, and made him suffer a thousand indignities.

"Look," Zachiel continued, "at those who men who seem to be tied together. They are Cassius and Brutus, two traitors who took up arms against the common father of the land—I mean Caesar. That Emperor was so fond of Brutus that he had named him as his heir, but the ingrate, believing that he would acquire immortal glory, took treason so far as to become the leader of a conspiracy, and although Caesar had received advice not to go to the Senate that day, Brutus took him there personally. As soon as the Emperor entered, sixty assassins surrounded him and struck him with their swords. Caesar defended himself courageously, but when Brutus had also struck him he ceased to defend himself. 'Oh, my son,' he said to him, 'in whom I have put all my confidence, is it necessary for you to give me death?' Caesar said no more, covered his head with his robe, and let himself fall against the statue of Pompey, pierced by twenty-three sword-thrusts, of which he died in the hall of the Senate. But Heaven avenged his death with that of all the conspirators, who are all buried here in the dust, and that same Brutus, after having lost a battle near the city of Philippi, fell on his own sword, and died instantly, killing himself with same blade that he had employed in the parricide that he had committed on Caesar's person.

"I would never finish," the genius added, "if I name for you all those you see here. It is true that some performed fine deeds, but they soiled them by actions even more barbaric; brigands rather than conquerors, it was their ferocity that animated them and not worth; they only sought to vanquish in order to massacre and pillage, and the name that they left after them is only immortal in the horror and execration of men, because they did not know the true path that leads

---

[15] This name is enigmatic, although the slightly-misrendered reference is obviously to Hermias of Atarneus, who was tortured by Memnon of Rhodes. Ovid records that he was sewn up in an ox-hide, but not by Memnon.

to the Temple of Glory and, although they took great steps in order to reach it, their faults and vices banished them from it forever."

"All these men horrify me," said Monime. "I find it repugnant to the society of reasonable beings that subjects dare to dictate the law to their masters and attribute to themselves to privilege of inflicting their punishments, since a sovereign is only accountable for the conduct to the tribunal of the divinity. However he disposes of our bodies and our wealth, one ought only to oppose to him submission and obedience; that has always been my way of thinking. I see it justified by the number of traitors, tyrants and the impious who, in seeking glory and immortality, have found nothing but opprobrium and scorn. One might think that tyranny is a species of rage, which is often pushed to the ultimate extremity. Oh, my dear Zachiel, let us flee, and no longer amuse ourselves with the contemplation of such monsters."

"I consent to that," said Zachiel, "but before going on, I want Seaton to look at this reef, which is scarcely confronted by except by those of his nation, and which is deadly to numerous Englishmen; its name is Suicide. Would you believe, my dear, that the greater number of all those you see are your compatriots who have been made enough to give themselves death? That kind of fury is regarded in England as a grandeur of the soul; it is a noble disdain for life, confusing despair with intrepidity, and that pusillanimity that allows itself to be felled by the slightest troublesome event, with the heroism that renders us superior to all the woes that surround us."

While Zachiel was making me that list, which I found very interesting, we saw a troop of individuals advancing toward us, very poorly clad and rather surly in appearance, who were holding large scrolls of paper, quills and writing desks. They saluted us in a pedantic fashion, and told us that they had come to offer us their services.

"I'm not dear," said one of them, who called himself a gazetteer. "For a small fee I promise to render you to the temple and sign you a distinguished place there."

Then a quantity of poets and historians presented themselves, to offer us immortality in verse and prose.

"Here, sirs," said one of the poets, "are poems that I have composed for the great conquerors, and here are some for great politicians; these are for the men of vast genius whose intelligence and enlightenment extend over all the sciences. I've left all the names blank; if you want to choose one, I'll immediately fill in yours, provided that you do me the kindness of making me a little present of a hundred guineas."

My curiosity excited by that singular compliment, I took one in order to examine it, but I only found it filled with enthusiasm and bloated verses; great words formed a complete collection of all the most anciently coupled rhymes: battles and chattels, sun and run, glory and victory, sublime and chime, hazard and Caesar, thunder and asunder, fights, mights, advantages, carnages, errors, terrors and many more. In the end, all those cadenced words, like a tune played on a pipe, which would be too long to reproduce here, appeared to me to signify very little. However, the poet offered nothing less than to put Monime at the rank of the goddess Pallas, and to make me occupy the place of the god Mars himself.

From the other side Monime was assailed by people presenting new pamphlets to her. "My Lady," said one of them, "this is new; if your grandeur will permit, I shall have the honor of dedicating this little work to you; it is bound in pink, which is the color in fashion."

"Take mine," said another, "it's in flax-gray, the delights of a tender soul."

"My Lady," said a third, "give preference to this collection; it's in green and yellow, to paint springtime; the book is sown with nothing but flowers and brilliant words; it's divine."

"Beautiful goddess," said a man with a languorous expression, "Allow me to present this elegy to you."

"And me these epistles, which are above those of Cicero."

Other brought odes, rondeaux and vaudevilles; those requested very little money. Afterwards however, came historians of great repute, who offered us the same services—which is to say, to have the most beautiful events in our lives inscribed in the book of bronze that is never erased. Oh, those were very dear!

I was tempted at first to place myself in that great book. The writer was already beginning to sharpen a fine quill, delicate and light, but when the hand posed on the paper, ready to trace my great deeds, he asked me under what title I wanted to announce myself. I confess that the question embarrassed me; I sensed internally that I did not merit any. After having thought for a moment, I said: "Give me whichever one you wish; perhaps hazard will enable you to encounter the right one, and if the zeal I feel to live up to it can substitute for merit, you won't be taking any risk."

Chapter II

Zachiel, who was present at that conversation, warned me that it was only by heroic actions that one could acquire the glory of occupying a place in the great book, without which whatever vulgar writers attempted to inscribe therein was easily erased by envy or jealousy, which pardon nothing, but the darts of which are blunt and cannot tarnish the reputation of individuals whom Heaven has endowed with true merit and invincible courage.

"The rank or the place that great men merit," added the genius, "can only be decided after their death, because there are some who lose in the last moments of their life a part of the glory that they acquired over several years, and others who become even greater in dying than they were when they enjoyed perfect health.

"Scipio, the father-in-law of Pompey, redeemed at the moment of his death the poor opinion that people had had of him; he showed by his confidence and boldness that the people who have seemed the weakest can sometimes raise themselves to the grandeur of soul of heroes. Having been cast up on the shore of Africa by a horrible tempest, and his vessel captured by enemies, Scipio wanted to save in his person the glory of his name, and could not suffer seeing the Africans, being accustomed to see them vanquished, put him in chains. As great as the vanquisher of Carthage, he tamed the horrors of death, by plunging his sword into his bosom. That example, my dear Seaton, ought to suffice to inform you that he last moments of life ought to be regarded as the touchstone that distinguishes the heroes and the true philosophers from those who have only usurped the name."

We were interrupted by a man, who came running toward us with a whip in his hand, saying: "Sirs, I am the English postillion; I guarantee to take you from here to the temple without spilling you; would you like a coach, a post-chaise, a two-wheeler, a cabriolet? Choose—we have vehicles of every sort here."

"Stand aside," said another, "you're nothing but a chatterbox. These gentlemen merit going forth on Pegasus; he's ready saddled and bridled, only waiting for you to depart; he's the gentlest animal in the world, and allows himself be mounted easily. Take advantage of it, beautiful goddess; I promise you that you'll arrive at the temple in the blink of an eye."

A runner advancing with a proud and audacious attitude told us, in a methodical tone, that he was the forerunner, who ordinarily matched his pace to the gifts that were made to him. He was followed by a quantity of scholars, who, all for a price of silver, cane to offer us immortality.

Aggravated by all these offers and that crowd of merchants of reputation, whose number was increasing at every moment, we made the decision to get rid of them, but we could only do so by accepting large volumes of praise, which they gave us very cheaply and which put us at least at the level of the most famous heroes and heroines of antiquity.

Renown immediately announced herself with her hundred mouths and her hundred trumpets, with which she intoned our pretended great deeds; at the same time her horse was hitched to our chariot; in a trice we were borne up to the clouds, and, without having touched the rocks, we found ourselves in the great square of the temple.

"I would prefer not to advance any further," said Monime, "with making a halt here. We're hungry, and I feel too weak to go on."

"What are you saying?" said Zachiel, interrupting her abruptly. "Is this the place to talk about eating and drinking? Know, beautiful Monime, that in the abode of glory, one only feeds on wind and smoke; one only gets drunk on one's own merit. Sleeping in the shade of those laurels, receiving incense, throwing dust in the eyes—that's the life and the sole occupation of immortal heroes."

Monime did not appear to have any appetite for that diet of immortality; she was already preparing to dip into her bag of dried fruits when we were suddenly invested by a swirl of exceedingly odorous smoke, Then came a gust of wind, which seemed to reanimate volcanoes of sulfur and saltpeter, which spread more smoke throughout the square. Combining with the other, it seemed to intoxicate all the spectators. Unable to sustain the force of that wind, Zachiel took us into a vestibule.

"Here you are," he told us, "in the midst of the most vaunted heroes in the universe."

Our astonishment at the sight of that singular company is inexpressible. Scarred faces, punctured eyes, slashed craniums, sliced ears, arms in slings, wooden legs, bodies covered in wounds and plasters, and women, one of whose breasts had been hacked off: such were the frightful sights that presented themselves to our eyes.

"Great God, where are we?" exclaimed Monime, utterly bewildered. "Oh, wicked Zachiel, you've deceived us; what pleasure have you gained in thus taking us for fools? Why have you forced me to undertake this long voyage? Why excite my curiosity with stories that have no kind of connection with what I see? Why, finally, have you claimed to be introducing us into the sanctuary of immortality, when I can see that all those magnificent promises have ended up bringing us to a hospital?"

The genius, smiling at her error, told her that he was sorry that these unfortunate officers had only excited her alarm, when they ought at least to inspire sentiments of admiration; and that it was only by way of such accidents that one could lay claim to glory."

"What!" said Monime. "You still expect to persuade me that we're in a temple here?"

"Assuredly," said Zachiel. "You're under one of its porticoes—but let's go into that vast colonnade on the left."

Frightened to see a large tower that was in the middle moving, Monime uttered a cry, dreading that it might fall on top of us. The tower, which machinery similar to our windmills was causing to rotate rapidly, showed us several figures that its movement appeared to animate. Monime's disturbance was augmented by that appearance, and in spite of the desire she had to discover what such an extraordinary decoration signified, I noticed that she would have liked to be much further away. However, Zachiel, attentive to all her movements, finally fixed her attention.

"Look at these different heroes," he said. The one that you see nonchalantly leaning on the arm of his squire is the great Cyrus, who transferred the empire of the Medes to the Persians, won an infinite number of battles and conquered entire provinces, who traversed Asia, Media, Hyrcania, Persia and, in sum, ravaged more than half of the world he inhabited."

"He was doubtless an ambitious Prince," said Monime, "who wanted all the earth to be submissive to him?"

"Not at all," Zachiel replied. "Amour alone prompted him to all that disorder. He only wanted to free the Princess Mandana, with whom he was passionately in love; but that Princess was snatched away from him eight times."[16]

"There," I said, "is a beauty that passed all proofs."

"That's true—but all her abductors were illustrious scoundrels, who nevertheless had virtue enough to respect her; they never dared even to lay a finger on her, and if her square could talk, he would recount marvels.

"The other who is appearing is Romulus, the first King of the Romans, whom he citizens put to death, and afterwards affirmed that he had risen up to Heaven. That one is Codrus, the King of Athens, who devoted himself to death for the service of the fatherland."

"I'd be curious," I said, "to know who that beauty is who appears with such a proud attitude."

"That's Cloelia, the most illustrious of all Roman ladies; she swam the Tiber in order to escape from Lars Porsena's camp."

"That one," said Monime, "appears to me to be a heroine very heavily armed; is she not some Queen of the Amazons?"

"That's the Maid of Orléans," said Zachiel. "You can't be unaware that she was the one who liberated France from the English yoke. The one that you see in the alcove is Zenobia, Queen of Palmyra, who governed that realm with as much wisdom and mildness for more than thirty years, until the time when Aurelian came to declare war on her. That Prince, after having vanquished her, took her as a captive behind his chariot of triumph. He had her two sons, Hernianus and Timolaus, killed.[17] There's Elizabeth, Queen of England; her glory would have been perfect if it had not be tarnished by the death of the Earl of Essex and that of Mary Stuart, Queen of Scots. It is claimed that jealousy had a great deal to do with the reasons that determined the pronunciation of those two condemnations."

Then we heard something akin to a hurricane excited by several winds that were in conflict. The wind of glory and that of immortality appeared to be struggling against that of jealousy. Renown was blowing from the south. To the north, the winds of envy and calumny were making such a frightful racket, shaking the edifice with so much violence, that they were bringing down various figures from the paneling and the colonnades, which were still attracting out curiosity.

---

[16] According to Herodotus, Mandana of Media was Cyrus the Great's mother, while his wife was Cassandane. How Madame Robert acquired this misconception is unclear.

[17] There appears to be no evidence of Zenobia having had sons with these names.

"There," said Zachiel, "is a King of Phrygia, who was the richest Prince of his time, and the one whose enlightenment, intelligence and politics were the most useful to his people, in enabling him to discover the secrets of his allies and the ruses of his enemies. That monarch profited so considerably from the gifts he had received from Heaven, in making them serve the glory of his realm, that he rendered his subjects perfectly happy. His name was Midas."

"What!" said Monime. "Is that the Midas who is depicted with asses' ears, and whom the indiscreet request he made of Bacchus to change everything he touched into gold caused him to die of starvation?"

"The same—which proves that posterity often spoils, by allegorical fables, the finest actions and embellishes pitiful ones; as witness the story of Lucretia, who has just fallen beside Midas; you're not unaware of the fashion in which her death was published; reading it ought to instruct you. Nothing, however, is as false as the story that is told of it; the truth is that Collatinus, her husband, having learned of her intrigues with the young Prince, stabbed her himself, and put about false rumors against the Tarquins, in order to take possession of the Republic conjointly with his colleague Brutus."[18]

"I suspected as much," I said. "Not that I presume that all women are coquettes, but that story of Lucretia always seemed to me to be a trifle apocryphal, in that it seems that it would have been more natural first to turn her weapon against the man who wanted to dishonor her, or at least not to wait until the crime had been committed to kill herself."

Aggravated by the fatigue of being obliged to struggle against the impetuosity of the winds that were blowing relentlessly, Monime asked the genius to take us into a building that was on the right.

The vault and pilasters of that building were made of glass; several columns of cardboard supported the edifice. On those columns, blackened by smoke and agitated by the winds, as in the other building, the great deeds of heroes—as many ancient as modern—were inscribed. It is true that when the gusts of wind became violent, some of those columns toppled, and although the poets and historian hired by the State to maintain the edifice applied an extreme attention to their reestablishment, it often happened, in the disorder, that they forgot a great many heroes, who, by virtue of that negligence, found themselves deprived of immortality in spite of the efforts they had made to merit it.

---

[18] The historical accuracy of the story of Lucretia's rape, which allegedly sparked the revolution that established the Roman Republic, as told by Livy and Dionysius of Helicarnasus, was always regarded with some skepticism; that did not prevent it becoming an oft-cited moral exemplar, employed by both St, Augustine and Dante, and a significant theme in Renaissance art and literature; English writers who employed it include Chaucer and Shakespeare.

We saw several people walking there who seemed to us to be greatly predisposed in their favor. One of those men approached me and asked whether I was newly arrived, and what was being said about him on our world.

"When you've told me your name," I said, "perhaps I'll be able to reply to the question you've asked me."

"I am Mucius Scaevola, a noble Roman, whom seeing my city besieged by King Lars Porsena, took my leave of the Senate and went to his camp with the intention of killing him; but as I did not know the King I was deceived and mistook one of his favorites for him, whose life I took. I was immediately arrested and taken before the King, but, without being astonished by any of the threats he made against me for daring to make an attempt on his life. I showed him how little I cared about the cruelest torments by putting my right hand into an ardent fire, and suffered the pain constantly until it was entirely burned. Lars Porsena, astonished by my firmness, could not help admiring my great courage and sent me away without doing me any harm. Scantly sensible to that generosity, I declared to him that I was not the only one that had conspired against his person, and that there were another three hundred Romans who had sworn his death. That was what determined him to make an alliance with the Romans, fearing their intrepidity because of the example I had just shown him."

"You horrify me," I said. "How dare you boast of the blackest of all attempted murders? Are those your fine exploits? What! After a cowardly homicide, you claim immortality? It isn't be treasons that one attempts to vanquish one's enemy. The action from which you want derive vanity would only be regarded today, in our world, as a model of rascality and ferocity, and you would have no other glory at present than being placed in the ranks of those bandits who hire themselves out as assassins and put a certain price on each murder proportionate to the difficulties they encounter in committing the crime. For myself, I do not see anything great in voluntary homicide. The basis of all the virtues is humanity; it flows like a pure and salutary stream that fertilizes everything it encounters; but you, vile assassin, if you have acquired any honors, they are illegitimate."

Mucius, very discontented by my reception, shrugged his shoulders and went away.

Soon afterwards I was surrounded by a large number of people. One of them told me that he was Achilles, another Caesar, and a third Alexander. I could not hear the names of a great many of those heroes because they were all speaking at the same time. As I saw that each of them was preparing to tell me his story, I interrupted them to beg them to explain themselves one at a time.

"I am Childebren," said a fat, wheezy man. "I would like to know what is being said about me."

"What is said about you? I can assure you that I've never heard your name pronounced on any world."

"And me," said another, with an air of generosity. "I am Montezuma."

"Ha! You, I know; you're an honest man to whom the Spanish did great injustice. But you, who announce yourself to be a Caesar, tell me what country you come from, which world you inhabited and in which realm you were born?"

"The question is singular; has there ever been more than one Caesar? You are an imbecile who only has a human face, and have not the intelligence of a carp."

"I have not learned to reply to invective, but I can assure you that there are at present on our earth more than a million Caesars and at least as many Alexanders, since the least of our officers, and even our soldiers, regard themselves as such."

I had no sooner uttered those words, which they doubtless took for as many blasphemies, than the entire crowd of heroes disappeared, to the great contentment of Monime, who was beginning to fear their petulance.

Zachiel then took us through a large hall filled with heaps of silk and cotton of different colors. Three old women seemed to be continuously occupied in spinning them. Monime and I looked at them very intently, without being able to discover the mystery. This is how the genius explained it to us.

"The three old women you see are the Fates who spin the lives of mortals. Humans can only remain on earth for as long as they take to finish each mass. When they have completed a skein, Destiny attaches a little gold, silver or lead plaque to it, which defines the good or bad qualities of person whose thread has just been cut; his name is engraved on the plaque and his virtues or vices traced in indelible characters. Then an old man, whose rapid course can never be halted, fills the flaps of his robe with them and goes to throw them in the river of forgetfulness, which you can see in the distance on the left flank of that hill.

"The old man comes back continually to take more, untiringly, without ever being able to diminish their number; but when, with an air of chagrin, he has discharged his burden, two swans whiter than snow, which float incessantly on the river, take care to detach with their beaks the names of the most illustrious mortals and put them in the hands of a nymph of ravishing beauty, whose unique employment is to carry them to the Temple of Glory, in order to consecrate them to immortality there. There she attaches them, with great care, to a simulacrum placed on a column elevated in the middle of the temple."

"It's easy to deduce," said Monime, "that the old man you have depicted for us is Time; but what do the swans signify, which, careful to detach the names of heroes from those of vulgar humans, prevent them from being swallowed up by the river of forgetfulness?"

"They represent the great poets and the best historians," said the genius, "who both, by their late nights and assiduous labors, serve to immortalize monarchs, princes, great politicians and all those who have distinguished themselves in the course of their life by heroic actions. The nymph depicts History, who, under that figure, represents the candor, purity, simplicity and above all the verity that a historian ought to employ in the pictures that he gives us in tracing the lives of the heroes that he sets out to put before our eyes."

After leaving that hall the genius took us across a large courtyard. We noticed that the sun, by the heat of its rays, had concentrated the smoke in the entrails of the earth; all the winds had dissipated; the only one that remained was that of glory, which, like all zephyrs, was only blowing to render the air milder and more agreeable.

"We have finally arrived," Zachiel told us, "at the Temple of Immortal Glory."

That temple, the dome of which appeared by its elevation to pierce the clouds, immediately fixed our gaze; we were enchanted by the beauty and the regularity of its architecture. Monime and I, dazzled by its majesty, felt a faint terror take possession of our souls; we approached it with the respect that divinity inspires.

Under the steps of the temple is a profound lair, in which we saw Vulcan forging, on an anvil, the redoubtable thunderbolts of which the Marcians[19] make use to sustain their rights and ensure the destiny of States. To one side of the door of the sanctuary was the divine Urania, a compass in one hand and a map in the other, one which were traced realms, cities, citadels, lakes and sea. On the other side, Calliope was holding a history book, using her finger to point out the finest features. Further away were ranged Intrepid Valor, Vigilant Toil, Tranquil Composure, Hope, Cunning, Deflection, Disguise and Imagination, who seemed to be occupied with a thousand brilliant projects that they were presenting to the confidant of Mars, whom Zachiel identified to us as Impenetrable Secrecy. The temple is surrounded by laurels, with which Pallas herself forms the crowns that Mars subsequently presents to his favorites.

---

[19] The original text employs both *Marciens* and *Marsiens* to describe inhabitants of Mars, although the former is employed to refer to a regional population, contrasted with the Salians and Bellonians, and might be derived from the name of the Byzantine emperor known in French as Marcien rather than the name of the planet. When first introduced, the latter seems to be used in a more general sense, but is subsequently used in the limited one. In consequence, I have maintained the inconsistency, transcribing the two terms as Marcians and Marsians, rather than unifying them or substituting the now-standardized "Martians." Some early English scientific romances employed "Marsians" rather than the more familiar term.

Chapter III

"You ought not to be proud," said Zachiel, "of the unmerited glory that you are receiving today in entering this temple. Covered by my wings, I shall render you invisible to the eyes of all these heroes, and those of Mars himself; I only want to excite in you the martial ardor and noble courage that animates and forms great captains in order to render you worthy of one day occupying a place beside these demigods."

Mars, seated in the middle of the temple on an elevated throne, sustained on the wings of the genius of war, appeared to be gazing at a hero placed beside him to his right, obligingly showing him several passages in a large book that Destiny was holding in front of him. I dared not ask questions of the genius for fear of being discovered, but he anticipated my desires and gave me an indescribable pleasure by telling me that the person who excited my curiosity by virtue of the preference he had obtained over the others was Henri IV, the good King of France, whom Mars was enabling to read, in the book of Destiny, the glory of his race and the striking actions that were to be accomplished by all his descendants.

"O gods!" said Monime, in a low voice, "What an amity I feel for that hero! He is the one, then, whose memory will be perpetuated eternally from race to race among the people as well as the great and sovereigns, who will always have the glory of being taken for a model throughout the universe? But tell me, my dear Zachiel—I'm curious to learn whether he knows how much his memory is revered in all the nations of Earth, and whether he enjoys here the renown that he so justly acquired."

"I give you my word," said Zachiel, "that what makes his recompense, and the proof that the divinity created him in an eminent degree of superiority of intelligence and talents in order to reign over all men, is that those who were most jealous of his glory are forced to admit today that he alone merits commanding the entire universe, since Henri IV has been placed above the greatest men that Rome produced in her greatest elevation.

"I hate flattery and false praise," the genius added, "and only ever applaud true merit. Scipio Africanus is, without contradiction, the greatest that Rome produced, but Henri IV required much more strength of genius, grandeur of soul, intrepidity and courage to reach the goal of becoming king of France than was necessary for what the Roman achieved.

"Scipio, supported by good troops, expelled Hannibal from Italy, reassured the Romans frightened by the loss of the battle of Cannes and carried to the Carthaginian lands the furies of a cruel war with which they had shortly before set all Italy ablaze; in sum, he liberated Rome from that proud and dangerous rival. But what puts the glory of Henri IV above that of the Roman is that, at the head of semi-naked soldiers, devoid of money and without any other aid than his courage and his right, he sets out to recover the crown; he is obliged to make the conquest of his own kingdom, usurped by the member of the Ligue, the Spaniards and others even more redoubtable. In spite of all his oppositions, Henri IV carried through his plans, and after having reestablished himself on the throne of his fathers he made those same Spaniards tremble who, a few years earlier, had combined scorn with presumption in merely referring to him as "the Béarnois."

"You see, my dear Seaton, the affairs of Henri IV were in much greater disorder on the death of his predecessor than those of the Romans after the battle of Cannes, since they at least had money and the means of reestablishing their army. Far from the king of France having the same assistance, I recall a letter that he wrote to one of his generals, in which he indicated that his finances were in a pitiful state, that his cooking pot had been empty for a week, that his suppliers had not had a penny, and that he was obliged to eat with the officers of his army."

I would have liked Zachiel to add to that account and summary of the lives of some of the heroes that I saw assembled in the temple, but Monime, who was beginning to weary of such a long fast, assured us that she did not have enough strength to want to attempt to resemble those great individuals, and that being unable to imitate Henri IV in his great deeds, she would still find enough glory in resembling him in his humiliation by going to ask for supper from some officer whose turnspit was not dismantled. It was necessary to satisfy Monime.

When we emerged from the temple we encountered a large number of troops, whose officers, dressed in different colors, were carrying on their flags or ensigns the emblems of battles they had fought. On some the depiction of an honorable retreat was seen; others described an advantageous capitulation; this one showed the conquest of an entire province; that one the destruction of a well-fortified city filled with all sorts of munitions; that other a naval combat that represented an entire fleet that seemed to have been dissipated or sunk. Further away, the standard of victory shone, borne on a chariot followed by various other troops; in fact, I cannot describe or enumerate the prodigious quantity of ensigns hoisted by the multitude of claimants of immortal glory, for it is necessary not to think that only military men can make the claim; all estates have the same rights, and Renown blows her trumpet for the favorites of Apollo as well as those of Mars, thus forming a perpetual competition in the vicinity of the temple.

As we advanced into the country we discovered a manor house whose form and structure indicated that it had seen several centuries; Zachiel took us to it. The manor house was occupied by an old officer who gave us a good welcome, but during supper he began giving us a account of the battles in which he had been involved, the duels in which he had been employed, the wounds he had received, the injustices that had been done to him in gratifying men far inferior to him, and a thousand other things just as uninteresting for strangers. That conversation bored Monime so much that she had the vapors. We took our leave of our host in order to depart at dawn the next day.

Zachiel took us in the empire of the Salians, where the fire of war was ignited everywhere. As we approached one of their cities we were obliged to pass through the middle of a camp. The officers, helmets on their heads and fully armored, were preparing to leave; the movement of the soldiers was already producing a cloud of dust that was rising into the air and the trumpets, fifes and drums were already sounding the march, when a courier arrived, bringing a countermand that stopped them.

Monime, observing their movements, seemed disconcerted at first by the sight of the blades of their bristling pikes and the brilliant gleam of weapons, which dazzled the eyes. Gripped by fear and dread, she begged the genius in a tremulous voice to take us to some other world, unable to bear the sight of those men, who seemed to be respiring nothing but death, blood and carnage.

"I see that you are still prey to unworthy weaknesses," said Zachiel, in a severe tone. "Ought you to dread anything while I'm accompanying you? Is this the fruit that I must expect from my care and my complaisance? Rid yourself of these vain terrors if you want to merit the gifts that I intend to make you."

Monime blushed; ashamed and confused by having attracted the reproaches of the genius, she dared not reply, and was constrained to follow Zachiel, who took us through the camp in order to enter the city, where we obtained a room in a lodging-house. We spent the reminder of the day resting, while listening to the instructions of the genius.

"These people are very different from the Marcians. Among the latter, morality, candor and good faith form the most solid foundations of their empire, and among the Salians those virtues have long been banished. You will see nothing in this realm but a tissue of false pretexts, vain arguments, frivolous complaints, crude and borrowed colors, muted and hidden intrigues, and artifices suggested by individuals interested in finding means to continue the war in order to enrich themselves at the expense of the people."

"I find the condition of humans very deplorable," I said, "especially when they take their own passions or those of others as guides for their conduct. If war is proposed, the soldier, dazzled by the lure of pillage, delivers himself to it with enthusiasm, and the citizens, seduced by the false pretext of conserving the fatherland and their liberty, seem to animate the troops; the officer, guided by another interest, encourages them, while he often runs to his own doom."

"It's true," said Zachiel, "that nothing is more persuasive for the persons one wants to rally to one's party than setting an example; that is an inclination attached to nature; it seems that humans are only made to imitate one another; an entire province observes what its neighbors do; the fire spreads, is communicated, and soon becomes a general conflagration. It is from those kinds of muted mines that one often sees an evil spring gush forth, and the politics of those who foment them often employs al the artifices that it has put to work until the blood

30

of the troops is shed. This realm has furnished a terrible example, since the war they have undertaken too lightly is reducing the State to cruel extremes. Imbecility, ignorance, corruption and debasement are the dominant vices of the Salians, the usual source of the poverty and misery of peoples; judge, my dear Seaton, whether they are to be pitied."

The next day we were visited by several officers. Monime's surprise was extreme when, instead of seeing robust men with martial features she only saw young Adonises, powdered, primped and perhaps painted, for they had complexions as fine as that of a woman who spends three-quarters of the day in her toilette. Those plumed demigods with red heels and doubly-ruffed sleeves did not have the slightest scent of gunpowder; ambered from head to toe they perfumed Monime's whole apartment. Those darlings of the god Mars doubtless made their principal occupation imitating him in his amours, leaving the care of their glory to hazard or fortune. They only talked to us about the favors they had received from their beauties, the feasts with which they had been regaled, and those they still proposed to give in the city, and invited Monime and me to take part in them.

That debut gave me a very poor idea of the prudence and talents of those young officers. However, curious to instruct myself regarding a profession of which I only knew the theory, which I soon hoped to put into practice, in order not to neglect anything, I asked them numerous questions about their manner of combat and certain rules that I thought necessary.

First I asked them whether they had a thorough knowledge of the map of the country into which they were about to go, and the character of the people they were going to attack, because I thought that knowledge very useful to facilitate the passage of their troops, taking precautions against enemy ruses and avoiding falling into the traps that might be extended for them. I added that I also thought that a good officer ought to know engineering, fortification, cartography and mathematics, especially the parts concerning the military art.

"Not a word of all that," replied one of the gentlemen, pirouetting on tiptoe. "Among us, courage and valor substitute for everything."

"But sir, valor that is not accompanied by prudence and composure becomes an impetuous courage that looks at danger from afar and wants to be at grips at the time when it is necessary to camp. Thus, I regard that valor as a false bravery or a blustering courage, instead of which a great soul, a penetrating genius and an intrepid heart sees peril at close range without being frightened by it."

"It appears to me," said the young officer, "that the men of your country are very phlegmatic; it's necessary to hope that a little of our way of operating can contribute to banishing useless reflections from your mind." Those words were pronounced in the most jovial tone, accompanied by a bow that announced their departure.

Surprised to see so much ignorance in an officer entrusted with an important position, I asked Zachiel whether the other officers were not more learned.

"It is necessary not to be astonished by the vivacity of the Salians," said the genius, "any more than that of all the peoples who inhabit this world. As this planet is much closer to the sun than the others, the influences that dominate them communicate the fire and petulance that often leads them to act without giving themselves time to reflect."

We spent a few days in that city, where we saw the most frenetic license reigning; pleasures—fine food, gambling, spectacles, concerts, balls and amorous assignations—were the sole occupations of a the officers; their tables, always served with profusion, represented nothing less than the calamities of war, always onerous for peoples. During those pleasures and that dissipation, however, the wretched soldiers who were camped in the vicinity of the city were exercising a thousand disorders therein, because of the poor discipline observed there.

Monime and I were invited to a great supper and to a masked ball that would be given thereafter by the steward of the province. That man, whom fortune had extracted from the most mediocre estate to raise him to the highest degree of favor, had rendered himself hateful throughout the city by the airs of grandeur that he effected with regard to the nobility and the scorn he displayed for the richest burgers. The women, piqued by the scant regard that he had for them, complained of it to the officers of the garrison, who promised to avenge them

The plan was to dress a dozen soldiers as women, magnificently dressed, who were to harass the steward all night long. The masque favoring that disguise, they had no fear of being recognized. We were only told about the comedy they intended to play two hours after the ball began. The pretended goddesses had already surrounded the steward, and were preparing to play a thousand pranks on him when a confused noise was heard of whinnying horses, men and women uttering frightful screams, and troops filing the air with bellicose roars. The alert was immediately sounded and the call to arms issued; the enemy had mounted a surprise attack on the city, and had entered through a passage that had not been guarded.

Then, all the young officers, without appearing to be frightened by the danger or the dolor of their beauties, calmly left them in order to run to give orders and assemble their troops. In spite of all their vivacity, however, and even though they deployed considerable bravery, their efforts were futile. The city was taken and put to contribution, in spite of all the efforts of the inhabitants, who defended themselves with courage and intrepidity.

Zachiel, who had anticipated that disorder, came to our rescue; he got us out of the city in order to take us to another province. I could not imagine that those pretty faces, which had been admiring themselves in all the mirrors a few hours before, had had the courage to precipitate themselves at the enemy squadrons; that appeared to me to smack of enchantment.

"After having thought about that event," I said to Zachiel, "I find the conduct of those men very imprudent. Since the guard of the city had been confided to them, why did they neglect to fortify the places at which it might be attacked?"

"It's because the enlightenment of those men is very limited," said the genius. "The majority have only one marked point of view, beyond which they cannot extend their penetration. They are, so to speak, enclosed in the darkness of human politics, which makes them blind to everything presented to them. They arm themselves with specious pretexts to embellish good or bad arguments in order to find the means of engaging their allies by motives of ambition or chimerical concessions, with which they are not miserly, but the ruses they employ often rebound on them."

During the journey the genius instructed us as to the religions and mores of the Marsians.

"Their way of thinking is free," he told us. "All the great men of this world prefer what they imagine to what they have seen or learned; all their sentiments belong to them; they think that in matters of opinions one should always follow the mildest and most moderate, and those which tend to conciliate minds and maintain social repose.

"There is nothing more absurd, say their pretended philosophers, than to try to subjugate beings who ought necessarily to be happy, in order to oblige them to regulate the celestial spheres and combine all the events that happen on earth in order to make gods of them susceptible to hatred and vengeance, who allow themselves to be moved by tears and prayers, and who can be offended by our disorders even though several among them furnish more than one pernicious example themselves; ought we, after that, to regard them as veritable gods? We ought, therefore to believe that if the world is submissive to the power of true gods, it would be much better guided, and that everything would happen in a manner worthy of those wise and enlightened gods who governed it. As we see the contrary every day, that is evident proof that hazard alone presides over everything that happens here.

"In spite of sentiments so contrary to their religion, one sees them regularly in the temple of Pallas in the position of suppliants, offering the goddess prayers and incense. As they relate everything back to union, they recommend to all the citizens to lend themselves to public ceremonies and the acts of religion that their mythologies impose, even when they are not penetrated by them to the depths of the heart, since persons of intelligence can scarcely be convinced of the verity of all the fabulous translations presented to them; but because the people believe them, and whom it is dangerous to disabuse, since they serve to maintain peace and mildness among them, the great are obliged to put at least their external appearance in uniformity with that of their compatriots.

"The most reasonable among their philosophers are convinced that good and evil are only vain or chimerical things that opinion has introduced. Good is, according to them, that which really augments the power one has to act, and that which can pass for a greater perfection; evil is the contrary and is that which weakens the same power.

"What, then, can nature offer more convenient to these different views than to attach them to pleasure? Is that not what inclines the soul toward good with all the more force because good is much more desirable than evil? When humans abuse pleasure and run after it blindly without any moderation, those are their crimes. But is nature not sufficiently avenged for that abuse by the sharp pains engendered thereby and remorse even more terrible than the pains? In general, one of the greatest obligations of humans is to watch incessantly over the safety and conservation of their being; that is a concern nature has engraved in every heart, even though they are persuaded that their days are numbered and that nothing can change their destiny.

"This world is divided, like all the others, into different sects. Some put their confidence in idols that they fabricate themselves; others address their prayers to divinities that the foolish imagination of their ancient mythologies have fabricated in order to trick the good faith of people who cannot be cured of their prejudices; but all the nobles and the majority of their scholars recognize no other divinity than Nature, which they regard as the invisible soul of the world; they say that she has a supernatural virtue, which produces, arranges and conserves all the parts of the universe.

"Those scholars distinguish two wills in Nature, one of which they suppose to be good and the other evil. They believe that there is a kind of equilibrium that enables everything to be balanced and remain in an equal proportion, and that it is absurd to think that a bountiful being created the world and that, able to fill it with all kinds of perfections, he set out to do precisely the opposite. But argue with those false scholars, ask them what that Nature is, of which the term seems so vague, and they will reply to you that it is an active principle, an economical entity that regulates all things with so much art that good does not surpass evil; it is, they say, a superb divinity, full of ostentation, powerful, which tries above all to hide its secrets in order not to be discovered."

"So, according to their system," I said to Zachiel, "Nature, fate and hazard are all the same thing?"

"You will see here," the genius went on, "almost all the great lords cultivating the sciences; they have books of morality, philosophy and history, which they conserve without any change or alteration; the foolish love of novelty does not impassion them, and what distinguishes them from other worlds is that the same language has been spoken here since their creation. That kind of immobility of language enables them to understand their most ancient authors, who are often not very reliable, whereas on your earth one sees the language of a people change entirely in less than a century; one might think that others come to establish themselves on the ruins of those that disappear.

"Music is regarded, throughout the extent of the planet, as a universal remedy capable of curing the worst diseases of the body and even of the mind; and the officers who command their armies draw infallible and incessantly present assistance from it, lifting the soul by means of noble chords in order to fortify courage and virtue, to govern and guide the passions at their will, to excite them and appease them at need. That is why all their exercises are preceded by agreeable and loud music that seems, in some way, to dispose the soul and render it bolder; for as the sound of the music penetrates it, they are transported, if one might put it like that, by a divine fervor, and believe that the god of war is entering via their ears to animate them to combat and better enable them to obey.

"The men who are born on this planet feel its influences very keenly; they are all bellicose, and when they are not making war on one another they compensate themselves by making it on animals; furthermore, their manners are always simple, frank and uniform in their societies. They guard their speech religiously, because lies are severely punished here. An officer who has broken his word cannot avoid the scorn of the entire nation; he will be stripped of his rank, expelled from his corps and forced to seek to hide his shame and humiliation abroad."

Chapter IV

We finally arrived in the realm of Bellonia, then governed by a tyrant named Tracius. That Prince, of a cruel and ambitious spirit, did not take pleasure in anything but blood and carnage. He was only occupied in seeking new ways of invading neighboring states and employing them to carry out the most unjust vexations there, while the legitimate sovereign, exiled, expelled from his kingdom, obliged to wander hither and yon in various states, groaned at the evils he saw overwhelming his people, especially those of which he anticipated that his unfortunate family would be the target.

Having arrived in the vicinity of the capital city, we were obliged to traverse a great plain strewn with dead and dying. One young woman whose sighs and sobs made the grief she was suffering manifest excited our pity and our interest in knowing her.

Monime, always full of zeal for the unfortunate, had our carriage stop and asked her what had occasioned the distress of which she was giving evidence.

"Alas, my Lady, you're doubtless unaware that a bloody battle took place on this plain yesterday. You see in me a spouse in despair, who bears in her womb the innocent fruit of a sacred union. Since daybreak I have been roaming this plain in vain; in vain I have visited all the bodies massacred by enemy fire; nothing has been offered to my frantic gaze, no hope has presented itself to my soul; disastrous fate has doubtless cut short my husband's days."

The young woman's tears redoubled. After having employed the consolations dictated by the generosity of her soul, Monime, touched by her distress, succeeded in calming her dolor somewhat. She invited her to take a seat in our carriage to return to the city, where we put her back in the hands of her family.

On the road we encountered a host of inhabitants who had come out in the hope of finding those who loss was exciting their groans.

There was an old man weighed down by the burden of his years; his organs, enfeebled by age, no longer permitting him to distinguish the objects surrounding him, he addressed himself to all those he encountered, asking them for news of his son.

"Alas," he said to one, his eyes bathed with tears, "the support of my old age has doubtless perished in the battle; I could not disarm or weaken his proud courage, but I lacked the strength to go with him and die beside him."

After those few words, suffocated by grief, his knees buckled and he was ready to fall, but, reanimating himself with a final effort, he approached the next stranger, and sighed as he gripped his arm. "Convey to my son," he said to him, "this last embrace; tell him never to forget an unfortunate father who only lived in him, and whom his absence has reduced to despair."

In other places, friends were searching urgently to procure some assistance for their friends. Elsewhere, young women could be seen running with great strides toward the plain, in the hope of encountering the young warriors who had promised them his faith.

When we reached the city, we learned the details of the battle, in which more than thirty thousand men had perished. To that bad news was added that of a complete rout of its navy. So many combined calamities spread consternation through all hearts. It seemed that such reverses ought to have corrected Tracius, or at least moderated his ambition, but in spite of those scourges, the tyrant could not resolve himself to abandon his foolish enterprises. Insensible to the calamities of the State, barbaric toward the people, he hid from them with a cruel concern the greater part of the disgraces that fortune had inflicted, and in spite of the number of troops already sacrificed in several deadly encounters, and the exhaustion of men and finances to which he was reduced, nothing could stop him.

An old officer whose acquaintance we had made assured us that for a long time, every step he had taken had always been stained with blood, obliged to go in search of the enemy in arid lands devastated by the number of troops who had already passed through it, who were accustomed to pillage because of the poor discipline maintains in the companies.

"To those difficulties can be added the misery of our soldiers, poorly paid, poorly dressed, poorly maintained and poorly assisted in their maladies by the fraudulent conduct of our entrepreneurs; that is what causes the defections in our armies; the majority of the soldiers, and even the officers, are going over to the enemy and increasing their numbers even further. All those malcontents then find themselves motivated by their own vengeance."

Dissatisfied with what we had been told, we left the city in order to continue our observations. As we advanced through the land, we encountered a multitude of poor peasants forced to follow a soldier what had just enlisted them, by surprise or by authority. Those wretches, in despair at quitting their cottages, even though most of the time they lacked the bare necessities of life, appeared to be in the utmost consternation.

I noticed one in particular who touched me sensibly; I approached him in order to ask him what reason he had to be so afflicted by following a métier that would at least provide him with the means of subsistence.

"Alas, sir," the young man replied, sobbing, "the excess of my despair will not surprise you when you know that I was snatched from the arms of a mother charged with eight children, of whom the oldest that remains is barely ten years old. In the eighteen months since I lost my father, I have at last been able to allow them to subsist by my hard labor; what completes my woes in that in taking me away from my family they have been deprived of all help, and I can assure you that very little can be expected from me in a métier that I do not know and for which I have no appetite—because, sir, I do not even know how to load a rifle, the sight of a sword causes me to treble and almost too faint. All my comrades are no braver than me; judge from that what troops can be opposed to enemies long accustomed to vanquish."

I left the young soldier after giving him all the money I had on me.

"It appears to me," said Monime, "that that troop of soldiers has no ambition to obtain a place in the Temple of Glory. I'd rather confront the enemy with a cardboard army, like those employed in our theaters."

"Which is to say," said Zachiel, smiling, "that you're comparing the Marsians to swarms of flies that one can frighten by presenting them with grotesque figures. But do you know that the Marsians are the most prudent men on this planet, the most judicious and he most intrepid in case of danger. Such are, my dear Monime, the enemies of the Bellonians. It is to their army that I am taking Seaton; it is there that I want him to serve his apprenticeship in the métier of war, under Prince Aricdef, who is the general commanding the army sent to combat that of Tracius. I presume, given the elevation of your sentiment, that you will not raise any objection to the design that I've conceived in order to enable Seaton to profit from this voyages."

Far from opposing the views of the genius, Monime, who only intended to render me worthy of one day occupying the rank destined for me, appeared, on the contrary to be charmed by the opportunity that was offered to me to distinguish myself by some action that would merit Zachiel's approval.

During our journey I could not help sighing at the thought that I was going to be separated from Monime.

"Why that expression of sadness?" asked the genius. "Are you insensible to the pleasure that a great heart ought to feel when it's a matter of acquiring glory?"

"Pardon the sigh," I said. "It does not come from a pusillanimous heart that fears danger, but may I give nothing to the dolor of being separated from you and Monime?"

"I dare not tell you that I am sensible to that separation," said Monime with tears in her eyes, "since it is necessary to your advancement."

"Calm yourselves, both of you," said Zachiel. "The separation will not be long; it's necessary, my dear Seaton, to show more strength and accustom yourself gradually to my absence; you will not always have me. I am only taking you into the midst of dangers in order to teach you not to be prodigal in shedding blood. Heaven has given birth to you in order to command one day, so remember that a good general ought to be model of all his officers; it is his example that animates the army. You will learn under Prince Aricdef to merit the title of a great captain.

"Remember, my son, that valor is perhaps only a virtue when it is regulated by prudence and moderation., without which it is merely an insensate scorn for life or a brutal ardor that only leads to doom. A man who cannot retain his self-possession in danger is more reckless than brave, because it seems that he needs in order to be animated to put himself beyond the dread that he cannot overcome by the natural situation of his heart.

"Know that by delivering oneself recklessly to dangers, one can trouble the order and discipline of troops; by giving an example of temerity, one often exposes an entire army to great misfortunes; so refrain, my dear Seaton, from seeking glory with too much impatience; the true means of finding it is to wait tranquilly for favorable opportunities. Remember, too, not to attract the envy of anyone; do not be jealous of the success of others, never seek to diminish its value; on the contrary, be the first to give praise to those who merit it.

"Consult the oldest captains; ask the most skilful to instruct you; show them meekness and docility in listening to their advice. It is necessary nevertheless to be on your guard, to convince yourself that even the most enlightened cannot see everything, and that the wisest often make gave mistakes when they only follow their impulses or their prejudices. Above all, avoid revealing yourself to certain flatterers who take pleasure in sowing division among the officers in order indispose the chiefs and profit from the disorder they create."

I listened avidly to these lessons from the genius, which seemed to pass into my soul like a stream of pure fresh water that one sees flowing between flowers. My tender Monime also appeared to me to be penetrated by the keenest gratitude. Until then I had only filled my memory with great names and great events, without giving myself the time to make any judicious reflection. That conversation—or, to put it better, the instructions of the genius—gave birth within me to an ardent desire to take as a model of my conduct the actions of illustrious men, to profit from their virtues and to avoid falling into their vices.

On arriving among the Marsians, we learned that their general was to leave the following day in order to put himself at the head of his troops. Without losing any time, the genius introduced me that same day to the Prince, who received me with marks of generosity that immediately attached me to him. He promised Zachiel to watch over my conduct, and to take care of my advancement. In order to begin giving me immediate proof of his benevolence he ordered that an apartment should be prepared for me to spend the night in his house, in order that I would be able to leave with him.

The genius left me after giving me a few more items of advice, and the strongest assurances that he would not abandon Monime—which tranquilized me considerably.

The sun had risen and was already gilding the summits of the mountains when Prince Aricdef departed to rejoin the army. I was by his side in the capacity of an aide-de-camp. When we reached the rendezvous, the Prince gave orders for the encampment. I had the advantage of being employed on several occasions that attracted praise on his part, and procured me his confidence and amity. I had the good fortune to accompany him into various actions in which the Prince gave evidence of his intrepidity and the invincible courage that never abandoned him.

I could not weary of admiring the advantageous situations that he was always able to chose for the encampment of his troops, either because of the forage or the necessities of fighting. I also admired the order and discipline that reigned in his camp, the intelligence and impenetrable secrecy necessary to the success of an enterprise, the care that he took in visiting his camp personally, the attention he paid to the least of the soldiers, in order that anything that could be useful to them, either for clothing or for nourishment, would not be lacking, and, finally, the obedience that they showed to the slightest indication of his will.

That first campaign had nothing remarkable except the capture of a few places that we took from the Bellonians. The Prince distributed his winter quarters and we went back to the capital city with a young officer who had acquired a considerable reputation among the troops. His modesty, his candor and the purity of his morals, rare qualities in a young man, had attracted all my esteem and confidence. We were soon linked by an intimate amity; I invited him to spend his winter quarters with me. I introduced him to Zachiel and Monime, who both appeared to confirm the choice I had made by the eulogies that they gave him. It is true that it seemed that he carried with him a charm that drew all hearts in his favor.

Out walking one day with that amiable chevalier, after a few vague remarks, I said: "How fortunate you are to have commenced so young a métier that has so often procured you opportunities to distinguish yourself."

"It's true," said the other, "that I entered the service very early, but my dear Milord, what do you expect a man of condition to do whom of fortune has, if I might put it like that, adopted the task of humiliating in the most sensitive places? The next campaign promises us a decisive battle; if I can only have the opportunity to acquire some glory therein! But what am I saying? Is it for me, alas, to dare to flatter myself? No, however things turn out, I shall retire after that action, and no longer think about anything but trying to procure a repose for which I've been searching in vain for a long time; for it's necessary to agree, my dear, that unless one has a great employment in the army, it's a métier that's scarcely attractive to those who can do without it. I can only regard it as a resource for poor gentlemen who have neither enough wealth nor enough authority to be considered, and the majority of whom don't know how to occupy themselves. It's assuredly the most honest profession that a man of condition can chose; I like it a great deal, and if it weren't for the annoyances I encounter at every step I'd have difficulty quitting it; pressing motives would already have forced me to make a different decision, if a secret penchant hadn't drawn me into Aricdef's army."

"You haven't always been with the Marsians?"

"No," said the chevalier, "I only arrived a short time before you did. I began serving with the Salians, but their service involved so many annoying things; one depends there on so many interested and ignorant people, incessantly the butt of brutes who are mostly scoundrels, debauchees, gamblers or drunks, that it became insupportable to me. In sum, those who have morals pass among them for pedants. Nothing compensates for the loss of one's wealth or repose. The injustices of the illicit favors are a more sensible aggravation. Among them, merit, great talent, prudence and valor count for nothing; all the positions are bought for money or by vile obligations—which means that in spite of the number of their troops and the superiority of their forces, it's often easy to defeat them, by virtue of the ignorance of their officers, who don't have enough prudence to be able to take full advantage of their strength. In any case, the alliance they've made with the Bellonians determined me entirely to go into the service of the Marsians.

"Don't believe, because of that, my dear Milord," the chevalier went on, "that the ambition or the desire to obtain a considerable post from the Prince attracted me to his army; I wasn't led there by any of those views, but only that of numbing myself to the misfortunes that had overwhelmed me. Yes, my dear, I want to try to vanquish the fortune that is the enemy of my happiness and my repose, which, in robbing me of the honors in which I was born, has been unable to change my heart. Powerful reasons don't permit me to tell you any more at present; let it suffice for you to know that it's neither the dangers nor the fatigues of war that have taken away my taste for it. I'm a man of sound constitution; I get by easily on very little; but I dread dependency and would greatly prefer death to renouncing my liberty."

"I feel sorry for you, my dear sir, and dare not enquire as to the reasons that occasion your distaste for military service; however, I find that war, in spite of the aggravations you've just represented, has many advantages that ought to counterbalance them; all the vices that you believe to be inseparably attached to it, are not innate, since there are laws that punish them severely, and you'll agree that the Prince who commands us is not stained by the vices that you say are commonplace in the officers at the head of the armies of the Salians and the Bellonians.

"What idea ought we to have of Prince Aricdef? Without pausing at that which only ought to dazzle vulgar minds, you can't disagree that one can't help admiring in him the true virtues that form heroes. It's not his invincible courage that charms me, not his scorn for death and danger that I admire; it's his presence of mind, that intrepidity, that coolness in the disorder of the most furious combats, the indefatigable activity that is the true character of a conqueror; the unexpected rapidity with which he falls on the enemy army and carries off a signal victory when he's believed to be dead or cut off in a gorge, or his entire army seems defeated.

"We've both witnessed in the last campaign that with a handful of men he rendered all the strength of the Salians futile and took from the Bellonians several well-fortified places. In sum, he has always denied his enemies the means to attack him. One can therefore say that it's by virtue of his talents and rare qualities that he has acquired the love and confidence of his troops. It's certain that the soldier who loves and can count on his general is invincible; instead of which, those who are commanded by cowardly courtiers that they cannot hold in high esteem, allow themselves to be defeated easily. It's only necessary to wait for the opportunity of some court intrigue, which sows division among their troops; then, when one has good spies that keep you informed, one can take advantage of their dysfunction. I've heard it said that Prince Aricdef never lets one of those advantages escape.

"One can also add to all his qualities his incorruptible probity, his love of justice, his liberality, his clemency, his inviolable attachment to his work, his good faith, his mild and amiable manners, his attention for the officers and his generosity to the soldiers. One cannot, therefore, without injustice refuse him the titles of great warrior, redoubtable captain, good politician and sage philosopher, since he's an honest and honest man and loyal to his friends. We see that he even cultivates with care those who are beneath him."

"I confess," said the chevalier, "that all these qualities are Aricdef's prerogatives, that he justly merits the praise and admiration of all men; the renown that has published them all over the world gave birth in me to the desire to come and participate in his glory; without that desire, my dear Milord, perhaps I would never have had the advantage of knowing you."

A sigh accompanied those last words, which, combined with those that had preceded it, appeared to me to enclose an impenetrable mystery. I dared not ask the chevalier the reason for it. Remarking a good deal of trouble and agitation in his eyes, I was anxious; in order to distract him from his melancholy I proposed that we should go to see Monime.

We were staying in the same house, and the chevalier rarely spent a day without seeing Monime; I even believed that I could perceive the pleasure he felt in her company, given the urgency that he showed to be near her. Monime also showed him a distinguished complaisance, which was only in accord with his true merit. The chevalier's character, mild without being insipid, attentive without any baseness, was combined with all the gifts he had received from nature and those that depended on a noble education; he possessed all sorts of talents, but he was naturally borne to melancholy. Zachiel, who was doubtless able to penetrate the reasons for his sadness, attempted, out of condescension for the chevalier and Monime, to give birth every day to new opportunities for amusement and dissipation.

We were scarcely approaching the welcome return of the season of flowers when Prince Aricdef was already preparing to reassemble his troops. I was ordered to join him near a frontier city belonging to the Bellonians, to which he intended to lay siege.

Engineers are surveying all the surroundings, drawing up plans; trenches are being dug and covered ways formed, and the Prince, always active, is supervising the work. He sees defects, he corrects them, doing everything that is to his advantage, following them and animating them in their labor, pressing the siege of the city with ardor, animating all his troops by distributing liquor to them, which he sometimes drinks with them, with the familiar air that, better than speeches and recompenses, often passes into the soldier's soul the noble ardor that animates the hero, who seems to be rendering himself their companion.

The enemy was unable to hold out against the valor and vigilance of Aricdef; the city was taken and he entered it in triumph at the head of his troops, received the oath of fidelity from the burgers, fortified the place, and, after having reestablished abundance and tranquility there, we emerged therefrom to follow the Prince, who went to take possession of an advantageous position in order to observe the enemy.

Surprised not to see the chevalier arrive, I began to fear that the secret chagrin I had remarked in him might have constrained him to withdraw. I was preparing to write to him when I received a letter from Monime which told me that he had been retained by a bad fever. Anxiety about my friend's illness, combined with the urgency I felt to see Monime, caused me to ask for a week's leave. I had difficulty obtaining it, at the commencement of a campaign in which our army, already victorious, was only waiting for a movement on the enemy's part to direct its march, pursue it or disrupt its projects, but I could not refuse myself the pleasure of seeing Monime again.

Her eyes, I said to myself, *will animate my courage; a word from her adorable mouth will fortify my virtue; Zachiel, by his sage advice, will contribute to enabling me to acquire glory; perhaps, too, I shall bring back the chevalier, who, I feel sure, is burning with desire to find a decisive action.*

I obtained relay horses, which I sent forth, and then presented myself to the Prince in order to receive his orders.

"I've just learned," he told me, "that the Bellonians are advancing, with the intention of forcing us back to our retrenchments. My duty is to anticipate them, and I presume that the battle will be bloody, so I believe there's no need to recommend you not to let any opportunity escape to signal your courage. I permit you to go where your affairs summon you, provided that you return by the time we set forth, in order to fulfill the duties of your employment."

After leaving the Prince I climbed into my chaise and traveled all night, in order to bring forward the moments of happiness that I anticipated. What sweeter charm is there in the world than that of the union of hearts?

Oh, dear Monime, you combine virtue and innocence with amity; no dread or shame troubles your felicity. I am sure of being loved without division by a sister, the most perfect of all women.

Those reflections enabled me to enjoy in advance the pleasure of surprising her.

I finally arrived at ten o'clock in the morning. I flew to Monime's apartment, where I thought I had been petrified. Great God, what do I see? The chevalier in her arms; she is holding him tightly, and seems to be reassuring him with regard to ill-founded dreads. She kisses him; I believe I can see their sighs confounded.

"Oh, perfidy!" I cry. "By what charm have you been able to seduce her? Your blood will wash away the shame I feel."

Those words, pronounced with vehemence, cause them to turn their heads. Surprised to see me, they both blush; I want to flee; the chevalier stops me without being able to pronounce a single word. Monime, trembling and bewildered, falls unconscious.

"I perceive only too well," I said to the chevalier, pushing him away with eyes full of the anger that is animating me, "by the disorder and trouble I am causing, that you have completed your treasons."

"No, my dear Milord," said the chevalier, in an emotional voice that was almost extinct. "In spite of appearances, refrain from daring to suspect two people who are equally attached to you. I shall leave instantly, and will tell you at the camp everything that is the cause of your surprise today. I shall wait for you there to give you the satisfactions you demand. Begin by helping Monime."

Zachiel, who appeared at that moment, followed by one of Monime's maids, extracted me with a single word from the new anxieties that that speech had just plunged me.

"No, my Lady," he said, stopping the chevalier, "you shall not leave. It's no longer in the danger of combats that you ought to seek glory; you've disguised yourself for too long; it's necessary to resume the clothing appropriate to your sex. Follow my advice and allow Zerbine to accompany you into this dressing room."

"Oh, my dear Zachiel," I exclaimed, "with what concerns are you occupying yourself? Alas, Monime is dying."

The genius went to her and made her swallow a spoonful of universal elixir. I was at her feet; I held one of her hands, which I moistened with my tears. She finally opened her eyes; her first gaze was for me; it was tender; its languor passed into my soul. I felt annihilated by the reproaches that she seemed to be making for my outburst.

"Is it really true, my Lord," said Monime, in a voice that was still ill-assured, "that you were able to suspect me? Alas, my heart is not yet known to you? But where is the Princess? She is the one who must justify me."

"You have no need of her, my adorable Monime; a single word from Zachiel has done that. But who will justify me to you for my unjust suspicions? Will you pardon me for an initial impulse of which I was not the master? It is honor that was responsible or my crime; that is what will judge me."

"Well," said Monime, "get up, amity pardons you."

"Oh, that admission restores calm to my soul," I said, kissing the hand that I had not released, delightedly.

"I agree," Monime went on, "that appearances must have alarmed you, not being disabused as to the sex of the pretended chevalier, whom you have always regarded s a man; so can I not support the idea of the suspicions that I perceive the situation in which you found us presented to our mind?"

We were interrupted by Princess Marsine, who came back in after having put on garments appropriate to her sex.

"You're doubtless surprised, Milord, only to rediscover in me an unfortunate woman, from whom fate has stolen everything. You have seen me fight in several encounters with some considerable advantage, which have attracted your esteem and amity to me. Do not reproach me for not having accorded you all my confidence at first; I know that you merit every regard, not only by your virtues but also by the thousand services that I have received from you on various occasions; be persuaded that I have always distinguished you from all the other officers. Had I told you about my birth and sex, however, it would have been necessary to explain my misfortunes to you, in order to justify in some measure the disguise that the austere wisdom that you profess might perhaps have disapproved. Besides which, I had promised myself never to reveal my secret to anyone.

"When the Prince's orders recalled you to him I was counting on joining you soon; stopped by a bad fever, I could not carry out my project. I owe the reestablishment of my health to the charming Monime; her kindness, her care and assiduous attentions, and that charm which enables the union of souls, finally extracted from me that which I believed was in my interest to bury eternally in a profound silence. She has repaid my confidence with a sincere attachment and the confession of the sentiments of esteem that link you to one another.

"Dispense me, Milord, from telling you the story of my adventures; I have hidden nothing from the beautiful Monime; I permit her to make you party to my secrets; the interest she has taken in my misfortunes, and the graces she puts into everything she says, will render them more touching, so I dare flatter myself that her account will reestablish me in your opinion."

Princess Marsine left without waiting for my response, leaving me at liberty to talk to Monime. After we had said all the most tender things that our two truly touched hearts could imagine, I begged her to acquaint me with the reasons that had engaged Marsine to maintain her disguise for such a long time.

Chapter V
(Which only contains an abridged history of Princess Marsine)

"Princess Marsine," said Monime, "is the daughter of Belus, King of Bellonia. That Prince chose for his favorite Tracius, whom one might deem to be one of those men born for great revolutions, who take and strikingly sustain roles on the world stage far above their birth. The King raised that favorite by degrees to the principal dignities in the realm. Tracius was so well able to take advantage of his favor and simultaneously hide the ambition that devoured him that the King did nothing without consulting him, regarding him as the most affectionate of his ministers.

"When Tracius saw that he possessed all his master's confidence, he got rid of all those who might clarify his conduct, and, making use of all his cunning, he succeeded so well by his insinuations, that he embarked the King on several false steps, the consequences of which he disguised from him with extreme care. His seductive intelligence even found the secret of causing him to envisage his treasons as signal services: the fatal blindness of a heart seduced by the poison of the most outrageous flattery, which unfortunately almost always surrounds a throne.

"The King, accustomed to the adulations of his courtiers, too prejudiced in favor of his favorite to listen to any complaints against him, was unable to perceive the precipice that was being gradually hollowed out in order to doom him. That monarch was ignorant of what the love of a people for their sovereign might be; he knew the art of vanquishing his enemies, of conquering cities, but he was entirely ignorant of that of winning the hearts of those he had conquered, which is the greatest advantage a Prince can obtain from his victories. He was all the weaker because he had too much faith in his strength and his own enlightenment—or, rather, those of his favorite.

"The newly-conquered provinces did not take long to revolt, and by virtue of the treasons of Tracius, several other more considerable cities followed their example. It was necessary to raise new troops to chastise the rebels and recall them to their duty. Those new recruitments occasioned excessive expenses; in order to meet them it was necessary to impose a number of taxes, which overburdened the people; but those impositions, far from swelling the public treasury, were merely torrents that carried away the substance of all Bellonians to disappear into the immense fortunes of those protected by Tracius—who were nevertheless obliged by secret treaties they had made to surrender three-quarters of it to him

"The tyrant employed a part of his wealth to win over the principal officers of the crown, who, seduced by his gold, had no difficulty in obtaining general command of the army for him. When Tracius was at the head of his troops, like a vulture falling on a dove or a wood-pigeon and dissipating its palpitating limbs in the wood after tearing it apart, the tyrant began pitilessly murdering the king' subjects. His parricidal hands, confiscating their wealth, sacrificed them to his ambition.

"Prolonging the war by means of his covert intrigues and underhand maneuvers, Tracius augmented the misery of the people and found the secret of multiplying his treasures. The tyrant's politics had doubtless engaged him to allow himself to be defeated in several battles, but, seeing his credit increased by those losses, the same politics inspired new projects. He began spreading his wealth among his soldiers, and then affecting to have only a very mediocre table, cutting back all his expenses. That conduct succeeded in winning him the hearts of the soldiers.

"The tyrant put about the rumor that a number of prodigies had appeared in the kingdom; it was said that on the frontiers the angry heavens had been seen covered in fire, and that on a tranquil and serene day the sun had appeared all radiant with flames; it was added that thunderbolts had fallen in several places, including the temples of Mars and Pallas, and that a statue of Hercules had been toppled.

"In spreading these rumors Tracius added hypocrisy to his villainy, pretending to be frightened by them. Bribed augurs consulted on his orders responded that a great swarm of wasps had flown around the square all day and had gone to settle on the temple of Hercules; it was said that it was necessary to consult the books of the Sibyls in order to try to discover the cause of the prodigies, and Tracius, continuing his false zeal for the worship of the gods, ordered sacrifices in order to appease them.

"Things being thus disposed, the tyrant then had further rumors spread that were very disadvantageous to the King, cleverly insinuating that the ambition, bad conduct and excessive expenses of Belus, and his lack of love for his subjects, were obstacles that would always serve as a barrier to their happiness.

That seditious discourse had all the success that Tracius expected; the troops began a mutiny, demanding their pay and wanting to lay down their arms.

Profiting from that disorder, Tracius distributed money to them, and, with a false zeal for the good of the State, ran through the ranks to encourage them. The soldiers, already won over by his liberality, seduced by his eloquence and the love he manifested for the public good, applauded him, and the army was then filled with a dull rumble similar to that heard after a tempest, when the recesses of rocks still retain the echoes of impetuous winds that have troubled the sea all night with their furious whistling.

"Such was the applause that they gave Tracius in choosing him for their King. He was first proclaimed unanimously at the head of his troops. In order not to let the ardor they had just manifested to die down, the tyrant advanced on the nearby city and had himself crowned with the ceremonies customary among the Bellonians. Then, pursuing his conquests rapidly, almost without encountering any obstacles, he came to besiege the King in his own palace. The unfortunate Prince was obliged to flee with Princess Marsine, the sole heir to the realm, who was then only four years old. It is certain that the monarch made an irreparable error in giving the tyrant time, by virtue of that flight, to fortify himself increasingly, and to engage several sovereigns in his party, which had become sufficiently strong to be feared.

"The unfortunate dethroned Belus, obliged to wander through various realms without being able to obtain any help, or even to dare to appear except under false name, finally terminated his sad destiny by a forced death. He commended his daughter, the Princess, to those of his faithful subjects who had accompanied him and who had never abandoned his party, preferring to sacrifice their grandeur and their fortune than to fail in their duty to their sovereign. They swore to the dying Prince to employ their zeal, their courage and their very lives in the service of the Princess, and to do everything possible to restore her to the throne.

"The unfortunate Marsine, reduced like her father the King to the sad necessity of hiding the majesty of the rank in which Heaven had caused her to be born, was thus forced to descend therefrom in order to drag out an obscure life in the world, subject to a thousand upheavals because of the intrigues of the tyrant, who took indignity so far as to put a price on the Princess' head.

"The resentment that Marsine conserved with so much justice, and the horror of the treasons that Tracius never ceased to exercise against her, had led her to adopt the disguise under which you have known her; it was in that costume and under a borrowed name that she distinguished herself in several battles, which acquired her a good deal of glory, while her faithful officers, dispersed in various provinces and States, tried by means of their friends to foment an uprising in favor of their sovereign, of which she might take advantage. Several were already ranged on the side of the Princess; they were only waiting for a favorable opportunity to allow their zeal and their submission to burst forth, when a countermove by a few traitors ruined al their plans; some were arrested and immediately executed; others more fortunate, took flight and Marsine did not know what had become of them.

"What completes the misfortunes of the Princess today, however, is that she has been unable to see Prince Aricdef without being touched by all the eminent qualities that shine from his person and all his actions. Although concern for her vengeance and her glory has never abandoned her, she has nevertheless admitted to me that she had only entered Aricdef's camp with a view to being noticed by him. Several occasions have arisen, when she might have been able to reveal herself without risk, if the dread of making known the sentiments that animate her in the Prince's favor had not retained her; but an unexpected event that caused today's disturbance and has augmented her despair forces her to retain forever a secret that was ready to escape her.

"A few months ago, Prince Aricdef was told that an envoy from Tracius was requesting a private audience. Marsine, who was engaged by more than one motive to inform herself carefully of the subject of that commission, learned from the Prince's squire that the Tyrant Tracius had offered his daughter the Princess to his master with the assurance of associating him with the crown, provided that he would immediately abandon the Marsian party and join his army to fight the Salians and the Ancides, with whom he had broken the treaties of alliance that he had contracted.

"The Tyrant judged the sentiments of the Prince by his own, not doubting that such a magnificent proposal would dazzle Aricdef and draw him into his party; but the Prince always unshakable in his duty, far from lending his ear to a treaty that could only be accomplished by a treason, could not help showing Tracius' envoy all the scorn and indignation that such a proposition excited in his soul; he sent him away, adding that if he ever had the audacity to show himself in his camp again, he would have him impaled.

"Marsine, who was entirely unaware of Aricdef's response, was in despair at the tyrant's plans; she feared that a general peace might contribute to their execution; her chagrin caused her to fall into a languor that soon damaged her health, and, her mind agitated by so many woes that had inflamed her blood, that is doubtless what brought on the malady from which she has just suffered.

"Although I still regarded her then as a simple officer, it was sufficient that she was your friend for me to take an interest in her fate. I begged Zachiel to visit her. The genius knew the subject of her woes immediately; he prepared for the soothing of her mind by making me the confidence. He revealed her sex to me, told me a part of what I've just told you, and advised me to see her frequently in order to try to reduce the bitterness of her troubles. I lent myself to that task with extreme care, and by that kindness, guided by Zachiel's advice, I acquired her full confidence, and was unable at the same time to refuse her mine.

"Alas, my dear Seaton," Monime continued, "when you came to surprise us it was at one of those frequent moments when reason buckles under the weight of her woes; the unfortunate Marsine, in a flood of the heart in which the soul is laid bare, appeared to be beside herself. As troubled as she was by the bitterness of her dolor, I employed all that amity could to do moderate its excess, convinced that a communication of hearts imprints on sadness something soft and touching that is the only thing capable of calming the greatest troubles.

"That, my dear Lord, is a succinct account of the disgraces of a Princess who merits, by her virtues, her talents and the grandeur of her soul, a more fortunate fate. Her beauty, although somewhat faded by her troubles, will resume all its brilliance when Zachiel has carried out his promises. I don't know what his views are for the happiness of the Princess, but he has assured her that her destiny will soon change. Marsine has for the genius all the deference that is due to him, but she is not informed of his quality; convinced that I owe my birth to Zachiel, as he has never assumed any other title, I often see her embarrassed as to those she seeks to give him. You have just been witness to the air of authority that the genius employed to engage her to quit her disguise. I know that her design was to go to the camp and do everything to try to distinguish herself in the case that there was a battle, or to conclude her sad destiny."

Penetrated by the misfortunes of the Princess, I went into her dressing room with Monime in order to offer her all the services in my dependency. We found her in her armchair, her head supported by one of her hands, plunged into a somber reverie; she looked up at us with languid eyes.

"I shall see you go with regret, Milord; alas, you are going to acquire glory while I am force to remain buried beneath the weight of my troubles."

"It is necessary, my Lady, "I said to her, "for you to make full use of the courage that has not abandoned you thus far. The grandeur of your soul ought to put you above the injustices of blind fortune. You have often honored me with your confidence; I leave you with a different self, who, penetrated by your woes, will employ all his care to help to support them. I also dare to combine my pleas with those of Monime, in order to determine you to follow Zachiel's advice. If his talents were known to you, I am convinced that you would have no difficulty in choosing him for the guide of all your actions."

The Princess, who was animated by a desire for glory and for vengeance, and perhaps even that of her love, seemed absorbed by her reflections; she did not think of making any response to me. Marsine was not unaware that a battle was about to be fought against the Bellonians; the hope of encountering Tracius, the author of all her woes, the advantage of fighting him, and the hope of defeating him, above all, were animated by despair. To those reasons was doubtless joined a keener sentiment: amour, the tyrant that respects neither scepters nor grandeurs, had also come to tyrannize her heart, in the hope of making herself known to Prince Aricdef by some striking action. All those thoughts were agitating the Princess when Zachiel came in, and, perceiving her trouble, hasted to extracted her from it.

"Moderate your anxieties, my Lady," said the genius, causing a divine fire to shine in his eyes. "Hide, if that is possible, the agitation of your soul. You know what I have promised you; rely on my word and my attachment until the complete accomplishment of your desires; the knowledge that I have of astronomy enables me to see distinctly that your troubles are about to come to an end, but if you are obstinate in wanting to risk yourself in combat, that same science predicts an inevitable death therein for you."

Such positive words produced all the effect that the genius had expected on the mind of the Princess. "I shall no longer resist following your advice," Marsine replied, "and will regard you henceforth as my father. My happiness and my glory are in our hands; I confide them to your wisdom and your experience. I only implore you to believe that everything I have attempted until now has merely been an enthusiasm caused by the ardor to die; I envisaged that as the sole means of delivering myself from a life that was a burden to me. What do I not owe to cares that are snatching me from a death to which despair was about to deliver ne! Fortunately, your discourse has imported gleams of enlightenment into my soul that have made me recognize that the benefits I receive from you are effective; I can only mark my recognition by an entire deference to your advice."

Zachiel told us then that Tracius' envoy, on returning to his court, had informed him of Prince Aricdef's response, painting in the blackest colors the scorn that he had showed for his alliance. That speech had thrown the tyrant into a fury; shame, honor, anger and despair had excited contradictory movements in his soul that almost caused him to lose control of himself. Fury got the upper hand and the barbaric tyrant, like those men who, for want to heroic virtues, have impetuous vices, abandoned himself entirely to all the sentiments that range cold inspire in him, in order to excite his troops to punish a proud individual who had resisted his power.

That news hastened my departure; it was necessary to tear myself away from Monime. The presence of the genius obliged me to constrain my dolor, but an expression of sadness spread over my face. My confused and inconsequential speech revealed more clearly what was passing in my heart than the most forceful eloquence could have done. Monime, whose trouble equaled mine, in spite of the efforts she made to try to hide it from me, could not help telling me, softening considerably, that she would renew her prayers to Heaven to augment my glory and conserve my days, to which her own were attached.

Without permitting me to respond, Zachiel drew me away to give me further instructions. "You're going to find yourself," the genius added, "in one of the most glorious occasions of your life. Never allow yourself to be frightened by the peril; let composure and prudence accompany all our actions. Above all, my dear Seaton, try not to be separated from Aricdef, and fight by his side; follow his orders; let false glory not prevent you from asking things you do not know; remember that the general is invested with all the power and authority of the Emperor, and that the authority in question is communicated like the sun's rays—which, immense and infinite as they are, do not diminish by their emanation the brightness of the star, the source of light. I shall not retain you any longer; go, my dear Seaton; victory will follow in your footsteps."

Chapter VI
Description of a Battle

I arrived at the camp at the moment when Prince Aricdef had just given the order to depart. The general had received certain news that the Bellonians were advancing with the design of fighting, that the conjunction of their army with the Salians would give them a numerical advantage, and that they had already taken possession of an advantageous terrain, which was a plain between two mountains, closed at the rear by a large wood, but spacious enough to contain an army in battle order. To that effect they had arranged all their troops in two lines; the first was backed up against the wood in order to prevent any attack from the rear; they also believed their right to be assured by a castle and the city whose masters they were; their left was closed by a chain of steep mountains that extended a long way. In addition to that, they had in front of them at the foot of the mountain a wide river and a substantial stream, which enclosed them on that side of the plain.

It was before that plain that the Prince led us, after several days of forced march. Aricdef began to reconnoiter the situation of the locale and the disposition of the enemy, which he could not attack from the right, because of the steep mountains, nor from the left, defended by the city and the castle. The only means of approach he could see was a defile alongside the city, which could scarcely contain four men abreast and was overlooked by the castle, so that one could only pass through it by taking control of the castle and the outskirts of the city, whose avenues were filled with market gardens, hedges, vines and little steams, which formed a marshy terrain in which foot soldiers would have great difficulty marching. All those locations were occupied by the Bellonians, who had stationed infantry there.

It was therefore necessary to expel that infantry, and pass over the stream and the river, which was deep, to reach the defile, at the far end of which it would be necessary to do battle on a very narrow terrain that was always rising, in which one could only deploy a front of six or even squadrons. It is true that the terrain broadened out after a certain distance, but also that the troops would then be within musket-range of the enemy. How could one have the audacity to form lines so close to a camp whose troops were still fresh, rested, and recently emerged from good winter quarters, while ours were extremely fatigued by a long march, without any rest and without carriages? Their cavalry was armored in metal; ours did not even have leather armor. Finally, from whatever direction one approached their army, it is certain that it not only had the advantage over ours of situation, but also that of numbers.

All these difficulties, far from stopping the Prince, only animated his courage. None of those advantages escaped his penetration; he envisaged them all, and also the dangers to which his troops would be exposed if they did not engage in battle before the conjunction of the enemy armies. The desire he had to signal himself in the campaign by a striking action determined him to fight, in spite of all the obstacles that seemed to deter him from doing so.

Such a bold resolution astonished all the officers, but the soldiers, accustomed to victory under the Prince, applauded the decision with cries of joy that were then regarded as a good augury; all of them zealously entrusted their destiny to the prudence, valor and great talents of their commander.

It was, therefore, that course that our general adopted. He arranged his troops in such a way as to provide mutual support, after having obtained an exact knowledge of the terrain. He was able to profit from his advantages, and the defects of the enemy, and to avoid traps with all possible activity.

Already he has taken possession of the heights overlooking the city and the castle, examined at the surrounding terrain, counted all the enemy's resources and discovered the points favorable for an attack. The night is destined to expel them from their positions, and the silence of that frightful night is troubled by the continual discharges of all our artillery.

It seems that the gods favor our designs; the sky is covered with clouds, lightning flashes mingle with the continual rapid fire of our batteries, and the noise of the cannons, combined with the increased outbursts of thunder, make the rocks resound; the ramparts crumble, and all the objects united in the obscurity of a dark night form a scene of horror and terror. The astonished enemy is forced to fall back to the torrent, felling after having surrendered all their riches to the flames.

Those unfortunates hastened to rejoin the bulk of their army. The vigor of the action spread alarm and fear in the Bellonian camp. We then attacked the castle overlooking the defile by mans of which we could reach the enemy army. When we had rendered ourselves masters of it, we dislodged them from all the heights, and the Prince passed his entire army, without any obstacle, into the terrain we had just gained, in order to take up battle order.

That terrain, closed on both sides by long hedges that extended all the way to the enemy camp, was guarded by our dragoons. The Prince had them advance to the left and the right of the infantry, which he placed in various locations, either in corps or detachments, in accordance with the disposition of the terrain, in order to cover the cavalry when it arrived, or to support it if the enemy charged. Those dispositions made, he had the cavalry units advance as they arrived, to arrange them in battle order. The restricted extent of the terrain forced us, initially, only to form very short lines.

The Prince then gave orders to the lieutenant generals who were each to command a position and placed himself in the center of the army, at the head of which he had placed his cannons. The Prince ordered that, above all, the cavalry should endure the initial enemy fire, and only charge with sabers in hand.

The Bellonians, who could see all our movements, came to fall upon us with all the advantage that the slope of the terrain gave them, and their infernal blades, quivering with rage, struck our soldiers, driving our first line back to the second. Confusion was already beginning to set in when Aricdef advanced his battalions, pikes lowered, to arrest the impetuosity of the enemies who were making every effort to make inroads into our lines; but those who were posted behind the hedge launched such furious discharges at them that they were unable to withstand the fire; they began to buckle in their turn, gradually retreating. We attacked them on the heights and gained enough terrain by the first impact to give a new form to our army.

Aricdef then placed his cavalry in the center, put four heavy battalions on the wings and platoons of infantry between the squadrons to support the cavalry when they came to blows. He placed his artillery at the head, made a third line, and ordered the other two to be extended.

Scarcely had our canons begun to fire than the Bellonians came back a second time, with the elite of their troops, folding us up and causing gaps to appear between several squadrons, which sowed enough disorder among our troops to cause fear for the outcome of the day, but the Prince had positioned his infantry so well that it found itself able everywhere to repair the disadvantage of the cavalry, with the result that our squadrons rallied. Aricdef set himself at their head, followed by his senior officers, who charged the enemy, swords in hand, with so much force and vigor that they folded up in their turn; that gave us the advantage again for the final action, which lasted until the end of the day, during which the Prince contented himself with going back and forth through the ranks encouraging the troops with words and gestures, animating them considerably by his example. The Prince was everywhere, not sparing himself any more than the least of his soldiers; he gave his orders with as much tranquility and composure as if he had been in his tent.

The Bellonians, dazzled by a phantom, followed the frightful death that covered their entire camp with funereal wings. At daybreak they offered us a combat far bloodier than the one the day before. Standards and flags were captured and recaptured on both sides. Our generals and other officers showed an equal courage in their conduct in the various encounters that took place.

The wind, which was then blowing impetuously, combined with the movements of the troops, raised such great amounts of dust that it was almost impossible to see, and the confusion almost inevitable in those circumstances contributed to the carnage. The battle was so furious that there were skirmishes everywhere. The fury unleashed became general; unusual clamors were heard; the noisy clash of weapons raised a frightful discord, and the scintillating wheels of the Bellonian chariots howled in their terrible impact. A multitude of flaming arrows was seen whistling frightfully through the air, covering the two armies with flames; and the noise of the cannons, similar to that of thunder rumbling in the clouds, added its threat to those who heard it at close range.

Meanwhile, our troops, animated by the presence of Aricdef, all knew when it was necessary to advance, to hold firm, to switch to the attack, to open or close their files; no one thought of flight or retreat; no action was marked with fear; everyone employed himself as if his arm were capable of deciding the outcome of the victory, In sum, everyone believed that they could see before them the death of their enemies getting closer.

That battle occupied an immense field; the face of the army was constantly changing, and fortunes still appeared equal, when Tracius, blinded by the fury and resentment that he conserved at the scorn Aricdef had shown for his alliance, advanced with the audacity that pride and presumption give; he was already envisaging the Prince as chained to his chariot.

"Tremble, perfidious one," said the tyrant, "at the horrors of this deadly war, which it only depended on you to end by advantageous propositions; these cruelties will only fall upon you and your accomplices; I shall send you fleeing to Hell to signal your furies there."

"Do not expect," Aricdef replied, "to intimidate by your bravado a man who is sufficiently scornful of you not to fear your blows. Have you put to flight the least of my soldiers? Do you think you can vanquish me any more easily, or do you have enough audacity to imagine that you can make me tremble? The justice that has put weapons in my hand is sustained by honor; such are my motives. Would you like to end this war by a single combat? Let us make use of our courage; it is for the god of battles to decide our fate."

They put an end to their discourse and, advancing toward one another with an equal ardor, they commenced a furious combat; they were seen to turn with equal rapidity, and their flamboyant swords traced horrible spheres of fire in the air.

That great spectacle suspended everything; the two armies, gripped by horror, fell back to either side to await the decision of that combat; their vigor, their skill and their agility seemed the same; but Aricdef had received from the hands of Mars a sword of such perfect temper that nothing could resist its trenchant blade; he broke his adversary's scimitar, and the second thrust inflicted a deep wound in his side. Tracius' buckler then became useless to him; he folded up and recoiled, tottering, and finally fell to the ground on his knees.

At that sight, the Bellonians, as if thunderstruck, shivered with rage and despair at the humiliating condition of their King. His bravest warriors ran to his aid, putting their bucklers over him and carried him to his tent, bewailing their misfortune. In fact, what a baleful augury for them, but what a triumph for us! Our soldiers uttered cries of joy that were simultaneously the signal for combat and the presage of victory.

The Bellonians, wanting to avenge the death of their King, did not remain inactive; their frightful cries were followed by a new attack. That last combat represented the image of Hell; iron and flames were glinting on all sides; they all fought, wounded and bloody, like ferocious beasts irritated by the sight of blood, unaffected by the fear of death. The cries of joy of victors were heard drowning out the plaints of the wounded and the moans of the dying.

We finally drove them back with so much vigor that they were entirely defeated, the majority hacked into pieces. A small number escaped by courtesy of the dust that hid their retreat from us.

Masters of the battlefield and their camp, which they were obliged to abandon, their artillery, their munitions and all their equipment were the prizes of victory. The soldiers made a considerably booty of them, which compensated them for the fatigue they had endured by a march of four days and four nights without having time to rest, followed by a battle whose second day lasted from six o'clock in the morning to five o'clock in the afternoon.

Prince Aricdef, without stopping, pursued his conquests with so much rapidity that he obtained the submission in very little time of all the cities that had allied themselves with the Bellonians, and those which had favored their passage through their realms. After having punished the chiefs for their rebellion, he no longer thought about anything but going to fight the Salians and the Arcians, whose army, he had learned was advancing rapidly to join that of the Bellonians, apparently unaware of their total defeat.

Aricdef caused his troops to retrace their steps, and in order to give them time to rest he took possession of an advantageous position, and distributed his army in various places from which it was easy to rally them, in order to attract the enemy into devastated terrains, to close the passages and be in a position to capture all the convoys coming after them. Those regions, inundated with blood by the ravages of the war, offered a frightful spectacle everywhere of the barbarity of Tracius. It was impossible for that multitude of poorly-hardened troops to resist an army of conquerors for long.

The Salians fell into the trap that Aricdef had set for them, and found themselves surrounded in spite of the number of their troops. The general of the Arcians, who perceived the mistake he had made, harangued his soldiers. He was eloquent, knew his men, and was able to exploit their weakness and master them, first appealing to their appetites studying them skillfully and adjusting himself artfully to the various movements that he observed passing through their souls.

The general was so well able to take advantage of his enlightenment that he made his troops see that the Salians had only been defeated by their own fault and the ignorance of their captains, who had not been able to make use of their numerical advantage or their strength. He gave reasons so manifest and so plausible for his sentiment that the officers and the soldiers were convinced; he invited them in consequence to make offers of peace.

"What augury," he went on, "ought we to take for the success of our forces and our courage, when the bravest of our allies have just been vanquished and reduced shamefully to flight? Are we, by our obstinacy, going to reignite the anger of the victors in the uncertainty of success? We have allowed ourselves to be seduced by the pernicious advice of Tracius, who has drawn us by means of the sights of ambition; we ought to have reflected further before taking up arms against such a dangerous enemy, but we delivered ourselves blindly to the impulses of our courage. You're not unaware that exile, ignominy and slavery are the inevitable woes of the vanquished. It is necessary to yield to fickle fortune and sue for piece; everything invites me to counsel peace, with regard to the condition to which you are reduced."

Scarcely had the general finished his speech than everyone applauded his advice. He was regarded as the pillar of the fatherland. Every soldier handed in his weapons, helmet, buckler and spear, in order to form a kind of trophy in his honor. One of the senior officers was delegated, with full powers to grant all the articles that Aricdef cared to demand.

The Prince received him as a generous victor, and although he was in a position to lay down the law, he accorded them reasonable conditions, and the peace was agreed at the foot of the mountain where the bloody battle had been waged against the tyrant Tracius.

The campaign ended with that peace; Prince Aricdef disbanded his troops and returned to the court, where I was constrained to follow him. After having received the honors of his triumph, the general introduced me to the King, and had the generosity to make my eulogy. The monarch heaped us with praise, and to conserve the memory of such a great success, he had a statue of Fortune erected facing his palace, holding a horn of plenty in one hand and a tiller in the other, at the top of which is a mural crown with these words around it:

The fortune of return brings us abundance.

Chapter VII
The Sequel to the Story of Princess Marsine

Hardly sensible of the praise I received from all the courtiers, I got ready to leave to return to Zachiel and Monime, from whom I flattered myself that I would receive the most sincere welcome. Marsine ought to have shared my concerns too, but I could not think about that Princess without feeling the most ardent desire to be of service to her being reborn within me. My urgency yielding to that desire, I did not want to quit Prince Aricdef without tell him the story of the woes suffered by the unfortunate Marsine, and to interest him more keenly in her favor I began by reminding him of the misfortunes of her father, the King.

"I'm not unaware," I added, "that the tyrant Tracius offered to share the empire he had usurped from Belus with you, by marrying you to his daughter, but the grandeur of your soul, your incorruptible probity and love for justice caused you to scorn propositions that could only be accomplished by unjust means. Permit me to dare to tell you, my Lord, that Fortune sometimes presents opportunities to us from which one can profit; such opportunities, far from tarnishing the glory of an illustrious conqueror, are only offered to make it shine with its full brilliance. You know all the treasons that the tyrant employed to render himself master of the realm of Bellonia, which belongs by right to Princess Marsine by virtue of the death of her father, the King."

"What are you trying to insinuate by this discourse?" said Aricdef, interrupting me. "I would have liked to be able to be useful to that unfortunate Princess, but since the flight of her father the King I have never heard mention of her; doubtless her misfortunes have precipitated her into her father's tomb."

"No, my Lord," I said. "She is still full of life; a disguise has hidden her for a long time from the unjust Bellonians; she is even known to you; her rare qualities cannot have escaped your eyes, since she has served in your army with the same employment that you have been kind enough to accord to me. Marsine and the Chevalier Meilly are one and the same person; you know what a reputation she acquired under that name."

"Gods, what am I hearing?" cried the Prince, extremely surprised. "Have I, then, been able to mistake for such a long time the heir to the throne of Bellonia? It is true that a secret penchant always led me to distinguish her from the other officers; I admired above all the candor, the verity, the generosity and the courage that are inseparable from great souls—but go on, and tell me what prevented her from joining the general action."

I then told the Prince about Marsine's illness, occasioned by the consequence of her chagrins, which I recounted to him in detail, combining them with the reasons that had engaged her to adopt that disguise, in order to evade the cruel tyrannies of Tracius.

"Why," said the Prince, "did she refuse to honor me with her confidence? Speak, my dear Lord; I implore you, in the name of our friendship, to tell me in what fashion I could have attracted her hatred—for what other reason could have prevented her from revealing to me the secret she confided to you? I know that you merit it, but in what way am I unworthy of it?"

"Oh, my Lord, how far away the Princess is from such an unjust way of thinking! It is true, my Lord, that Marsine permitted me to be informed of all her secrets. There is another that your generosity doubtless ought to have extracted from me, but permit...."

"I permit nothing," said the Prince. "Once again, speak, my dear Lord. I wish it; I demand it, not as a Prince but as a friend."

"It's too much," I aid. "I cannot resist that excess of bounty." Then I revealed to the Prince the tender sentiments that the Princess had conceived for his rare virtues, the renown of which was incessantly published throughout the world. Nor did I believe that I ought to hide from him the combats that had taken place in her soul between the desire to declare herself, the dread of saying too much, and that of a peace that might ruin all her hopes.

"I was unable to see that unfortunate Princess," I added, "without being touched. An impression of languor and abasement, extinguishing the vivacity of hr physiognomy, renders her more interesting; her eyes, tarnished by dolor, like rays of sunlight filtering through the clouds, launch, like them, the most piquant gleams; her humility still has the graces of modesty; one cannot see her without feeling compassion for her, or listen to her without admiration."

I had the good fortune, by my story, of inspiring Prince Aricdef with an ardent desire to see the Princess and offer her all the services within his dependency. The Prince went to take his leave of the King. That monarch, who loved him dearly, surprised by such a precipitate departure, wanted to know the reasons that obliged him to leave the court so soon.

Aricdef, who had been expecting the question, did not hesitate to satisfy the king. He told him all the details of the misfortunes that had afflicted Princess Marsine in the course of her life; then he begged the king by all the arguments he thought most capable of touching him to accord his protection to the illustrious unfortunate, who could not be abandoned without injustice.

The monarch, surprised that the Princess had been able to resist so many troubles, not only granted him what he desired but obligingly added that he could not give better recognition to the services that he had just tendered the State than by employing all his power and the most convincing reasons to determine Princess Marsine to share her crown with a Prince who would sustain its majesty with as much justice, prudence and glory as he had acquired by his courage and his talents in all his campaigns.

A grace accorded with such flattering eulogies on the part of a King full of justice and bounty, whose merit alone had a right to claim all favors, filled the heart of Aricdef with joy; his gratitude was manifest by assurances of a respectful attachment and an entire submission to His Majesty's orders. The King instructed him to assemble his troops and depart immediately, in order not to give Tracius time to form new intrigues in Bellonia.

After Prince Aricdef had taken his leave of the King, animated by a new desire for glory, and perhaps that of a nascent amour, the prince easily recalled the features and majesty of bearing of the false chevalier; he already sensed the seed of a passion attracting him toward her, which he would conserve until death. The lure of a crown that was almost on offer also had attractions for a heart made to reign.

His orders having been given to his officers to gather the troops, we got ready to leave. I dispatched a courier to the Princess to announce the Prince's visit and the grand designs that he had formed to reestablish her on her throne; but we proceeded with such great diligence that we arrived in advance of the courier by an hour.

As much for the sake of decency as amity, Marsine had continued to share Monime's apartment. The two charming individuals were together when we arrived; I introduced them to the Prince. Marsine seemed a little troubled at first, but Monime caused joy to shine in her eyes, and the Prince, surprised by their striking beauty, was rendered momentarily speechless.

Pulling themselves together, however, the two of them had a long conversation together, in which the Princess displayed the nobility of her sentiments, the grandeur of her soul, the extent of her intelligence and the courage that she had show in so many adversities. Aricdef, already prejudiced in Marsine's favor, conceived in that first conservation as much amorous sentiment as she desired to inspire in him.

While the Prince and the Princess were so agreeably occupied I retired with Monime to the embrasure of a window in order to be able to talk more freely. We said everything tender to one another that amity can inspire in two truly fond hearts that have not seen one another for some time. Monime expressed herself with the energy that characterizes the sentiment of a noble soul. She told me about all the care that Zachiel had taken to ensure Marsine's happiness.

The genius had made several journeys with the design of disposing the Bellonians to receive their legitimate sovereign, and in consequence of his moves those subjects who had remained faithful to the Princess and had been obliged to wander hither and yon in various realms had been reassembling when they learned of the death of the tyrant Tracius, which was followed by the defeat of his entire army. Their zeal enabled them to seek out all those whom fear, or perhaps interest, had caused to support the tyrant; the banished their fears, reanimated their zeal and their fidelity, so successfully that in very little time they were able to form a considerable body of troops.

Zachiel came in, and brought my joy to a peak by his presence; he received me with the love and cordiality of a father who cherishes his son. After certain conventional politenesses due to the noble, he confirmed to the Prince everything that Monime had just told me. That news reanimated the hopes of the Princess. It was decided to set out the very next day to join up with those troops and stimulate them by the presence of their sovereign.

Monime wanted to accompany the Princess; Zachiel, far from opposing it, seemed charmed by her resolution. He had no doubt that Marsine's example would serve to dissipate all fears.

Prince Aricdef, at the head of an army of thirty thousand battle-hardened—and even better, victorious—troops, soon joined the supporters of the Princess. Once the conjunction of the troops had been made, they entered Bellonia, but the Princess, who wanted to spare the blood of her subjects, sent a herald to announce her return and published a general amnesty in favor of all those who wanted to return to their duty and rally to the standards of their sovereign. That mark of clemency swelled her army considerably.

However, Princess Faustine, the daughter of Tracius, who had just been crowned, had a strong party; her generals employed all the forces of the realm to maintain her on the throne, but Aricdef took away all their means of taking him by surprise and obtained information about all their moves. The Prince distributed men in Faustine's camp, her court, her Council and everywhere else who observed, discovering her views, her designs and her projects, and then informed Aricdef. In spite of the rigors of the season the Prince advanced into the country, withstood several attacks, subjugated cities and pursued the rebels. The surprised Bellonians, confused by his audacity, fled precipitately, conceding him victory everywhere, and were finally constrained to surrender and ask for a pardon that they had no difficulty obtaining.

After having reconquered her realm, Princess Marsine received a magnificent embassy on behalf of the Emperor of the Marsians. The ambassador had orders to congratulate her on her fortunate accession, to assure her of his friendship, and to negotiate a treaty of perpetual alliance, the principle article of which was to accept Prince Aricdef as a husband.

Marsine gave the ambassador the most pompous reception and with the approval of all the nobles of the court she replied that she was delighted that the Emperor's wishes accorded so well with her own; that she could not better recognize the protection he had accorded her and the services that Prince Aricdef had rendered her than by sharing with his a crown that he had already acquired by his intrepid valor, his rare virtue and his talents, so worthy of reigning; that in addition, the prince having the honor of belonging to him by blood, she would always glory in the alliance that gave her the right henceforth to regard the Emperor as a father attentive to the happiness of his children. She added, with infinite grace, that she begged him to assure the Emperor that, in spite of all the advantages she found in the union, interest had less part in it than the choice of her heart. The Prince, a witness to that conversation, felt penetrated with the keenest gratitude; love and joy gleamed in his eyes.

The Queen did not want to send the ambassador away until he had witnessed her marriage to the Prince. The ceremony took place with a pomp and magnificence worthy of the two spouses. It was learned a few days later that Princess Faustine, in despair at her fall, had shut herself away in the temple of Pallas, in order to devote the rest of her days to the worship of the goddess. Finally, the amiable peace so long desired closed the temple of Janus, reestablished confidence, and banished envy and jealousy. Commerce acquired new energy, talents and the arts were reborn, the dismissed troops were no longer occupied in anything but combining myrtle with their laurels, and no one as thinking about anything except enjoying the fruits of glorious labor.

Aricdef and Marsine, peaceful in their estates, are only concerned with rendering their subjects happy. The Prince, ever humane and very wise in his projects, is attentive to all the parts of the economy, all the objects of public administration and everything that might ensure or augment the power, the glory and the wellbeing of his subjects; he could be compared to a Proteus, taking on a thousand different forms. His life is a book that all the generals, even the great Princes, ought to study.

That conduct makes him adored by his people, who count his days by as many benefit. It can also be said that the Fates, attentive to their common happiness, have been glad to elongate the weave of his days, in order to give his subjects time to admire his virtues and allow them to germinate in their hearts.

Chapter VIII

We could not refuse the pleasure of waiting for the return of spring to Aricdef's court. The Queen, attached to Monime by the bonds of the most tender amity, wanted to ask her to take up residence with her, and made her several brilliant proposals on that subject for my establishment. The King joined forces with Marsine, and it would have been very difficult to resist their urgency without the eloquence of Zachiel, who made them sense the necessity of our continuing our voyages.

Although lodged in the royal palace, we were nevertheless obliged to go through several courtyards and a prodigious number of apartments to arrive at the Prince's study. Those apartments were always full of people who had come to solicit pensions, a government post, or the guard of a fort; some were from companies, and a large number requested little gold plaques representing the face of the god Mars surrounded by glory; that plaque as a mark establishing their courage, which ennobled them and made them respected by soldiers and the people. That procession of petitioners formed a crowd that it was difficult to penetrate.

Others—old officers no longer fit for service, purveyors of news—assembled, cheerful or taciturn in spite of the rigors of the season, in platoons in the palace gardens; there, without fear of the north wind, they warmed themselves by regulating the State, arguing about the judgments that each one brought to all affairs. The extent of their sight pierced the cabinets of princes and seemed able to discover the most impenetrable secrets there.

Curious to hear them arguing, I went into the garden one day. I accosted an old military man, who seemed to me to be full of common sense. After a few turns around the path I asked him what the laws of the Bellonians were.

"Our laws," said the officer, "go back to before the war. Our legislators had no goal in mind but victory; that it why they recommend us always to keep our citizens occupied with military exercises, without permitting them to devote themselves to any other profession, except for those who had grown old in the métier of arms and whom the feebleness of age or the wounds they had received rendered them incapable of serving. So, when we were at peace, they had to study with the same diligence all the means of making war advantageously, by carrying out without delay all the orders of their commander—for troops are a body of which the general is the head; it is necessary that he animates his efforts, since their destinies are committed to his prudence and skill, which remain awake while they sleep. The safety of his soldiers depends on him alone. He has to establish good discipline and oppose cruelties. Any general who suffers carnage, who pillages, ravages and permits excess, even if he conquers half the world, is seen as nothing but a tyrant and a bloodthirsty tiger by the voice of people, united against him, forgetful of all his exploits."

"With such extensive knowledge of the military arts, sir, you merit a command."

"Those principles," he went on, "were never to the taste of Tracius; too full of pride, he didn't take advice from anyone; that was what led to his downfall."

"The King who governs you now has always followed those maxims exactly; he renders justice to merit, and only accords military honors to those who have distinguished themselves by striking actions, without regard to birth."

"I know," said the officer, "But I'm too old now to bother paying court to him. I yield to the young courtiers the precious advantage of meriting his benefits."

During our sojourn at the court we were regaled with several lavish feasts, in which Monime made her graces shine and captivated more than one heart. Occupied the rest of the time in paying our court, receiving visits or rendering them, it is certain that we did not have time to get bored.

In the number of Monime's suitors I remarked one who appeared to me to be more assiduous then the rest; he was a young colonel, very full of himself, who turned his eyes and mouth methodically, always equipped with little items of news and gossip, which he recited in terms typical of individuals of his species. We could not take a step without encountering him; I believe that he had the gift of multiplying himself.

One day he came to the house of a woman who had invited us to supper; after he had reeled off a tissue of nonsense devoid of common sense he got up to leave. "What," said the mistress of the house, "you're not saying for supper?"

"No," he said, "I have to go and see the marshal, who, as you know, honors me with his esteem. In truth, I'm in despair at not being able to take advantage for longer of such radiant company, but visits exhaust me; they petrify me, although no one renders or receives more of them than me; my secretary can't keep up with them and my horses, which I force to be martyrs to fashion and good taste, are dead on their feet, as is my runner."

"What do you think of that amiable cavalier," Monime asked, maliciously, of a woman who had never ceased applauding all his stupidities.

"He's charming," said the lady. "It's necessary to agree that he's an adorable man, full of wit, replete with graces, as amusing as possible, who sets off a tapestry nicely, matches porcelain astonishingly, has an exquisite taste in ornaments and is always radiant in his costume, his furniture and his carriages; in sum, he's divine."

"It's true," I said, "that those are rare and useful qualities in a military man."

I noticed that the occupations of almost all the young officers who inhabit the world of Mars resemble closely enough those that had just been offered for our admiration. Those occupations are analogous to their character. Their first concern on waking up is to think about their adornment. The morning goes by without their being able to determine what coat to put on; the choice of color embarrasses them. There are some that heighten pale complexions, others serve to diminish and soften the redness of those the previous days excesses in gabling, dining and other exercises. It is therefore necessary to consult one's mirror; one has difficulty making up one's mind. If one is spending the day with the beautiful Julie, whom the vapors cause to faint continually, one must necessarily put on something tender and serious, but is the amiable Dorine is encountered, one must also please her, and a sepulchral tone would amount to torture.

The valet, who does not understand any of this reasoning, is convinced that his master's irresolution is only caused by the embarrassment of choosing a coat that does not outshine the women to whom he intends to give preference today. He admires that expert delicacy in his master. Accustomed to speak his mind freely on much more serious matters, he extracts him from his anxiety. "Put on a blue coat, sir; that color goes equally well with a blonde and a brunette."

That oracle determines his decision; it is worth a part of his wardrobe to his domestic. The toilette continues; one gives orders to one's runner, whom one dispatches pitilessly to the four quarters of the city to pay compliments to women one quit at five o'clock in the morning and one is counting on seeing again in the evening. Meanwhile, one occupies oneself with one's purse, whose strings must be knotted in the latest fashion; but the wig, the arrangement of the curls, takes much longer than the coiffure of a woman who has a new net for her chignon.

When he has taken all possible trouble and care to decorate his face, all of the features of his visage being his own composition, the various attitudes of which that ought to render him more agreeable he has studied in mirrors, our young colonel believes himself to be more charming than Adonis. He departs like lightning in a magnificent carriage in order to have himself admired by several women, to each of whom he recites a epigram on all the others, relates an anecdote that he has just made up and which does not make sense; he mingles a few insipid compliments in the conversation, which he reels off with a distracted air, takes a hand, kisses it, while looking to see whether the kiss has made an impression, protests that he has never seen a woman as radiant, interrupts himself, sighs mechanically, bows and flies to the home of another in order to repeat the same comedy scene.

Monime's beauty attracted the homages of all the nobility. We were visited one day by one of those men that hazard has been pleased to elevate above their birth; his name was Doronte. His fortune had been established during the reign of the tyrant, who had raised him from a simple soldier to the highest dignities. Constrained to abandon them under the new regime, he nevertheless enjoyed certain honors and the immense wealth with which Tracius had heaped him. Full of pride and conceit, however, he was sovereignly scornful of people he had known in his mediocrity.

He had completely lost his reason, and was barely vegetating; his judgment gone astray, he recalled his initial condition dolorously; half of his life was, for him, a frightful torture that might cause him to die of vanity; in sum, he was seen to be succumbing under the weight of the pride that the post he had occupied had given him—but he was not the only one whom Fortune deprives of judgment by virtue her dangerous charms. There are few people strong enough to defend themselves from the traps that she sets for them.

Zachiel pointed out to us that experience shows us that in all times, the greatest of men have been subject, like the vulgar, to the fault of allowing their fortune to blind hem. They have justified what Hasdrubal said in the Senate when he established as a certain maxim that one very rarely sees judgment in company with good fortune. Those who have applied themselves most assiduously to knowing the human heart regard the union of wisdom and prosperity as something almost impossible. Self-esteem has too much influence over men not to persuade them very easily that they owe to their merit alone that which is often a pure effect of hazard. The greatest men are subject to the same faults. On examining ancient and modern history, one finds that the characters of those who have been favored by fortune almost always become more ill-natured as a result of the success they have had.

Alexander, on leaving Greece, was virtuous and humane; when he had defeated the Persians, he became debauched and cruel, had several of his captains put to death, ordered that Lisimacus be exposed to ferocious beasts,[20] killed his favorite Cleitus during a feast, and took the eunuch Bagoas, who belonged to Darius, in order to make him serve a shameful usage; in sum, the pride that inspired his good fortune rendered him sufficiently insensate to want to regard himself as a divinity.

Sulla only committed the cruelties that he exercised against his compatriots after having bee heaped by the favors of fortune in all the wars he had undertaken; the proscriptions with which he filled Rome and all of Italy were the consequences of his fortunate success.

"Several more examples could be cited," the genius continued, "but those ought to be sufficient to make you see that high birth does not always protect from the reefs those whom good fortune favors. A man elevated above others often believes that he in entitled to permit himself all kinds of excess; he forgets

---

[20] In the tragedy *Lisimacus* (1755) by David Augustin de Brueys, an entirely fictitious story. Cleitus and Bagoas, on the other hand, are both cited in Plutarch's *Life of Alexander*.

that his birth is an elevated rock, where he appears uncovered, where his designs and the motives that make him act are visible, and where the public, an impartial judge of his actions, pronounces sentence on him with impunity. The mask of virtue only deceives for a while; its penetration allows the depths of the heart to be read, and with a supreme air, the great are all condemned: dignities, wealth, honors, nothing stops censure; their glamour decries them; a false step dooms them; informed of all their deviations, they are published; their virtue are effaced and the brilliant aurora that seemed to presage fortunate days is soon eclipsed by bad politics. There are few princes who carry to the tomb the regrets of the nation, whose attachment they warranted at the beginning of their reign.

The term that Zachiel having accorded to the King and Queen having expired, we got ready to follow the genius to the fifth heaven. I shall not report the final conversation that we had in taking our leave of Their Majesties. That somewhat halting conservation made us know the dolor that they felt at our separation by the violence they put up in contesting our departure. Indifference and coldness find words easily, but sighs, tenderness and tears are the true language of amity. Monime could not employ any others, and the sensibility of her heart had more impression on those of the King and Queen than the most eloquent speech.

We left that realm more flourishing than anyone had ever seen it. The throne had never been filled by a King as wise in the art of reigning. Uniquely occupied with the aggrandizement of his realm, he did not lose sight of the desire to extend its domination; his affability and the facility with which he expressed himself won him the hearts of all those who approached him, and his liberality attached them to him without return. The proofs that he had given of his intrepidity in danger, and his unshakable firmness in difficulties attracted their full confidence. The Prince was inexhaustible in his resources; one can say that he most complicated designs were, for him, merely the play of an imagination that, as vast as it was fecund, procured him the means of executing them with as much rapidity as ease of projection.

The arts, children of repose and abundance, reappeared at the court of a Prince who had become, by his conquests, powerful enough to protect them. He loved letters, and knew their price, recompensing those who cultivated them and often applying himself to them personally.

Nicolas-Edmé Restif de la Bretonne: *Posthumous Correspondance* (excerpt)

Les Posthumes: Lettres reçues après la mort du mari par sa femme, qui le croit à Florence, par feu Cazotte *[The Posthumous: Letters received after the death of a husband by his wife, who believes him to be in Florence, by the late Cazotte] was originally published in Paris by Duchêne in 1802. Its actual author was baptized Nicolas-Edmé Rétif (1734-1806) but styled himself, with satirical pretentiousness when he began his career as a professional writer, "Restif de La Bretonne."*

Les Posthumes, *after a number of false starts, was never the project that Restif had envisaged, partly because it was too difficult and partly because external circumstances defeated it. In purely literary terms, the work is rambling, prolix, frequently self-contradictory, sometimes incoherent, and riddled with errors. But within it, still strikingly visible in spite of its fragmentation, is the ultimate version of Restif's speculative cosmogony, and the graphic literary illustration of some of the consequences and corollaries of that thesis. It is also the archetypal, and by far the most extreme, example of the modern genre of superhero fiction—which must qualify, today, as an asset, although it would not always have appeared so.*

The book changed direction and focus several times while Restif was writing it, probably for his own amusement and was written throughout 1787 and 1788. It is evident from the first few "letters from the tomb" that formed the first version of Les Posthumes *that Restif's initial intention was to focus narrowly on the relationship between the letter-writer, Monsieur de Fontlhète, and his beloved wife Hortense. At some point, however, the author apparently realized that his initially-intended scheme was too complicated and confusing to be viable as a project; and that his format, vaguely planned in the image of the* Thousand-and-One Nights, *might benefit from a much closer resemblance, in the sense that Fontlhète, instead of devoting himself to an overcomplicated analytical remembrance of things past and anticipation of the future, could become a storyteller instead.*

For that reason, therefore, Restif changed the direction of his self-indulgent whimsy, and began to develop the sequence of letters as a sequence of fantasies with the underlying subtext of trying to convince Hortense that death was not to be seen as a bad thing but rather an entrance into a wonderland of posthumous opportunity. Fontlhète does that by allegedly making contact with two discorporated souls who have remained closely united after death by virtue of the fact that they were accidentally slain on their wedding night. When that narrative sequence became too silly, Restif apparently had another change of heart, and abruptly, without bothering with any explanation, gave Fontlhète a pair of wings, thus enabling him to become a nocturnal vigilante. Then, the amazing Duke Multipliandre made his entrance into the scheme, taking up where Fontlhète left off, and began narrating his adventures, including visions of the future from the end of the eighteenth century until the death of the Earth, when it is swallowed by the Sun, .and dealings with "angels."

B.S.

Letter CCXI

F.m.T. 30 August.

Buffon has said that life has ceased on Mars. That is because he has not been there. Multipliandre doubted it strongly. But eventually, not seeing any animal, he did not really know what to think. He plunged a little way into the very humid atmosphere of the planet. He found that it was almost entirely covered, where it was not sea, by exceedingly muddy marshes, scarcely garnished with a few aquatic plants. It was there that he perceived an ugly amphibious animal with large eyes and a gaping maw. He was reluctant to enter the brain of the monster—which was doubtless not one for the planet—but he lodged there anyway.

He was scarcely any further advanced. He only found obtuse ideas there, no knowledge of other beings, and he was especially embarrassed in trying to move. It appeared that it was a species of Martian crocodile.

While the Terran man was in that perplexity, two sea-swallows—or, rather, two flying fish—which were pursuing one another, launched themselves almost as far as the crocodile, which had reared up slightly. The Terran man did not miss his chance; he threw himself on one of them, disanimated it, and substituted his own soul for its vital force. When that operation was complete he searched for a more perfect animal.

All of Mars is a single flat country, with the exception of a few mountains that are not very high, which form islands in the middle of the sea or the marshes. A multitude of hideous reptiles live in those marshes, which devour one another. The Terran, having reached a large island, dry by comparison with the marsh that surrounded it, searched there for the most advanced of its animals. He saw nothing resembling humankind, or that had a comparable intelligence.

Eventually, he perceived what he considered, in his sea-swallow-cum-fish body—which was obliged to plunge into the water from time to time in order to be able to fly—to be a kind of winged hippopotamus that was traveling underwater, and sometimes coming up for air with the aid of two enormous wings, like those of our water-fowl.

He quit the body of the diver to enter into that of the hippopotamus. He found a kind of reasoning there closely akin to our own. He also understood that by allowing the material memory to operate, he would find a language, mores and customs there, if the animal were the most advanced on the planet.

We shall see about that tomorrow.

Response to Letter CCXI

12 September.

So, in all the theological debates about the habitation or non-habitation of the planets, no one knew what they were talking about. For what assured our theologians that humans had been put on the other planets? It is astonishing what false thinkers and poor reasoners people are who see all of that as it is not, or who, for the pleasure of making an argument that they believe to be over-whelming, elect expressly to contradict what is said to them. It appears that Mul-tipliandre, in spite of yesterday's reasoning, will place beings that are different from one another on all the planets. He is not taking any risk; no one will be able to contradict him.

Letter CCXII

F.m.T. 31 August.

The language spoken on Mars is uniform, as that of Earth once was, very coarse and imperfect but nevertheless more extensive than that of the Rondins of the Moon. The creatures there have a head and limbs. The terrestrial philosopher sought an individual of the same species, other than the one he was inhabiting, in order to be able to converse...

He discovered one, but stouter, more hideous and much more ferocious. That animal, known on Mars as Nüsüsümü—pronouncing the *ü* as the French do, which is to say, like the Greek ypsilon, rolling it—threw itself upon him and said to him: "Mümüarümü"—which means, in Martian, "I want to possess you."

That was because the poor Duc had just taken over the body of a Nüsüsümü that pleased the hippopotamus more, and he was therefore possessed. He even felt all that a female Martian amphibian would have felt on such an im-portant occasion...

After this operation, which lasted rather a long time, the Nüsüsümü made his mistress, or his spouse, kiss his posterior, effected a few heavy capers and plunged into the marsh, where he disappeared. In order not to be exposed to these rather disagreeable assaults any longer, the terrestrial soul entered the body of a young male, very cheerful and playful, which appeared to be at the end of its adolescence.

He found then that the community of Nüsüsümü, of which he had the honor of being a member, labored on its aquatic habitations much as our beavers do. Their nourishment consisted of a fleshy herb like the thick and leafless plants of our hot countries; the bark of a tender cabbage-like tree; large citrus-like fruits that tasted like cooked apples, which came from soft palm-like trees; and almonds as big as pumpkins, borne by trees resembling walnuts, which made a whole meal for a female although it took three of them to satisfy a male. They also ate dried fish, sometimes living ones, commencing with the head, as we eat a piece of bread. The most delightful meal was serpent, or eel.

What the Earthman found most advantageous about these amphibians, which ruled the animal kingdom, was that no other species was stouter, stronger, more courageous or more voracious than them. They made all others tremble and flee.

Multipliandre saw animals of a thousand species; all of them were smaller than a female Nüsüsümü. As for the males, they were enormous in size; they went into the sea to seize the largest fish and serpents whose length exceeded six hundred feet. They broke them up as they are them, and every female that followed them got a twelve-foot section for her meal.

Response to Letter CCXII

13 September.

Oh, poor Multipliandre! He has played a funny role there, with that naughty hippopotamus—which is to say, quasi-hippopotamus. Filète is still laughing at it.

So everything on Mars is either fish or amphibian. Apparently, the scholars of our society say, that planet, which was originally fluid, like all the others, has not yet dried out sufficiently, and it is necessary for it to arrive at the location of the Earth in order to have dry monobies,[21] as the purely terrestrial animals are here. For they have explained to us very well, according to Euler, how all the planets, since their origin as comets, draw gradually closer to the Sun and replace one another, and how the nearest are eventually absorbed by the sun.

Letter CCXIII

F.m.T. 1 September.

The tranquility that the Nüsüsümü enjoyed seemed perfect to them. Undoubtedly it was the Golden Age of Mars. He saw other Nüsüsümü, which were

---

[21] This improvisation appears to have had no other existence at the time outside the present work.

called simply Nüsü, which were much smaller and were so disproportionate, although they resembled then as small dogs resemble big ones, that there could be no alliance between the two species, except accidentally at the two extremes. That sometimes happened, before the eyes of the Terran, but Multipliandre perceived that the little Nüsü were much less benevolent than the giants.

Alas, he said to himself, *that is the image of what has happened on the Earth. The Giants were good, and the little humans of my species have been very nasty. Mars is happy, whereas, when it encounters a comet that it incorporates or satellitizes, that will lead to the destruction of the large beings, which have perhaps been preceded by others even larger.*

"While I was making that reflection," Multipliandre told me, "I perceived a heavenly body that was drawing nearer and nearer. I saw that it was a comet almost as large as the Moon. I had no doubt then that Mars, which was more powerful, would have the honor of victory in the encounter, and that it would acquire a satellite.

"At that moment, however, I sensed the atmosphere becoming agitated, as if before a terrible storm; the waters of the seas became turbulent, and formed liquid mountains which collapsed thereafter by virtue of their own weight. They furrowed Mars in a frightening manner, and when they had all withdrawn, to go and ravage the hemisphere to which they were being attracted by the comet, the surface of Mars, almost uniform before—and, for that very reason, marshy—appeared to me to be so ravined and jagged that a corporate being, a monobie would not have been able to cover two leagues in succession.

"I went to the other hemisphere, and I saw the same ravages, which soon recommenced on the first. The planet was furrowed in every direction. That tempest lasted until the moment when the comet began to draw away by the force of its natural movement—but it found the attraction of Mars much more powerful..."

Until tomorrow, my beautiful love.

Response to Letter CCXIII

14 September.

I see, good husband, that you are going to give us the story of the acquisition of a satellites by a planet. So here you are, cast into high physics!

What I like, in your letter, is that, independently of the personal interest that they have for me, they are always amusing. I see that by the manner in which they are awaited by our society...by the joy of the lovable and naïve Filète, when the seal is broken. It appears, too, that you regard the huge Nüsüsümü as the equivalent of our giants, and that our species, ourselves, are on the Earth what the Nüsü are on Mars, wicked, like all weak beings. However, strong beings are wicked too, toward the weak. They crush them pitilessly, as if they were nothing—as witness humans with regard to flies, ants, etc.

Letter CCXIV

F.m.T. 2 September.

"The moment when Mars retained the comet by the force of its attraction was terrible. It pirouetted upon itself, as did its satellite, which removed a great deal of its humidity. That pirouetting occasioned a great singularity, which is that the Sun appeared, during several days, to rise as all the points of its circumference—which is to say, in the south, the west, the north and all the intermediary points: a phenomenon that once occurred on Earth, according to the report that the priests of Egypt gave Herodotus. Voltaire, in his *Philosophie de Newton*, says that Herodotus is mistaken, that it is impossible, unless it was two million years ago, for that to have happened to our globe in few days during the satellitization of our Moon. Before denying, though, it is necessary to look at everything...

"Finally, things settled down and resumed their ordinary progress. That does not mean that everything was as it had been before, but that everything was regulated. I cast my eyes over the new surface of Mars; there were profound valleys, steep mountains, and rocks with sheer peaks. All of that was not crystallized thus, any more than on the Earth, but tranquilly, in horizontal layers."

It was the subsidence of the waters raised by a satellitized, or not-yet-satellitized, comet that had furrowed our globe, just as Multipliandre saw that of Mars furrowed, so to speak. Here, a volcano erupted; further away, a mountain fell into a valley.

Multipliandre observed the poor giant Nüsüsümü for a while. They were languishing, or had disappeared. He saw many of the small ones that had been shielded from the fall of the waters toward the poles. Those unfortunates were astonished, and trembled when they looked at their Moon, before which they prostrated themselves. They were only gradually reassured, and while becoming absolutely savage. They only preserved a confused tradition of the giant Nüsüsümü. The necessity of nourishing themselves, and that of defending themselves against more powerful animals, big fish, big birds and serpents, absorbed them entirely.

It rained. Streams formed, and rivers, at the feet of high mountains. Mars was then very nearly similar to what the Earth had been several hundred thousand years ago, after the acquisition of the Moon; it had two warming stars, the Sun and its new satellite, which had acquired, at its perihelion, and enormous degree of heat. Its surface is now covered with comets, which renders Mars less brilliant because it is becoming less appropriate to reflect light.

That history of Mars is, with slight differences, that of our globe.

Response to Letter CCXIV

15 September.

That is a revolution that gives me an idea of the one that happened on the Earth when we acquired our moon. It appears that it was in that epoch that the giants disappeared. Apparently, they needed a marshy terrain and an atmosphere thickened by abundant vapors. The aridity of the Earth has shrunk all the animals there, as aridity will shrink them on Mars. It appears from your letters, dear husband, and the commentaries of our reasoners, that there is a uniform progression by which the existence and the conservation or the destruction of all living beings, no matter what their nature, is directed.

"It is a relief," says Monsieur de La Grange, "to have a rule, and it makes it easier for limited beings like us to grasp the ensemble of the operations of Nature."

Letter CCXV

F.m.T. 3 September.

The forests that cover the mountains of Mars contribute to conserving their primitive height, which the exception of the sheerest, on which, when the snow melts, ravines are hollowed out, which furrow them.

The little Nüsü will multiply gradually, and, as they will hold the scepter of animality, they will become much more perfectible than when they had the Nüsüsümü above them, who crushed them or treated them as we treat bees, from which we steal wax and honey. The Giants had entire villages of Nüsü which they robbed from time to time of all their provisions, and the little species had to begin all over again.

They will be civilized in two or three thousand years. The existence of the giant Nüsüsümü will then be called into doubt, and the Nüsü will claim that Mars has always been as it will be in that epoch.

Meanwhile, the rain will gradually wear away the mountains, which will be slightly diminished, and will become less steep; the valleys, in consequence, will be less profound. The streams and rivers will diminish in the same proportion.

The Nüsü, having become comfortable, improved by the invention of various arts, will invent a religion; but they will follow in our footsteps. First they will worship the Sun and their Planet. Afterwards, refiners will make them ashamed of that; they will transform the Being-Principle into a person, and they will make it an anthropomorphic being, who will have created the Sun and Mars. Ingrate children, they will say: "We were not born of the Sun and the

Planet, but of God." Like the child who beats his father here, they will say: "I am not your son but God's." That is a felony!

Multipliandre examined the march of Nature on Mars. It resembled ours perfectly. He foresaw an epoch similar to that of the Trojan War, another resembling that of 1792.... He had the faculty of seeing the future, by a contension[22] of prolonged intelligence, which allowed him really to perceive all the events consequent upon one another—with the result that, in accordance with him, I could conduct you reliably all the way to the absorption of our globe by the Sun.[23] He saw his Julie and her two companions, forever young, thanks to the precautions he had taken, forever pretty, forever eighteen, and forever virginal.

Beautiful Hortense, the head is losing itself a little, but the heart, the heart....is always burning with love for you.

Response to Letter CCXV

16 September.

All your consequences are reasonable, good husband, and the men of our society admire the accuracy of your views in physics. Everything is in accord; nothing is disparate.

But what you say about religions has been found sublime! How humans have debased themselves and denatured themselves in ceasing to recognize their mediators, the Sun and the Earth! There is no other direct and immediate god for humans but the Sun, and then while regarding the Earth as the mediator. The Earth and Sun are but one relative to us, as the father and mother are but one single productive being relative to their child.

The sole reasonable religion to establish, according to our friends and ourselves, is the cult of the Sun, that of Vesta or the Earth, and that of the Ancestors, much as in China. That is the kind of religion, of worship, that it is necessary to introduce. Once a year, one should pray to the Earth and the Sun to take our homage to the Being-Principle, their immediate father, or at least of the Sun.

One should adore the Sun every month and the Earth every tenth day; the Ancestors should be honored every day at midday; at the sound of a bell, one should render one's homage to the Ancestors. That would be far better than the Angelus. That is a cult, since one is necessary, and the only reasonable one.

---

[22] I have assumed that Restif invented this word, and that it is not a misprint; he uses it again.

[23] Author's note: "See that in *L'Enclos et les oiseaux*." Alas, we cannot: the entire future history of Earth was lost to posterity because the author, beset by the diffidence and persecution of his contemporaries, could not scrape together the money to publish the work in question in 1796.

X. B. Saintine: *Astronomical Journeys*

X. B. Saintine was the by-line used by a prolific dramatist and novelist who was born Joseph Xavier Boniface (1798-1865). Although he is largely forgotten today, two of his works, both fact-based novels, remain fairly well-known: Picciola, *about a political prisoner who conserves his sanity by investment in the fate of a flower growing in a crack between the stones of his prison; and* Seul! [Alone!], *which purports to tell the true story of the castaway on whose experiences Daniel Defoe based the story of Robinson Crusoe.*

The fascination with strategies of psychological survival exhibited by these two novels resonates in many of Saintine's other works, including a curious book of visionary fantasies, ostensibly (and perhaps genuinely) drawn from a notebook in which the author had long compiled a record of his dreams, La Seconde vie *(1864).[24] The following two-part episode is taken from that book, where it forms chapters IV and V; the second is there separately titled "Une Autre visite! Une Autre planète!" [Another visit! Another Planet!]. It is not the only dream recorded therein that is of interest in the context of scientific romance; others deal with hypothetical microscopic life-forms named "animules."*

Most of the dreams related in La Seconde vie *are earthbound fantasies mingling broad comedy with sly philosophical and psychological speculations, but this brief cosmic odyssey, while remaining as cheerfully nonsensical as any of the other dreams narrated in the book, boldly involves itself with contemporary debates regarding the evolution of the Earth and its living species. Camille Flammarion employed similar visionary artifice in some of contemporary popularizations of astronomy and discussions of the possible habitation of other worlds, especially* Lumen *(1866-69; 1872 in* Récits de l'infini; *revised for separate publication 1887), but Flammarion's evolutionism was responsible for a sharp ideological contrast between the imaginary excursions described in* Lumen *and those detailed by Saintine.*

Saintine's fantasy, which takes some inspiration from the endeavors of followers of the anti-evolutionist anatomist Georges Cuvier, makes an interesting comparison with Eugène Mouton's "The Origin of Life," whose inspiration was similar. Its graphic depiction of animate matter anticipates the imminently-impending public clash between Félix-Archimède Pouchet and Louis Pasteur regarding the viability of the theory of spontaneous generation—an issue not yet regarded as conclusively settled at the turn of the century, when Gustave Le Bon wrote L'Evolution de la matière *(1905; tr. as The Evolution of Matter) and Gaston de Pawlowski dramatized its substance in* Voyage au pays de la quatrième

---

[24] The Second Life, Black Coat Press, ISBN 978-1-61227-750-9.

dimension *(1912; revised 1923).*[25] *Saintine does not, of course, attempt to ad-dress these issues seriously, but his flamboyant celebration of their potential as aliments of nightmare testifies to the extent to which thinking men of the time were haunted by the possibilities that contemporary scientific research and speculation were releasing into the public domain.*

B.S.

1.

Where am I? What eager whirlwind is carrying me into the depths of the Heavens? I am floating, rising up with a speed that only the rapidity of the electric current can approach. The Earth vanished from my sight some time ago: poor wretched little Earth, I watched it shrink, gradually diminishing until it seemed no more than a schoolboy's ball, rotating after having touched the ground—and my heart was touched, my eyes moistened. Poor, poor little Earth, where so many grand passions seethe—and vanities no less grand!—little grain of sand from which I saw the Sun for the first time, on which I have loved and suffered, shall I ever be allowed to return to you?

My emotion was not long delayed in changing its object. Still rising up, I was swallowed up by profound darkness, and the dread took hold of me that I might crack my skull on some unperceived celestial body. A feeble radiation dissipated the obscurity around me somewhat; I glimpsed a sort of reddish globe that was heading towards me. Was it a comet ready to crush me in its passage? What could I do to avoid it? I had no wings to regulate and direct my course.

With a vivid sentiment of joy, I then perceived that my own will was adequate in itself to move me the direction I desired. At first I had difficulty believing myself to be endowed with such power, but what could be more logical and natural, in accordance with the universally established order? When I was an inhabitant of the Earth, could I not cause my limbs to move solely by means of a mental instruction? Now my thought—my will, in the final analysis—was similarly steering my body: a body freed from the bonds of gravitational attraction, and consequently almost weightless.

Assured of this precious faculty, after having tacked back and forth for a while, gently cradled by the waves of the ether, intoxicated by that pure essence of life, I was emboldened to resume my ascent, continuing my course through the higher regions of space.

I saw that same reddish globe again, my first discovery in my voyage through the Heavens. It seemed paler to me. Whatever it was, it was definitely not a comet; it had neither the dazzling head nor the long atmospheric tail that is the obligatory accompaniment of all comets; no more was it a star, properly

---

[25] *Journey to the Land of the Fourth Dimension*, Black Coat Press, ISBN 978-1-934543-37-5.

75

speaking, no scintillation within it indicated an active flame. What was it, then? Suddenly, a sort of grotesque face turned towards me; I recognized it. My reddish globe, my tail-less comet, my ray-less star was the Moon!

On that subject, I had read all that dreamers had thought and all that thinkers had dreamed, from Pythagoras to Seneca, and from Cyrano de Bergerac and Fontenelle to Humboldt and Arago.

Among the scientists, one alone had not been content to think and dream; he had wanted to see with his own eyes.

> *From Easter to St Michael's Day,*
> *He built a telescope*
> *So large, so large, that Herschel's*
> *Was myopic by comparison.*[26]

Then, he saw…what did he see? Huge bats in human form, *Homo vespertilio*—and I was consumed by desire to know that which all these scientists had thought, dreamed or seen, in the direct line of incontestable truth, Could I ever hope to have a better opportunity to clear up my doubts? The Moon was there, right there in front of me, accessible to me!

Exerting all my will-power to one unique purpose, combining all its force into a single impulse, I precipitated myself in headlong flight, and a few minutes later I touched down on a high mountain that presented hardly any other view than that of immense glaciers. The natural location of glaciers is on high mountains; I was not surprised.

I left these lunar Alps, or Cordilleras, to descend to the plain. There, the soil was covered with snow of dazzling whiteness, doubtless fallen the previous day; I had presumably arrived on our satellite in the winter season.

Winter could not be manifest everywhere, though. I visited the Moon's four cardinal points; I descended into its valleys, and also into the craters of its volcanoes. I traveled over its seas, its gulfs. Everything there was rigid, motionless; it was all frozen. The place was fully illuminated by the Sun, but the Sun's light did not brighten or heat up anything there; its rays arrived there chilled, without the power to melt a snowflake, without awakening an atom of life. On the plains, there was not a tree; on the receding flanks of the rocks, there was not

---

[26] The first line of this verse, "De Paques à la Saint Michel" is a popular way of indicating the summer months in France. Subsequent references to "Monsieur Nicolet" are presumably to the author of the poem, but I can find no reference to any lunar fantasy written by a man of that name or to any contemporary work that populates the moon with giant bats; it might have been a fashionable *complainte* whose popularity proved brief. The term *Homo verspertilio* was once used in a German work by Heinrich Hoffmann, but I cannot find any French reference to it.

a blade of green grass or patch of moss; in the air, which was so clear that I could see every planet gravitating around its orbit, there was not a cloud, nor a bird in flight; no cry or insect hum could be heard there!

I could only perceive a single breath—that which emerged from my own breast.

The Moon is dead, dead, dead!

"Has it, at least, lived its planetary life? Was it once inhabited?"

To that double question, I can give a bold affirmative response.

The cadavers of cities lie upon its plains; though covered by their shrouds of snow, the remaining indications of rounded shapes and rectangular lines are sufficient testimony to the hand of a constructor. Now, was this constructor Fontenelle's human being or Monsieur Nicolet's bat?

To decide the matter, it seemed at first that I would only have to dig down into the layers of snow, to go into one of the houses, which must surely have retained traces of heir inhabitants, even better than those of Pompeii. Any tool that came to hand, of iron or wood, would be sufficient to the task. But one does not travel through the impalpable ether with arms and luggage—except in extraordinary cases, as we shall soon see.

I had brought with me neither a spade nor a pickaxe, and I could not excavate a path through those towns and ice-sealed tombs with my fingernails. Besides which, the land's more-than-Siberian cold rendered me incapable of action. I was already thinking of leaving, and in thinking that, became depressed. Had I, then, undertake this long journey only to register the Moon's death-certificate? Would nothing help to enlighten me as to the nature of its former inhabitants?

Providence came to my aid!

Numbed by cold, with frostbitten fingers and chattering teeth, I was on the point losing all hope and was about to resume my flight, when a large corridor formed by high white rocks, decorated externally by a layer of ice that gave them the appearance of immense blocks of porcelain, opened before me. On the hardened ground and along the walls, a series of objects were scattered, the nature of which it was impossible for me to make out. I drew nearer, only expecting to find a few outcrops of rock or a few tree-trunks not covered by the snow—which would have been a victory in itself—but a much greater surprise and an unexpected triumph awaited me! I had before my eyes a complete specimen of the ancient population of the Moon. These sad specimens of an entire vanished race must have taken refuge there at the very moment of the great cataclysm. There were there still, conserved intact by the cold, with their last anguished expressions and in their final stances, perhaps hundreds of centuries old.

I therefore found myself in a position to answer, with complete authority, the great question of the inhabitants of the Moon—a question that had so keenly preoccupied the scientific world and myself!

The Moon had once been populated, not by giant bats, as Monsieur Nicolet had believed, or pretended to believe, but by beings much closer to the form and nature of humans, although they were quite different in certain essential respects.

The double man, Plato's *homo duplex*, brought back into favor in our time as an anatomical reality by the savant Dr Serres of the Institut, was displayed there in the full expansion of his duplicate individuality.[27] Male in the right half of the body, female in the left side, the lunar human possessed two arms and two legs, exactly like the humans of Earth, but had in addition two distinct and separate heads, elegantly rising from articulated clavicles, capable of certain movements that are forbidden to us. Each of these heads had an elongated neck for a stem, which drew apart progressively from their bases. Evidently, this neck, instead of supporting only seven vertebrae, as ours do, must have accommodated at least 22, like those of birds.

The broad chests of these strange beings presented, not quite in the middle but slightly to the left, two breasts, to which the double mouth of a bicephalous infant could be simultaneously applied. To the right, there was no trace of the vestigial nipple with which nature has decorated us, more in accordance with harmonic law than the law of necessity.

A double spinal column, branching from a junction, permitted the conjoined individuals to look one another in the face in order to smile, to talk—for I cannot doubt that they were possessed of the gift of speech—and to put their hand on one another's shoulder in a sign of friendship. That affectionate pose must have been habitual to them in moments of great stress. Almost all the poor coupled creatures that I had before my eyes gave me evidence of that.

The inhabitants of the Moon were certainly the most complete hermaphrodites among the superior races, and love, among them, must have been practiced according to the strictest rules of moral hygiene. Brother and sister at first, later husband and wife, linked by custom and by blood, exempt from suspicion and jealousy, since they were never apart, unable to take a single step without one another, since they were born together and would die together, can they not offer perfect models of conjugality? If there were ever a Golden Age of happy households, it must surely have been on the Moon.

At this point, before having reached my conclusion, I felt my thoughts clouding over because of the intensity of the cold, and I suddenly lost con-

---

[27] Plato's *Homo duplex* conceives humans as duplicate beings in terms of body and soul, although Plato did also speculate about sexuality in terms of the figurative division of a hypothetical hermaphrodite form. The anatomical observations of Étienne Serres (1786-1868)—in accordance with the remainder of the passage—had more to do with bodily symmetry. A similar calculated ambiguity forms the ideative basis of one of the chapters in Pawlowski's *Voyage au pays de la quatrième dimension*, which might owe something to Saintine.

sciousness. I only recovered when I heard two voices: two quarrelsome voices, which increased in volume as they argued, replying to one another in the angriest possible tones. To the extent that I could understand, at first, the argument concerned furniture (how strange dreams are!). One of the voices was that of my upholsterer; my upholsterer as arguing with someone, and that someone, who was shouting the louder, was me!

And yet, my astronomical voyage continued.

This is what happened.

2.

Chilled to the bone, half-frozen, almost as dead as the Moon itself, I took advantage of the feeble residue of my will to head for the first available planet. Desirous above all of warmth, rest and comfort, I had told my upholsterer—don't ask me how!—to send me all the furniture in my bedroom.

My upholsterer is punctiliousness personified. When I arrived at my planet, I found him waiting at the landing-stage with his baggage. It was the dead of night; without listening to his observations, of which I heard not a single word, and without even bothering to find out whether there was a hotel in the vicinity, I instructed him to set it all up in a beautiful grotto of slate-colored basalt, whose entrance, in the form of a portico, opened on to a lake.

Nothing was lacking in my improvised apartment, not even central heating; I perceived a gentle warmth there, which did not take long to bring me out of my glacial torpor. I could have believed that I was in Paris, surrounded by my furniture in the Renaissance style—I had a penchant for the Renaissance at that time.

Monsieur Durand, my upholsterer, had brought my old Gobelins tapestry, decorated with great characters of mythology, my Palissy faiences ornamented in relief with lizards, snakes and frogs, and even my famous Giotto canvas, *The Massacre of the Innocents*. I could certainly have been satisfied with less, but, I repeat, Monsieur Durand is punctiliousness made man; I had asked him for all my furniture, and he had brought it to me complete—and if he had not delivered the doors and windows along with the furniture, it was doubtless because the landlord had opposed it.

I threw myself on my bed, where I went to sleep immediately.

In the middle of the night, dull cracking sounds became audible above my head. The walls of rock seemed to be splitting noisily—and, from time to time, small flakes of basalt were falling on to my bed. Twenty other noises were not long delayed in mingling with these sounds; I heard sighs and all sorts of murmurs—even the murmur of water, which seemed to be lapping spasmodically against the entrance to my grotto.

"A fire has broken out, caused by my central heating, and the firemen are in the process of putting it out." That was my first thought.

Frightened, I hurled myself out of bed in order to get out of that inferno as quickly as possible. The exit was closed! The tall portico of rock had subsided, now leaving only a narrow aperture at its base, through which the hissing waves were coming.

"If it's not a fire," I said to myself, "then a storm has broken out over the lake—a tempest, most certainly, complicated by an earthquake!"

My situation, already terrible, was about to get even worse.

On going back into my room, I stood petrified by the spectacle that offered itself to me, which a phosphoric leakage from the frock permitted me to contemplate in all its marvelous horror.

All my furniture had come to life. Just as the high basaltic mountain into which I had come in search of shelter was cracking and moaning, and just as the little lake, my neighbor, had come swirling to besiege me in my refuge, every item of my household goods was playing an active role in its turn.

My four-poster bed, made of old oak-wood, entirely disarticulated in its limbs and joints, was attempting to return to its primitive and natural state. Its twisted feet and pillars were unrolling their spirals, standing upright, digging into the ground in order to implant themselves there; they were also implanting lively cuttings, by means of roots abruptly emitted by their nether parts, while a thin layer of bark began to cover each new stems as soon as it set itself upright.

Inlays in mother-of-pearl or tortoiseshell were detaching themselves from other items of furniture and becoming curved, rounding themselves off, acquiring the forms of shells and carapaces. The leather and morocco upholstery of chairs was distending and taking on the appearance of the animals that had furnished it. The horsehair with which the armchairs were stuffed was escaping in order to attach itself to strange animals, comprising their manes or fleeces.

All around me, everything that was conscious of a previous organic life, animal or vegetable, seemed to be trying to return to it. Nor did the miracle stop there. My night-stand started to dance; one by one, with a menacing air, it lifted each of its feet, which terminated in powerful eagle's claws—and these claws were opening and closing again as I approached, as if to seize their prey.

Further amazement! The mythological characters depicted in my Gobelins tapestry—Mars, Pallas and other gods of the first rank—were suddenly taking on a frightful three-dimensionality; their eyes were lighting up, their muscles stirring, their mouths murmuring confused threats. The lightning-bolt that old Jupiter was holding flashed momentarily, and three times the mountain trembled on its base. Then, all those fallen gods began to flex their backs and stretch their arms in order to rid themselves of the weave that retained them—but they could not complete the task.

Less encumbered than the gods, the Roman soldiers in Giotto's painting launched themselves out of the canvas with wild-eyed gazes in pursuit of poor little innocents; I saw the blood running, and heard the screams of the victims and the imprecations of their executioners....

By means of a bizarre phenomenon, already observed by Pascal, I was momentarily conscious of my sleeping state. "I'm dreaming; it's a dream: a frightful nightmare, which my dear doctor would not hesitate to class among his *symplegadics!*"[28] I told myself—but after due consideration, I replied in the negative; "No, I'm awake, I'm fully conscious; it's all true, all real!"

And I continued to be subject to my dreamer's torment.

A formidable cracking sound warned me of the imminent collapse of that fatal rock, under which I had voluntarily imprisoned myself. From the obscure corner in which I curled myself up, with sweat on my brow, a violent shaking threw me back to the middle of the grotto; the cave, doubtless in consequence of an upset effected within the mountain, became narrower, gradually closing in until I was only left with just enough space to avoid contact with all the monsters by which I was surrounded.

Soon, enormous blocks of basalt detached from the ceiling fell upon the gods of old Olympus, who were more entangled than ever in the threads of their tapestry, and the infamous Roman soldiers, who had not relented in their massacre of innocents. The trees and animals of my furniture, crushed and broken, were no longer anything but shapeless debris. Only my distraught night-stand, as if overcome by madness, ran away from that rain of rocks, using its powerful eagle's claws to clamber up the wall, scaling it all the way to the top.

To cap it all, the frightful reptiles—Palissy's lizards, snakes and frogs—which had retained for some time in the torpor habitual to them, were now sliding, running and hopping through the bloody debris; impregnated with that blood, they were swarming around and crawling up my legs, mingling their sinister hissing and frightful croaking with my cries of distress.

It was horrible!

However, the greatest suffering I endured did not arise from the perils I was running, nor from the spectacle before my eyes, nor from the venomous touch of the serpents; it came from the intolerable heat that reigned within the grotto. I was suffocating, choking; I thought I was dying.

In that supreme moment, a resounding voice burst out, overwhelming all those noises, all those rumblings and all those sobs.

The voice was my upholsterer's. "Quickly! Quickly!" he cried, seizing me by the hand. "The way out has been opened up for us again by a landslide. We haven't a moment to lose—hurry up!"

---

[28] The Symplegades are two rocks featured in the story of Jason and the Argonauts, which periodically smash together; that term is thus used metaphorically to refer to any course steered between two parties in imminent danger of clashing violently. I cannot find any evidence of the term being incorporated into 19th century psychology to describe a category of nightmare, but it could have been, although it is also possible that Saintine, who was obviously very interested in oneirology, might have improvised the term himself.

Would you believe it? At the very moment when I owed my salvation to the honest Monsieur Durand, I elected to inflict upon him the most unjust outbursts of temper. All my fears and all my suffering had just degenerated into furious anger. I reproached him for his disloyalty; I accused him of knavery. The furniture he had brought me could not be mine; it was bewitched! He swore to me by his greatest gods that he had never played a practical joke in his life. I replied that he was a miserable liar! It was with malevolent, criminal intention that he had fired up the central heating to the point of asphyxiating me. I finished up threatening him to take him to court.

O triple Hecate! O Bombo, Mormo, Gorgo![29]

Fortunately, my brave upholsterer continued to drag me along with him, without paying overmuch attention to my recriminations.

Once outside the grotto, I looked for the lake that bathed its edge and could no longer see it. The lake had evaporated into steam, and now formed a large dark red cloud, in which the glow of a fire seemed to be reflected.

I scanned the high mountain of which my grotto was the base; it had been turned upside-down and 20 craters now open simultaneously along its torn flanks. The horizon traced in front of us was nothing but a circle of volcanoes.

"Where are we?" I asked, gripped by terror.

"On Monsieur Le Verrier's planet, incorrectly called Neptune," Durand replied, with the utmost calm. "You've come from the Moon, haven't you?"

"What! You know that?" I cried, interrupting him. "My dear Monsieur Durand, do you also know how the Moon died?"

"That's an old story," he answered. "After having created the terrestrial globe. God put the Moon at the service of the Earth, in the capacity of its satellite. It was charged with restraining and moderating the seas by means of its gravity, and for a few centuries things went according to plan—but the day came when, weary of turning on it axis, the Moon broke its chain and tried to wander away from its regular orbit. Then there was the Deluge; in addition, to punish it for its disobedience, God struck it dead; since that time, it accomplishes its duties as a star entirely automatically, no longer doing anything but obeying the general laws of gravitation. Now, my dear client, let me resume what I was saying. Yes, as you have been able to verify for yourself, the Moon is dead, and

---

[29] Hecate is called "triple" here because she was thought by some writers to have three different aspects, being Selene or Luna in the Heavens, Atrtemis or Diana on Earth and Persephone or Proserpine in the Underworld; she was thus represented, on occasion, with three bodies or three heads, one of a horse, one of a dog and one of a lion's and afforded such epithets as Tergeminus, Triformis and Triceps. A supposed hymn to Hecate exists in which the three aspects of her personality are addressed as Bombo, Mormo and Gorgo, although the last of the three terms is more commonly associated with the gorgon better known as Medusa—who was also part of a set of three, according to Hesiod.

quite dead; here, entirely to the contrary, you have before your eyes a world in formation, where the forces of organic life are presently constituted with a frightful intensity. Here, due to the excess of heat, solid bodies liquefy and liquids evaporate into gaseous form, thus forming the atmosphere indispensable to every planet that wishes to live."

I stood in front of my upholsterer, rapt. Never had I suspected him of being well-informed on these sorts of things.

"The brute matter has now been sufficiently warmed up and ground down," he went on. "Some of these volcanoes are beginning to die down; their fire is becoming central. The moment has arrived when the germs of animate beings can develop here, and they will develop, at first to excess and with prodigious rapidity. Examine the terrain on which we're treading at this moment; every atom of matter here is restless, avid for friction. Throw down an acorn here and it will germinate instantly, immediately growing and pushing up towards the heavens; tomorrow there will be an oak-tree, which will have taken on immense proportions in no time at all—but that gigantic tree will soon perish, empty and flaccid, exhausted by its effort.

"Instead of an acorn, set down the egg of a lizard here, or that of a hummingbird; out of it will come an eagle or a crocodile. This is the phenomenal epoch of monsters, of which Monsieur Cuvier had spoken to you, and the Marquis de Laplace before him. Here the globe is so avid to produce that everything that has form is alive. Here, a wooden horse will become a horse of flesh and bone, a doll will become a woman—and we ourselves, if we prolong our sojourn here imprudently, might well be transformed into giants."

I took three steps backwards. Monsieur Durand took hold of my arm again, with a smile full of irony. "Now, my dear client," he continued, "do you understand why, without any witchcraft on my part, the mother-of-pearl and tortoiseshell of your bed, the leather and horsehair of your chairs, the feet of your nightstand and Bernard de Palissy's frogs and serpents, as well as the people in your tapestry and Giotto's painting, tried to recreate their life, their form, their activity? And also why, without any other central heating but the volcano that warmed the ground beneath your feet, you almost died of asphyxia? Whose fault is that? Is it mine, who was only carrying out your instructions, eh? Answer me."

I gave him no answer; I had none to give. Besides, I was quite out of breath, with my tongue stuck to the roof of my mouth. The open air had become as hot as that of the grotto. Having almost died of cold on the Moon, I didn't want to meet my end by virtue of an excess of heat; in any case, the prospect of turning into a giant was not at all tempting to my vanity.

I looked down at myself…my feet had already begun to develop considerably; my knees seemed to me to be more highly placed than before…

I hastened to quit Monsieur Le Verrier's planet, my mind anxiously full of the idea that creation is not yet terminated, and that God, instead of being at rest, as tradition affirms, is actively continuing his work.

Guy de Maupassant: *Martian Mankind*

Guy de Maupassant (1850-1893), the foremost French short story writer of his admittedly-brief era, became famous as a naturalist by virtue of pioneering the development of anecdotal slice-of-life stories and calculatedly low-key contes cruels, *which helped define the narrative method of the modern short story, but the range of his work extended much further.*

His most famous alliance with speculative motifs was the classic and much reprinted Le Horla *(1887), an ambiguous story whose distressed narrator becomes convinced that he is being tormented by an invisible creature, which must have come from Brazil on a passing ship, and that its species may be in the process of displacing humankind on Earth.*

In the same year, he produced L'Homme de Mars*[Martian Mankind], which complemented Flammarion's speculations—most elaborately fictionalized in* Uranie *(1889)—regarding the forms that Martian life might have taken in adapting to the physical conditions of the planet's surface.*

Although it still retains an echo of the apologetic formula used by Louis-Sébastien Mercier and Eugène Mouton—which Maupassant had brought to a kind of perfection in Le Horla—Martian Mankind *is a fundamentally earnest story, which is prepared to take its central hypothesis seriously, and the scientific data it quotes were all deemed accurate at the time. Its suggestion that Mars might be a warm world despite its distance from the Sun, by virtue of the influence of the greenhouse effect, proved dead wrong, but its underlying logic deserves some credit. Its account of a brief glimpse of alien life—remarkably similar to modern day UFO reports—strikes a subtle note of exotic poignancy that was to become one of the keynotes of 20th-century science fiction.*

B.S.

I was busy working when my servant announced: "Monsieur, there is a Monsieur asking to speak to Monsieur."

"Show him in."

I perceived a small man, who bowed. He had the appearance of a puny and bespectacled assistant schoolmaster. His clothing was too large, hanging loosely from his thin body at every point.

"I beg your pardon, Monsieur," he stammered. "Forgive me for disturbing you."

"Sit down, Monsieur," I said.

He sat down, and continued: "*Mon Dieu*, Monsieur, I am deeply troubled by the step that I am about to take, but it is absolutely necessary that I fix upon someone, and there is no one but you, only you... Finally, I have plucked up the courage, but to tell the truth... I no longer dare."

"Then be bold, Monsieur."

"You see, Monsieur, the problem is that as soon as I begin to speak, you will take me for a madman."

"*Mon Dieu*, Monsieur, that depends on what it is you have to say to me."

"Exactly, Monsieur. What I have come to tell you is bizarre. But I beg you to consider the possibility that I am not mad, for the very reason that I admit the strangeness of my story."

"Well then, Monsieur, get on with it."

"No, Monsieur, I am not mad, but I have the distracted appearance of men who are more thoughtful than others and who have gone a little–so little–beyond the limits of the average mind. Just imagine, Monsieur, how few people in this world ever think about anything. Everyone is occupied with his own affairs, his own fortunes, his own pleasures–with his own life, in sum–or with petty and trifling amusements like the theater, painting, music, politics–the greatest nonsense of all–or matters of trade. So who really thinks? Who, exactly? No one! Oh, pardon me... I'm getting carried away! I'll get back to the point.

"It was five years ago that I came here, Monsieur. You don't know me, but I know you very well... I never mingle with the crowds at your beach or your casino. I live on the cliffs. I positively adore the cliffs of Etretat. I know none more beautiful or healthier–I mean healthy in a spiritual sense. There's an excellent pathway between the sky and the sea, a verdant route that runs along the great wall of white rock, which takes you along the rim of the world, the rim of the land, above the Ocean. My best days are those I have spent stretched out on a grassy slope, in broad daylight, a hundred meters above the waves, dreaming. Do you understand what I'm saying?"

"Yes, Monsieur, perfectly."

"Now, would you be kind enough to let me ask you a question?"

"Ask, Monsieur."

"Do you believe that the other planets are inhabited?"

"Certainly I believe it," I replied, without hesitation or any evident surprise.

He got up, moved by vehement joy and seized by a manifest desire to clasp me in his arms, then sat down again. "Oh, what luck!" he exclaimed. "What a blessing! I can breathe! But how could I ever have doubted you? A man would not be intelligent if he did not believe other worlds inhabited. He would have to be a fool, a cretin, an idiot, a brute to suppose that the myriads of the universe shine and spin solely to amuse and astonish that imbecile insect man, to fail to understand that the earth is nothing but an invisible mote in the dust of worlds... that our entire solar system is naught but a handful of molecules of sidereal life, which will perish soon enough.

"Look at the Milky Way, that river of stars, and realize that it is nothing but a smear on the expanse that is infinity. Only think about that for ten minutes and you will understand why we know nothing, we divine nothing, we understand nothing. We know only one place, nothing of anything beyond or outside it, of anywhere else–but we believe and we have faith. Oh! If it were suddenly revealed to us, the secret of the vast extent of extraterrestrial life, how astonished we would be!

"But no... no... it's my turn to be stupid. We don't understand it, because our mentality is crafted to understand none but earthly things. It cannot extend much further; it is limited, like human life, trapped on this little globe that carries us, and it judges everything by that standard. So you see, Monsieur, that the whole world is stupid, narrow-minded, and fully persuaded of the power of our intelligence, which scarcely surpasses that of animal instinct. We do not even have the capacity to perceive our infirmity; we are shaped to know the price of butter and corn, and–at the most–to haggle over the value of a couple of horses, a couple of boats, a couple of ministers or a couple of artists. That's all.

"We are just about fit for tilling the land and clumsily making use of that which lies upon it. Having only just begun to construct working machinery, we are childishly amazed by every discovery that we ought to have made centuries ago, had we been superior beings. We are still surrounded by the unknown, even at the moment when, after thousands of years of intelligent life, electricity has been discovered. Are you and I of the same opinion?"

"Yes, Monsieur," I replied, laughing.

"Very well, then. Well, Monsieur, do you ever pay any attention to Mars?"

"To Mars?"

"Yes, to the planet Mars?"

"No, Monsieur."

"You know nothing at all about it?"

"No, Monsieur."

"Will you permit me to tell you a little about it?"

"Yes, Monsieur, with great pleasure."

"You know, presumably, that the worlds of our solar system, our little family, have been formed by the condensation into globes of rings of primal gas, detached one after the other from the solar nebula?"

"Yes, Monsieur."

"It follows from this that the most distant planets are the oldest, and in consequence, must be the most civilized. This was the order of their birth: Uranus, Saturn, Jupiter, Mars, the Earth, Venus, Mercury. Will you admit that these planets must be inhabited, like the Earth?"

"Certainly. Why suppose that the Earth is an exception?"

"Very well. The man of Mars will have a longer history than the man of Earth... but I'm going too quickly. First, I want to prove that Mars is inhabited. Mars presents to us something very similar to the aspect that Earth presents to

Martian observers. The oceans there take up less space and are more widely scattered. They are identifiable by their dark hue, because water absorbs light, while the continents reflect it. Geographical modifications of the planetary surface are frequent, thus proving that its life is active. It has seasons like ours, snow at the poles that can be seen to grow and diminish with the passage of time. Its year is very long: 687 terrestrial days, which is 668 Martian days. That breaks down as follows: 191 days of spring, 191 of summer, 149 of autumn and 147 of winter. Fewer clouds are seen there than here; there must, in consequence, be greater extremes of cold and heat."

I interrupted him. "I beg your pardon, Monsieur, but as Mars is much further from the Sun than we are, it seems to me that it must always be colder there."

My bizarre visitor exclaimed very vehemently: "Wrong, Monsieur! Wrong, totally wrong! We ourselves are more distant from the Sun in summer than in winter. It is colder on the summit of Mont Blanc than at its foot. I refer you, moreover, to the mechanical theory of heat of Helmholtz and Schiaparelli. The heat of the Sun is principally dependent upon the quantity of water vapor contained in the atmosphere. This is why: the absorbant capacity of a molecule of aqueous vapor is 16,000 times more than that of a molecule of dry air, so water vapor is our storehouse of heat. Mars, having fewer clouds, must be both much warmer and much colder than the Earth."

"I no longer contest the point."

"Very good. Now, Monsieur, listen to me with the utmost attention, I beg you."

"I am all ears, Monsieur."

"You have heard talk of the famous canals discovered in 1884 by Monsieur Schiaparelli?"

"Very little."

"Is that possible? Well then, in 1884, while Mars was in opposition to us, separated by a distance of no more than four million leagues, Monsieur Schiaparelli, one of the most eminent astronomers of the century and one of the most adept observers, suddenly discovered a large number of straight and broken black lines forming constant geometrical patterns, crossing the continents to link the seas of Mars! Yes, yes, Monsieur: rectilinear canals, geometrical canals, of a similar width throughout their course, constructed by living beings! Yes, Monsieur, the proof that Mars is inhabited, that there is life there, that there is intelligence there, that there is industry there... which can see us. Do you understand? Do you understand?

"Twenty-six months later, at the time of the next opposition, these canals were visible again, Monsieur, even more numerous–and they are gigantic, no less than a hundred kilometers wide."

I smiled as I replied: "A hundred kilometers wide! It must have required strong workers to dig them."

"Oh, Monsieur, what are you trying to say? You do not know, then, that such labor is infinitely easier on Mars than on Earth, since the density of its material constituents is only 69% of ours. The intensity of its gravity is scarcely 37% of ours. A kilogram of water only weighs 370 grams."

He threw these figures at me with such assurance, with the confidence of a businessman who knows the value of a number, that I could not prevent myself from breaking into laughter, and I was tempted to ask him how much sugar and butter weighed on Mars.

He shook his head.

"You are laughing, Monsieur; instead of taking me for a madman, you take me for an imbecile–but the figures I have quoted you are those that you will find in every specialist textbook of astronomy. The diameter is nearly half as much less than ours; its surface area is only 26% of ours; its volume is six and a half times smaller than that of the Earth and the velocity of its two satellites proves that its mass is ten times less. Now, Monsieur, the intensity of gravity depends on the mass and the volume, which is to say on the mass and the distance of the surface from the center, so the indubitable result is that on the planet there is a state of lightness that makes life completely different, regulating mechanical actions in a manner unknown to us, which must lead to a predominance there of winged species.

"Yes, Monsieur, the Ruling Being of Mars has wings. He flies, passing from one continent to another like a spirit, all around his world, although he is unable to move beyond the vestiges of its atmosphere...

"To conclude, Monsieur, can you imagine this planet, covered with plants, trees and animals whose forms we cannot even suspect, and inhabited by great winged beings like our artists' images of angels? Personally, I see them flying over the plains and cities, in the gilded atmosphere that they have there–for although it was believed in former times that the Martian sky is red while ours is blue, it is actually yellow: a beautiful, golden yellow.

"Are you still amazed that such creatures as those could hollow out canals a hundred kilometers wide? Then again, just think what science has achieved for us, in a single century... in a hundred years... and remind yourself that the inhabitants of Mars may well be far superior to us..."

He fell abruptly silent, lowered his eyes, then murmured in a very low voice: "Now the time has come that you will take me for a madman... When I tell you that I have glimpsed them myself... The other night. You may or may not know that we are in the season of shooting stars. On the nights of the 18th and 19th, especially, they are seen every year in innumerable quantities; it is probable that we are passing at this very moment through the tail of a comet.

"I was, therefore, sitting on the Mane-Porte, that enormous sheer headland that juts into the sea, watching the rain of little worlds overhead. It's prettier and more entertaining than any artificial fire, Monsieur. All at once, I perceived, directly above me, very close, a luminous transparent globe, surrounded by immense beating wings–at least, I thought I saw wings in the semi-darkness of the night. It was fluttering like a wounded bird, turning on its axis with a loud, peculiar noise, seemingly breathless, dying, lost. It passed in front of me. One might have taken it for a monstrous crystal balloon, full of panic-stricken creatures, scarcely discernible but excited, like the crew of a ship in distress, no longer under control but rolling from wave to wave. And the strange globe, having described an immense curve, came crashing down into the sea some distance away, where I heard it plunge into the depths with a noise like a cannon-shot.

"Everyone for miles around heard that mighty impact, which they took for a thunderbolt. I alone have seen... I have seen... If it had fallen on to the shore beside me, I would have met the inhabitants of Mars.

"Don't say a word, Monsieur. Think it over. Think it over for a long while... Then tell the story, one day, if you wish. Yes, I have seen... I have seen... The first spaceship launched into the infinite by thinking beings... Unless I have merely been present at the death of a shooting star captured by the Earth. For you may not know, Monsieur, that the planets hunt the wandering worlds of space as we pursue vagabonds down here. The light and feeble Earth is only able to intercept the smallest of infinity's passers-by."

He stood up, delirious with excitement, opening his arms wide to describe the march of the stars.

"The comets, Monsieur, which roam the frontiers of the great nebula whose condensates we are; the comets, free and luminous birds, coming towards the Sun from the depths of infinity. They come towards the radiant star, trailing their immense tails of light; they come, accelerating so forcefully in their bewilderment that they are unable to unite with their summoner; after the merest brush with it, they are hurled back into space as rapidly as they fell. But if, in the course of their prodigious journeys, they pass close to a powerful planet, if they feel its attraction and are drawn from their route by its irresistible influence, they return then to their new master, which renders them captive henceforth. Their unlimited parabola is transformed into a closed curve, and it is thus that we can calculate the revisitations of periodic comets. Jupiter has eight slaves, Saturn one, Neptune one also,[30] and its exterior planet one again, plus an army of shooting stars... Then... then, perhaps I only saw the Earth intercept a little wandering world...

"Goodbye, Monsieur, make no reply. Reflect, consider, and tell the whole story one day, if you wish..."

That was all. The lunatic seemed to me less stupid than some mere man of independent means.

---

[30] Although I have left it as it is, this reference to Neptune must be an error. Maupassant must have meant to name Uranus, Neptune–discovered in 1846– being the "exterior planet" mentioned immediately afterwards. (Pluto was not discovered until 1930.)

Georges Le Faure & Henri de Graffigny: *The Extraordinary Adventures of a Russian Scientist*

(excerpt)

The first of four volumes of Aventures extraordinaires d'un savant russe, *signed "G. Le Faure and H. de Graffigny" was published by Guillaume Edinger in 1888.*[31] *That first volume was an unusually lavish book illustrated with astronomical photographs, maps and drawings by various hands, and a preface by France's best-known popularizer of science, Camille Flammarion, who is also the novel's dedicatee. The second and third volumes of the original version appeared in a slightly less lavish format in 1889 and 1890, but Edinger appears to have ceased trading as a publisher thereafter, either because his enthusiastic political activities proved too much of a distraction, or because his recently-established and highly ambitious publishing program had stretched his finances to breaking point; at any rate, the assets of his firm were acquired by Arthème Fayard. After a long delay, Fayard issued the fourth and concluding volume of the* Aventures extraordinaires *in 1896, with illustrations distinctly inferior to those in the earlier volumes. The story told in the four volumes is a single continuous narrative whose subdivision was entirely arbitrary.*

The two authors of Aventures extraordinaires d'un savant russe *were both at the beginning of their careers in 1888, having published relatively little before that year, at least in book form. Whether they formed their partnership spontaneously or were brought together by Edinger to execute a plan formed by the publisher, it appears that theirs was a literary marriage of convenience; the evidence of their separate careers strongly suggests that Le Faure was appointed to be the provider of the action/adventure component of the work, while de Graffigny was to supply the science content. There is no way to be certain, but de Graffigny might well have provided a rough draft that was then given to Le Faure for expansion and melodramatic enhancement—a pattern of production*

---

[31] Many bibliographical sources give 1889, that being the date on the copy currently available in electronic form, but several copies offered for sale on the internet at the time of writing are dated 1888, and one is described as being dated 1889 but actually published in October 1888 (it was not uncommon for volumes published late in a calendar year to be dated for the following year). Flammarion's preface is, however, dated November 1888, so it is unlikely that the book was published before then. The first volume was certainly reissued when the second volume was published, and the copies dated 1889 might be a second edition. Sources also differ as to the date of the third volume, some giving it as 1891.

employed in other notable partnerships in French scientific romance, including three collaborative works by between Paschal Grousset (alias André Laurie) and Jules Verne and the two-volume Martian Epic *credited to Octave Joncquel and Théo Varlet.[32]*

The senior writer of the present partnership, Georges Le Faure (1858-1953), went on to become a prolific writer of popular fiction, especially for younger readers. Much of his work was in a vaguely Vernian vein, although he never did anything else as ambitious as the Aventures extraordinaires, *and he became conspicuously more modest in his imaginative reach once the four-volume novel was complete. While the early volumes of the* Aventures extraordinaires *were in progress, however, he was extremely enthusiastic in his production of scientific romances—so much so that when Fayard took over Edinger's assets, he was able to reissue a three-volume omnibus of Le Faure's other* Voyages scientifiques extraordinaires *in 1892-94, containing nine novels originally issued in 14 volumes. Le Faure became a regular contributor to the Vernian* Journal des Voyages *thereafter, sometimes using the pseudonym Georges Faber, but most of his contributions were non-speculative adventure stories.*

The most successful of Le Faure's scientific romances was probably Les Robinsons lunaires *[The Lunar Castaways] (1892), but once he had completed the nine novels reprinted in the Fayard omnibus, and had belatedly put an end to* Aventures extraordinaires, *Le Faure seems to have decided that speculative work was not worth the necessary imaginative effort and abandoned it, although modest speculative technologies are featured in peripheral roles in some of the adventure stories he produced in the 1920s.*

"Henry de Graffigny" was the pseudonym of Raoul Marquis (1863-1942), an engineer by training and a popularizer of science by vocation. The idea of writing the Aventures extraordinaires *is likely to have been his, if it was not Edinger's. De Graffigny had made his first tentative foray into the subgenre of Vernian romance in 1887, with* Voyages fantastiques *[Fantastic Voyages], which he followed up with* De la Terre aux étoiles *[From the Earth to the Stars] (1888)—a work that is not as extravagant as its title promises, only taking in the Moon, Venus and a ride on a comet, although it might be regarded as a preliminary prospectus for* Aventures extraordinaires, *whose early phases follow the same route.*

Both these works, aimed at a juvenile audience, were awkwardly didactic, so it is unsurprising that Edinger thought that de Graffigny was in urgent need of a collaborator skilled in melodrama if he were ever to produce something that aficionados of Vernian fiction might actually enjoy.

Although he worked for much of his life as a scientific journalist before "retiring" in 1920, ostensibly to dedicate his life to "electroculture"—the application of electricity to agricultural endeavor—de Graffigny did make further

---

[32] Black Coat Press, ISBN 978-1-934543-41-2.

excursions into Vernian romance following the conclusion of the Aventures ex-traordinaires. *Like Le Faure, however, he stuck to inventions that were, by comparison, conspicuous by their modesty.*

The most imaginative work of the latter part of de Graffigny's career, Voyage de cinq Américains dans les planets *[A Voyage to the Planets by Five Americans] (1925), appears to have been directly inspired by André Mas'* Les Allemands sur Venus *(1913)[33] and he maintained a steady flow of non-fictional publications on the possibility of interplanetary travel, culminating in the speculative enquiry* Irons-nous dans la lune? *[Shall we go to the Moon?] (1932).*

The historical importance of the Aventures extraordinaires d'un savant russe *is primarily derived from the fact that it was a determined and highly ambitious attempt to hybridize action-adventure fiction and the popularization of science to produce a new kind of fiction: one that had much in common with the "hard science fiction" that aficionados of the American-born science fiction genre distinguished when they thought it politic to discriminate between stories that were fundamentally faithful to known science and those which merely used a lexicon of imaginary entities—spaceships, aliens, robots and so on—as standard props of futuristic costume drama or as metaphorical and symbolic devices.*

It was the first scientific romance to attempt a tour of the entire Solar System, and the first to venture outside by means of faster-than-light travel. Only a handful of subsequent scientific romances made similar attempts, and the fact that writers active in the American science fiction genre eventually grasped the nettle of interstellar navigation more firmly and more securely is largely responsible for the eventual triumph of that genre over its European rivals—which entitles Aventures extraordinaires d'un savant russe *to be one of the most important proto-science fiction novels produced by the earlier genre.*

B.S.

Chapter XXXII

As the comet carries the celestial voyagers away from the Sun towards its aphelion in the vicinity of Saturn's orbit, Ossipoff looks forward to a long sojourn there and a chance to observe the planets beyond Earth's orbit. Fricoulet, however, formulates a plan to use the selenium sphere as a balloon to make a relatively short journey between the comet and Earth as it crosses that orbit. That plan does not work out, but is cleverly reformulated as the comet approaches the orbit of Mars.

Farenheit, who still harbors murderous intentions toward Sharp, falls out with him yet again over a huge piece of diamond found on the comet, with which the millionaire hopes to recover his losses but which Sharp judges too heavy to be transported in the makeshift balloon's gondola. When the time

---

[33] *The Germans on Venus*, Black Coat Press, ISBN 978-1-934543-56-6.

comes to take off, however, Farenheit takes the diamond and saves the necessary weight by stranding Sharp on the comet. Even so, the descent to Mars goes awry and the balloon is forced to land on Phobos instead. There, a further accident

When Ossipoff's timetable marked midnight, they had traveled about 4000 kilometers and were virtually weightless, to the extent that the Terrans had to attach themselves to the gondola to avoid being thrown overboard by their slightest movement. Suddenly, the apparatus appeared to perform a pirouette, and the appearance of the sky suddenly changed.

"We've just penetrated the Martian zone of attraction," Ossipoff told Gontran, by way of his speaker.

"And that's doubtless Phobos that we see beneath us," Flammermont replied, by the same means, pointing to a little ball a few 100 kilometers away in space, which seemed to be enveloped by a reddish radiation.

The old scientist nodded his head affirmatively. Suspending himself from the metallic wire that controlled the valve, he opened it all the way, thus permitting a certain quantity of gas to escape. Immediately, the heavier balloon began to descend and the star they had to reach increased in size with a vertiginous rapidity before the Terrans marveling eyes. It seemed that they were immobile in space and that Phobos was racing to meet them.

"How long do you think the descent will last?" asked Flammermont.

Ossipoff darted a rapid glance at his instruments. "About an hour," he replied.

For a while longer he left the valve half-open, then closed it. He dropped a metallic cable overboard, to which a selenium bar curved in the form of a hook had been fixed, by way of an anchor.

Suddenly, the gondola received a shock; it had just touched the ground. Then, after lifting up again, the balloon fell back a few 100 meters further on, to rise up and fall back once again. After that, it began sliding on its side, dragging the gondola—to which the voyagers, roughly shaken, clung with all their might.

Finally, they came to an abrupt and conclusive halt. The anchor had evidently just dug in and immobilized the sphere—which, retained by its cable, swayed back and forth a few meters above the soil. Leaning over the edge, the Terrans examined the strange configuration of the new world on which they had landed, with anxious curiosity.

By virtue of a singular optical illusion, it seemed to them that the ground was covered with a sort of net, with a regular and rather narrow mesh, which extended as far as the eye could see.

"Oh!" Ossipoff said, immediately, to Gontran. "We must lose no time investigating one of the most interesting questions of astronomy." In response to the young man's interrogative expression, he added: "I'm talking about the canals of Mars. Perhaps what we see here, beneath our feet, will serve as a clue to resolve that curious problem right away."

Meanwhile, Fricoulet, aided by Farenheit, had thrown the rope ladder that would enable the voyagers to leave their vehicle out of the gondola. The American went down first; then it was Selena's turn. After that, Ossipoff and Gontran also climbed over the edge to rejoin their companions. Fricoulet was about to follow them when, all of a sudden, the sphere—which the old scientist had not completely drained of hydrogen and which had just been lightened by the departure of the greater part of its load—exerted such a formidable tension on its cable that the anchor broke free and it regained its liberty. Before the Terrans had time to realize what was happening, the metallic balloon was no more than a dot in the sky.

"Fricoulet! Fricoulet!" cried Flammermont, waving his arms desperately in the direction in which his friend had just disappeared—but the young man's voice did not get past the envelope of his respirol.

"Don't be afraid," said Ossipoff, putting a hand on his shoulder. "The young man may not be very knowledgeable but he's very courageous. Besides, he knows more about balloons than astronomy…I have an idea that he'll get himself out of this." Then, drawing Gontran's attention to the ground with a gesture, he asked him: "What do you think of this?"

He showed him a veritable metal net on which he had set his foot, in one of the knots of which the balloon's hook had taken hold. What was the net covering? It was impossible to get an idea, by reason of the relative darkness that reigned on Phobos; it seemed that a perpetual opaque fog hid the appearance of the little world on which they had landed from the Terrans' eyes.

Receiving no answer, Ossipoff repeated the question. Gontran remained mute, plunged as he was in profound reflection. In addition to the fact that the accident that had overtaken Fricoulet was troubling him greatly, he was not without anxiety with regard to the modification that the sudden disappearance of his source of inspiration would bring to his relationship with the old scientist—not to mention that the gondola had carried off, along with all the luggage, the blessed copy of *Les Continents célestes* that had rendered him so much service. Deprived at a stroke of his prompter and his *vade mecum*, Flammermont thought it would be absolutely impossible to continue to play the role that he has sustained so cleverly for several months. Was it necessary for him, after so many proofs, to renounce the hope of ever becoming Selena's husband? No, that could not be, that would not be! And he begged the Martian divinities to send him an inspiration.

Amazed by this mutism, Ossipoff shouted at him with all the force of his lungs: "Are you deaf?"

Gontran shook his head negatively and placed his index finger on the point of his respirol corresponding to his mouth.

"Mute!" exclaimed the old man. "You're mute?" Turning to his daughter, he said: "The poor boy! How exquisitely sensitive he is! The loss of his friend has produced such an upset that he's suddenly lost the power of speech."

The young woman threw herself into her father's arms. Her rubber mask prevented anyone from seeing the tears that were running down her cheeks, but it was easy to divine from her breast, which was rising and falling in abrupt jerks, that she was sobbing.

"There, there, darling," said Ossipoff, softened by that great distress. "It's the initial emotion…with time, it will pass."

Suddenly, Farenheit—who had remained silent until then, positively dumb-founded by the loss of his precious diamond rock—began to gesticulate, waving his arms about wildly.

His companions ran to him, and uttered cries of horror on perceiving that one of the American's feet had been gripped by claws of some sort emerging from inside the net. These claws were fitted at the extremity of long membranous wings, which themselves belonged to a hairy body, along which they extended, attached to the anterior and posterior limbs, which closely resembled the arms and legs of the human species. To a rather long neck was attached a proportionate head: a completely hairless head in which two animated glaucous eyes gleamed between lashless lids. The nose was long and mobile, like a tapir's trunk; the mouth, entirely round, was rimmed with powerful lips, partly opened to reveal formidable jaws. Hanging on to the metallic net by its claws, this strange and horrible being had seized the American by the lower leg.

Finally, with a violent effort, Farenheit freed himself, leapt 20 feet into the air, and came down again 50 meters away.

"A singular world and singular inhabitants," muttered Ossipoff. He drew his daughter away, half-dead with fright

Gontran, who was only partly reassured, followed them. *Perhaps*, he thought, *the net is designed for no other reason than to transform Phobos into a vast aviary…* And he added, with a profound sigh: *O imperfection and inanity of human science! What would the gentlemen of the Observatoire de Paris say if they could see through their telescopes that the Martian satellite is surrounded by a net like a vulgar chignon!*

"If you ask me," said Farenheit to the old man, "We should try to get away from this cage thing; apart from the fact that these vile beings inspire a profound disgust in me, walking on it isn't at all easy, and to maintain one's balance it's necessary to perform acrobatic exercises that have never been my forte."

"Bah!" replied the old scientist. "So far as this world's inhabitants are concerned, what have you to fear? By reason of our weight, which is 100 times less than on the Earth's surface, our strength will be 600 times greater. You could break the skull of one of these individuals with a flick, as if with a sledgehammer blow. As for walking, if you care to try it out, you'll see that a simple pressure of the foot will carry you like a bird for four kilometers. Go ahead and try it, if you're not convinced."

The American shook his head. "I'd be too scared of losing you," he replied.

"On the other hand," Ossipoff went on, "I'd like nothing better than to walk for a while. Firstly, it would get the numbness out of our legs, and secondly, I wouldn't be displeased to get a better idea of this microscopic world...."

"Microscopic!" Farenheit repeated.

"Why, yes! What other label would you put on a worldlet that we could explore in its entirety in ten hours?"

For five hours the Terrans marched, or rather advanced, at a steady speed, by a series of successive bounds of equal height. Suddenly, however, without any transition, night fell and thick darkness overtook Phobos. At the same time, an enormous sparkling star rose above the horizon, similar to a gigantic Moon.

"Mars!" Ossipoff declared.

"Phobos has rotated," said Selena.

"No, darling," the old man relied. "Like all satellites, Phobos always presents the same face to its planet. We're the ones who have turned, having just passed from the solar face to the Martian face."

"It's frightening to see!" cried the young woman, hiding her face in her hands. "One might think that the mass is about to fall on us and smash us to pieces."

The old scientist smiled gently and shook his head. "The sensation you're experiencing doesn't surprise me at all," he said. "It would be the same for the inhabitants of our planet if they suddenly saw the apparent diameter of the Moon become 24 times larger and its volume 6400 times greater."

"6400 times!"

"Yes, that's the exact proportion of Mars by comparison with the Moon...it would be enough to make Mr. Farenheit fear for his beloved United States."

Eventually, after an hour's progress by Marslight, the voyagers came to a place where the metallic mesh seemed to come to an end. It was near the summit of a hill, which Ossipoff immediately declared to have an elevation of 100 meters, and on which they decided unanimously to get a little rest.

"Tomorrow," Ossipoff said to Gontran, who was still struck dumb, "we'll continue on our way, and perhaps we'll obtain news of Monsieur Fricoulet."

A few moments later, in spite of his anxiety, Flammermont was sound asleep—in which he was imitated by his dear Selena and by Farenheit. As for Ossipoff, gently taking possession of the marine binoculars that the American was wearing around his neck, he aimed them at the Martian landscape displayed before his avid eyes.

Chapter XXXIII
Six thousand kilometers in eight hours

One of the most singular and remarkable things about the celestial system is the difference that exists between the movement of the two satellites of Mars around their planet. While one of them, Deimos, orbits in 30 hours 17 minutes and 54 seconds, the planet itself rotates in 24 hours, 37 minutes and 23 seconds; in consequence that satellite appears to move slowly from east to west in the Martian sky. If the duration of its revolution were equal to the duration of Mars's rotation, it would be constantly visible to the inhabitants of one hemisphere, and unknown to the inhabitants of the other. The difference between that revolution and that rotation being 5 hours 41 minutes, the result is that Deimos seems to accomplish its circuit of the Martian sky in 131 hours—which is five Martian days. If, therefore, the inhabitants of the planet have, like their terrestrial brothers, a calendar regulated by the revolutionary period of their satellite, the months would be no more than five days long—which, for a year of 608 days, gives a total of 133 months.[34]

Very different conditions apply to the revolution of Phobos, the nearer satellite, which completes its entire orbit in the space of 7 hours 39 minutes. From the difference between this movement and that of Mars, which rotates in the same direction in 24 hours 37 minutes, it results that the satellite rises in the west and sets in the east, after having traversed the Martian sky with a velocity corresponding to the difference between the two movements—which is to say, about 11 hours. This is a unique example in the system of the world.

This special condition of revolution was particularly favorable to the examination of Mars that Mikhail Ossipoff wanted to make; carried by Phobos as if by a celestial racehorse at the gallop, he would race all the way around the new world, whose faces would file past his delighted eyes.

The Sun was rising on the part of the continent Huygens that is bathed by the Huggins Sea, and the satellite, overtaking in its rapid course the more slowly-rotating planet, followed the day star. As if he were in a balloon, the old scientist floated above bizarrely outlined oceans in the midst of yellowish continents, striped haphazardly by numerous streams extending in every direction. In the equatorial region, the continents Herschel and Copernicus appeared to him clearly; then to the north the Lands of Fontana. Laplace and Le Verrier; to the south the isles of Green, Jacob, Cassini, Rosse, Secchi and the isthmus of Niester attaching the Land of Hall to that of Green.[35]

---

[34] The Martian year is approximately 687 terrestrial days, or 660 Martian days, in duration.

[35] I have transcribed the names employed by the authors, which derive from Flammarion's maps, although modern maps of Mars use a terminology derived, with appropriate modifications, from the competing maps drawn up by Schiaparelli. The authors occasionally acknowledge the competition by citing Schiaparelli's names as alternatives to Flammarion's.

Dark amid the brighter oceans, bathing the equatorial coasts, the Newton Ocean and the Maraldi and Flammarion Seas extended. Then there was the strange Sablier Sea, which, after winding its bizarre contours between the continents Herschel and Copernicus, was linked to the Delambre and Beer Seas. Eventually, shining in the sunlight with an admirable brightness, the white patch of the polar snows extended from the fiftieth degree, almost at the tip of Le Verrier Land, to the South Pole.

For long hours, the scientist remained motionless, his chest strangely constricted, his gaze fixed in a sort of hypnosis on the world he had studied from the Pulkova Observatory at a distance of 19,000,000 leagues, from which he was now separated by only a few 1000 kilometers. Successively, he saw the Kepler Ocean, with the Kaiser Gulf and the curious Mediian Bay, so bizarrely cut out by the waters, and then the continents of Galileoi and Huygens, bathed to the south by the Schiaparelli Sea and to the north by the Oueman Sea, appeared and disappeared in the oriental occident.

At that moment, Phobos, drawn by its rotation, presented the face on which the Terrans had stopped to the Sun, and day dawned abruptly, without transition. Mikhail Ossipoff released a sight of regret at having been thus interrupted in his contemplative studies. Then he straightened up, and only then did the memory of his companions return to him. He turned to look at them, lying on the ground in the same positions in which drowsiness had taken them by surprise a few hours earlier, still asleep.

For a moment, he hesitated over waking them; unlike him, they did not have the passion for science that devoured his entire being to make them forget their fatigue; they were exhausted—but he thought about Fricoulet, who, given his knowledge of aerial navigation, might perhaps have succeeded in landing on the world on which they were located, and in search of whom it was necessary to set out as soon as possible. He went to Farenheit, who happened to be nearest to him, and applied his speaker to the sleeper's helmet. "Ahoy!" he cried. "Get up!"

This summons resonated in the selenium helmet with a terrible loudness—so terrible that the frightened American bounded to his feet. That same bound, though, by virtue of his body's scant weight, launched him 1000 meters into the air. "By God!" grumbled the citizen of the United States, on perceiving his companions below him, who seemed to him to be reduced to half their size, "I'm a dead man, or at least badly damaged!"

Instinctively, he closed his eyes so as not to witness his fall. To his great surprise, though, several seconds passed, then one...two...three...four minutes, and no point of contact had yet been made between Phobos and himself. Then he risked opening his eyes. How great was his amazement and bewilderment on observing that he was still at least a dozen meters from the ground, and that he was descending no more rapidly than a feather released in mid-air. Beneath him, Mikhail Ossipoff, Selena and Gontran were waving their arms desperately.

Finally, with a slowness that did not lack majesty, the American arrived within range, and was immediately grabbed by the feet by the Comte de Flammermont, impatient to regain possession of his traveling companion.

Immediately, Ossipoff signaled that he wanted to enter into communication with the young man. When the two speakers were adjusted, the old man exclaimed, victoriously: "Hey! Mr. Farenheit has just given us proof that Proctor was correct in his prognostications regarding the satellites of Mars."[36]

Gontran felt a slight shiver run down his spine at the thought that Ossipoff might take it into his head to engage in an astronomical discussion; he had already opened his mouth to reply with a non-commital "Ah!" when he suddenly remembered the mutism with which his prudence had suggested to him that he declare himself afflicted the day before. He therefore suppressed the interjection that as ready to escape his lips and contented himself with sketching a vague gesture with his head, which might have passed for an affirmation as easily as a negation.

Ossipoff, however, gripped by the urge of scientific communication, continued. "On the basis that the diameter of Phobos might, at the maximum, be 32 kilometers—which is to say, 100th of the lunar diameter—the English astronomer established that the surface area of Phobos must be 1/10,000th that of the Moon and that it volume, compared to that of the Earth's satellite, must be in the proportion of one in a million."[37] He paused momentarily, then added: "You can see the consequences immediately, can't you? The intensity of a world's surface gravity being proportional to its mass and density, as Proctor takes the Moon as a term of comparison with respect to the volume of Phobos, it is not unreasonable for us to imitate him with respect to its mass and density. It therefore follows that the intensity of gravity here is 100 times weaker than on the surface of the Moon, or 600 times weaker than on the Earth's surface...have you got that?"

Gontran nodded his head several times.

"That's why Mr. Farenheit," Ossipoff said, by way of conclusion, "whose terrestrial weight is 74 kilos, weighs no more than 115 grams here—which permits him to jump, as he has just done, by the simple pressure of his feet..."

The old man, taking his fact as his point of departure, was undoubtedly about to launch into one of those philosophical dissertations to which he was accustomed, when a hand falling on his shoulder made him turn round. He found himself face to face with Farenheit—who immediately put himself in

---

[36] Richard Anthony Proctor (1837-1888), a prolific popularizer of astronomy, produced the first good map of Mars in 1869; like Asaph Hall, he took advantage of conjunction of 1877 to make an assiduous search for the planet's satellites, and eventually observed one of them, but not in time to claim credit for its discovery.

[37] The actual diameter of Phobos is 27 kilometers, at its longest (its shape is rather irregular).

communication with him and said in a surly tone: "What are we going to do now?"

"Continue our exploration. We can't think of leaving Phobos without having done everything in our power to retrieve Monsieur Fricoulet. Don't you think so, Mr. Farenheit?"

"How can you ask me such a question?" replied the American. "Not only does humanity make it our duty to conduct such a search, but our own interests concur."

Misunderstanding the meaning of his words, Ossipoff shrugged his shoulders and replied in a scornful tone: "On that score, you have nothing to fear; from the viewpoint of our personal interests, it's 1000 times preferable that Providence has separated us from Monsieur Fricoulet and left us Gontran, whose science and ingenuity have got us out of trouble several times. Monsieur Fricoulet is, perhaps, a charming fellow, but he's the fifth wheel on a cart..."

Farenheit shook his head. "You haven't understood me. I meant that by finding the engineer, we'd also be getting back our food stores. Now I don't know if your stomach is mute, but mine is claiming its due with unparalleled energy. By God! 16 hours without eating!"

The old man slapped his forehead despairingly. "My poor Selena!" he murmured. Then, to the American, he said: "Let's get going! We need to march until our air-supply is exhausted. Let's hope that Providence, which has not abandoned us heretofore, is still watching over us, and that we'll find Monsieur Fricoulet before it's too late." With these words, he adjusted his respirol and gave the signal to depart.

In a few bounds, they descended the side of the hill on the summit of which they had spent the night, and found themselves on a plain of strange appearance. Immense fields extended as far as the eyes could see, churned up and turned over from top to bottom, occasionally forming hillocks 12 to 15 meters high. They were reminiscent, albeit on a gigantic scale, of the waste ground in the suburbs of large towns into which detritus of every sort is tipped—but it was all deserted, sterile and uncultivated; here were neither vegetables nor animals. A profound, sinister, implacable silence covered these disordered plains with its heavy and terrifying wing.

For several hours the Terrans struggled through the midst of this inextricable chaos. Their strength ran out, however; in the meantime, they were tormented frightfully by hunger, and above all by thirst—and into their breathless lungs, a thin and polluted air no longer transported life, but asphyxia.

Leaning on Gontran's arm, Selena dragged herself painfully along behind her father, who seemed not to be feeling any of the suffering endured by his companions, and marched with a light step. Bringing up the rear, stumbling at every step and complaining incessantly, was Jonathan Farenheit.

Finally, they came out of that desolate and devastated region, and walking became less difficult. Suddenly, Gontran uttered an exclamation and stopped.

Selena's hand had jus released the arm that had been supporting her, and the young woman, sliding to the ground, remained lying there, motionless. Alarmed, Flammermont fell to his knees. Hastily unscrewing the selenium apparatus that imprisoned her, he perceived her pale and discolored face, her closed eyelids—whose long lashes cast a shadow over her cheek—her blanched lips and her slender nostrils. The contours of the immobile nostrils were slightly blackened by the commencement of asphyxia.

"Selena!" he moaned. "Selena!"—but this tender appeal was arrested by the walls of his selenium helmet. At the same time, a thick veil descended upon his eyes. With an incredible effort, his lungs dilated to breathe in the last puff of respirable air—but in vain. The supply had run out. The respiratory bellows expanded, closed again, expended anew. His face contracted and his fingers clenched upon the ground in a gesture of agony; then he fell backwards. Even at the approach of death, his last thought was to seize his fiancée's hand once more and to press it to his breast.

"By God!" groaned Farenheit, who had fallen some way behind the little troop but reached the two young people in a few bounds. "They're dead! They're dead!" Forgetting that his respirol would stifle the sound of his voice, he set about shouting at Mikhail Ossipoff with the full force of his lungs. The latter, not knowing what was happening behind him, continued placidly on his way.

Torn between the desire to alert the old man and a perfectly understandable reluctance to leave Gontran and Selena alone, the American stayed where he was, hesitating over the two bodies extended at his feet. All of a sudden, he saw Mikhail Ossipoff stop, totter as he put his hands to his head, then beat the air with his arms and spin around several times before finally falling down.

Farenheit thought that he was going mad, and was abruptly gripped by the sensation of the frightful solitude in which he found himself, on this unknown world, between the corpses of his companions. In a movement of despair, he raised his eyes to the heavens to beg for divine mercy.

As if in response to his prayer, a black dot appeared in the east, visibly increasing in size, seemingly heading toward Phobos. "My God!" murmured the American, his heart wrung by an inexpressible anguish. "May that be help that Your generosity and benevolence is sending us!" As he finished this speech, he found incredible difficulty breathing, and his lungs produced a sort of hiss as they collapsed, empty.

By God! he thought. *That's how these unfortunates died—and what I'll die of too...lack of air.* He looked back at the black dot and his eyes, already obscured by a light mist, thought they could distinguish, in the midst of the solar radiation, a strange apparatus moving through space with a magical rapidity.

"As long as they see us!" he murmured. "A few minutes' delay could cost all four of us our lives."

An idea came to him then—which was scarcely his habit, but the instinct of self-preservation let a light into his thick suet-merchant's skull. Rapidly, he unbuttoned his vestment and unrolled a long, wide strip of flannel that was wrapped around his body in the manner of our zouaves—except that, by an eccentricity that could only be entertained by a man as excessively full of patriotic pride as Farenheit, this girdle was colored blue and sprinkled with stars, as was the flag of the United States.

He waved this makeshift flag desperately, at arm's length, exhausting the strength that the asphyxia had left him in one last effort. Then his mind was illuminated, as if by lightning; he suddenly remembered the adventure that had overtaken him a few hours earlier, by virtue of his incredible lightness.

He bent his legs and put all his remaining strength and courage into straightening them, launching himself into space like an arrow, dragging his long girdle behind him. With the little lucidity that his frightful agony left him, he had thought of doing that, not so much to reach the savior dot that was advancing towards Phobos as, at least, to be more easily visible to it.

Had he calculated correctly? That was what he could not know, for, suddenly defeated in his struggle against asphyxia, having exhausted the last gasp of air contained in his respirol, he closed his eyes and opened his mouth wide in one last intake of breath. Then his convulsed limbs stiffened in the immobility of death—and the body of Jonathan Farenheit, rolled up in the folds of the starry girdle as if by a shroud, began its slow and almost imperceptible fall upon Phobos.

"By God!" said the American, sitting up on his elbows and rubbing his eyes energetically. "What a terrible dream I've just had!"

"A bad dream! Not at all, my dear Mr. Farenheit—you've very nearly gone west!"

At the sound of this voice, Farenheit shivered and rubbed his eyes harder. "I'm dreaming now, then—for I'm damned if that isn't Monsieur Fricoulet's voice that I thought I heard."

"Don't think, but be certain, my dear Mr. Farenheit—for it's certainly Monsieur Fricoulet in the flesh and bone who's speaking to you." So saying, the engineer—smiling mischievously, as was his habit—shook Farenheit's hand energetically.

The latter leapt down from the seat on which he was lying and looked at the young man with eyes full of bewilderment. "My word, it's true!" he murmured, as if he had needed the testimony of his eyes in order to believe the engineer's words. Then, after a moment of astounded stupor, the American looked around, and his face reflected the most profound astonishment. "Where am I, then?" he said.

"In an apparatus belonging to the Martians."

"Then the black dot that I saw in space…"

"The black dot was me, racing to your rescue. Thanks to your ingenious idea, I had no need to devote myself to a long and dangerous search to find you."

Farenheit's features darkened with an anxious frown, and he asked: "What about the others? What's become of them? Did you manage to bring them back to life, as you did me?" As he posed that question, the American's voice had a slight tremor.

"Would you see me in such good spirits, Mr. Farenheit," Fricoulet replied, a trifle dryly, "if anything had happened to our friends?" Extending his hand toward a dark corner that had escaped the American's investigations, he said: "There's Monsieur de Flammermont, for one. He's resting at the moment, for he suffered more than the others from the crisis, and even I was afraid that I might not be able to bring him back to life. Fortunately, thanks to his strong constitution, I've snatched him back from Pluto's somber realm."

"What about Monsieur Ossipoff and his daughter?"

"They're in the next room, where it's necessary that I pay them a visit now."

"I'll accompany you, if you'll allow it."

"Unfortunately, I can't allow it. For one thing, you're very tired and a little nap will do you the world of good; for another, being forced to absent myself, I don't want to leave Gontran all alone."

The American stifled a formidable yawn. "By God!" he murmured, "I'm as hungry as all the devils in hell!"

Fricoulet went to a shelf, on which stood a little flask. He picked it up and uncorked it. "Here," he said, holding it out to Farenheit. "Drink a mouthful of this—but only one mouthful, or you'll give yourself indigestion."

The American thought that the engineer was about to laugh, but the other spoke very seriously as he added: "It's in this liquid form that the Martians absorb the substance necessary to the support of their muscular strength. It's the quintessential product, raised to the highest power, of one of the aliments in use on the planet."

Farenheit looked suspiciously at the flask he was holding in his hand. "These people aren't gourmets," he said. "By this method, they deprive themselves of one of greatest pleasures there is on the surface of our world—the pleasure of the table."

Fricoulet shook his head. "These people have but one passion, albeit a mad and excessive one, pushed it its ultimate limits: curiosity. To extract from Nature the greatest possible number of secrets—that's the goal to which, from generation to generation, over the centuries, their efforts are devoted." He uttered a little mocking laugh and continued: "Ah, Mr. Farenheit, despite your pragmatic outlook on life, how far distant you are from these people, and how antiquated your famous motto *Time is money* sounds beside theirs! Which is to say that, compared to the Martians, the most agile, hard-working, restless Yankee is nothing but a dormouse…or a snail."

"Hang on! Hang on!"

"For them, time is so precious that they scarcely rest. As for meals, they do without, replacing them by what you hold in your hand—just time enough to uncork the flask, to bend the elbow, and it's done…to go more quickly, in fact, they've refined the liquid to its quintessence. Try a little."

The American said no more; he was convinced—and, deep down, a trifle humiliated. The activity of the citizens of the United States had been surpassed. He put the flask to his lips and swallowed a mouthful of it contents. He pulled a face and gave it back to Fricoulet.

"I'll put it up here," said the engineer, replacing it on the shelf. "If Gontran wakes up before I come back, make him drink the same, for he too must have prodigious hunger pangs." With that, the young man headed for the far end of the room.

He lifted the curtain and found himself face to face with Mikhail Ossipoff. The old man immediately asked, anxiously: "How is Monsieur de Flammermont?"

"Have no fear, he's resting—but I don't see Mademoiselle Selena."

"Here I am," said the young woman, appearing in the doorway. Then, putting her hands to her abdomen with a painful expression, she moaned; "My God, I'm hungry!"

The engineer nodded his head in an understanding manner and, as he had done with Farenheit, made Selena and her father drink a mouthful of the contents of a flask that he took from his pocket. "Now that you're fed…" he began.

Ossipoff did not let him continue. "Before anything else," he said, "tell me where we are."

"On the national balloon that maintains a service between Mars and its satellites."

The old man started in amazement. "Really!" he said. "It's a balloon? But I see nothing that resembles one."

The engineer smiled, took out his notebook, and rapidly scribbled a sketch on a blank page, which he showed to Ossipoff.

The old scientist's faced reflected the most profound bewilderment.

"Certainly," declared Farenheit, "this is an apparatus that will have the same effect on you that it had on me at first—this species of large cylinder defies all the ideas of aerial navigation that we have on Earth…and yet, do you recall the numerous models affecting the form of a cigar that you might have seen at various expositions? There's some analogy between them and the apparatus that's carrying us."

"That's quite possible," murmured Ossipoff.

"I'll resume my explanation," said the engineer. "The cylinder that you see there, which appears to me to be made of a sort of metallic fabric, measures no less than 60 meters in length by 12 in diameter. Its various sections are traversed along its entire length by a tube, in which there's an axis around which the apparatus—driven by an electric motor placed in the gondola—turns at a rate of between four and five cycles per second. What you see there, on the external surface of the apparatus, is a propeller 25 meters in diameter, making three complete turns, which gives it a span of 50 meters. The result is that the apparatus advances at about two meters a second, or about seven kilometers and hour."

Mikhail Ossipoff was literally stunned, as if hypnotized by Fricoulet's drawing.

Selena whose ignorance sheltered her from excessive astonishment, and who had, in any case, had a surfeit of the extraordinary, asked the engineer: "Have we left Phobos, then?"

"Yes, Mademoiselle—about three hours ago…with the consequence that we'll arrive on Mars in about five hours.

The young woman clapped her hands. "We've left Phobos! What luck! We're no longer running the risk of seeing those frightful creatures!" Then she interrupted herself abruptly. "That's right," she said to Fricoulet, "you don't understand—you haven't seen them. Can you imagine that we landed, not on the actual ground of the satellite, but on a sort of gigantic cage in which hideous monsters were enclosed?"

The engineer burst out laughing. "Yes, yes," he said. "I know what it is—or, at least, I think so. If I've understood what was explained to me, Phobos is nothing but a penitentiary colony: a sort of celestial convict prison, where the Martians send those among them whose vices render them dangerous to society."

"But what's the purpose of the net?"

"To prevent the prisoners from flying to the planet. Being equipped with wings, that probably wouldn't be impossible for them."

"In that case," cried Selena, her hands meeting in a gesture of fright, "those winged monsters with the sinister appearance are the Martians?"

"Yes, and despite the disgust and terror that they appear to inspire in you, Mademoiselle, these monsters seem to me to have arrived at a degree of perfection much superior to that of our world. It won't be long, in any case, before you have proof of it—but it's probable that the types glimpsed by you through the latticework are the sum of all the moral and physical ugliness of the globe."

"But how can they live in air so rarefied?" the young woman went on. "Without your miraculous appearance, we'd have been done for."

"Your reasoning might be false, Mademoiselle, in the sense that the lungs of these folk are doubtless less demanding than ours. On the other hand, it might perfectly well be that they're sent to Phobos precisely because of the rarefaction of the air, in order to relieve them, gradually and without suffering, of all muscular strength. The asphyxia that renders the convicts apathetic and devoid of energy might be a punishment like any other."

"My dear Monsieur Fricoulet," said Ossipoff at that moment, "Would it be possible to make a tour of this vehicle?"

"Certainly—but for that, you'll have to put on your respirols."

"What?" said Selena. "It's necessary to imprison ourselves in those helmets again?"

"Undoubtedly—but this time there's nothing to fear, for we have our supply of solidified oxygen with us. Then again, your father's curiosity will be satisfied in a few minutes." As they went to put on their respirols, the engineer added: "One last recommendation: be as sober as possible in your movements, for a single slightly-exaggerated gesture might throw you overboard—and this time, you'd be irredeemably lost." With these words he climbed a small ladder, followed by Ossipoff and Selena. A few moments later, all three found themselves standing on a sort of deck serving as the roof of a lodgment, from which and around which ran a metal border.

Above their heads, turning with vertiginous rapidity, the gigantic cylinder extended its enormous moving mass, which surrounded the propeller that appeared to them as a diaphanous outline. In a forward direction, the gondola narrowed like the prow of a ship and the balloon was elongated into a point, cleaving through space almost soundlessly. It was there, by courtesy of a little ladder about 30 meters high, that the Terrans went into the tube in the middle of which the central axis rotated; then, having passed along its entire length, they reemerged at the rear, near the rudder—a vast circular surface that could be tilted at will in any direction.

Once there, Ossipoff put himself in communication with Fricoulet. "But this apparatus can nether move not steer by itself…it must have a crew?"

The engineer signaled to his friends to follow him and went inside through a narrow opening pierced in the stern of the gondola, hermetically sealed by a sort of lid. Once here, all three took off their respirols and Fricoulet then invited Ossipoff to admire the engine-room, in which incomprehensible machines—bearing no resemblance to any that the old man had seen on Earth—were manufacturing, without heat or sound, the electricity that activated the motors in order to make the gigantic cylindrical balloon rotate on its axis and spin its helical aerofoils.

Half a dozen strange beings were coming and going around the machinery, seemingly indifferent to the Terrans' presence. As the engineer had suggested, there was a considerable difference between the convicts of Phobos—the vile creatures, half-reptile and half-bird, that they had glimpsed through the mesh of the protective net—and the individuals that were in front of them, with their proud bearing, their noble gait and the remarkable intelligence readable in their gaze. They were a little more than two meters in height. The round head was attached to a powerful neck and the remarkably large eyes shone with a vivid gleam which became fatiguing at length. The toothless jaws projected forwards in the form of a beak. The short and profound ears were hairy, as were the cheeks and the skull. The limbs were long and seemed robust, although slender, and a membrane similar to those of bats joined them together.

Fricoulet explained that this membrane served them as both wings and a parachute. At rest, as they were at present, the membrane completely replaced clothing for them, rather like a sort of toga in which they draped themselves, not without nobility. The engineer added that some among them, who moved in the highest intellectual circles, painted the membrane with highly artistic colors.

"And you dared to say, just now, that these creatures are not ugly!" said Selena.

"From your point of view, without doubt, they're frightening," replied the engineer, "but beauty isn't everything, not only in this world but in the Universe entire. Now, what I've seen of their planet has been sufficient to convince me that these people have attained a degree of civilization that we shall not attain for several centuries."

While chatting, the Terrans had gone into the interior of the gondola again and were heading toward the cabin in which Gontran had remained, in Farenheit's care. Fricoulet, who went ahead of the old man and Selena, was about to cross the threshold when the sound of raised voices reached him and immobilized him. He gestured to his companions to remain silent and all three of them pricked up their ears.

"By God!" howled Farenheit, "I tell you that it was an American who discovered these satellites…or Monsieur Ossipoff doesn't know what he's saying."

"Agreed," replied Flammermont. "Who would think of contesting that Hall deserves credit for that discovery? I'm merelly saying that although he, being favored by the maximum proximity of the Earth and Mars, actually saw the satellites of the latter planet, others before him had foreseen them."

"Get away!"

"There's no *get away* about it, and these lines I find quoted in my illustrious namesake's *Les Continents célestes* were certainly not written by Hall…they're from the pen of Voltaire, who wrote them in his romance *Micromégas* in 1750: 'On leaving Jupiter, our voyagers crossed a space of about a 100,000,000 leagues and skirted Mars. They saw two moons serving that planet, which have escaped the eyes of our astronomers. I know that Père Castel will write to dispute the existence of these two moons; but I am in agreement with those arguing by analogy. These good philosophers know how difficult it would be for Mars, being so distant from the Sun, to have less than two moons…' "[38]

---

[38] This quote from *Micromégas* (which was actually published in 1752) omits one minor phrase, which offers Père Castel a backhanded compliment in suggesting that he will write "pleasantly enough." The use of the future tense may seem odd; the reference is inserted because the Jesuit mathematician Louis Bertrand Castel (1688-1757) had published a *Traité de physique de la pesanteur universelle des corps* [Treatise on the Physics of the Universal Gravitation of

Gontran shut the book firmly and asked, ironically: "What do you think of that, Mr. Farenheit?"

"I think that Voltaire, not being an astronomer, said that at random, and that an unexpected stroke of luck made his prediction come true."

"It must be admitted, at any rate," Gontran retorted, "that it was a truth that was in the air—no pun intended—for Swift, the celebrated author of *Gulliver's Travels*, not only mentions two 'lesser stars or satellites, which revolve around Mars,' but even gives precise information about one of these satellites; thus, according to him, the one nearer to the planet 'revolves in the space of ten hours, and the more distant in 21 hours.' "[39]

"I'd make the same reply as for Voltaire—Swift said that at random."

"Not so," declared Flammermont. "They both worked by analogy."

"What do you mean by that?" Farenheit complained.

"I mean that from the fact that Earth has one satellite, Jupiter four and Saturn eight, it is presumable that Mars, situated between Earth and Jupiter, would have two. That's mathematics."

As if blinded by the evidence of this reasoning, Farenheit fell silent for a few seconds; then, finally, he muttered: "It doesn't alter the fact that it was a man from America who discovered the satellites of Mars."

The door opened then and Ossipoff replied: "Not a man from America, Mr. Farenheit, but a woman from America. It's an authenticated fact that, after having spent several nights fruitlessly searching for the presumed satellites of Mars, Hall was about to renounce the continuation of his search in despair, when his wife arrived and insisted firmly that he devote 'one more evening' to it."

"That's not important," the American replied. "What has to be established is that the honor of the discovery reverts to the United States."

"No one thought of denying it," my dear Mr. Farenheit, said Fricoulet in his turn.

"The moral of the story," said Selena, darting a malicious glance at the engineer, "is that wives can sometimes be useful."

Bodies] (1724) that opposed Isaac Newton's theory, without reference to empirical data, on the grounds that it was irrational and overcomplicated, and Voltaire—one of Newton's chief defenders in France—is suggesting that Castel was the kind of man who would routinely deny facts if he found them unesthetic.

[39] The second of these quotes from Chapter III of Part III of the book generally known as *Gulliver's Travels* is slightly mistaken; the figure Swift gives is actually "21 and a half hours." The great satirist goes on to explain that the squares of these times are in proportion to the satellites' distances from the planet, thus providing an illustration of the universal law of gravitation—that being the principal importance of the discovery, from the viewpoint of the astronomers of Laputa.

Fricoulet was doubtless about to reply, but Gontran advanced toward him and hugged him. "Ah!" he said, in an emotional voice. "I didn't expect to see you again."

"A miracle!" cried Ossipoff. "You've recovered your voice!"

"In recovering Fricoulet," replied the young Comte, with a smile addressed to Selena, "I've recovered everything that I had lost." Then, after a further accolade, he added: "But by what miracle have you rejoined us?"

The engineer shrugged his shoulders slightly and replied in an affected tone that brought a slight frown to Ossipoff's face: "No need for miracles, my dear chap; a little intelligence and skill were sufficient. Scarcely had the metallic balloon taken to the skies again than I perceived the material impossibility of my being able to come down again to join you, so I abandoned myself to Providence and let myself be carried along for a few hours. Having traveled a few 100 kilometers, the balloon turned a somersault, by virtue of which I recognized that I had just penetrated the attractive zone of Mars. From that moment on, I had a chance of being saved."

"What—of being saved?" Farenheit interjected.

"Assuredly—for, instead of Phobos, I would be able to land on Mars. I immediately maneuvered in that direction. I pulled hard on the cable controlling the valve, opening it wide enough to let three quarters of the gas escape. Then began a frightful, vertiginous, formidable fall; in less than half an hour I fell 5000 kilometers. I was obliged to put on my respirol in order not to be stifled. As I clung to the edge, it was as if I were fascinated by the world whose force of attraction was increasing with every second, on which I would inevitably crash."

"Poor Monsieur Fricoulet," murmured Selena. "What terrible emotions you must have experienced..."

"My God, Mademoiselle, would I seem boastful to you if I were to confess, in all sincerity, that the thought of death never crossed my mind for an instant? On the contrary—I was very calm, and while falling, I calculated the velocity at which I was about to establish contact between my poor body and the surface of Mars. I also tried to extrapolate what the result of that encounter would be."

"Ah, that's the man I know you to be!" cried Gontran, taking pride himself in his friend's courage.

"In brief," the engineer went on, "I was barely 100 meters from the ground when my vertical fall was suddenly halted and I found myself drawn along horizontally by an unknown force with uncommon velocity. I covered 40 kilometers thus, and a vast extent of water soon appeared beneath me, shining in the sunlight. It was the Kepler Ocean. If hazard dictated that my fall would be completed in that liquid element, I had a chance of getting out of it..."

"The element?" asked Gontran.

"No, the situation I was in. Unfortunately, I continued to fly horizontally and, after crossing the ocean, began flying over solid ground again. Gradually, however, my speed relented, and I arrived at a sort of metallic apparatus, where I stopped."

"What was it?" Ossipoff asked, with keen interest.

"I understood, from some summary explanations that were given to me afterwards, that the Martians have established a means of very rapid locomotion on their world, based on the formation of violent air-currents that push vehicles from one relay station to another. I had been caught in one of these air-currents and my balloon, forming a vehicle, had thus miraculously escaped the death that awaited me. As you can imagine, my first concern was to try to rejoin you. That wasn't easy, I can tell you; finally, after much effort, I succeeded in making these people understand the situation you were in. I then persuaded them to charter this balloon in order to permit me to search for you...and here we are..." Then, letting himself fall into a chair, exhausted by his narration, the engineer added: "That, certainly, is a story compared with which that of Théramène[40] is nothing at all; I'm completely out of breath."

Farenheit, who had listened to all these explanations with great attention, went over to Fricoulet. "My dear sir," he said, "I'd like to ask you a question."

"Ask, Mr. Farenheit, ask."

"You mentioned an ocean just now...so they exist on this world?"

"Indubitably, my dear Mr. Farenheit. Their areography has been known to everyone for some time."

"Areography?" Selena repeated, interrogatively.

"The geography of Mars, if you prefer, Mademoiselle—from the Greek Ares, equivalent to the Roman Mars."

Farenheit sniggered audibly. "The geography of the Moon was known for a long time too—selenography, as you call it in that impossible language of scientists. Seas are found there on the maps that were drawn up, but it seems that words change their meaning in astronomy, since the spaces designated on the lunar map by the name of 'seas' are only immense arid and desiccated plains, without the slightest trace of water..."

"But since I tell you that I have seen the Kepler Ocean with my own eyes..." protested Fricoulet.

"You're like Saint Thomas, Mr. Farenheit," Mikhail Ossipoff put in, mockingly, "you only believe in things you've seen...but if it had ever occurred to you, during your terrestrial existence, to look through a telescope, you would have been convinced of the existence of the Martian seas without actually needing to make the voyage."[41]

---

[40] Théramène is a character in Racine's *Phèdre*; the narration that made his name proverbial in this fashion was his account of the death of his pupil, Hippolyte.

[41] This may seem odd to the modern readers, but it was not until the observations made from Percival Lowell's Flagstaff Observatory in the 1890s became

"A little voyage," Flammermont sniggered, "of some 19,000,000 leagues."

"14,000,000 only, if you please," observed the old scientist. "To study a world, one does not choose the moment when it is furthest away."

"Let's say 14,000,000," said Farenheit, folding his arms. "And you want me to believe that it is possible at such a distance to establish the presence of water on a planet?"

"You admit yourself that one of your compatriots has discovered Deimos and Phobos—two worldlets a few kilometers in diameter—but you doubt that it has been possible to study Mars, whose diameter is nearly 1700 leagues and its circumference of 5375 leagues? If you take the trouble to reflect a little, you'll avoid many unnecessary words."

The American stamped his foot violently. "Don't put words into my mouth that I haven't said," he muttered. "It's one thing to recognize bodies existing in space—that's what telescopes are made for—and another thing entirely to claim to study infinitely petty details."

"But my dear Mr. Farenheit," aid Gontran, maliciously, "telescopes are made for that too."

"Monsieur de Flammermont is right," Ossipoff added. "Thanks to the marvelous instruments that progress has put at the disposal of modern science, one can affirm the existence of facts occurring millions of leagues away with as much certainty as if one could lay a finger on them. Thus, I will go further still in my affirmation; not only is there water on the surface of Mars but that water has the same chemical composition as ours. Not only are there seas, but we also know their depth. We know, for example, that the deepest are in the vicinity of the equator and the torrid zone, like the Schiaparelli Sea, the Flammarion Sea, the Kepler Ocean and the Newton Ocean, while those in the polar regions, such as the Mädler, Faye and Beer Seas, are not as deep."

Farenheit's amazement was indescribably profound.

"On would think, I'd swear, that you've never gone up in a balloon!" Ossipoff exclaimed.

"My word, no," Farenheit replied. "My trade in animal fats does not require ascensions, and my liking for solid ground has always prevented me from indulging in such perilous exercises."

"Well, my dear Mr. Farenheit, if you had gone up in a balloon, you would not be surprised that, in spite of the 14,000,000 leagues that separate us from

---

the basis for the elaborate mythology of the canals of Mars that the idea took hold that Mars was a world that had become direly arid, whose inhabitants had been forced by necessity to transport water from the poles in order to sustain their decadent civilization. In the 1880s, Camille Flammarion's writings, and those of other popularizers, not only still held to the notion that the Martian "seas" really were vast expanses of water, but took it for granted that the fact was manifest to the eye of the experienced observer, as Ossipoff here maintains.

Mars, one can know the relative depth of its seas. It depends on the relative darkness of the color that the appearance of large masses of liquid present. The darker the hue, the greater the depth."

"Can one not equally deduce," asked Fricoulet, "the degree of salinity of the different seas, for it's proven that the saltier an expanse of water is, the darker it seems? Now, as the salinity depends on evaporation, it's quite natural that the darker seas—which is to say, the saltiest—are found in the equatorial regions."

Ossipoff inclined his head slightly, in a movement full of approving condescension.

The American remained silent for a few moments, then suddenly clicked his fingers. "Anyway," he said, "it doesn't matter to me whether the seas are salty and deep or not. The man thing, for me, is that we can breathe at our ease, freely, without being obliged to shut ourselves up again in those selenium cages." He favored the respirols piled up in a corner with a dirty look.

"In that regard," said Fricoulet, laughing, "you can be tranquil, my dear Mr. Farenheit—the planet Mars is provided with an atmosphere whose composition is identical to ours. Spectral studies leave no doubt on that subject. If you like rain and cloud too, you will have what you need to be content, for the Martian atmosphere is rich in water vapor."

"But in view of the lesser intensity of gravity at the Martian surface," Gontran objected, "the density of its atmosphere must be almost ineffectual, and it probably follows that there is a rarefaction similar to that on the summits of the highest terrestrial mountains."

The American's radiant expression darkened again. "It's respirols again, then?" he groaned.

Fricoulet clicked his tongue impatiently. "If what you say were the case," he replied to Flammermont, "the Martian seas would be dry, all their contents having long been volatilized into space, instead of being transformed, after their evaporation, into vapor—clouds and fogs—to fall again thereafter on to the surface of the planet in the form of rain. Then again, the snows that surround the poles, instead of being simple caps in the polar regions, would bury the entire planet in a shroud, transforming Mars into a block of ice."

Gontran seemed rather annoyed by this explanation, furnished in front of Ossipoff; as for Farenheit, his expression cleared again.

"Now that you've reassured Mr. Farenheit," said Selena, in her turn, with a smile, "I'd like you to reassure me too, Monsieur Fricoulet."

The engineer bowed. "Entirely at your disposal, Mademoiselle," he murmured.

"You know that I'm sensitive to cold," the young woman said.

"Yes, I know—and your cometary sojourn must certainly have developed that natural disposition further—but why mention it to me?"

"Because I suppose that it can't be very warm on your Mars."

The engineer's eyes widened. "I'm curious to know on what you base that supposition?"

"On what I was told by Gontran."

Scarcely had the engineer posed the question than he regretted it, for he had anticipated the response almost immediately, so he muffled the final words of her reply with a loud and obstinate fit of coughing. Then he said: "Yes, yes, I see where you're coming from. You're one of those who believe that the temperature of the planets is determined by their distance from the Sun and that Mars, in consequence of being 19,000,000 leagues further away from the central star than Earth, must enjoy Siberian temperatures."

The young woman indicated with a nod that this was correct.

"Well, that's a mistake," Fricoulet continued. "The temperature depends on the composition of the atmosphere, which acts as a greenhouse. With respect to the solar heat, it allows it to reach the surface of the ground, and then retains it, opposing itself to its dissipation in space. Air, properly speaking—that is to say, oxygen and nitrogen—only plays an insignificant role in the mechanism that I've just explained; only water vapor has an influence on heat, by reason of its absorbent power, 6000 times superior to that of dry air."[42]

Selena clapped her hands. "I get it!" she exclaimed. "You said just now that the spectroscope had discovered a considerably quantity of water vapor in the Martian atmosphere, so the temperature…"

"May be colder or warmer than on Earth, or perhaps even equal to it, depending on circumstance—but in any event, I don't think we'll have to suffer overmuch."

"Besides," Farenheit said, "if these Martians are as advanced in their civilization as you claim, they must certainly have infallible means of protecting themselves from cold and heat."

"It's probable." Having said that, Fricoulet put on his respirol, screwed on his selenium helmet and went up on deck, looking for Ossipoff—whom he found leaning over the rampart, devouring the landscape extended beneath them with his eyes.

"How well one can take account of the Martian topography, eh?" said the scientist, immediately putting himself in communication with the engineer.

"It's true," the young man replied, "that from a few 100 kilometers one has things more clearly in view than one has from several million leagues."

---

[42] The "hothouse effect" by virtue of which atmospheres may act as heat traps was first described by Jean-Baptiste-Joseph, Baron Fourier (1768-1830); unlike Fricoulet, however, Fourier recognized the importance of carbon dioxide as well as that of water vapor. When the authors wrote this passage, however, they were unaware of the calculations made in the 1890s by Svante Arrhenius, who asserted in consequence that doubling the amount of the carbon dioxide in the Earth's atmosphere would result in a mean temperature increase of five degrees Celsius.

"How different it is from our globe! While three-quarters of the terrestrial surface is covered with water and our vastest continents are, properly speaking, only gigantic islands, here it's the other way around. The seas and the continents are in almost the same proportion, but in favor of the continents."

"And in consequence, curiously enough," Fricoulet continued, "all its seas are, in effect, Mediterranean." As he finished these words a hand fell on his shoulder. He turned round and saw Gontran, who signaled that he wanted to talk to him. Immediately, the two speakers were adapted to the two helmets.

"What is it?"

"It's just," replied the young Comte, "that I'm straining my eyes in vain to discover the bloody gleam that has made Mars the warrior planet, of which I can see absolutely nothing."

"Which isn't at all surprising, given that the reddish—or, to be strictly accurate, orange-yellow—tint is more appreciable to the naked eye than through a telescope. It has been remarked in observatories that the tint diminishes in intensity the more the instrumental magnification increases. That's why you can't even make it out."

"A reddish atmosphere ought, however, to give everything it surrounds an appearance of the same hue."

"Heresy, dear chap, heresy—for, if the coloration were due to the atmosphere, it would be more intense at the edges than in the center, by reason of the atmospheric thickness traversed by the luminous rays."

"Is it necessary to attribute it to the soil itself?"

"If Ossipoff heard you, he'd have a fit," said the engineer, "for that hypothesis is in flagrant contradiction with what we know about the world of Mars. How, indeed, can we admit that the age-long effect of the four elements that engender life—water, air, earth and fire—have remained ineffectual, and that no vegetation has dressed the surface of Mars?"

"So it's the vegetation! But you must know something about that, since you arrived there."

"On that subject, I can't give you any information. For one thing, I landed on Mars at night—but even if it had been broad daylight. I'd have been too overcome by anguish to take any notice of it."

Gontran remained silent for a moment. "In that case," he said, "pending further instructions, what I'd better do is to adopt the vegetation theory, if Ossipoff interrogates me?"

"Pooh! It's of little importance. Just remember that Mars is 5375 leagues in circumference, and that, by comparison with the terrestrial globe, its surface area is 27%, its volume 16%, its weight a fifth and its density 69%—which means that the intensity of gravity at its surface is a third of what it is on the Earth's surface. Can you remember all that?"

"I think so—but is that all?"

"No, remember this, too: that Mars rotates on its axis in 24 hours, 37 minutes and 27 seconds, and around the Sun in 660 days—which makes its year twice as long as ours."[43]

"And consequently, its seasons…"

"I'll stop you there, for that's one of the characteristic differences between this world and ours. Not only is the duration of the seasons longer, but it's unequal, by reason of its elongated orbit. Thus, while spring and summer last 191 and 181 days, autumn and winter only last 149 and 147 days."

The engineer was doubtless about to continue his explanations when a Martian approached and signaled to him that it was necessary to descend into the cabin.

Chapter XXXIV
The Warrior Planet

"On landing on this new world, the first impression received by our mind is not very different from the impression that the spectacles of nature impose upon us. We find ourselves transported to a world strangely analogous to ours. The edges of its seas receive, as they do here, the eternal plaint of the waves that break and die on the shore—for there, as here, the breath of the wind wrinkles the face of the waters and gives birth to waves that follow one another and fall back. If the sky is pure and the atmosphere calm, the mirror of the waters reflects, as it does here, the dazzling Sun and the luminous sky.

"The European villager who, cast up by the wave of emigration on the shores of Australia, wakes up one fine day in the midst of an unknown country where the soil, the trees, the animals, the seasons and the courses of the Sun and the Moon are very different in appearance from what he has previously seen in his native land, is no less surprised and lost than we are on arriving in the planet Mars. To be transported from the Earth to Mars is simply to change latitude."[44]

Thus, with regard to the planet on which our voyagers were landing, the celebrated propagator of astronomical science expresses himself—and Gontran, analyzing his own sensations, could not help recognizing how concordant they were with the thoughts contained in the passage from *Les Continents célestes* reproduced above.

It was night when a sign from the Martian who appeared to be the captain of the vessel invited them to come out of the gondola, and the entire landscape surrounding the Terrans was immersed in profound darkness. Here and there,

---

[43] These figures are all reasonably accurate except the last, although the figure of 660 is closer to the actual number of Martian days in a Martian year (670) than the figure of 608 previously given.

[44] This quotation is an abridged version of the first paragraph of Chapter II of *Les Terres du ciel*, pp.20-21.

however, thicker shadows stood out, confused but intriguing by virtue of their mass or their height. Our voyagers' eyes strained in vain to pierce the obscurity. The only thing of which they were truly conscious was a sheet of water that extended to their feet, making soft sounds like those of the minuscule waves of our Mediterranean impelled by a spring breeze. In the water, as in a burnished silver mirror, the sky was reflected, with its myriad sparkling stars. One might have thought it a silken cloth sprinkled with gold.

Instinctively, our friends looked up.

"But the sky hasn't changed!" Gontran exclaimed. "There are the same stars, the same constellations...that one sees from the Paris Observatory."

Ossipoff turned to him enthusiastically, retorting: "The same stars, perhaps...but the same planets?" By the tone in which these few words were pronounced, the young Comte scented an ambush, and prudently uttered a little dry cough to attract Fricoulet's attention—but the engineer was much too busy studying the maneuvering of the balloon to think about his friend, so the latter's embarrassment increased.

With his nose in the air and his gaze fixed on the starry vault, Gontran slowly pivoted on his heels, summoning to his aid all the gods with whom mythology had been pleased to populate the sidereal immensity. The gods were doubtless asleep, though, for no inspiration came to the unfortunate ex-diplomat. Suddenly, though, a voice as light as a breath whispered behind him: "Over there, on your right...Jupiter, then Saturn...and then on the other side...the Earth."

Meanwhile, astonished by the incomprehensible silence, Ossipoff uttered a "Well?" replete with suspicion.

As if gripped by a dream, Flammermont shivered. He passed his hand over his forehead, redirected his gaze to the old man and said, in a vibrant voice: "Excuse me, Monsieur...but the sight of my native planet evoked memories that took entire possession of my mind."

"Only memories?" asked Selena.

"Naughty!" he replied, taking her hand and kissing it affectionately. "Not only memories, but hopes too...since it's there alone that our happiness will become complete..."

Ossipoff coughed lightly, for he was always rather embarrassed when Gontran made allusion to his problematic marriage to Selena. Then, to change the subject, he pointed toward the brilliant star. "In truth," he said, "would one not swear that one were looking at Venus? It's the same soft light...the same situation..."

"We probably play the same role for Mars?"

"If, by that, you mean that the Earth is the Martian evening star, you're right."

"Evening?" said Jonathan Farenheit. "Do you think that star you're admiring is an evening star?" And, without waiting for a reply, he held up his chronometer. "It's 1:30 p.m. in New York," he said, after a momentary pause.

"6 p.m. in St. Petersburg," added Selena

"5 p.m. in Paris," said Gontran, in his turn.

"With the result that it's 4 a.m. in the morning here," concluded Mikhail Ossipoff. "You're right, Mr. Farenheit."

"Isn't that the Earth, then?" stammered Gontran.

"What's problematic about that? Isn't Venus both an evening and morning star for us? It precedes the dawn and follows the dusk...it depends..."

"Yes," Gontran repeated, mechanically. "It depends..."

"Depends on what?" Farenheit asked him.

The young Comte found himself suddenly embarrassed, all the more so because Mikhail Ossipoff was staring at him. Instinctively, he leaned backwards to put his ear within rang of Selena's lips. Then, straightening up, he replied: "It depends on the seasons, of course, my dear Mr. Farenheit. We've been leading such a singular life for so long that I scarcely know what month it is."

"It's May," replied Ossipoff. "May 8. Yesterday, the Earth was at its greatest occidental elongation, 37 degrees and 37 minutes, and it will remain the morning star until October."

Oof! thought Flammermont, uttering a slight sigh. *That's the Q.E.D. of the problem. This oral exam is interminable.*

Fricoulet arrived at that moment. "My friends," he said, "we'll get under way, if you're ready."

"Where to?" the Terrans immediately asked, with one voice.

"To the City of Light, as the planet's capital is called."

"And is your City of Light far from here?" asked Farenheit, already alarmed by the prospect of making use of his legs.

"If I've understood Aotaha's summary explanations..." Fricoulet began.

Gontran interrupted him. "Who's Aotaha?" he asked.

"A very friendly and learned Martian whose acquaintance I have made, and who seems to fulfill the role, on this planet, of Grand-Master of the University."

Flammermont could not help emitting a short burst of mocking laughter. "If you've understood, you say; do these people talk, then, as one does on the Boulevard Montparnasse?"

"Pooh!" said the engineer, with a moue of disdain. "It's a long time since the Martians left syntax and everything connected with it behind; time being, for them, the most precious thing in the world, they've sought a linguistic system permitting the expression of thought as rapidly as it springs to mind."

"A sort of stenographic language?"

117

"Precisely; the five vowels serve as the basis for this very simple system, in such a way that, according to the tone in which they are pronounced, they express some thought or another."[45]

"But that gives them a very restricted vocabulary," Mademoiselle Ossipoff objected. "Remember that the voice only has two and a half octaves—which gives, by its division into semitones, a total of 30 different sounds. These people would only have very imperfect means to express their thoughts."

The engineer smiled. "You can't be unaware, Mademoiselle," he replied, "that it's vibration that forms sounds; thus, the deepest note of the human voice corresponds to 160 vibrations, while the most elevated is 2048. Well, in going from 160 to 2048, the sound is modified by each added vibration, which gives 1888 different sounds. You see that the Martian language is richer than you think."

"What you say is quite accurate," Flammermont riposted. "Unfortunately, the human ear is unable to grasp such subtle nuances."

"The human ear, agreed—but these people's ears are subject, from birth, to an education that even permits them, after a certain number of years, to achieve a truly marvelous perception. Young Martians are taught to distinguish the vibrations that compose a sound just as we learn to discover the subtle beauties contained in a text by Virgil, Homer or any other ancient author."

"But we have grammars, dictionaries and a whole host of instruments..."

"Just as they do..." The engineer took a rather singular apparatus out of his coat; it resembled a helmet ornamented on each side by who appendages similar to the funnels of hunting-horns. "This," he said, "is what infants of the most tender age carry; these shell-like items, made of a metal that has the property of vibrating with extreme facility, are fitted over the ears and transmit the vibrations stored within them to the eardrums. As the child grows, the size of the shells diminishes, to disappear entirely when education is complete."

With an easily-imaginable curiosity, the Terrans studied the bizarre instrument, which each of them tried out in turn.

"Myself," said Gontran, rather ironically, "I find that it distorts speech."

"Because we don't make use, as these people do, of monosyllables to render our thoughts; the vibrations of each of our speech-acts are confused with one another."

"Ending up as an incomprehensible cacophony," said Farenheit.

"And you already understand what they're saying?" asked Selena, ready to fall at the engineer's feet in admiration.

"Oh!" the latter replied. "You have too high an opinion of my intelligence—which is to say that the excellent Aotaha, with a patience beyond all

---

[45] The reader might wonder how "Aotaha" and the other Martian names subsequently recorded in the text are derived from this system; Fricoulet is however, rather economical with his explanations.

118

praise, has enabled me to make use with him a sort of pidgin, by pronouncing certain monosyllables and then showing my the object to which he is referring. I only know the ABC of the Martian language; as for the theory I've just outlined, I deduced it from what I could understand of Aotaha's language."

"Well, old chap," said Flammermont, "from this day forward I nominate you as my private interpreter...for I've never had a liking for vocalization exercises, having always had a tin ear."

"To get back to your City of Light," said the American, "you were saying..."

"That the city is located at the extremity of the continent Kepler, on the 195th degree of longitude."

The American uttered a dull groan. "That's all very well—but first, where are we?"

"Not far from the Lake of the Sun, on the continent that Schiaparelli baptized with the name Thaumasia."

"Which is to say," added Ossipoff, "on the 90th degree of longitude. We have, therefore, about 105 degrees to travel...which is 6800 kilometers."

"I'll never do that on foot," Farenheit complained.

"Who said anything about that?" asked Fricoulet. "We have a vehicle ready, and if you'd care to follow me..."

Marching on the engineer's heels, the Terrans moved back toward the place where the national balloon had set them down. To their great surprise, they saw the gondola in which they had made the crossing from Phobos to Mars standing on rails of some sort. The enormous cylinder that had surmounted it had disappeared, however, along with the propeller and the rudder. As it now was, it had the exact appearance of a gigantic shell—or, rather, a monumental Lebel rifle bullet.[46] Its tip was directed toward a metallic mass about ten meters high and as many wide, which had suddenly extended from the ground to an extent of 30 or 40 meters.

"Devil take me!" said Farenheit, who had approached the monstrous apparatus and was examining it closely. "It's highly reminiscent of the breech of a cannon."

As he finished these words, a sort of electric bell rang and the object that the American had just compared to the breech of a cannon opened up, displaying a profound cavity sparkling with light. Taken by surprise at first, the Terrans took a step backwards.

"What's that?" murmured Selena, in a fearful voice.

"Nothing very frightening, Mademoiselle," replied the engineer.

"What, then?"

---

[46] The Lebel Model 1886 rifle, introduced in that year, had a distinctive "boat-tailed" bullet. The narrative voice is probably entitled to make the comparison for the benefit of its 1889 readers, even though the scene is set in 1884.

"I've told you about the inestimable value that time has in the Martians' eyes. You'll not be astonished to learn, therefore, that all their efforts tend to shorten distances—which is to say, to travel the said distances as rapidly as possible."

"Don't their wings enable them to do that?" objected Farenheit.

"Just so—but because their muscular force isn't much greater than ours, relatively speaking, they can't accomplish much more in flying long distances than we Terrans could by walking. They have therefore been obliged to invent systems of locomotion…and this is one of them, which will transport us to the City of Light."

"That doesn't explain…" said Selena.

"Listen," said Fricoulet. "You know the pneumatic system that transports dispatches enclosed in little vessels resembling rifle bullets through a network of underground tubes? What you see here is a system of locomotion based on the same principle…"

Mademoiselle Selena's slightly anxious face cleared as if by magic; without waiting any longer, she leapt on to the platform of the gondola with a single bound and disappeared inside.

Less than two minutes had elapsed since Fricoulet, who was bringing up the rear, had rejoined his companions, when a dull noise was audible outside.

"That's the doors of the tube closing again," the engineer replied, to the mute interrogation in Selena's eyes.

For a few moments, a profound silence reigned in the cabin; each of them, absorbed in personal reflections, was silent.

Farenheit was the first to speak. "One thing that astonishes me, my dear Monsieur Ossipoff," he said, "is that this world, which the Creator has endowed with two satellites, should be worse lit by night than the Earth, which has but one."

"One thing that astonishes me more," retorted the old scientist, with a smile full of condescension, "is your astonishment. Two reasons, in fact, prevent Mars from receiving a very bright light from its satellites. The first is the distance that separates Mars from the Sun, which appears to the planet only in the form of a circle 21 millimeters in diameter, whereas its disk, seen from Earth, is between 31 and 32 millimeters…an appreciable difference, you'll agree."

"I agree to that, but you'll also agree that the difference might be counterbalanced by the proximity of the satellites to the planet they ought to illuminate. While the Moon orbits the Earth at 90,000 leagues, Phobos traces its orbit at 6000 kilometers and Deimos at 20,000…that's also appreciable."

Ossipoff nodded his head. "Undoubtedly!" he said. "But you're forgetting one thing, which is that, even at 6000 kilometers, the disk of Phobos is no larger than seven minutes, and that of Deimos only two minutes; that of the Moon is 31—which is to say, three and 15 times larger…"

"And in conclusion from these figures," Fricoulet said, in his turn, "do you know how much difference of light-intensity those differences of distance give? As the light received from the Sun varies according to the position of Mars, the result is that the brightness of Deimos is between 1/400 and 1/675 of our moon-light and that of Phobos between 1/45 and 1/67. Is that clear?"

"Clearer than the light of the Martian satellites," Farenheit replied, laughing, "but if they don't serve as illumination, what are they useful for?"

"Regulating clocks and longitudes with remarkable precision, thanks to the rapidity of their rotation," Gontran replied, half in jest and half seriously.

Fricoulet wagged a finger at him. "That's not yours," he whispered in his ear.

"Not mine!" relied the young Comte, almost offended.

"You memorized *Les Continents célestes* with such great ardor that you've ended up appropriating its contents and, without being conscious of it, offering us the theories of your illustrious namesake as your own..."

"That's quite possible," muttered Flammermont.

"Now then!" cried the American, suddenly. "Will we be leaving soon?" He consulted his chronometer and added: "It's nearly 20 minutes since we got in, and we haven't budged."

"There's every chance that we've arrived," replied Fricoulet, seeing the door open and Aotaha beckoning to him from the threshold.

There was a rapid and animated dialogue between the Terran and the Martian, mingled with expressive gestures on the part of the latter and curt monosyllables pronounced with bizarre intonations on the part of the former.

Afterwards, the engineer came back to his companions. "I guessed right," he said. "We've arrived."

"Arrived where?" asked Gontran. "At the City of Light?"

"No, we've only traveled 400 kilometers and we're on the shore of the Lake of the Sun."

"Or Terby Sea," Ossipoff rectified.

The America's amazement was profound. "But that's magical," he stammered. "We didn't experience any shock on departure or arrival...even better, we heard neither the rolling of wheels or the friction of the vehicle's walls against those of the tube."

"There's a very simple explanation for that," replied the engineer, smiling. "First, the vehicle has no wheels; second, its walls have no point of contact with those of the tube in which it circulates."

"That's a fairy tale!" exclaimed Flammermont, involuntarily. "You want us to believe that our vehicle is suspended in the middle of the tube without touching it at any point?"

"I don't want you to believe it—I affirm it."

"What about the wind?" added Flammermont. "What do you do about that? If things were as you say, the compressed air propelling the vehicle would pass into empty space and there'd be a considerable loss of force."

The engineer shrugged his shoulders and replied: "Your argument lacks common sense; even so, when I have a minute to spare, I'll refute it. For the moment, we have to disembark."

As he spoke, he went to stand underneath the aperture pierced in the cabin's ceiling and, with a slight thrust of his feet, leapt outside. At that moment, the Sun appeared over the horizon, and its golden darts split the somber mantle of the night, causing a liquid immensity whose surface was rippled by a slight breeze to sparkle before the Terrans' marveling eyes.

"The Lake of the Sun!" exclaimed Mikhail Ossipoff, in a ringing voice. With his elbows on the rampart, he sank into ecstatic contemplation.

Meanwhile, with a curiosity not exempt from suspicion, his companions examined a host of individuals similar to Aotaha, who were surrounding the vehicle, pressing together, jostling one another and pointing at the strange beings gathered on the footbridge, with forceful gestures and exclamations.

"Great God!" moaned Selena. "Just as long as they don't come any closer."

"Don't be afraid, Mademoiselle," said Fricoulet. "Curiosity alone impels them."

"It's singular," Gontran murmured, "that the extreme civilization you claim for this advanced Martian race doesn't render them more beautiful than they are."

"And why do you expect this world to be different from our own? To take but one example, compare our ancestors, the ancient Frankish warriors, with the coxcombs that we are."

"So you say," Gontran retorted, jokingly. "Speak for yourself."

"Assuredly," said Selena, "I don't find Monsieur de Flammermont to be as much of a coxcomb as you might think…"

The engineer shrugged his shoulders casually. "Just put a heap of weapons into his arms, and chain-mail from the Middle Ages on his torso, and you'll see how freely and easily he carries himself."

"What are you getting at?" asked Flammermont, in a bittersweet voice, not very pleased at being subjected to ridicule in the presence of his fiancée.

"I'm trying to make you understand that the more a race advances in civilization, the more it atrophies…the brain monopolizes vigor, to the detriment of the rest of the body."

At that moment, Ossipoff released a cry of terror. A host of those strange creatures had suddenly risen from the ground, spiraling in the air above and around the group formed by the Terrans. One might have taken them for a flock of immense birds, whose wings beat the air almost silently.

At a gesture from Aotaha, all that ceased, as if by magic. Folding their wings, their curiosity doubtless satisfied, the Martians drew away.

"Our guide is signaling to us to follow him," said Fricoulet, touching Ossipoff on the shoulder.

The latter raised his head and saw Aotaha—who, deploying his wings, flew rapidly down to the ground.

"Follow him!" muttered the old scientist, his mind still full of the dreams he had been entertaining. "That's easy to say—but how?"

"By the same route!" retorted Gontran. Tensing his leg, the young man jumped over the side and landed lightly beside the Martian. One by one, his companions did likewise.

Moored to the shore, a singularly-shaped boat was bobbing. It attracted the attention of the Terrans, especially Fricoulet, who ran to it in a few strides. "Hey!" he exclaimed, summoning his companions with cries and forceful gestures. "Hey! It's Raoul Pictet's apparatus!"

"What do you mean by that?" asked Ossipoff.

"I mean an apparatus equipped at the rear, like this one, with a vast plane surface forming a keel, permitting the boat to glide over the surface like a sleigh over ice."

"A boat on skates, then!" said Gontran.

"Very nearly."

"And what results from that?" asked Farenheit.

"Considerable speed—something like 40 or 50 knots."

"That's prodigious."

"I don't know whether it's prodigious," Gontran said, in his turn, "but it's a very graceful navigation apparatus, at any rate."

And he was certainly right; the bow, highly elevated above the waves, was curved in the fashion of the gondolas plying the Venetian lagoons; the rounded stern rested on the vast triangular platform spread out over the liquid sheet like a gigantic peacock's tail. On the poop and along a third of its length stood a cockpit pieced by portholes, and a floor had been built on to that cockpit at prow level, forming a second deck—which was itself covered by a light roof designed to protect the passengers from the ardor of the Sun. In the posterior section of this deck, enclosed by the boat itself and partly resting on the cabin on the lower floor, was a launch, which a simple spring could dispatch into the water in a matter of seconds.

Once the Terrans had taken their places aboard this strange vessel, Aotaha gave a signal. Driven by a propeller set beneath the launch in the middle of the platform, the boat drew away from the shore. As Fricoulet had explained, it skimmed the crests of the waves like a seabird, with incredible velocity, without any pitching. In less than an hour, the coast disappeared over the horizon.

"At this rate," murmured Ossipoff, who had unfolded one of Schiaparelli's maps, "we'll have crossed the entire width of the ocean before nightfall."

"Do you know that the width in question is 600 kilometers?" Flammermont asked.

"If you'll take the trouble to make the calculation," the old scientist retorted, "you'll see that I'm not exaggerating."

All day they glided over the waves without any incident breaking the monotony of the voyage. Ossipoff, whose eyes never quit the map, declared that they must be approaching the equator, not far from Schiaparelli's Nodus Gordii.

The Sun, almost at its zenith, directed its rays vertically, and the heat was fearsome. Suddenly, there seemed to be an extraordinary animation aboard. The Martian crew, grouped on the deck, were arguing enthusiastically and pointing into the distance as a point invisible to the Terrans, but which the Martians, with their acuity of vision, could make out clearly.

"An accident, no doubt," grumbled Farenheit. "You'll find that we'll be obliged to continue the journey on foot."

"We'd have to begin by continuing it by swimming," Gontran retorted.

"I don't know," Ossipoff murmured, shaking his head, "but all that fuss doesn't augur anything good."

Fricoulet, who had gone to find Aotaha at the very first moment, came back with a grave expression, seemingly annoyed. On catching sight of him, Gontran exclaimed, jokingly: "Here he is, his misfortunes written on his brow/He has the face and the manner of the first to fall."[47]

"Given that my misfortunes are yours too," complained the engineer, "I think it's ungracious of you to mock."

"Really? What's happened?"

"We can't go any further."

There was a general exclamation. "No further!" said Ossipoff. "Now then, what sort of joke is this?"

"It's not a joke—the canal is closed."

"The canal!" cried Farenheit. "What canal are you talking about?"

"The one we're on, of course."

"This is a canal?" exclaimed the American, indicating with a sweep of his hand the sheet of water that extended as far as the eye could see in every direction."

"Yes, a canal...a simple canal 500 kilometers long."

Farenheit stood still, his eyes wide and his mouth wide open, so profound was his amazement.

Gontran, no less astonished, hid his amazement beneath an apparent indifference. "Admit, my dear Mr. Farenheit," said the engineer, clapping the Ameri-

---

[47] Gontran is quoting from Jean-François Regnard's comedy *Le joueur* [The Gambler] (1696); the dialogue in which it features was often reprinted in collections of homilies, thus becoming familiar to many readers who never saw the play.

can on the shoulder amicably, that Suez and Panama are child's play by comparison with this canal."

"But you can't persuade me that this ocean—for I persist in giving it that name—was hollowed out by the hand of man!"

"It's necessary, though, that I make you believe it, since it's the truth. Besides, you'll be able to convince yourself with your own eyes before long. They're in the process of hollowing out one at right angles to it, and that's why we can't go on."

Ossipoff had abandoned his companions and gone up to the bridge in order to be the first to establish, with his own eyes, the truth about the famous Martian canals—one of the largest question marks posed by the scientists of the entire world.

For an hour, the old man waited, his chest constricted, his heart beating rapidly and his eyes obstinately staring into space.

Finally, in the far distance, a vague line appeared, which gradually became distinct, grew, lengthened, and finished up barring the uniformly blue horizon, with a slight tint of yellow ocher. It was the eastern bank of the canal, where the boat was not long delayed in landing.

"Well?" asked Farenheit. "What are we going to do now?"

"We're going to continue the journey," Gontran replied.

"Like these folk, no doubt," said the American, ironically, pointing to the Martians, who were taking flight on every side.

"Certainly not—*pedibus cum jambis*," riposted the young Comte, who was greatly amused by Farenheit's reluctance to make use of his natural means of locomotion.

Ossipoff intervened. "Before anything else," he said, "I want to see the works of the canal that's being dug at present."

"Another detour that will delay us," grumbled the American.

Without reacting to this manifestation of bad temper, the Terrans set off walking, under the guidance of Aotaha, who fluttered alongside them. Suddenly, they perceived a veritable swarm of living beings tearing formidable masses of earth from the ground, which they were loading on to balloons similar to the one that had searched for the Terrans on Phobos. Enormous machines were running silently, each activated by some sort of thermoelectric pile that transformed solar radiation into electrical energy. As far as the eye could see, they perceived the same swarm, occupied in digging a trench several kilometers wide across the Martian continent.

"A strange notion, to cut their planet up like this," muttered Farenheit.

Meanwhile, Fricoulet was listening in amazement—which grew with every passing second—to the explanations that Aotaha gave him in his laconic language.

"It appears that they're carrying out this gigantic task in anticipation of an imminent war," the engineer said, responding to the American's explanation.

"A war?" cried Ossipoff. "A war, did you way? That scourge, which I considered as the fatal consequence of the state of barbarism into which we are plunged! That terrible, hideous, abominable scourge exists in these lands—which, I thought, had reached the summit of progress and civilization!" And the old man, prey to a strange discouragement, let his head fall into his hands.

In his capacity as an engineer, Fricoulet was prodigiously interested by the works that were being carried out in front of him—before his eyes, so to speak. Suddenly, a question crossed his mind, which he formulated immediately.

"What do you do with all the displaced earth?" he asked the Martian.

"You see those balloons," replied Aotaha. "As soon as they are loaded they depart for Phobos. Phobos was once one of the asteroids that exist between Mars and Jupiter; it was a rock measuring no more than half a league in diameter. When it was captured by our attraction, we thought of utilizing it by establishing a dump there for the waste generated by the digging of the canals."

"Something like a rubbish-tip for the dirt and refuse of a great city," murmured Gontran, for whom his friend had translated the Martian's reply. "But if they go on like that indefinitely, the entire planet will end up being transported to its satellite."

Fricoulet laughed. "Fortunately," he said, "the apogee of these great works has passed."

"How do you know?" asked Flammermont, skeptically.

"Schiaparelli found out for me," the engineer replied. "His studies, during the last conjunction on Mars, revealed to him that the number of canals remained stationary and that…"

His sentence was cut short by an exclamation from Ossipoff. "I deeply regret," the old man said, rubbing his hands together, "that Fedor Sharp is not here. When I think that one day, at the Institute of Sciences, he bored us for several hours in order to prove to us that the Martian canals were nothing but a sort of land-register of collective farms on a globe 'that has attained the era of harmony'!" He paused, rubbing his hands energetically, and added. "What a long face he would have if he knew the bellicose purpose of these works, so peaceful in nature—according to him!" Then, after a second pause, gripped once again by humanitarian ideas, he murmured, bitterly: "So they still make war on Mars!"

Fricoulet, to whom Aotaha had just furnished a long explanation, turned to the old man. "It's not, as you might think, a residuum of barbarism," he told him, "but a fatal, inevitable product of civilization exaggerated to the degree that it has attained on this world."

"That's a paradox, or I don't know one," said Gontran.

"I share Monsieur de Flammermont's opinion," said Farenheit, in his turn.

"Before pronouncing judgment," said Ossipoff, sententiously, "it's necessary to know the facts."

Then, repeating what their guide had said, the engineer explained that war, on the world of Mars, was necessary and indispensable, made by common agreement between the populations of the planet. Several centuries before, at a conference held by delegates of all the Martian nations, the abolition of war had been decided; an international tribunal had been appointed, charged with judging, as a last resort, all the differences that might arise in future between fraternal populations. For a long succession of centuries, the decisions of this tribunal having legal force, the world of Mars lived in unalterable peace and devoted all its efforts to the perfection of arts and sciences, especially sciences, which were solely capable of permitting humanity to reveal the secrets of nature.

Unfortunately, thanks to the progress accomplished in all things, medicine became so powerful that all diseases—all the scourges that had once inflicted terrible but necessary ravages upon the planet—became impotent. There was no need even to combat them; they were prevented. That led to a terrible excess of population. The continents, which began by being too small to nourish all their inhabitants, ended up having an insufficient surface even to contain them. Maritime cities and aerial agglomerations were created; artificial aliments were invented by extracting the nutritive principles indispensable to the renewal of Martian strength from air, water and minerals. Soon, all these expedients became insufficient, and the disasters once produced by war were nothing compared to those that famine engendered.

Then, as had happened several centuries previously, all the nations of the Martian globe sent delegates to a conference in the City of Light; they decided unanimously to re-establish war. As people had been habituated for a long time to consider one another as brothers, however, and, on the other hand, civilization had expelled from the souls of sovereigns all the sentiments that had formerly caused some to take up arms against others, the conference decided to regulate war. It was, in consequence, established that, four times a century, two nations designated in advance by an international assembly would pit themselves against one another, in such a way as to bring the Martian population back to a figure in rapport with the continental surface.[48]

"That's why," Fricoulet said, concluding his story, "every 50 years, after having fixed the number of victims by means a census, the two nations designated by lot are put into a closed field designated for that purpose, and slaughter one another for the good of humankind."

"That's horrible!" said Selena.

---

[48] The modern reader might think it strange that the highly advanced Martians never thought of birth-control as a humane alternative to mass slaughter (just as modern readers are sometimes surprised that Thomas Robert Malthus, who originated the argument extrapolated here, never mentioned it). The fact is that in both Protestant England in the 1790s and Catholic France in the 1880s, birth control—though widely practiced in both nations—was literally unmentionable in print, especially in a book intended to be read by children as well as adults. Insane and absurd mass murder, by contrast, was perfectly acceptable.

"I don't agree with you," the engineer replied. "In these humanitarian wars there are neither victors nor vanquished; the lure of glory doesn't enter into it at all, but only the desire to live—and once the number of victims is achieved, they live in peace, cultivating the arts and sciences until the conference decision brings them face to face again."

"At least, in that fashion," Gontran said in his turn, "those who fight die without ulterior motives, without fear of leaving their home and family at the mercy of a pitiless conqueror."

"Very true," muttered Farenheit, "except that I don't see what the story has to do with the canal."

"The canal is quite simply designed to transport the combatants designated by the supreme tribunal to the battlefield."

A gleam appeared in Flammermont's eye. "So there's going to be a war here quite soon?" he said.

"Next month, according to what our guide told me."

"We'll be here, eh, Mr. Farenheit!" cried the young Comte.

"By God!" growled the American clenching his fists. "It reminds me of the Civil War!"

While talking, the Terrans had started walking in the direction of Holion, an important city where, their guide said, they would find a means of locomotion to transport them to the City of Light.

"Do you see?" Ossipoff suddenly said to Gontran, showing him the map he was holding. "The canal that brought us this far was the Oreus. A few degrees further to the left is the Pyriphlegeton, and we'll cut across the equator in order to descend towards the land of Amazonia."

"I don't know whether we'll cut across the equator," Farenheit muttered between clenched teeth, "but I do know we're cutting across fields and that my legs are exhausted."

They were crossing an immense field, which was not verdant but the color of rust. There were occasional clumps of small trees with orange flowers, bearing clusters of pink or scarlet fruits. The plants that covered the ground with a soft carpet were all red, and their large leaves spread out in marvelously graceful plumes.

"Hey!" Fricoulet murmured in Gontran's ear, as he pointed at this singular vegetation. "Do you understand now why the Martian atmosphere seems red to terrestrial astronomers?" Then, turning to the American, who was whining incessantly, he said: "What's the matter, my dear Mr. Farenheit?"

"I...I...need a road. My feet can't do any more."

Fricoulet laughed. "A road!" he said. "We could, I think, travel all over Mars without finding a single one, given that, for people traveling by water and by air, the ground has no utility from the viewpoint of locomotion."

"I declare," said the American, stopping on the edge of a wide ditch that had to be crossed in a single bound, "that I'm stopping here, even if I have to sleep under the stars."

Ossipoff looked at Selena, who, although she was not complaining, was giving evidence of great fatigue. "Ask the guide," he said to Fricoulet, "whether it would be inconvenient for us to spend the night here. We'll resume the march tomorrow morning."

Aotaha, for whom the engineer translated the old man's question, uttered a few guttural sounds, then deployed his wings and flew off into the sky, which dusk was already darkening.

"Now then!" said Farenheit. "Is he abandoning us?"

"No, he's going to enquire about a means of locomotion, and will return at dawn." As he spoke, the engineer took out the flask of nutritive liquid with which he was equipped—cautious man that he was—and passed it to Selena. "The honor is yours, Mademoiselle," he said.

Chapter XXXV
The truth about the series 4, 7, 10, etc.

The first rays of sunlight were already gilding the high Martian clouds when the voyagers woke up. Some ten meters above their heads, a strange apparatus was suspended, motionless, as if it were attached to the ground by an invisible tether. It was a sort of mast that appeared to be about 15 meters high, and which bore, on its upper section, a helical rotor with eight blades, each of which was at least as large as the sail of a windmill. Above that, on the same prolongation, but around an axle concentric with the first, were two small superimposed helices with only four vanes, turning in the opposite direction to the larger one.

50 centimeters lower down, the two axles went into a sleeve on which metallic arcs were fixed, sustaining a kind of folded tent. Further down, supported by hoops, were ten seats somewhat similar to those of bicycles, with the difference that they were equipped with backs. Finally, the bottom section of the apparatus terminated in two cylinders, doubtless containing the motors operating the rotors, and also activating a horizontally-placed drive-shaft, at each extremity of which was fixed a little paddle-wheel serving as a propeller.

"Either I'm very much mistaken, or that's a helicopter!" cried Fricoulet, who had been looking up for some time studying the machine attentively.

"Helicopter!" murmured Gontran. "I knew that...hang on..." After a pause, elevating his voice in order to be heard by Ossipoff, he said: "Why, of course! It's Ponton d'Amécourt's apparatus."

The old scientist turned round. "You mean Philips' apparatus."

"I beg your pardon," replied the young Comte. "I said Ponton d'Amécourt; I even recall that I was able to see his model...in some museum or other...it was made of aluminum."

"So you've only seen the model," Ossipoff riposted. "Personally, I've seen the apparatus itself. I remember having witnessed the trial of a steam helicopter whose inventor was named Philips; it was in 1845, in Varsovia."

"Come on," declare Fricoulet. "I'll put you in agreement. I've also seen an apparatus very similar to this one, but it was due neither to the inventive genius of Ponton d'Amécourt nor that of Philips; the inventor was the Italian Forlanini." So saying, the engineer flexed his legs, reached the apparatus with a single jump, and took his place there. "A charming country!" he said, leaning over his seat. "Lower the stairways and ladders!"

Gontran and Ossipoff joined him immediately, and were soon followed by Selena, to whom the Martian had gallantly offered a hand, and who had been effortlessly transported to her seat by the guide, with his wings deployed.

That left Farenheit, who considered the strange vehicle suspiciously, his feet nailed to the ground.

"Well?" Flammermont shouted to him. "Aren't you coming up?"

"Those perches are only good for monkeys or parrots," retorted the American.

The young Comte frowned. "So you say, Mr. Farenheit," he muttered. "It seems to me that you're scarcely polite. Besides, do you think that the United States would be more dishonored by your presence than France and Russia are by ours?"

"Anyway," added Fricoulet, "each of us is free to choose the mode of locomotion that suits him. We've chosen the air…you prefer dry land. You're free to do so—but I advise you to stretch your legs if you want to arrive in the City of Light at the same time as us." With that, he made a sign to Aotaha, who pressed a lever to put the helicopter in motion. "If you lose your way," the engineer shouted, jokingly, to the Yankee, "ask the first policeman you meet…"

This sally provoked a general burst of laughter, which was lost in the air as the apparatus rose up rapidly. They were already three of 400 meters from the ground when they saw Farenheit brace himself, launch himself like an arrow, and attempt to rejoin his companions with a single prodigious leap.

"The poor fellow!" said Selena, putting her hands together. "He'll never get this far!"

Scarcely had she uttered this exclamation than the Martian pressed a switch that immobilized the apparatus, while he opened his own wings and took a header—as the vulgar expression has it—into the etheric element. A few seconds later, he was beside the American, whose leg-muscles had been insufficiently powerful to take him all the way to the helicopter, and who was slowly falling back to the ground, shouting and desperately waving his arms and legs. Aotaha seized him by one of his side-whiskers and, steering his flight toward the apparatus, soon rejoined it, dragging Farenheit—who seemed to be floating in mid-air like a blow-up doll—in his wake.

"By God!" the American complained, taking his place on a seat between Fricoulet and Ossipoff. "I thought you were going to abandon me…"

"I don't know," riposted the engineer, "how awkward perches like ours appear to you to be, but I must tell you sincerely that, as seen from a height, even though you were on firm ground, you gave a paltry impression of American dignity."

Farenheit muttered a few words whose meaning Fricoulet could not catch, then abruptly turned his back on the engineer and addressed his left-hand neighbor. "How long will we have to spend on this machine?" he asked.

Ossipoff transmitted this question to Fricoulet, who translated it for the Martian. The latter, after a few seconds of reflection, replied: "If the wind continues to be favorable, we shall arrive at about midnight."

The old man unrolled his map and measured the distances carefully. *Damn!* he thought. *We won't be wasting any time, for we still have more than 500 leagues to cover.*

"What I don't understand," said Gontran to Fricoulet, "is why we couldn't arrange matters so as to come directly from Phobos to the destination of our journey. By landing where we did, we've been forced to undertake a journey of 1800 leagues—quite gratuitously, it seems to me."

The engineer darted a sideways glance at Ossipoff; the old man was so absorbed in studying the map that he had not heard a single word of his future son-in-law's observation. Prudently lowering his voice nevertheless, he replied: "If you think about it for a moment, you'll immediately realize that it was impossible, by virtue of the motion of Phobos around the planet, to land anywhere else."

"Ah!" said Gontran, with an intonation that made it easy to understand that the engineer's words were only vaguely meaningful to the young Comte.

"During our journey, Mars has rotated on its axis, with the result that the objective had drawn away. To arrive directly at the City of Light, it would have been necessary to calculate the rapidity of rotation of the planet and the speed of our balloon, and to direct our course 300 or 400 kilometers in advance of the place we wanted to reach."

Gontran shrugged. "Pooh!" he said. "I knew that—it's the ABC of the manual of the prefect hunter; when you aim at a partridge, it's necessary to aim at the head to hit the wing or the leg."

"It's the same thing. Now, the most urgent thing was to save you, wasn't it? Not to mention that, by means of this voyage made as a bird flies, you can take account of the areography."

"Oh," Flammermont replied, "*Les Continents célestes* suffices for me…" Pointing at the immense panorama that was unrolling beneath the vehicle with vertiginous rapidity, he said: "It's always the same; the countryside is depressingly uniform."

"Exactly like the Moon," said Farenhheit, in his turn. "Except that there were volcanoes there, and here there are canals."

"That animal is never content," muttered the engineer.

"By God!" riposted the American, "Try to see things from my point of view. What am I doing here? Nothing—absolutely nothing. Don't you think that, instead of dragging my gaiters through the celestial worlds in your company, I'd be much better off in New York?"

"What would you be doing in New York, then?" demanded Fricoulet. "Do you think that the United States are marching any less straight along the path of progress because one of their citizens is missing?"

"No, of course not—but my shareholders will say to one another, at their general meeting in June, that they don't see me at my post. Then again, the Eccentric Club's elections take place in July…where will I be in July? Oh, by God! By God!" And the American fell silent, his fists clenched and his lips taut with impotent wrath.

"Monsieur Fricoulet," said Selena, who was sitting with her elbows on the back of her seat, observing with intense curiosity the landscape extended at their feet, "Are all these 'canals,' as you call these seas that criss-cross the planet in all directions, known to terrestrial astronomers?"

The engineer smiled enigmatically. "Your question, Mademoiselle," he replied, "proves that you don't know our scientists very well. Yes, all these canals are known, catalogued, baptized…they even have the advantage over a great many Christians of having been baptized several times over."

"Why is that?"

"For the very simple reason that fate has dictated that the same canal has been discovered at the same time by astronomers of different nationalities, who have hastened to give it a name in accord either with their own personal or national pride, or with their own imagination."

"How does one get one's bearings, in that case?" the young woman asked, ingenuously.

"One doesn't get one's bearings, Mademoiselle," replied the American, with comical gravity.

"Mr. Farenheit goes too far," Fricoulet declared, "but it's certain that the hastiness of certain astronomers to baptize their discoveries has rendered sidereal maps confusing to the *vulgum pecus*."

Throughout the day the helicopter flew from north to south, following a line almost strictly parallel to that track of the Oreus, sometimes passing over red-glowing fields enameled here and there with grayish patches that Aotaha declared to be towns and villages, sometimes above silvery threads glittering in the sunlight, which extended away to the right and the left and were nothing but canals intersecting with the Oreus at right-angles.

The principal characteristic of the countryside, as Fricoulet noted in his observational log, was a depressingly monotonous flatness—not the slightest mountain, or anything more than the smallest hill, emerged from the waves that bathed it. When Selena expressed astonishment, the engineer explained this lack of relief in the topography by the erosion resulting from the friction of the Martian surface against the molecules composing the ambient atmosphere.

About 6 p.m., as the Sun was about to disappear over the horizon, the voyagers perceived beneath them, extending as far as the eye could see, an immense liquid sheet from which the last rays of the day star were reflected.

"That's the Trivium Charontis," declared Ossipoff, who was following the progress of the apparatus on his map. "It's a sort of lake, or rather Mediterranean, into which several canals discovered by Schiaparelli flow, including the Oreus, the Laestrygonians, the Cerberus, the Styx, the Hades, the Erebus..."

In a matter of seconds, the helicopter was flying over the ocean, and the continental coast vanished from the Terrans' sight. Suddenly, without any transition—as occurs in our equatorial regions—night succeeded day, and our voyagers found themselves enveloped by a vague darkness into which the surface of the planet melted, becoming confused and indecisive.

The Sun had just disappeared beneath the horizon after having reddened the atmosphere for a few seconds with its final rays; immediately, though, at the precise point where it had just sunk into space, a star rose, shining with a soft clarity that cast a strange melancholy over the seascape.

"The Moon!" exclaimed Gontran.

Ossipoff started so violently that he would have fallen off his seat if Fricoulet had not grabbed him by the arm.

"What did you say?" the old man exclaimed, in a strangled voice.

This attitude amazed his future son-in-law and made him indignant, but a kick dispatched by the engineer by way of advertisement warned the young man about the heresy he had just committed. "Yes," he said, with marvelous self-assurance, "the Moon of Mars—or rather one of its moons...isn't that the role that Phobos plays?"

Ossipoff inclined his head affirmatively.

"Quite right," he murmured. "I thought..."

"What did you think?" asked Flammermont, affecting a slightly haughty stiffness.

"Nothing, nothing," the scientist hastened to reply. "The expression you used made me think...but it was a mistake..."

Fricoulet laughed covertly, so amusing was the worthy scientist's embarrassment. Fortunately, an exclamation from Farenheit put an end to the difficult situation. "Another moon!" he cried, pointing to the east.

"Well," said Gontran, "what's surprising about that? It's Deimos."

"But that moon there isn't moving in the same direction as the other one."

"As you can see."

"They're going to meet, in that case."

"It's bound to happen sometimes."

"What will happen then?"

"An eclipse, quite simply," replied Fricoulet. "Partial or total, according to the positions of the two satellites in the sky. That's another originality of this world...and you'll admit that it's worth the journey."

For three hours the apparatus streaked through the sky beneath the gentle clarity of Phobos and Deimos—which did not afford the Terrans the spectacle of an eclipse that evening.

Finally, in the distance, piercing the light mist that floated above the surface of the ground, a spray of light became visible to the voyagers. In a few moments, they were floating 800 meters above the City of Light, the intellectual capital of Mars.

Viewed from that height, the spectacle was magical, reminding each of the Terrans of the capital of his own fatherland. Gontran and Fricoulet declared that they recognized the Opera quarter, sparkling with its many lights and its extraordinary animation. For Selena and her father, it was the Nevsky Prospect whose shining image extended at their feet. As for Farenheit, he proclaimed immediately that New York, with its rectilinear avenues and brilliant lighting, must certainly have that appearance from the gondola of a balloon. What gave the City of Light a strange and fantastic aspect, however, was not so much the numerous lights that carved the very carcass of the city out of the shadows of the night, with its streets and its monuments, but more especially the many sparks streaking through the air in every direction, like myriads of will-o'-the-wisps dancing over the surface of the ground.

"Uh oh!" said Flammermont, in a bantering tone. "The Martians are going in search of their pleasures."

"Or to work!" Farenheit put in.

"The night isn't usually the time that one chooses to go to work," the young Comte replied.

"Business!!!" the American replied, sententiously. He turned to Fricoulet. "Didn't you tell me, only yesterday, that these folk, even more than us, conform to the motto *Time is money*?"

"Certainly—but I didn't tell you that they dedicate the time that is so precious to them to business affairs."

Farenheit opened his eyes wide. "With what, in that case, do they employ their time?"

"I told you—the Martians, endowed by nature with a considerable amount of curiosity, dedicate their lives to satisfying that curiosity. To them, everything is a problem...and every time they succeed in solving one—however petty it might be—they're convinced that they've taken another step toward absolute perfection...so all their efforts are directed toward science, the only key that can open the doors of eternal mystery to them."

"Then you're convinced that all these individuals aren't in search of pleasure?" said Gontran.

"And you believe that they're not attending to their affairs?" Farenheit added.

The engineer smiled and shook his head. "You're both right with regard to the expressions themselves, but you're wrong in the sense that you mean them. By affairs, I, personally, mean the employment of time. Well, when one employs one's time following one's tastes and aptitudes, doesn't one experience true pleasure?"

At that moment, Aotaha uttered a guttural exclamation, extending his hand toward a sparkling aggregation of light in the very heart of the city.

"What's that?" asked the engineer.

The Martian's reply provoked a sharp surprise in him.

"What's the matter?" asked Ossipoff.

"If I've understood correctly, that illuminated monument is both a kind of Institute and a Governmental Palace."

"What!" said Gontran. "Politics and science lodge under the same roof?"

"For the simple reason that they're one and the same thing…or, rather, that the former is absorbed by the latter. In a world as advanced and civilized as this one, the special Earthly tribe known as 'politicians' must have disappeared a long time ago. It must certainly have existed, but in an epoch that is, so to speak, prehistoric—perhaps corresponding to our present."

"Ah, the happy nations!" Flammermont sighed, satirically.

"Happy because they're practical; and then again, it's another consequence of their *Time is money*. Time in their eyes, is too valuable to be wasted in politics. Besides, among us, politics always conceals personal interests, and these people have minds too deep and hearts too large for any similar pettiness to find a place therein."

"Ah!" cried Gontran. "If my love for Selena did not make me desire ardently to return to Earth—since only there will I find the municipal sash indispensable to my happiness—I'd pitch my tent here…for a country in which no one talks politics, especially one in which politics does not even exist, is Paradise!"

During this conversation, the apparatus had quit the heights at which it had been flying and descended gradually to 100 meters above the city. Aotaha pronounced a few monosyllables, which Fricoulet presumably understood, for he got up and took the Martian's place as the latter deployed his wings and left the machine.

"Where is he going?" the Terrans asked.

"He's going to notify the authorities of our arrival," the engineer replied. "He'll come back shortly."

Soon, indeed, a sound of wings cleaving space was heard, and Aotaha rejoined them. Without saying a word, he seized the control lever and the helicopter headed for the monument described by Fricoulet as "the Institute." Once there, the large upper rotor came to a stop; sustained only by the two smaller ones, the apparatus fell vertically, like the bob of a plumb-line.

Then the voyagers passed through a sparkling zone—so sparkling that they closed their eyes against the pain; without being immediately capable of figuring out why, they heard an indescribable tumult of noise.

Suddenly, a slight shock made them jump on their seats and they opened their eyes tentatively. The apparatus, now immobile, was suspended by its large rotor from the vault of a vast hall—a transparent vault, for the starry skies were visible through it, although it simultaneously mirrored the many lights sparkling everywhere. Beneath them, a restless and gesticulating crowd was looking at them in astonishment, emitting brief interjections amid a precipitate fluttering of wings.

"Damn!" said Fricoulet. "We seem to be having a certain effect."

"Yes," riposted the American, sarcastically. "The effect of a theater chandelier."

"My word, that's true!" said Gontran in his turn. "It's only regrettable that we aren't incandescent. We resemble a cluster of Jablochkoff lamps!"[49]

Mikhail Ossipoff swelled with pride, convinced that this whole multitude had gathered to acclaim him and his companions. "This is what glory is," he whispered in Flamermont's ear.

The latter shrugged his shoulders imperceptibly. "Don't be under any illusion, my dear Monsieur," he replied. "If what Fricoulet had told us about these people is accurate, we can't be anything more than little children to them...compared with thinkers who have extracted such a large fraction of nature's secrets, we've scarcely reached the scientific alphabet."

"Look who's talking, my dear Gontran," said the engineer, "and you're all the more correct because they aren't waiting for us; all these people are scientific delegates from different districts of the equator, who have come to hear interesting communications regarding the impending war."

Aotaha touched Fricoulet with his finger to impose silence on him; then he launched himself on to a tall column topped by a sort of platform, where he folded his wings again. Once there, he pronounced a few guttural sounds, which appeared to make a profound impression on the assembly, and then rejoined the voyagers.

"What did he say?" asked Selena.

"He's playing Barnum, introducing us to the Martians just as some deformed monster or inhabitant of an unknown country is presented to the public in the circuses of Paris. From his viewpoint, at any rate, we're perfectly ugly and we represent a very backward species of Universal intelligence."

---

[49] Paul Jablochkoff (1847-1894) invented an early electric arc-lamp in 1876, which was usually known by the slightly derisive nickname "Jablochkoff's Candle."

"But what did he say at the end, which appeared to excite the hilarity of the audience?"

"He made an allusion to our inferior limbs—thanks to which, he said, we're so disgracefully late. He declared that many canals would be hollowed out on the surface of their world before we grow wings."

"Wings...wings!" growled Farenheit. "Do they consider wings to be the summit of perfection, then? They seem reminiscent to me of enormous birds."

The American's indignation amused the voyagers greatly; they burst out laughing. Their hilarity was drowned out by the unimaginable racket that greeted the appearance on the column that served as a pulpit of a Martian whose ponderous flight and entirely white down gave him the appearance of an old man. Fricoulet, told by his guide that this was, indeed, one of he oldest and most renowned scientists of the Equator, got ready to listen attentively.

Soon, his companions saw him smile pityingly. "Parbleu!" he murmured. "That's a rather ridiculous idea—which, in any case, ought not to be too lethal: cannon loaded with air."

"Indeed," said Gontran, "as an engine of war, that seems to me rather Platonic."

"More Platonic, to be sure, than fine 24 inch field-pieces loaded with good 500-pound cannonballs," Farenheit muttered.

Fricoulet put a hand on his arm. "In fact, no," he replied. "They'd be even less lethal than the air-cannons about which that individual is talking."

"Why's that?"

"Because, by reason of their lack of weight, your good 500-pound cannonballs would never come down and would fly forever into the sky...unless a portion of the combatants had taken a position on Deimos or Phobos, and then..."

The Terrans' attention was drawn back to the orator, whose speech seemed to be having an effect one the audience diametrically opposed to the one he had expected. He gesticulated in vain, holding up a glass tube nearly 50 centimeters long by 20 centimeters in diameter. In vain, too, he uttered exclamations that, on occasion, attained the intensity of veritable screeches; the efficacy of the system he was proposing seemed less than proven. Then he suddenly aimed his tube at the part of the room where the opposition was most heated and, without saying a word, directed a flaming jet into the tube. This demonstration was conclusive; all those who happened to be in that direction were knocked down, collapsing like cardboard monkeys.

For a few moments, there was indescribable confusion: a concert of cries, groans and fearful flutterings; in the sudden chaos of individuals, families dispersed, became muddled up and confounded, trying to sort themselves out—and as soon as the husbands found their wives, the fathers their children and the children their mothers, their wings opened up and they fled through the open bay windows with which the hall was dotted.

The other audience-members, convinced by this striking example, gave voice to a slight clicking of tongues by way of applause, then slowly withdrew. Then darkness fell, and the Terrans, overcome by fatigue, fell profoundly asleep aboard their apparatus.

Fricoulet was the first to wake up. Already, the sunlight had penetrated every part of the immense hall, which Farenheit alone filled with the sound of his snoring. As soon as he opened his eyes, the engineer thought of investigating the neighborhood in which he found himself, so he ran to one of the openings through which he had seen the crowd of Martians fly on the previous evening. He uttered a cry of surprise that woke his companions and brought them running to his side.

"But it's Venice!" exclaimed Selena.

Instead of being solid, the streets were, indeed, liquid; the houses were reflected in the water.

"How do they get about?" asked Farenheit.

"As one does in Venice, of course!" riposted Gontran. "They go by boat."

"That's hardly necessary…their wings suffice."

"That's true; I always forget that these folk have the ability to fly—but that must modify their architecture strangely."

"No need for staircases, in fact."

Flammermont folded his arms in a comic gesture. "Ah, the lucky people!" he sighed.

"What's so lucky about that?"

"That they're unfamiliar with one of the worst scourges invented by our civilization: the concierge! Because the houses have no doors, there's no need for anyone to guard them. The tenants go in and out, and receive guests, without being obliged to pass before the eyes of that Argus/Cerberus hybrid. Oh, the lucky people!"

Fricoulet—who, although he liked his friend, never neglected an opportunity to torment him, murmured in his ear: "Unfortunely, if the Martians don't know the concierge's sash, they're equally ignorant of the mayor's tricolor version…"

The young Comte's smiling face darkened immediately.

Aotaha arrived at that moment.

"A world as advanced in progress and civilization as this one must possess marvelous telescopic instruments?"

These words, pronounced by Ossipoff, were addressed to Fricoulet. "Undoubtedly," the latter replied—and he immediately transmitted the old man's reflection to the Martian.

Aotaha pointed to the enormous column at the top of which the Martian inventor had experimented with his air-cannon the previous evening, and the Terrans noticed, to their great amazement, that this column—which was 24 meters long and measured almost three meters in diameter—was nothing but a gigantic equatorial. Ossipoff uttered a cry of joy and admiration; in one bound, he was next to the instrument.

"What do you expect to see in light like this?" asked Fricoulet.

"I want to resolve one of the most interesting problems of modern astronomy," the old man replied. "From here, with an equatorial this powerful, one ought to be able to penetrate the veil that envelops the minor planets." Rubbing his hands together raptly, he added: "Eh, Gontran? The minor planets?"

The young man searched Fricoulet's face; the later laughed covertly.

"Ah yes, the minor planets," Gontran repeated. "What a magnificent treat!" And again he implored the engineer for help.

While Ossipoff maneuvered the equatorial to aim it in the desired direction, Fricoulet leaned toward the Comte. "Minor planet observation is impossible at this moment," he whispered.

Gontran immediately repeated: "But, my dear Monsieur, you can't devote yourself to any study of that subject at present."

The scientist straightened up. "And why not?" he asked.

Gontran looked at Fricoulet; the engineer directed his attention to the Sun, whose gilded rays were irradiating the sky.

"Simply because it's daylight," replied the young man, affecting a slightly mocking tone.

Ossipoff slapped his forehead. "My word, that's true!" he said. "There are moments, I swear, when I don't have my wits about me." Then he added: "Well, I'll wait for nightfall. There'll be no shortage of objects to observe, thank God!" And, with a cheerfulness all the more ineffable because he had not enjoyed it for such a long time, he stuck his eye to the ocular lens of the equatorial.

When he saw the old man depart into space in the wake of his line of sight, Gontran drew Fricoulet aside. "Tell me about the minor planets, please," he said. "What are they?" Taking is head in his hands he groaned: "My brain will never be strong enough to withstand all the work I'm making it do."

"Is all this changing it?" the engineer joked.

"Too much..."

"Well then, renounce your marriage plans, and become the Gontran of yore again."

The young Comte made a forceful gesture. "Never! I prefer to swallow the planets, small and giant, after having devoured the medium-sized ones—even if I have to die of indigestion!"

"In that case," said Fricoulet, laughing, "get your stomach ready...the astronomic crammer is about to start...."

"I'm listening—speak."

The engineer took his inevitable notebook from his pocket, gave it to his friend, and said: "Write down the following numbers: 0, 3, 6, 12, 24, 48, 96."

"I've done that—now what?"

"Now, what do you notice?"

The young man's eyes widened at this question, and his tongue became mute.

Selena, who had just joined them and was looking over his shoulder, murmured: "That each number is double the one preceding it—is that it, Monsieur Fricoulet?"

"Mademoiselle," replied the engineer, "I have rarely seen a person of your sex endowed with an observational sensitivity as intense as yours."

The young woman blushed. "It's not very difficult," she stammered, "and if Monsieur Gontran cared to take the trouble to pay attention…"

"Now," said Fricoulet," to each of those numbers add 4."

Gontran started. "But this isn't astronomy," he aid. "It's one of those petty party games to which bourgeois families devote the kind of soirées they call 'social evenings,' and in which…"

A formidable yawn interrupted him. "Come on," said Fricoulet. "Have you added 4?"

"Yes—there, it's done. Now I have 4, 7, 10, 16, 28, 52, 100."

"That's very good. Now, do you know what each of those numbers represents, approximately?"

"You're asking preposterous questions. These numbers might represent any number of things…it depends what one's talking about…"

"I don't know that we're talking, at this moment, about anything other than astronomy. Well, since you don't know, I'll tell you. Each of those numbers represents the mean distance of a planet from the Sun. Write this: Mercury 3.9, Venus 7.2, Earth 10, Mars 15, Jupiter 52, Saturn 95."

"Indeed," Gontran observed, "they're almost identical…"

"But in comparing the new numbers with the first, you don't notice anything?"

The young man was silent for a few moments. "My word, no," he said. "I don't notice anything."

"What about the number 28?"

"Yes, that's right! It doesn't correspond to any planet."

"It's precisely that lacuna that Kepler pointed out in his *Harmonies of the World* and the existence of which Titius and Bode later confirmed. Besides, when Herschel discovered Uranus in 1781, it was located at the distance that continues the series, 196…"[50]

---

[50] Johannes Kepler (as he signed such Latin texts as *Harmonies Mundi*, first published in 1619) spent a great deal of time searching for mathematical order in the layout of the Solar System, in the course of which he discovered that the planetary orbits are elliptical rather than circular, thus solving some of the mathematical difficulties associated with the Copernican model. His attempt to explain the distances of the various planetary orbits from the Sun by reference to

Flammermont listened to his friend speaking without appearing to under-stand much of his explanation. "Then," he said, "the number 28..."

"Is one which represents the distance at which, between Mars and Jupiter, there ought to be another world, which has thus far escaped human observa-tion..."

"That's odd," murmured Flammermont. "I haven't seen anything similar in *Les Continents célestes*."

"Your memory is at fault. There's the question of the minor planets."

"Indeed—I've seen a chapter bearing that title...but it didn't seem very important and I passed on to Jupiter."

"Well, you were wrong...for it's precisely these minor planets that repre-sent the number 28."

"The minor planets!" repeated the young man. "How many are there, then?"

Fricoulet pushed out his lips in a dubious moue. "Pooh!" he said. "Some-thing like 234, I think...but more are being discovered every day."

Gontran started in fright. "You don't imagine," he complained, "that I'm going to stuff the names of 234 planets into my head?"

"It's not just their names; there's also their fundamental data—which is to say, their diameter, surface area, density, and the orbits they describe around the Sun, with their aphelia, perihelia, etc..."

"And there's an etcetera!" groaned Gontran. "No, as you can see, I'm go-ing mad!" And he held the borrowed notebook out to Fricoulet.

"However," the engineer persisted, "prudence demands that you don't al-low yourself to be taken by surprise by the questions that Monsieur Ossipoff will surely not neglect to ask you this evening."

Gontran assumed an air of resignation. "Go on, then, executioner," he murmured. "Murder me with your 234 planets...even if each of them is only as large as the Earth, you'll have enough to crush me."

"What!" replied the engineer. "See how right I was to insist! You've just committed a formidable heresy. According to the general theory of the planetary system, the total mass of these 234 planets can't be more than a third of the ter-restrial mass..."

Plato's set of "perfect solids" was less successful, and is generally regarded by modern astronomers as a mystical wild-goose chase, but it was carried on by other seekers of arcane order, including Johann Daniel Titius (1729-1796), who came up with the arithmetical sequence cited here, long known as "Bode's Law," after its subsequent popularizer, Johann Elert Bode (1747-1826). Fricou-let refrains from pointing out that Neptune's eventual discovery was an embar-rassment to those convinced that the Titius-Bode sequence had some as-yet-undiscovered significance, because its mean orbital distance does not fit the se-quence.

"Why is that?"

"To reply would delay me needlessly. It's sufficient for you to know that it is…later, when I have a moment, I'll explain…"

"Explain to me, then, why this sidereal zone was considered for such a long time to be deserted."

"Because of the infinite smallness of these asteroids, of which the most important are 500 kilometers in diameter at the most, and which appear to us as stars of the 11th magnitude. On the other hand, you must have noticed that there's a much greater chance of finding something that is known to exist than one for which one must grope without any precise indication or certainty."

"That's true."

"Well, on the day when number 28 was declared by Titius to have no celestial representation, an association of 24 astronomers was formed to search space and find the world that evaded human curiosity in this fashion."

"And did they find it?"

"Themselves, nothing at all—but an astronomer in Palermo, who was observing the smaller stars of Taurus, discovered by chance, precisely at that distance of 28, a new world that he baptized with the name of Ceres."

"By chance!" exclaimed Gontran. "Was it really worth the trouble of constituting a society of 24 scientists?"

"Many great discoveries of which humankind is proud are due to chance, my dear Gontran," said Mikhail Ossipoff, who had come to rejoin his companions.

The young Comte shivered and leaned toward Fricoulet. "Above all, don't abandon me," he whispered in his ear,

"In any case," the old man went on, "although the first was discovered fortuitously, it wasn't the same for the following ones, which were all the result of relentless study and resolute research."

"There are astronomers," Fricoulet said, in his turn, "who have, so to speak, made a specialty of minor planets. Palisa has discovered 40 of them; Peters—one of your compatriots, Mr. Farenheit—has discovered 34; we owe 14 to Prosper Henry of the Observatory of Paris, and another 14 to a German painter, Goldschmidt…"[51]

The engineer would have continued in that vein for longer if Ossipoff—convinced, as ever, that the young man was making a boastful display of superficial science—had not cut him off with an impatient gesture. "Since this is the

---

[51] The last two figures in this sequence, referring to the discoveries credited to the two brothers Prosper Henry (1849-1903) and Paul Henry (1848-1905) and to Hermann Goldschmidt (1802-1866) remain the same today, but Johann Palisa (1848-1925) eventually totted up the record total of 122 asteroids discovered, while Christian Peters (1813-1890) eventually scored 48.

subject of conversation," he said, addressing Gontran, "I'd be grateful if you'd give me your opinion."

"My opinion about what?" asked Flammermont, silently adding: *Here it comes.*

"Your opinion on the formation of the planets, of course," said the old man.

Gontran was momentarily cornered by his ignorance; nervously, he tugged his moustache, while um-ing and ah-ing in a revealing manner, and his desperate gaze was settling on Selena when he saw the young woman take out her watch and drop it.

Ossipoff exclaimed in surprise and leapt forward—but the young woman beat him to it and, gathering up the pieces, showed them to Flammermont with a singular smile. This gesture lit up a sudden inspiration in his brain. "Of course!" he said, with assurance. "All these minor planets can only be the fragments of a world that must have broken up, for some reason still unknown—but which science will discover."

Ossipoff shook his head. "Yes," he said, "I know that opinion has fervent supporters—but it's not mine."

"And why is that?" asked the unfortunate Gontran, still with assurance.

"Because a zone as extensive as that occupied by the minor planets is absolutely unnecessary to a single world of a mass equal to scarcely a third of the mass of the Earth." And he looked at the young Comte, waiting to see what he would say to refute this argument.

It was Fricoulet who replied, before the old man could stop him. "What you just said would be logical if that fragmentation had not been successive and if Jupiter were not there to explain how the orbits of the fragments became so widely dispersed." Seeing Ossipoff stamp his foot impatiently, he hastened to add: "I don't have any ideas of my own on the subject—I'm only repeating, word for word, what Gontran said to me just now…"

The old man's irritation was appeased; nevertheless, he replied in a slightly dry tone: "All opinions are free; for myself, on the contrary, I consider that, far from being the fragments of a planet, these asteroids are the constitutive elements of one, detached from the solar equator by the powerful attraction of Jupiter and prevented by that same attraction from ever uniting to form a whole."

Gontran shook his head in a knowing fashion.

"That theory is at least as plausible as yours," said Ossipoff, in a slightly bitter tone.

"Undoubtedly…undoubtedly…."

Fricoulet, who had noticed how his interventions irritated the old man and took a mischievous pleasure in exasperating him, asked in a naïve tone: "How do you explain in your theory, the particularity that the orbits of these minor planets all intersect at one point? Isn't that a proof supporting ours? As you know, a law of mechanics specifies…"

Ossipoff looked daggers at him. "Ah!" he said. "You're very glad to have learned that a little while ago, in order to parade it now."

Fricoulet frowned slightly.

"Alcide!" murmured Gontran, in a prayerful tone.

"Monsieur Alcide!" implored Selena, who dreaded that the engineer, exasperated by the old man's acerbic manner of speaking, might let slip some imprudent comment.

Fricoulet, however, having already collected himself, made a sign with his hand to tell them to have no fear.

"On the other hand," Ossipoff continued, this time addressing himself directly to Flammermont, "the largest of these worlds are spherical: Ceres, Pallas, Juno, Hebe, Psyche, Calliope…"

Yet again, Fricoulet intervened. "What about Camilla, Sylvia, Zelia, Lumen and Gallia?" he asked. "What do you think of their form?"

The old scientist smiled scornfully. "My dear Monsieur," he retorted, "when one butts into a conversation, one must at least know something. Now, you imagine that you possess astronomical knowledge, because Monsieur de Flammermont has told you a few things from time to time; unfortunately, that layer of scientific varnish cracks of its own accord. With respect to the bodies that you've just named, Gontran has perhaps neglected to tell you—or, more plausibly, you have neglected to remember—that they are so small that they only appear as luminous dots in the most powerful telescopes."

"It's exactly that on which we base our claim," Fricoulet declared, striking a pose of comic importance, "that these worlds are little splinters of polyhedral form—fragments of a destroyed world."

Ossipoff burst out laughing. "If that's your reasoning," he muttered, "all discussion between us is futile."

To create a diversion, Selena said: "If these worlds are so tiny, there's very little chance of their being inhabited."

Gontran, to whose memory the philosophical theory of his illustrious namesake suddenly returned, replied with an authority that impressed Ossipoff: "And why is that, my dear Selena? What basis do you have for proclaiming that these worlds uninhabited? Their exiguity—but I don't see how that can prevent them from taking part in the concert of universal life. Have we not proofs even on Earth that I might cite? Was not Greece, that territorially-trivial land, the torch of Antiquity for many centuries?"

"Except that," Fricoulet objected, mischievously, "the gravitational conditions on Greek terrain are very different from those on the surfaces of these globules in which you appear to be enormously interested—I don't know why."

"Nothing proves that humankind can't be colossal; on the contrary, everything encourages us to think so—the stature of inhabitants being in inverse proportion to he intensity of gravity." Satisfied with this formula, which had just germinated in his head, Gontran leaned toward Selena with a gracious smile on his lips.

"Do you realize where you end up with such reasoning?" Ossipoff said, then. "With inhabitants who are larger than the worlds on which they're summoned to live!"

Gontran shivered, and looked at the engineer, who signaled to him that the old man was right.

Fortunately, a group of Martians had just landed in the observatory, soon followed by another, and then yet another, setting up a sequence that soon formed a long queue similar to the human ribbons that extend every evening from the doors of our theaters. One odd thing, which Selena was the first to notice, was that children were in the great majority.

"Doubtless there's a matinée performance by some conjurer or circus troupe," said Flammermont, jokingly.

"The best means of finding out what's going on," proposed Fricoulet, "is to follow these people. Given that we're on a world in which curiosity is the motive for all actions, they can't begrudge our being curious."

This opinion was judged sound, and the Terrans joined the queue without delay.

After a wait that was not long—the Martians bringing an unusual rapidity to all their actions—our voyagers arrived at a doorway, whose threshold they crossed in the wake of those preceding them. They immediately found themselves enveloped by dense shadows—so dense that they were not only unable to distinguish what sort of place they were in, but even whether they were alone or not.

Suddenly, without their having moved, it seemed to them that they were being transported through space, beneath the celestial dome strewn with a myriad of stars, among which sparkled the easily-recognizable constellations and planets.

Then, one of these worlds—which had appeared until then as a luminous point—increased in size, racing toward the spectators with a vertiginous rapidity, to be transformed, as if by some miracle, into an enormous sphere that soon filled the entire sky. Now, the Terrans—mute with amazement, with their chests constricted by a singular anguish—were able to distinguish, as powerfully as they could have done with a powerful telescope, the bizarre topography of this unknown world. It was an inextricable confusion of land and ocean: of lands that seems to be ardent furnaces and oceans that seemed to be agitated by waves of liquid fire. There were also dark holes, as well as volcanic craters and peaks sparkling like the summits of snowy mountains; greenish clouds arrayed in parallel bands at the equator formed a sort of screen over that region.

Gontran felt someone jog his elbow and a voice—Ossipoff's—murmured in his ear: "I no longer know where I am, my dear friend. What about you? No celestial map mentions such a planet. What do you think?"

His last sentence ended with an exclamation of simultaneous surprise and fright. Just as it seemed to the Terrans that the colossal sphere, still advancing toward them, was about to crush them with its mass, it burst, like those beautiful multicolored rockets bursting in mid-air that usually conclude firework displays—except that, instead of dissolving like the infinitesimal debris of rockets and becoming invisible, the fragments of this world, driven away by a force interior to the sphere, fled in every direction into darkened space. Soon, there remained nothing but a bright small sun, which slowly continued its march into infinity.

Then the stars appeared to fall back into darkness; everything disappeared and the shadow thickened around the Terrans again.

"By God!" complained Farenheit. "That's a very interesting trick, which would be a great success in New York."

"Pooh!" replied the skeptical Fricoulet. "It's nothing but the magic lantern complicated by phantasmagoria and melting views. Gontran was right just now to say that the Martians were going to a matinée performance; one might think that this was a conjurer's tent."

"But what was that supposed to show?" asked Ossipoff.

"Planet number 28, no doubt," Fricoulet replied.

"You're mad."

While talking, the Terrans had retraced their steps; on re-entering the observatory, they found Aotaha.

As might be imagined, Fricoulet's first impulse was to ask him for an explanation. Having listened to the Martian's brief and rapid speech, the engineer turned to his companions. "My dear Gontran," he said, "they're right to say: 'to innocents, full hands.' "

"What do you mean by that?"

"Quite simply that what we have just seen is confirmation of your theory of the minor planets."

Ossipoff started violently. "How do you know?"

"Because Aotaha has just told me."

"How does he know?"

Fricoulet's only reply to that question was a shrug of his shoulders. To Gontran, he said: "Thousands of years ago the Martians discovered a means of recording light, just as we have found, in the phonograph, a means of recording sound. The gripping spectacle that we have just witnessed was photographed from Nature, and the break-up of that planet appeared to us as it appeared, centuries ago, for the Martians."

"That's incredible!" muttered Farenheit.

"These living images, so to speak, serve for the education of the young. That explains why the crowd that we followed was almost exclusively composed of children."

Ossipoff, very thoughtful and somewhat humiliated, said nothing.

"Monsieur Fricoulet," said Selena, "you know so many things—explain to me how such a result could be achieved."

"My word, Mademoiselle, with regard to the Martian system, I can't answer you, not having studied it; as to what master-conjurer did, it's quite simple: by rapidly drawing away from a screen extended between the spectator and the optical apparatus, the illusion is created of the approach of the apparition, by the opening of a second lantern which lights up gradually as the first goes out, the projection of the subject in view is changed."

"It's what they call *dissolving views*," said Farenheit.

"Or *melting views*," added Gontran.[52]

"Monsieur Fricoulet, I'd like to ask you something else."

"Go on, Mademoiselle."

"These people have photographed a planet that no longer exists; perhaps they're sufficiently interested in the Earth to have created images of it by similar means."

The engineer turned to Aotaha and translated the young woman's question. The Martian inclined his head slightly and signaled to the voyagers to follow him.

As before, the Terrans stopped in a dark room; then, suddenly, a veil was removed, revealing the immensity of the heavens, in the depths of which a slender crescent appeared, shining with a soft and feeble light. Gradually, this crescent grew, extending it two immense horns over the entire horizon; then its dimensions became such that the horns themselves disappeared, and only a part of the planet was framed by the view.

"By God!" muttered Farenheit. "But that's London we can see there...look, there's the Thames on the left...and all those chimneys...all the masts of the ships..."

"It's very odd," said Fricoulet, in his turn. "One would think that we were floating in a balloon a few kilometers above the ground."

An emotional exclamation burst forth almost immediately. "France! France! Oh, how fast it's going! It's Paris that's emerging from the mist...Paris!" A formidable sigh escaped Gontran's breast; along with the vision of the city of his birth, the young Comte had just seen unroll before his eyes the

---

[52] The trick of substituting one lantern-slide by another by means of two projectors, as Fricoulet describes—exploiting the persistence of vision to give the impression of a transformation—was a popular device in the years before the invention of cinema, which made much more striking substitutions possible. Although de Graffigny and Le Faure were writing only few years before the invention of cinema, it is not surprising that Fricoulet could not describe "the Martian system" in more detail, and the anticipation of such cinematic effects as the zoom—which have now become perfectly familiar but were then hard to imagine—is striking even in the absence of a hypothetical mechanism.

silhouettes of all those he had left behind there—relatives, friends and comrades—and he wondered whether he would ever see them again.

"Parbleu!" sniggered Fricoulet. "I bet you're looking for the Rue d'Anjou."

"Why the Rue d'Anjou?"

"Isn't that where the town hall of the eighth arrondissement is? The most fashionable arrondissement in Paris?"

Flamermont squeezed his friend's arm forcefully. "Shut up," he said. "Your jokes are ill-timed."

Successively, the panorama of Central Europe passed before the eyes of the mute and marveling Terrans: Switzerland exhibited its glaciers, ravines and snowy peaks, Germany its old ruined towns and its mysterious forests, Italy its gilded countryside and blue coasts. Then the white immensities of Russia appeared, the gilded cupolas of Moscow, the icy Neva in St. Petersburg, the minarets of Constantinople...then there were the Siberian steppes, the jungles of India, the Chinese paddy-fields and the cities of the Celestial Empire, with their bizarrely-carved monuments...then another expanse of water, which appeared to extend as far as the eye could see but whose limit nevertheless appeared in a few minutes.

Then a formidable "By God!" suddenly burst forth—it was Farenheit, testifying to his joy at seeing New York and its harbor swarming with steamers. "Ah!" he said, sighing deeply. "Haven't the Martians—these people of progress and civilizations—got some means of sending me back to Fifth Avenue?"

"They've just done it," Selena replied. "Hasn't their visual ray transported you to your native city?"

"Look, but don't touch," Flammermont added, jokingly.

"It's the torture of Tantalus," Fricoulet concluded.

H. Gayar: *The Marvelous Adventures of Serge Myrandhal on Mars*

Aventures merveilleuses de Serge Myrandhal sur la planète Mars *by H. Gayar, here translated as the first part of this novel, was first published by L. Laumonier et Cie, on 18 June 1908. A second volume followed,* Aventures merveilleuses de Serge Myrandhal: Les Robinsons de la planète Mars, *dated 15 July 1908.*

There is no evidence of the existence of a "H. Gayar", although Pierre Versins' Encyclopédie *records a death-date of 1937,. Francis Lacassin alleges that the author's name was actually Gaillard, and given that one of the two Henri Gaillards who published work under that name parallel with Gayar's career did die in 1937, Versins and Lacassin might both have been assuming that he was "H. Gayar." However, that Henri Gaillard (1869-1937) was a scholarly Orientalist who is highly unlikely to have committed the many naiveties featured in* The Adventures of Serge Myrandhal, *and even less likely to have been responsible for the other conspicuously downmarket works signed with variants of the H. Gayar pseudonym. The other Henri Gaillard (1866-1939) whose career ran parallel to Gayar's was a notable advocate for the deaf and an important pioneer of the teaching of sign-language, again highly unlikely to have been responsible for H. Gayar's publications.*

It does, of course, seem likely that "Gayar" was derived from "gaillard," but is perhaps more likely to have been taken from the common noun—especially the familiar usage that renders it parallel to the American "good guy"—rather than the surname. A search for the name Gayar on the Bibliothèque Nationale's website gallica *turns up references in theater advertisements from the mid-1890s and early 1900s to a "comique" (comedian) employing that stage name, in one instance apparently featuring in a double act, Gayar et Gerdal. In isolation, that observation might be reckoned trivially coincidental, but it seems a little more significant in conjunction with the remarkable and highly distinctive literary style in which a substantial fraction of Serge Myrandhal's story is narrated. Once the introductory phase is complete, much of the consequent narrative consists almost entirely of dialogue seemingly taking place on a series of imaginary stage-sets—apparently the work of someone who thought entirely in dramatic terms, with a pronounced inclination to vaudeville humor, even in an ostensibly earnest melodrama.*

Gayar's literary career, insofar as it can be mapped through periodicals currently reproduced on gallica, appears to have begun in 1899. Between then and 1903 he contributed numerous short stories to two periodicals available on gallica, the short-lived Arthème Fayard periodical Les Romans inédits and the weekly literary supplement of the daily newspaper La Lanterne (not to be con-

fused with the Belgian satirical publication of the same name). The signature frequently appears in both periodicals simply as "Gayar," but is sometimes rendered as "H. Gayar" and sometimes—slightly more often—as "P. Gayar". The reason for the variation is unclear, but it is possible that there were two individuals involved, who sometimes worked together and sometimes separately, in the same fashion as "J.-H. Rosny"—a signature shared at the time, with much publicity, by two brothers.

The short stories produced under the variants of the Gayar name are lightweight works often echoing, with no great distinction, the fashion for ironic "contes cruels" that was then at its height, routinely featuring lurid crimes, broken romances and unfortunate misunderstandings.

Les Aventures merveilleuses de Serge Myrandhal appears to have been a new venture, representing a definite change in direction, perhaps in response to a marked contraction in the market for short fiction. It was not, however, a successful venture in commercial terms, the books being somewhat fugitive. Its publisher, L. Laumonier et Cie., seems to have vanished after 1908, and only published a handful of titles while it existed. At any rate, Gayar fell silent for more than a decade thereafter.

The pseudonym reappeared in 1921 when La Lanterne ran a feuilleton novel "Cindrella" [sic], signed M. Gayar. It is unclear whether the M. simply stands for "Monsieur" or whether it is supposed to be the initial of a Christian name. The expanded version of the pseudonym, "Henri Gayar," made its first appearance in 1927 on a short novel published by Arthème Fayard, La Fiancée veuve [The Widowed Bride], and appeared on a number of other similar cheap publications, alongside others signed simply "H. Gayar"—there appear to be fifteen in all. The last, La Remplaçante [The Replacement], signed H. Gayar, appeared in 1937.

In between "Cindrella" and La Fiancée veuve, however, Serge Myrandhal made a curious reappearance, in an extensively rewritten version of his adventures entitled Les Robinsons de la planète Mars and signed with the pseudonym "Cyrius," which initially appeared in 1925 as a feuilleton in Le Magazine Illustré and was reprinted in book form in 1927.

Much shorter than the two-volume original, only retaining thin slices of the 1908 text—amounting to less than a quarter of the total—those slices are reconnected by new text that makes the whole a markedly different story, about which I shall provide more detail in the afterword. The Cyrius version provides the narrative with a conventional ending—something that was conspicuously missing from the original version, perhaps having been postponed until a projected third volume that never appeared. Given the return of H. Gayar/Henri Gayar to regular publication in 1927, there seems to be no obvious reason to doubt that the author of the second version was the same person as the author of the first, although the use of a different pseudonym seems odd, and it might be as well to bear in mind that there could have been two Gayars from the start.

150

Because of the potentially-interesting symbolic interpretation of the dream-like development of the story, and its odd quasi-religious elements and remarkable surrealism, and the peculiar symbolism of Serge's, and it is possible to see Les Aventures merveilleuses de Serge Myrandhal *as an extension of a long tradition of mystical interplanetary fantasies, particularly strong in France, which integrate visionary interplanetary journeys into some kind of cosmic scheme of moral evolution, usually involving some kind of "cosmic palingenesis," in which the worlds of the solar system are arranged on a scale of existential perfection, in such a way that souls reincarnated in other-worldly bodies can pursue a quest for ultimate enlightenment for which an Earthly lifespan leaves insufficient scope.*

That idea had been memorably incorporated into the medium of post-Voltairean conte philosophique by Louis-Sébastien Mercier in "Nouvelles de la Lune" (1768)[53], further elaborated by Bernardin de Saint-Pierre in Harmonies de la Nature *(1815; tr. as The Harmonies of Nature) and redeveloped in a more informed cosmological context, initially in* Lumen *(1866-69), by Camille Flammarion, who shared with Jules Verne the honor of being a cardinal influence on the late-19th century development of the* roman scientifique.

Gayar's particular fusion of such ideas is, however, more idiosyncratic than the relatively conventional spiritist adaptations of Camille Flammarion, notably in his embryonic representation of Martian evolution—the evolution of the Zoa, that is—as a physical as well as a spiritual evolution toward a strangely unsustainable perfection. It is not obvious from the existing text whether the author intended to make anything significant out of the characters' decision to refer to the last Martians as Elohim, and there are very few clues as to what the consequences of their awakening might be (the tame return to Earth featured in the Cyrius text is clearly a minimal improvisation and offers no clue as to the possible development of a third volume of the 1908 text, had any been produced), but it is at least possible that an elaborate scheme of moral evolution might have been developed, transfiguring further elements of the Judeo-Christian mythos.

Perhaps the author was not capable of doing that, and was already painfully conscious of having extended his narrative reach much further than his imaginative grasp, but at least he left scope for the reader's imagination to obtain a measure of stimulus—and in that respect, the deliberately teasing ending of volume two might be reckoned preferably to the summary dismissal of the Cyrius text. The author of Serge Myrandhal *might have been doing the reader a favor by leaving the symbolism of the birds with human faces and the apparent absence of the Zoa previously-advertised wings from the dormant Elohim unspecified, along with numerous other teasing issues. In the same way, it might be reckoned a blessing in disguise that the reader, after finishing the extant text,*

---

[53] *News from the Moon*, Black Coat Press, ISBN 978-1-932983-89-0.

has no idea whether the names of Tao and Zoa have any connection with any other uses of the terms in question. That way, we can at least conjecture that the answers he could have provided, given the chance and the inclination, might not have been tamely bathetic. In the same way, we remain free to wonder what Serge Myrandhal and his beloved Anna would have found when they eventually did what they were surely always destined to do, once their discoveries on Mars were in the bag, and set a course for sovereign Jupiter instead of limping home.

B.S.

Book One: On the Planet Mars

I. A Great Event!

"Where are you off to in such a hurry, Mr. Grok?"

"I'm doing what everyone else is doing, of course, Monsieur Durand—going to the *Athenaeum*."

"Well, that's a coincidence—I'm on my way to the famous lecture myself."

"Let's hurry, then. It's almost impossible already to find room in the fifty electric elevators going up to the great hall."

This dialogue was exchanged between two individuals who were correctly shaved, in the Yankee fashion, and wearing smoking jackets. The former was none other than the great American industrialist Joe Grok, the wealthy owner of copper mines. His interlocutor was Professor Justin Durand, a French chemist passing through New York. The two men had met the previous evening in one of the most exclusive drawing rooms on Fifth Avenue. They exchanged a cordial handshake and drew together in the midst of the dense crowd that was pouring in continuously from the staircases of the aerial railway, ferry-boats, electric cars and other public and private vehicles with which the Yankee capital is so abundantly provided.

That crowd, rumbling, whistling and roaring like a stormy sea, was about to unfurl between the walls of the vast building of the Athenaeum. It was engulfed, with formidable eddies, beneath the fifty monumental arcades, each of which terminated in the cage of an elevator able to accommodate fifty people.

Jostled, confused and bruised, Joe Grok and his new friend nevertheless succeeded in taking their place in the steel basket of one of the vast electric elevators. The operator pressed the button.

The elevator rose up to the thirtieth floor of the gigantic building with the reckless rapidity of which one can have no idea unless one has visited America.

"Do you are least have a ticket?" the professor asked his companion, who was wedged, as if in a vice, between an Englishman with a poppy-red complexion and a kind of Canadian giant with a red beard.

"Of course," said Grok, ill-temperedly. "But I couldn't get one for less than five hundred dollars."

"Damn!" said the professor, admiringly. "That's steep! I have a ticket too, but I confess that it didn't cost me anything. It was a gift from the lecturer himself. If I'd had to part with five hundred dollars, I'd have deprived myself of the pleasure of attendance, attractive and sensational as it promises to be."

"Well," said the millionaire, in a tone of conviction, "personally, I'd have paid a thousand if need be. Serge Myrandhal's lecture will be the great event of the season."

"I can understand your enthusiasm," the Frenchman replied, enthusiastically. "Just think of it! An engineer who claims to have found a means of condensing psychic fluids, storing them, and using the prodigious latent force enclosed within them—and is talking about nothing less than reaching distant planets by that means!"

"It's a dream," murmured the skeptical billionaire. "A beautiful dream, worthy of Edison, but..."

"Who knows?" the chemist interjected, excitedly. "In any case, our Edison—you'll soon have the tangible proof of the fact—has already completed half of his program. He's invented an engine capable of utilizing the imponderable forces in question, including that of will, the most powerful of the 'animic energies.' Since the day he published his first book, *Psychic Mechanics*, translated into twenty languages, he hasn't ceased working on his great project—and today, if I'm not mistaken, my friend's goal is within reach."

"So," the American scoffed, "you think we're going to see your compatriot rise up before our eyes and launch himself toward the stars like the prophet Elijah, in a chariot of fire?"

"We're not there yet. The engine—or, more precisely, the amplifier—that will function before you is only an experimental model: a laboratory model, as we say. To construct the definitive apparatus, capable of launching a projectile through sidereal space, money, and more especially the fluid agent, is necessary. Think of the colossal quantity of animic energy required to vanquish terrestrial gravity for a projectile weighing several tons. It's in order to procure that fluid that my compatriot is traveling from one continent to another and lecturing.

"Already, on his way across the world, he's recruited four remarkable producers of energy—four 'human piles' as Annabella Carpenter very aptly calls them in her article in this morning's *Herald*—who have caused a sensation, as you can see from the crowd that's pressing around us. You know that your learned female reporter, the gracious Annabella, has taken the invention under her wing."

"And the inventor too," the American added, in a tone full of implication. "So it's said, anyway. What's certain—and it's not the smallest attraction—is that she'll be in the press ranks at the lecture. Take note that it's the first time that the haughty young lady—who was worth a dowry of twenty million not so long ago—has appeared in public in the exercise of her new profession. That must flatter your compatriot, no matter how little conceit he has..."

"Serge Myrandhal is the most modest man I know," protested Justin Durand, sharply.

"Pardon me," the Canadian giant interjected, "but who is this Annabella whose name is on everyone's lips? Is she the daughter of the billionaire whose bankruptcy was in all the papers, along with his picture, the other week?"

"That's right," said the American. "Miss Annabella Carpenter. It's this evening, as I was saying, that she's ostensibly making her debut in the career of reportage—in front of the whole of New York society, which will have all eyes fixed on her. She's a proud and courageous young woman! She wrote several astronomical novels when she was rich, in an amateur way, for her own pleasure. She thought of utilizing her writing talent without wasting another day. The editor of the *Herald*, who had been one of her father's friends, didn't hesitate to hire her, at a decent salary. Everyone knows that, and as many people have come to see her as the lecturer. And don't forget that there's going to be another celebrity in the hall as well!"

"What celebrity?" asked the Canadian.

"Neither more nor less than the mysterious Ely,"[54] Joe Grok relied, proudly. "The Maharajah Indraghava and his son, the handsome Prince Djalor."

On hearing those names, the chemist had pricked up his ears. "I've heard a great deal about Prince Indraghava," he said. "He's one of those rare sovereigns of the peninsula who's been able to keep his independence intact under the English protectorate. He's famous for his fabulous wealth...and for something else: a rather strange legend.

"It's said that every time His Britannic Majesty's sepoys have tried to penetrate into his domains, they've been forced to retreat almost immediately, for reasons that have never been entirely clarified. There's been talk of inexplicable epidemics that suddenly strike all the officers, the ill will of the soldiers, and mysterious phenomena that stop the expeditionary forces at the Rajah's frontier.

"As a result, Prince Ely Indraghava is famous throughout the Orient. He's reputed to be one of those who have conserved the pure doctrine of the Buddhist religion, at the same time as the gift of operating certain prodigies that modern science is forced to admit, although it hasn't yet been able to explain them.

"Will my friend and compatriot Serge Myrandhal be more fortunate and stronger than these fakirs, whose age-old secret—the means of commanding matter—he claims to have usurped by purely scientific methods? I hope so, ardently. I'd even say that I'm counting on it, knowing the great intelligence of the

---

[54] The author might mean this word as a title—in the Biblical sense of "high priest," although that appellation is more usually rendered in English texts as Eli—rather than as a proper name. Either way, it eventually vanishes from the text.

lecturer. I don't believe that I'm going too far in telling you that we're going to see experiments that will amaze us at the Athenaeum.

"But let's not anticipate, and get back to the Rajah. As I was telling you, he's a strange individual. When he travels, he does so in the greatest luxury; his richly-costumed crews and servants give him the appearance of one of those fairy-tale princes that one only finds in India or the Arabian Nights. On the other hand, I'm told that in his own kingdom, he sometimes lives for months in the ascetic and vagabond fashion of the yogis who beg for bread on the roads and at the crossroads in cities. Many of his subjects have never seen him, and even go so far as to claim the Indraghava, Rajah of Kampour, and the Great Lama, the all-powerful Buddhist pope, are one and the same person."

"You seem very well-informed," Joe Grok put in.

"Yes, I spent some time in the vicinity of his small kingdom during my last mineralogical expedition."

"If all that's true, he's a very fantastic individual!" said the Canadian.

"There's a great deal of truth in it, at least."

"What's certain, said the billionaire, who did not want to be left out with regard to rare and precise information, "is that Rajah Indraghava is causing quite a stir in New York. Everyone is talking about his fabulous generosity, his eccentricities and the mystery that surrounds him. It appears that since yesterday, his servants have been busy preparing a private box for him in the Athenaeum, where we're going, made of cloths of unusual magnificence.

"An hour ago, his litter, carried by ten slaves—ten statues of black bronze—went through the city, heading for the Athenaeum. It goes without saying that the extraordinary individual in question doesn't take the elevator but the stairs—a staircase specially enlarged for him, for which he's had several walls knocked down! But Serge Myrandhal's impresario—because our lecturer has an impresario, like a great tenor—doesn't recoil before any sacrifice. He knew that the presence of the mysterious Nabob would be enough to fill the hall.

"Take note that the numerous spectators who have come here solely to see the 'Mendicant Prince' won't see anything. The Rajah only goes out veiled, like a sultana! And what's more, his box will be closed on the side of the auditorium by a triple curtain of gauze, permitting him to see without being seen."

"It's a box with a lid!" joked the Canadian with the carroty beard.

"Exactly," Grok continued. "That's one of the conditions imposed by the Prince, who doesn't want his august face to be soiled by the gaze of infidels. He's said to be old and very ugly, but so far, the only person who's seen his face in Annabella Carpenter, who made her debut in the interview game with that masterstroke.

"How was Miss Carpenter able to obtain that audience, solicited in vain by so many others, including important people? In the simplest fashion—she had a very powerful intercessor with regard to the Rajah: his own son, the handsome Prince Djalor. Since the last ball hosted by the wife of the English ambassador, you see, when he danced with Miss Carpenter, the Prince has been madly in love with her. People were even anticipating a marriage, when the girl suddenly found herself ruined. I hasten to add that Djalor, who is rich enough for two, is courting her as before, but I doubt, Prince as he is, that he'll arrive at his goal, since he has a rival..."

The American was abruptly interrupted in his explanations, however. The elevator had just stopped at the thirtieth floor, and was rapidly unloading its cargo.

It is perhaps necessary at this point to offer a few details regarding the purpose of the Athenaeum.

It was one of those gigantic buildings that the Yankees proudly call "skyscrapers." Its thirty stories were built with steel beams; no wood or stone was employed.

The major part of the monstrous edifice was occupied by lecture and conference rooms, and libraries open to the public night and day. The Athenaeum, which was decorated by a stature of Minerva of colossal proportions erected on the principal facade—hence its name—was a kind of grandiose "Temple of Knowledge." Each of its ten topmost floors was devoted to a different science, but it was the last, dedicated to astronomy and equipped with an observatory, that offered the most luxurious accommodation.

Under the immense cupola with crystal panes was an amphitheater disposed in such a way as to allow more than ten thousand spectators to attend lectures on cosmography and astronomy in comfort. On the stage that occupied the back of the gigantic vessel, all the instruments designed for the study of the stars—equatorial and meridional telescopes, etc.—were deployed. Under the pressure of a simple electric lever, the immense glass dome opened, as if one were removing a quarter of the peel of an orange, allowing the vault of the heavens to be seen.

Finally, there was a powerful cinematographic apparatus, which permitted the photographic magnification and reproduction of various celestial phenomena for the benefit of the audience.

Placed at the summit of the skyscraper, that observatory was surrounded by a kind of terrace, as vast as many public squares of the Old World, which permitted the easy operation of the fifty elevators previously mentioned.

One detail worth remembering, and citing as an example to the bankers of the Old World, is that the Athenaeum had been donated by a group of powerful capitalists, each of whom had furnished one floor, in order to stimulate education in the democracy.

In that era, Annabella's father, the honorable Allan Carpenter, had been making his second billion. In order to please his daughter, rather than to obey the need for expense and ostentation that is one of the notable traits of the American character, Allan Carpenter had given the Athenaeum its topmost floor and its magnificent observatory. Needless to say, Annabella, who had always had a great enthusiasm for astronomy, had had a great deal to do with that generosity.

In the young woman's soul there was a little of the mystical poetry that sees in the stars, doubtless with reason, worlds inhabited by beings similar, and perhaps superior, to humans. She had been scarcely twenty years old when she published *The Celestial Garden*, an astronomical novel which, luxuriously published, had obtained a considerable success in the drawing rooms of Fifth Avenue. Then there had been *The Soul of the Stars*, welcomed by the world of American letters with equal success. On several occasions, Annabella had given lectures herself in the hall donated by her father, and an elite audience had come to applaud her.

Then the bad times had come. Allan Carpenter's bank had been one of the first to go bust in an American crash that claimed many victims. In forty-eight hours, Carpenter—who had reimbursed all his clients in full—had nothing left but his daughter's dowry, two hundred thousand dollars, which Mrs. Carpenter, on her death-bed, had placed on deposit in the coffers of the State, having feared—with reason—that her husband might overextend himself.

In spite of his daughter's urgent solicitations, the father had refused to touch that sum. Burning with the desire to remake his fortune, he had departed for the Far West, while his daughter, eager for the challenge and wanting to show that she was worthy of her father, had announced her intention of living solely by her pen. That resolution, and the unexpected disinterest of the young woman, no longer rich—one is not rich in American with two hundred thousand dollars—but comfortably off, had occasioned great enthusiasm in New York society.

And indubitably, that day, as the estimable Joe Grok claimed, as many people had come to the Athenaeum to see her as to hear the exciting lecture advertised by the engineer Serge Myrandhal, the future conqueror of the "Earths of the Heavens."[55]

The impatience of the crowd, swarming under the harsh light of electric lamps, had almost reached the point of exasperation. The impetuous were shaking the grilles serving as guard-rails. Already, a few bars had come loose. Joe Grok and his two companions were beginning to feel anxious. If one of the barriers gave way, there would be a catastrophe. Hundreds of people would fall thirty stories to be crushed on the pavement.

---

[55] *Les Terres du Ciel; voyage astronomique sur les autres mondes et description des conditions actuelles de la vie sur les diverses planètes du système solaire* [The Earths of the Heavens: An Astronomical Voyage to the Other Worlds and a Description of the Present Conditions of Life on the Various Planets of the Solar System] (1884) was one of the most sumptuous and imaginatively ambitious of Camille Flammarion's popular astronomical texts, used as a guide book by more than one *roman scientifique*.

The cries and vociferations continued to grow louder, however. At one time, a frenetic gang shoulder-charged one of the massive doors of armored steel disposed around the observatory like the vomitoria of ancient circuses, of which there were fifty, each one facing an elevator. Others attempted to smash the panes of the cupola, which still remained feebly illuminated, with revolver shots.

Cries of "Death to the Frenchman!" began to rise up.

"He's mocking us!"

A few people of good will pointed out that the advertised time of the lecture—eight o'clock—had not yet arrived, but their voices were drowned out by those of the malcontents, who were becoming increasingly excited. There is nothing as turbulent as an American crowd.

The French chemist, who had never seen such chaos, was almost repenting of having come when eight o'clock chimed on the Athenaeum's electric clock.

The eighth stroke was still vibrating when the cupola lit up with the glare of a thousand Edison lamps, abruptly switched on.

At the same time, the fifty doors slid in their grooves, thanks to an automatic switch installed in case of fire or riot—and the crowd poured through the fifty entrances, uttering howls of joy, disappearing, to the very last man.

II. An Eccentric

The interior of the Athenaeum lecture room, with its elegant spans of cast bronze and its gigantic crystal-glazed dome, is one of the masterpieces of metallic art. Everything has been arranged with a view to the security and well-being of the spectators. A fire would be impossible; there is not a single cubic centimeter of combustible material to be found therein. Even the cushions garnishing the ten thousand comfortable armchairs arranged in tiers are made of fireproof fabric that is absolutely uninflammable. In addition, numerous circular corridors and the fifty doors previously mentioned ensure that the hall can be evacuated in a matter of minutes.

Above the spacious boxes of the first row, all the seats are equally good. One can see and hear what is happening on the vast stage, at the front of which stands the lecturer's podium, equally well from all of them. Everything has been anticipated to prevent disorder, jostling and encumbrance.

In spite of the architect's prudence, however, and in spite of the fifteen squads of Herculean policemen wearing leather helmets and armed with truncheons, that evening, the hall contained almost twice as many people as there were seats. They were climbing on to the entablatures and perching on the balustrades; a few had even climbed up to the ledges and were sitting astride the bronze beams of the framework.

All of that multitude, panting with curiosity and impatience, had succeeded in squeezing into the immense auditorium. The human waves were breaking against the walls and flooding the upper tiers.

Gradually, the racket decreased. From the crowd, finally heaped up, a dull murmur arrived, as confused as that of the sea when the tide is going out.

Suddenly, that rumor ceased, and two thousand pairs of opera-glasses turned almost simultaneously toward the summit of the cupola. Up there—two hundred feet above the floor!—a man had suddenly appeared, tranquilly seated on one of the giant branches of the electric chandelier.

"Who's that?" demanded anguished women, seized by vertigo.

"He's mad!"

"He's going to kill himself!"

From a box decked with flags—the box of the Splendid Club—a formidable burst of laughter emerged at that moment.

"No!" cried the clubmen, who had just recognized an Englishman, a member of the club as famous for his fortune as for his practical jokes.

"It's our dear and perverse colleague, Sir Washington Pickman!"

"The Baronet."

"The Eccentric!"

"He bet ten thousand dollars that he'd be the first one in, without paying for a ticket!" said one of the group.

"He's won his bet!"

"And magnificently!"

"Except that he risked his neck scaling the dome!"

"Only one man has attempted the adventure before, and he broke his neck! And he was a professional, a roofer charged with placing a flag up there on the day the news came through of the annihilation of the Spanish fleet."[56]

"Just think that, by virtue of an inexplicable omission, he has neither a ladder, nor crampons of any sort—that in consequence, the Baronet must have made a long journey on a frightfully dangerous track, with no support, over a slippery, concave crystal ball, with no footholds..."

"A fly would have broken four of its legs doing that. Only the Englishman, the first man to climb the great glacier of Everest, could pull off that feat."

"Hurrah for the English!"

"Hip, hip, hurrah!"

However, Pickman, who still had within reach the knotted rope that had permitted him to descend from the summit of the dome on to the chandelier, seemed to be paying little heed to the ovation of which he was the object.

The Eccentric, who, having been on his perch for hours, was doubtless feeling the spur of hunger, took a vast handkerchief in the colors of the Union Flag from one of his numerous pockets, and carefully spread it out over his bony knees.

He was having a snack!

---

[56] At the Battle of Santiago de Cuba (1898).

On his improvised tablecloth he placed a paper plate containing a slice of roast beef and a slice of bread with a gilded crust. Then the original individual set down his traveling knife and fork, in order to extract from another pocket of his jacket-cum-haversack a jar of "mixed pickles," with which he seasoned his slice of beef.

Then it was the turn of a tasty chicken sausage—a "Cambridge roll"— which he devoured hungrily, while unceremoniously dropping the peelings, with utter scorn for what the cheering crowd might think.

Not a muscle in his face twitched. He appeared as much as ease on his aerial perch as if he had been sitting at a table in a restaurant. His legs, clad in knickerbockers and protected by brown leather leggings, were crossed with a casual negligence.

When no more roast beef and sausage remained, the eccentric diner opened a box of what the English call "biscuits." He seemed to have a complete food-store in his pockets. After the biscuits, which had doubtless given him a thirst, he displayed a gutta-percha cup, of the kind that can be flattened to the size of a shilling in order to be more easily transportable, and filled it with the contents of a flat bottle, doubtless full of whisky.

This time, the picnic a hundred feet from the ground was complete. The unknown man gravely shook the crumbs out of his napkin, lit a gold-banded cigar, and started smoking it with an imperturbable phlegm, which redoubled the joy and clamors of the crowd.

Justin Durand and his two companions, sitting side by side, continued to comment on the event.

"I wonder how he's going to get down?" said the French chemist.

"The same way he got up," Joe Grok replied. "That's a condition of the bet. Besides, there isn't any other. It seems that the scaffolding...."

The Frenchman interrupted abruptly. "Look—there's Miss Annabella coming into her box. She's never looked as charming. And see how fickle and easily bored the American crowd is! Already, they're no longer paying any more attention to the Eccentric, sitting up there like a parrot on a perch. They only have eyes for the brave and beautiful Annabella!"

It was indeed the young female reporter who had made her entrance in the hall.

Annabella Carpenter, clad in an elegantly-tailored costume, with suede gloves and a felt hat of severe form, offered in all her beauty a type-specimen of the Anglo-Saxon race. The careful simplicity of her clothing only made her dazzling beauty stand out more.

Very tall, with an admirable figure, she possessed a complexion of dazzling whiteness, blue eyes that were almost green, and hair with the golden glints that English painters affect in their portraits. Her high and slightly bulbous forehead, however, and the slightly willful curve of her nose, would have revealed to any observer that her beauty was combined with energy and intelligence, just as the rapid quiver that caused her perfectly-designed nostrils to vibrate from time to time indicated the keenest and most feminine sensibility.

With a courage devoid of affectation, her eyes scanned the entire hall, in which every gaze was aimed at her. In the audience, which included the most brilliant New York society, there were many of Annabella's old friends, former rivals in elegance and beauty. For some of them it was a genuine feast to see the beautiful and incomparable Annabella fallen from the rank of socialite, reduced to a salaried profession, having become a mere employee.

"She hasn't sold her big diamond yet," said one old lady, bitterly. "When one's ruined, one doesn't wear jewelry of that value."

"Especially in such a profession," said another.

"Look," added a third. "She doesn't even seem discountenanced. She's smiling."

"She's taken her ivory notebook out of her briefcase and her golden pen, and she's already started making notes."

"She definitely has a certain aplomb."

At that precise moment, a box that had remained obscure between two columns suddenly lit up.

An "ah!" of disappointment sprang from a thousand throats. A curtain of impalpable gauze—woven mist—masked the mysterious box completely.

It was there that the Rajah Indraghava, who had arrived an hour before with his son Djalor, was waiting for the session to commence.

In vain, the opera-glasses sought to explore the cloud behind which the invisible star was hiding.

A few murmurs rose up, and feet were tapping impatiently, but already, the public was offered compensation. The spectacle now passed to a box at the front of the stage, the most spacious in the entire hall. A grave individual with a pale complexion and long white hair floating over his shoulders—the head of a true prophet—and a Quaker-style coat had just entered it with a hesitant step. Behind him, at a respectful distance, came a string of women, just as soberly dressed but almost all delightfully pretty.

It was the venerable Mormon Eliezer Pellmann, the bishop of Salt Lake City, making his entrance, followed by his three wives and eighteen favorite daughters. The others had had to stay at home, for lack of room.

Thus, the Mormon patriarch, the holiest of the Latter Day Saints, had yielded to the attractions of the advertised lecture, just like a simple Fifth Avenue snob.

The American cheered the antique gentleman, the Biblical individual whose love of science had driven him to brave ridicule. The unexpected ovation made the holy man blush all the way to his ears, and no more was needed to change the disposition of the crowd, which immediately started joking at his expense.

Troubled as he was, Eliezer Pellmann did not beat a retreat. Standing up to the quips and jibes, he leaned his elbows on the front of the box and remained there, his eyes fixed on the podium decorated with the American and French flags, at which the impatiently-awaited lecturer would soon appear.

Let us leave him to his meditations and transport ourselves into the box where the Hindu princes are waiting with at least equal fever.

The Maharajah, for anyone who had seen him once, was an unforgettable individual. His brown, parchment-like epidermis, as if stuck to his bones, and his black and desiccated hands, would have caused him to be taken at first for an old man, almost a centenarian, but for the strange expression of vitality in his eyes. When one had seen those eyes, one remained indecisive, almost fearful of the strange suggestive power that emanated from them. They penetrated you— burning you, so to speak—and produced a sensation of unease comparable to that caused by vertigo.

Then too, there was a disquieting nervousness in his long stiff hands. At times, they extended with the suddenness of a spring, then to remain pendant, as if dead. Another deceptive detail was that his teeth, like his eyes, remained intact and youthful, of an ivory whiteness, in a mouth as shriveled as that of a stuffed monkey.

That bizarre individual was, moreover, sumptuously clad in a silk robe with wide sleeves and a waistcoat whose fabric disappeared beneath golden embroideries sown with precious stones. His large turban of white cashmere was surmounted by a cluster of diamonds, and his bony fingers sparkled with the rarest gems. Those on his person—about his neck, his wrists and on the hilt of the khanjar he carried in his belt—were of inestimable value; everywhere, there was a stream of stones that comprised something akin to an aureole, placing a halo of light around his spectral face.

As if to contrast with that Oriental pomp, Prince Djalor was simply dressed in the European fashion. Without his coppery complexion and a pin in his excessively gaudy cravat, he could have passed for the most correct gentleman in Paris or London. There was also a determined simplicity about the young man. Prince Djalor had been brought up in London and Oxford; he spoke English with an extreme purity, and only held European mores and ideas in high esteem. He had even made rather advanced scientific studies, devoting himself, on the advice of his father, to chemistry, physics and, most especially, electrical mechanics. We shall soon discover why...

Physically, he was a young man of aristocratic bearing, with supple and sinewy movements, symmetrical features and a slender dark moustache; his slightest gestures revealed an impeccable social and sporting education, but nevertheless combined with the secret languor, indolence and air of ennui—almost of spleen—that is the prerogative of the last descendants of ancient sovereign races.

At that moment, the father and son seemed preoccupied and worried. That was because the Rajah Indraghava had long been nurturing grandiose projects that the discovery of the French engineer, if it was real, might upset completely. The last inheritor of sciences all but lost today, which permitted fakirs to work miracles of will-power, he had broadened their scope by means of the reasoned study of modern science. No man was more up-to-date than him with the slightest discoveries made in Europe or America.

The goal of his research was to restore the all-powerful theocracy of the ancient mages, who, according to the sacred books, could resuscitate the dead, extinguish fires and calm the furious waves with a few words and gestures.

In that order of ideas, he had obtained astonishing results, but he was far from having attained, or even approached, the immense goal that he had set for himself. He too, like Serge Myrandhal, dreamed of conquering one of the worlds that twinkled so softly in the azure of the evening sky, of being the Argonaut of some planet of which his son might become the Adam of a new race, strong, happy, powerful and almost divine, leaving the old Earth prey to the struggles of gross material science, the limited and finicky science of the Occidental barbarians.

The announcement that the lecturer possessed the means of accumulating the force of the will, like vulgar electrical fluid, and of utilizing it on a large scale, had troubled and irritated the Maharajah, who had been pursing similar research for many years, to the highest degree. That, he felt more than ever, was the only means of realizing the fabulous dream of celestial migration that he had been pursuing all his life.

Had the Frenchman not announced that he had found, thanks to his machine, his "condenser-amplifier," the means of reaching the planets? So, this accursed engineer, this Occidental dog, had not only stolen his idea, the great idea of his life, the fluid motor, but also the grandiose utilization of which he had dreamed: the conquest of the Earths of the Heavens. And that thought caused the Maharajah's eyes to flare up, and his emaciated breast with its jutting ribs to swell with rage beneath the precious fabrics.

"Curse him!" he murmured. "Curse the man who has dared to get in my way, to place himself between me and the Stars! By Brahma! He shall be swept away like a snowflake torn by the wind from the icy slopes of the Himalayas!"

The fever burning the aristocratic Hindu, long accustomed to seeing everything bend to his will, is now comprehensible. He did not take his eyes off the podium at which the engineer as about to appear, and the stage where his demonstrations would take place. He frowned, as if he wanted to hasten the progress of the hands of the large electric clock by the power of his will.

Prince Djalor, for his part, was looking at the opposite side of the hall. He was invincibly attracted toward the box where Annabella, without even glancing in his direction, was continuing to make notes, under the admiring and inquisi-

163

tive gaze of the multitude. He was attentive to the beautiful woman's slightest gesture, her most fugitive expression. He drank her in with his eyes!

For him, Europeanized and Anglicized, she represented the most complete ideal of feminine beauty. He wanted her for his wife, with the passionate, volcanic violence that is the foundation of the Hindu soul, simultaneously indolent and full of indomitable ardor.

The Maharajah Indraghava noticed the direction of his son's gaze, and the emotion by which he was agitated. He had known for a long time about Djalor's love and his projects, and if he had pretended to oppose them, it was solely to exasperate the passion in question, which was profitable to his future plans. From the very first day, he had had designs of his own upon the beautiful American. For other reasons—which we shall soon know—he wanted to see Miss Carpenter enter his family as ardently as his son.

Aware of the favorable impression made at first by the handsome Prince Djalor on the young female reporter, and believing, on the other hand, that he was able to incline any will before his own, he considered it as already settled, and a miscalculation in that direction on his part would have been one more disappointment to add to the others. Nevertheless, he grimaced sourly on seeing his son's dilated pupils sparkle, and extended his bony finger toward Annabella.

"You know," he said, in Pali, "that I don't want you to think of marrying that girl. She's neither of your blood nor or your rank. I've made bigger plans for your future."

"The best plan of all would be to be happy," the young Prince replied, with a melancholy smile.

"You'll be much happier if you follow my advice. I'm only asking you for a little patience."

"I doubt that. It's been a long time since you told me about your magnificent dreams. Do you think they'll ever be realized? In spite of all the respect I have for you, I confess that they seem to be to be almost impossible."

The Rajah's glare was charged with lightning. "Nothing is impossible for whoever has the will," he said, severely. "Faith moves mountains! The will creates! Haven't you seen me work authentic miracles?"

Prince Djalor could not suppress a gesture of impatience. "Those miracles, astonishing and inexplicable as they are," he said, "haven't yet permitted you to..."

The argument would doubtless have continued in that bittersweet tone, but three brief rings of a bell announced that the session was about to begin.

"Finally!" said the Maharajah, with a shiver of impatience.

A lateral door slid sideways, and eight men appeared, pushing a heavily-laden trolley covered with a sheet. The cart stopped in front of the podium and was immediately surrounded by a cordon of policemen.

When the sheet was lifted off, an enormous aluminum box in the shape of a cube became visible. Inside it, shielded from all excessively curious gazes, was the amplifier: the mysterious and prodigious machine, transported at great expense by special trains and ships from Paris to New York. All that could be seen of the apparatus were two laterally-situated handles, the purpose of which we shall soon see.

On top of the box the aides placed a light wicker bench, with insulating glass feet, on which three people could easily sit. That was what was known as "the saddle," the term having been borrowed from aviators.

Curiosity was excited to the highest degree; everyone was waiting, heart pounding with an almost painful anticipation, wondering what the result of these singular preparations would be.

Even the Eccentric finally seemed to emerge from his indolence. Clinging to his aerial observatory, he leaned over to get a better view.

III. Human Piles

It was known throughout New York that the bizarre machine that had just been brought out represented an invention of unparalleled importance. The newspapers had advertised it with an unusual luxury of attention.

The excitement of the spectators, therefore, at the sight of the singular machine that might perhaps be about to modify the conditions of human life completely, was as intense as at the most suspenseful moment of the finest of dramas.

Murmurs of astonishment rose from tier to tier, but resounding "Shhs!" were heard. Attention was over-excited, exasperated to such a degree that two men fell from a cluster that had climbed on to a ledge without anyone taking any notice.

Three men came forward through the same metallic doorway from which the trolley had emerged.

Everyone knew that these were the "human piles"—the producers of cerebral energy whose combined will-power was about to charge the machine, whose story had been widely told.

The engineer Myrandhal had chosen them from among a thousand, discovered with great difficulty in the course of his voyages, and persuaded to follow him more by virtue of the superiority of his own will than the rather high wages that he paid them.

The one marching in the lead was tall and muscular, in the full flush of youth. With curly hair and a curly moustache, he was clad in a braided sky-blue Brandenburg dolman, soft boots and knee-length deerskin trousers. He was an Italian animal-tamer named Giulio. A former street-urchin with no education and not much intelligence, he possessed an inexplicable power over all animals. An anecdote was related in his regard worthy of comparison with the legend of Androcles.

During a voyage he had made to the Italian colony of Eritrea, he had been taken by surprise in the desert by a lion. He had returned to the camp, followed by the lion, which had attached itself to his heels like a well-trained dog, and which he had immediately put in chains without he animal protesting even in the most benign fashion.

There was in that brutish brain—for outside of the gift that he possessed, Giulio was the worst of the ruffians of the Naples docks—an intense production of the will-power that Balzac called a "real substance."[57]

Behind him marched a person of the most enigmatic appearance. Barefoot in threadbare slippers, tall, thin, coifed with a pointed astrakhan cap in the Armenian style, he had a tapering nose, hollow cheeks and large, shining, almost liquid eyes, ascetic and mystical. He belonged to the sect of "whirling dervishes" and his name was Phéliny.

He realized with a surprising facility all the miracles of the Aissawa.[58] In the course of crises of ecstasy that followed his hysterical gyrations, he broke pieces of glass between his teeth and swallowed them; he lay down on beds of nails, passed a stiletto through his nose or ear-lobes, or marched over red hot coals, smiling.

He also possessed the magnetic will-power for which the engineer had sought assiduously. Without turning round, Phéliny could force passers-by to follow him, to sit down, to share their purses or their meals with him. However, he only used that prestigious power to satisfy his needs in the strictest fashion.

There was a certain analogy between the whirling dervish and the third human pile. There was the same thinness, the same frowning eyebrows, the same somber and concentrated expression, the same feverish gestures—except that, instead of being Persian, as Phéliny was, he was a peasant from the Cévennes, Mathieu Maugars.

Residing in a ruined hovel, a kind of cave in a desolate mountain ravine, a kind of living anachronism, he had been living like the sorcerers of the Middle Ages. A spell-caster of sorts, a bone-setter, an assembler of storms over his enemies' fields at harvest-time and a poisoner of wells, he had the reputation, first and foremost, of being a "wolf-leader"—a terrible individual who still inspires terror in certain remote rural areas, who only has to make a sign to deliver those he detests to the wild beasts whose sovereign he is.

But there was a fourth human pile.

To the increasing emotion of the spectators, four of the Athenaeum's waiters, in their spangled blue livery, appeared carrying a flat pedestal on which was propped a grotesque individual, a kind of human debris. He had neither arms nor

---

[57] In *Eugénie Grandet* (1833) as well various works written in his mystical phase.

[58] Aissawa is a Sufi sect founded in the early 16th century, famous for its uses of music and dance to achieve trance states.

legs: just a formless trunk in a sheath of black serge, and above that trunk an enormous, fearful head.

Of the eyes nothing remained but bloody cavities, two raw wounds, of the nose, merely a short stump; the cheeks and lips, gnawed and corroded, left teeth of dazzling enamel bare. The ensemble affected the sinister rictus of a death's-head, a specter whose vital spark had triumphed over the putrescence of the sepulcher.

A frisson of horror ran through the room, quickly repressed by a kind of respectful terror.

Thanks to the newspapers, people knew, broadly, the story of the terrorist Rywal Goledgine, whom the lecturer—at the risk of his life—had brought out of the ruins of a dynamited railway station at Weresli, near Arkhangelsk, almost a cadaver, and saved from the hands of the Russian police.

Rywal Goledgine, a knowledgeable chemist before becoming a militant revolutionary, had tried three times to kill the Tsar. With a single bomb the size of a fist, filled with a special nitrate of mercury of which he had found the formula and had contrived to manipulate without danger, he could reduced an entire block of houses, a fourteen-million-tons ironclad or a railway viaduct to rubble, but he had fallen victim to his own discovery.

The bomb that he had been carrying to blow up Weresli railway station and facilitate the pillage of the imperial finance wagon had exploded a few minutes before the intended time, doubtless by virtue of one of those little-known molecular modifications produced in explosive materials by trepidation, heat or other ill-defined agents. It was a veritable prodigy that he had not been killed instantaneously, that he had survived frightful mutilation and burning by the explosive.

In the hospital in which Myrandhal had placed him, illustrious physicians had cared for him because his was a unique case, almost out of professional dilettantism, for the love of the art. They had succeeded in saving his life, but he had emerged a blind, disfigured amputee, reduced to muteness by the loss of his tongue, which had been resected for fear of gangrene.

Rywal Goledgine had vowed an unrestricted devotion to his rescuer. That audacious individual, who had commanded almost all Russian terrorism, had come to obey the slightest order of the engineer, in whom he had absolute faith.

The reader might be wondering how the mutilated man could communicate with his fellows in that lamentable condition. Hearing was the only sense that remained intact within him. He could hear, and he replied by means of a series of hideous contractions of his ravaged face.

Without even raising their eyes toward the hemicycle crowded with squinting eyes, the first three human piles came to take their places on three crystal armchairs symmetrically placed at each face of the mysterious cube, which the blue-clad waiters had just brought. The same waiters carefully posed the pedestal to which Rywal Goledgine as attached on the fourth of those seats, doubtless designed, in the thinking of the engineer, to insulate the producers of will from certain injurious fluids.

Almost at the same moment, the engineer—the lecturer awaited with so much impatience, the hero of the day—appeared and sat down, slightly nervous but nevertheless calm, in the chair imitative of a Gothic pulpit that had been reserved for him.

Serge Myrandhal was about thirty years of age. Tall in stature, with broad shoulders and prominent biceps, he bore no resemblance to the professional scientists who are conventionally represented as stooped and hollow-chested, with spectacles and ridiculous mannerisms. He had a high and bulbous, slightly pensive, forehead surmounting a perfectly oval face with symmetrical lines but by no means insipid. His eyes were dark, ardent and avid, his nose and chin imperiously curved, his moustache proudly turned up at the tips. Everything about him testified to a formidable energy. His gestures were precise and sober, of masterly exactitude, and he had the clear, frank, almost harsh gaze of a technologist accustomed to maintaining his composure at all times.

Such as he was, he was a magnificent specimen of the Latin race.

A thunder of applause rose up from the crowd at the sight of the young engineer, the mere sight of whom had immediately conquered all sympathy. The women were particularly enthusiastic. Serge felt thousand of pairs of opera-glasses aimed at him with ardent curiosity.

Among the large number of billionaires' wives and daughters in the audience, many could not help thinking that, poor as he was, the young Frenchman would have made the most charming of husbands, if he had only possessed one of those titles—Duc or Marquis—of which the heirs of parvenus are so fond.

But Serge Myrandhal had already arranged the sheets of paper covered with figures that comprised his notes on the hinged table in front of him. He was about to begin, when Annabella Carpenter suddenly leaned forward in order to hear better,

Their gazes met—and then something strange happened. Serge Myrandhal, that man so chilly in appearance, felt his heart lurch. Annabella, disturbed without knowing why, lowered her eyes.

Those two souls had penetrated one another, as if in a double thunderbolt, as their gazes met.

But two other men had noticed that rapid drama and that instantaneous exchange of mysterious effluvia. They were the Rajah and his son. The latter had immediately bowed his head, his heart painfully constricted. As for the Rajah, he gripped the curtain with a nervous gesture, as if enraged.

IV. The Miracle

Making a violent effort of self-control, Serge Myrandhal overcame the emotion that had gripped him.

At a gesture from him, the applause died down. It was in the midst of a respectful silence that he began: "Ladies and gentlemen, permit me first of all to thank you—not on my own behalf, but that of science, of which I am a modest representative—for the applause with which you have just welcomed me.

"I salute, in the American nation, the youngest and most energetic people in the world. Others have qualities more refined, but America has the uncontested privilege of audacity and strength. It is the great realizer of the boldest chimeras—the chimeras that will be realities tomorrow, soon surpassed by the ascendant march of eternal progress. That is why it is not to the peoples of the Old World that I am addressing myself. It is to America that I want to submit my projects, which are called—as I hope to convince you—to change the face nor merely of our petty globe, but the entire solar universe..."

That opening had been pronounced in a warm voice, vibrant with conviction and sincerity. One sensed that the orator was not saying a single word that he did not believe. Already the audience was conquered, subjugated, persuaded in advance. Its members all recalled that the engineer Serge Myrandhal was the author of the famous treatise on *Psychic Mechanics*, already translated into twenty languages, commented on and passionately discussed by the intellectuals of all nations, which had had the shattering effect of a thunderbolt in the nebulous skies of official science.

Further applause drowned the orator's voice. There was a veritable tempest of bravos, a roar of hurrahs.

When silence was reestablished, with great difficulty, the orator got to the meat of the subject with a clarity and simplicity which demonstrated that he combined with the gifts of the scientist those of the writer and the orator.

Avoiding technical terms as much as possible, he found the means of making the theory he was presenting, as original as it was abstract, perfectly comprehensible. Above all, he separated himself from the spiritualists and occultists, etc. Without claiming that all of them were charlatans, he insinuated that a great number of them were. He, Myrandhal, had nothing in common with them; he was, primarily, a man of exact science, a mathematician who abandoned nothing to crazy hypotheses, only making use of pure logic.

"Mind acts upon matter—*mens agitat molem!*"[59] he exclaimed. "That cerebral energy, that animic fluid, which produces so many marvels, is a mechanically usable force, like all the forces of nature.

"It is this power, the most formidable of all, that has given the surface of the globe the aspect that it presently possesses, raising cities, piercing isthmuses and drying up seas. It is this force, which is truly the living and active soul of the planet, that it is a matter of applying directly, of harnessing like a horse of prodigious velocity..."

---

[59] The Latin phrase is taken from Virgil's *Aeneid*.

Now, he went on to affirm, that omnipotent force had been captured, channeled. The miracles of the yogis and thaumaturges of all times and all countries would be surpassed, reduced to triviality, considered as simple child's play. Humans were about to reconquer the fraction of divine sovereignty that they had lost in catastrophes obscurely designated in ancient books, in the annals of vanished peoples...

The frisson of the eternal mystery passed through the crowd like a storm wind over the sea. Grandiose perspectives opened up.

Those American materialists and skeptics widened their eyes, prey to a kind of sublime horror, so emotional that no one applauded.

After a few minutes of vertiginous silence, in which all hearts could be heard beating as one, Myrandhal resumed the course of his lecture. He spoke about the prodigies—very simple, according to him—that certain Indian fakirs accomplished. He emphasized one of the best-known: the "levitation" that consists of rising into the air to a certain height without any point of support, by the force of will alone.

"It is that prodigy," the lecturer said, "which science has not yet been able to explain in any satisfactory fashion, that I propose to reproduce, but not in the paltry, rudimentary fashion that consists of rising a few centimeters into our heavy atmosphere.

"Thanks to my discovery, humans will be endowed with the prodigious wings of the will, compared with which balloons and airplanes, all the machines constructed with difficulty by technologists, will no longer exist. Humans will not only move at will though the gaseous layers that surround the planet, only a few leagues in thickness, but will be able to risk themselves without peril in the gulfs of the cosmic beyond, on the imponderable waves of the interplanetary ether.

"What I propose to realize is perhaps the most sublime and most grandiose enterprise that has ever been attempted. It is a matter of nothing less than taking possession of the entirety of our solar domain, of colonizing all the planets that emerged, along with ours, from the sovereign star...

"From there, who can tell what heights humankind might reach?"

After this almost lyrical passage, Myrandhal went into more positive details. What he claimed to be able to accomplish was no hazardous hypothesis; it was an exact and definite matter. If he only had the necessary capital—for it would require money, naturally, and a great deal of it—he would immediately commence the construction of his apparatus. He would find the indispensable human piles—perhaps that was the most difficult part, but it was not impossible—and he would immediately attack the heavenly body that would reach its greatest proximity to the Earth in a few weeks' time: the planet Mars.

This time, the applause resumed with increasing force, which went as far as delirium. The idea of colonizing the planets turned the Yankee brains upside-down. The enthusiasm was white hot, reaching an almost dangerous level of intensity.

The spectators uttered hoarse and guttural hurrahs, so much had they already shouted and applauded. Some threw their hats and canes into the air. The whole assembly was sweating, panting and gesticulating, quite out of breath. In spite of the ringing of the bell and the calls for "Silence, gentlemen, please!" howled by a powerful megaphone placed within arm's reach of the orator, whose vibrations were veritably thunderous, it was only after a long quarter of an hour that the lecturer was able to continue.

"As you are going to see with your own eyes, the problem has been solved—not on paper, in theory, but in a real and tangible fashion. It is true that I have only been able to realize my idea on a small scale. The condenser-amplifier—the engine, to use the more easily understandable language of the newspapers—is merely a laboratory model. As such, however, it is sufficient to convince the most incredulous."

Myrandhal then went into a few explanations of his human piles.

Those four men, of a terribly active will, were about to direct the waves of their animic fluid toward the apparatus. And it was the force in question, thus captured, but employed integrally and, in a way, multiplied tenfold, that the engineer would be able to employ at will, thanks to the secret that constituted his invention.

In addition, he made it understood that, for the full-scale construction of the ingenious machine hidden behind the sparkling walls of the vast cube, precious metals—radium, vanadium, helium and iridium—and rare sera were necessary. It is well-known that some of those newly-discovered metals are worth hundreds of thousands of francs per gram. That already gives an idea of the fabulous price that the imagined machine would cost.

Furthermore, to reach the planet Mars, a projectile would be required of large enough dimension to carry, along with the indispensable food supplies and instruments, sufficient reserves of fluid to be able to accelerate the progress of the outward journey, and then effect a return journey, if necessary.

But the money—the lecturer came back to that point—was not the only thing. It would require thousands of brains of considerable will-power to charge the animic accumulator with volitional fluid and communicate to the engine the impetus necessary to reach its goal...

At that moment, an incident occurred.

In the great silence of that select auditorium, suspended, so to speak, on the orator's lips, a woman suddenly raised her hand to point at the top of the cupola, and uttered a piercing scream.

The spectators, momentarily distracted, looked in the direction of the chandelier where the Eccentric was sitting. Caught in an electrical short-circuit, the rope that the audacious individual had employed to reach the chandelier had begun to smoke and slowly to burn.

The Englishman did not appear to have attached any importance to it, however. While listening with all ears, he was occupied in peeling an orange—a refreshment doubtless necessitated by the enormous heat of the chandelier—and was negligently dropping the peel on the spectators in the hemicycle beneath him.

A murmur of stifled laughter ran through the hemicycle. The audience members wondered how the obstinate individual would get out of this predicament. They were amused in advance by the ridiculous situation in which he would find himself in consequence of the loss of his rope.

"We spoke too soon," said Joe Grok to his two companions. "The Englishman has lost his bet."

"How's that?" asked the Canadian.

"Remember what I said a little while ago. The Eccentric undertook to penetrate the Athenaeum by surprise and get out by the same route that he took to get in. That route—the rope—is now cut behind him, and unless someone sends him up a new rope by means of a kite, I don't see..."

"Why a kite?" asked the professor. "There must be a movable scaffold here, or something like it, which is used for cleaning the chandelier."

"There is—or rather, there was," the American replied, "but that's where the story gets complicated. A few days ago—during the last visit to the chandelier and the ventilator that surrounds it—the scaffold broke..."

"It's merely a matter of building another. Nothing simpler."

"Not as simple as that, by Jove! I'm not talking about the cost, of course—ten thousand francs at the lowest estimate; that hardly represents the Englishman's daily expenditure—but the time it would take to set up the new apparatus. It would take twenty four hours, at least. Now, during the preparations, the Eccentric might very well get hungry..."

"What an adventure!" exclaimed the Canadian. "And what an unexpected result of a crazy bet! If he's going to die of starvation up there...it would, after all, be a death worthy of a millionaire, especially an original of his sort!"

The new diversion provoked by the Englishman had not occasioned such amiable commentaries elsewhere. From a box partly occupied by scientists from Berlin, with blue-tinted spectacles, square foreheads and pale hair, brutal protests rose up, directed simultaneously at the lecturer and the Eccentric.

"That man perched on the chandelier," shouted one, "is a clown—a sidekick of the other, the engineer."

"*Tarteifle!* This is a trick!" complained another. "They're making fun of us. They're going to create an illusion with some clever conjuring. We thought we were coming to a lecture, but it's a circus performance they're putting on for us."

These objections and other similar ones, however, proffered in loud voices and demonstrating evident jealousy, whipped up a storm of protest. Cries of "Shut up!" came from all directions, punctuated with: "Throw the Germans out!" The latter hastened to beat a retreat into the depths of their box, and the crowd calmed down.

Again the entire hall became attentive. The incident was forgotten. With one word, Myrandhal had succeeded in calming things down.

The experiment awaited with an impatience that was tending to anguish was about to begin.

The moment was solemn. The engineer had got down from his pulpit. He whispered a few words into the ear of each of his producers of animic fluid.

Phéliny and Mathieu Maugars had each seized one of the movable handles that emerged from the cube, while they placed the third on the shoulder of the Russian Rywal Goledgine.

The animal-tamer Giulio, turning his back to the audience, had placed one of his large hands on the shoulder of the dervish and the other on that of the "wolf-leader." In that fashion, the psychic chain was complete.

The four men darted "volitional fluid" at the mysterious cube with dilated, seemingly radiant pupils. Under Myrandhal's gaze, animated by a somber flame, they emitted the *summum* of their will.

As handsome as an archangel in command of the thunder and lightning, the engineer stood tremulously within arm's reach of the strange machine, ready to intervene in case of catastrophe.

Now he was brandishing a kind of tuning-fork with a glass hilt and spiral prongs, which he was doubtless using to orientate the fluid at his whim. One of the prongs was formed of metal rods soldered together; the other was merely a crystal tube filled with a blue-tinted liquid.

The sight of that strange double wand could not fail to simulate the curiosity of the spectators considerably. A great silence reigned beneath the immense cupola. Several minutes went by, which seemed as long as centuries to the breathless spectators.

The four mediums, their faces contracted by a dolorous rictus, maintained an absolute immobility. Their pupils were phosphorescent. Myrandhal was pale, and his face too was contracted by the tension of his will.

Suddenly, a hum, imperceptible at first and then more distinct, was heard inside the mysterious cube. Little green sparks appeared at the corners. An indefinable odor, like that of a distant storm, spread out into the hall.

Myrandhal extended his wand.

In response to his gesture the "saddle" placed on top of the cube first began to oscillate, and then, with extreme slowness, rose into the air. One might have thought, to begin with, that there was something hesitant about its ascent, but eventually, it flew like a bird toward the summit of the cupola.

It arrived a few feet from the chandelier on which the Eccentric was perched, toward whom attention abruptly reverted.

The latter, having finished the cigar that he was smoking, made as if to drop it overboard, like everything else. Still as impassive as ever, he stretched out his arm, while protests went up from the spectators placed beneath the chandelier, who had been receiving the Eccentric's detritus since the beginning.

"No, no!" they cried. "Enough!"

"Not here."

"Get out, Englishman!"

"Get out, or we shoot…"

Two of the most excited spectators were already raising their revolvers.

Without any emotion, the Englishman gazed curiously at what was happening down below. An imperceptible smile illuminated his face.

Suddenly, as the saddle arrived within reach, he stretched out his hand and delicately deposited the litigious cigar on the seat, which seemed to have been sent expressly for that purpose.

That solution, as elegant as it was unexpected, unleashed a gale of mad laughter, which put an end to the incident. In any case, attention was now solicited elsewhere.

Serge had extended his wand. The saddle descended again with a gradual and decreasing movement. Without the slightest sound or shock, it returned to settle gently on the top of the cube, in the location it had occupied a few moments before.

This time there was a new thunder of applause. The most skeptical were convinced.

The experiment was complete and conclusive. The lecturer had provided the proof of what he had asserted. The man capable of such a miracle, operated without any possibility of deception, merited that people should listen when he spoke of conquering the empire of the terrestrial earths. Now, it was no longer merely admiration, but a veritable respect that they felt for him.

He understood that. He took account of the fact that the entire crowd was his, that it belonged to him body and soul, and that he would, so to speak, do with it as he wished. He sensed the ecstatic eyes of Annabella upon him, and felt an indescribable intoxication. At a glance, he glimpsed the realization of his grandiose projects, a glory of which no man had ever dreamed. Annabella's radiant face, which he perceived as if surrounded by an aureole in the semi-darkness of the box, became an integral part of that future happiness.

For a second, he closed his eyes, as if prey to a strange drunkenness, but he opened them again immediately. It was in a grave voice—an almost blank voice—that he resumed speaking in the midst of an imposing silence.

"Ladies and gentlemen, you have just witnessed for yourselves that the volitional fluid produced by four human piles"—he pointed to the four mediums whose faces were contracted with effort—"and stored by my apparatus is capable, at my behest, of lifting that saddle, the weight of which is thirty kilograms.

"That is merely the beginning of the experiment to which I have invited you.

"Three people from the audience may take their places on that bench, if there are any—as I do not doubt—who will consent to lend themselves to the demonstration. Those three individuals will, by virtue of the energy of the fluid alone, be raised to the summit of the cupola, and then returned to their point of departure.

"The volitional waves emitted by the human piles are sufficient in intensity to obtain that result without an accident or jolt.

"In brief, the saddle, laden with three people—which is to say, a weight of at least two hundred kilograms—will repeat the ascent and gradual descent through the air that has just been carried out before your eyes.

"It only remains, now, to select the three individuals who will lend their collaboration to the experiment."

These words provoked, beneath the sonorous cupola, a veritable storm of cries, howls and the stamping of feet. Myrandhal's proposition was so much to the Yankees' liking that they all wanted to take their places on the apparatus. They raised their arms and shouted. A few even began to insult one another and adopt fighting stances. The same exasperated cries rose from al throats.

"Me! Me!"

"No, me!"

"We'll see about that!"

Some brandished their check-books, howling numbers. "A thousand dollars! I'll buy a place for a thousand dollars!"

"Two thousand dollars!"

"Ten thousand dollars!"

"Fifteen thousand..."

There was a crazy auction, bids howled at the top of the voice by the agitated crowd, which could have been mistaken for the population of a lunatic asylum.

The honorable Joe Grok was shaking an enormous wad of banknotes like a distress flag; already, he was so hoarse that it was only in a raucous croak that he succeeded in articulating: "Twenty thousand! Cash! Twenty thousand dollars! All right!"

There was a din, a disorder, a chaos of which it is difficult to form the slightest notion. The bell and the megaphone could not make their voices heard in the midst of that pandemonium, although they were as powerful as that of a steam siren.

The four human piles remained impassive, absorbed by their task.

Myrandhal feared, however, with a legitimate terror, that the composure and volition necessary for his experiment might be corroded by that delirium. He could see the moment coming when he would no longer be able to control the fanatics. The worst catastrophes were to be feared. In their furious desire to be the first to take their places on the apparatus, they were capable of fighting, of breaking the precious machine that represented so much work and so much effort.

Already, some of them were coming to blows.

Under the pressure of necessity, Serge had a good idea, calculated to please the Yankees. He spoke rapidly into the ear of one of the waiters. A moment later, the thunderous voice of the megaphone drowned out the rumor for a few seconds, uttering the magical words: "The three places will be chosen by lot. Your seat numbers will play the role of lottery tickets..."

That proposal had a prodigious success. "Very good!" was shouted on all sides

"That's it!"

"That way, there's no privilege for anyone! Everyone will have an equal chance."

Only a few billionaires, who had hoped to win the game with banknotes, looked sullen. The majority had been won over to the lottery plan, however, and they were obliged to yield the point.

Already, with the rapidity of improvisation that is only found in America, the waiters in blue costumes were collecting the seat numbers. They deposited then, folded into four, within sight of everyone, in a large aluminum bowl placed on the edge of the stage.

In five minutes, the bowl was full. All the numbers were deposited. The audience waited, panting with a genuine fever of anguish. In the silence that had been reestablished, there were a few seconds of recollection, such that nothing could any longer be heard but the slight sound emitted by the machine, still surrounded by the four ecstatic human piles.

Slightly emotional, Myrandhal unfolded one of the squares, taken at random from the bowl.

He read: "Two thousand four hundred and nine."

A cry of joy went up from the third row of seats, and the winner, a pale and thin young man, came forward, trembling and intimidated, toward the center of the hall, under the curious gazes of all the spectators. He was the son of a rich cotton merchant, very well-known in the drawing rooms of the Five Hundred.

Already, Myrandhal was unfolding the second piece of paper. It bore the number 3,007. This time, the winner was a member of the Splendid Club with a slightly deformed shoulder.

"A hunchback," said one joker. "That's a good sign—he'll bring good luck to his traveling companions."

It only remained to draw the third number. This time, the spectators had arrived at a paroxysm of emotion. Hearts were leaping in bosoms.

Serge hastened to take a piece of paper from the bowl, and announced the number 990.

A few cries of disappointment were heard, but everyone was primarily curious to know who the last of the fortunate competitors might be.

A waiter armed with a seating list called out the name of the Reverend Eliezer Pellmann. It was the Mormon patriarch whom we saw installing himself in his box with his wives. That discovery excited the joy of the crowd to the highest degree.

"Is he going to take his seraglio into the air with him?" someone asked.

"He won't dare!" sniggered another.

"So much the better, then," said a third. "The place can be allocated by another draw."

"Pardon me," objected a fourth, "but since he's won, the Reverend Eliezer is free to do whatever he wants with his place, even—and especially—to sell it."

"Never in this life!"

"Of course!"

During this exchange of exclamations, the venerable Eliezer Pellmann stood up. At the sight of his round face, red with surprise and—even more so—timidity, vociferations burst forth from all sides, and from the upper tiers.

"Climb on!"

"Don't do it!"

The bishop, whose anxiety and confusion were increasing by the second, took a step forward, as if making and abrupt decision, and was immediately surrounded by the women of his entourage.

Then there was a colossal wave of Homeric laughter throughout the hall.

"Hold him back!"

"He'll come to harm!"

"It's his bedtime!"

These sarcasms had a decisive effect on the Latter Day Saint. With an abrupt, violent gesture—the gesture of a man making a heroic decision—the bishop pushed away his wives and daughters and, stepping over the rim of the box, he advanced toward the engineer, who was waiting for him, smiling, encouraging him with his gaze to brave public malignity.

Myrandhal held out his hand to the Mormon, delighted and confused by such an honor, and that gesture had the sudden result of imposing silence on the mocking laughter. Scattered applause burst forth.

"Hurrah for the Frenchman!"

"Bravo for the bishop!"

"He's no longer trembling. He's a worthy fellow."

In the meantime, the waiters had rolled a mobile staircase up to the cube, which was part of the observatory's equipment.

After a few words pronounced in a low voice by the engineer, the three willing volunteers climbed the steps and installed themselves, not without a certain emotion, on the saddle.

Tall and proportionately corpulent, majestic and Biblical, the Mormon patriarch had taken his placed between the other two; he was a head taller than either of them.

"Ladies and gentlemen," said the engineer then, in an imperious tone, "the second part of the experiment is about to begin. The slightest disturbance or cry might cause an irreparable catastrophe..."

After this warning, with had its importance, Serge set the human piles in action again with a gesture of his strange wand.

There was a deathly silence in the vast dome. All hearts were oppressed, all bosoms breathless. It was no longer a matter of an experiment that might be more or less interesting to see, but of the lives of three men.

The producers of volitional fluid now had bulging eyes, clenched jaws and foreheads furrowed by the terrible effort they were making. A kind of immaterial mist lifted up their hair, making it bristle like the fur of an angry cat. Their ears and nostrils vibrated rapidly, agitated by nervous tics.

A few minutes went by, as long and tortuous for the public as for the three experimental subjects. Then the upper wall of the mysterious cube emitted a crackling sound. The crystal feet of the bench creaked.

Finally, with the same slowness as before, the saddle, laden with its three passengers, was detached from the cube. It rose up, with an ascending movement whose smooth regularity had something frightening about it.

The spectators could clearly see a phenomenon that had not been observed the first time: between the cube and the saddle there was a kind of phosphorous green-tinted fog, luminous at the base but scarcely perceptible at the summit.

Carrying all gazes and all hearts with it, the bench rose toward the terminus of its ascent.

From the height of his perch, the Eccentric watched it rise toward him, with an expression that was both amazed and attentive—and the saddle continued rising, accelerating as it went.

The fluidic mist now formed a long phosphorescent column.

The saddle was no more than a few feet from the chandelier on which the eccentric Englishman was perched.

Suddenly with a movement that no one could have foreseen, let alone prevented, Pickman grasped the branch of the chandelier that was supporting him and swung on it, like a trapeze artist about to launch himself into space.

The members of the audience shivered, holding their breath.

Then there was a scream: a single scream of horror springing from twenty thousand throats.

The Englishman, letting go, had just dropped, to sit astride the shoulders of the Mormon, dragging the overloaded bench downwards with his weight.

There was a plummeting vertical descent.

Already, the saddle was only a few yards from the floor, into which it was about to crash with its four passengers—and then the sudden miracle occurred.

With a fulgurant gesture, Serge Myrandhal had extended his magic wand, bringing the bench, from which cries of fright were emerging, to a dead stop.

The aerial chariot oscillated for a few seconds, and then began to climb again, very slowly.

The mysterious cube was suddenly sounded by a blue aureole, and a dull hum, like the rumble of distant thunder, emerged from its sides.

Finally, at a gesture from Serge, the saddle began to descend again.

Delicately, it settled on to the cube, while a sigh of deliverance, a great "Ah!" rose up all the way to the chandelier.

Suddenly, as the waiters were liberating the still-impassive Eccentric and his three companions, the latter blue with fear, a thunder of applause burst forth, in a delirious manifestation of enthusiasm.

The spectators broke the metal chairs, struck the ground with frenetic blows of their canes and fired revolvers as a sign of delight.

It was a colossal success for the engineer, surpassing all anticipation: an eruption of madness, impossible to hold back.

Too emotional to pronounce a single word, Serge made a gesture of thanks and, with one last glance toward Miss Carpenter's box, slipped away. He made his escape while the waiters took away the four human piles, the four producers of psychic energy, inert and inanimate, wrapped in blankets, their features drawn by frightful contractions and their eyes bloodshot.

If Serge had been less absorbed, less distracted and less fatigued by the terrible experiment he had just carried out, he would have seen, at the edge of the curtain of gauze masking the Maharajah's box, a black and desiccated hand, rutilant with gems, extended toward him in a gesture of menace.

A quarter of an hour later, in the vast and elegant hall that served as the Athenaeum's foyer, in the bustle of the exit, an interminable queue formed around the engineer. Hundreds of hands shook his as if to crush it. He was complimented, he was acclaimed. A few people, even more enthusiastic, talked about lifting him on to their shoulders and carrying him back to his hotel in triumph. Others embraced him.

Serge was half-stifled by these excessive manifestations. Without energetic resistance, he would have been at risk of being torn to pieces by his frenetic admirers. Already, his shirt-front was in tatters. A Yankee had carried off his gloves, which he ripped apart with his pen-knife and distributed to his friends.

Meanwhile, the crowd, rushing for the elevators, gradually dispersed.

At a given moment, he perceived Annabella a few yards away, advancing toward him, cleaving a path through the mass; he hastened to go to meet her.

The young woman's cheeks were colored by a slight blush.

"*Monsieur l'ingénieur*," she said, in French that was almost devoid of an accent, "I'd like to ask you for a favor."

"I'm entirely at your disposal."

"You've doubtless guessed what it is. I've recently been employed by the *Herald...*"

"You want to interview me—here?"

"No, sir; I don't want to tear you away from your admirers," Miss Carpenter replied, graciously. "If you'd care to indicate a more favorable time..."

"Any time that suits you," Serge Myrandhal hastened to reply, "will suit me too. I'll hold myself at your disposal all day tomorrow. I'm staying at the Atlantic Hotel, fifth floor..."

Scarcely had these words been pronounced than Serge stopped, hesitantly. Imbued with French notions regarding the education of young women, and, on the other hand, being aware of Miss Carpenter's delicate situation, he was fearful of having humiliated her by giving her his address, as he would have done to a tradesman. "No," he resumed, almost immediately. "Better than that—I'll come to the newspaper. Would you care to tell me what time I'll find you there?"

This proposal was undoubtedly not the result for which she had hoped. Annabella raised her head proudly. "No," she articulated, precisely, as if offended. "I'm the one who ought to take the trouble. After mature reflection, I've adopted a profession of which I intend to fulfill all the obligations..."

Before the young man's distraught expression, however, the haughty young woman softened rapidly. "Besides," she added, settling her frank and candid gaze on Serge, "I'm used to operating in the open. I know that you're being considerate, but you've judged me a little too much by French standards." She held out her hand to Myrandhal and continued, laughing: "No hard feelings, though..."

Myrandhal was so distraught that the reporter, self-possessed as she was, felt a similar disturbance invading her.

There was whispering around them.

Again the two young people exchanged a handshake, but their fingers were tremulous, and their palms scarcely made contact. They had understood that they loved one another, and that, as solemnly as if they had sworn an oath, they had promised, with a glance, that they would only ever belong to one another.

Serge was still under the influence of the disturbance caused by that encounter when a Hindu—whose white cashmere turban and rich silk costume made him easily recognizable as one of Indraghava's servants—handed him a letter bearing the Rajah's seal, with all the marks of the most profound respect.

In a few lines, the Mendicant Prince congratulated Myrandhal on the prodigious results he had obtained and the composure with which he had given proof of them. At the same time he asked him to come and see him at his villa, for an important communication.

After having read it at a glance, Serge slipped the missive negligently into his pocket. As is easily understandable, he had other things on his mind: the radiant image of Miss Carpenter.

He had no suspicion of the implications of that fatal letter, and would have shrugged his shoulders disdainfully had anyone told him that at that moment, it was his destiny that was close at hand.

V. Father and Son

It was at Chipside, a few kilometers from New York, with a delightful view over the banks of the Hudson, that the villa built by the Rajah Ely Indraghava was located. It was entirely constructed from cedar logs cut on the slopes of Mount Almowrat, in the sacred forest that surrounds the monastery of that name. The villa, which only one person, Annabella Carpenter, had obtained the privilege of entering, was justly deemed to be one of the curiosities of New York.

The Rajah and his son Djalor were standing in a large drawing room whose veranda, with stucco colonnettes, overlooked the Hudson. The almost dazzling magnificence of Indian taste was displayed there in all its splendor. Golden lanterns encrusted with opals and rubies hung from the vault, divided into sculpted sections, which formed as many mini-cupolas separated by pendentives. The floor was strewn with the skins of lions and royal tigers, carpets from Iran and Turkestan, and draperies of Indian brocade, cashmere and Chinese silk, ornamented with dazzling embroideries, lent the room a magical sparkle. From high-set incense-burners, benzoin, myrrh and cinnamon—perfumes cherished by Orientals—spread their fumes, creating a kind of mist of dreams.

There was material there to furnish a fine room in the richest of museums. There were idols removed from the secret crypts of some Ellora, statues of the wise Ganesh, the goddess with an elephant's trunk, Shiva the destroyer, and Kali, the protectress of the assassins known as thugs or stranglers. Further away, there was a whole collection of pipes: Persian chibouks with cherry-wood or jasmine stems; narghiles and hookahs in glass annealed with golden arabesques, with slender necks, interminable tubes; and opium pipettes like flattened mushrooms, with all the supplementary apparatus of pots, lamps, boxes and needles.

In one part of the room, a panoply that would have done honor to the royal armory of Madrid or the Louvre displayed khanjars, poisoned krises, damascened swords, rifles and pistols with jeweled butts, which put the glare of fireworks in the shade. On the ceiling, a punka—a kind of fan with vast flaps—inert for the time being, its silk cords tied up, was reminiscent of a gigantic motionless butterfly. Because of the fumes, gems and radiance, the atmosphere of the room seemed to be composed of a golden and nacreous mist.

The dominant note was struck by a gigantic gilded Buddha squatting on the symbolic lotus flower, one finger raised, with an eternally smiling expression. At its feet, sticks of perfume were burning, as in Chinese temples. A large candle of vegetable wax, graduated and divided in such a way as to measure the progress of the hours as it burned, was lit to its right.

The entire backcloth of the room gave the impression of a strange and sumptuous temple. On the side of the veranda with bright windows open over the Hudson, however, certain details modernized the appearance, displaying the commencing fusion of the calculating and practical Occident with the contemplative and mystical Orient. A bookcase full of volumes with rich bindings, and a few scientific instruments in a display case, testified to a preoccupation with the exact sciences.

Prince Djalor was dressed like a correct British gentleman, as we have already seen him at the session at the Athenaeum. Sitting in a rocking chair of American manufacture, he was sipping perfumed tea while savoring one of those delicious Indian cigars, some brands of which equal, if they do not surpass, the finest Havanas.

A "houseboy" clad in white silent and agile, had just taken away on a silver tray the remains of the oyster soup, pheasant curry and lobster cooked in champagne that had comprised the Prince's lunch. Fruit, pale ale and Stilton cheese stepped in Madeira had completed the thoroughly Anglo-Indian menu, to which the prince did not appear to have done great honor.

Djalor seemed somber, nervous and melancholy.

A few feet away from him, his father the Maharajah, squatting on a simply bark mat, wrapped up in a Tibetan goatskin, had also finished his meal, but it had been much more modest in kind, solely composed of grains of dourah, wheat, barley and other cereals, which the old yogi seized one by one in his fingertips with simian dexterity. One might have thought that he was some strange bird in the process of pecking. He seemed plunged in profound meditation. From time to time his gaze went, with visible preoccupation, toward a large crystal sphere set on a bronze tripod, almost hidden in an obscure corner. Then he shook his head, and remained pensive, as if the presence of the iridescent globe was both something heart-breaking and consoling.

Abruptly, he got up, and with a slow, sinuous movement that revealed an infinite lassitude—an age-old lassitude—he went over to the mysterious crystal globe in which there was something paternal and heart-rending. He reached out to it with his desiccated hands, as if to warm them at some unknown flame.

A frisson of wellbeing agitated his skeletal carcass and he breathed more deeply. Truly, benevolent effluvia seemed to be emanating from the sphere, which had now become much darker, as if the Rajah's presence had drawn off a part of the light and infused it into his own molecules. The Rajah seemed reanimated and rejuvenated. He took a few strides across the luxurious room.

"Yes," he murmured, speaking to himself. "I anticipated, and partly realized, with that sphere, the idea that the accursed Frenchman has just stolen from me...I was on the track. With Djalor's help, I would have ended up finding what Serge Myrandhal has found! I was on the brink of success, and everything has fallen apart. I've been overtaken, frustrated."

The father and son looked at one another.

"Do you know," murmured Djalor, in a dull voice, "that the news I mentioned to you yesterday is exact, confirmed in every point. It isn't official yet, but in a few days it will be. The *Herald*, the great American newspaper, has assumed all the expenses of constructing the Frenchman's machine. The Metal Syndicate is putting all the necessary metals at his disposal, gratuitously, from the most common to those that are worth hundreds of thousands of francs per gram, which have only just been discovered by chemists."

"The beautiful Annabella Carpenter," interjected the Rajah sarcastically, "doubtless has much to do with that favor. She's all-powerful at the *Herald*."

"Perhaps," said Djalor, with an angry gesture, "but that's not all. The proprietor of the *Herald*, the famous Norton Bennett, wants to maintain the traditions of the newspaper, which sent Stanley to search for Livingston and organized the celebrated and tragic expedition of the *Jeanette* to the North Pole, and has devoted himself entirely to the new project.[60] At this moment he's putting him up in a cottage not far from here, on the Hudson, where he's providing the engineer with a laboratory. They're in the process of building a high protective wall around it and installing the necessary equipment, at considerable cost. The engineer left his hotel to take up residence in Norton Cottage the day after the famous lecture."

"You don't know everything," the Maharajah interjected, again.

Prince Djalor shuddered. "What else is there?"

"You'll see that I'm better informed than you are. In certain circles, an obstinate rumor is going round. It concerns a projected marriage between the engineer Serge Myrandhal and the very charming Annabella Carpenter."

Prince Djalor had clenched his fists angrily; his eyes had flared up, but he did not say a word.

"Well," the Maharajah went on, with a diabolical smile, "is that what you were thinking about just now?"

"Yes and no," the young prince replied, his eyebrows furrowed. "I was thinking more particularly about Serge Myrandhal, that petty penniless low-born engineer, who has put you and me to shame, wrecking our most cherished projects, forestalling us and humiliating us in everything..."

Prince Djalor hesitated.

"What were you going to say?" asked the Rajah.

"Well, Father, I confess that I don't understand why you've invited that man—our most redoubtable adversary—to come here, to your home. What do you intend to do?"

The Maharajah smile enigmatically.

---

[60] The proprietor of the New York *Herald* who sent Stanley to find Livingston in 1869 and sponsored George DeLong's ill-fated polar expedition of 1881 was actually named James Gordon Bennett, Jr., although he was generally known as Gordon Bennett to distinguish him from his father. The surname of the present character is rendered as Bonnell once in the first volume, and on the several occasions when the character is mentioned in the second volume, but I have unified the references by selecting the more frequently-employed name.

"There are two things," he said, sententiously, "that the engineer Myrandhal lacked in order to succeed in his projected voyage to the planet Mars. The first is money—a great deal of money. That difficulty has been ironed out for him, thanks to the enthusiasm he was able to whip up in the Yankees. But there's still one element that he lacks, unless I become involved: what he calls 'human piles'; producers of energy sufficiently numerous and powerful to furnish the indispensable volitional fluid. All of Uncle Sam's dollars can't give him thousands of wills, both supple and powerful, overnight. I alone..."

"So, Father," Djalor interjected, "you want to associate that man with our sublime projects?" The young man's voice was tremulous with indignation.

The Maharajah's gaze was sharply ironic. The wrinkles surrounding his bright eyes deepened, and the whole of the old man's physiognomy revealed a profound and concentrated cunning. He shrugged his shoulders imperceptibly, as if pitying the naivety of his son, too honest to have guessed the treason that was already planned. "You don't understand, Djalor," he said, in a calm voice. "I don't want to associate him with my projects. I only want to make use of his discoveries to complete ours. He's an instrument that the Invisible Powers have sent me."

Prince Djalor scowled dubiously. Although he did not know the details as yet, his father's plan was repugnant to his honesty. "But later," he said, "when the Frenchman has collaborated with our work and has communicated his discoveries to us, how will you get rid of him? You can't dismiss him after having...robbed him like that."

The Maharajah uttered a little sarcastic ripple of laughter. "Once in my realm," he murmured, "in the Monastery of Almowrat, where I'm the absolute master, he'll be at my discretion. Willingly or not, he'll have to submit to my will. I want him to become similar to one of the slaves who answer to me, bowing down to the ground when I give them an order."

Prince Djalor remained silent for a few moments. Then, abruptly dropping his cigar into a jade ashtray, he said: "I take back what I said to you just now. Even if everything happens as you anticipate, though, there's one thing for which I can't console myself—this marriage, about which people are already talking."

The Maharajah straightened up slowly. "The marriage between Annabella Carpenter and the Frenchman, about which people are talking, will not take place," he declared, in a dry voice that was almost a hiss. "I promise you that."

"Who will prevent it?"

"Me."

"You, Father!" exclaimed the Prince. "I thought that, on the contrary..."

"I'll prevent the marriage—but on one condition, which is that you do *everything I wish*, that you obey me without question, and, if necessary, without seeking to understand."

The young man was violently disturbed. "Father," he said, eventually, "I accept. I'll obey you."

The Maharajah had a triumphant gleam in his brought eyes. He sat down again on the mat, from which he had got up in order to go and obtain a little vital warmth from the sphere charged with effluvia, and in a vibrant voice, he began to speak: "Today, Djalor, I want you to know a little more about my vast hopes. I've already told you, more than once, the doctrine that I've been able to extract from our sacred books.

"Man is a child of the Sun and of the Earth, but he is not born on the Earth. He arrives there from a nearby planet, probably Mars. And it is that voyage which it is a matter of remaking, in the reverse direction.

"For us, Mars is the most accessible and the most habitable planet. It is a miniature Earth, we are assured by the scientists of the Occident, all of whose treatises I have read. There is, however, for the conquerors who have the audacity to land there, a marvelous realm there, an entire treasure of sentiments, thoughts and unknown sciences! Other plants, other animals, new minerals and unknown metals await the bold explorers of the celestial earths.

"On Mars, a human race, doubtless once superior to us but now decadent and moribund, is calling to us and extending its arms to us across the infinite ocean of the ether. It's there that I want to transplant our religion and our civilization, to create a new, regenerated, immortal race, liberated from disease, vice and hatred.

"And do you know who will be the Adam—as the Christians put it—of that new race? It will be you, Djalor! It is you, my son, who are called to become the ancestor, perhaps the god, or at least one of the gods, of Martian generations!"

Djalor looked at his father. The young man was stupefied, as if trembling with sacred horror.

"I knew a large part of your plans for astral colonization," he murmured, lowering his head, "but I didn't know that you had designated me for the august role of the ancestor of peoples."

"In my mind, I've always seen you as the root-stock of new posterities— but I have another surprise in store for you. Do you know who your companion will be—the Eve with fecund loins who will collaborate with you in the great work?"

Djalor had gone pale. "I...don't know," he stammered.

"It will be the woman you love, Annabella Carpenter, that perfect, robust, almost unique exemplar of a strong race. Yes, it will be Miss Annabella herself."

"Then you consent...?" stammered Djalor, stunned by joy.

"Not only do I consent, but I wish it! Annabella is the woman selected by me from among all the daughters of the earth. It was a long time ago that I cast my eyes upon her."

"But only yesterday, that marriage displeased you."

"Child! It has never displeased me. My resistance was merely feigned. I wanted to be certain of your love for her. Now, my paternal dissimulation has become unnecessary. I have studied Annabella in accordance with the principles of the seven sacred sciences. She unites the nineteen perfections. I have interrogated by the future by means of sand, water and the stars. It is Annabella who must be the mother of the supreme race."

Djalor listened to these words as if he were hearing celestial music. He was enraptured, ecstatic. Of all that the Maharajah had just said to him, he only retained one thing: his father was permitting him to love Annabella Carpenter; that had been granted to him. The rest did not matter, so far as he was concerned. To depart for the planet Mars in Annabella's company seemed to him to be perfectly simple.

Let us admit that beneath his grave Anglo-Indian indolence, Prince Djalor concealed an enthusiastic and ardent soul. For many years, his father had trained him only to be moved by the most extraordinary things.

Why should he have had any doubt?

He saw his father, whose power and immense knowledge he respected, whom he had seen performing, in his own fashion, the celebrated miracles of the yogis, adding a blind faith to the audacious project. He knew what a profound affection the old man had for him, the last scion of an illustrious, privileged race...

Besides which, the opinion of a man of high scientific worth like the engineer Serge Myrandhal had made a deep impression on him. It must be possible to reach Mars, since the two men he held in the highest esteem—his father and the engineer—had arrived at the same conclusion, having departed from opposite poles. The yogi and the mathematician came together at that point.

Djalor was at that point in his reflections when the note of a gong resounded and a white-clad houseboy came in.

"The engineer Serge Myrandhal," he announced.

"Show him in!" exclaimed the Rajah, his pale eyes sparkling.

VI. The Association

Having come from New York to Chipside on one of the gigantic multistory ferry-boats that travel up the Hudson, the engineer Serge Myrandhal had no difficulty finding the way to the villa inhabited by the Rajah Ely Indraghava. The first idler on the quay had immediately pointed out an elegant and sumptuous construction on the edge of town, whose gilded turrets emerged from a wood of cedars and plane-trees. It was surrounded by a high wall, fitted with sharp spikes that would make climbing over impossible.

At the end of the deserted road that wound around the princely property the engineer found himself confronted by a massive door made of thick oak planks joined together by strips of wrought iron. He rang a bell, was examined through the grille of a judas-hole, and was eventually admitted by two white-clad sepoys armed with curved swords.

He went through the grounds behind them, climbed the marble stepped to the front door and went into a waiting room furnished with the luxury that was displayed everywhere in that sumptuous dwelling. Serge Myrandhal only stayed in that room for a few minutes. Almost immediately, the Rajah's houseboy came to fetch him in order to show him in.

On hearing his rival's name, Prince Djalor had risen to his feet with an abrupt surge of anger. The two men met on the threshold and the Prince, after a glacially correct bow, stood aside to let the engineer pass. Their eyes had met, however, and Djalor, whose impetuous temperament was incapable of dissimulation, had revealed a somber gleam of hatred.

The engineer, still under the influence of other preoccupations, had not noticed.

Already, the Rajah was advancing to meet him, his hand extended in a princely gesture of courtesy and nobility. He invited the engineer to sit in one of the vast Chinese armchairs made of porcelain that are so comfortable in hot countries.

"Be welcome, *Monsieur l'ingénieur*," he said, in perfectly correct French. "I'm happy and proud to receive your visit. You amazed me the other night, at the Athenaeum." And he added, with an amicability that was truly seductive on the part of such an individual: "Even though I'm blasé with regard to miracles."

And as Serge Myrandhal excused himself modestly, attributing the merit of his discovery to the hazard that sometimes favors seekers and gives them more than they had hoped to find, the Rajah went on, with the same princely affability: "No, Monsieur Myrandhal, don't talk about hazard…there is no such thing. Refer instead to your tireless labor, your marvelous qualities of calculation and intuition, and the patience of your research."

In that atmosphere of apparent cordiality, the visitor quickly felt at ease, almost at home, in spite of the fantastic décor that surrounded him. The conversation immediately took on a familiar, almost confidential tone.

"What if I told you," the old man said, having squatted down on his mat again, "that I too have dreamed many a time of utilizing the prodigious energy of human brains to reach the neighboring planets?" As Serge Myrandhal made a gesture of astonishment he continued: "Yes, many a time, in the golden mourning-dress of our beautiful Indian nights, motionless on the high terraces of the Monastery of Almowrat, it has occurred to me, while contemplating the infinite swarm of stars, to think about means of reaching them. I've always thought that the animic fluid was the only possible means."

"I'm glad," said the engineer, inclining his head, "to have been anticipated in my work by Your Highness."

The Rajah smiled with feigned bonhomie. "Let's not exaggerate," he said. "I wouldn't want to claim the role of precursor of your admirable discoveries. My idea remained in the state of a dead letter. I never sought to realize it. It was merely a vague dream hatched in the mystical mind of a contemplative old man, who does not know the first thing about modern science."

The old man had spoken in that fashion in order to reassure the scientist completely, and convince him that he was not dealing with a rival. At that moment, however, his sparkling pupils had strayed involuntarily toward the crystal sphere, and a grimace of hatred had curled the corners of his parchment-like lips.

Entirely overwhelmed by the charm of the welcome he had received, the engineer had not noticed that fugitive expression. He was a thousand leagues away from supposing that the ostentatious Maharajah could be harboring any evil intention toward him.

"At any rate," the old man said, "thanks to you, the chimera has become a reality. You would not believe how interested I am in your grandiose project. I intend to give you proof of my esteem for you and my admiration for your work. When I asked you to come to see me, it was not to satisfy a vain curiosity. I wanted to help you in the measure that is possible, and I believe that I can do so better than anyone else. That said, I shall get straight to the point. This is what I propose: that you come and carry out your experiment in my realm, at the monastery of which I am the high priest."

"But what difference would that displacement make to the prospect of success?" the engineer could not help objecting.

"Patience—I'll tell you, and I'm certain that you'll share my opinion. You possess the engine, but you don't possess a sufficient quantity of the fluid required to activate it."

"That's true," the engineer admitted. "It will certainly be very difficult to find the enormous number of human piles that I need. I've known from the outset that that would be the greatest difficulty. I was sure of finding the money sooner or later, but the fluid..."

"Well, I'm in a position to remove that obstacle and solve the problem at a stroke."

"How?"

"The monastery of Almowrat, in the Himalayas, is a veritable city, and it contains no less than ten thousand fakirs, or penitents, all trained to the most difficult exercises of the will, and who are all obedient to me, as their spiritual leader as well as their temporal sovereign."

"They would be the ideal human piles," the engineer put in.

"That's what I thought—but that's not all. You know that all the monasteries, all the bonzeries, and all the cells of the contemplative yogis perched in the inaccessible caverns of the Himalayas or the Shivalik mountains are in constant psychic communication. Without messengers or telegraphy, we can transmit news or instructions to one another with the speed of thought.

"In brief, I can organize matters in such a way that thousands of the faithful of mystic and contemplative India will pray simultaneously, and transmit the effluvia of their will, refined by meditation and privation, to your receiver. The volitional fluid will radiate from those purified brains in powerful waves, like those of a majestic river, with such intensity and abundance that it will triumph over space and time. All that depends on me, and me alone.

"Well, that formidable power, I will put at your full and entire disposal. In exchange, perhaps I shall ask you one day to take advantage of your marvelous discovery."

The Rajah had pronounced these words with an impressive nobility and simplicity. He had spoken like a true sovereign. His thin figure had straightened; his physiognomy reflected a majestic affability.

Serge Myrandhal was profoundly moved; his heart was overflowing with gratitude and joy. Thanks to the unexpected collaboration of the Maharajah, the problem was now completely solved. The energy source had been found; success as assured.

"You're doing me a service of inestimable value," he stammered.

"You accept, then?"

"With enthusiasm. But how can I repay you?"

"Firstly, by succeeding. You and I are working for science and for humankind." A glint of savage joy had appeared in the old man's fickle pupils. He went on, very calmly: "So, Monsieur Myrandhal, you and I are now collaborators. My opinion is that we should set to work as soon as possible."

"That's necessary," the engineer relied, becoming pensive. "It's in three months—which is to say, in the second fortnight of August—that the planet Mars will be in the proximity most favorable to our attempt.[61] Unless we put off the realization to an indeterminate and distant epoch, we need to be ready in three months."

Rapidly, Serge Myrandhal brought his new protector up to date with the situation. He told him about the generous decision made by the directors of the Metal Syndicate and the commission furnished by the *Herald*, whose proprietor had put an entire laboratory at his disposal.

The Maharajah listened with extreme attention, and refrained from saying that he already knew most of the details in question.

Without surrendering his secret, the engineer added a few technical explanations regarding his engine-amplifier and the vehicle in which he intended to travel.

---

[61] Mars and Earth were in conjunction on 22 August 1908, and would not be again until 27 September 1910.

"But that's not all you need to succeed," said the Rajah, not without a perfidious hidden agenda. "It's necessary that your discovery isn't stolen from you at the last moment; it would be as well to take minute precautions, and to be extremely suspicious."

"Don't worry—all imaginable precautions have been taken, or will be when the time comes. The model you saw at the Athenaeum is guarded night and day by a squad of policemen, watched themselves by two incorruptible detectives. The Norton villa is surrounded by good walls that are in the process of being further reinforced, and the workshop in which I shall manufacture certain components personally is a basement inaccessible to indiscreet gazes.

"The components of the apparatus for which I shall be forced to have recourse to industry will each be cast by a different company—one piece, for example, by Krupp, another by Creusot, a third in England, at Maxim's, a fourth at Carnegie's, and so on. I alone, which one carefully-chosen assistant, will carry out the final assembly. To complete the precaution, components that do not respond to any need, items of pure fantasy will also be ordered here and there, to deflect curiosity and espionage. I've thought of everything, you see."

The Rajah remained silent for a few seconds. If he had thought momentarily that the engineer might reveal his secret at the outset, he had been mistaken, but he did not let anything show. His manner conserved the same affability and sovereign cordiality.

"How long will the construction of the apparatus take?" he asked

"About a month. As for the voyage from here to the monastery of Almowrat, I don't have a very exact idea of that."

"That's the first thing we'll have to examine together," murmured the Rajah, counting on his meager fingers. "A week to get from New York to San Francisco. That's not too much, with the bulky material that will be accompanying us, and over which we'll have to stand guard ourselves."

"Let's say a week, then. From San Francisco to Calcutta, even by chartering a special steamer, will require a fortnight."

"Even more, as we have every interest in navigating with extreme prudence. A shipwreck or serious damage to your apparatus would annihilate all your hopes. From Calcutta to the city of Karputhala, the capital of my realm, is four full days by rail. This is perhaps the first time I've rejoiced about having allowed the English to link my capital to the railway network of the Indian peninsula.

"It's from Karputhala to the monastery of Almowrat that the transportation will be most difficult and awkward. No more railway, and hardly any roads. Fortunately, we have elephants, the most practical means of locomotion in that region. I estimate that it will take at last a week to cross those fifty leagues in mountainous country, still covered in large part by virgin forests of cedar, fir, Aleppo pine and ilex."

"That's a total of thirty-six days. That's a long time, for the final assembly, preparation and calibration, and the trials, will require a month, if not more, and we're running the risk of being caught short. It's at the last moment, most of all, that we need to have plenty of time, not to be rushed, if we want to succeed in our difficult enterprise. So, the slightest negligence, the slightest omission, might have terrible consequences..."

"I agree, Monsieur Myrandhal," the Rajah interjected. "So let's try to gain a week or ten days on the approximate figures we've just established. Don't forget that in Karputhala you'll be my guests—which is to say, the Maharajah's guests—and that I possess absolute sovereignty over all my subjects there. You'll see what I'll be able to do to accelerate the transportation. But while I think about it, I forgot to ask you what the weight of the apparatus will be."

"About a hundred tons, but it can all be dismantled, and hence easily transportable."

"It's not as much weight as I'd anticipated. In that case, we'll doubtless gain some time. I'll occupy myself immediately with the organization of all that. I'll leave today—tomorrow at the latest."

"Already!" murmured the engineer, a little surprised.

"Yes," said the old prince, smiling. "In a week's time I ought to have reached my realm. I confess to you, in all sincerity, that it's solely because of you and your experiments that I've prolonged my stay in New York. In your own interest, however, in order to prepare the way, I need to leave as quickly as possible."

Myrandhal thanked his protector warmly, knowing him to be as interested in science as only princes can be, when they wish to dabble in it.

It was agreed that the engineer would embark for India and reach Karputhala with the shortest possible delay.

The young man had already stood up to take his leave when the Rajah, taking his hand in his own mummy-like hands, placed a ring ornamented with a beautiful diamond on one of his fingers. "You know, *Monsieur l'ingénieur*," he said, with his most gracious smile, "that India is the land of precious stones par excellence. I possess in my treasury a collection of these brilliant pebbles that is said to be incomparable. You will permit me, I hope, to give you this ring in memory of your visit and the pleasure I have had in conversing with you."

Once again, Serge Myrandhal thanked the man he regarded as the most loyal of friends and the most magnificent of monarchs, and bade him farewell. He was guided from room to room by the servants who had introduced him, with all the minutiae of Oriental ceremony.

His heart was afloat in joy. In accordance with a very apt popular saying, he felt as light as a bird, almost drunk on the unexpected good fortune that seemed to be attached to his enterprise.

The door-curtain had scarcely closed behind him when Prince Djalor came in through the other door. He was immediately struck by the expression of diabolical satisfaction radiating from the old prince's features.

Personally, he was dejected and consternated. "I chanced to hear the last few words of your conversation," he said. "We're leaving, then?"

"You misheard," the old man replied, cheerfully.

"What do you mean?"

"I said that I was leaving—me, which is quite different. I didn't mention you. I can see that you're already in despair at the thought of quitting the beautiful Miss Carpenter, but you can be reassured on that point. I'm not taking you with me. You can stay here, to watch over your interests and mine. You'll come to join me at the same time as the engineer, with whom my plans are proceeding admirably. Until then, and while making yourself useful, you'll have the leisure to pay court."

"Father!" stammered the Prince, dazed with gratitude—and he kissed the old man's hand, in the Indian manner.

At the moment, Djalor was giving no thought to the perfidious and criminal aspects of his father's plans. He only saw the pleasure of remaining near his dear Annabella. In order to win her, he was ready to accept tasks entirely contrary to his honest and gentlemanly character, and his Asiatic princely indolence. Carried away by passion, he did not reflect. He did not even perceive that he had just involved himself in a complicated scheme from which he might not be able to disengage himself subsequently.

For the moment, he was entirely given over to his dreams of happiness and the magical vision of Annabella Carpenter.

VII. In the American Style

On emerging from the Rajah's villa Serge Myrandhal headed toward the center of the town, where he had noticed an electric car station. He had almost got there when he heard an unusual rumor of voices behind him. The explanation did not take long to become clear.

"It's him!" cried one.

"Who?"

"The famous Frenchman, of course, who's going to travel to the planets."

"Serge Myrandhal!"

"Where is he?"

"Are you sure?"

"I was at the Athenaeum."

"Hurrah for Serge Myrandhal!"

"Myrandhal forever!"

Myrandhal knew from experience how rough Yankee enthusiasm could be, so he hastened to leap into a passing electric cab.

Half an hour later he got out in front of the door of Norton Cottage, the property placed at his disposal by the proprietor of the *Herald*.

The engineer was radiant. He could not remember a day as happy in his entire life. Everything was going as he desired. He had found the psychic energy that he had so far lacked; at the same time he had won the amity of a Prince, an Asiatic autocrat, who was putting his sovereign power at his service. Furthermore, he had a rendezvous with Annabella that very evening.

Before going through the gate, the engineer could not help casting a glance over the works with which an entire army of laborers was occupied, and which were advancing with prodigious velocity.

A mere day earlier one entire side of the property had only been enclosed by an acacia hedge, and in its place a wall was emerging from the ground that was already a foot high. Stimulated by the exorbitant wage of ten dollars a day, the workmen were laying bricks with fantastic rapidity. As soon as a section of wall was finished, another crew, with the aid of huge trowels, coated it externally with bituminous cement that dried almost as soon as it was in place.

In addition, on the top of the existing walls, a third crew—this time composed of metal-workers armed with a powerful acetylene torch were setting in place a metal grid whose stout bars, barbed at the bottom and the top, ought to defy any attempt to climb them.

Serge Myrandhal was wonderstruck. He could see that improvised construction rising up visibly, under the pressure of dollars. He had never had such a clear and exact idea of the power of American activity. Evidently, the Yankees, spurred by the spirit of competition, had resolved to dazzle the man who had astonished them first.

All round the cottage a host of idlers, whose patience was inexhaustible, were watching the also emerge from the ground with profound attention. They were held back by a cordon of policemen who would not let anyone approach. The precaution was not superfluous. In the crowd, a hundred reporters, notebooks in hand and pencils behind the ear, were stirring, jotting down everything they saw or heard. Others were brandishing their kodaks and taking snap after snap. The ensemble exhibited the animation of a Babelesque hive.

As the engineer cut through the crowd with the aid of two policemen, he thought he recognized therein two of the Germans who had raised such coarse and maladroit opposition to him at the Athenaeum. Evidently, the prodigious discovery was being watched, attracting the espionage of all the great industrialists of the Old and New Worlds.

The engineer smiled. His invention was one that was almost impossible to happen upon by chance.

He went through the gate and into the narrow grounds that surrounded the cottage, where detectives were patrolling gravely, accompanied by mastiffs with terrible jaws, which made the ideal guard dogs.

The engineer headed directly for the laboratory situated in the basement of the cottage. There too an almost ferocious activity reigned—the kind of activity that only the divine dollar can stimulate to the point of exasperation.

In the vast room, entirely lined with porcelain tiles, a squad of highly-skilled metal-workers was hastily connecting up the stout copper cables that terminated in a powerful electric furnace. A forge and various machines—tools adequate for the manufacture of metallic components of medium dimensions— were already in place, with crucibles, hammers, cupolas and all the indispensable equipment. Employees of Steever & Co., suppliers of chemical products, were noisily unpacking crates and arranging bottles and jars on the shelves of glass-fronted cupboards.

It was a rapid, almost instantaneous visible change of décor.

Dusk was falling.

Delighted by what he saw, and having given his instructions and darted an expert eye over everything, Myrandhal climbed the stairs going up to his bedroom.

When he got there he was blinded by a dazzling glare. Fifty electric bulbs had just been switched on in the grounds, illuminating the various worksites, where the labor would continue until dawn. New crews were arriving to replace those who had finished their shift.

Serge noticed, among others, a whole squad of gardeners and nurserymen, graduates of the New Jersey College of Horticulture, carrying flowers and green plants in pots, including saplings, already considerable in size, with which they set about feverishly establishing patterns, beds and lawns.

Captivating as the spectacle was, the young man, who had not stopped thinking about the anticipated visit for a moment, soon moved away from the window and took out his watch.

"Just time to change into something appropriate," he murmured. "Annabella will be here in a quarter of an hour."

He went into the dressing-room, to which a bathroom was adjacent, equipped with the latest improvements in hydrotherapy. He emerged again shortly afterwards, showered and shaved, clad in an elegant smoking jacket.

To moderate his impatience he spent a minute running though the voluminous correspondence piled up on his desk.

The bell at the main gate rang. A minute later, the well-trained servant that Norton Bennett had placed at his disposal brought in a visiting card inscribed: *Annabella Carpenter. Reporter, New York* Herald.

VIII. *"To be Continued on Mars..."*

It was the first time the American woman had come to the young man's home.

The interview arranged at the Athenaeum—which, our readers will remember, was supposed to take place at the Atlantic Hotel—had not happened.

In fact, the day after the famous lecture, the proprietor of the *Herald*, adroitly stimulated by Annabella, whose article attracted a great deal of attention, had precipitated himself into Serge Myrandhal's room while the latter was only half-awake and taken him away in his automobile, with all his luggage, and had installed him half an hour later at Norton Cottage, immediately setting in train its transformation in view of its new destination.

The journalist and the engineer had met before, either at the *Herald* or at the home of their common patron Norton Bennett, but this would be the first time that they young couple had found themselves alone with one another, and the thought of that *tête-à-tête* filled the Frenchman's heart with a tender emotion.

"Send her in," he ordered—then changed his mind. "No! One moment. I'll go to her."

He ran out. He arrived at the door in time to greet Miss Carpenter, who had just got out of a forty-horsepower vehicle with copper trim.

"Monsieur Myrandhal," she began, in a teasing tone, "you thought that I wouldn't dare to face the lion in his lair, but here I am. I've even chosen dusk— a particularly dangerous time, if we can believe French novels. But duty before all, and I need more information from you regarding the great invention. I used up the last lot in yesterday's article, and our readers, ever more avid and insatiable, expect their daily fodder. For that reason, I had to take the risk..." She paraded an amused glance around, and concluded: "Fortunately, I see that there are considerable police forces here. That's reassuring."

At these words, a shadow of melancholy had passed over Serge Myrandhal's face; he had been hoping for something else.

Miss Carpenter noticed that, and held out her hand to him in a spontaneous gesture. "Come on," she said. "You're not going to sulk over a ridiculous joke. It's easy to see, Monsieur Inventor, that you've never flirted—and I congratulate you for it. Personally, I'm the least flirtatious of American women, but I'm a tease—a terrible tease. Life will doubtless punish me for it, but what do you expect? I've been so spoiled until recently, that my faults have only increased and run wild. You must think, with good reason, that I'm a detestable woman?"

"Oh!" exclaimed the Frenchman, awkwardly. "You know that's not so, Miss Anna...you're an exquisite adorable woman!"

While conversing, the young couple had moved toward the house that served as Serge Myrandhal's lodgings, but as they were about to cross the threshold the young woman paused involuntarily. For the first time, in spite of her self-confidence and in spite of her ironic opening, perhaps uniquely designed to conceal her anxiety, the American hesitated. She had been brought up in the liberal Yankee fashion, accustomed to pay little heed to obsolete prejudices and conventions, but she suddenly experienced an insurmountable embarrassment at the idea of going inside the dwelling in the engineer's company.

With the divine instinct of love, she had understood that Serge Myrandhal was in love with her, and she had sworn to herself that she would never have any other husband. That no doubt, was the source of the strange emotion by which she was agitated.

At that moment, however, one of the detectives patrolling the grounds approached the engineer and Annabella, not without having taken the precaution of typing the redoubtable mastiff he had been holding on a leash to a plane-tree.

"What is it?" Myrandhal asked, impatiently.

"I believe, sir," the detective replied, in the calm tone particular to Yankee policemen, "that it's my duty to warn you. You can do as you please, but the locality is swarming with spies of all nationalities. They want to have your secret at any price. Be sure of your guards. I wouldn't be surprised if an attempt is made tonight to get into the cottage."

"Thank you," Myrandhal murmured. "I'll be doubly vigilant."

He was about to go on when another interruption arrived. This time it was a policeman, one of those charged with guarding the gate. His arm was in a sling, and a trickle of blood was running from his hand, which was wrapped in a handkerchief.

"What's that?" exclaimed Myrandhal. "You've been wounded?"

"Yes sir, but it's not much—a thrust from a stiletto in the flesh of the hand. It was in trying to arrest a malefactor, an urchin not much taller than my boot. Can you imagine that the scoundrel was in the process of sawing through one of your beautiful new bars? I'd grabbed him in the act, and didn't think I had anything to fear from the runt, but the kid suddenly shook himself free and scarpered, not without sticking me first. Oh, the little rogue! The most annoying thing is that we haven't caught him. He had accomplices who helped him get away."

"It doesn't matter," said Myrandhal. "You've done your best, and I thank you." At the same time, he slipped a banknote into the policeman's good hand; the latter caused it to disappear adroitly.

"And now," said Miss Carpenter, smiling, "the most urgent thing is to bandage your wound. I'll do that. Have you a first aid kit, Monsieur Myrandhal?"

"Yes—in my study."

"Well, lead the way."

Ten minutes later, the detective and his subordinate, whose hand Annabella had bandaged with professional dexterity, withdrew, proffering lavish thanks.

Serge and Annabella scarcely perceived that they were now alone in the study. The incident, in giving them a diversion from other thoughts, had had the advantage of putting them perfectly at ease with one another. Now they were talking with the utmost cordiality, with the camaraderie full of frankness and gaiety that is so easily established, in America, between young men and women.

Annabella had taken out her propelling pencil.

"Now, Monsieur Serge Myrandhal," she said, "I have to acquit the duties of my profession. I'm going to interrogate you..."

"At your orders...and you've arrived at just the right moment. I have some big news to give you..."

And in a single rush he told her about his meeting with the Rajah and the extraordinary proposal the latter had put to him.

"Needless to say," he concluded, "I accepted. You can imagine with what joy and what enthusiastic gratitude. But there's one person to whom I owe an even greater gratitude—that's you, Miss Annabella."

"You're exaggerating my small role," the young woman murmured, smiling.

"No!" Myrandhal exclaimed, forcefully. "No, it's you to whom I owe all my good fortune. Your smile, your grace—that's the charm, the magic spell that has opened all doors to me. Without you, without your notoriety, without your sensational articles, which have stirred up the public, raised Yankee enthusiasm to white heat and forced your editor's hand, so to speak, I would never have obtained the precious collaboration I now have.

"And since, for the first time since these definitive events, we find ourselves alone, let me lay at your feet the tribute of my infinite gratitude. You have been more than a help to me, more than a collaborator: a veritable associate. You have been—and, I hope, will continue to be—my Lucky Star!

"Henceforth, thanks to you, I'm sure of success, sure that, in a matter of weeks—mere days—I'll reach the mysterious planet that we're about to see lighting up in the Orient."

"What a prodigious dream!" exclaimed the young woman, adroitly deflecting the conversation. "And to think that the dream will soon be a reality—in a matter of days, as you say. You have no doubts, then? You're entirely confident?"

"Totally, absolutely confident," Serge Myrandhal replied. "A confidence such that if I had beside me a dear individual, a sister or a brother..."

"You'd offer to take them with you?" said Miss Carpenter sharply, her beautiful face illuminating suddenly.

"No, Miss Anna," Serge replied, calmly. "Great as my chances are, that would be too grave a matter for me to take the initiative. But if that person, dearer to me that my own life, were, by virtue of her anterior studies, to decide for herself in full knowledge of the circumstances...if, after mature reflection, she asked to accompany me, I would accept without any hesitation, any remorse..."

Before the sentence was finished, the reporter had turned her head away, her soul full of a delightful anguish. She had immediately understood that the "dear individual" in question, able to decide in a full knowledge of the circumstances, to whom the inventor was referring, was her. And that indirect invitation, the idea of accompanying the man she loved on that prodigious voyage, made her amorous heart, fond of adventures, beat in the most delightful fashion.

At that moment, she was studying her companion between half-closed eyelids; and Serge Myrandhal, with his handsome face to which genius added its flame, appeared to her to be more handsome than any of the heroes of history or legend: more handsome, in spite of his unromantic costume, than Christopher Columbus standing on the deck of his caravel, or Lohengrin towed by his swan…more handsome than Prometheus, the vanquisher of gods!

She collected herself momentarily, and then, with a slightly mocking accent of coquetry, belied by her gaze, she said: "*Monsieur l'ingénieur*, it seems to me that we're straying from our subject. Let's not forget that I'm a reporter on a mission. As I told you when I came in, the *Herald*'s readers, ever more numerous since your lecture doubled our print run, are expecting their daily pittance.

"It's a matter, if not for you, who have nothing more to desire, but for me, who might never have such an opportunity again, to maintain the vogue on which my future as an independent woman depends. This evening, I propose to announce your association with Indraghava—which, unfortunately, is taking you away, stealing you from young America!" The young woman pouted adorably, in a coquettish fashion, and continued: "As an American, I'm jealous, and I warn you that my dear compatriots are going to murmur. They had hoped that it would be from New York that you would launch yourself toward the stars. To appease them, to create a diversion, I'll talk to them about our preparations for your imminent departure. It would be useful if I could fix an approximate date. That's why I'm asking you: when do you expect to get under way?"

"For India?" asked Serge, smiling, "or for Mars?"

"For India, to begin with."

"In a month, or thereabouts—which is to say, in mid-June. If things continue to progress as they've begun, in the American fashion, all the apparatus ordered from various factories, on which people are working feverishly, will be ready three weeks from now. A week should suffice for me to assemble and adjust them, and carry out a preliminary trial.

"For my part, I'll employ that time in producing certain components that constitute the delicate and secret part of the invention—components that only I can manufacture. So, announce boldly that in a month's time, everything will be ready, and that on the fifteenth of June at the latest, we shall take the train to San Francisco."

"Good!" the young woman replied. "The Transcontinental Railway—in which I still have a few shares, left over from the crash—will bank colossal receipts, thanks to you. Similarly the Trans-Pacific Company, which operates the service between San Francisco and Calcutta. I'm sure that thousands of tourists will invade India in your wake."

"What's the point, since they won't see anything? Apart from two or three privileged friends, the list of whom I shall have to submit to the Maharajah in advance, no one will be admitted into the monastery. The experiment must remain secret. That's one of the conditions imposed by my all-powerful collaborator, and I didn't put up any argument. So, if you think it appropriate warn your compatriots..."

"God forbid!" the young woman cried. "It's obvious, Monsieur Scientist, that you've never been a journalist or a novelist, like your humble servant and admirer. Otherwise, you wouldn't suppress so unceremoniously the principal, if not the only, interesting link retaining our readers.

"But now let's talk about the other departure—the great departure for the stars! Just now you mentioned a few weeks. I didn't think things would move so fast. You must be in a great hurry to leave us!" Miss Carpenter raised her eyes to look at her interlocutor tenderly as she concluded.

"It's necessary!" Myrandhal replied, in a profound voice. "As you know, you who read the heavens like an open book, in a few weeks the planet Mars will be in an eminently propitious situation, which won't recur very soon. That will last until the fifteenth of August, the twentieth at the most. It's necessary that I bid adieu to the Earth before that deadline.

"Then again, I have another reason, just as pressing, which incites me to make haste. You know the Rajah, since you've interviewed him. You've doubtless been struck by his truly alarming state of decrepitude. Remember that the old man in question, the moribund, might die at any moment, and everything would be compromised."

"I don't think there's any danger of that," Miss Carpenter replied, slowly, as if weighing her words carefully. "Either I'm much mistaken, or there's a vitality in that shriveled body that will surprise us all. What struck me most of all is the extraordinary vivacity in his eyes—that sharp, troubling gaze. Were it not for the fear of declining in your esteem, of passing for a nervous girl, I'd almost say that the old man frightened me..."

The Frenchman smiled indulgently. "That's the first impression I had, too, but it dissipated quickly before my host's amiable manner. As for the precariousness of his health, it's Indraghava who mentioned it first and gave me that further reason for hastening our departure for India—so insistently that we divided up the remaining time without further ado: one month for the construction of the machine, as I said at the beginning; one month for the journey from here to Karputhala; one month for the ascent to the monastery and the final preparations. That brings us to the beginning of August, which is the crucial time.

"That's when Mars passes the meridian at midnight: the fatal hour, the signal for the great *forward ho!* My heart shivers at the thought...and it seems now that time is passing very quickly...too quickly..." Serge hesitated, as if fearful of saying too much, and then went on, almost immediately: "My dear collaborator, I dare to hope that until that fateful day you'll continue to lend me your precious concourse...that you'll come with us to the monastery."

"That's a promise!" said the American, impetuously. Then, taking hold of herself, she continued: "Do you imagine that I'd leave the glory of such sensational reportage to anyone else?"

She rose to her feet then. "Now, Monsieur Myrandhal, you're going to accompany me to my carriage. It's getting late and I have a long article to write."

"You're going already?" the engineer murmured.

"I must."

"So be it. But before you go, at least let me show you how the various enterprises are progressing. That's part of your job—isn't it necessary for you to inform the public and your employer as to the fashion in which his orders are being executed?"

"Well, all right," the young woman said, taking the Frenchman's arm. "Let's make the proprietor's tour."

The two young people went out.

Night was falling gradually in the garden, drowned by a violet mist. The first stars were lighting up in the firmament. Here and there, enormous electric globes were sizzling, illuminating the work-sites, where the labor was still continuing. Workmen were coming and going, attentive and mute, but neither Myrandhal nor Miss Carpenter, absorbed by other thoughts, seemed to be paying any heed to that hive of activity.

Instinctively, they had steered away from the light and the noise, toward a small clump of parasol pines planted at the back of the garden. They moved forward, invaded by a strange anguish, a delightful disturbance, which they did not have the courage to break through. They were silent, fearful of disturbing the divine silence in which their entire souls were in communication with words.

Suddenly, Annabella, feeling Serge's arm trembling under hers, pulled away gently and let herself fall on to a stone bench nearby. "I'm a little tired," she murmured, very softly.

As Serge, very pale, sat down beside her, she suddenly extended her arm toward the Orient. "Oh!" she exclaimed, delightedly, almost ecstatically. "There's Mars, there's the star…the star that is showing you the way!"

Serge had raised his head immediately, and both of them, their faces radiant and transfigured, contemplated the golden planet, which seemed to be giving them a sign, summoning them across the sidereal immensity.

There was a long silence, during which the lovers could hear their two hearts beating in unison. Then, suddenly, Serge's pale forehead slumped, while a hoarse and profound sigh, almost a sob, was exhaled from his bosom.

Immediately, Annabella put her white hand on the young man's tremulous shoulder. "What's wrong, Monsieur Myrandhal," she stammered. "What are you thinking about?"

"I'm thinking," the engineer murmured, in a lugubrious voice, "that in a few weeks, I'll be far away from you, lost in the heavens…that I might not see you again…ever…*nevermore!* I was so happy yesterday…why have you come?"

That dolorous voice, the secret that had suddenly escaped, in a few halting words, from that heart swollen with love, moved Annabella to the deepest fibers of her being. Her heart raced, and a vivid incarnadine colored her cheeks.

"Calm down, my friend," she began, in a hesitant voice.

"No," Serge replied, somberly, almost grimly. "No, Miss Anna, it's necessary that I speak." in a supplicant tone he continued: "Listen to me, Mademoiselle, I beg you. Don't interrupt, or I'll never, never have the courage to confess the secret that's crushing me! Listen to me…and help me…otherwise, I'll never dare to tell you that I love you…that I love you madly."

"My friend…" Annabella tried to begin.

"No, don't interrupt" Myrandhal repeated. "Don't disturb me…or I'll no longer have the strength to finish. You can reply afterwards, and I accept in advance your sentence of life or death. Remember that I'm not a sociable man. Apart from the time devoted to indispensable sports, I've lived my life buried in laboratories. I don't know how to talk to women, and this is the first time I've talked to a young woman, a real young woman…hence my religious, sacred disturbance on the threshold of mystery, before the great Isis...

"Oh, poor scientist that I am, I thought I knew nature and life. For years, I've studied the celestial infinity, and I was ignorant of the other, the one contained in each of your glances, in the blink of your luminous eyelashes. But I feel now that I would no longer be able to live without you…that it's necessary, here or on that distant earth shining in the Orient, that I have you by my side—or else I'll die.

"Miss Anna, will you be my wife?"

After that last sentence, uttered in a breathless voice, Myrandhal straightened up. Now that he had spoken, and unburdened his heart, overflowing with love, he dared to look his destiny in the face. Suddenly, his convulsed features relaxed, and an expression of ineffable bliss illuminated his face.

Annabella, her eyes moist, smiled, and extended her arms to him in an adorable gesture. "My friend," she said, "this is my response..."

Serge had seized the American woman's trembling fingers, and was covering them with kisses.

"Finally," he murmured, "I can breathe! How small a thing is a man, and what magic there is in love! I was dying just now, and one word from you has sufficed to bring me back to life. Once again, I've recovered my zest for life and my work…the work that will no longer separate us, since..." The Frenchman hesitated.

"Since I'm going with you!" cried the young woman, with juvenile enthusiasm.

"I daren't ask it of you..."

"But yes! It's entirely understood! Are you unaware, my husband, that a wife ought to accompany her husband everywhere? Or is it, perchance that you're thinking of abandoning me...already! So it's decided, irrevocably. As soon as our marriage is consecrated, I go with you. A honeymoon trip to Mars! That won't be banal!"

And as, at that explosion of child-like joy, a shadow passed over Myrandhal's face, Miss Carpenter rose to her feet. "Come on, Monsieur Scientist," she said, gaily. "Don't be jealous. The adventure enchants me—certainly, the prodigious voyage is well designed to tempt an American, but what pleases me even more is my traveling companion. That's a declaration, it seems to me! And on that note, I must run..."

The American woman was already moving away toward the gate, laughing tremulously.

Two minutes later, Myrandhal helped her into her car, and how his lips lingered over his fiancée's hand!

"Come on," said the young woman, wagging her finger at him. "Finish, Monsieur Scientist. To be continued in the next issue, as the feuilletonists say. Or, rather, no...to be continued on Mars...!"

IX. Pickman

Scarcely had Miss Carpenter gone than the detective responsible for the security of Noton Cottage, whom we have already seen at work, appeared before Serge Myrandhal.

"Monsieur Engineer," he said, pointing toward the study window overlooking the garden, "you have a visitor."

The Frenchman, still under the spell of his conversation with his fiancée, was dreaming, with his elbows on the desk. He could not suppress a gesture of annoyance.

"A visitor?" he said. "But I'm not expecting anyone. I don't understand why you let him in. The orders don't permit any exceptions..."

"Pardon me," stammered the agent, who, to boost his audacity, was fingering in his pocket the large tip that had just been surreptitiously offered to him. "Pardon me, Monsieur Myrandhal, but the gentleman who asked to be let in is a very rich man...I mean, very influential, an important person. That's why I didn't think I should turn him away. Besides which, it would have been a waste of time. When one thrown him out of the door, that one, he comes in by the window, or else the chimney. You can guess who I mean—the Eccentric...the Eccentric, in the flesh."

"The Eccentric..." said Serge distractedly, his thoughts elsewhere. "What's that you're saying, Mr. Stick? Who's he?"

"The Englishman—you know! The one who was perched on the chandelier at the Athenaeum. The millionaire fantasist, the Baronet, Sir Washington Pickman." And the detective, wanting to prove that he was a polyglot capable of making a pun in French, added with a sly smile. "Pickman...the *pique* man...as you can see from here."

Serge looked in the direction indicated, and saw a man, a tall long-legged fellow marching placidly back and forth along a path. It was the Eccentric, wearing his invariable Alpinist's costume: leather leggings, knee-length trousers, a reefer-jacket with countless pockets and an alpenstock.

"You see," the detective continued, ironically, "that our Eccentric has gone to some trouble for you. He's renounced his helmet and put on a bowler hat, which doesn't suit him. As for the alpenstock—the *pique*, as I said—don't be surprised to see it in his hand. The Englishman is never apart from it. Every day, that mania gets him stopped at the doors of theaters, churches, even some restaurants, and there are indescribable scenes over that pikestaff. It's a fetish, according to rumor.

"In the course of numerous perilous ascents, that bit of wood has saved its master's life on several occasions, it's said—but he'll tell you that himself. I'll go fetch him, shall I, sir?"

Myrandhal had gradually relaxed. He smiled, interested by these details and by the memory of the scene at the Athenaeum—a scene that had certainly caused him a terrible emotion, but which, by way of compensation, had multiplied his triumph tenfold.

On the other hand, distracted as he was, his natural intelligence had immediately divined the secret motive for the agent's zeal.

"Well, go on," he ended up saying, "if you must."

Less than two minutes later, Pickman made his entrance, alpenstock in hand. He nodded his head curtly by way of a salute, stretched himself out unceremoniously in the rocking chair that Serge indicated to him, set his long staff horizontally upon his lap, and then, in a voice devoid of inflection—a nasal voice like that of phonograph, which lent itself to facile mockery—he started speaking in French with a strong English accent..

"I beg you to excuse me, sir, not for forcing my way in—I had no alternative—but for approaching you without having been formally introduced. Alas, I couldn't find anyone to do that for me. My friend Prince Djalor, on whom I was counting, told me to go to the Devil, as you say in France—but he'll pay for that. I'm related to the Viceroy of India, and I'll get my own back once out there. I can assure you, believe me, that the saffron-faced little fop will pay. I swear by John Bull!"

The Eccentric twirled his staff nervously. "And Miss Carpenter!" he said, suddenly. "Another one who let me down! She promised to bring us together, and then changed her mind at the last minute. She laughed in my face—and the worst of it is that I can't hold it against her. I'd forgive the little minx anything...she's like my protégée, or my ward, at least...I knew her father well, and I was to have been her godfather, but God damn it, I was on the other side of the world at the time, lost on the Antarctic ice-sheet. I'd wagered that I could climb Erebus, the famous polar volcano. Won the bet, of course—that's my game, climbing, and what I say, I do, always! Doesn't affect the fact that I broke my promise—so, you understand, one has obligations...

"Let's understand one another; it's the other way around, the opposite that happened. One isn't used to contradiction, and it makes me angry. So, when the crash happened, I tried save her father, and he flew into a temper. A self made man, he doesn't accept help. Then I fell back on my god-daughter, I learned that she was working for the *Herald*, and I was humiliated, heart-broken. Can you imagine? A beautiful young girl, well-educated, one of the queens of Fifth Avenue, the ward of Washington Pickman—an old madman, but who has a heart—doing a pauper's job! I hastened to write to her immediately, to put myself at her service. I offered her a dowry, so she could marry anyone she wished...her Prince, young Djalor, or anyone else..."

At that name, Serge had pricked up his ears. "Is she in love with him?" he asked, his expression troubled. "I mean...*was* she in love with him?"

The Eccentric shrugged his shoulders. "No," he said. "You're insane...pardon me, you're in error...that's it. Her, love that fop with painted fingernails! You don't know her. She's an American, a virile person. Too effeminate for her, the Hindu. Oh, she was flattered by his suit, obviously. She might be an American, and money doesn't turn her head, but she's a woman...but as for what you suggest, no, don't make me laugh!

"Where was I? It's your ludicrous question that made me lose my thread. I was explaining to you that I'd sent a letter to Miss Anna, in which, as a last resort, I offered to marry her. I'm a good catch, you know! A hundred thousand pounds a year. And that was a sacrifice—for me, I mean. I love my ward, but not in that way, you understand? And then, a globetrotter, always on the road, doesn't marry...or, to put it better, I'm already married. Look, here's my wife!"

The Englishman, gradually becoming excited, held up his alpenstock.

"This cane, you see—that's my wife. Perfect! I put her under my arm, and she goes with me everywhere, as a good wife should. She sustains me in the difficult passages. If an unsafe glacier presents itself, or a shaky rock, or a suspect snow-bridge, I put out my cane to sound it. I interrogate her, and she replies—all right! Apart from that, she never says a word. She's a model wife.

"Because, you see, I'm like Socrates, myself. The babble of women—Anna excepted, of course—their henhouse clucking, gets on my nerves. Add that my cane, the one you see here, has saved my life. So, we're never apart. We've slept together in the snows of the pole, and the torrid sands of the Sudan. We'll sleep together under the grass of Kentucky—that's my parish in Essex. All that's to explain to you that I've come with..." Abruptly, the Englishman passed his hand over his brow. "Damn!" he said. "There I go, losing track again. Excuse me, sir, I'm not in the habit of getting confused in my speech...

"Oh yes! So, I was saying that I'd offered to rescue my ward in that fashion, but she received me even more poorly. Papa had been content to look at me with his American eye, but with the little one, it was another song entirely. You'll never guess, sir, what she said to me in reply."

"What did she say to you in reply?" asked Serge, who as decidedly intrigued by the conversation.

"Nothing at all! She didn't reply at all. She simply sent me her seconds—two friends from the Ladies' Club! The little scatterbrain claimed that I'd insulted her gravely and wanted to kill me without further ado. And she would have done it, I can assure you...

"You're laughing. There's no reason for that. You don't seem to be aware that Annabella can handle a foil and a pistol like a master. So much so that I made my apologies. I'm sixty years old, so you ought to understand...and since then, I, who've always loved and adored my god-daughter—who have no one but her in the world—have been literally mad! I'm talking about her to you, as I talk to everyone, like an old fool.

"Oh, sir, what a brave and honest girl! What a noble heart and soul! She really is her father's daughter. She only lacks one thing, and that's being English!"

Serge Myrandhal drank in these words.

The Eccentric, who was nothing less than an "old fool," and who, beneath a somewhat rebarbative exterior, hid a great finesse, had immediately, and at the first stroke, been able to find the way to Serge Myrandhal's heart.

"Of course," Pickman continued, "my beautiful ward is a trifle stubborn, and quick to take offense...and in that regard, a piece of advice: you're paying court to her...yes, it's futile to deny it, you're paying court to the beautiful Annabella; the whole of New York is talking about it...well, be circumspect. Whoever rubs her up the wrong way gets stung, as you've seen. So, be prudent—if not, do you know what will happen one fine morning?"

"I can guess," said Serge, smiling. "Two envoys from the Ladies' Club."

"Exactly. Two seconds! And as you aren't her uncle, and aren't sixty years old, you'll have to go to the dueling-ground, if only out of gallantry. Three bullets in the chamber—those are the conditions of our chivalry. And once on the meadow—I mean, in the field—do you know what will happen?"

"No, but I have my suspicions."

"Not at all!" cried the Eccentric. "You're going to say that you'll apologize, or refuse...or that you'll fire into the air. You won't have time, Monsieur Frenchman. As soon as the *go* is pronounced, your pistol will be shot out of your hand! Then, disarmed as you are, you'll still have to face two more shots from your adversary, and it's the conclusion you can't guess.

"Coldly and calmly, at thirty paces, my terrible god-daughter will trim your moustache with bullets. One to the right, *zim!* One to the left, *vifft!* You'll hear them whistle. After which, Monsieur Conqueror of the Stars, dishonored and shaven, there'll be nothing left for you to do but take the first steamer back to France!"

Having said that, Pickman uttered a shrill laugh, like the cry of a corn-crake, with which the Frenchman joined in with the best will in the world.

"Thank you for warning me," Serge said, almost immediately, "but I don't suppose that it's purely for that reason that you're here. It still remains for me to discover to what I owe the honor of your visit."

"The thing is," the Eccentric replied, having resumed his customary impassivity, "that my god-daughter, who has been interested in astronomy since early childhood, is enthusiastic about your project, and even, a little, about you...yes! One can say that. She's no longer merely dreaming, under the pretext of reportage, of accompanying you to old Indraghava's monastery...but further still, perhaps...all the way to Mars!"

"Did she tell you that?" asked Serge, sharply.

"Well, no!" exclaimed the Englishman. "But I guessed it, by Jove! I'm an old fool, and I've never had a child, but all the same, I can read the heart of a girl I love. Oh, believe me, she's burning, *dying*, with the desire to go with you. It's obviously not her father who'll stop her—another eccentric, old Allan, a cold hothead immune to astonishment, who doesn't suspect a thing, and has as much idea about his daughter as a trout about an orange. You'll have some idea when I tell you that, compared to him, I'm practically a sage. Don't laugh—it's the truth.

"Look, I can hear the dialogue between the daughter and the father as if they were here.

"'I need to leave you, Papa.'

"'All right, dear. Where are you going?'

"'Mars.'

"'All right then. Are you coming back'

"'I hope so.'

"'Good. Bring me back a stone for my collection. I don't have one.'

"Anna has doubtless told you that her father collects aeroliths—'moonstones,' as they were once called."

The baronet made a grand gesture, and, with comical explosiveness, said: "There's a screw loose in that family, I tell you! So what's clear is that it's not the father—an old madman, in truth—who'll put up any opposition. Provided that decency is saved, that before you nestle down in our chariot, your celestial sleeping-car—where you'll be alone in somewhat close company, I expect—you've appeared before the minister of the parish, and provided that you also promise him a pebble for his display-case, Anna's father will give you *carte blanche*...

"There remains her guardian..."

"Ah!" murmured Serge, thus far delighted with what he had learned, but seeing the first obstacle rear up. "Miss Carpenter has a guardian, then?"

"Yes, sir."

"Who is…?"

"Me!" said the Englishman, touching his breast in an important manner. "Oh, I'm a guardian in much the same way as I'm a godfather, unofficially…nothing in writing. When Mrs. Carpenter died, and it was necessary to choose the family counselor whose functions were rightly mine…"

"I can guess," Serge interjected, smiling. "You'd gone to the Devil…lost on the Antarctic ice sheet."

"No," said the Englishman, "not exactly. I was at the other end of the world, at the North Pole. I'd wagered that I could cross a glacier that no human foot had tried before me. If you ever pass that way, you'll find my name engraved on a stray block of stone, with the date. That's what I always do—you'll find my signature in the four corners of the globe…

"But to get back to my ward…as chance would have it, I was in New York when the crash happened, and before he left for the Far West, my friend Carpenter confided his daughter to me. He asked me to look after her."

"Which means," said Myrandhal, looking his interlocutor full in the face, "that you're presuming a duty, albeit rather vague, to thwart your pseudo-ward's plans."

"Me!" the Baronet protested. "Never! Agree, however, that I don't have the right to disinterest myself in her completely. Oh, I don't want to tyrannize her—I'd come unstuck. She's an *enfant terrible*, an indomitable young woman who can only be guided on condition that she doesn't feel the bridle…so, don't worry, and don't look at me sideways like that. My god-daughter is free, as free as air! She can go to the Himalayas, to Mars, and then to Saturn, further if you want. I only put one condition on that."

"Which is?" Serge asked, impetuously.

"That I go with you…"

Serge Myrandhal made no reply. He was thinking.

Here we are, he said to himself. *Here we are, at the goal of that long conversation. Pickman's telling the truth in representing himself as Anna's friend and protector. I remember now that she mentioned him to me, and their statements are concordant. So it's necessary for me to treat him carefully, to gain time. Later, we'll see…*

"Well?" said the Baronet, brusquely. "You're not saying anything? Is that a refusal?"

"I'm neither refusing nor consenting…yet. It depends on too many things. Your proposal has taken me somewhat by surprise. You have a way of gripping people by the throat. I need time to think."

"Take your time," said the Englishman, phlegmatically. We're not leaving for another month."

The engineer darted a sideways glance at his interlocutor, wondering whether he was bluffing or speaking seriously, but Pickman's physiognomy was impenetrable. Before going any further, Serge wanted to discuss the matter with his fiancée, and sought a means of getting rid of the Eccentric without offending him.

I believe I have it, he thought. Aloud, he said: "Assuming that Miss Carpenter does go with me, from the moment that she sets foot on the *Velox*—that's the name of our craft—Miss Anna will be the captain of my ship; she'll be in command. It's therefore up to her to decide whether..."

"I'm doomed!" cried the Englishman, getting to his feet abruptly. "Not daring to refuse me yourself, you're sending me to my god-daughter. You know my weakness for the child, who abuses it. You also know that, just as I can't do anything to oppose her, she won't do anything without consulting you. Well played, Monsieur Frenchman! But I'm tenacious, you know—as tenacious as an Englishman, like Wellington at Waterloo, and I won't resign the game as easily as that. I have another proposition to put to you, and this time, I'll put my cards on the table.

"Before going on, I ought to tell you that I'm...I'm reputed to be an eccentric, but I'm not; I'm simply obstinate, a stubborn man who always finds the way to get what I want in the end. What I say, I do, always! Understand that—it's important.

"Thus, I said that I would get into the Athenaeum before anyone else, and gratis...and I got in through the roof..."

"You very nearly stayed there," murmured Serge Myrandhal, amused by the memory.

"No," said the Englishman, imperturbably, "The difficult part, believe me, is climbing up. As for coming down, that always happens. Thanks to you, I even made a very graceful descent...agreeable, I must say. It was the first time I'd sat on the wind. It's very good—no jolts, soft as a feather. I'd have liked it to last longer, if it hadn't been for that old fool Pellmann, gnashing his teeth and biting me in the calf. In fact, that's perhaps what you have against me?"

"Me?" exclaimed Serge, with an explosion of cordial hilarity. "Believe me, no! Oh, I'd have consigned you to the Devil for a second or two. You nearly compromised my experiment, and you gave me a terrible fright."

"There was no reason. Personally, I'm never afraid."

"You were risking your neck, though."

"Risk calls to me, attracts me. Then again, I had confidence."

"Confidence in what? In me, or the apparatus? You didn't know one or the other?"

"No, not in the apparatus, in you. At the first glance I could see that you were a man, Monsieur Engineer, and that one could count on you...rely on you...so I sat on your bench, that that's that!" The Englishman was becoming excited as he jabbered on. "And then again, there was something that couldn't be said—that people had traveled on the fluid but that I, Pickman, hadn't!

"It isn't your reputation that's at stake here, but mine, that of my exploits, permit me to say. I know you, and I render you justice—you, on the contrary, don't know what you ought to make of me, not at all. I'm a fanatical globetrotter. At twenty, I'd been around the world three times, and since then, I've found the world too small, and I'm looking for something else. Do you understand?

"In the meantime, to occupy my legs, I started climbing; there are a few fine ascents to my credit. I was the first to climb Gaurisankar, the highest peak in the world, 8,840 meters, between India and Tibet. It's been done since, but I hold the record. My celebrity dates from then.

"I was also the first to climb Aconcagua in the Andes, 6834 meters. If you ever go there you'll see my name, with the date that confirms it. I won't mention other mountains, which are molehills. In truth, I think that the Earth is a ridiculous ball, with its mountains. Talk to me about the moon, with its fifteen-thousand meter volcanoes. That's a nice height, by Jove! Since I read that in my almanac, I've only had one dream: to take a trip up there. And I count on succeeding, now that I know you. We'll go together..."

"I've never said anything about that," Serge objected, swiftly. "The moon doesn't interest me—for the moment, at least."

"Yes," said the Englishman, "you'll go. You'll go with me—to please me!"

"You're admirable!" exclaimed the engineer, laughing in spite of himself at that formidable aplomb. "You have no doubt about anything..."

"A man who has doubts is doomed. It's written in the Bible, if you recall: 'No man, having put his hand to the plough, and looking back...'[62] I forget the rest—not important! Now, a good Englishman never doubts. He goes straight ahead—all right!

"That posited, I arrive at the proposition that I put to you just now. You don't want me as a traveling companion, as a passenger—very well, that's you're right. Take me as an associate, then, let's make a contract. Wait—you'll understand!

"You already have two associates: one for the money, Norton Bennett; the other for the fluid—the animic force, as you put it—the Rajah. Well, you're going to break with them and take me in their place. Yes, I alone can supply ten times more force and money than them. I have in England a company formed as a Trust; the government is involved. We'll have as much money as necessary. As for the fluid, its better still, as soon as we—the English—take a hand in it.

"The English are the masters of India, masters of the fakirs—can you imagine how many? Indraghava has ten thousand yogis in his convent; we, in the whole of India, Tibet and Ceylon, have more than a hundred thousand, and it's that tenfold force that I'm offering you. We'll gather all the wretches together on

---

[62] "...is fit for the kingdom of God." Jesus, quoted in *Luke* 9:62.

the banks of the Ganges, the sacred river, and make them pray by means of force."

At that, Myrandhal burst out laughing, frankly. "Not a bad idea, in fact!"

"Then you accept?" said the Englishman, impetuously.

"No, I can't. You've come too late. But for that, perhaps...but there's no point in examining your proposal. I've made commitments."

"To whom?" cried Pickman. "To the Hindu? He doesn't count, and will do what we want. He's an English subject. As for the proprietor of the *Herald*, we'll compensate him, that's all."

"You think he'll agree?"

"He'll have to! If he makes difficulties, we'll force him by buying his newspaper. I've already acquired a hundred shares. You haven't signed anything, I know. So, you see, there's no objection."

"There is for me," the Frenchman replied, forcefully. "Those gentleman have my word. So..."

"So you're refusing!" cried the Baronet, furiously. "You're refusing to let me set foot on Mars with you. However, in addition to Anna, there's one other that you've accepted."

"Who told you that?"

"I guessed. I know that you've ordered two shells, two *Veloxes*—a small one first and then a larger one, capable of carrying two people. It's *Velox* number two of which my little madcap ward is dreaming. I conclude, therefore, that there will be two voyages."

"It's possible," Myrandhal agreed, "but nothing is certain yet. The truth is that, in view of certain circumstances and the Rajah's assurance that we'll have all the fluid necessary at our disposal, I ordered a second *Velox* of less restricted dimensions, with more room inside. As for the first, the smaller model, I had intended to leave it here, until Prince Djalor's father asked me via his son to take it with us."

"He's the one who intends to make use of it?"

"Yes—or, rather, his son. Nevertheless, it's only a very vague and very distant project. It will be necessary, for either of them to risk it, that the news I send back from up there—for we have a means of maintaining correspondence—should be particularly favorable."

"And that second voyage doesn't offend you?"

"Not at all. It's one of the clauses of our association with Indraghava, and I couldn't refuse anything to a man who is bringing to the common enterprise the most important element after the invention, properly speaking. I'm the one who will depart first; mine will be the honor of being the first to set foot on the unknown planet. That's the limit of my ambition for the time being."

"Well," said Pickman, who had listened to these details with a marked attention, "too bad—and since you're intractable, I'll try to reach an understanding with the Rajah. But I hope to do better...much better...

"As it's necessary to anticipate everything, though, one more question. Once up there, to whom will the planet belong, you or the Rajah?"

"My word," said Serge, smiling. "We haven't thought about that yet. Anyway, Mars certainly being inhabited, the question doesn't arise."

"Yes it does!" cried the Baronet, furiously. "It does, damn it! Oh, that's the French all over…always the same. Whether Mars is inhabited our not, it's a colony for the taking, and we'll be there, we English."

"A colony! You want to colonize Mars?"

"Why not? You were the first to mention it, at the Athenaeum."

"That's true, but I was talking about the future—a future that I don't see, as yet. The time is a long way off when there'll be pleasure trains circulating between the planets."

"Who's talking about trains? One man's sufficient…one man with a flag. He plants it, and that's that: the claim's made. So, I have another proposal to make to you—the last. I assume that you'll arrive on Mars first. Whether the planet is deserted or not, you have the rights of the first occupant. What are you going to do? Are you going to take possession of it in the name of France?"

"In truth, I don't know. Perhaps, perhaps not. I've told you that in the circumstances—given the impossibility of exploiting the heavenly body in question, except for the good of science—such a formality seems to me to be futile, and, to tell the truth, rather ridiculous. I'll be content to give French names to the lands and seas I discover. Thereafter we'll see; it's not probable that I'll have any competitor up there, any rival with whom I have to reckon."

"Who knows?" the Eccentric murmured. "At any rate, you're hesitant. Well, I have an idea—a bizarre idea, but practical. Mars will belong to you, and you don't know what to do with it. Sell it! I'll buy it. How much?"

Again Serge Myrandhal burst out into child-like laughter. "You really are unbelievable!" he said. "Sell a planet—that's very English."

"Are you refusing?" the Englishman interjected, bitterly.

"No."

"Finally!"

"I believe that on that terrain we can make a deal. You've opened my mind, and since the realizations of which you're dreaming are possible, in sum, and since we're under the regime of the *entente cordiale*, I can't see any objection to giving you a share in my future domain!"

"That's the ticket!" cried Pickman, a vague smile illuminating his bony face. "That's straight talking. We'll draw up a contract and, as soon as possible, we'll go to the embassy to get it signed."

"That's moving a little rapidly. How the devil are you going to divide up a planet as little known as Mars? How can the frontiers be drawn? We really ought to wait until we possess a map more precise than those of the astronomers—a map made on the spot…"

"No," groaned the Baronet. "No need for a map! I have another means, much simpler, which will suppress any objections. Would you like to hear it?"

"Go on."

"Here goes—listen carefully, with all your ears. On Mars, in contrast to our globe, there's much more land than sea. Those lands, those continents, will be the property of France, the terrestrial power; the seas will remain communal and undivided, as is only fair. For us, the English, we'll be content with a parcel to be determined, slightly larger than the present United Kingdom. In exchange, the canals—the famous canals of Mars, where they be natural or artificial, will be England's with a strip of land to either side."

"Damn!" said Serge, who could see the imperialist ears of John Bull looming up. "But, according to the configuration of Mars, it's the empire of the seas that you're attributing to yourselves, nothing less. The means of opening and closing the gates to them at will. It's Gibraltar and Suez all over again..."

"You don't want it?" cried the Eccentric, breathlessly.

"Perhaps," Myrandhal went on, a gleam of malice having just appeared in his eyes. "All things considered, I accept. It only remains to agree on the price."

"Hurrah! That's settled, then. As for the price, it's not a trivial thing like that which will set us at odds. If you want billions, you'll have them. Speak bluntly. Name your figure, I'll accept. Old England is rich."

"So am I," Serge replied, proudly. "Richer than you...a thousand times richer. Up there, on Mars, I own gold mines, diamond mines, unprecedented, fabulous wealth! So it's not money I'll ask of you, but something else."

"What, then?" asked the Englishman, slightly anxious.

"Very little. Simply return to us one or two of the colonies you've taken from us—Egypt, for example, or India."

This time, Myrandhal had found the means to drive his visitor away. At the mere mention of India, the Englishman, his face scarlet, had taken a step toward the door.

"Monsieur," he grumbled, in a restrained tone. "You're joking. Know this: the English take, but they never give back. That said, I'll retire; I sense that I'm about to do violence, and tomorrow, the little one—I mean that little pest Anna—would force me to apologize to you. But you were wrong to make fun of me. I have a great deal of sympathy for you, myself."

The Eccentric was already moving toward the exit, followed by Serge; he went through the garden with long strides. When he reached the gate he turned round suddenly, and in a voice still trembling with anger, he said: "Sir, one last word, to recapitulate. So it's clear, is it not, that you're refusing to take me with you?"

"Address yourself to Miss Carpenter..."

"No point; I know her response. Similarly, you don't want me as an associate?"

"I'm committed elsewhere...."

212

"Good; let's pass on. Finally, you're refusing to sell me Mars?"

"For money, yes."

"Well, I know what I have to do. I came to you honestly, my hand extended. You want competition, war—you shall have it! And you'll lose everything. Oh, you great French fool, you presumptuous young man! You think you're sure of your success—well, hear this: the last thing I shall say to you..."

The Englishman had struck an earnest, solemn pose, and his little colorless eyes had a strange gleam, a flash of steel blue.

"Hear this," he repeated. "This is what I, who never lie, am telling you: *There is a man who will reach Mars before you!*"

"Who?" asked Serge, incredulously.

"Me."

"You?"

"Yes."

"How?"

"I don't know—but I know that I shall go. I've said so, and what I say, I do. *Au revoir*, sir!"

X. Velox no. 2

A fortnight had gone by. Serge Myrandhal's success was assuming enormous proportions.

It had required heroic courage and an entire squadron of servants and detectives to resist the frantic enthusiasm of his admirers, not to be submerged by the heaps of letters and telegrams that arrived by every post from all over the world and not to be stifled by the embraces of the "fans" who lay in wait for him every time he stepped outside the grounds of Norton Cottage.

Every morning, the *Herald* published a front page article on what was already being called "the great enterprise," curiously documented and illustrated with photographs. In a matter of days, the newspaper had multiplied its circulation tenfold, and three European editions were being sold in Paris, London and Berlin with the same success as the American edition.

The signatory of those articles, which were producing such a great sensation in public opinion, was always Annabella Carpenter, and that circumstance was appreciated all the more by the public because the engagement of Annabella and the young man was already almost official. For the readers, the sentimental charm of a love story was added to the powerful attraction of the audacious interastral flight.

The work, driven by the kind of furious ardor that we have already witnessed, was approaching its conclusion. Already, in the middle of the enclosure, the metallic vehicle that was to traverse space, the *Velox no. 2*, was completely assembled and fitted out, hoisted on to the truck that would transport it to San

Francisco, from which it would be embarked for India. The day fixed for that first departure was a veritable scientific solemnity.

At two o'clock in the afternoon, several electric coupés came to a halt one after another outside the gate of the cottage. They were bringing the few privileged individuals admitted by the engineer to visit the *Velox* before is embarkation.

Among them were President Rosenfeld, the most popular politician in the United States;[63] Norton Bennett, the proprietor of the *Herald*, accompanied by Annabella and a few of the newspaper's major shareholders; three directors of the Metals Trust; and a small number of scientists and artists.

Finally, it would be unjust to forget, among the individuals we have already encountered at the beginning of the story: Prince Djalor, always impeccable, although a trifle melancholy since the news that Annabella's engagement had become semi-official; and the honest Canadian Ned Friedlander, beside whom advanced, alpenstock in hand, our friend Pickman, who, although annoyed with Myrandhal, had not been able to resist the attraction of the sensational ceremony.

Let us add that the Frenchman, full of disdain for the man who had dared to pose as his rival to his face, had put the coquetry of a good sportsman into the insistence that the Eccentric should accompany his ward to Norton Cottage. He wanted to show him that he had nothing to fear, and nothing to hide.

Also among the small number of the elect were His Excellency the Plenipotentiary Minister of the French Republic, who was escorted by the chemist Justin Durand, a friend of the inventor, and his inseparable companion Joe Grok, the industrialist.

No other guests had been admitted, in spite of the most urgent solicitations. The discontented were, therefore, numerous. In the street, a turbulent crowd was being held back, with great difficulty, by fifty vigorous policemen.

The spies, reporters, curiosity-seekers and everyone else who had hoped to penetrate into the mysterious cottage, were profoundly disappointed. Without the energetic attitude of the policemen, they would certainly have attempted an invasion by force.

Meanwhile, Serge Myrandhal had come to met his guests and conduct them personally to the *Velox no. 2*.

They found themselves in the presence of a cigar-shaped metal hull, blue-gray in color, which was somewhat reminiscent of an enormous torpedo or a small submarine. Let us say immediately that, like a submarine, the *Velox* was designed to maneuver in the seas or the famous canals of Mars.

About forty-five feet long, the *Velox* measured exactly eleven feet three inches from its base to the hatch on top. Apart from the conning-tower on top—

---

[63] The actual president of the U.S.A. in June 1908 was Theodore Roosevelt.

a tower partly retractable for movement while submerged—the only other swellings in the hull were enormous portholes with lenses of rock crystal.

"Gentlemen," the engineer began, I'll show you in detail all the interior components and fitments of the *Velox*. As you can see, the apparatus resembles a miniature submersible. I have particular reasons for giving it that form. My intention is to fall directly into one of the seas or one of the vast canals that furrow the planet Mars. The *Velox* is, therefore floatable and submersible.

"After having served me as an aerial vehicle, as an 'aeronaut,' this *psychoscaph*—which is to say, a container moved by psychic force, if you will permit the slightly barbaric neologism—will serve me as an aquatic vehicle. It is not without reason that I've adopted this amphibious system, imitative, in a way, of flying fish.

"We know nothing about the nature or the character of the inhabitants of Mars. They might be barbaric, bellicose and formidably armed. Enclosed in my *Velox*, I can, in any case, hold them off and, thanks to the canals, transport myself rapidly, in total security, from one part of the planet to another. With that objective I am taking a propeller and a rudder that are easy to fit, and even an automobile, for excursions on the continents..."

"But what will you do," asked President Rosenfeld, very interested, "if you ever take it into your head to come back?"

"I'm counting on doing that, Mr. President. I wouldn't go if there were no hope of returning. I believe I've resolved the difficulty; I shall take with me a sufficient reserve of animic fluid to regain our old planet whenever I wish."

"Marvelous! You'll be awaited here with impatience, and welcomed with the enthusiasm merited by an argonaut of the earths of the heavens, a Christopher Columbus of the planets."

At this compliment, punctuated by an approving murmur from the audience, the engineer bowed, blushing slightly. Then, after a slight pause, in the midst of a religious silence, he continued.

"The hull, formed of an alloy of chromium, steel and vanadium, is capable of resisting the most formidable pressures. It is doubled, in any case, and there is a gap between the two hulls filled with an appropriate insulating substance. I won't say much about the conning-tower, which scarcely protrudes and is hermetically sealed. The hatch will only be unscrewed after my arrival on the planet.

"Now you're going to be able to take account of the interior fitments. We'll go inside the *Velox* and visit the five compartments composing it, in succession."

That announcement caused a considerable stir of interest and curiosity. At a signal from the engineer, one of his assistants attached a ladder to the narrow walkway situated at the rear of the psychoscaph. Then he operated the manual control of the seal of the hatchway. The hatch opened and a narrow opening appeared, a kind of miniature cylindrical bay, just sufficient to allow a single person to pass.

"This way, gentlemen," said the engineer, cheerfully. "Follow me, without fear. I'll go first to lead the way."

While speaking he had climbed the iron ladder and inserted himself into the narrow passage. One by one, with the President in the lead, the guests followed in Indian file.

"As you can see," the engineer said, "this first, rather narrow compartment serves as both a kitchen and food store and as a store-room for instruments, tools and weapons. Here, in a very small volume, are enough concentrated food supplies for several weeks. This is an electric cooker with saucepans, equipped with a graduated semi-circular dial and a needle..."

"But why is the cooker electric?" asked the President, and added, not without a touch of humor: "Couldn't it be animic, or fluidic, like the rest?"

"Undoubtedly," said the engineer, undisconcerted. "Cerebral energy, once captured, can be subjected to any application, just like any other force, but as I have just explained, I need to be extremely miserly with the fluidic reserves that will permit me to make the return journey. That's why I'm not only taking accumulators and an electric motor, but a steam engine and an internal combustion engine. All of them will prove useful on Mars, where combustibles and electricity ought to exist in as great abundance as on Earth."

Now the engineer indicated a host of objects stowed in thick leather sheaths along the walls, all the way up to the rounded ceiling of the compartment. "I won't list all of this paraphernalia," he murmured. "You can see that not an inch of space is wasted. There are indispensable precision instruments, tools of primary necessity, weapons of every sort and caliber, including two mountain machine-guns, which will make our automobile, if the need arises, into a formidable war-machine."

Serge had opened a metallic door fitted with a rubber rim that ensured a perfect seal. By the soft light of a small electric ceiling light, a cabin appeared. It was fitted out with comfort of luxurious simplicity: furniture of light lemonwood, a thick carpet, furs, a few bronzes, two or three precious trinkets and a low bed with lacy pillows made it into a retreat that was entirely feminine in its elegance. A bathroom with a minuscule tub and shower-head was hidden behind a vast curtain of the same mauve blue as the rest of the hangings. The cabin was evidently designed for a woman.

While the engineer gave a few hasty explanations, all gazes instinctively went toward Annabella, who, apparently very calm, and slightly hidden behind the group of guests, seemed to be absorbed in making notes. A slight blush, however, and an imperceptible tremor of the lips showed that her indifference was not as complete as she wanted everyone to believe.

Prince Djalor had looked successively at Serge Myrandhal and the young woman, and had gone pale.

216

Already, though, the engineer, opening another door, was introducing his guests into the next compartment.

"This room," he explained, "occupies the exact center of the vessel and is situated immediately beneath the conning-tower, to which the spiral stairway on the left gives access. It's there that the passengers of the *Velox* will spend most of their time. It will be the dining room, the study and the living room.

"I forgot one important detail. You see that platform at the top of the stairway: it's the station of the captain and helmsman, when the Velox is navigating on the surface of the water. From there, thanks to the electric panel fixed within arm's reach, I can control the entire machinery of the submersible: the various accumulators, dynamos, propeller, rudder, etc. I can open a porthole, release the lead counterweight in the form of a sheath that protects our external keel, fill or empty the ballast-tanks. Even so, it's only case of extreme danger that I'll have recourse to those maneuvers, always hazardous even on the best-equilibrated submarines.

"The other apparatus—valves to evacuate detritus and vitiated air, liquid air inhalers, diving-suits, etc.—isn't much different from the apparatus in use in all submarines. One point to note, however: my compass, thanks to a process of magnetization that I'll keep to myself, doesn't obey terrestrial magnetism, too weak and uncertain over the distances we're traveling, but solar magnetism, much more powerful. That way, I'm sure of not losing north."

The guests marveled as they examined all the equipment, so complete and soberly comprised, and so ingeniously packed into such a small space. They looked at all the objects and utensils, simultaneously light, solid and comfortable, which represented, in terms of square feet, the last word in progress and perfection.

Among the visitors, however, there was one who was studying everything with avid, almost hypnotic attention. That was Sir Washington Pickman, the Eccentric. From time to time he dropped back slyly behind the group of guests, took a pencil from his pocket, and rapidly noted a few figures or a diagram on his impeccably bleached shirt-cuffs. Annabella's notes were certainly not as complete as his. He did not miss a single word of the engineer's explanations.

Serge Myrandhal had already passed into the fourth compartment. It was a very simple cabin. A narrow bunk, a bathroom equipped with the strict necessities, a bookcase full of books, and a few strangely-formed instruments, formed its entire furniture.

"I infer that this is your cabin, Monsieur Engineer," murmured the President.

"It's not very sumptuous, as you see, but nothing essential is lacking."

"Would it be indiscreet to ask," the President said, "what that bizarre machine is, with the multitude of small levers, and that globe in which gold leaves radiate from a crystal coil in a spiral, seemingly agitated by a continual tremor?"

"There's no indiscretion. That apparatus, which I call, perhaps a trifle presumptuously, a *telepath*, is a kind of telegraph moved by animic energy and based on the same principles that led me to construct my condenser of volitional fluid. Thanks to the telepath, I expect to remain in communication with my friends throughout my voyage from the Earth to Mars and my sojourn on the planet..."

"And able to keep the readers of the *Herald* informed!" proclaimed the honorable Norton Bennett, in a thunderous voice.

"Of course," said the engineer, smiling, not without exchanging a furtive glance with Annabella, "the *Herald* will continue to be the best-informed newspaper, not only on Earth but in the solar system. It's a record that it will hold for a long time, if it only depends on me!"

Then he continued his explanations.

"As you've noticed, the *Velox*'s compartments are equipped with electric radiators. It's thanks to those and the double hull that we can resist the absolute cold of interplanetary space, 270 degrees below zero..."

"Pardon me," Washington Pickman interjected, striking the floor with his alpenstock in a mulish automatic gesture that amused the audience, "But you've forgotten to tell us what's underneath this."

"Simply our provisions of water, liquid air and electricity..."

By way of thanks the Eccentric uttered a kind of approving grunt, and hastily scrawled a note on his sleeve.

Serge Myrandhal had already opened the final door. "It's this compartment, the equivalent of the first you visited, that contains the animic condensers and the steering mechanisms. This is where the pilot is stationed who will guide the *Velox* through the sidereal ether."

The engineer closed the door of the redoubt almost immediately, cutting off the questions that the Eccentric was doubtless already preparing to ask.

The tour of the *Velox* was concluded.

The guests, marveling at what they had seen, emerged one by one from the hull of the psychoscaph, where they had seemed to be living in a dream for a few minutes.

A surprise was awaiting them.

While they were inside the aerial ship, the décor of the grounds had been modified, as if in response to a stage-manager's whistle in some great theatrical extravaganza.

The *Velox*, decked from one end of its hull to the other with French and American flags and gigantic bouquets of magnolias, roses, orchids and camellias, had been hitched to a powerful traction engine.

A few paces away, a table was waiting, laden with all the elements of a light lunch.

"Gentlemen," said the engineer, not without a certain restrained emotion, "the *Velox* will depart for San Francisco in a few moments. It's the first stage of the journey that will end on Mars! I thought that it would be nice to baptize her in your presence—all of you who have supported, helped and encouraged me, permitting me to realize my dream, who have been my friends and collaborators, of unwavering devotion."

An energetic hurrah from the entire audience punctuated those final words.

"The godparents are both here," the engineer continued, when silence was reestablished. "They will be, if they will do me the honor, President Rosenfeld and Miss Annabella Carpenter."

"I'm very flattered," the President relied, gravely, "personally and on behalf of the people of America, by the great honor you're doing me. I accept with great pleasure."

Shortly afterwards, the President led Miss Carpenter to a small podium set up in front of the *Velox*. There, Annabella took a bottle of champagne from a servant and broke the gold-sheathed neck against the pointed prow of the psychoscaph. A flood of blonde foam inundated the metal of the hull. The *Velox* was baptized!

A triple salvo of hurrahs welcomed the young woman's gesture.

At the same moment, after a signal from the engineer, the *Velox* moved off.

A strong picket of guards was waiting at the gate. The escort surged forward, opening a way through the frantically clamoring crowd, and then disappeared in a cloud of dust.

In the meantime, in the grounds, the toasts commenced. President Rosenfeld stood up, glass in hand.

"Gentlemen," he said, with a delicate smile, first I propose we raise our glasses to the heroine of the day, the first and most gracious collaborator of our hero Serge Myrandhal, the godmother of the *Velox no. 2*. Miss Carpenter, I drink to your honor and your happiness!"

A concert of applause welcomed this allusion, and the rest of the toast was downed by the acclamations.

Early the next morning, at the Palace Hotel, Justin Durand was taking his bath when Joe Grok hurtled into the bathroom. He was brandishing an issue of the Herald striped with enormous headlines:

PLOT FOILED

THE HERALD ON THE ALERT

etc.

"You haven't read the news that has all of New York in uproar?" he exclaimed. "Yesterday evening, almost immediately after the presidential visit, the inventor and Miss Anna secretly took the train for San Francisco.

"An earlier train had left an hour before carrying all the equipment—so we've been robbed! The great projected ceremony, the triumphal procession that ought to have accompanied Myrandhal, is off. And I'd paid a thousand dollars to hire a simple balcony! Well, what do you think? You don't seem surprised at all."

"I knew all that," said the chemist, smiling.

"What! You knew?"

"Yes. You're forgetting that Myrandhal is my friend, and that, thanks to one of his marvelous telepaths, I'm in communication with him."

"In that case," cried the billionaire, hotly, "you'd do well to inform him as soon as possible of what's happening at Norton Cottage."

"What is happening, then?"

"Something terrible and unexpected, which demonstrates the determination of certain people to steal your compatriot's secret. At midnight, three hundred masked men descended on the villa. They overwhelmed the police, broke down the gate and invaded the basement. Fortunately, they didn't find what they were looking for. The laboratory was empty, dismantled. That doesn't affect the fact that there's still a battle raging around Norton Cottage. The villa is on fire!" The American concluded, triumphantly: "That's something you certainly didn't know!"

"But we knew perfectly well that our enemies, after having failed in their attacks several times, were about to attempt a violent blow—hence the clandestine departure arranged a week ago."

"A week! And you never said anything to me! You let me hire a balcony! You even accepted a place on it."

"I'd given my word."

"Yes, I understand. By way of compensation, I hope you'll be less secretive in future and make me party to the news you receive, thanks to the famous telepath."

"I would, but there again my hands are tied. My compatriot has a formal contract with the *Herald*."

"That's true," said the American. "Business is business."

Nevertheless, doubtless in the hope of learning some unpublished detail that would win him glory in the drawing rooms of Fifth Avenue, Joe came to his friend's residence almost every morning to read the *Herald*.

Every day, the dispatches became more interesting, and the public literally snatched the newspaper's four editions out of the vendors' hands. At certain hours there were veritable mobs outside the *Herald*'s offices.

One of those dispatches, covering several columns, excited honest Joe's admiration especially. It was the description of Karputhala, the city of pink marble, the Maharajah's capital, and its palace.

"To cap it all," he exclaimed, "there's the nocturnal festival held by the nabob in his gardens prior to his departure for the convent of Almowrat. Oh, if only I'd been able to leave New York!

"Frankly, I'd have given half my fortune to see such a magical spectacle: the Rajah scintillating with precious stones like an idol; the bayaderes, the marvelous park where tigers with velvet and silk coats, more diamond-laden than the greyhounds of our elegant strollers, wander at liberty among the rose-bushes and jasmine!

"Then, the complete change of scene at the departure: a stroke of a gong, and everything's extinguished. In the immense courtyard paved with cedar-wood, the caravans—two hundred elephants and as many camels—are lined up, waiting for the master…people are already anxious…

"Suddenly, a man appears, barefoot, clad in sackcloth, with a pilgrim's staff in his hand. It's the Mendicant Prince! He takes the bridle of the first camel, and the entire column moves off in the midst of a religious silence.

"What do you say, eh? Another eccentric, that one!"

The chemist smiled. "By the way, do you have any news of Pickman?"

"No—he's disappeared, but no one doubts that he's on his way to the convent of Almowrat. Your friend and his associates, who avoided him the first time, might have brought off that coup, and taken the strictest measures, but they won't stop him. No one's ever stopped the Eccentric, anywhere. There'll be one man there to witness the departure of the *Velox* for the stars, and that's the Baronet!"

"I doubt it."

"You're free to do so. Pickman hasn't taken me into his confidence, but I know him well enough to guess that he hasn't said his last word. According to rumor, the Steel Company—the Trust's rival—has constructed a second *Velox* in great secrecy, which can only have been commissioned by him. What would you say if he arrived on Mars before your friend?"

"I defy him to do that! It's impossible!"

"Impossible for us, but for him…who can tell? If you knew him as I do, you'd know that it's necessary to expect anything from the old devil."

XI. At the Monastery of Almowrat

When she woke up that morning, Annabella took some time to get her bearings.

Having arrived at the monastery of Almowrat the previous evening, in pitch darkness, she had immediately been taken to the apartment specially fitted out for her. Falling asleep, she had gone to bed immediately, and her new abode was now appearing to her for the first time.

The sun, already high, was shining through the arched windows.

Before her, there was a horizon of somber forests and ruddy, jagged mountain, which surrounded the plateau on which the monastery, as vast as a city, had been constructed.

In the background, the snowy caps of the last peaks of the Himalayas were sparkling with an immaculate whiteness.

Annabella felt enormously distant from the world she knew. The civilized world seemed as remote as a mist of dreams; she thought that she had been transported centuries back in time.

Her room, however, without offering the luxury of the palace of Karputhala, presented all the necessary comfort and elegance.

After a rapid lunch, the young woman went into the room that served as a drawing room, and from there on to the balcony, protected by a cloister of colonnettes, that extended externally.

She found Serge Myrandhal there; he had already been up for two hours, and was in the process of bringing his travel journal up to date.

The two young people greeted one another effusively, and Serge Myrandhal deposited a respectful kiss on the hand that his fiancée held out to him. Then they both spent a few silent moments contemplating the heavy black stone cupolas of the monastery-city, perched like an eagle's nest on a plateau halfway up a giant mountain.

Suddenly, Annabella smiled.

"I mustn't forget my professional duties, though," she said. "The *Herald* must be waiting impatiently for my dispatch. The last time I telegraphed was from Karputhala, where the line stops. Since then..."

"Don't worry, my dear Annabella," the engineer interjected, hastily. "I've thought about you. Your telepathic apparatus was the first I unpacked and set up. It's in the antechamber, from which you only have to transport it to your bedside, so as to be always ready to respond to the first appeal. That's what I've done with mine, and I've already given my news to my friend Justin Durand."

The American woman frowned.

"Oh! Are you, by chance, going into competition with me, Monsieur Engineer? You must remember that the *Herald* ought to be the first..."

"Don't worry!" Myrandhal hastened to protest. "I know and respect the rights of our all-powerful collaborator. My old comrade is a discreet man, aware of the agreements that bind me, and incapable of abusing a confidence. I'll add that my dispatch, were it to become known, would only serve to inflame the curiosity of your subscribers, given its concise and incomplete form. The proof is that it read: *Monastery of Almowrat. Arrived safely.* That's all! I agree, nevertheless, that, strictly speaking, I ought to have submitted my telegram to your inspection. I hope you'll forgive me."

"I forgive you," the young woman replied, smiling. "But only on one condition..."

"Which is?"

"That you don't do it again."

"That's a promise."

"And that you help me telegraph the newspaper. I'll talk, and you can operate the controls."

"At your orders."

Serge Myrandhal preceded the young woman into the room where the telepath was. He switched it on, and the gold leaves began vibrating.

An hour later, the writer specially delegated by the *Herald* to keep track of the audacious enterprise knew all the details of the latest stage of the journey and was able to give its countless readers a first description of the famous monastery of Almowrat.

Once that was done, the two fiancés returned to the balcony. A shadow had suddenly troubled the young woman's bright eyes.

"Serge," she murmured, in a low voice, "I want to tell you something that's been bothering me, rightly or wrongly. I've wanted to raise the question for some while, and the time has come.

"I might be mistaken, but my woman's instinct makes me dread that your Hindu associates, who have never inspired much confidence in me, might attempt to take possession of your secret, supplant you and depart before you. I might be wrong, but I sense around you an atmosphere of espionage and treason. In particular, I'm worried about the first apparatus you constructed, the *Velox no. 1*."

"My dear Annabella," the engineer replied, swiftly, "you know that the first model was commissioned for me alone, when I was unaware of the happiness that awaited me. After that, it was necessary to make one that was larger and more comfortable..."

Annabella blushed imperceptibly.

"I intended to leave the *Velox no. 1* in New York," the engineer went on. "It was on the insistence of Prince Djalor, who asked me on his father's behalf, that I was obliged to bring it here. They thought, as is their right, of coming to join us up there later—much later—but I doubt that they'll ever attempt the adventure. The Rajah is too old and his son too effeminate for such an enterprise. Nevertheless, they talked to me about it again yesterday evening, and I promised—it was an implicit clause of our contract—to furnish them with the means. Note that I couldn't do otherwise. I need them..."

Miss Carpenter shook her head. "I understand," she said, "but I mistrust your generosity and your frankness, which prevent you from seeing treacheries of which you're incapable. Would it not be possible, without annoying our associates, to proceed in another fashion? Thus, all the components that you've manufactured in duplicate, the engine that is now, and will remain after our departure, in the Rajah's possession...once again, have you no anxiety?"

"I can assure you that I have nothing to fear. You can see for yourself. I had the duplicate components of which you speak made in my own—our own—interest. It's necessary to anticipate everything. What if, in this inaccessible place, far from cities and factories, one of the complicated and delicate mechanisms were to fail, for some unknown reason, or sustain some damage...?"

"There'd only be a delay."

"Yes, but as our days are counted, the delay would take on catastrophic proportions. It would be a fatal and definitive check. With my duplicate components, it's a risk I avoid.

"Besides which, it's necessary not to forget that the Rajah and his son have rights over my invention, which they've so fortunately completed. I'm bound to them by a contract, which is no less imperative for not being written down. I won't be the first to break my word, and you've been impressed yourself, in the course of our journey, by the urgency and zeal with which our friends have supported me."

"That's true," said the young woman, still unconvinced. "But it's precisely that excessive zeal that sometimes worries me. These people are too polite..."

"Listen," said the young man. "Would you like me to reveal my secret to you in its entirety, as I've already offered to do many times?"

"No," Annabella replied, forcefully. "You mustn't. It would be a further imprudence, perhaps the gravest..."

"A further imprudence!" exclaimed the engineer. "What do you mean? Explain yourself, please."

"It's rather difficult. For some time, my nights have been troubled by strange nightmares. I sense confusedly that I'm the object of a kind of suggestion, that a will as strange as it is foreign is trying, in some way, to violate my thoughts, my mind...to introduce itself into my mind as if breaking into a house...and I think about the burglars that were swarming around Norton Cottage..."

"We're no longer in America."

"How do you that those who want to frustrate you haven't followed you? But let's leave that and get back to the nightmares I was talking about. Astonished by the bizarre phenomena—absolutely new to me, who have always slept like a baby—I've searched for the cause, and this is the reasoning I followed, going from deduction to deduction.

"Let's not name anyone, but you have envious, jealous, determined enemies—bandits who won't stop at any crime to obtain possession of your invention. These enemies suppose that I, your fiancée, know the secret of the engine-amplifier, and, not being able to attack you, whose powerful brain is proof against such maneuvers, they thought of getting it from me.

"They hope, by means of the mysterious key known as suggestion, to open the most secret compartments of my mind. Perhaps they've succeeded, but they haven't found what they were looking for. The drawer was empty. And that's why I don't want to put anything in it, why I refuse to know your secret."

"As you wish," the engineer murmured, impressed in spite of his optimism by the justice of her reasoning. "Nevertheless, while accepting your thesis and not giving you anything that might be stolen from you, I intend to reassure you. Although I'm as unsuspicious as you judge me to be, I've also taken my precautions, and a theft—even operated in the subtle manner that you dread—is almost impossible."

The engineer took his wallet out of the inside pocket of his jacket. "You'll understand..." He opened the wallet and took out a pinch of minuscule filaments, gold-green in color. "The entire secret," he said, "the entire mystery, resides in these fibers of an alloy whose preparation requires an exceedingly delicate dosage and a twist that only I know. It's this filament that I introduce into the apparatus every time, which is then ready—loaded. Without that, nothing functions, and after every experiment, the filament, melted and volatilized by the enormous power of the animic fluid, has disappeared without leaving any analyzable trace. Do you understand now?"

"I feel reassured," said the young woman, smiling again, "but hush— here's Prince Djalor coming toward us, at the far end of the gallery."

The fiancés advanced to meet the Prince, who greeted them with his habitual correctness, always imprinted with a kind of melancholy, which was accentuated as soon as he found himself in Annabella's presence. He asked the two young people if they were satisfied with the first night they had spent at the monastery of Almowrat, and almost immediately offered them a tour of the old monastery.

"My father," he said, "sends his excuses for not serving as your cicerone himself, but he's particularly absorbed at the moment, as you'll understand. I'll try to stand in for him, although his explanations would doubtless be more interesting than mine."

"I suspect," the engineer murmured, "that we'll be able to see marvels equaling those we were able to contemplate in Karputhala, which my memory retains in dazzling fashion."

"They won't be marvels of the same sort," Prince Djalor replied. "I'll show you—it's necessary for you to see—what prodigies the will can accomplish. It will give you an idea of the prodigious psychic power stored here." He turned to the young American. "I don't know, Miss, whether I ought to ask you to come with us. You'll see some horrible spectacles." Pensively, he added: "Except that there'll be the elements of a sensational article for the *Herald*. No one has ever seen at close range what I'm about to show you."

"If there's an article for the *Herald* in it," Annabella replied, bravely, "I won't hesitate. Professional duty before all! I'll try to be courageous."

Following the Prince, the fiancés went down a staircase with heavy banisters sculpted with interlaced snakes, and steps worn down by the centuries. They went through several courtyards with dilapidated colonnades. There was not a soul to be seen.

The sculpted façades displayed upright hieratical figures of mystical rigidity, like certain palaces of ancient Egypt. Their features, scarcely sketched in the black rock, had expressions of pitiless ferocity.

"Those," the prince explained, "are statues of some of our primitive gods, whose all-powerful will extracted the world from chaos." He put a finger to his lips. "In the place we're about to enter, I recommend the most profound silence and firmness. Do your best not to seem affected by what you see."

He opened a bronze door. A majestic courtyard appeared, surrounded by a forest of pillars. In the center was the sacred pool that is invariably found in all Hindu temples.

Annabella and Serge went pale, scarcely able to suppress an exclamation of horror.

On the edge of the muddy water, where the Brahmins made their ablutions and washed the statues of the gods in a ritual manner, a hundred men were heaped up or laid out in contorted and grimacing poses.

Annabella was gripped by anguish. She thought for a moment that she had been transported into one of the circles of the Chinese hell, the most complicated and most ingeniously barbaric of all.

"Where am I?" she asked Prince Djalor, who remained impassive, like a man long accustomed to such spectacles.

"This is the place where the fakirs reside, the yogis who—of their own free will, don't forget—submit themselves to tortures and ordeals with the objective of making themselves agreeable to the divinity and being admitted more rapidly to the ineffable nirvana.

"Look! Here's one who, in order to remain faithful to a vow of silence, has sewn up his lips with silver thread, leaving nothing but a minuscule opening. He can't eat anything except a little thin rice broth, which he sucks through a straw.

"This one has nailed his ears to the trunk of a tree. He's been there for years. Slowly, the trunk has grown and has stretched the lobes, which now resemble the wings of a bat.

"This one has kept his hands joined together and bound with cords for so long that the fingernails have driven through the flesh, at the almost inevitable risk of perishing of gangrene. He has doubtless only escaped death because of his frightful thinness. The putrescence can find nothing to devour in that mass of bones. At present, though, he's obliged to crawl like an animal to his bowl and lap up his rice like a dog.

"What do you think of such stoicism?"

Annabella made no reply. She thought she was the victim of the most abominable of nightmares.

Meanwhile, Prince Djalor continued to move forward cautiously through the squatting or sprawling bodies, as if he were walking through a battlefield strewn with the dead and wounded.

A little further on he pointed out a fakir so perfectly motionless at the summit of a column that his body, naked and skeletal, the color of old ivory, seemed to be carved of stone itself. One might have thought him devoid of life. His white beard hung down to his navel and little birds had built nests in his bushy hair, without being disturbed. Little golden lizards ran over his thighs, scarcely as wide as an ordinary man's wrist, and darted between his mummified toes.

Further on, other fantastic individuals agonized beneath piles of stone slabs or were buried in the mud, where insects were devouring them, without a muscle in their face quivering or any contortion betraying their suffering.

A few were writhing on beds of hot coals, which they had to extinguish with the blood oozing hideously from the burns with which they were covered.

There were several who were lying on sharp spikes, which penetrated profoundly into their flesh.

Annabella turned away in horror at the sight of a huge bamboo wheel that was turning with extreme rapidity, bearing the bloody bodies of three old men, whose hips and shoulders were traversed by iron hooks. Wherever she directed her gaze, however, there were similar spectacles of horror, similar scenes of horrifying torture.

"Let's get out," Serge Myrandhal murmured in Prince Djalor's ear. "I think that Annabella is feeling sick."

"You're right. I've been used to these spectacles for such a long time that I didn't calculate the effect that they might have on an impressionable feminine nature."

"Yes, I beg you," the young woman murmured, "let's go. I'm running out of strength."

The Prince hastened to satisfy Annabella's desire, stammering vague apologies. In his urgency, however, he tripped over one of the bodies lying on the ground.

One might have thought it a mutilated cadaver rather than a living human being. His blinded eyes were no more than two bloody holes, two frightful gaping wounds. He had cut off his nose, his ears and, more frightful still, his lips and part of the musculature of his mouth. His teeth were bare. He was reminiscent of some character in the *danse macabre* or one of the most terrible tales of Edgar Poe.

It was more than Annabella could bear.

She fled, closing her eyes, chilled by horror, all the way to the bronze door that had given the access to that terrible place.

The prince and the engineer hurried to catch up with Annabella, who, leaning against a pillar in the neighboring gallery, gradually recovered, breathing in one of the revulsives most effective in such instances from a bottle of "lavender salts."

"I never imagined that such frightful things existed beneath the face of Heaven!" she exclaimed, after a brief interval. "How can your father, the Maharajah, tolerate such horrors, Prince?"

"He doesn't tolerate them," the Prince replied, a trifle embarrassed. "He doesn't have the power to prevent them. He would lose a great part of his authority over his subjects if he tried to stop these fanatics torturing themselves so cruelly. You'll see in due course, in any case, that the Rajah has done a great deal to restrain and moderate these futile martyrdoms..."

"I can't help feeling sickened and indignant," said the engineer in his turn.

"Do you want to know what I think?" said the Prince. "To be sure, I disapprove of the excesses, the abuses of that exaggerated exercise of the energetic faculty, but you'll agree with me that it's thanks to that power, that methodical training of the controlled will, continued over the centuries, that certain marvelous results have been obtained. Isn't it thanks to the psychic contention of thousands of poor yogis that you're going to be able to realize your marvelous project? It would certainly be impossible to do it with the brutalized wills of Occidental individuals, disseminated in a thousand futile preoccupations."

"That's an argument *ad hominem*," said the engineer, smiling. "I have no reply to such an argument, since I shall be one of the first to profit from the meditations of these fanatics."

"In any case," the prince continued, "We don't only have hideous spectacles to offer you. There are less frightful ones." Pushing a cedar-wood door ornamented with pentagrams that was facing the bronze door, he went on: "Come into this room with me and you'll see something that, although it's not terrible, is just as marvelous."

"Let's go in," said the engineer.

"Let's go in," repeated Annabella, after a slight hesitation.

The room into which they went had a high ceiling, and was absolutely bare, with paving-slabs of black porphyry covered with ancient Sanskrit inscriptions.

At first, Annabella did not perceive anything extraordinary, but, having raised her eyes, she uttered a cry of astonishment.

Grouped slightly below the center of the ceiling, slightly hollowed out in a vault, three human beings were suspended in mid-air with no kind of support.

"You see here," Prince Djalor explained, "a manifestation of a phenomenon well known to scientists under the name of levitation. It's by the power of their will alone that these three monks have risen from the ground and can maintain themselves in the air for as long as they wish."

"I've read accounts of the feat related by a large number of trustworthy travelers, but I've never witnessed it," said Annabella. "I don't deny that I much prefer this strange miracle to those I've just seen in your torture garden..."[64]

At that moment, the solemn sound of a gong rang out.

---

[64] Although this phrase is *jardin des tortures* in the original, it nevertheless re-emphasizes an echo in the previous scene of the descriptions contained *Le Jardin des supplices* (1899; tr. as *Torture Garden*) by Octave Mirbeau, one of the classics of Decadent prose.

The prince made a gesture. "My father's summoning us," he said, in a respectful tone. "Come with me—I believe he needs to talk seriously to Monsieur Myrandhal."

XII. In Which Events Move Rapidly

A fortnight had gone by. It was the thirtieth of July.

That morning, Serge Myrandhal and Annabella had just come down from their apartments. They were in the first courtyard of the monastery when the entrance door, opened by the old bonze who was in charge of it, gave passage to a Hindu whose meager torso was only protected by a scrap of cloth covering his loins. Over his shoulder was slung a brown leather bag. In his left hand he was waving, with an incessant and automatic movement, a sheaf of metallic rods whose sound was supposed to drive away rattlesnakes. His body was streaming with sweat.

"The mailman!" said Annabella, joyfully. "There ought to be a letter from my father."

The young woman was not mistaken. The Hindu took a large envelope from his bag covered with multicolored stamps and handed it to its addressee in exchange for a silver rupee.

The young woman scanned the missive at a glance; her cheeks colored with a blush of pleasure.

"Good news!" she exclaimed. "Father tells me that the Reverend Jonathan Burrett, who is to bless our union, is on his way. As long as he arrives soon!"

"He'll arrive," the engineer replied. "I'm confident—your father understands the situation. Remember that in one of my previous letters—the one in which I asked him to accept me as a son-in-law—I explained to Mr. Carpenter that the most favorable interval for our departure was between the first and the fifteenth of August. Remember, too, his enthusiastic response. He hoped to be able to come, and he was already talking about chartering a special ship."

"Yes," the young woman murmured. "And the Reverend Burrett is just as resolute, it seems. He's a missionary, a man hardened to all fatigue, as my father says. He'll travel night and day. Read it for yourself."

"All's well, then," said the young man, after having perused the letter. "I see, too, that your father has succeeded in beginning to rebuild his fortune."

"And my guardian," the American woman went on, laughing in a child-like fashion, "the eccentric Pickman—do you think he'll arrive in time? He's promised to be my first witness, but since his last dispatch, not a word…might he be annoyed with us?"

Serge laughed too, at the memory of the famous conversation. "I'm not worried about that," he said. "As a good Englishman, Pickman is a slave to his word and his rendezvous. Time is money...

229

"He's an excellent fellow, fundamentally, in spite of his manias and his slightly...brusque manners. Besides, I'll wager that, like all eccentrics, he's mathematically exact in his punctuality.

"Then again, he loves you too much not to be present on such a solemn occasion. Come on, everything's going well, and it's up to us to make haste now. For the first time, work will continue all night if necessary."

"As it did back at Norton Cottage..."

"Yes. It's necessary that the track from which the *Velox* will be launched is finished before tomorrow. Now, if you wish, let's go see our workmen; our presence stimulates them."

A few hours later, shortly before midnight, the old monastery presented an unaccustomed activity, which would have made the old monks shiver in their tombs.

A long line of Jablochkoff candles departing from the breached ramparts scaled the steep slope of the mountain to a culminating point four kilometers away. By the electric light that patched the darkness with long bright beams, twenty elephants specially trained for the work, like those owned by all the Anglo-Indian railway companies, were finishing placing cross-ties and rails of the track.

Everyone knows the promptitude and precision with which the intelligent pachyderms lift up rails or cross-ties with their trunks and set them down gently in the correct location, without missing it by a centimeter. Behind the mahouts who were encouraging them with their cries and caresses, a crew of coolies were rapidly tightening the wedges and bolts.

Already, the steel ribbons raised toward the sky—toward Mars—at a forty-five degree angle, were cutting through the darkness like twin lightning-bolts.

Departing from the summit, the line went down to the monastery situated below, and terminated inside a profound high-ceilinged crypt whose walls and vault had been partially demolished to accommodate the track. That was where the *Velox no. 2* was, installed on the launch-truck that would roll all the way to the top of the mountain, from which it would take off for the Empyrean.

Behind the long metal vehicle was situated the engine-amplifier, similar to the first experimental apparatus that we saw in the hall of the Athenaeum, but much larger in its dimensions.

The strange wand of which the engineer had made use during the memorable ascent of the three spectators was there again, considerable enlarged and fitted by a knee-joint to the upper wall of the cube instead of the "saddle." It was extended vertically, but it sufficed to fold back the "trolley" to put the *Velox* in contact with the propellant machine that was to project it toward the stars.

Finally, half way along the side of the motor, a large metallic wheel could be seen, fitted with controls somewhat reminiscent of steering-wheels, moving in front a graduated circle. This was the "activation wheel"—the device that, when the moment came, would open up a fluidic current of formidable power.

Another important detail: all the walls of the vast subterranean chamber were lined with long silky threads of all colors, which gave the crypt the appearance of a marine cave with walls covered in extremely fine algae. Strangely, these threads seemed to have a life of their own.

Some of them, gray in color and initially dull, suddenly took on a bright coloration, of orange, red or blue. They began vibrating, slowly bristling until they were perpendicular to the wall, standing up like the hair of a terrified man. From their tips flowed a soft yellow and blue phosphorescence, which filled the entire crypt with gleams that had something magical and immaterial about them. These gleams converged, attracted by a superior force, on the cube, which seemed to be absorbing them avidly, penetrated by them.

The reader has doubtless guessed that these threads, several thousand in number, all planted in miniature ampoules, were nothing other than receivers of the animic fluid emitted by the innumerable penitents and fakirs under the Rajah's orders and directed by them toward the crypt. The differences in brightness and rigidity were due to the various degrees of material displacement or intensity of the human piles.

There was something grandiose and terrible about that crypt, with its sculpted arcades of grimacing gods, where the energy of thousands of human brains was being stored.

Meanwhile, the intensity of the light was increasing by the minute, until it became fulgurant; at the same time, the temperature was rising. The cube now seemed to be aureoled by a kind of luminous mist, like the smoky vapor emitted by retorts of phosphorus.

At that moment, the only door of the *Velox*, the automatic valve situated at the rear, opened with a dry click.

The engineer Serge Myrandhal appeared in the narrow passage that served as a threshold of his strange dwelling. With one hand on the brass rail, he started climbing down the metal ladder hooked on to the guard-rail,

Half way, he turned round.

"Well," he said, "are you coming, my dear Annabella?"

"I'm following you," said a voice that came from inside the psychoscaph, "but whatever you say, I'm sure I'm not mistaken. Something abnormal is going on here. There are objects that seems to me to be out of place. Something's amiss."

Annabella, entirely devoted to her investigation, continued to remain out of sight.

"My dear friend," replied the ever-confident Serge, "I can't see what you're worried about. Everything seems to me to be in its place."

Suddenly, however, the young woman uttered an exclamation of surprise, and in a tone of annoyance she said: "This time, it's too much. I'm not the victim of a hallucination. I came smell a pipe. Some insolent individual has been smoking in my bedroom. *Shocking*, as my old governess would say."

The young woman had just appeared on the walkway. She tapped her foot, pointing an accusing finger at the Frenchman, in a manner that was supposed to be menacing. "Do you, perchance, smoke a pipe, my dear fiancé?"

Myrandhal smiled. "I'm not afflicted by that vice," he protested. "I only have the occasional cigar—but I'm quite ready to give it up, to please you. In any case, I very much doubt that the plant Mars is provided with tobacconists."

Again Miss Carpenter tapped her foot. "That's the French!" she exclaimed. "Laughing at everything. I persist in my affirmation. It reeks of pipe-smoke, horribly."

"Pure imagination, I swear. No one here, so far as I know, enjoys that odious instrument. It's probably the emanations of the accumulators, which..."

"You can say what you like!" cried Anna, impetuously. "And getting back to it, I insist that there are objects in the cabins that are no longer in the same place. Someone's been in here..."

"There's nothing extraordinary about that, my dear Annabella. It's Prince Djalor or his father. They come here every day, as is their right."

"Exactly. It's to them that I'm alluding. I think they prowl around too much, observe too much. I sniff some treason on the part of that old Maharajah, some sly scheme..."

"My dear, I assure you that your suspicions are unfounded, and exceedingly unjust. The Rajah has rendered me the most eminent services."

Pointing at the walls of the crypt, streaming with light, he said: "It's thanks to him that this river of energy is flowing in here, like the water of a thousand streaming feeding a lake. Haven't I explained that, even if the Maharajah had evil intentions, he couldn't discover my secret. You've seen the filaments without which the rest of the apparatus is useless."

Annabella took hold of her fiancé's arms, gently. "I'd really like to believe you," she said, submissively. "Does a woman have the right to an opinion? In France—I'll be French soon—a wife only has the right to shut up. You're the stronger, and you've abused that to martyrize me already. What will be, will be, great Lord! But be careful, Monsieur Frenchman, be careful. I'm American, myself, and the fatal *yes* hasn't yet been pronounced."

She burst into joyous laughter, with which Myrandhal joined in chorus.

Then, abruptly passing on to another idea, she menaced him with her gloved fingertip again. "I have a complaint to make," she said. "I want to know what's in the little box that you received so mysteriously from New York the other day. Why haven't you shown me?" Pulling a face she added: "Perhaps I'm being indiscreet?"

"No," Serge replied, embarrassed. "I swear to you..."

"Don't swear!" said the American, petulantly. "I can see by your confused expression that you don't have a clear conscience. After all, it's none of my business. You doubtless have your reasons, and I can only bow down to them for the moment. I'll see later what there remains for me to do." Annabella had suddenly struck the offended pose of a jealous woman.

Myrandhal did not know what to think. "I wouldn't want, for all the world, that you should think me capable of finding something from you," he declared. "I'll tell you everything, but it will spoil the surprise I wanted to give you on your birthday..."

"Which is the day after tomorrow, August the first..."

"I haven't forgotten. Do you still want to know my secret?"

"More than ever!" exclaimed the fiancée, whose lovely face lit up with a smile.

Myrandhal took a morocco-leather jewel-case out of his pocket and opened it.

"A watch!" the young woman exclaimed, not without a hint of astonishment.

"Yes," said Myrandhal, smiling. "A watch—but not an ordinary watch."

"What's different about it?"

"My dear Annabella, it's a Martian watch. The hours are regulated as on the planet to which we're going, where the day is thirty-seven minutes longer than ours. Look, it's a small masterpiece of scientific jewelry; the movement of the two moons of Mars, Phobos and Deimos, is reproduced here in these little lateral dials..."

Annabella was profoundly moved; her large blue eyes had suddenly misted over. "I beg your pardon," she murmured, enveloping her friend with a tender gaze. "I wanted to tease you a little..."

"You're completely forgiven."

The young woman had taken the Martian watch in her hands. She examined the elegant trinket curiously, whose case, artistically carved, represented the *Velox* afloat in a sky constellated with diamonds and rubies.

"It's adorable!" she murmured. "The winder has the form of a sun, and the whole circle is sown with little stars." With the gesture of a curious child she put it to her ear, and pouted prettily. "But it's not going."

"Big baby! It won't go until we're up there. Its first tick will coincide with our first step on the planet."

Annabella was still listening. "Yes!" she suddenly exclaimed. "It is going! I can hear a tick-tock..." She lowered her head, and with a tender coquetry, she whispered: "No, it's our hearts beating...quite loudly, in fact..." Piously, she kissed the watch and slipped it into her bosom. "I'll keep it there forever!" she said, gravely.

Serge, too emotional to speak, thanked her with a squeeze of his hand.

"How, in the midst of all this turmoil," Miss Carpenter added, "did you remember my birthday? I'd almost forgotten it myself, and the surprise is all the more agreeable for it."

"I hope that it would be even more complete. I dreamed of landing on Mars on your birthday—and that's the day on which I would have given you the watch. From that moment on, given the annual rotation of Mars around the sun, which is 669 days, you'd only have had a birthday every two years..."

"That's exquisite!" cried the American. And how lovely it would have been to get there in time! I would have been so happy to begin my twentieth year up there, with you! Is it impossible, then?"

"It's very difficult."

"Even if we leave right away? What if we try? Don't you want to?"

"I want whatever you want, but I repeat, it's almost impossible. You can see for yourself—only I'd be obliged to give you the figures, and I'm afraid..."

"Don't be afraid. Figures don't frighten me now, and besides, I'm so interested..."

"In that case, I obey. Anyway, I'll simplify. We'll leave out the fractions and the quarter-seconds with which some astronomers abuse us. Thus posed, these are the givens of the problem: at this moment, the most favorable, and until August fifteenth, Mars it at its minimal distance, fourteen million leagues. Light, at the formidable rate of eighty thousand leagues per second, takes three minutes to cross that distance, but the *Velox* is far from possessing that velocity—which isn't one, properly speaking; it's a long vibration, without real displacement.

"Add that, with regard to us, it's difficult to evaluate the exact potential of the mysterious agent that will project us toward the Empyrean, and difficult to estimate the depreciation to which that force will necessarily be subject on the highways of the Ether.

"At a rate of two hundred and fifty kilometers per second—a frightful, mortal speed—the *Velox* would take four days and fifteen hours to reach Mars. If we could go fast as five hundred, it would take two days seven and a half hours.

"As you see, even by doubling..."

"Well," cried Annabella, enthusiastically, "let's triple it, and arrive in time to celebrate my birthday on Mars! Note that you'll need flowers, and as I only like roses and orchids—doubtless unknown species up there—you'll have to bring a bouquet from here. Now, if you want to give me pleasure—the greatest in my life—and not to give me flowers that aren't very fresh, you'll have to resign yourself to going seven hundred and fifty kilometers a second...or a thousand, if necessary."

"That's the velocity of a comet..."

"Then we'll play the comet. You know that I'm being serious, and that what I want, I want! So, tell me frankly: is it impossible—absolutely impossible—to arrive on Mars the day after tomorrow?"

Miss Carpenter was speaking with such fire, such enthusiasm, that Serge felt shaken, infected by the intoxication of speed for which so many automobilists pay with their lives.

"No," he replied, "not absolutely. But in all probability, the fluid of our terrestrial factory wouldn't be sufficient, and we'd have to have recourse to our accumulators, to squander precious reserves..."

"Well, squander away," said the young woman. "Burn out the machine—what does it matter, provided that we get there? It's a matter, as my worthy guardian would say, of setting a record that won't soon be beaten. Doesn't that tempt you?"

"Yes, but I'm hesitant. To dip into our fluidic reserves...we need them in order to remain masters of the *Velox* in case of an accident. Most of all, we need them to get back."

"We won't come back, that's all."

"And if Mars is uninhabitable..."

"Impossible! As long as we're together...you see, I have an answer for everything. In consequence, enough discussion. We're wasting time, when we could be *en route*. In a word...and just say yes or no, nothing more...is it possible?"

"It's possible."

Increasingly carried away, the American clapped her hands. "In that case, Monsieur Frenchman, I'm taking you away...abducting you...we're going right now"

She had grabbed her fiancé by the shoulders and was dragging him. Bewildered, bowled over by the young woman hanging on to him—entwined with him, as it were—Serge Myrandhal allowed himself to be dragged. He followed her lead, without knowing, and without even asking, whether his fiancée meant what she was saying or not. It was one of those moments when the most earnest of men can commit the worst imprudence.

As for Miss Carpenter, simultaneously impetuous and reflective by nature, her enthusiasm, real and spontaneous as it was, lacked foundation. The time it took her to traverse the crypt was sufficient for her to get a grip on herself and envisage the incredible folly of her first impulse.

She hesitated, and sought a subterfuge—an escape route—which her alert mind rapidly discovered.

Having reached the foot of the ladder, she released Myrandhal's arm, and changed direction yet again. He expression suddenly severe, she pointed at the *Velox*, and in the coquettishly quarrelsome tone that had already enjoyed so much success, while she frowned and a gleam of malice appeared in her eyes, she said: "Tell me, Monsieur Frenchman, do you imagine that I can go in there and leave, just like that, alone with you? But we're not married, and you'd compromise me horribly! Now, I don't like that. My dear guardian must have told you that I know how to make a man respect me! Tomorrow, you'll receive a visit from my seconds. Here's my card!"

She held out her hand to Myrandhal—who, utterly nonplussed at first, soon smiled, delighted to see the incident resolved in such a fortunate manner.

"What a pity!" cried the American, who could not let it go so easily. "What a beautiful dream destroyed! Oh, if that honest Jonathan Burrett had only had the good idea of arriving today. If he were here, the situation would be saved! But we can't think about it anymore, and will have to content ourselves with leaving in time, before the fifteenth of August. Just as long as the venerable clergyman gets here before then!"

"As to that," Serge replied, "I'm not worried. The pastor will be at the monastery in a week, perhaps sooner if, as your father hoped, his friend was able to take the first ship leaving for India."

At that moment, a man in a turban appeared at the entrance to the breach, illuminated by the phosphorescence of sorts that the fluid-saturated crypt was projecting. Recognizing the foreman of his Hindu workmen, Serge advanced to meet him, followed by Annabella.

"Sir," said the man, in English, "Allah has sustained our efforts. The track is complete." And he pointed along the central pathway at the elephants, who were coming back, carrying the tools, piles, cross-ties, wheelbarrows etc. that were no longer necessary on their backs.

Myrandhal congratulated his overseer and bade him farewell, after giving him a golden rupee.

In the meantime, Annabella contemplated the sky, as she frequently did, with a wondering, almost ecstatic gaze. The stars were shining with an incomparable gleam through the pure air of the mountainous region.

A little below Mars, ready to cross the meridian in its turn, Jupiter, the monarch of the heavens, was advancing at the head of a cortege of stars, which it eclipsed with its white fire, and in the distance, toward the Orient, the pale light of distant Saturn could be distinguished.

As soon as they were alone, the young woman lowered her gaze, and in a voice charged and vibrant with the ream she had just had, she said: "Do you know what I'm thinking about, my friend?"

"At a guess, you're thinking about Mars."

"No, my dream took me much further—all the way to Saturn and beyond, to the extreme limits of the solar system; and I hope that dream will be a reality one day, that the *Velox* won't stop half way."

"I'd like nothing better."

"In that case," the young woman continued, studying the shining words—the giant Jupiter; Saturn wearing its beautiful rings like a Moor's head-dress; old, cold Neptune, lost so far from the sun, condemned to eternal polar night—"I was thinking that those planets, so dissimilar to ours, are certainly inhabited, but by beings very different from us."

"No doubt about it. Creation—life—is everywhere."

"Yes—but what life? What are the beings that are stirring, who might perhaps be looking at us at this moment and asking themselves the same question? Are they beings composed of an ephemeral body and an immortal soul, who are, like us, only passing? Do they live, and die…do they love…up there?"

"Certainly," the young man replied, impetuously. "Love, the attraction of souls—like gravity, the amour of matter—is a universal law. It's even the one and only law, the one that has populated infinity, that has caused those billons of stars, of suns, to spring from the burning bosom of God, every one of which, like ours, illuminates an entire world, an entire universe…

"Now, what are the beings that gravitate up there? That something impossible to know, and which it would be madness to imagine in accordance with the few data that we possess. That would be wanting to match our feeble imagination against the resources of Nature, which are infinite in every respect.

"Perhaps, one day, it will be given to a human, a privileged being, to see those distant relatives…"

"Oh!" declared Miss Carpenter, in an ardent invocation. "If only it could be us!"

"Until then, we can't know anything about them—I mean, nothing about their bodies, perishable things condemned in order to live, to perpetuate themselves, to submit to the humiliating functions of animality, to model themselves according to their environment, their climate…

"It's quite different for the soul, the pure essence, freed from matter and death, and one can assume that the soul of a Jupiterian, for example, only differs from ours in the degree of its perfection, by virtue of a more or less complete knowledge of the god, the true and he beautiful.

"Personally—although I wouldn't want to seem too mystical—like the Rajah, I'd willingly admit the theory of spiritual reincarnation, already glimpsed by Pythagoras, our old master in mathematics. I firmly believe that our sun is not only a planetary center, but a psychic nucleus, around which our immortal but perfectible souls rise by degrees, transmigrating from planet to planet, getting closer at every step to the superior beauty that is nothing other, according to Plato, than the splendor of the truth."

Serge raised his inspired face toward the firmament, and continued: "No, those sparkling heavenly bodies—Jupiter, even Neptune—are not empty. The heavens are not empty! No, those planets are not the desert worlds that some people imagine, from the little that we know. There are superior races up there, which once came to the Earth. It's the abode of the fortunate, and that's where we shall rediscover those we have loved!"

At these last words, pronounced in a warm. Vibrant voice, the young woman sensed her yes moistening with tears.

"Oh, my sweet friend," she murmured, "now much good you do me! You've never spoken better in accordance with my heart. It seems to me that it's my late mother, so tender, who's expressing herself through your mouth, and like you, I firmly believe in the migration of souls. Our relatives, our friends, are up there in the heavens. They're waiting for us! And look, my dear fiancé—it's necessary that I tell you an idea that I've had many times since we've been here, far from the world, confined in this somber monastery with that enigmatic and all-powerful old man.

"You've soothed all my anxieties, but our happiness is so great, that it seems to me impossible, and I sometimes have the sensation of living a dream whose awakening will be terrible! A woman's imagination, no doubt, the fear of a woman in love trembling for her happiness; but there's one thing that consoles me, and that's my belief in the immortality of the soul. I say to myself, my dear friend, that nothing can separate those who love truly; that if ever you succumb to some ambush, I shall fight to save you to begin with, and then to avenge you—after which, my work done, I shall be able to join you. I shall find you up there, on one of those bright planets, where those that we have loved live!"

Serge Myrandhal took his fiancée's hands and pressed them to his lips. "My dear Anna," he stammered, "my sweet and tender love!"

Already, however, Miss Carpenter, fearing that she had softened too much, was gently pulling away. Becoming mischievous again, she exclaimed: "Oh look! A shooting star!"

"Make a wish."

"It's made."

"What is it?"

"I'll tell you. My first wish, to land on Mars the day after tomorrow, my birthday, is no longer realizable. But if, at least, we could be married by then..."

At that precise moment, one of the monastery's servants, clad in one of the buttonless black robes, maintained only by a belt, that Buddhist priests wear, came into the crypt, seemingly a little frightened by the strange phosphorescence.

He handed the engineer a black-framed visiting card: that of the individual awaited so impatiently, Jonathan Burrett.

Serge showed it to his companion. "Victory!" he exclaimed. "The star has granted your wish."

And with a spontaneous, irresistible impulse, the fiancés fell into one another's arms.

"Victory!" exulted the American. "We'll marry tomorrow—and on the day after, *en route* for the stars!"

"And now," Serge concluded, "let's go and greet the worthy gentleman. He must be getting impatient..."

The young people had scarcely drawn away when, behind them, in the *Velox*, a head appeared, slipping prudently out of the partly-open door.

The eyes of the unknown man, all that were visible in a bushy black beard that rose all the way to the eyelashes, reflected a malign joy. Bent double, one might have thought him a hunchback afflicted with an enormous belly, swaying like a bladder inflated with air. He emerged silently from his hiding place and started coming down the psychoscaph's iron ladder.

Having reached the bottom and looked around carefully, the false hunchback straightened up. "By the horns of Beelzebub!" he groaned. "I need to stretch my bones. It's really not comfortable in that storage-locker. On the other hand, I've learned some interesting things. I'll be glad to be able to sleep in a bed like everyone else—but I'd better keep my eyes open, al the same. It's necessary to expect anything from a lunatic like that little Carpenter girl, the Eccentric's ward. Oh, the little minx—what a tease!

"There was a moment just now when our love-birds nearly flew the coop without saying goodbye to anyone. Fortunately, I was there, as I shall be the day after tomorrow…and with that, let's get some sleep! I'm sure now of not missing the bus!"

XIII. "Forward Ho!"

In the meantime, the Mendicant Prince's narrow cell was the theater of another, no less important, scene.

Djalor, who had been living in mortal apprehension since being informed of the arrival of Jonathan Burrett, had just come into his father's room. He sat down in the Oriental fashion on the fiber mat comprising the only furniture of that monastic interior, and waited.

Squatting at the other extremity, his back to the wall, his knees under his chin and his eyes tightly closed, the Maharajah seemed to be asleep, but he had seen the other come in, for almost immediately, and without deigning to raise his withered eyelids, he said, in a shrill tone as distant as a dream: "You again! Why are you disturbing my nirvana?"

"Father," murmured Prince Djalor, "you know I'm suffering…"

A shiver of impatience agitated the old man's skeletal body. "I was decidedly mistaken," he interjected, in a sarcastic tone, "to send you to the home of the English who dare to call themselves our masters. I hoped to infuse you with some of their virtues, but you've only picked up their vices."

"You're cruel, Father. You love me, I know; you can see my anguish. You're the only one who can lighten it, but you remain silent. You shut yourself away in tragic silence. Why won't you…"

"Why do you doubt?" cried he Mendicant Prince, coming fully awake this time. He had folded his arms over his meager chest, and a flame of life colored his prominent cheekbones. Angrily, he repeated: "Why do you doubt? I've promise you that Miss Carpenter will never be the Frenchman's wife. Have you ever known me break my word?"

"No, Father, but something might happen at the last moment, some unexpected intervention, that can disrupt the best-laid plans. As long as we were alone here, where you're the absolute master, I've had confidence in you, and obeyed you in every detail. I've put a brake on my passion and a seal on my lips. I've smiled at my rival and condemned my eyes no longer to see the one of whom my soul is full.

"But it's no longer the same today!

"An Englishman, an unknown—and doubly dangerous, in consequence—has introduced himself into this abode under a name and a pretext that are both undoubtedly false, and for a week, he's been hiding from everyone...

"The monk who received him at the secret door, who only perceived a fraction of a beard beneath the pulled-down hood of his robe, and you are the only ones who have seen this strange individual's face. All I know about him is what you've deigned to tell me: that his name is Archibald Denvalor and that he was sent here by the district governor—who wants, he claims, to be represented at the marvelous experiment we're preparing.

"All that is extraordinary, to say the least. The delegates of the English government usually behave in a far more cavalier fashion. Ordinarily, it's in broad daylight, with a large cortege, that they come among us. This one, by contrast, has slipped in like a thief...

"But what surprises me most of all is that you, so jealous of your slightest prerogatives, have welcomed this intruder without a murmur; that, far from forcing him to explain himself, you're helping him to hide. I know that a man who has reached the level of sanctity where you exist receives enlightenment from on high refused to mortals still retained by the bonds of the flesh, but I have my lover's instinct, which warns me...

"Believe me, Father, this man is dangerous!

"Is he a friend, a relative of our guests, who is attempting to watch over them, to protect them in secret? Might he not be one of these innumerable detectives hired by the *Herald,* who pullulated back there, around Norton Cottage, who has caught wind of our plans and has come here incognito in order to defend the invention of which we intend to take possession?"

The Rajah shrugged his shoulders imperceptibly. "My child," he jeered, "I'm glad that your love has not put your vigilance completely to sleep or obscured your understanding. Your mistrust, although misguided, is legitimate; in sum, I congratulate you on it.

"As for the Englishman, banish all anxiety on that subject. Denvalor isn't dangerous. He knows nothing of our plans, but I've known his since the first day. He had scarcely crossed the threshold of this cell than I read his face and his heart like an open book.

"For now, I'll only tell you one thing: Archibald Denvalor is neither a friend nor an enemy. We could make him an associate, but that would do him too much honor..."

That superb indifference reassured Prince Djalor. He was about to reply when the sound of a gong suddenly rang out in the nearby corridor.

Djalor shivered and leapt to his feet with the agility of a young jaguar.

"That's for me," he said, in an anguished voice. "There must be some important news. Excuse me, Father."

He launched himself toward the door...

When he came back, a few minutes later, his face was distraught, his eyes hollow, burning with fever. "Father!" he said. "All is lost! The minister, Jonathan Burrett—may Hell confound him!—has just arrived, with the authorization of Annabella's father. The Frenchman and his friend are mad with joy. They've announced that they'll marry tomorrow, and launch themselves into the heavens the day after!

"The Frenchman's already giving orders, as if he were at home. He's just instructed that the crypt and the *Velox* should be decorated with flowers. It's there, in front of the apparatus, that the nuptial service will take place..."

Despairingly, Djalor wrung his long, slender hands, whose bones clicked. In clipped sentences he gave a few more details, and then, with his throat tight and his mouth convulsive, he groaned: "No, it can't be! I love her too much..."

A cloud passed over the decrepit face of the Mendicant Prince. The man, in whom almost nothing human remained, had felt a string vibrate in his shriveled heart.

"Djalor," he said, in a grave, almost gentle, voice, "Djalor, my child, the hope and pride of my race, calm down and listen. Nothing is lost, and the pastor's arrival will have no other result than to hasten our triumph. We are the masters here. The inventor, his invention and his fiancée belong to us. I've promised to give you the woman you love, to throw her into your arms a virgin, and I will keep my word. You know on what condition..."

The Prince lowered his eyes in shame. "Yes," he said. "You want me to help you rob my rival. I shall obey! For you, for her...I shall go as far as dishonor, as far as crime..."

"Pusillanimous soul!" murmured the Rajah, scornfully. "Heart of a jackal! There is neither dishonor nor crime for men such as us, acting in the name of a superior principle. It is Brahma who commands, and delivers our adversaries to us, bound hand and foot. It is necessary to act..."

"Command," said the young man, convinced. "I'm ready. But how can we prevent what is in preparation? Tomorrow, or the day after, at the latest, the Frenchman will depart, taking his fiancée...his wife...and his secret with him..."

"No! declared the father, curtly. "The secret—the secret that will give us a world—will remain here, in our hands. I have discovered it; I now possess it in its entirety. As I no longer have any need of the inventor, I shall kill him...or, even better, get rid of him by sending him far away, to a place from which he will only return with our permission...which is to say, never.

"As for Miss Carpenter, who is your destiny, she too will remain in our hands."

"How?" asked the Prince, feverishly. "How will you do that?"

"What does it matter?" said the Rajah, with a sudden abruptness. "I can only tell you one thing Tomorrow, when the moment comes to embark, the Frenchman will have changed his mind. He will depart alone, leaving us his invention as the price of our aid, and his wife as a hostage.

"It will be thus because I wish it, because it is right that it should be thus. We are hesitating because everything is in our favor. Another few hours, one more move, and the game is won, all along the line. I am taking possession of what I consider to be my property, and getting rid of an inconvenience: an inconvenience that I am making into a collaborator—a test subject, as you say in your laboratories—who will inform us as to the habitability of the planet."

"Are you sure?" asked Djalor, already half-convinced by his father's unshakable assurance. "Myrandhal might suspect our ruse, our treason, and refuse to communicate..."

"He will suspect nothing," the father replied, his lips pursed, "and it doesn't matter; I've anticipated the possibility and I have the means to constrain him."

"What means?"

"There are several. The simplest is that the lovers, as soon as they are separated, will certainly communicate via the telepath, of which I too know the secret. What is simpler than eavesdropping on their communication? If necessary, we shall only have to suggest certain questions to Miss Carpenter, who will become our unwitting and benevolent secretary..." The Mendicant Prince concluded, with a ferocious snigger that showed his sharp teeth: "Everything is already planned and weighed, you see. In making your rival depart alone, I shall strike a double, a triple blow! I shall conquer a woman for you, and a world for me, of which you will be the first couple...and I shall be avenged!

"I shall be avenged for that which was stolen from me by the victor of the Athenaeum, who will become once again what he should never have ceased to be, an instrument of our service, a lowly creature on which we shall carry out our experiments *in anima vili* as you say."

"What about the other one?" objected Djalor. "This mysterious Denvalor? What will you do with him? You have no fear of him, you say—I have no difficulty believing you, but still... Judging by his letters of accreditation, this Englishman, whoever he is, has connections, and authority with which we have to reckon. If he's there are the moment of departure, he'll discover our trick; he might become inconvenient. Suppose he sides with Miss Carpenter..."

"The Englishman will not be any hindrance," Indraghava declared, in a peremptory tone. "If he takes it into his head to see too clearly, he can be eliminated, sent far away like the other. In any case, the hypothesis is gratuitous. Far from getting in our way, Denvalor will assist us, if he is asked. It will be sufficient to associate him with our work—to make him believe that he is an associate—and he will do whatever we wish.

"Do you doubt that? Well, you can judge for yourself. You shall see"—an enigmatic smile creased the terrible Rajah's parchment-like lips—"that, like that ridiculous Eccentric, *what I say, I do*...always!

"For nearly a week, Denvalor has been asking for a second meeting, always refused. Go out and give the order that he should be fetched as quickly as possible. Then, hide behind that curtain"—the mage pointed at a door-curtain of coarse fabric masking the entrance to a second cell—"and from there you shall listen, and you shall see...

"I want to give you that further proof of my power over the other Aryans, those ingrate and degenerate sons who, because they have made a few improvements of the science we discovered thousands of years ago, think themselves our equals, our masters. How ridiculous! I hope that, after that, you will no longer doubt me, and will obey me blindly."

"Yes, Father."

Less than ten minutes later, the man we have just seen sliding out of the *Velox* made his entrance, followed by a silent monk carrying a poorly-wrought stool, which he placed in front of the Master's mat.

Archibald Denvalor, interpreting to his advantage the long-desired meeting that had suddenly been accepted, seemed very proud, inflated by his sudden importance. He paraded his arrogant, provocative gaze over the bare walls, and the sordid old man, still ensconced, his eyelids lowered, who had not deigned to greet him even by means of a gesture.

When the mute servant had withdrawn, the Mendicant Prince pointed to the seat and, in excellent French—the Rajah never spoke the language of the abhorrent conqueror—said in an indolent tone: "Sit down, Mr. Pickman."

His visitor started and blushed. That simple sentence had sufficed to deflate the presumptuous individual, who let himself fall on to the proffered stool rather than sitting down.

"What's that?" he stammered, passing his strong hands over his moist brow. "What, that, sir? You say...by Jove! If you weren't an old man... You're joking, I think..."

"It's you who are joking," the mage replied, curtly and harshly. Then, abruptly changing his attitude and in his most amiable manner, he continued: "Come, come, my dear Baronet. You've lost. Be a good sportsman. You've lost, but your honor is safe. Your disguise was superb. Even my son, your fellow for more than a year in the Splendid Club, was taken in, like the rest. With the father, it's not so easy, and I'm astonished that you haven't approached me, at least, without your face uncovered, without that beard and your fake paunch.

"Come on, my dear Pickman, you're an Englishman, and a man of intellect in consequence; you know India and its yogis; you've witnessed incontestable instances of 'second sight'—and it's in the presence of one of those thaumaturges, and not the least, that you attempt a childish, comical trick?"

The Eccentric was on the spot. Angrily, he twirled his absent alpenstock on his knees.

"As for me," his mocking interlocutor continued, "I haven't even taken the trouble to see you, remember. You hadn't even crossed the outer wall when I was aware of your coming and your plans, Mr. Pickman."

"My plans!" stammered the Englishman, increasingly bewildered. "You know what I've come to do here? No! That's impossible. Everyone thinks I'm in San Francisco. I telegraphed..."

"Another trick that stuck out a mile, that dispatch. It would have been sufficient to give you away to Serge Myrandhal if he were not distracted—doubly distracted, as a scientist and a lover. Otherwise, given the overtures you made to him—for you've spoken to him, that's obvious—he would have seen the trap right away."

"That's true, murmured the Eccentric, red with confusion. "I'm an old fool, yes—a lumbering brute, that's what I am. So you know my plan."

"For a long time."

"And you're going to stop me?" Pickman said, anxiously.

"I didn't say that."

"Oh!" The Eccentric's eyes lit up with hope.

"I didn't say that," the mage repeated, still smiling. "I'm not a jealous man, myself—not ferociously jealous, like my associate—and I haven't taken sides in your personal competition. Until now, I've remained neutral, and I'll continue to do so—always provided that you don't harm the common enterprise."

"I've no intention of doing that!" the Englishman protested, striking his breast with demonstrative violence. "I'm a gentleman, a pure soul, by Jove! All I ask, personally, is a place on the *Velox*...that's all."

"Then we might...yes, we might, perhaps, come to an understanding," the Mendicant Prince insinuated. "I like you..."

"You too...I like you!" exclaimed the Eccentric, impetuously. "You're a good chap, a fine fellow...I mean, a worthy man...a generous heart, that's it. Apologies...I've lost the thread. I must seem stupid to you..."

"Not at all," the Rajah replied, with a thin smile. "I'm not suspected of affection for your people, but your enthusiasm appeals to me. I like your juvenile valor, your style, your 'forward ho!' attitude, as you say, and I might even help you..."

"You'd do that!"

"Perhaps...if your intentions are pure. Before anything else, let me tell you that your means—the idea of leaving hidden in the *Velox*'s hold—is no good. For several days you've been slipping in there every night, at the risk of being asphyxiated by the emanations of the accumulators. You haven't been caught so far, but that couldn't be long delayed. A man of your size doesn't hide easily, and although our scientist is distracted, Miss Carpenter has an American eye. Beware...

"Why, since that inconsiderate fellow Myrandhal was so intractable in your regard—which is hardly gallant toward your god-daughter—didn't you address yourself to me boldly and frankly? You know that my son and I are also planning to make the great voyage..."

"Yes, I know—the *Velox no. 1*. I know about that. Serge—that inconsiderate fellow, as you put it—told me about it. But can you launch it? That's the objective...I mean, the objection..."

"What a question! You're forgetting, my dear Pickman, that it's me who supplies the fluid..."

"No, only the motive force—but the amplifier, as he calls it: do you know its secret?"

"I know enough to be able to make use of it whenever I please, if that's sufficient for you. It was one of the clauses of our association, and if your intentions are honest, I'm ready to let you take advantage of it."

"All right!" cried the Eccentric, leaping off the stool—but he sat down again almost immediately. "Except," he went on, "that there's a catch...I mean a hitch...

"According to what he told me, Myrandhal is going to leave first and arrive on Mars first. Isn't that so? If it is, then I'll lose the record. That's the question, you understand?"

"I understand perfectly. Myrandhal does, indeed, have to depart before anyone else; that's specified in our agreement, which I intend to honor strictly, to the letter—nothing more and nothing less.

"As for landing on Mars first, that's a different matter. There, the field is free, open to competition. With the means at our disposal, provided that we don't leave it too long, we might well be able, not merely to catch up with him, but—who can tell?—perhaps even overtake him."

At that idea, the Eccentric leapt up again, mad with you, his eyes wide. He applauded with his strong hands, as large as shoulders of mutton.

"Bravo!" he cried. "Hip, hip, hurrah for Old England! A steeplechase to the planet! That's magnificent...fantastic! No such thing has ever been seen. A handicap through the stars, and it's the outsider, the Englishman, who'll win! Rule Britannia! It's prodigious! Well done! Oh, if they knew about this at the Splendid Club, what colossal bets they'd be laying! Look at the odds! I'll take ten to one, and I'll bet..."

The Eccentric continued in this burlesque manner for another full minute. Then he calmed down slightly. "You're sure of success, then?"

"As much as one can be. I've told you that we have immeasurable reserves of force here. Take note, too, that the *Velox no. 2*, even far away, outside our sphere of gravity, will still remain subject to my psychic influence, and that very probably, in spite of the fully-charged accumulators he's carrying, I can still, if not stop him, at least slow him down..."

"No! Shocking!" cried the Englishman, hotly. "It's necessary, sir, not to do anything felonious. We must win the great battle by playing straight. And we *shall* win—hip, hip hurrah for England!"

On receiving that admonition, the Rajah had frowned momentarily, but now he was smiling. *That's right*, he thought. *Enthusiastic and honest, in the English fashion—that's the man we need.* "So, my dear Pickman," he said, "you agree to join forces with us against Myrandhal. You're with us?"

"Yes I am," declared the Eccentric. "I'd risk my life for that. That Frenchman offended me gravely; I'm going to…what do I have to do?"

"Very little. As with you, Myrandhal has offended me, with his pride, and his mistrust. While respecting our contract to the letter, I want to teach him a lesson in modesty. To do that, I need someone, an associate…"

"And you thought of me! Thank you!"

"Exactly. I'll even say, although you'll accuse me of bluffing, that it was me who suggested to you, at a distance, the idea of coming here…"

"No! That's true!" the Eccentric affirmed, becoming a flatterer for the first time in his life. "That's true, by Jove! I remember now…you're a prodigious man. Well done!"

"As for what you have to do," the mage continues, "very little. Continue hiding, playing dead, and wait. The *Velox no. 1*, ours, is ready and provisioned. An hour after the Frenchman's departure, it will be hoisted on to the rails…and on its way!"

"All right!" howled the Englishman, applauding loudly again.

Shortly afterwards, he withdrew, enveloped by the Rajah's indefinable gaze.

XIV. Married!

In accordance with Annabella's wishes, the marriage was celebrated the following day at midnight, twenty-four hours before the departure for the stars. The young woman had wanted those two events, the crucial turning-points in her life, to take place at the same hour: the moment when Mars passed the meridian.

The ceremony, a very simple one, had just concluded. Annabella and Serge were alone with Jonathan Burrett in the *Velox*'s crypt, decorated with flowers—roses and jasmine.

The Rajah, still impenetrable, and Prince Djalor—the latter livid beneath the make-up with which he had coated his cheeks—had retired discreetly as soon as their royal signatures had been added to the document drawn up by the pastor.

The Reverend J. Burrett, a stout man with a jovial face, but endowed with an exquisite tact and delicacy, closed his Bible and led the newlyweds to a bench situated a few yards away, at the entrance to the garden. He invited them to sit down beside him, and then, in a paternal tone, he said: "My friends, I have only a few more things to say to you, and one desire to express, and then I too shall leave you to your happiness, blessed by God.

"It's no longer the pastor who is speaking, but the friend, the man who represents, for the moment, your whole family, Indeed, I'm not only replacing your guardian but your father, who is struggling out there in the Far West. He's already received the telegram sent this morning, and he's thinking about you at this solemn moment. He'll be thinking about you even more tomorrow, at the moment of the great Exodus...the moment when all eyes in America—what am I saying? in the entire civilized world—will be upon you.

"But it's not your glory, which will be great for centuries to come, but your happiness with which I'm concerned, and I want that happiness, my dear children, to be as complete as your valor, as vast as your enterprise, deserves...

"You are a privileged couple, elected among thousands to realize the most prodigious conquest in human history. The Eternal has chosen you both; he has given you beauty and strength. He has marked your young foreheads with the sign of heroes and prophets, in order that you might go on high to carry the good word.

"Tomorrow, beautiful with youth and faith, radiant with love, you will quit this Earth, you will fly like the angels through the constellations, realizing the most marvelous endeavor, living the most sublime dream that the human mind has ever conceived.

"At the mere thought of that marvelous adventure, my mind is troubled and my heart fills with a patriotic pride. I am proud, as a humble associate, an old priest brought from afar to bless you, that it is my country, America, that has given a hero like you a companion worthy of him. And I think, with a thrill of enthusiasm, of that unknown planet to which you are going, a new Adam and a new Eve, to be fruitful and multiply, in accordance with Jehovah's command.

"But I'm talking too much, talking about glory to you who have happiness, and in the meantime, the minutes are going by, the golden sand of Time is flowing. This is the august moment: on high, angels are passing, bearing in their arms the souls of generations to come. This is the moment celebrated in the Song of Songs, at which the shadows bow down and the husband goes to the wife...

"It seems to me that a few moments ago, I perceived behind you a grave and tender face: that of the angel of holy love, who will conduct you to the nuptial chamber. It's to him that I confide you, after having blessed you one last time!"

Jonathan Burrett placed his hands on the heads of two spouses, and withdrew.

Left alone, the young people remained silent, listening to their hearts beating precipitately. Serge had taken Anna's tremulous hand and was squeezing it gently.

Around them, in the age-old gardens, an indefinable odor was floating, and the foliage, bathed in moonlight, was stirring. From the overheated crypt, the scent of jasmine and roses drifted on the breeze. Under the bench, a cricket sang, seemingly counting the seconds…such brief seconds, and yet so full, enclosing an eternity…

Suddenly, the young woman rose to her feet.

Serge leaned toward her, his face ecstatic. "I won't say adieu," he murmured, in a breath.

She turned away, her face pink with modesty, and fled, leaving a kind of wake behind her.

Her dress gleamed one last time, then disappeared in a moonbeam.

Myrandhal, his heart overflowing with an ineffable joy, lingered for a few moments more. Then he got up in his turn and headed through the garden to the wing of the convent that had been prepared for them. In a few strides he had negotiated the pathways and had climbed the stairs leading to his wife's apartment.

Once there, his pace slowed. He wanted to anticipate his happiness…

His soul rhapsodized, he went along the corridor at a supple, elastic pace, barely skimming the floor.

The décor, which was not unfamiliar to him—the old walls illuminated by lamps burning in front of statues or covered with pious, even sinister, inscriptions; the bas-reliefs in which yogis writhed in torment; the thicket pillars whose heavy shadows were projected by the moonlight coming through the narrow windows on to the flagstones worn away by the bare feet of monks; the whole severe and disquieting ensemble of a Buddhist cloister—had the effect on him of an enchanted palace.

Like Victor Hugo's lover, he marched, "fully alive, through his starry dream."[65]

Once or twice however, he thought he heard the noise of sandals, and stopped, gripped by an obscure presentiment.

There's someone here, he thought. *Someone's following me…might it be Prince Djalor?*

Serge turned round, clenching his fists, ready to defend his happiness. At that moment, between the pedestals of two gigantic Buddhas, a man emerged from the shadows and threw himself upon the Frenchman, gripping him with his thin arms.

It was the Rajah.

"My friend," stammered the old man, distressed. "Where have you been? I've been looking for you for an hour!"

---

[65] The original quotation "*Donc je marche vivant dans mon rêve étoilé*" is from Hugo's *Ruy Blas* (1838), but the addition of *tout* before *vivant* was supplied in a secondary rendition of the quote by the composer Hector Berlioz.

248

"What's happening?" exclaimed Serge, distressed in his turn. "Has Anna...?"

"No! Madame Myrandhal is in her room. It's not to do with her but you, your invention, ours..." While speaking, the Mendicant Prince had seized Myrandhal's arm and as dragging him through a labyrinth of corridors and staircases toward the pitch dark gardens. "Come quickly," he sent on, breathlessly. "There's someone...a malefactor...down there in the crypt, in the *Velox*...someone's trying to rob us! What can I do? I'm an old man, and my son—you can guess why—left the convent an hour ago..."

Myrandhal had drawn a revolver from his pocket and was running, followed close behind by the mage, who was wheezing ominously.

The crypt, into which he soon hurtled, was in exactly the same state as he had left it a few minutes earlier. Two torches were on the point of going out. The flowers and green plants, strewn on the ground all the way to the ladder of the *Velox*, had not been disturbed.

"I don't see anything..." Serge began.

"Yes! The trolley!"

The arm connecting the motor to the *Velox* had been lowered, as if someone were about to depart...

One twist of the wheel, and the projectile would be shot into the sky like a bullet.

Myrandhal raised his hand to push back the lever connecting the current, but the Mendicant Prince stopped him with an abrupt gesture,

"Look!" he said, his teeth chattering. "Look at the door"—he pointed to the valve at the rear of the *Velox*, which was open. "There's someone in there—our thief! I can hear footsteps..."

Already, Myrandhal had climbed the iron ladder and gone into the psychoscaph.

Indraghava followed him at an unsteady pace, and stopped on the top rung. "Well?" he asked, in a choked voice, quavering with alarm.

"I can't see anything," Serge said, having already gone through the first two compartments.

"Look out!" recommended the mage, increasingly anguished. "Be careful!"

Because of his excitement and the precipitate run, the old man was tottering on his emaciated legs. In order not to fall, he had to grab hold on the lever controlling the seal of the valve.

There was a dry click. The door had just closed behind the inattentive Myrandhal, and Indraghava's face had suddenly become terrible. As nimble as a monkey, with an agility that made his old skeleton creak, he bounded to the activation wheel, which he began to turn...

What followed—a drama that unfolded in less than a second—is indescribable.

A convulsive face appeared at one of the portholes of the *Velox*, and then flew away at a vertiginous acceleration. A horrible scream, a superhuman scream, caused its sides to quiver.

Almost at the same moment, the *Velox*, reaching its full speed, appeared to extend, to stretch, covering the entire course of the track, all the way to the summit...

Then the rails reappeared, shiny and empty.

High above, in the sky, there was a strident whistle, the cry of a steel bird cleaving through the air at the speed of a bolide—and that was all.

As for the Rajah, he was still turning the control-wheel

As the needle on the dial completed its rotation, providing the full intensity of the current, the entire crypt became incandescent. Wires melted, and were volatilized; tongues of fire licked the walls, while a steel bar left on the edge of the track, weighing a hundred kilos, began to twist, coiling like a snake around a centenarian oak tree.

At the same time, fiery sparks sprang from the Rajah's hair, beard and eyelashes, so that he seemed momentarily to be enveloped by flames. Terrified, and burned all over, he was obliged to let go of the wheel.

Staggering, half-killed by the frightful discharge, he slumped against the back wall. He remained there for a long moment, his throat and lungs contacted, his body shaken by titanic convulsions.

Soon, however, life reappeared; his diaphragm dilated like a bellows filled with air. As his respiration returned, a ferocious smile creased the terrible old man's desiccated lips. His bright and terrible eyes were flamboyant with pride.

"That went well!" he murmured. "I promised the Frenchman a wedding night without parallel, and I kept my word. If my son hadn't left, like an idiot, like a coward, he would be delighted! We'll finish the job without him. To the other now—Miss Anna!"

He was still speaking when he perceived the American woman, fully illuminated by the glare of the of the phosphorescent crypt.

Clad in a simple peignoir, her beautiful hair braided for the night, her brow furrowed, she had just emerged from the breach in the wall through which the machine had taken flight.

Standing at her window, gazing at the stars, she had heard and seen—insofar as it was visible—the steel bird plunge into the darkness.

Sensing treason, she had run through the gardens. The disappearance of the *Velox* confirmed her fears, but she was far from suspecting the truth, of glimpsing the full horror of the situation she was in.

She looked around, her eyes full of menace, and said, I an imperious voice: "What are you doing here? And where's Serge my husband?"

A sadistic joy was sparkling in the Mendicant Prince's cruel eye. "Your husband," he said, gesturing toward the gardens, "has gone."

"Gone!" murmured the wife, struck full in the heart, but not yet understanding.

"Yes," the sinister old man continued, sarcastically. "It was an accident. He came with me to cast one last glance at it. Someone—a bandit—had primed the apparatus. Then..."

A hoarse sob cut off his speech. Annabella had understood, and put both hands to her breaking heart. Her eyes turned back, biting her lips, digging her fingernails into her flesh in order not to scream in front of her enemy, she tottered, as pale as candle-wax.

Then, making a prodigious effort of will, of pride, she succeeded in overcoming her horrible anguish. Her eyes blazing, full of lightning, menacing and terrible, like a wrathful archangel, she took two steps toward her torturer, who beat a retreat.

Before that superb creature, magnificent in anger and in love, the mage, in spite of all his psychic power, was momentarily overwhelmed.

"You're lying!" she said, in a vibrant voice.

"Well, yes," the Rajah replied, suddenly assuming a soft, compassionate voice, toying with his prey. "I wanted to spare a newlywed a painful truth, but you're forcing me to speak. There was no accident. Your husband left because he wanted to, and because he had to, because it was the only means of breaking an engagement made too lightly."

The Rajah's accent was so sincere, and Annabella's distress so great that she did not protest immediately.

She lowered her head, and was thoughtful, her mind and heart crushed. With a mechanical gesture, she had undone the cord securing her peignoir, and was swinging it in front of her like a sling.

"You understand," the Hindu continued, his tone gradually becoming ironic, "that my friend Myrandhal never seriously intended to take you with him. What childishness! It would have been contrary to our agreement. However, he needed you; you've been very useful at the *Herald* and elsewhere, so he promised you everything you wished—marriage and the rest—but it was only a lure, a pretence, one of those promises one makes to little girls.

"Your marriage isn't even valid, and I assure you, Miss Carpenter, that you'll never call yourself Madame Myr..."

He could not finish the insulting assertion. Brandishing the cord like a whip, the American had just truck him across the face.

"Wretch!" she howled. "Don't insult the man I love! You're lying, and I know everything. I guessed it all, suspected it for a long time. I even warned my husband! Poor and loyal friend, who didn't listen! Nevertheless, don't be too hasty to gloat. You haven't won yet. Serge is up there—I'll go to join him if he doesn't come back; but nothing—*nothing*, you hear—will prevent us from seeing one another again, from loving one another."

"As for you, your crime, your abominable treason, you won't profit from it. You think you know our secret, but you're mistaken. Our precautions have been taken, and well taken. You won't have Myrandhal's invention, or his wife! And it's his wife who will punish you, who will avenge him, you hear! I'll denounce you to the English authorities."

Indraghava, who was calmly wiping his swollen eyelids, from which a trickle of blood as running, laughed shrilly and hoarsely.

"I pity you, Miss Carpenter," he sniggered. "You're forgetting that I'm the master here, and the only master! You've entered this convent, and you'll only leave dead or submissive, accepting all my conditions. You're my prisoner, my hostage, and I'm keeping you."

At that threat, Annabella made a superb gesture of defiance. Her only response was to hurl a gaze of crushing scorn at her enemy. Then, disdainful, as haughty as an offended queen, still brandishing the whip with which she had just chastised her insulter, she went back to her apartment.

For his part, the mage had run into the corridor adjacent to the crypt. He struck a gong suspended from the top of a column. Almost immediately, the monk who always followed him in more or less considerable proximity, emerged from the shadows, and the two men embarked on a feverish conversation.

For her part, Madame Myrandhal, who knew that she must be ready for anything, went into her apartment, all the doors of which she bolted carefully. At the sight of her empty bedroom—the bedroom of a virgin wife and widow!—all the courage and pride she had sustained thus far suddenly collapsed. She fell on to her bed, in tears, and writhed there, biting the pillows in order to stifle her sobs.

Two brief, imperious raps on the door of the antechamber, recalled her to herself. Then there were furious, muffled blows. Action was following close behind the threat, and her domicile was about to be violated!

Frightened, she looked around, and saw the telepath that Serge had given her a few days before—and a gleam of joy, of love, lit up her ravaged face.

"Let me warn him, at least!" she sighed, running to the apparatus. "Let me talk to him one last time!"

Close at hand, however, the blows redoubled on the door to the corridor, which would soon be broken down.

Panic-stricken, the American had seized the signal-key, which she was manipulating with a feverish finger.

My dear husband, she began…and at that word, so sweet, her tears sprang forth again…

XV. The Great Dark

Meanwhile, the *Velox*, launched at prodigious speed, had traversed the terrestrial atmosphere.

With one bound, it had cleaved through the illusory blue vault that we call the firmament, which is nothing but an optical effect produced by the form of our eyes and the color of the gas in which we bathe.

After a few seconds, the horrible whistling and the suffocating heat caused by the friction of air on the hull had ceased completely.

Now, the psychoscaph, having arrived in the absolute void—the interastral void—was flying soundlessly, without a shudder. To the person inside it, it seemed to be motionless, just as the Earth does not reveal its enormous speed of thirty kilometers a second. And yet, a human eye capable of perceiving it at that moment would have seen something frightful: a black dot, a long dark streak, traversing the sky from end to end in less than a second and flying on and on, madly!

Leaning against the wall of the central compartment, against which he had been thrown at the moment of the fatal launch, Serge Myrandhal had not uttered a word or made a movement. He seemed thunderstruck, flabbergasted, like the upright cadaver discovered among the still-smoking ruins of Martinique, who fell into dust at the first touch...

His stunned brain, as if paralyzed, as devoid of thought or definite sentiment; but before his wide eyes—the vitreous, atonal eyes of a madman—there were two terrible, tortuous images.

There was a man, a stranger, whose name he did not know—a little, diabolical old man—maneuvering some kind of wheel.

Then, beyond that, on the far side of the tall trees swaying gently in the embalmed nocturnal breeze, a lighted bedroom...the bedroom of a young woman, glimpsed from afar, like a paradise—and in the middle, all alone, seemingly waiting, a woman, weeping...

His wife!

"Anna!" he moaned.

Suddenly, emerging from his stupor, he uttered a terrible roar, the cry of a wild beast whose nourishment has been snatched away.

She's calling to me, he thought.

And the desire to save the woman he loved, to race to her aid, vanquished the crushing torpor by which he had been overwhelmed. His face, distraught, almost cadaverous a few seconds earlier, was now fulgurant. The hero, the man who had vanquished nature, had just got a grip on himself, drawn him upright, ready for the fray...

With long strides he headed for the forward compartment. It was there, it will be remembered, in the "engine room" of sorts, that the recording apparatus was, the accumulators and, above all, a priceless resource, the reserves of psychic fluid stored for the return to Earth, and which could—which had to—permit him and his wife to come home...

By the light of the radiant walls, the young man consulted a dial indicating the velocity of his invention, and could not suppress a shudder of horror.

"Thirty-three kilometers a second!" he murmured. "And as it's a matter of a supraphysical force, which doesn't decrease, or only decreases very slightly, with distance, I'll be on Mars in a matter of hours—and that's not what I want!"

While reflecting, Serge had rotated a commutator with an anxious finger. Again he consulted the dial, and went pale. The needle indicating velocity was leaping madly.

"Seventy-two!" he stammered, fearfully. "Ninety-six...a hundred and twenty...a hundred and thirty-two. We've quadrupled our speed in a matter of seconds. The contest is impossible—I'm beaten!"

Gripped by rage, he seized another lever with both hands. He clung on to it, accumulating all his will-power, extending all the energy of which he was capable in the opposite direction to the force that was driving him on with lightning speed.

Almost immediately, however, after a final glance at the counter, he let go of the commutator and, from the depths of his bosom, from the depths of his entrails, twisted by a nameless anguish, a hoarse plaint emerged.

"It's all over!" he croaked. "I'll never be able to oppose the psychic current that's driving me. I'm no longer master of my ship. My terrestrial force-factory is overwhelming me, and will do so until the end. I should have anticipated that danger and forestalled it, but it's too late.

"Only one man—the mage—might perhaps be able to bring me back, and even then, who can tell? My momentum is such that, by the time it relaxes slightly, I'll have fallen into another sphere of attraction—that of Mars. I ought to have foreseen this, and not trusted the sinister old man!"

At the name of Mars, great as the distress of the lover was, the curiosity of the scientist awoke again.

He searched for the planet through the little porthole to the right, but only saw a black wall, nothing but a black wall. The star, placed on the axis of the *Velox*, which was heading directly toward it, was invisible from that position.

Then, with the scarcely-conscious desire to find another observation-post, he went back to the central compartment. He went at a mechanical, quasi-somnambulistic pace. His brain, woken up momentarily, was gradually falling back into is initial stupor. The instrument of thought, so powerful in our hero, was no more than an organic mechanism, so to speak, an automatic recorder of sensations and numbers, something like one of the multiple counters that could be seen hanging on the walls of the *Velox* on all sides.

As he went into the compartment, Serge uttered an exclamation of surprise. The large portholes were veiled with a fine lacework of frost, which, at that moment, had something lugubrious about it. One might have thought that they were dead eyes, petrified by horror.

"It's the cold," he said, drawing nearer. "We're traveling at this moment through absolute cold, 270 degrees below zero!

"A few minutes have sufficed to refrigerate the *Velox*, which was red hot a little while ago. In another few seconds if I don't open the radiators, the thermometer will fall to fifty below, then a hundred, and I'll die. The numbness is starting already, cerebral anesthesia...and it's doubtless thanks to that that I'm still alive. My paralyzed brain is hardly thinking, and I'm suffering less."

While speaking, he wiped away the layer of ice blurring the crystal with his sleeve. He leaned forward to look through and recoiled, shivering, at the terrible appearance of the sky that he had just glimpsed.

A funereally black sky...a cataclysmic sky!

Toward the pole, the Great Bear shone menacingly. Here and there, a few stars, and everywhere, darkness, opaque darkness, the Great Dark of which the Bible speaks.[66]

All around him, the firmament extended like a mortuary drape studded with gold. Serge Myrandhal had reached the regions "mute of light," according to Dante's expression, the terrible sky that "knows neither dusk nor dawn."

Another phenomenon: the luminous beams spring from the portholes, which, a little while before, in the terrestrial atmosphere, had given the *Velox* something akin to wings of flame, had also disappeared. The luminous current, invisible because it did not encounter any reflective matter, was lost; or rather—since nothing is lost—went a long way, to the end of the world, to be reflected by who knew what distant planet!

For a long minute, Serge contemplated the tragic scene.

The universe is terrible, he thought, *and the firmament is not what poets and lovers imagine. Scientists know that truth, but they scarcely suspect the horror of it!*

What is the World, in fact—our world? A bubble of gas, a grain of dust, lost in the ether...

What is daylight—our daylight? What is the dawn, the light with its thousand fires? What is the rainbow? An optical affect.

---

[66] The phrase employed in the original text, *Grande Ténèbre* [sic] does not appear in any French version of the Bible that I can identify, in which darkness tends to be signified, as is usual in French, by the plural *ténèbres*. It does crop up in the singular form, however, in some Christian mystical writings in French, where it refers specifically to the "superior obscurity" of the "inaccessible light"—i.e., to God in essence, beyond all names and forms, stripped of His attributes. I have translated the phrase as Great Dark rather than Great Darkness to stress that a particular meaning, albeit not a Biblical one, is probably intended.

Oh, how formidable Creation is, looked in the face, outside the frame, the milieu of illusion in which we were situated by an unknown law!

For hours, perhaps days, I shall travel without encountering a ray of light, one of the sunbeams that rejoice the human heart! And yet everywhere around me, near me, there are stars: the moon, the planets, which are shining but without illuminating!

There is, above all, the sun, which no longer sets for me, which will never set again until my arrival on another world. At this moment it is shining out there, silvering my hull, but between us, all around us, there is night...implacable and opaque night!

I knew that, personally. I knew, in theory, that nocturnal, sinister aspect of the universe. Whence, then, comes this tremor, these cold droplets trickling over my temples? I knew the spectacle that awaited me, and yet my mind is troubled. My blood is chilled and my hair is bristling. It's the frisson: the great frisson of the abyss! The one that gripped the wicked angels precipitated by the archangel Michael, who fell for seven times seven days through the void.

Decidedly, the space, not only space but interplanetary space, that I declared to be our domain, is forbidden to humankind. I thought in my pride that man was the glorious son of the sun, the master of all the worlds that gavotte around the sovereign star. I was mistaken! Man is only the child of the Earth, the humble product off vile clay, condemned to crawl eternally through the primordial mud.

I wanted to break the divine order, to brave God, and that terrible and jealous God has punished me as he punished Lucifer!

In Serge's mind, those thoughts and impressions, which we have taken a long time to describe, presented themselves almost simultaneously, in a rapid and confused fashion.

Suddenly, his face convulsed.

"Insensate that I am!" he groaned. "I was about to associate a woman with my folly. She would curse me if she were here...but no, I'm blaspheming, and I want to believe in God, in love...I don't want to doubt either her or myself. The two of us would have succeeded, vanquished Nature, or we would have died together!"

The window had misted over again. Serge stifled a sigh and shook himself, as if to tear himself away from the tortuous thoughts that were invading him.

I need to see! he said to himself. *I need to embrace my distress in all its sinister splendor. I'm going out, climbing up on to the walkway...*

He took two steps and stopped, abruptly.

"My diving suit!" he exclaimed. "I forgot that, outside the hull, there's no longer any air, that there's an absolute void. This is the moment to test my machine."

Immediately—driven as much by a confused curiosity, which, in spite of everything, survived in the scientist, as by an obscure need to create a diversion from other anguishes—he went into his cabin in quest of one of the items of apparatus with which he had equipped himself in case the atmosphere of Mars was not breathable.

It was a simple diving-suit helmet, but improved by Myrandhal, equipped with an ingenious reservoir of liquid air sufficient to maintain respiration for more than twenty-four hours.

Serge screwed the enormous copper ball over his shoulders. As usual, it was fitted with three powerful lenses like the eyes of some marine monster. Then he wrapped himself, from the nape of his neck to his heels, in an ample fur with long silky hair, designed to protect him from the terrible intersidereal cold. It was one of those cloak-bags divided in the bottom half of which people make use in Alaska, and which is secured at the wrists and ankles by means of drawstrings.

Thus equipped he headed for the door—so tragically closed a little while ago!—opened it resolutely, and advanced on to the narrow landing from which the *Velox*'s ladder, dispatched with him, still hung.

He had scarcely grasped the frail guard-rail than his garments, saturated with interior moisture, bristled with icy needles, but Myrandhal took no notice of that. He leaned over avidly, his mouth twisted by a cry of amazement: "The sun!"

It was, indeed, the sun—but a terrible, tragic sun! A bald star, devoid of radiance, devoid of a halo! A dead sun, invincibly giving rise to the idea of an immense putrefied and phosphorescent cadaver.

It appeared in the distance, at the limit of the horizon, like a large incandescent millstone,[67] with an unsustainable glare that did not illuminate. That glare, like that of the *Velox*, that vibratory movement, for lack of a substance, any reflective matter capable of vibrating in unison, was lost in the void.

And it really was a frightful, sinister thing, that white sun, devoid of radiance and glory...

"One might think it were the end of the world," Serge murmured. "The wan 'great Star' that will see the death of the Earth."[68]

Sometimes, all around the disk, brief pink or crimson flames rose up vertically, giving the impression of some formidable explosion.

"Solar eruptions," murmured Myrandhal, moved in spite of himself by the prodigious spectacle of those fiery tempests.

Abruptly, he had to bow his head, his eyes being dazzled, burned by the ardent nucleus. He turned his back on the star, and for the second time, uttered a cry of surprise.

---

[67] I have translated *meule* as "millstone" because that seems a likelier intention than the word's other meanings, which refer to hayricks or round cheeses.
[68] The reference is to *Revelation* 8:10.

In front of him, the *Velox*, bombarded by the obscure effluvia emitted by the sun, was shining like the moon on its fourteenth day, and that contrast between the ambient night and the long, rutilant copper spindle had something fantastic about it.

One might have thought it a golden olive magically ripened by the black wall of night.

Serge had bowed his head, and was thinking.

"What a silence!" he murmured, pensively. "What calm! No sound, no breath, not a quiver. We seem to be motionless, and yet...

"It really is nothingness, the void, death.

"What is the Ether in which I'm floating? What is that mysterious, imponderable, invisible fluid that fills the whole universe—not only space, but substances themselves?

"What is the nature, the essence, of that fluid, which is nothing and perhaps everything...which, awakened, condensed, vibrating in a certain way, becomes of Force and Matter, which creates the Universe entire?"

While raking over these philosophical theories, already envisaged many times over while he was working on his great endeavor, Serge Myrandhal raised his head.

For the second time, the terrifying, pitiless aspect of the abyss through which he was flying aimlessly terrified him. With a strange gesture of sudden dementia, he shook his fist at the stars.

"No!" he cried. "God doesn't exist, and the heavens lie! What calls to us thus is nothing but a frightful desert! Nature is accursed and the universe empty. Everywhere, there is nothingness, death. Death, the final refuge..."

He fell silent; then, with an abrupt, reactive, angry movement he turned round again. With one hand over his eyes, to avoid sunburn, he inspected the sky, trying to get his bearings.

"What's that?" he suddenly exclaimed "The moon! It's not in its place!"

Far away, beneath his feet, he had just perceived a long, broad and bright strip, with a cold steely glare: a gigantic scythe slicing the horizon, the scythe of Time floating in the void.

"The Earth!" murmured the engineer, going pale. "It's the Earth. Earthlight! I can only see a crescent, a spindle, but that's exactly what I wanted."

At the sight of that world, from which he was banished, exiled forever, he started trembling in every limb; his teeth chattered.

"Earth!" he repeated, in an agonized voice. "And that continent there is Asia. It's the Himalayas! The convent is there, there, in the center of that dark patch. That where *She* is waiting for me, where *She* is weeping!

"I want to go there...I want to get her back...and I can! We're still under the influence of the planet; it's attracting me. I only have to let myself go, to fall! I'll never see her again, but what does it matter? At least I'll sleep my final sleep close to her, in the same region of the heavens! We'll be buried in the same soil, and perhaps, one day, the wind—the wind that marries the flowers and transports the pollen—perhaps the wind will mingle our ashes..."

Serge interrupted himself mentally to devote himself to one of the calculations of which he had the habit.

"It's really true," he resumed, almost immediately. "We're still in the grip of terrestrial gravity. No other star in the vicinity to deflect me from my terrible trajectory. Like Lucifer cast down, I can fall, travel through the nothingness, the night, for days, and toward the middle of the fifth, or thereabouts, already pulverized and reduced to the state of vapor, I'll arrive. What a fall, and what a prodigious, unique death!" At that thought, his tormented heart swelled up with a noble joy. "Finally," he concluded, in an explosion of pride that terminated in sobs, I've found an end worthy of me! A death equal to my dream and my superhuman love!"

Immediately, with a wild frenzy, he overstepped the fragile barrier that separated him from the abyss, launching his head forward, but he could not tear his body free, weighed down—solidified, so to speak—as it was by frost. His limbs, his joints, the entirety of his human machine, stopped by the sidereal cold, refused to obey.

He could only succeed, with difficulty, in liberating his fingers, hooked around the protective rail.

As the same time, a sharp, intolerable burning sensation ran through his whole body. His skin, his cheeks, sunburned and frozen at the same time, split and burst beneath his mask; his eyes were bleeding, blurring his vision.

Simultaneously, his breath failed. The air in the reservoir of his diving helmet must have solidified.

Half-asphyxiated, incapable of thinking, he went back inside precipitately, closed the door, and took off his helmet. It took him several seconds to recover consciousness fully.

He was coming round, crushed, exhausted and shivering, when, close at hand, in the central compartment, a bell rang.

The young man shivered, as if in response to an electric shock, and like a madman, he leapt up and ran.

"A dispatch!" he howled. "A dispatch from Earth! It's her, it's Anna! Thank God! I knew that she was thinking about me, as I was about her. Except that the dispatch, launched in my pursuit, has taken a certain time to reach me."

The strip of paper in the Morse apparatus was already unrolling, and Serge read it, desperately.

My dear husband,

I know everything. I have just caught the mage in the crypt, and he has confessed, with horrible threat.

Don't worry, my beloved, I'm not afraid, and it's not for myself that I'm weeping...

But time's pressing...already they're breaking down my door. I'll only tell you one more thing: the bandits won't take me alive.

I'll die before...remember what we said yesterday about the migration of souls...I'll go to join you.

Soon, on Mars! I give you my lips.

My door's giving way...au...

There was a nervous tremor, a few disordered clicks, and the apparatus became still.

What did that tragically interrupted *au* signify? *Au revoir? Au secours?* A maddening mystery.

Meanwhile, Serge Myrandhal, his face convulsed, was still listening, his ears pricked, his eyes fixed on the telepath, as if to hypnotize it, to command the miracle that he wanted from it...

It seemed to him, in that minute saturated with anguish, that the apparatus, which he knew to be extremely delicate, almost alive in its sensitivity, was about to obey, like a telephone...

A few seconds went by; then, with a haggard expression, in a demented voice, he croaked: "Ah! They've killed her. She's dead! My turn!"

Head down, he rushed at the wall, and fell back, his scalp cut open, bleeding.

In the meantime, deprived of its captain, the *Velox* continued its implacable course, moved by a superphysical and vertiginous force.

It flew like a lightning bolt from one sky to another, carrying toward infinity and eternity the man who had created it, already moribund, in his rigid shroud of hardened steel, writhing in a pool of blood.

XVI. The Dove of the Ark!

How many hours that unconsciousness lasted, Serge was never able to calculate exactly...

He stirred momentarily, doubtless awakened by an incomprehensible noise coming from outside, which was communicating strange trepidations to the *Velox*.

Everything aboard the psychoscaph, which shortly before had been floating mutely in the silence of the interplanetary void, was now vibrating.

The hum, however, muted at first, was gradually rising up the sonic scale, sometimes rising to shrill notes.

Soon, there was a resounding howl, plaintive and disturbing, like the noise of the winter wind in the trees. Serge half sat up and passed his hand over his head, which was no longer bleeding.

"Anna!" he moaned.

A piercing clamor, an authentic whistle-blast, strident and sinister this time, drilled into his ears. Almost immediately, three more blasts resounded, brief and urgent…genuine cries of alarm!

One might have thought that the *Velox*, that marvelous machine animated by a mysterious force, "thinking," in a sense, was warning its master, signaling a danger, an obstacle into which it was about to crash, with a formidable impact.

That was Serge's impression. He leapt to his feet immediately. He moved back and forth across the compartment, parading his gaze from right to left.

"It's stifling in here," he murmured. "Where are we?"

Suddenly, above a porthole, russet smoke rose up; long red tongues sprang forth and flowed, licking the ceiling.

"Fire!" he stammered. "The *Velox* is burning!"

He seized a vaporizer of liquid air, and directed the glacial jet at the fire, with immediate effect. There was a crackle, a rain of ash and sparks, and through the half-consumed curtain the incandescent wall appeared.

"The hull!" Serge exclaimed. "It's the hull that's red hot! We're traveling through a gaseous mass, but what kind? If it the vivifying air of a planet, or the asphyxiating tail of some vagabond comet? What is this unknown world precipitating itself upon us with lightning speed?"

At the thought of the prodigious encounter, the frightful collision, Serge felt his hair stand on end around his white forehead.

For a second time, before the inevitable, certain catastrophe, he thought about death, about Anna, whom he was about to rejoin…

A further brief, imperative whistle-blast stopped him on that fatal slope. All his energy had suddenly reawakened. The instinct of survival, the love of danger, the desire to fight, to vanquish Nature—the dream of his entire life—was suddenly resuscitated, abolishing all other sensations.

He closed his eyes, as if no longer to see the sweet phantom, and swore that he would not think about her again until he was out of danger. Then, stimulated by that virile resolution, gathering all his physical and mental strength for the supreme struggle, he headed at a firm pace toward the "compass" suspended nearby, in its crystal case.

"That's bizarre!" he said. "The direction needle isn't even oscillating, and we haven't deviated from a straight line. The world on which we're arriving must be semi-fluid, extra-light, devoid of sensible attraction. Is it a matter of some gaseous comet or one of those minuscule planets that circulate around the sun, fragments of some shattered globe, too weak to capture us as we pass by?

"In that case, the most favorable, a fall might be avoided, thanks to our formidable speed, and our fluidic reservoir, which I'll unleash in its entirety in order to struggle against the new attraction. We'll pass by then, shaving the obstacle."

Almost immediately, however, he shivered, a cold sweat on his temples.

"Unless," he stammered, "that planet, that gigantic bolide, is directly ahead of us, in a straight line. In that case, our direction can't vary, but with the aid of its attraction, our speed will increase in frightful proportions!"

Fearfully, Serge consulted his counter—and stood there stupefied.

Far from increasing, the frightful velocity of the beginning of the voyage had suddenly fallen to fifty meters a second, the speed of a swallow on the wing.

The needle of the speed gauge, whose mad leaps had frightened the traveler during the departure from Earth, was now trudging over its dial. One might have thought that the *Velox*, having reached some crowded intersection of the universe, was moderating its pace of its own accord, like a well-trained horse.

Nevertheless, under the influence of the star in view, an acceleration was becoming manifest, albeit scarcely sensible as yet.

Serge started counting. "Fifty-one...fifty-two...fifty-five meters... We've taken more than ten minutes to gain a few meters per second. I was right; the strange world we're approaching unexpectedly is very light, or very distant. We're not falling yet, and there's still hope...

"In spite of that, the situation is grave; the peril, although less immediate, persists in its entirety, and I only just have time to do everything possible to avoid it. Above all, I need to know where I am, and what the gas is through which we're presently flying."

Immediately, without pausing for a second over the multiple dangers of the maneuver, Serge, with hasty, feverish gestures, put on his diving suit and headed for the rear compartment.

As he was about to release the valve, he hesitated. He had just remembered the terrible, dark scene that had frightened him so much a little while ago: that glacial, funereal sky, that star of terror contemplating the disaster with its pale eye. But curiosity and the thought of the approaching, imminent peril quickly got the upper hand.

Serge opened the door and launched himself out on to the walkway—and, for the first time, his contracted face relaxed, animated by a furtive joy.

"The star has disappeared!" he exclaimed, suddenly relieved of an enormous weight. "The Great Star that seemed to be illuminating the end of the world! And the sky is immediately softened, humanized, after a fashion. There's no longer that opaque night, that sinister, implacable aspect that caused me to blaspheme."

In fact, the atmosphere in which the *Velox* was bathing, doubtless little different from terrestrial air, was producing the same optical effects. The stars were twinkling gently in the dark blue of the Empyrean.

"Finally," Myrandhal murmured, his soul dilating and his heart beating more rapidly. "Finally, I've found the heavens again, the deceptive azure vault, as tender as a woman's gaze...the dear, gentle firmament of poets and lovers— and they had the right of it, against science...

"Here I am, back in the world of 'illusions,' the only habitable one. I was wrong to revolt just now. God is good and the universe isn't empty. Creation is beautiful, except, like the Egyptian deity Isis, she doesn't like to be looked in the face. Woe to whoever dares lift the redoubtable veil of the goddess!"

While his thoughts agitated, Myrandhal, his mind freer, his brain more lucid, observed and compared.

Evidently, he thought, *all my sensations prove—the azure vault, the air that's caressing my hands—that I've arrived in proximity to a planet, but which one?*

Mars is still millions of leagues away. What if it were Earth, toward which some miracle had brought me back while I was asleep? A prodigy of love, Anna's appeal, more powerful than all the volitional power of the Mendicant Prince?

Serge was about to soften, forgetful of the still-imminent peril, but he started.

"No," he said. "I've sworn not to think about that." And he launched himself back inside the *Velox*.

At that precise moment, the psychoscaph, as if it wanted to recall its master to duty, began to produce the murmurous sound, like the buzzing of an irritated bee, that was its alarm signal of sorts.

Serge ran to the recording apparatus.

"Still the same direction," he murmured, "but the speed is increasing slowly, proof that the star is getting closer. The situation isn't critical yet, but it's getting worse by the minute. It's necessary to act. Let's take care of myself first, my wound. I'll need all my physical means, and more; we're arriving at a perilous moment…perhaps the last!"

He took off his helmet, and observed that it was full of blood. His wound had reopened, doubtless under the weight of the apparatus, and was causing him pain.

Rapidly, Serge washed the wound, and wrapped an antiseptic and anesthetic bandage around his head. Then he drank a large glass of a kola remedy that he had prepared personally for such extreme cases. Immediately, a gentle warmth spread through his arteries.

His injured brain, animated by blood loss, and his entire physical and mental state, exhausted by his unparalleled traumas, were about to acquire an artificial vigor that might save his life. Already, Serge could feel that wellbeing, that fever of life, similar to a slight intoxication, which infuses the veins with a new ardor and shows everything in the most propitious light. He was not far from seeing the wound he had received as one of those mysterious aids of Destiny.

"Who knows?" he said to himself. "But for that bleeding I'd be dead, struck down by congestion. Now for the *Velox*! First of all, I have to identify the nature of the gas through which we're flying, which will be the first datum regarding the mysterious world that has thrown itself into my path. It's obviously a matter of a considerable gaseous mass, afflicted by violent currents—veritable storm-winds. Just now, when the Velox whistled so obligingly, we must have been passing through one of those cyclones. Now, is this, gas—this atmosphere—breathable?"

Serge was thinking about making a quick analysis of the ambient air when a cooing coming from a storage locker caused him to change his mind. He ran to it, and came back carrying one of four turtle-doves, which, in imitation of Noah, he had planned to send out when the moment came.

From his watch-chain he detached a minuscule seal that his fiancée had given to him, bearing an interlaced A and S, moistened the indelible ink, and stamped both of the bird's wings.

Having done that, he carefully opened one of the small portholes in the central compartment and deposited the messenger—which he scarcely hoped to see again—on the narrow sill. Dazzled by the light projected through the lenses, but glad to be free, the bird flapped its wings joyfully and flew off. It let itself fall along the luminous beam, at the end of which it disappeared.

The proof was there!

Incapable of waiting any longer, Serge opened the window wide and stuck out his head, his neck and the whole of his upper body.

His cheeks whipped by the wind of the course, with blood infusing his skin, he plunged himself with delight into the beneficent gaseous shower and bathed in it.

"It's air! Pure air!" he murmured, filling his lungs with an indescribable voluptuousness. "It's terrestrial air—but a trifle cold."

Indeed, snowflakes were floating around him.

Serge hastened to close the porthole, and then suddenly froze, his feet nailed to the floor, his eyes haggard, as if fascinated by horror. In front of him, five meters from the window, a terrible face had just appeared: a monstrous face, part-human and part-owl, with a mouth equipped with sharp teeth, a stiff moustache like a hog's bristles and large staring eyes like the large bright golden eyes of nyctalopes...[69]

---

[69] By "nyctalopes" the author presumably means nocturnal animals. Given that the next sentence refers to an impression of a giant vampiric bat, however, it is not inconceivable that there might be something more to the peculiar coincidence of imagery, given that Gustave Le Rouge's similar Martian fantasy features giant vampiric bats and that Jean de la Hire made mention in the second feuilleton he published in *Le Matin*, in 1908 of a human "nyctalope"—meaning someone capable of seeing in the dark—a new version of whom was later to feature in a long series of *feuilletons*. Given that this episode is entirely gratuitous, serving no function within the story, one is tempted to wonder whether Gayar might have known something about the contents of works by Le Rouge and La

Serge was put in mind of a giant bat, of some prodigious vampire—but the horrible vision had already disappeared.

He passed his hand over his forehead, moistened by fear.

"It's an illusion," he said, "A creation of my overworked brain. Indeed, I remember that when I was asleep jut now, I dreamed about similar beings. Besides, how could such a monster be sustained at such a height? We'll go take a look, though. I'll go out and look for the monster in the sky—but I know it doesn't exist. It's pure and simple auto-suggestion."

His disturbance had almost dissipated, and yet, in spite of himself, he thought about the flying demons that, according to one tradition, inhabit certain accursed planets. He thought, in particular, about the authentic monstrous flying creatures that had populated in Earth in the early ages of the world, such as the pterodactyl.

He thought it prudent, in consequence, to arm himself. At hazard, he picked up a Colt revolver and a solid dagger with a short triangular blade, put his marine telescope under his arm, and went out, leaving his helmet—unnecessary henceforth—in the wardrobe.

He opened the valve and paused, as before, shivering, his heart inundated by a joy that almost caused him to faint.

To the right, as if at the wave of a magic wand, the sky had just brightened abruptly. Day was breaking, still pale, but more beautiful than ever.

Immediately, everything was transformed, everything was smiling: the air, the heavens...

The Orient, in the distance, was decked in crimson and gold; glorious rainbows rose up, sparkling with all the colors of the prism, and along that triumphant road the light advanced, strewing rises beneath its feet...

Backed up against the metal hull, Serge contemplated the ineffable spectacle, which would have caused the knees of the most insensitive person to buckle.

"It's Aurora!" he stammered. "The divine Aurora, the daughter of God, that I thought I'd never see again. I'm saved! Thank you, almighty God!

He had completely forgotten the still-impending catastrophe, the errant star into which he was perhaps about to crash...

Soon, coming from the depths of the horizon, a streak of fire, a fluid golden arrow traversed the sky, and a star appeared: a glorious fulgurant disk, from which torrents of multicolored flames flowed.

It was the sun, rising over the unknown planet!

Myrandhal had fallen to his knees, and the most ardent prayer that had ever sprung from a human breast was exhaled by his heart.

Hire that had not yet appeared in print but were soon to do so, and was deliberately dropping a hint to that effect.

He remained collapsed in that fashion, prostrate before the sovereign star, for some time, stammering the bewildered hymn that "cavemen" murmured every time the sun returned, which they had believed to be lost forever.[70]

Finally recalled to reality, returning his attention from the heavens to the "earth" that he sensed getting nearer and nearer, suddenly monopolized by an intense curiosity, he leaned over the frail guard-rail and contemplated the unknown panorama emerging from the darkness...

Beneath his feet, less than a mile away, and immense white, moving extent, a sea of clouds, was agitating, pierced by the sunlight and tormented by a rising wind. Here and there, immense vortices were hollowed out, immense funnels animated by a king of gyratory movement. Serge aimed his telescope at one of these vertiginous gulfs with crumbling walls of vapor and gazed into it avidly, his eyes bulging, injected with blood like those of a man threatened by apoplexy.

His temples were buzzing, his arteries throbbing as if to burst, and yet he could not make anything out as yet—nothing but a flat chestnut-brown plain, still drowned in shadow.

Gradually, however, the interior layers of the atmosphere brightened in their turn, the last mists disappearing.

Now, Serge perceived a boundless desert, a kind of red-tinted Sahara furrowed by long rectilinear valleys, trenches of a sort extending geometrically from north to south.

Then the landscape was suddenly illuminated, the trenches sparkled, and Serge, his face transfigured, uttered a cry of triumph.

"The canals!" he shouted. "The famous canals of Mars! I've arrived!"

As before when he had rediscovered the radiant star, Serge Myrandhal took some time to recover from the immense joy that overwhelmed him.

So, he had succeeded; he had reached his goal without knowing it.

The unknown, redoubtable world that had frightened him a little while ago was the one that he had been inclined toward for months. He had succeeded in his prodigious adventure, and had reached the planet about which he was no longer thinking, after so much anguish!

Leaning over the rail, his hair whipped by the wind of the abyss, his body lifted up by a delightful vertigo, he contemplated his conquest

Through his joy, that world, which his telescope had just shown him to be arid and desolate, now appeared to him as a magical land, like the terrestrial par-

---

[70] The idea that primitive cave-dwellers were amazed by every sunrise, having become convinced during the night that the sun would never reappear, makes little sense, but it is memorably featured in a strikingly bizarre short story by the Symbolist writer Bernard Lazare, contained in the collection *Le Miroir des Légendes* (1892).

adise to which the venerable Jonathan Burrett had made allusion a few hours earlier in his Biblical homily.

Suddenly, his heart lurched. He thought about his companion, the promised Eve, his wife, who was moaning out there in the depths of the sky, perhaps lying dead, having the horrible weight of the monastery, her tomb, above her young head"

Instantly, he shook his head.

"No," he murmured, "she's alive! The Hindus wouldn't dare. She's too precious a hostage, and they need her, especially now that they know—they must know—that my secret has escaped them...

"As for Anna, I know her virile intelligence, her courage, her cleverness, her prudence! Why didn't I listen to her sooner! So long as a glimmer of hope remains to her, she'll defer her fatal resolution to put an end to her days...

"So she's alive! Besides which, if it were otherwise, I'd know. Liberated from terrestrial chains, her soul would have come through space and time to find me. I would have felt her passing around me.

"She's alive...and I'll find her again. Launching myself from Mars as I did from Earth, I'll go to find her, to rejoin her!"

He started; a rush of blood colored his cheeks.

"What if I were to go, to try right away?"

Immediately, though, the folly and futility of that attempt became apparent to him, and his eyes, momentarily dazzled as if by the sight of the sun, closed again.

"No," he said, "I don't have sufficient means. If I want to get my wife back, to avenge myself on the mage, I need to go about it another way—and I shall. I want my revenge!

"I'm arriving on a habitable world, older than ours and hence more advanced in its civilization, in its science. I shall find, among our Martian cousins, all the help and assistance I need to attempt the return journey with every chance of success. It's a new game that's beginning between the Hindus and me. They've won the first round, but I'll have my turn, and it will be terrible!

"And I have confidence; I'm hopeful! The mysterious forces that have seconded me thus far won't suddenly withdraw. If I've survived, avoided the frightful catastrophe, it's because God in on my side...

"I shall return. I shall see the sweet Earth, the abode of my human brothers, again. And that's what it's necessary to tell my dear wife as soon as possible. I'll tell her that I to have been saved...that I'm thinking about her, that I love her more than ever...forever!"

He hastened to the central compartment, but by the time he had reached the telepath, ready to activate it, he had already changed his mind.

"What's the point?" he murmured, with a grimace of discouragement. "If Anna hasn't telegraphed me again, it's because, as her dispatch anticipated, she's a prisoner, at least kept out of sight. What good will it do, then, to send another dispatch, intercepted in advance, that can only end up informing my enemies, warning them of my intentions. The first and most important precaution is to mistrust the mage, whose psychic superiority and supremacy probably remains redoubtable in spite of the distance, even on another world. Patience! My time will come…"

Comforted by this prospect, his soul caressed by a first ray of hope, a ray sweeter than "the first fires of Aurora," Myrandhal envisaged, incontinently the means of realizing his second voyage, the return to Earth—the more difficult of the two.

Before thinking about that, he ought to set foot on Mars, and he could not attempt anything on that sort as long as he had not reacquired mastery of the *Velox*. It was necessary, first of all, to make sure that the apparatus had finally escaped the potential superiority of its terrestrial powerhouse, and take advantage of it to redirect the psychoscaph—which, influenced by gravity, was tilting forward—and moderate its velocity, which was increasing in a worrying fashion.

Swiftly, the young man went into the helmsman's chamber, moved a few controls, consulted various indicators and came back radiant.

"That's it!" he sang. "The sinister Rajah has forgotten me, or is no longer able to do anything, and the *Velox* will henceforth be obedient only to me. Finally, I can take the tiller again!

"On the other hand, I still have sufficient fluid to fly for some time yet, and to 'make a parachute' when I go down. I can land whenever and wherever I wish, in the most propitious place. In order to decide that judiciously, the first thing to do is to determine which region of Mars I'm in—to take a bearing, as mariners say. It's high time, after all these shocks, to get a grip on myself, to *situate* myself in time and space.

"First of all, what time is it? How long did it take me to accomplish my formidable journey?"

Myrandhal took out his watch. It had stopped. He consulted the two precision chronometers installed nearby in a suspended frame.

"Also stopped," he said, disappointed. "That's strange. What can have caused that accident? It only required a slight push of the pendulum to start them going again, proof that nothing is broken. Perhaps the interruption was only due to some magnetic phenomenon, which I don't have time to investigate. Whatever the reason, I'm deprived of an important notion, and in consequence, I can't tell how long it took me to get here. Twenty or thirty hours, undoubtedly. That represents a formidable velocity: the velocity of one of those 'moonstones,' which are instantaneously melted and vaporized on impact with an atmosphere. The smallest bolide, one of those grains of sand drifting in space, would have sufficed to pulverize me, but an unknown power is watching over me…"

During this monologue, Myrandhal had picked up his marine telescope again. He opened one of the large portholes in the central compartment and set about examining the Martian landscape over which he was flying.

The dome of vapor that had intercepted his view a little while ago had completely disappeared, dissipated by the sun that was rising rapidly over the horizon.

At that moment, according to the indications of the measuring device, the *Velox* was flying at an altitude of about twenty-two thousand meters. In two hours of flight he had only descended three thousand meters, and the reserves of fluid measured by the psychometer had only decreased by a negligible quantity. Thus, Serge observed mentally once again, given the relatively weak intensity of weight on Mars, about a third of Earth's, the descent was taking place in the best conditions for which one could wish.

From the considerable altitude at which he was flying, and thanks to the greater curvature of Mars, Serge could see a considerable fraction of the planet, a "cap" almost as large as Europe. With his telescope he could make out the contours of seas and continents, the lines of gulfs and straits, and the pattern of the canals, perfectly. As he knew the map of Mars by heart, he quickly got his bearings.

"There's no doubt about it," he soon cried, joyfully. "We're floating over the Mädler Sea in the northern hemisphere—and, in consequence, at the very spot I anticipated and chose. While I was agonizing, the marvelous machine that the *Velox* is flew to its destination without any deviation.

"That heart-shaped land is Laplace Land.[71] We're in the polar circle, but even though it's claimed hat Mars is an old, frozen world, I can't see the slightest trace of snow or ice. It's true that I've arrived in summer.

"Everything seems empty and uninhabited—the land, the sky and the water. No trace of any city or civilization. A desert—I'm sure of not being greeted by arrows!

"It's now a matter of landing, of launching the psychoscaph into the open sea, for I must certainly stick to my plan of diving. It's the surest means of deadening the fall, of protecting my precious and delicate vehicle, on which I'm counting more than ever, by means of that liquid mattress. The slightest shock or rip made by those sharp rocks I can see down there would suffer to compromise me return for a long time, if not forever."

Increasingly reassured by what he could see and what he hoped, Serge Myrandhal closed the porthole again and occupied himself with the descent. He consulted the sun with a slightly artificial gaiety.

---

[71] There is a *Mer de Mädler* [Mädler Sea] and a *Terre de Laplace* [Laplace Land] in the far north of Camille Flammarion's map of Mars, as reproduced in *Terres du Ciel* and elsewhere, but the author seems to have made an error of transcription, as the "heart-shaped" body of land adjacent to the "sea" in question on Flammarion's map is *Terre de Lalande* [Lalande Land], while *Terre de Laplace* is a peninsula attached to *Continent Copernic* [Copernicus].

"It must be about nine o'clock," he said. "I'll try to land of Mars on the dot of mid-day…lunch time!"

He went into the engine room and set about diminishing the resistance of the psychic accumulators considerably. Immediately, the *Velox*, subjected to the preponderant influence of weight, accelerated its fall.

Two hours later, he was flying eight hundred meters above the Mädler Sea, a few miles from Laplace Land.

Serge slowed his descent then and, armed with his telescope, began to examine the Martian sea with all the attention of which he was capable. In fact, one hast question remained, on which the issue of the descent depended. Was that liquid splashing less than a kilometer away water—water such as it exists on Earth, with the same density, and hence capable of supporting the *Velox*, whose floatability had been regulated in accordance with the weight of terrestrial water?

Everything seemed to indicate as much: the gradually increasing humidity of the atmosphere, as revealed by the hygrometer; the whiteness of the surf, the movement of the waves and the play of the light on their crests, sometimes iridescent with all the colors of the prism.

"Let's go," our hero ended up concluding. "The proof is there. I could investigate further, but there's no need. Besides, my *Velox* is also a submarine, of the most advanced sort. I have the means to refloat it almost instantaneously, if it changes to plummet beneath the waves. It only remains, therefore, for me to transform my aerial vehicle into an aquatic vehicle. My preparations are made and it won't take long."

The engineer went into the rear compartment, where, along with food supplies and weapons, the tools and other equipment necessary for the landing were stored. He soon emerged, carrying over his shoulder a light rudder made of a sheet of steel and an electric control mechanism. He opened the valve and attached the precious apparatus to the brackets set up in advance for that purpose at the rear of the *Velox*, just above the walkway.

Setting up the propeller below the walkway presented a few more difficulties, but the inventor's foresight had reduced them to a minimum. First he set about freeing the axle installed in the hold under the floor of the psychoscaph. When the steel rod was extended to the required length, Serge fitted the helix to it. It was difficult for one man working alone—constrained to operate with one hand, in order to be able to hold on with the other—to put that relatively heavy piece of equipment in place, but the circumstance had been anticipated and the propeller could be dismantled. The engineer only had to screw on the hub and then the three blades, one after another, and the operation was concluded in ten minutes.

That done, Serge climbed the narrow ladder permitted access to the central dome and installed himself on the little platform fitted here, just below the conning-tower. It was the control-station for the electric motors installed in the forward compartment.

Myrandhal moved the levers on the control panel in front of him and made sure that the propeller and the rudder were working perfectly. In the same way, after having established the necessary contacts, he tested the various mechanisms that would permit him to control all the complicated machinery of the *Velox*: the psychic and other accumulators; the back-up dynamos installed in the hold, the automatic latches of the portholes and the hatch, and the release-mechanism of the counterweight—in case of an unexpected plunge.

After that he went back inside and carried out a minute inspection of the *Velox*, now mutated into a submersible, checking the seals on the portholes and the ballast tanks.

During these preparations, the psychoscaph, which had not cased its slow descent, arrived within a few feet of the Mädler Sea, whose waves occasionally lapped its hull sonorously.

Myrandhal put on a lifebelt, went back up the stairway to the captain's bridge, and took up his station at the electric control-panel.

The solemn moment had arrived.

It only required a momentary distraction, one false move or an error of calculation—some trivial forgotten detail—to bring about a catastrophe. Serge knew that, but he was confident. Even so, he was a trifle pale; his eyes were anxious and his throat was dry.

As he reached for one of the levers, he heard a flutter of wings immediately overhead. He looked up through one of the narrow crystal slits arranged around the perimeter of the conning-tower, and perceived, flying only a few meters away, the pigeon that he had launched as a scout a little while before.

"The dove of the Ark!" he cried. "It's a good sign."

He gave one last thought to his wife, and then pulled the lever.

"Adieu!"

The *Velox* dropped vertically and disappeared into the waves.

Two hundred meters away it resurfaced, white with foam, and, with its top opened, proceeded with its first trials of navigation.

The submersible steered marvelously. He increased its speed, stopped, swerved to port and starboard. One might have thought it an enormous strangely-formed Martian fish, or some amphibious monster emerged from its grotto and frolicking in the sunlight.

Then the *Velox* set a course southwards, toward Laplace Land, and set off at top speed. It moved as smoothly, as nimbly and as joyfully as a young shark beginning its first voyage around the world...

XVII. Wedding Night

Less than forty minutes later, Serge Myrandhal saw land surge forth a quarter of a mile away: a desolate, arid land, always the uniform color of brick. Only a few scattered red tufts represented the Martian flora.

Serge would have liked his first steps in his new domain to be in a more engaging landscape. In any case, there was no urgency about going ashore; it was better, taking advantage of the marvelous means of locomotion that the *Velox* provided, to explore the planet a little more first.

He searched for one of the canals he had glimpsed during the descent, and soon found one. It was an arm of the sea about a hundred kilometers wide, so far as he could tell, and it headed southwards as far as the eye could see. Serge moved along it, searching for a more inviting location: a bay or a port worthy of the beautiful name of Anna, which he gave it in advance.

The *Velox* progressed at a good speed for two hours and the country did not vary. The right bank, which was about a cable away, unfolded flat and bleak, the color of rust, suggestive of an immense sheet of lava frozen by a gust of the wind of chaos.

Standing on the walkway, with his upper body protruding from the conning-tower, Myrandhal, more disappointed the further they advanced, contemplated the panorama, which seemed to him to be desperately monotonous.

"What solitude," he thought aloud, "and what silence! It seems that Mars really is a dead world. Not a tree, not a bird, not a spring, not a valley, not a hill, not even a cloud...nothing to animate the landscape. The rivers have dried up, the mountains have been leveled, the valleys filled in. Time has passed this way, polishing the planet, making the ruddy surface into an immense bleak expanse of desert. It will be the same for the Earth one day.

"Even the sun—the sun that seemed so beautiful this morning—produces les light. It's only been three hours, but one might think that the light has diminished already. It's true that I'm twice as far from the star, whose diameter, if I could look directly at it, would seem to be reduced by half. It's also true that we're in the shorter days of the Martian summer in this hemisphere of the planet.

"Decidedly, Mars is a world, if not dead, at least uninhabited. I was congratulating myself a little while ago, but I'm almost grateful now. There's something anguishing about this funereal silence. I'd have preferred, at the risk of my life, to have to confront, if not other humans, then animals—something alive.

"I would have liked, at least, to have to contend with mysterious forces, with one of those phenomena with which writers of fantastic fiction populate unknown planets: sky-piercing volcanoes, cataracts of fire...but there's nothing!

Nothing but placid deserted canals, which inevitably make one think of some sandy town in Holland or Bruges-la-Morte."[72]

Then, suddenly, he said: "Hold on! One might think that life is reawakening. The current, imperceptible a little while ago, is increasing rapidly, and the sky is changing too. Is there going to be a storm, a cyclone? So much the better! The *Velox* has nothing to fear, and it will break the monotony."

Swiftly, Serge grabbed the telescope that was suspended from his belt and directed it southwards. In the distance, cutting into the implacable blue of the sky, a small white patch had just appeared, with coppery glints.

"It's not a cloud," Serge soon observed. "It's too low...it's more reminiscent of mist rising from the ground. What can it be?"

To content his thirst for marvels, at least in imagination, he set about building the most extraordinary conjectures, which he eliminated successively.

Soon, he slapped his forehead. "Of course! It's a city. It's smoke—I should have thought of that sooner. All great cities—Paris, London—have that roof of mist, and to judge by the dimensions of that one, the city it marks must be colossal in size!

"Who knows, perhaps I'm arriving at the Martian capital, in some gigantic agglomeration where Martians from all over the world, having abandoned the sterile countryside, have taken refuge, and where they live in some strange fashion. That dome of vapor in the respiration of an entire humankind, the breath exhaled by billions of engines that are whirring and pouring out there. It seems to me that I can hear the hum of a great factory."

In fact, for several minutes, a dull rumor had been audible in the south. At the same time, while Myrandhal gazed into the distance, the rapidity of the current as increasing in a disquieting fashion. Too absorbed, however, Serge paid no heed to it. Meanwhile, waves were beginning to rise. The water was boiling, steaming. Although the sun was already low on the horizon, the heat was becoming oppressive.

Very surprised, Serge got down from the bridge and, through one of the upper portholes, plunged his hand into the water; he snatched it back immediately.

"It's hot water," he murmured. "I've just encountered a 'gulf-stream'...or rather—and the volcanic appearance of the landscape is another indication—a hot spring with a considerable flow..."

Serge stopped the engine and, increasingly intrigued, recommenced examining the cloud, which he could now make out more clearly.

---

[72] *Bruges-la-Morte* (1892) is a novel by the Belgian writer Georges Rodenbach, nowadays hailed as one of the archetypal products of the Symbolist movement, the protagonist of which a grief-stricken widower, with whom Myrandhal might well have found some reason to identify.

"That's bizarre," he thought. "The cloud's floating on the water. So it's not a city. It might be an island, it's true, or a volcano…but no; at this distance, I'd be able to see its sides. And now the speed of the flow is beginning to take on menacing proportions. The noise is getting louder too. What a racket! I think it might be as well to stop."

Rather anxious, Myrandhal restarted the propeller and put the engine in reverse. Carried on by its momentum, the *Velox* covered a further two hundred meters and then stopped, paralyzed, incapable of going upstream. It pitched and creaked impotently, threshing the water with its hectic propeller, tossed by the waves, still increasing in force, surging upon it from all directions.

Soaked by the spray and whipped by splashing water. Serge felt a frisson run through his flesh. Immediately, he released all the available current, harnessing at a stroke all the electrical force stored in the hold.

This time, the submersible succeeded in extracting itself from the liquid grip. Panting like a wrestler, its four dynamos roaring, it had begun to describe the arc of a circle with a large radius when a big wave hit it directly in the side. The frail vessel heeled over, and was dragged a hundred fathoms further the middle of the stream—and all was lost! It was a flight toward catastrophe, toward the unknown, a race to the abyss!

Serge only just had time to close the conning-tower. His face on fire, his eyes glued to the visor, he looked out, convinced that he was the plaything of one of those mysterious forces that he had provoked a little while before, against which human beings can do nothing.

"No," he said to himself, "there's nothing to be done. The Nature that I challenged is taking her revenge. I have an anchor, but the cable would break like a thread. As for diving, why? The current is obviously faster down below than on the surface, and, if it's a choice of deaths, it's better to finish in daylight. That way, at least I'll know the name and see the face of the phenomenon that is dragging me away and is going to swallow me! The cloud's still growing…it's coming closer, racing, flying toward me like a cyclone…!"

The sun had set when, after a vertiginous course, Serge Myrandhal arrived within a quarter of a mile of the prodigy, still invisible, hidden behind its cloud like thunderous Jupiter.

The din, which had not stopped increasing, had now become something extraordinary, without any possible comparison to terrestrial sounds. Ten simultaneous thunderclaps would only give a feeble idea of it. At every crash the ground trembled and the *Velox* vibrated like a gong. Serge felt that his temples were shattering, and his eyes were bloody, as if a ten-ton cannon were being fired next to his ear.

Dazed and stupefied, invaded by such strong curiosity that he almost forgot the imminent peril, with his eye to the visor, Serge contemplated the monstrous and inexplicable phenomenon.

"No," he repeated, for the hundredth time, "it's not a volcano. It's almost dark now; I'd be able to see the flames." He interrupted himself abruptly. "A cataract!" he cried, going pale. "It's a waterfall! A Martian Niagara! Why didn't I think of that?"

He shivered. Up above, at the top of the cloud, there was a stir. Soon, a prodigious spray of water appeared, inclining graciously, describing a spiral. One might have thought it the crumbling arch of some gigantic viaduct. The fall lasted for several seconds, and then the mass fell into the sea, raising a formidable wave.

Launched like a bullet, creaking in every joint, the *Velox* ran over the crest of the wave.

"It really is a cataract," Serge stammered, "but instead of falling down it rises up. It's the world upside-down!"

At that precise moment, a final explosion, more powerful than all the rest, swept the sky clear, and the Prodigy appeared.

"A maelstrom!" Serge howled, his hair rigid with horror. In front of him, beneath his feet, a precipice half a league wide, a liquid gulf with spinning walls, had just opened up. From the depths of that abyss, forming the axis of the whirlpool, a prodigious column of water—a monstrous, spitting, fuming jet—launched into the sky!

It was a geyser and a volcano at the same time. A Geyser-Volcano!

Now, night having fallen completely, tongues of fire could be seen furrowing the geyser at its base. Jets of lava were melting; enormous blocks were soaring like bomb to explode in mid-air. One of them passed, whistling, within a matter of inches from Serge—who, clinging to his porthole, fascinated, paralyzed by the horrible spectacle, was still watching.

Meanwhile, the *Velox* had climbed the cushioning rim surrounding the whirlpool and had begun to descend the fatal slope. Again it was gripped, hurled like a roulette ball, spinning around. The violence of the maelstrom was so great that, swept by the centrifugal force, the solid bed of the gulf appeared at times: a rubble of volcanic rocks from which flames were spurting

One might have thought it the fuming gateway to Tartarus.

Sometimes, one of those rocks, torn away, seized by the geyser, shot up vertically. Serge saw one block of several tons fly toward the zenith.

Suddenly, the *Velox* was seized in its turn and projected to the summit of the geyser, in mid-air. For a second, it danced up aloft like an egg-shell in a fairground shooting range. Then everything collapsed, and everything seethed before Serge's eyes, blinded by the blood of his reopened wound.

When he was able to get a grip on himself again, the *Velox* was floating in calm water, a cable from the shore.

A further prodigy: the geyser-volcano had disappeared, and once again, there was silence—a funereal silence.

In the sky, there was a huge cloud, and on the water, enormous high waves—indications of continuing submarine explosions—were the sole indication of the place, a mile away, where the Prodigy had been.

Darkness had fallen, and millions of stars were dotting the azure mantle of the firmament.

Serge did not even ask himself what had happened, and how he came to be still alive. He no longer had the energy to be astonished. Snatched from his post, he was lying at the bottom of the staircase, half-unconscious.

Around him, wings were fluttering. It was one of the turtle-doves, escaped from the broken cage, which was fling about madly, bumping into the walls.

Almost at the same moment, something warm and flaccid slapped Serge in the face.

"Water!" he croaked, raising himself up.

It was, indeed, water. Split by the shock and already three-quarters full, the *Velox* was sinking.

A few seconds more and its captain, buried alive, screwed into the steel helmet, disappeared under the waves.

Serge only just had time to climb up, open the hatch atop the conning tower, take two steps along the hull and dive.

Danger gave him a supreme burst of energy. In any case, the shore was nearby, and the current was running toward the land. A few swimming strokes sufficed for him to reach the shore, where he let himself fall down, exhausted, in a faint.

He shivered, gripped by the nocturnal cold after his long immersion in the hot water of the canal.

At the same time, an anguish, dull at first, but becoming sharp and painful rose up within him, climbing from his loins to his empty, buzzing head.

Soon, a plaint sprang from his tortured entrails: the moan of a defeated man.

"I'm hungry," he murmured, in a faint, child-like voice, while two large tears ran down his emaciated cheeks.

Throughout his long voyage—which is to say, for thirty hours, perhaps more—Serge had only consumed a cordial, the glass of kola, whose comfort, although artificial, had lasted a long time.

"I'm hungry," he repeated.

And from then on, everything was wiped out, abolished. Serge was no longer anything but an unconscious creature, a famished animal in search of fodder. His head empty, he dragged himself along on all fours, turning over stones, digging in the sand, in search of one of those mollusks that abound on the shores of terrestrial seas.

There was nothing—not even a sprig of weed—to put into his mouth. Mars really was a dead world, decidedly an accursed planet.

After a time, he perceived one of the ruddy tufts he had glimpsed before, and dragged himself toward it, at the cost of enormous effort. His hands and knees were bloody, and a pink sweat was oozing from the pores of his distended skin.

Finally, he reached the plant, the object of his ardent covetousness.

It was a bouquet of rigid stems bristling with coarse hairs, devoid of flowers, leaves and fruits, a harsh, sterile herb, a true plant of the dunes.

Serge grabbed it in both hands. Devoid of roots, the plant came away in its entirety, and he perceived a brown bulb with a layered rind, reminiscent of an onion, which he stuffed into his mouth.

Sand grated between his teeth, but he paid no heed to it, any more than to the slightly bitter taste. Afterwards he attacked the stems, from which a milky sap oozed, similar to that of a poppy.

Either because of the effect of the sap—perhaps narcotic—or because he no longer had the strength to suffer, Serge sudden felt an immense relief. His numbed intelligence revived, throwing off gleams like a dying lamp. He sensed that his end was near, and his tormented face lit up with a smile of joy, of deliverance.

"I've found the remedy for all my ills," he stammered. "I've been poisoned. Thank you, kind plant, relief of castaways! I have nothing more to do than dig my grave."

In the course of this monologue he set about digging in the sand with his trembling hands. In a matter of seconds he had opened a cavity a few inches deep, into which he started feverishly putting his papers and his jewelry.

This way, he said to himself, *those who land here in years to come—when nothing remains of my bones, absorbed by the soil—will know where I died. Anna, if she ever comes, will know where to kneel.*

He filled in the hole, and rolled a few blocks of lava on top of it to build one of the cairns with which explorers lost at the pole strew their funereal route.

After which, holding a photograph of Anna in his hands—the only thing that he had kept—he lay down on the strand, waiting to die.

Above him, the sky scintillated; a calm, an august serenity, fell from the stars, filling the heart of the dying man with an infinite bliss. His emaciated face was radiant with tenderness and joy. He thought that he had accomplished his duty and was about to rejoin the woman he loved.

He lowered his gaze from the ethereal vault to the photograph of Anna, which he pressed against his lips.

"My work is done!" he murmured. "The task has been hard, but I've toiled well. I've toiled for Science and for Humankind. I've shown the way to the stars!"

He raised his gaze to the stars again. "The heavens haven't budged," he went on, "or rather, it's me who hasn't budged. What is the distance between the Earth and here?—a single step in infinity! Our firmament—that of the sun—

hasn't changed much. The moon has disappeared, replaced by two other satellites, Deimos and Phobos. One other change. Jupiter, which we were contemplating yesterday evening at the convent, is closer…it really is the monarch of the heavens, and perhaps Anna is contemplating it at this very minute.

"As for the Earth, it hasn't yet risen, but it's coming…it's coming to bid me adieu…

"And now, everything is finished…

"I'm going to rejoin my beloved…"

Serge shivered suddenly, and raised his head, lifted up by a titanic convulsion.

"Who's calling me?" he croaked. "Anna! Is that you?"

His eyes wide, his mouth agape, as if in ecstasy, he went on: "Yes…yes, I recognize you…your voice…your sweet face! I knew you'd come…I was expecting you!"

Suddenly, though, his voice was extinguished.

He fell back, breathless, his face a frozen mask.

Was it a mirage, or one of those miracles engendered by love, which can also move mountains?

Was it the living spouse, or her spirit, her soul, which came through space for the eternal marriage, to fuse with the disincarnate spouse?

Perhaps, one day, some telepathic message launched from on high will permit us to inform our readers, and unveil for them, by the same token, other secrets of the planet Mars.[73]

---

[73] The volume concludes at this point, but the author adds a footnote subverting the seemingly-conclusive ending: "Coming soon: *Les Robinsons de la Planète Mars*, a sequel to the adventures of the principal characters introduced in this volume."

Book Two: The Castaways of Mars

I. A Martian

When, after quite a long time, Serge Myrandhal recovered consciousness, and perceived the person who was lavishing cares upon him, he uttered a hoarse shout:

"Anna!"

And again he fainted, not having the strength to support such happiness.

The American woman took advantage of it to pour another mouthful of cordial between his teeth. Then she made him breathe from a bottle of lavender salts.

The injured man shuddered; his eyes opened again, but closed again almost immediately, full for fear.

"It's a shade," he muttered, "a phantom. She's dead. But me, am I alive? Am I dreaming? Anything's possible. I don't know any more; I can't see any more. Everything's dancing, whirling around me.

"I'm in a whirlpool. The maelstrom! Do you hear it? You can hear the monster roaring. It's claiming its prey...

"How cold it is! And that odor of sulfur! It's the very breath of Hell, the wind from the abyss. And yet, it was so beautiful a little while ago in the garden. The birds were singing in the foliage, and I was sitting with my bride..."

He fell silent.

Anguished, Anna leaned over him.

"Mercy!" she murmured, in a faint voice. "Has he gone mad? It's doubtless that wound on his head. Oh my God, has he been returned to me only for me to lose him immediately?"

She stood up suddenly and turned round, as if to ask for help.

A hundred paces away, a man, who was doubtless watching, immediately emerged from behind a heap of sand. He took two long strides and stopped.

"No!" shouted the American woman, abruptly changing her mind. "He's better. Go away. It's best he doesn't see you."

In fact, Myrandhal's face was transformed, illuminated, as it had been a little while before, when he had uttered Anna's name.

He had gripped the young woman's skirt, and was feeling it, rubbing it with trembling, feverish fingers.

"It's you," he stammered. "It's really you I'm touching! Am I still dreaming?"

Madame Myrandhal leaned over the young man and her lips brushed his burning forehead. "Yes, it's me, my friend Wake up."

Serge began trembling in his every limb.

"Her voice!" he stammered. "It's her voice!" Suddenly, with a single bound, he was on his feet. He had embraced his wife and he was covering her with bewildered kisses.

"Anna…it's you…my bride…my wife! It's you!"

"Yes, Serge, it's me…my love…my dear husband! Finally, you're awake…you're awake. Oh, how fearful I was!"

They hugged one another ardently, madly; then, mutely, their faces bathed with delicious tears, they stood there, intertwined, for a long time, living one of those moments that cannot be described.

Finally, Anna disengaged herself gently. "Come on," she said, in a soft voice. "Let's not stay here any longer."

She tried to draw him away, but Myrandhal's feet were nailed to the ground.

"Just a moment," he murmured. And, placing his hands on his wife's shoulders, he said: "Let me look at you, fill my eyes with you. How beautiful you are! I've never seen you like this. So it's you—it's really you!

"Is it possible? Yesterday, we were talking in the garden, and now, here we are on Mars, together, as we were back there. Is my dream continuing? But no…all this is real. When I doubt, I have only to look up at the sky. The stars are there to bear witness! There are the two moons, Deimos and Phobos. That golden globe rising slowly toward the zenith is Earth…

"What silence! What joyful peace!"

Myrandhal stopped, as if seized by a sudden idea, and looked at the sea.

"Nothing there any longer," he went on. "The thunder is silent. How strange it is! The prodigy was there just now, the maelstrom. It was roaring…"

"What are you talking about?" he young woman exclaimed, prompt to take alarm. "That's twice that…"

"Don't worry," said Serge, smiling. "I'm in my right mind. I'll explain it to you later. Besides which, you'll doubtless have the opportunity to see the terrifying phenomenon for yourself before long. It's obviously one of those intermittent geysers, like the ones on Earth—but what violence! What a mighty jet! I'm still wondering how I was able to escape it. I'm utterly bewildered, as if I were emerging from some frightful nightmare…

"Except for you, who have always been present, I don't remember anything—or almost nothing—of what preceded the catastrophe, and I'm trying to remember…

"How do you come to be here? It's a mystery, a miracle! But I'm no longer astonished by anything. For twenty-four hours I've been living in the midst of the fantastic, the plaything of prodigious forces. I have you: that's sufficient for me…"

"So you don't remember anything?" Anna said.

280

"Yes, but it's distant, vague. As soon as I try to fix an idea, everything trembles, spins, like the maelstrom just now. I can't distinguish the true from the false, the real from the imaginary."

"Try. I'd like to know so much myself—to know what happened to you, what harm you've sustained, in order to care for you better. How were you wounded?"

Serge put his hand to his head. "Yes," he said. "Why, you've bandaged me! Fortunate wound! Without that, I'd probably have gone mad."

"How did you do it? Was it the geyser?"

"No, it was in the *Velox*, after the departure from the convent. I'd just read your dispatch…"

"You received it?"

"Yes. Then, I thought you were dead, murdered by the bandits, and I felt on to a sharp panel."

Anna shuddered, and enveloped Serge with a loving gaze. "And afterwards?" she said.

"Afterwards, it's more confused. I remember that it was black, ever more black…a funereal, horrible black. A terrible sky! And in it, a pale, wan sun…"

"Oh yes," the American murmured, shivering again. "It's frightful. I was there, and I saw it myself."

"Hours passed," Serge continued, "and then the star disappeared. What a relief, what a sigh! It wasn't as black. The stars were shining, as they did back there is the garden, and I thought of you."

"Dear soul!"

"Meanwhile, the sky gradually changed. The tender blue vault reappeared. Then I saw the dawn, the rising sun, and I prayed."

"Me too!" Annabella murmured.

"Mars was before me," her husband continued. "I was almost happy. Something told me that we'd see one another again. And I came down in the sea. The *Velox* swam like a fish. And suddenly, the catastrophe…a kind of submarine volcano, a waterspout, threw me up into the clouds. How is it that I wasn't crushed, pulverized a hundred times over? I don't know.

"Shortly thereafter, the *Velox* sank…poor *Velox!* I was able to escape, to reach the shore…and there I collapsed, out of strength."

"And afterwards?" asked the American, breathlessly.

"Afterwards it's even more confused. I dragged myself over the sand. I was dying of hunger…atrocious hunger. Finally, agonized and defeated, I lay down to die. I called to you, and suddenly I saw you, as if in a mist, but I didn't recognize you. I was delirious."

"Yes," said Anna. "Oh, how I trembled."

"And when I came to, I thought the delirium was continuing. I thought I was mad—proof that I wasn't, but my reason was jibbing before the miracle. I wondered whether it wasn't in the other world that we had found one another. I was convinced that I was dead."

As he pronounced that word, Serge turned round and pointed at the cairn. "Look," he went on. "I was so convinced that I was dead that I'd built my tomb in advance, after a fashion...that heap of stones you see there. It's under there that I buried my papers, my jewelry. I wanted to make sure that, once my body had disappeared, if you ever came—for something old me that you would me—I wanted you to know where to pray, for you to have a souvenir. I'd only kept one thing: your dear image. I looked at it while I was dying!"

While speaking, Serge had drawn his wife toward the cairn. He knelt down, moved away the blocks of lava and started feverishly digging in the sand, from which he soon pulled out the various objects he had buried half an hour before.

"Look," he said, "here's my notebook, my watch, and the seal you gave me. Here are your letters...all my life, my heart, my soul! I was there, in my entirety. What does the rest matter, the perishable flesh, fodder for grave-worms?

"Oh, how happy I am! How good it is to live, to stir this soil into which I felt myself descending forever, dissolving, as it were. How good it is to believe, to love!

"I was dead! An angel came, touched me, and I'm alive! I'm alive! What intoxication!

"A man buried alive, who gnaws his fists, and suddenly sees the tomb open, and the light shine...the sweet light...must experience what I'm experiencing."

Serge Myrandhal seemed completely recovered now. The cordial, wine and concentrated meat extract he had absorbed a little while before had done him a great deal of good. He was talking and acting like a healthy man.

Nevertheless, his weakness persisted, and the effort he had just made had exhausted him. He was out of breath, and drops of sweat were trickling down his thin cheeks.

His wife became anxious. "Leave it at that," she said. She took a tablet from a box. "Here, chew this—it's concentrated peptone."

Serge pulled a face, like a capricious invalid. "No," he said, with a sort of puerile stubbornness. "Why do you want to make me think that I'm ill? I don't like taking medicine."

"It's not medicine," said the American. "It's food. I take one every day; that's what keeps me going. You ought to have done the same—but there's still time." She suddenly changed her tone, becoming coquettish, as in the garden at Almowrat. "Go on, to please me, take the tablet."

"Since I tell you that I don't need anything, I don't want..."

"But I do want," Anna interjected, stamping her foot. "And then, Monsieur Myrandhal, you promised to obey me, in everything and always. Do you remember?"

Serge's gaze softened immediately. "So be it," he said. "But after you. Taste it first..."

The young woman understood. She broke the tablet, keeping one piece and holding out the other to him, on which her teeth had left a damp trench. "You now."

Avidly, Serge seized the tablet, which he chewed joyfully. "There!" he said. "You're a sister of charity, an angel, an enchantress! That tablet was nothing but a piece of dried gelatin, but you touched it with your lips and made it a balm, a marvelous elixir. I can feel it gliding through my veins like a subtle fire. I was still weak, although cured, but all my strength has suddenly returned. My blood is pulsing more rapidly. I feel rejuvenated, ready to brave anything!"

And to prove that he was telling the truth, he took his wife in his arms and, setting off at the double, ran to deposit her ten meters away.

"Well?" he asked. "Are you convinced now?"

Serge was bathed in perspiration, and his eyes were shining; the American was slightly anxious about that excitement. "Yes," she said, "and the proof is that I'm taking your arm to support myself. I'm the one who's weary. I've been searching for you all day; we've been wandering along the shore for an hour. It's late, and we ought to go back."

"Go back where?" Serge asked, distractedly. "And why? It's so nice here. If you're tired, let's sit down and talk."

Madame Myrandhal uttered a brief mutinous laugh. "Are you making fun of me, Monsieur my husband? Do you take me for a little savage, who sleeps in the sand? I told you that we're expected. We have to go back."

"Go back?" said Serge, scanning the nocturnal landscape with a circular glance. "Where to?"

"Home."

"Home...this is getting stranger and stranger. You have a domicile here, in this desert?"

"Yes...the *Velox*."

"The *Velox*? I thought it was at the bottom of the sea. Have you recovered it, then?"

"Yes, but not yours—the other one, the *no. 1*."

"The *no. 1*?"

"Yes—the one that the Mendicant Prince was to use."

"Ah!" Serge exclaimed, his face clearing. "That's the means that brought you here, then? He was afraid...he's repented..."

"Not exactly. There was a fight, but we won. It's a long story, which I'll tell you shortly, at table. I didn't want to tire you out."

"Always that idea. But I'm not ill, my dear Anna, I swear. I've never been ill. A nervous disturbance, the effect of emotion, and weakness too. I was wrong not to take anything. As for this wound, it's nothing. There'll be no sign of it tomorrow." Another idea suddenly made him start. "Then the other ship's here!"

he exclaimed, his face radiant. "The *Velox no. 1*. We're no longer castaways deprived of everything. We can navigate, come and go, explore the planet, search for more hospitable terrain! We can leave if necessary. Quickly, tell me: is the other *Velox* intact?"

"Entirely intact. Not a plate out of place."

"That's marvelous. Take me to it right away. I'm in haste to see it, to touch it. Why can't I see it? Where is it? Is it far away?"

"No—about a mile."

Serge stood on tiptoe. "I can't see anything."

"The sand's hiding it. There's nothing as deceptive as shifting dunes. Just now, while looking for you, I almost got lost once or twice. Fortunately, we have an excellent reference-point. You see that rock over there, that sort of obelisk overlooking the beach?"

"Perfectly. One might think that it was a bell-tower..."

"That's the word—I'll keep that. It will be our bell-tower. Well, it's there. The *Velox*—or, rather, the *Annabella*, since that's the name it's been given..."

"A beautiful name!" Serge murmured.

"...is beached a little further on, about three hundred meters..."

"Let's go, then. It must be late—what time do you think it is?"

"My watch has stopped."

"Like mine. I suspected as much."

"And not only mine, but all the clocks on board."

"When did they stop? On arrival...?"

"I don't know. I'd lost all notion of time, and I didn't think about consulting the chronometer once. Our journey might have lasted twenty or thirty hours; is it the first or the second of August? I can't tell. And what does the terrestrial time matter? We're on another world, on Mars."

"We're on Mars," Serge repeated, like an echo. "I need to repeat that in order to believe it. You said just now that you'd been searching for me all day; in consequence, we must have arrived, together, almost at the same time, at dawn."

"That's right. And what a dawn!" the young woman exclaimed. "I'll never forget it. What a shiver, when I recognized the famous canals. So, the *Annabella*, left to her own devices, as it were—for I had nothing, or almost nothing, to do with her direction—had continued on its route without deviation an inch. She steered like a living being who knows where she's going—unless she was drawn, attracted to Mars by some unknown force, by some occult power that will reveal itself later. Several times, during the journey, I had the sensation that a mysterious will was watching over us."

"Me too."

"It's like our arrival at the same point, almost at the same time. Doesn't that make you believe in that intervention, in some mysterious protector who was bringing me to you? God was evidently on our side."

"Yes," the engineer murmured. "Take note, though, that the thing might have a simpler explanation. Launched from the same point, in the same direction, by an identical force, the two psychoscaphs were bound, like two bullets, to end up at the same place. We had the same itinerary; in a word, we followed one another. Notice too that I'd often mentioned the Mädler Sea to you, where I counted on coming down. You might have remembered that, and unconsciously, without being aware of it, steered the apparatus in that direction."

"It's possible. In any case, from that moment on, I started steering in an effective fashion. I was familiar with the various items of apparatus."

"You didn't have any difficulty?"

"Not once. You had explained those in the *Velox* to me so often, and they were the same. Of course, from then on your itinerary escaped me. First I searched for you in the air with the telescope. The *Annabella* flew at a considerable height for some time, in order to see further.

"Then, not having discovered anything, I concluded that the *Velox* had come down right away, and that it was already heading for the shore, so I came closer to the sea and started to described concentric circles of increasing radius. But I couldn't see any more trace of the *Velox* on the water than in the air. It's true that so little of the vessel protrudes that the slightest wave might hide it.

"That's why I'm so late. Finally, as the sun was setting, I set forth along the canal. Something told me that you must have gone in that direction...

"It was getting dark rapidly, and I was beginning to despair. Briefly, I heard a horrible noise..."

"The maelstrom," Serge murmured.

"Yes I understand now. Darkness had fallen, though, and my anguish was increasing. One hope remained, though. A presentiment—one of those mysterious warnings in which you and I believe, told me that you were there, nearby, struggling against some incomprehensible phenomenon. I wanted to call out to you, to shout: 'Be brave! Someone's coming to your rescue...' And once again, I looked for the telepath, and I found it behind a divan, where it must have slipped when we took off. I called to you, but you didn't reply..."

"That's explicable," Serge replied. "At that moment I was in the middle of an atmosphere saturated with electricity, in the middle of a storm. The feeble waves of the apparatus must have gone astray..."

"That's what I thought, too. In fact, the racket suddenly became frightful. One might have thought it an artillery battle between two fleets. Suddenly, everything went silent...a deathly silence...and I let go of the steering wheel. *It's all over*, I said to myself. He's doomed... "

"I'd just saved myself."

"I was sobbing. Suddenly, my companion uttered a cry that I can still hear: 'A wreck, there, near the bank!'

"It was the *Velox*, coming back up to the surface. It sank again almost immediately, but the hatch of its conning-tower was open, and I realized that you must have escaped that way and swum to the shore.

"Close by, there were shifting dunes. I sailed straight for them and our ship ran aground gently on the sand. A few moments later, we were beside you, and you opened your eyes."

Serge hugged his wife impetuously. "What you have done is marvelous—marvelous, for a woman..."

"I wasn't alone."

"That's true...I saw someone a little while ago. I remember now...a man. Where is he, so that I can thank him? Why has he gone away?"

"For the sake of discretion. And then, I feared that his presence here might displease you. I remember that you were determined to be the first man on Mars, and I feared that you'd see him as a competitor, a rival for glory."

"Glory," Serge murmured. "What a vain word, after such ordeals." Again he embraced his wife. "This is my glory, and I want no other. The man who has brought you to me will never be a rival. I feel that I love him already. So you can name him without fear. Who is he?"

"Guess," said Anna, who was reassured.

"How do you expect me to guess? Is it someone I know?"

"Yes."

"And who was at the convent with us?"

"Obviously."

"It's not at all easy, you know...we were alone, with no friends. I can only think of the reverend. That's it. You already mentioned abducting him..."

"No, it's not him."

"Then I give up. And what does it matter? I have no need to know him to love him. Take me to him so that I can take him in my arms. Where has he gone? He was here just now, behind that heap of sand. Where do you think he is?"

"Back at the ship, no doubt. I expect we'll find him setting the table. Perhaps he's scold us a little for being so slow. We've been wandering in the moonlight for more than an hour. We've taken the lovers' route...

"Our friend is a hearty eater—one of those imperturbable Anglo-Saxons whom nothing troubles. At the battle of Tsushima[74] he was aboard the Japanese flagship, and at the height of the battle, when hundred-ton cannons were blazing, do you know what he was doing?"

"No."

"Eating lunch sitting astride a yard-arm."

"I've got it!" cried Serge, laughing. "This time, I've got it. It's Pickman."

---

[74] The major naval battle of the Russo-Japanese War, fought in May 1905. The Japanese won.

"The very same."

"What a man!" Myrandhal continued. "And what a good companion, what a jolly fellow! He swore to make the voyage and he's kept his word, to our great good fortune."

Again he burst out laughing. His wife did likewise.

"I can breathe easy," she said, then. "Just as long my dear guardian is as agreeable. I can't help feeling a certain anxiety, I confess. You know his mania for setting records. This morning, when we spotted you, he didn't want me to hurry the landing, so that he could mark the record and the time. Fortunately, our watches weren't working.

"Until then, he'd convinced himself that the *Annabella*, being lighter than the *Velox*, would arrive first—and now we don't know what time it is, and have no way of checking the time. Imagine his disappointment! He's heart-broken, and I'm wondering how he'll greet us. It's necessary to expect anything from an eccentric of his stripe. He's capable of not wanting to recognize you."

"Don't worry," said Serge. "I'll soon soften him up. I'll make concessions..."

"No!" cried the American. "That's exactly what I don't want. Let me handle it. My guardian is a good man, in spite of his manias. If you'd seen his emotion just now, when we found you lying on the sand. He loves you, deep down..."

"And I adore him! But where is he? Where's the *Annabella?* We're only a short distance from the 'bell-tower' and I can't see anything."

"Come on," said Madame Myrandhal. "We're nearly there."

After having gone around one last mound of sand, the two young people stopped in amazement.

In front of them, at the foot of the obelisk, the Eccentric, holding his alpenstock in one hand, on the end of which a lantern was swinging, and a brush in the other, was in the process of applying red paint on the base of the monolith. Already, an inscription was displayed in letters a foot high:

SIR WASHINGTON PICKMAN
1 August 19**

On hearing the sand creak, he darted a glance sideways, and calmly continued his task.

Discontented with this welcome and losing patience, the American ran toward him.

"My dear guardian," she said, "may I introduce my husband, Monsieur Serge Myrandhal..."

"Your husband?" said the Englishman, without turning his head. "What's this nonsense? God damn it! Have you lost your mind, Miss Anna?"

The final digit had been filled in. Unhurriedly, Pickman wiped his hands, turned round, and at the sight of Myrandhal, muttered: "Why, who's this gentleman?" Then, addressing the young woman, he said. "Well, Miss Anna, be polite. What are you waiting for? Introduce me to this young Martian."

II. Peace is Made

The bluff was so colossal, and so unexpected, and the Eccentric had said it so seriously, that the American, who had been on the point of getting annoyed, was gripped by irresistible laughter.

Her husband was also making superhuman efforts not to burst out laughing.

The Englishman was still waiting, impassively. "Shocking!" he ended up saying. "Miss Anna, you're a silly girl, and unseemly. I forgive you because the voyage has troubled your mind slightly. It's stupid to laugh like that."

Myrandhal feared that the Baronet might really be offended, so he took a step forward.

"Monsieur," he said, courteously. "Believe that..."

"Prodigious!" cried the eccentric. "They speak French on Mars! It's bizarre, but everything is upside-down here." Becoming amiable, he went on: "In any case, sir, I'm delighted to make your acquaintance. You can serve as our interpreter. Furthermore, I'm delighted that your wound is better. You were wounded in combat, I suppose? You must tell us all about it at table, for I'm inviting you to dinner. I'm keeping you. You're our guest, our hostage. Oh, don't worry—you'll be well treated...

"As soon as possible, we'll exchange you. There would be a preferable arrangement, and we'll make it with great pleasure—I and my ward, Miss Anna Carpenter, whom you see here. That would be, if it's agreeable to you, for you to stay with us..."

"But I'd like nothing better," said Myrandhal, with the utmost seriousness.

"All right! I can see that we'll get along. You understand that we're a little like castaways here, like Robinson Crusoe, the great English hero. We need someone who knows the country, the indigenous customs—a Friday, in sum. Would it please you to accept that role?"

"Gladly."

"All right!" the Eccentric repeated. "And now, my friends, to table. I'm as hungry as a shark."

Madame Myrandhal observed this scene without saying a word. She was thinking, wondering what her guardian was playing at, and not knowing whether to laugh or get annoyed.

Myrandhal, for his part, was avidly contemplating the psychoscaph lying about a quarter of a mile away.

The Englishman took a step. "Forward march!" he commanded, dryly. And, in a lower voice, as if he feared being overheard by his ward, he added: "My dear Friday, I have something delicate to discuss with you."

"Speak, my dear Robinson."

"This is it. You seem like a gallant man. In fact, perhaps you're not as Martian as you'd like to have us believe. Well, you see that young woman—the one who bandaged you and brought you here. She appears to be quite rational..."

"Indeed."

"Wrong! My ward's mind is severely deranged. I'd already perceived it during the voyage, but it has suddenly taken on greater, yes, unexpected proportions. Reasoning is futile. Best, I think, to explain the matter to you.

"So, my ward is a lunatic, as I said. She's seeing double, and mistakes you for her boy-friend, a certain Myrandhal, who's a long way away. So, you understand, it's necessary to do as I do, to lend yourself to the game, otherwise she might easily..."

The American was not listening. Her brows furrowed, she was looking at the rear of the *Annabella*, where something was floating that puzzled her: a square piece of muslin with orange stripes, which was difficult to make out in the gloom.

She suddenly stopped. "That's too much!" she exclaimed. "An English flag!" And she turned to her guardian, her eyes blazing. "Mr. Baronet, you're going to take down that rag right now. I stopped you a little while ago, and you've taken advantage of my absence. It's naughty! It's a crime, an infamy!"

"An infamy," muttered the Eccentric, disconcerted by the abrupt attack. "What do you mean? What's biting you, Miss Anna?"

The American stamped her foot. "First of all, I forbid you to call me Miss Anna."

"Forgive me, Madame Myrandhal. I forgot..."

"And then, I told you that I don't want that flag. There's only one man who has the right to plant his flag on Mars, and that's my husband, here present."

The Englishman nudged Serge with his elbow. "You see, sir? That's what I was saying. I'll try to reason with her. Help me...

"By Jove, my dear Anna, you're making a mistake. You've forbidden me to raise my flag on Mars, and I respected the order. I'll respect it as long as it isn't proven that I set foot here first. But on the *Annabella*, it's a different matter. God damn it. I have the right. The ship belongs to me..."

"Oh!" said Anna, calming down. "It belongs to you..."

"Yes. I conquered it in battle. You were there and can bear witness to that. I'm entitled to say: the *Annabella* belongs to me; it's English territory, on which I have the right to plant my flag. Don't you agree, sir?"

"Entirely. In your place, I wouldn't have been so pernickety. I'd have hoisted my flag on the land itself, boldly. I can assure you that no one would have protested."

Pickman had pricked up his ears, wondering if he had heard correctly. "Not even you? And yet you might, perhaps...you're the first occupant...as a Martian, I mean..."

"Oh, I'm a very recent Martian," Serge replied, smiling, "and perhaps I won't be one for long. I have a revenge to take on Earth, and am only waiting for an opportunity to quit this excessively inhospitable world. Don't worry, sir, it's not possession of this desert, these few square feet of sand, that will cause us to quarrel."

"A few square feet of sand!" murmured the Eccentric, delighted by what he heard. "That's the way they talk...always the same, these crazy Frenchmen. Good for puling chestnuts from the fire. So, I only have to wait...he goes, I stay, and once alone, I annex! All right!" In a louder voice, indifferently, he added: "So you're going to leave Mars?"

"As soon as possible."

"And if others take it?"

"What would they do with it? I once said to someone, who looked a lot like you, that the time is a long way off when pleasure trains will be circulating between the planets."

"Yes," said the Englishman, feigning a detachment that he was far from feeling, "You're absolutely right. There's no point envisaging such a fugitive prospect. I agree with you, my dear Friday."

The American shrugged her shoulders at that word. "What a ridiculous joke," she murmured. "I warn you, my dear guardian, that I'm going to get annoyed if this goes on."

"But I'm not joking, I'm being serious..."

"Thank you very much! Then it's seriously that you're claiming that I'm mad?"

"No!" protested the Englishman, swiftly. "I was wrong to say...yes, I was joking then. You're not mad, Miss Anna...Madame Myrandhal, I mean."

"It's you who's an old madman."

"No, me neither. However, we don't see things the same way. So, there's a mystery..." The Englishman slapped his forehead. "I've got it!" he cried. "I've found it!"

"What have you found?"

"The key to the mystery. We're both in our right minds. It's not us who's seeing double—no, it's this gentleman, quite simply."

"You're being ridiculous," said Anna.

"Wait," said the Eccentric. "Let me speak—I'll prove it. You'll be forced to agree, since I'm reasoning in accordance with your own ideas. A hundred times, Anna, you've said to me that each of us has a double somewhere, another self, on another planet, who calls to us...

"So, everything is explicable! You're right, and I'm not wrong. Or, to put it better, we're both right, since Monsieur Myrandhal, as you call him, and Friday, as I call him, are one and the same…why are you laughing? Does that seem ludicrous to you?"

"Indeed."

"No. It's true—perhaps, at least…let's suppose that it is, that it's the only way of reaching an agreement. You can see that I'm making concessions…"

Madame Myrandhal shrugged her shoulders without making any reply.

"You're sulking!" said, the Englishman, crestfallen. "And yet, I'm doing what I can! I take our guest as my witness that I'm doing what I can—aren't I, sir?"

"Absolutely."

"Ah! You see, Miss Anna…I only want to reach an understanding with the two of you—with you, sir, even though I have reasons for holding a grudge against you. Let's leave that aside, though, and make peace. I'd like that. But it's still necessary that I know your intentions. The first point that might have set us at odds, the possession of Mars, is settled—or rather, set aside. The question doesn't arise for the moment—but there's something else that bothers me."

"What's that?"

"This: whether you're Myrandhal or his double, the matter concerns you intimately, and you're certainly aware of it. You've heard mention of the great enterprise, the great race organized by an American newspaper: the race from New York to Mars."

"Indeed."

"You know that Myrandhal—the one in New York, I mean—and I were competing to win the cup…"

"I know."

"Well, now that everything can be explained…Anna's holding it against me that I'm not stepping aside in favor of her 'dear heart.' More than that, she's accused me of having lacked honesty, and yet, I swear to you that I've never done anything incorrect. I'm a gentleman…"

"I never doubted it," Myrandhal protested.

"Thank you," said the Englishman, immediately. "Oh, the battle has been rude, and if we've achieved a dead heat…you'll permit me to suppose that until the negative is proved…"

"I permit everything."

"Thank you! So, I was saying that, if we'd arrived neck and neck, I'd have merit. You ought to understand that if the struggle was unequal between me, an old globe-trotter, and that young man, who is a famous scientist…you can see that I'm rendering the same justice…"

"Thank you," Serge murmured, in his turn.

"So, I repeat, I've done nothing improper; I've only taken advantage of opportunities. A Rajah I know had a psychoscaph, another *Velox* that he could launch second. He ceded his right to me, one way or another—that's between us—and I got aboard with my ward. The *Annabella* departed, according to the agreement, a long time after the *Velox*—almost two hours—it remains to be determined which of the two machines won the race. One, the *Velox*, was giving weight, but receiving time; the other was doing it the other way around, to equalize the chances—a handicap, what! Launched with the same force, but lighter and faster, the *Annabella* ought to have overtaken her competitor. Did she succeed? That's the question. Which arrived first? That's what it's necessary to establish, to prove..."

"It's proven," Serge replied. "It's the *Annabella*. Her name has brought her luck."

Pickman's face lit up. "Do you have proof?"

"No, but it's probable, as you say—so probable that I'm ready to concede it..."

"God damn it!" exclaimed Pickman, raising his arms in the air with a furious expression. "That's not the point at all! It's a matter of sport, this issue, and it's necessary to proceed properly. War and business are one thing, but sport is another. Here, honesty is required. I'd be delighted, and I'd give my fortune and my head together, to be able to put on my card: *First man on Mars*—but I need it to be the truth. I don't want a title accorded by kindness, by gallantry.

"You can understand now why I'm in a hurry to discover who the record belongs to, and I think you can help us. So, I'm asking you a question that's been burning my lips for a long time: what time was it—I mean, the terrestrial time—when you arrived on Mars?"

"I don't know. All the chronometers on board had stopped.

"God damn it! Just like ours. Tell me, then, what time was it on Mars, according to the sun? You must have measured its height."

"In truth, no," Serge replied, insouciantly. All that I can say is that the sun had risen. As for measuring its height above the horizon, I didn't think of it..."

"I thought of it!" cried the Eccentric. "It was all I thought of, throughout the voyage. So, as soon as we recognized Mars, I measured the height of the sun—exactly two and a half degrees—and ours as well. Those two measurements combined permit the specification of the time—the Martian time, if course. If you'd done the same, the problem would be resolved. We'd only have to compare them...

"What a pity, sir! You've done us considerable harm. You don't think you can repair that omission?"

"It would be difficult. If I had my ship, my apparatus, perhaps it would be possible, by a sequence of deductions...unfortunately, they're at the bottom of the canal. I'll try, though. I'll do everything I can to give you satisfaction. Rely on me, my dear Robinson."

"Thank you, my dear Friday!"

They were only a few meters from the psychoscaph now.

Suddenly, Serge, leaving his companions, ran toward a nearby sandy mound. He had just perceived a sprig of the "castaways' herb" to which he might have owed his life. At the top of the ruddy stems a few pale flower-heads were swaying, reminiscent of lilies of the valley.

"Flowers," Serge murmured. "I want to be able to celebrate my wife's birthday."

He picked the most beautiful stems, tied them up with a twig, and hid the bouquet in his bosom.

As he completed that operation, he heard an altercation flare up between his companions.

When he came back, the Eccentric was alone. Head bowed, his expression crestfallen, he was scratching the sand with the tip of his alpenstock.

"Where's Anna?" the engineer asked.

The Englishman pointed to the young woman, who was on the walkway of the psychoscaph. "She's gone," he said, piteously, "and I think she's really angry."

"Angry with whom? Me?"

"No, not you—quite the contrary. Me. She's just been quarreling with me again."

"About what?"

"You. She wants me to apologize to you…or at least give you an explanation."

"But I won't allow…you don't owe me any explanations."

"Yes, let me do it. There's no inconvenience, now we're in accord about everything. Obviously, I was a little ill-tempered at first. You hadn't been friendly toward me—but since then, you've made amends. Above all, you've promised me to establish the true record. I was annoyed with you just now—hence that ridiculous bluff."

"Not at all. On the contrary, your idea was very amusing..."

"Bah, you understand the joke—but she doesn't want to. She's just told me. So, it's necessary to put an end to it. There's no more reason for it, anyway."

Leaning on the rail of the walkway, the American was waiting. Her guardian shot her a sideways glance.

"You see," he murmured. "She doesn't trust me. She wants to make sure that I'm making amends. She's a tyrant! Just as long as she stops sulking once the ceremony's over and done with..."

Abruptly, like a man submitting at his cost, the Eccentric held out his hand to the engineer. "With that, let's end the joke. Monsieur Myrandhal, I offer you my apologies; let's make peace."

"I'd like nothing better."

"Me too. I hold you in high esteem. We should have been friends for a long time It's you who..."

The Eccentric could not complete his sentence. From the walkway, making a bound of thirty feet, a dog had just leapt upon Pickman's shoulders. He nearly fell over.

The animal—a Saint Bernard of considerable size—continued its hectic bounds, raising clouds of dust every time.

"It's Stop," grumbled the Eccentric. "Peace, Stop! What a crazy devil! He doesn't understand that on Mars, his weight of hundred and thirty pounds becomes barely thirty. It's the second time that the satanic fellow has knocked me over. Anna knows it, and I'll wager that the little pest has unleashed him deliberately."

In fact, on the walkway, Madame Myrandhal was laughing uproariously. She clapped her hands.

"Let's eat!" she cried, joyfully. "The table's laid. Let's not wait any longer. I'm as hungry as a wolf, God damn it!"

The Eccentric had raised is head. "Good," he said, joyfully. "That's much better. She's making fun of me. Peace is made! To table, sir!"

III. The Drama of Almowrat

The *Annabella*, into which we are introducing the reader for the first time, had the same dispositions as the *Velox*, except that it was smaller by a third and did not have separate cabins. From the store-room one passed directly into the central compartment beneath the conning-tower, and from there into the engine room.

"Sir," said the Eccentric, "Before anything else, I'll do you the honors of our dwelling. I'll show you, not the vessel itself, which you know as well as I do, but its equipment. You'll be astonished by the cargo that I've succeeded in lodging in this egg-shell. It's a masterpiece of stowage, without boasting. I was a midshipman once, and it's served me well. So, before sitting down at table, I'll give you the proprietor's tour, if you wish."

"I was about to ask you," Serge replied. "I'd be interested to see how this machine, which appeared to me to be a trifle fragile, stood up to the journey."

"Marvelously," replied the Englishman, triumphantly. "It's true that we had a master pilot: my ward, here present. She manned the helm, and by Jove, she astonished me—and I'm not easily astonished. I wish you could have seen her, especially during the landing. She executed a descent and a swerve at top speed that were a veritable marvel."

Myrandhal squeezed his wife's hands. "My dear Anna," he murmured. "Where would I be without you?"

Meanwhile, the Eccentric had started walking the young couple from one end of the submarine to the other. They lent themselves to that whim with a good grace, but were scarcely listening to the former midshipman's expert explanations, spiced with marine terminology. Entirely devoted to their happiness, they were whispering in one another's ears.

Nevertheless, as they went on, one thing that surprised Myrandhal was the enormous quantity of food supplies and machinery of every sort heaped up in the three compartments. They were everywhere.

"That's surprising" he murmured in the American's ear. "For the worthy Pickman to have accumulated so many provisions, he must have been certain of making the voyage."

"He says so," the American replied, smiling, "but he's boasting. He merely hoped so, and had, entirely at hazard, packed his bags. It appears that, the day after his entry to the monastery, an entire caravan arrived for him, more than fifty camels..."

"Fifty camels," murmured Serge. "In that case, we can only see part of the cargo here. What could there have been in all those crates? All that is strange, as is the presence of the Eccentric in the convent. What was he doing there and why was he hiding? Obviously, he was preparing a coup—as was his right. I should have suspected it, and my word, I agree that he employed his time marvelously. Perhaps he intended to leave before us—before me. In fact, the *Annabella*, you said, left the monastery an hour after the *Velox*?"

"An hour and a few minutes."

"It's necessary, then, that the *Annabella* must have been fitted out without our knowing it, fully loaded—ready to depart, in sum. That's a mystery."

"Yes," said the American, not without a certain hesitation. "That's a mystery. During our journey, I tried to make my guardian confess, but he seemed so embarrassed, and ashamed, that I thought I ought not to insist...

"To tell the truth, and to deal with the delicate subject in one go, my feeling—which, I divine, is also yours—is that an association had been formed, a conspiracy against you, between my guardian and the mage, that horrid monk who had inspired such a revulsion in me from the very first day..."

"How right you were," Serge murmured.

"Except," Anna went on, "that as soon as the Baronet—a gallant man with a great heart, in spite of his passion, which sometimes blinds him—saw his accomplice's infamy, he pulled himself together and made an about-turn, in such a way as to redeem the situation entirely.

"What his exact intentions were, it's probably best not to inquire too closely, and only to see one thing—his subsequent conduct. He's fully repaired the wrongs that he might have done. After all, it's Pickman alone who has saved us—you and me. Without him, we'd be separated forever."

"That's true," Serge murmured, raising his wife's hands to his lips.

Shortly afterwards, the tour concluded, the voyagers returned to the central compartment, where the table was laid.

"That's enough for this evening," said the Eccentric. "I'm hungry. Tomorrow, we'll make a more detailed tour, for I have many interesting things to show you. I've thought of everything—there's everything, all the way to radish seeds and special thread to make fishing lines."

While talking, the Englishman had opened various tins of food. As they were taking their places at the table, Serge leaned toward his wife and took out the bouquet he had picked and hidden.

"My dear Anna," he said, "permit me to wish you happy birthday. It might be a little late, and these flowers are very modest, but they're the only ones I could find on this arid world..."

Tenderly moved, the American had thrown herself into her husband's arms.

As for the Eccentric, seized by a sudden enthusiasm, he applauded with his huge hands and became excited. "Hip, hip, hurrah!" he cried. "Well said! Bravo, sir! I'm entirely of your opinion. Perhaps it's not as late as you think, and there's always time to do the right thing. Imagine that I didn't think of it! I'm an ass!"

In his turn, Pickman threw himself upon his ward and hugged her whole-heartedly. He was so emotional that he nearly hugged Serge too. Then he ran to the store-room and came back carrying a bottle of champagne, which he immediately uncorked.

"To the health of Madame Myrandhal!" he declared. "To our all-round success! Today is a great day, and it's necessary that the celebration should be complete. Wait!"

Again, the Englishman ran to the store-room. He soon emerged again, brandishing a large flat tin, which he set about opening.

"A plum pudding!" the Eccentric howled, having arrived at the peak of his enthusiasm. "I was keeping it for a special occasion; what better one could there be? And it will be excellent, by Jove, although tinned...besides, I have a means of making it new...fresh, I mean."

The Baronet poured half a liter of rum over the pudding, and set fire to it.

The young couple looked on, amused and bewildered.

"But where the devil did all that come from?" asked the engineer. "This ship is a veritable treasure-trove—a Mère Gigogne's cupboard!"[75]

Meanwhile, the Englishman had stuck a knife into the national pudding.

"This is some party!" he murmured. "I'd give a great deal for the members of the Splendid Club to be able to see me now."

"And the *Herald*, which we're forgetting!" cried the American, suddenly remembering her duty as a reporter. She was already sitting at the telepath's signal-key and spelling out the dispatch that she was sending: "*Mars, Mädler Sea. Arrived safely. Desert world. Details tomorrow*...and that's enough for now. Will the dispatch arrive, though?"

"I hope so," Myrandhal replied, "but I can't be certain."

---

[75] Mère Gigogne [Mother Ginger] is a stock character in French puppet shows, who has a large number of children and works wonders in order to feed them. She might be a version of the character in the English nursery rhyme "There was an old woman who lived in a shoe...."

"My dispatch reached you, though."

"Yes, but that was a much shorter distance. Until now, the newspaper telegraphed us every day, but it's been at least twenty-four hours since we received anything. That gives me doubts. I wonder whether the apparatus really has as much power as I hoped. In any case, the paper's reply, or its silence, will settle the matter. We have only to wait."

"That's right," the reporter replied. "If the apparatus is defective, we'll have to improve it. Is that possible?"

"I'll try, if you insist."

"I do insist. Don't forget, my dear husband, that you've made a formal promise not to impede my career."

Once their initial hunger had been appeased, Madame Myrandhal began to relate what she called "the Drama of Almowrat."

"I'll resume, she said, at the moment my dispatch left off: '*my door's giving way. Au revoir.*'

"It was *au revoir* that you were trying to say?" asked Serge, swiftly.

"Yes, but I didn't have time to finish. The horrible Rajah had just grabbed my hand, and a dozen monks with ugly faces were surrounding me, dragging me toward the antechamber."

"The wretches!" murmured the young man. "Where were they taking you?"

"I was wondering that when a formidable growling resounded and I saw a beast, which seemed at first to be frightful and monstrous, bounding into my room..."

The Englishman laughed. "It was Stop," he explained. "The old fellow, coming on the scene."

"At the same time," the young woman continued, I saw the men who were holding me leap into the air, their faces crushed, gnashing their teeth..."

The Eccentric extended his bony fist like a boxer.

"That was me," he said, simply. "Three punches, and they were sorted..."

Myrandhal seized the Englishman's hand, and pressed it in his own. A little more and he would have raised that fist, bristling with russet hair, to his lips. "My dear Robinson," he said, "I owe you more than life. You risked being killed..."

"Pfft!" said the Eccentric, disdainfully. "It was nothing, really—the monklings knew nothing about boxing. My only merit was arriving in the nick of time, like Blücher at Waterloo. I'd heard the screech, you see—the whistle of the *Velox*—and immediately thought of some trickery, some dirty deed on the Rajah's part. I'd seen him prowling around too much, that night. I called my dog—he always sleeps with me—and forward ho! There were monks running ahead of us and I only had to follow them to find the right place.

"God damn it! When I saw what was happening...those dozen apes attacking my ward...my heart leapt in my breast like a football. If Anna hadn't held me back I'd have massacred the lot..."

"I was just in time," Madame Myrandhal resumed, unable to help smiling. "My guardian already had the Mendicant Prince under his knee. The monk was choking, sticking his tongue out."

"The vile beast!" muttered the Baronet. "One second more, and I'd have strangled him like an owl..."

"Fortunately," the American continued, "I'd recovered my composure. I threw myself on my uncle like a fury..."

"A fury, in truth," the Eccentric approved. "I'd never seen anything like it in my life..."

"'Let him go!'" I howled. "'Let him go—I need him!'

"'Why?' my guardian asked, amazed. 'Pull yourself together, Miss Anna. Explain yourself. What do you want to do?'

"'What do I want? I want to go in search of my husband. First, get everyone out.'

"The Baronet distributed a few punches, which cleared the place completely. Left alone with my guardian, and the mage, to whom he was still holding on, I went into the dressing-room to change. Less than ten minutes later, I came out full dressed, my suitcase in my hand, ready to depart.

"'Where are you going?' Pickman asked. 'I don't understand. Explain, by Jove.'

"'I've told you—I'm going to Mars. There's another psychoscaph—the *Velox no. 1*. The Rajah has to give the order to get it ready. We're going, and I'm taking you with me.'

"At that announcement, the Baronet uttered a cry of joy, a veritable roar. At the same time, he picked up the mage, tucked him under his arm, and held him there effortlessly. 'All right!' he shouted. 'It's settled. I'm with you—all the better, then, that the *Velox* is all fitted out, ready for take-off. Indraghava was going to leave tomorrow, and even proposed to take me with him. Oh, the wretch—I understand now. It was just a pretext to make use of me...'

"At that moment, there was a racket in the corridor. It was Jonathan Burrett, arriving in his turn, knocking everything over as he came. He came to place himself at my right hand, taking an enormous revolver out of his Quaker overcoat, a pocket machine-gun...

"My two defenders looked so terrible that no one in the convent, that city of more than ten thousand monks, dared to raise a hand against us..."

"Pardon me," the Eccentric interrupted, pouring himself a glass of old whisky. "It's necessary to get things right. In truth, you're making us look too good, my dear ward. Probably, the Rajah only had to raise a hand to launch all those thin apes against us, and there would have been a massacre, but he was too sick. He sensed, too, that at the first gesture, I'd crush him like a viper. So he preferred to negotiate. That was better for him and for us, who had need of him, after all."

"It's possible," Madame Myrandhal went on, "but reflection only came later. It was you, my dear guardian, and the worthy Burrett, who won the game by your attitude. It was only in the crypt, where we'd just arrived, and you'd relaxed your grip slightly, that Indraghava thought about negotiating.

"My guardian had put the revolver to his head, with that concise persuasiveness of which he has the secret. 'Now,' he said, 'You have the coolies, the rails, the elephants. Set it up. Have them bring the *Velox* out, put it in place. If it isn't done in thirty minutes, I fire!'

"The mage reflected for a moment, and then asked: 'Is the pastor going with you?'

"'No,' the Reverend replied, divining the Rajah's thinking. 'I'm going back to America. As soon as my friends have gone, I'm leaving the monastery. And don't try to get rid of me. My whereabouts are known, and there's an American consul in Karputhala. On the other hand, if you accept our conditions, and fulfill them to the letter, I promise, on my word of honor, not to breathe a word about the drama. No one will know about your crime but God, who will punish you in His own time.'"

"That's right!" exclaimed Serge. "That's what it was necessary to do. The mage belongs to me, and I'm the one who'll punish him."

"The Rajah hadn't said a word," the American continued, "nor sketched a gesture...except that he must have done something, for one of the monks, who was trembling with fear, suddenly made off. A few minutes went by, and then the coolies suddenly appeared, dragging rails and cross-ties.

"The Rajah had accepted!

"Entrusting the mage to the pastor, Pickman took command of the crew, and they set to work feverishly. It was a matter of placing twenty meters of rail to the cellar next to the one where the *Velox* was stored. An hour later, the track was in place, the needle was brought into play, and the *Velox*, sliding on its truck, came to take its place in front of the engine-amplifier.

"Pickman came to me. 'All aboard for Mars!' he joked. And, seeing tears in my eyes: 'Pardon me, Miss Anna, but you mustn't cry. You mustn't, by Jove! It's not the time. We need you. I believe you know how the machine works better than I do. My part's done—it's up to you now. You're our captain. Be strong, a true American, by the living God—or we're doomed. Is everything ready?'

"Those forceful words recalled me to my duty. At the same time, I shivered, gripped by a sudden anxiety. 'No,' I replied, 'Something's missing.'

"'What?' asked Pickman, suddenly anxious.

"'Come on—I'll explain on the way,'

"You'll have guessed, my dear Serge, where we were going—to your room, to search for one of the filaments needed to arm the engine. I'd suddenly thought of that, and shuddered. If, by chance, the wallet in which you kept the precious filaments was on your person at the moment of your departure, ours would be impossible.

"'By Jove,' groaned the Eccentric. 'We'll see about that. We only have to ask the mage. He's bound to have what you're looking for.'"

"No," said Myrandhal. "I'd taken my precautions too, and the filament was only to be given to the Rajah later. The wretch wanted to play false, and fell into his own trap..."

"The scoundrel!" murmured the Englishman, between his teeth. "He'd told me that the possessed the secret in its entirety. He was lying, the blackguard!"

"It's the biter bit," Madame Myrandhal went on. "I knew that myself, and you can imagine my anxiety as we went up to our apartment. Fortunately, the wallet was there, on the night-stand! It was the first thing I saw when I went in. God was with us! That idea restored all my courage, all my presence of mind. Less than five minutes later, the engine was armed and I went into the psychoscaph.

"I had no trouble finding my way around. All the apparatus I saw there, I knew. I'd seen it already on the *Velox no. 2*; you'd shown me how it worked, and I remembered every last detail. Your voice had engraved a course in mechanics in my memory, in my heart, and I found it when the moment came.

"An immense confidence had invaded me. I was in haste to launch myself on your track, and yet I remained calm and lucid. The consciousness of my responsibility had made another woman of me."

"Yes, Anna," the Eccentric said, approvingly. "You've been marvelous from that moment on. A captain, a true captain, that's what you've been, and there aren't many captains of your caliber in His Majesty's fleet. I know that, by Jove! I'm proud of you, my dear Anna—you're worthy of being an English-woman."

"However," the young woman continued, "I went up on to the walkway in order to give the indispensable instructions to Pastor Burrett. He was the one who had to open the formidable current, when the time came, that would project us into space.

"He listened to me attentively and went to his post beside the engine. Pickman, who was there, whispered a few words into his ear and then came to join me. My worthy guardian was seething with impatience and rambling: 'Well, are we going? I've found a name for our machine that will bring her luck: the *Annabella*. Only, get on with it—it's a matter of catching up with that damned Frenchman. Fortunately, I've had a word with the Reverend, He's going to stoke up the power...'

"That statement didn't strike me at the time, any more than the signs the Baronet was exchanging with Burrett. I was too absorbed—so absorbed that it was only then that I noticed that the mage was with us on the platform. Pickman was still holding him by the throat. 'What are you doing?' I said, nonplussed. 'Let that man go.'

"'No,' he said. 'I need him.'

"'Why? What are you going to do?'

"'Make sure he keeps his word. Who can tell? Perhaps the thin ape could stop everything with a sign at the last moment? So, you understand…once we're off, the current on full, I'll throw him overboard. Too bad if he breaks.'

"'But he'll be killed! I don't want that. Let him go,'

"'No,' said the stubborn old fool. 'Don't worry—I'll let go of the old man in time. Go on. Forward ho!'

"I didn't have time to reply, gripped by a shudder of horror…can you imagine that our worthy Burrett, at that 'Forward ho!' which was doubtless a signal between the two conspirators…"

"Oh!" the Eccentric protested. "Conspirators! You're harsh, Miss Anna…Madame Myrandhal, I mean."

"I stand by the word, my dear Pickman. Your impatience nearly cost us dear. You'd thought it a good idea to give the pastor instructions contrary to mine, and catastrophe was hanging by a thread. One second more and the *Annabella*, instead of launching slowly and progressively, would have departed like a cannonball and we'd have been crushed, broken…"

"No," the Eccentric relied, "you're exaggerating, Anna. I've been imprudent, certainly, but it's Burrett who's a mollusk, a cephalopod. I'd told him to stoke it up, yes, but not to that point. He should have known that a machine that travels a hundred thousand a second doesn't move off like a sixty horse-power, at top speed. That's obvious."

"So be it," the young woman went on. "At any rate, the honest pastor didn't have the slightest idea of the formidable implement he was handling. At Pickman's command he had brought down the trolley and grabbed the wheel in both hands; already he was putting all his weight on it…

"Evidently, he was about to open the current at a stroke, and that was catastrophe, instant death. I uttered such a scream that the pastor stopped dead. He looked at me, saw my distraught face. 'What is it, Milady?' he asked. 'Are you ill?'

"'No…only, you're doing it wrong. This is how we need to proceed…you see this hand that I'm lifting up; I'm going to lower it slowly, and you have to follow the movement with the wheel. It needs to take at least ten seconds. Do you understand?'

"'Yes, Milady.'

"'Go on, then…by the grace of God!'

"'All right!' howled the Baronet, stretching out his arm to let go of the mage.

"We left...we left at a moderate speed at first, but which increased in a frightful fashion. We hurried down into the central compartment, and then there was the void, the starry night.

"I'd put my hands over my ears, ripped by a frightful screech, the horrible whistling that had made me shudder an hour earlier.

"It was the *Annabella*, bidding adieu to the Earth!"

Madame Myrandhal stopped, palpitating, carried away by the memory.

Her husband was breathless. "And then?" he asked. "Go on, my dear Anna..."

"And then, my dear Serge...there is no *and then*. At least, it's very confused. From the departure to the arrival, until the moment when we discovered the canals, it seems to me, as to you, that I've been living a dream.

"I can only remember one thing, about which I'd rather not think: that sinister firmament, that wan sun that seemed to be looking at us, following us in our audacious flight. What a frightful spectacle that implacable sky was...that *atheistic* sky, so to speak! I was really desperate then, and for the first time, I doubted God! I'm still shuddering over it.

"As for the rest—our arrival on Mars, our search up to the moment we found you, I've already told you about that."

"There's one thing," Pickman added then, "that Madame Myrandhal hasn't said and that I want to tell you about myself. It's her courage, her valor during the journey, and especially on arrival, when we finally saw the *Velox*. As soon as we understood that you were still alive, that you were there on the beach...

"It was a matter of getting down as quickly as possible, but where and how? On land or water? Taking a plunge into the water was the safer course, but also the longer. It would have been necessary to close up the *Annabella*, transform her...you'd have had time to die a hundred times in the interim.

"It was then that your wife had an idea of genius. Close by, on the coast, there were shifting dunes, and our captain threw us at them at top speed. The *Annabella* went through the first one like a bullet, traversed the second less rapidly, and came to a stop without any fuss or damage. I wanted to say that...

"And now, my friends, it's time to sleep. It must be late, and I can see Anna's eyes fluttering. What's more, my dear Friday, you need rest, and personally, I'm exhausted. We'll resume tomorrow...you can tell us your story, which I'm dying to hear. Then we'll hold a council to decide what to do next. Now, good night; I'm falling asleep, in truth."

The three castaways immediately made their arrangements for the night. While the young woman lay down on the divan that was the vessel's only couchette, her companions, rolled in blankets, lay down side by side on the floor.

A sonorous snoring soon announced that the Eccentric had departed for the land of dreams.

Anna too, worn out by fatigue, went to sleep almost instantaneously. Then Serge became drowsy in his turn.

IV. The First Excursion

When Serge opened his eyes the next day, it was broad daylight. He propped himself up on his elbow, and almost immediately, a burst of youthful laughter resonated in his ear. It was Annabella, coming back from the kitchen, carrying three silver bowls on a tray, from which an aromatic odor was emerging.

Sitting at the table, Pickman was making sandwiches, which he was piling up methodically in front of him, building an appetizing pyramid.

The Eccentric raised his head.

"Good Morning! *Bonjour!*" he said. "Did you sleep well, sir?"

"Marvelously, thank you. But I'm truly confused. You should have woken me up."

"Why? Sleep is good and you have a right to it."

"Yes," said Anna, setting down the tray. "How is your wound?"

"Couldn't be better. I can't feel it anymore."

"To table, then! What would you prefer, husband? Coffee, chocolate, sandwiches, cold meat?"

"Your husband will take all of them," the Englishman replied. "He needs to get his strength back. Yesterday was hard work, and today will be no less so. So we have a right to double rations."

"I think you're being very prodigal," said the engineer. "It's probably the opposite that we need to be doing."

"What do you mean? Explain, my dear Friday."

"I mean, my dear Robinson, that we ought to eke out our provisions wisely. We don't know when we'll find others, in fact."

"Pshaw! Bah!" the Eccentric expostulated. "It's our first breakfast on this new world—and then, Mars is a big place; we mustn't judge it by what we've seen so far. You seem to think that Mars is a dead, sterile world."

"I never said that. I only think that it might be best to anticipate the worst. One thing is certain, at any rate, and that is that the desert surrounding us extends for a long way. You must have seen that, as I did, when you were flying..."

"That's true," said Anna. "This is a black spot..."

"Bah!" said the Baronet. "We were too high up to judge. We need to take a look at closer range, and explore. Only then will we have an exact idea of the country and its resources. That's what we ought to do first. Do you agree?"

"Entirely."

"Furthermore, there's the sea. One can always find food on the edge of the sea. I'll get my fishing tackle out this evening. By the way, did you know that we were nearly carried away last night?"

"Carried away?" exclaimed Myrandhal. "How? By what?"

"By the sea—or rather, by the tide. We ought to have thought of that."

Serge ran to the porthole. In front of him, the beach was still occupied by the waves, which were seething as they retreated. Nevertheless, thanks to the position of the vessel, the danger identified by the Baronet had only been momentary. In fact, the border of foam and mud left by the sea as it ebbed was still three hundred meters from the submarine.

"That's bizarre!" murmured Serge.

"Isn't it?" said his wife. "I thought that on Mars, given its distance from the sun and the smallness of its moons, the tides would be much less noticeable."

"That should be the case, in fact. There must be another cause."

"What?"

"Jupiter. At least, our colossal neighbor surely has something to do with it. As you know, the enormous planet is quite near to Mars at the moment, and will still be getting closer for a few days.[76] That will cause increasingly powerful tides, and perhaps other, less anodyne phenomena."

"What phenomena?"

"Earthquakes. Already, last night, in my sleep, I felt two or three shocks.

"Me too," said Madame Myrandhal, "and the last was very sensible. At the time, I attributed it to the piles of sand that we're resting in, and didn't attach any importance to it. Do you think there's any danger?"

"Danger...no...not immediately, at least. Nevertheless, it would be a reason not to linger in this locale, which has nothing delightful about it. Then, as I've told you, the volcanic nature of the region worries me. Just now, when I woke up, my first thought was to consult the seismograph, to see whether the shocks were continuing."

"And are they?" the American asked.

"Yes, in a peculiarly characteristic fashion. A series of undulations, all in the same direction."

"From which you conclude?"

"I conclude that we have beneath our feet a considerable quantity of lava, a kind of sea of fire. Take note that the influence of Jupiter will make itself felt on that sea like any other; hence the shocks, which will increase from day to day. When Jupiter reaches its greatest proximity, a formidable tidal wave will occur down there."

"Damn!" muttered the Eccentric. "In other words, we're on top of an overheated pressure-cooker, which might well boil over one of these days. You're sure about that?"

---

[76] There was a conjunction between Mars and Jupiter on 14 August 1908, although the tidal effects of the conjunction would not have been very great, given the distance between the two planets—more than twice as far as the distance between Mars and the sun.

"Yes—and the more I think about it, how else can we explain the abnormal temperature we're enjoying? Given the season and at the latitude where we are, it ought to be frozen already."

"However," Madame Myrandhal put in, "you said just now that there's no immediate danger..."

"I still think so. The dangerous—the critical—moment will be when Jupiter arrives at its shortest distance from us, but we'll be far away by then, I hope."

"When will that eventuality occur?" asked Pickman.

"In a few days time. I don't know exactly...I'll only be able to reply in a precise fashion when I've made the necessary calculations. In any case, a wise precaution to take would be to refloat the *Annabella*."

"Already!" complained Pickman. "So you really think that we ought to leave right away—that it's urgent?"

"The sooner the better. Nevertheless, the day hasn't come yet. Personally, I have an excellent reason not to hurry."

"What reason?"

"The *Velox*."

"You hope to recover the *Velox*?"

"I want to try, at least. It's a project that I mulled over for some time yesterday, before going to sleep. I regret my valiant ship...and what it contains even more: the provisions, the food supplies."

"I understand," said the Baronet. "Still the fear of dying of hunger. What a task, though! If we only knew where it had sunk, into what depths..."

"I do know. Yesterday, on the way here, I was looking at the place. As for the bed, it ought to be quite accessible. In fact, the more I think about it, the more convinced I am that it's a rip in the keel that caused the catastrophe, so the vessel should be caught at present on reefs that aren't very deep. As she went straight down, she should still be there. In consequence, it will be easy to find her."

"I agree. But what will you do then? You don't suppose that you can refloat her?"

"Obviously not. The ship is lost, as I explained; it's the cargo I want to get, at least in part."

"Well. I understand the utility, but how are you going to do it? Do you have a means?"

"Yes. As I told you, the tides will increase in violence. It's probable that the submarine won't resist the thrusts of the sea for long. Once the hull's broken, we'll only have to pick up the flotsam."

"Yes, we'll be our own wreckers."

"That's right. If necessary, we can hurry things along."

"How? I don't see..."

"In the simplest fashion. A stick of dynamite should suffice. You have some, I suppose?"

"Yes," said Pickman. "A full case. I like your idea. One question, though: how are we going to leave here. You don't have the intention of taking the aerial route again, I same?"

"That would be difficult. We don't have what we need for that. The *Annabella* was flying for an entire day, and her psychic accumulators must be exhausted. We'll use her as a boat, therefore. The transformation has been anticipated, and will soon be carried out."

"Well, everything's ready for that. There's a gasoline engine, fuel..."

"How much?"

"A hundred gallons."

"That's about four hundred liters. It's not much, and we won't get far with that meager provision. Oh, if we could only recover the *Velox*'s fifteen hundred liters..."

"Perhaps we will recover them. Then again, we can rig up a sail if necessary."

"That's true, but I hope for better. On Mars, as on Earth—more so than on Earth, given the disposition of the oceans—there are numerous marine currents. It will doubtless be easy to discover one that heads in the direction we want to go. But we're wasting time talking. It's better to do something. We'll talk about all this again this evening, when we've explored the surroundings. Perhaps that reconnaissance will turn up something new. That's why, if Anna isn't too tired..."

"Not at all. On the contrary, I'm in haste to get going. I've just loaded my Kodak. So, whenever you wish, gentlemen, I'll be delighted to stretch my legs."

"Me too," said Pickman, "but not so fast! You're forgetting, sir, that you owe us a story, that it's your turn. We're eager, Anna and I, to know how that rascal of a Rajah caught you, in order to send you away—and then your arrival here, your shipwreck. You can tell us while emptying a glass of whisky. We'll leave afterwards."

Myrandhal complied with a good grace.

"Prodigious!" exclaimed the Englishman, when he had finished. "That Geyser-Volcano is a prodigious, astonishing thing. We heard it, but didn't see it. What a marvel, and how lucky you were. I would have liked to be in your place when you were dancing up there, at the summit. Do you think the prodigy will reappear?"

"Undoubtedly. When we were no our way here, we could see the deep-originated waves—indubitable proof that the volcano is still active."

"I don't care about the volcano—I've seen one of those. It's the geyser that interests me. It'll come back, you say—but when, do you think?"

"It's difficult to be precise. It's necessary to allow time for the reservoir that aliments it to fill up again..."

"Yes, I understand. It's doubtless a matter of the phenomenon known as 'communicating vessels'."

"Probably, although there's no proof. The propulsive force might be quite different. Nevertheless, if we assume that it's simply a matter of a difference in level..."

"Let's assume so. In that case, the reservoir, as you call it, is placed high above sea level."

"Evidently."

"In consequence, Mars isn't a flat world, as you claimed a while ago. There are mountains, and I'll have an opportunity to climb. There's one more thing that's necessary to consider before we set out. All three of us are going, you say—is that prudent? Wouldn't it be better for one of us to stay to guard the ship. I'll offer, if..."

"Guard the ship?" the engineer interjected, nonplussed. "Against whom?"

"Against thieves."

"What thieves? What do you mean, my dear Robinson? You're joking..."

"I've never been more serious. You seem to believe that we're alone here, but are you sure? Are you sure that there aren't any inhabitants in the vicinity, any Martians?"

"Martians!" exclaimed the American. "Where do you get that from? We've been here for twenty-four hours, and we haven't seen the shadow of one. Anyway, it's sufficient to look around: not the slightest trace of inhabitants or habitations."

"That's not proof."

"It seems to me that it is."

"And I say that it's not. You're reasoning as if we were on Earth, my dear Anna. Simply consider that you know nothing about the Martians, their nature, their mores. Perhaps they're nocturnal beings, some sort of vampires, which sleep underground by day, and only come out after dark. In fact, last night, I saw..."

"You saw Martians?" exclaimed the American incredulously.

"No, not exactly, but I saw signs that they made...well, signals."

"Signals!"

"Yes. I went out to answer a call of nature, and as I was coming back, I perceived a glimmer over the sea...oh, very small, like the flame of a match. It happened so quickly that I thought it was an illusion, or some kind of phosphorescent fish, as exist on Earth. I wouldn't have attached any importance to it if a similar gleam hadn't appeared at the same moment over there, on the lava. That one blinked twice, as if it were replying to the other. One might have thought it was an optical telegraph. That's proof—or a strong probability, at least. Don't you agree, sir?"

Myrandhal reflected. "No," he said, after a few seconds. "I thought the same, at first, but the hypothesis doesn't stand up to examination. In fact, why would Martians—if there are any Martians—who have any facility of communication, use that complicated means? It would be necessary to believe that they're impeded. Now, I can't see how, or by what."

"Even so," the Englishman objected, "those flames really did seem to be communicating."

"It's a coincidence. As for the flames themselves, as you thought at first, it's evidently a matter of a natural phenomenon: phosphorescence, spontaneous combustion of an inflammable gas on contact with the atmosphere—how do I know? You don't seem to be convinced."

"No. Scientists have an answer for everything, but I have my own ideas. Then again, there's Stop, who knows more than any of us, and who agrees with me."

"What makes you think that?" asked the young woman.

"Lots of things—and if you knew him as I do, you'd think the same. Stop has a way of sniffing the ground at intervals, growling, and then looking at me in a significant way. He's scented an enemy, I'd swear, and when he looks at me, do you know what I read in his eyes?"

"No."

"I read: *Beware! There's an enemy out there: Martians.*"

"That's implausible, inadmissible," replied Madame Myrandhal. "Why would they be hiding? It would be necessary to suppose that we intimidate them greatly—proof, at any rare, that they're not very redoubtable. First of all, where are they hiding? The country is as bare as my hand. Unless they live in the water like fish, or in the air like birds. But those—the flying men, that is—we'd be able to see passing overhead, soaring in the sky..."

"You're forgetting one thing: under the ground. Perhaps the Martians live underground. An English astronomer claims that on certain cold worlds, like Mars, the inhabitants live underground, like Siberian bears during the winter. Anyway, what's the point in arguing about it? The best thing is to go and see. Stop has a marvelous nose; I'll take you to where I saw the light, and get him to sniff the holes and fissures we encounter; if he doesn't find anything, I'll agree that I was wrong."

The Eccentric stood up. "And now, let's go. I'll get my equipment."

"You're going with us," observed the young woman, not without malice. "So you don't believe in Martians as much as all that?"

"Yes, by Jove. Except that, on due consideration, I don't think the thieves would take the risk in broad daylight. Besides which, the *Annabella*'s visible from a long way off; it'll be sufficient not to lose sight of her.

"At any rate, I'll bring a carbine and cartridges with explosive bullets—and you ought to do the same, my dear Friday, or at least take a hunting rifle. If any game appears within range, you'll easily be able to pot it."

"Indeed—but I doubt that I'll have that agreeable surprise. It seems to me that the region is absolutely deserted, and I'm sure in advance not only of returning empty-handed, but of not even having had an opportunity to fire a shot."

After that, the three castaways discussed the itinerary of their first excursion on Mars.

"To begin with," Pickman proposed, "we'll beat the surroundings. If we don't see anything suspect, we can chance going a little further, perhaps even not coming back until nightfall. In that case, we'll have lunch out there, when we rest. That's why I've made so many sandwiches."

Madame Myrandhal had retired momentarily to the forward compartment, in order to change her clothes.

Once they were equipped, with their knapsacks on their backs and their rifles slung over their shoulders, Serge and Pickman emerged from the submarine. The American joined them soon afterwards. With her felt hat, ornamented with a cockerel's plume, her bicycle shorts and her Kodak attached to her left hip, along with a small keg containing food-supplies, she looked both martial and mettlesome. The engineer was advancing to compliment her when she suddenly burst out laughing at the sight of her guardian, who had put on what he called "full kit": leggings, short trousers and a khaki jacket, with an enormous knapsack, to which an ice-ax and two coils of rope were attacked.

"Ropes!" she said. "What are you expecting to do with ropes and that ice-ax? One might think that you were getting ready to climb Mont Blanc."

"You're a little fool, Anna," the Englishman replied. "An ice-ax is always useful, if only to test the ground. Ditto the ropes. We might encounter crevasses, or precipices. Besides, your husband is almost as heavily laden."

"It might all prove useful," said Serge, smiling.

"As you please, after all," the young woman continued. "When you're too tired, you'll only have to put your bags down on the ground."

"Enough chat! Let's get going."

"Not before I've taken a photograph. Stand over there, both of you, under the platform. Take Stop with you. That's right. Now, don't move!"

Then the American posed in her turn.

"Those," she said, when it was done, "are photographs for which our friend and sponsor Norton Bennett will pay dear. By the way, we still haven't had a reply from the *Herald*. I fear that our dispatch hasn't reached its destination."

"That's probable," he engineer replied. "As soon as we have time, therefore, I'll try to improve our telepath."

"Let's go!" said the Eccentric, becoming impatient. "I have ants in my feet, and so has Milady."

"Milady?" queried Serge.

"Yes," said the Englishman, displaying his alpenstock. "Lady Pickman. Remember what I told you in New York. Milady is my cane. She's getting impatient too. She's fidgeting—as fretful as a sorcerer's magic wand—and that's an indication. She's sniffed something. I'm telling you the truth: there's an enemy lurking nearby."

Meanwhile, the excursionists had already set off over the plain of lava that extended behind the *Annabella*. The dog ran back and forth around them, making furious bounds.

"You see," said the American, eventually. "Stop isn't showing the slightest sign of anxiety. In consequence, there's no one here—no Martians!"

"That's not proof," Pickman replied. "I agree, however, that there's no danger for the moment. The Martians who were prowling around here yesterday must have gone. Thus, we can venture further. It remains to decide which way. I can't see any reason for turning right rather than left."

"My opinion," said the engineer, "is that we should continue westwards. The terrain slopes upwards slightly in that direction, so we're sure of not losing sight of the ship."

"All right," said the Eccentric—and the excursion continued, without incident.

Madame Myrandhal's Martian watch, set at the moment when the sun passed the meridian, marked two o'clock when the castaways stopped for lunch.

Almost without perceiving it, so gently did the terrain slope, they had reached a kind of ridge, from which the view extended a long way into the distance. For a few moments, they contemplated the immense plain of lava that extended all the way to the horizon.

"Still the same thing," Serge murmured. "The proof is there; there's nothing to be obtained from this desert, and the sooner we leave it, the better."

The Eccentric shook his head in a melancholy fashion. "Yes," he said. "I'm beginning to believe so myself—but I'm not giving up yet. We might be able to get something out of the sea. I propose that we investigate that tomorrow. I'm a great fisherman, you know, and I have everything necessary aboard: lines, nets, etc. I'll go on campaign tomorrow. If I'm lucky enough to catch a fish, that will give us some encouragement, and permit us to vary or menu."

"Oh, I doubt that there are any fish," the engineer replied. "Not here, at least. They must stay away from the shore—far from the geyser, whose hot water, saturated with more or less toxic gases, would scarcely suit them. It's necessary, in consequence, to be able to fish in the open sea, and I don't know how you're going to manage that."

"It's easy," the Baronet replied. "I've anticipated the circumstance; I think of everything. We have a rubber dinghy; it only has to be set up. I'll do that this evening."

While conversing, the excursionists had set out their meal on a block of lava. After lunch, they spent a further hour "prospecting" in the vicinity; then, as the sky was clouding over, they decided to go back.

Although the sun was low on the horizon the heat had become oppressive. Large black clouds were accumulating in the west. Gradually, the wind rose, lifting up clouds of dust and sand. From time to time there was a rumble, like that of distant thunder.

"There's no doubt about it," said the Eccentric. "It's a storm—a squall, as mariners say. What fools those astronomers are! I've heard one of them affirm that it hardly ever rains on Mars. I won't complain, though; it will settle this dust, which is rather tiresome."

The little troop contained to advance. It was about a quarter of a mile from the *Annabella* when the dog, which had been frolicking joyfully until then, suddenly changed his attitude. He went back and forth with his nose to the ground, sniffing the lava and growling dully.

At one point he stopped, uttered a brief bark and started scratching furiously. His behavior was so characteristic that Serge and his wife were impressed. As for the Eccentric, he was exultant.

"Well," he demanded, "are you convinced now? It's obvious...this is the very spot where I saw the light shining. It's impossible to doubt it: there were indigenes here last night, and they'll probably come back tonight, to spy..."

"Are you sure?" asked the American.

"Yes," said Pickman. "So sure that I'm going to stay on watch myself. There's an excellent observation post near the boat: the obelisk. I'm going to climb up it. It won't take me long to discover what these bipeds look like."

"But there's no proof that it's a matter of bipeds," Madame Myrandhal replied. "The way that Stop is scratching the soil is suggestive of something else. In my opinion, he's simply detected some bizarre animal lurking underground— a mole or a mouse..."

"A mole!" the Englishman muttered. "As if Stop doesn't know what a mole is—and as if I could make a mistake about his manner of expression! But there's no point arguing. Let's see what happens. This is no weather for talking—I have a mouth full of gravel. What a filthy country! It's definitely a storm—more than a storm, a cyclone—that's coming. What a wind! One might think it were the simoom!"

Indeed, the violence of the wind was increasing by the second. Clouds of sand and dust were swirling everywhere, making the march increasingly difficult.

The sea, which was beginning to get choppy, took on livid tints in the red light of the dusk. The storm was gathering rapidly, and the darkness was soon complete. The thunder was getting closer, but flashes of lightning were still sparse. The fuliginous darkness of the sky seemed to brighten somewhat, however, toward the pole. There, an orange gleam with red fringes was gradually growing.

"What does that presage?" the Englishman asked Myrandhal.

"I don't know. The light is reminiscent of certain magnetic phenomena. Perhaps it's simply a kind of aurora borealis."

"I thought, myself, about an earthquake."

"That was my first idea too, and anything's possible. What astonishes me is that the ground isn't even trembling. It's true that there are sometimes deceptive calms just before..."

The engineer was still speaking when the Eccentric, who was marching on the right and slightly ahead, suddenly turned round, gesticulating.

"A cyclone! Lie down..."

At the same time, an explosion resounded, illuminating the sky all the way to the zenith, and knocking the three voyagers flat on the ground.

Around them, everything shook, and there was a terrible din. One might have thought that the carcass of the planet was disintegrating.

It went on for a few seconds, and then stopped. The whirlwind had passed over.

The excursionists were already getting to their feet, astonished to have got away with a fright.

"It's over," said the engineer. "I mentioned a pressure-cooker this morning—it's just boiled over. Look..."

Ahead of them, a few miles to the north, a hill had just surged forth, surmounted by a red plume.

"A volcano!" exclaimed Madame Myrandhal. "We can see the lava flowing. As long as it doesn't get this far..."

"Don't worry," said Serge, swiftly. "Major eruptions start differently, and this one's already calmed down. Look—the plume is falling back. As for the lava, see how it's changing color and slowing down. Tomorrow, that volcano, sprouted as suddenly as a mushroom, will be cold, and we'll be able to climb up it, as one can climb Mount Vesuvius."

"By Jove!" cried Pickman, enthusiastically. "That would be a fine ascent! So you think, sir, that there's no more danger?"

"No. Fortunately, the pressure-cooker had safety-valves, and one of those that has just come into play, that's all. The danger has passed, in consequence—and for proof, look at your dog. So turbulent a little while ago, he's observed that it's calm now. Thanks to his instinct, he divined the phenomenon long before us."

"Hmm!" grunted the Eccentric. "There's something else."

"You're sticking to your Martians?"

"Yes. Stop couldn't be mistaken about that. If he barked for a man, it's because there are men here—well, Martians. Let's just wait and see!"

V. The "Red Men"

"By Jove!" said Pickman, feeling the lava. "The ground's still hot. Are you sure that there's no danger? That the volcano is really extinct? It's not for our benefit that I'm asking, but for Anna..."

312

"Utterly extinct," Myrandhal replied. "The fumaroles that always precede eruptions disappeared several hours ago—but that doesn't mean that there's no danger climbing up there. The ascent, over those fractured, collapsed rocks, needs to be carried out prudently."

"Good—that's familiar. I've climbed much harder. I'll get over."

The castaways, having set out at dawn, had arrived at the foot of the Norton Bennett, as they had baptized the miniature volcano that had surged forth a few hours earlier.

"Before anything else," the engineer continued, "We're going to make a tour of the cone, as much to get an idea of the whole as to identify the most accessible slope."

They set off again, and when they were on the far side of the peak Serge took advantage of the shadow projected by the volcano to measure its height.

"What is it?" demanded the Eccentric, who had taken out his notebook in order to record the altitude of the mountain on which he was about to accomplish his first Martian ascent.

"Three hundred and a few meters."

"That makes nine hundred feet in English measurements. It's a good size for a new-born mountain."

"Indeed!" exclaimed the American, laughing. "If it continues to grow at that rate, more than a hundred fathoms every twenty-four hours, it'll be a fine mountain, capable of surpassing the famous Gaurisankar. I hope, my guardian, that you're happy now and won't make any more difficulties about telling us what you saw last night. I'm eager to know what it was. What little you have said has excited my curiosity to the highest degree."

The Baronet shook his head.

"There's no urgency. It would start endless arguments. Better to act. I won't talk until we've explored the volcano. I have a suspicion that we'll discover things here that will support what I say."

"Does that mean that it was on Norton Bennett that you saw Martians? For you have seen some?"

"Perhaps. I'll tell you later."

"In that case," the American said, teasingly, "these people live in fire. Who knows? Perhaps they came out of the crater. They're no longer humans but salamanders."

"Yes, salamanders," muttered the Englishman, sulkily. "Let's climb first; we'll argue later. This isn't the time for joking. Just follow me."

"I'll be quiet. But how susceptible you are this morning, my dear guardian! It's easy to see that you slept badly."

In fact, the Eccentric had slept with one eye open that night. Several times, he had got up and made a tour of the boat's surroundings, taking Stop with him. At dawn, when his companions woke up, the Baronet had already been up for

313

two hours. His attitude was simultaneously delighted and anxious, but he refused to explain himself.

"You'll see," he contented himself with saying, "that Stop and I were right. Either I'm nothing but an old fool, or the day won't go by without our having news of the Martians."

The Englishman's confidence and his mysterious expressions intrigued Madame Myrandhal increasingly, but it was in vain that she tried to discover more.

Meanwhile, the little troop led by Pickman, after having followed the base of the volcano for about a quarter of a mile, discovered a fairly easy path. There was a heap of fallen rocks forming a kind of gigantic stairway, which they immediately set about climbing.

The Eccentric marched at the head, testing the ground with his alpenstock, sometimes turning aside to examine the rock. He seemed to be searching for something, but he did not say what. He was heard muttering from time to time, like a disappointed man.

Half an hour later the excursionists arrived, without any hitch, at the summit of Norton Bennett. It was an almost circular plateau measuring about a hundred meters in diameter and bristling with enormous blocks of quartz and granite, still warm.

In the middle was the chimney, a partly-obstructed excavation, from which a stream of lava the width of an arm was slowly trickling.

"You see," said Myrandhal. "The volcano is in the process of gently becoming extinct. All danger from that direction has vanished, for the moment."

"You don't think it will wake up again?" the Baronet asked.

"Not soon, at any rate. We have several days before us, of which we'll take advantage by going away. This new excursion confirms the opinion I'd already formed: the sooner we leave, the better."

"What about you, my guardian?" said the American. "You're not saying anything. You have a serious communication to make to us, though—remember?"

The Eccentric had lost the serene confidence he had had a little while ago. "Yes," he said, nodding his head. "But I haven't found what I was looking for—the traces…you're going to mock me again, and yet, there were people here last night."

"People!" exclaimed Serge and his wife.

"Yes. Stop saw them too. We ought to have brought him; perhaps he would have found something."

"You're the one who wanted to leave him to guard the lodgings."

"That's true," said the Eccentric, increasingly discountenanced. "You're definitely going to think that I'm going senile…"

314

"Not at all," the engineer replied, wanting to put the Englishman at his ease. "On the contrary, I understand your disappointment. After all, there might well be Martians in the vicinity…doubtless some nomadic family."

"Why are they hiding?" asked the American, swiftly. "That's what it's necessary to explain. Do we frighten them?"

"Perhaps," the engineer replied. "The arrival of the psychoscaphs must have struck their imagination. They might be afraid of men coming from the sky, which is easily explicable on the part of primitive, uncultured, semi-savage individuals, like the land they inhabit. They might have taken advantage of the darkness to come and take a closer look at the *Annabella*."

"In consequence," Madame Myrandhal continued, "you're admitting our friend Pickman's thesis. You believe that Martians appeared here last night? What the devil were they doing? Don't you think that it was more probably an animal of human appearance—some anthropoid?"

"No—climbing the volcano is a reasoned action. Animals guided only by their instinct would only have thought of running away."

"That's what I told myself," murmured the Englishman. "Only the thing is so extraordinary and incredible that I'm now beginning to doubt what I saw…"

"You don't say. One might think, my dear guardian, that you're taking pleasure in keeping us in suspense."

"No, believe me—but it was so improbable that I preferred to wait. I thought we were going to find Martians here, and that they'd introduce themselves. Since they haven't, and it's what you want, I'll talk…

"It happened last night, when my watch marked one o'clock. I woke up in response to a dull growl from Stop…"

"We didn't hear anything."

"It didn't last long. I was sleeping with one eye open—like a gendarme, as you put it—and as soon as he heard me move, Stop shut up. He knows his business as a guard dog, and that there are times when it's necessary not to bark—necessary not to alert the prowlers who are approaching…

"I picked up my revolver and went out. One on the walkway I looked around, and didn't see anything suspicious. The moon—the smaller of the two—was shining between the clouds, enough to see for about a hundred meters, and besides, it's difficult to hide on that bare ground.

"Stop was trying to drag me toward the obelisk. I followed him, thinking that I might find something behind it. There was nothing there, but I discovered what was troubling him. It was the volcano in the distance. When I looked in that direction, he twitched his ears in the way he has, and I understood that he was saying: *yes, that's it*—but I still couldn't see anything.

"After a few minutes though. I saw a bizarre individual emerge from behind a rock near the summit, then another, and then a third. They were little men with enormous heads and straight limbs. Thickset dwarfs of a sort: red, or, rather, the color of brick…"

"But how could you make them out at that distance?" the engineer interjected. "Were they carrying torches?"

"No," said the Eccentric. "That's where it gets complicated. It was pitch dark here, and the red men weren't carrying any kind of torches, and yet I could see them! I could see them because the dwarfs were, well, luminous...there's no other explanation! Just luminous enough to stand out against the dark background.

"Remember how a firebrand that's about to go out, still shines sufficiently for one to make it out. It was exactly like that. At first, I wondered where that fantastic light could be coming from..."

"From the volcano," said the engineer. "Doubtless the reflection of a stream of lava."

"I thought so too, at first, but no; there was no doubt about it, the little men were luminous themselves—yes, phosphorescent. Sometimes, one of them gave off a brighter gleam, a flash—something akin to what I'd seen the previous night. Meanwhile, there were now five of the red men. They seemed to be consulting one another, holding a discussion. In the end, one of them climbed on to a rock and looked in my direction, toward the sea."

"What did it look like?" asked the American, increasingly interested. "Did you see its face?"

"No. Impossible at that distance."

"Could it see you?"

"No...at least, I don't think so. Stop and I were in the shadow projected by the obelisk—but it must have seen the *Annabella*, which was fully lit by the moon at that moment. So far as I could understand by its gestures, that as what alarmed it. It soon went back to its companions, and they began to go back down. When they got half way, they stopped in front of some kind of grotto, and suddenly, I couldn't see them anymore. It was as if they'd put out their lights—switched themselves off, as it were.

"What do you think of that, my dear Friday?"

The engineer, who was afraid of offending the narrator, hesitated momentarily.

"I don't think anything yet," he said. "It's necessary to verify certain things. Can you find this grotto again?"

"I understand. You think I've gone crazy. I'd think so too, in your place. As for the grotto, yes, I made a mental note of the spot and went straight to it just now, but nothing—the cavern has vanished. That's what's fantastic. Another mystery!"

"No," said Serge. "Your imagination's panicking. Nothing extraordinary about that. A landslide, such as must be occurring all the time on this crumbling slope, might have blocked the cave. When we go down again, we'll all look for it.

The Englishman had a constrained smile. "You don't think I'm completely mad, then?" he murmured. In a louder voice, he continued: "Personally, I never doubted for a minute that they went underground, into the grotto, and I sometimes wonder whether it might have been them who blocked the opening by rolling a rock over it."

"Anything's possible."

"Yes...just s it's possible that I've been duped by an illusion, a phantasmagoria. This morning, I hoped to find traces of the red devils—that's why I preferred to wait before speaking, and now I'm hesitant...

"Last night, at the moment when they went back underground, I didn't have the slightest doubt about it. There are still moments when it all seems true. I remember the way in which Stop, moving ahead, looked through the ground, his eyes shining as if he could see men moving beneath it...

"After all, why not? Perhaps there's nothing on Mars, no race of inhabitants or civilization, because all that's in the interior. An English scientist claims that that's the case on some planets, and his opinion seems to be confirmed here. I said to myself that it must be hot there, under Norton Bennett, but that was reasoning by Earthly standards. The Martians might be a different species, different in nature from us—incombustible, something like salamanders...

"Then I recalled the theories of one of my friends, who believes in metempsychosis, the plurality of worlds and so on. According to him, humans don't invent, they remember. So, still in accordance with our philosophy, all the beings in tales and legends—genies, fairies, monsters—existed on some other planet.

"In fact, my red men bear a strong resemblance to certain blacksmith-dwarfs, the gnomes and kobolds who are both the spirits of mines and the guardians of subterranean treasures. So much so that if we were to see one of those fellows emerge from the ground right now, and invite us to visit his palace, it would seem quite natural to me...

"You might think that's absurd, and so do I...perhaps I saw all that in a dream. That's possible too.

"After that, once the dwarfs had disappeared, as I didn't want to go back to sleep, I sat down on the bridge, with the dog beside me, and I dozed off momentarily...let's say that I was dreaming...and yet...but it's better to talk about something else. That's what I'm beginning to think. It's suggestion, in fact! There's only one means of fighting it, and that's to think about other things, and there's no lack of those at present.

"Now I think about it, I remember that I was going to inflate the dinghy and take a trip. It's necessary, then, not to waste any more time. I think we'd better go."

Pickman, who had never made such a long speech, ran out of breath and stopped, surprised by the attention that he was being accorded.

"Well," he added "you're not saying anything. When are we leaving?"

"Right away, if you like. Nothing is keeping us here."

"Just a minute," said Pickman, opening the knapsack he had deposited at his feet. "I have something to do first, which I never miss..." almost immediately afterwards, he added: "God damn it! I've forgotten my red pot."

"You're red pot?"

"Well, my pot of red paint—you know, the vermilion, with which to write my name and the date on the rock."

"It doesn't matter," said Anna. "You can come back later."

"No," the globetrotter grumbled, "it's not the same. The inscription needs to be made now, or never. That no longer works the charm. For want of paint—of ink, so to speak—one can try to engrave, but I don't have any tools, and this rock is as hard as metal."

While the Englishman was lamenting, Serge whispered something in his wife's ear. She smiled.

"My dear guardian," she said, "come this way. Just now I saw a soft rock that will suit your purpose perfectly."

As soon as they had gone, Serge went to the place where the stream of lava was emerging. There was a layer of clay nearby, still moist. He hollowed out grooves in it, forming crude letters. Then, with the tip of his cane, he caused lava to flow into the improvised moulds.

Shortly thereafter, the Eccentric came back, brandishing his broken ice-ax. The American was following him.

"You call that soft rock!" he complained. "You have the audacity! I broke my implement at the first stroke."

Suddenly, he stopped, amazed. At his feet, in the sand, an inscription was outlined in letters of fire:

PICKMAN
August 1908

"Prodigious!" he exclaimed. "Fantastic! Who did that?"

Madame Myrandhal was laughing covertly. "It's the red men," she replied, "the kobolds. They know your name and they've written it there, with lava."

The Eccentric's face had contracted. "You're being ridiculous," he said. "You shouldn't joke about such things. I shan't say anything from now on. I'm going back."

And the Englishman turned on his heel. He really seemed to be in a bad mood, and his ward, regretting her innocent joke, tried in vain to strike up the conversation again.

Serge, who strove to appease him, had no more success.

The descent continued in silence.

Suddenly, the engineer, who was bringing up the rear, uttered a cry of joy.

"The grotto! I've found your grotto, my dear Pickman—come and see!"

The Englishman's physiognomy was suddenly transformed. He came running. "I knew it..." he murmured.

"Well," Serge said to him, "do you recognize it? This opening corresponds quite well to the description you gave. You mentioned a narrow passage, a kind of fissure between two blocks of lava. Is this it?"

The Eccentric hesitated. "Perhaps," he said, eventually. "I don't recognize the entrance, exactly, but it was certainly hereabouts—I mean, on this slope and at this height—that the Red Men suddenly disappeared."

"That's sufficient," said Serge. "On this shifting ground everything is modified from one minute to the next. Then again, the tunnel might have several exits. We're going in—I've got a candle."

"A candle!" said the Eccentric, disdainfully. "I've got something better than that." He had already unbuckled his knapsack and taken out a small acetylene lamp, which he lit immediately. "In addition," he went on, "I have magnesium wire in my pocket, and you know how brightly that burns. One can take photographs with it. You can get your apparatus ready, my dear Anna. You'll have pictures to take—beautiful pictures—for the *Herald*."

The Englishman was visibly delighted by the turn that events had taken, no longer giving any thought to the young woman's mockery. Before going into the grotto, he turned to the engineer.

"Let's understand one another," he said. "I'll go first. You take care of your wife. You have your revolver—keep it in your hand."

"Why?" asked Serge, surprised. "Against whom? You're still thinking about last night's Martians, the Red Men?"

"About them—but there are other perils to anticipate: gulfs, shafts opening unexpectedly, labyrinths where there's a risk of getting lost..." The Eccentric lowered his voice. "As for the red devils, listen, sir...either I'm an old fool, or they really exist, and if they do, I have to find them...even if I have to go looking for them in the depths of Hell!"

Pickman's eyes were shining with fever. "One more recommendation," he whispered. "If, by chance, I get too far ahead and you don't see me reappear, don't wait for me. Leave—that would be better. I'll make my own way back, if I come back at all...now, let's go."

The grotto into which our heroes slid was a tunnel offering a complicated series of chambers of various sizes, with galleries and corridors intersecting it from every direction.

"It's a veritable labyrinth," said the Baronet. "A warren for elephants."

They spent nearly an hour exploring the principal ramifications. After that lapse of time, the engineer proposed that they go back.

"You can see," he said to the Baronet, "That the cave has nothing special to offer, and it's beginning to get terribly hot under these low vaults. We could do with a change of air."

"Go," said the Eccentric. "Me, I'm staying. There's obviously another exit; I want to find it. I've just discovered a new corridor that extends for a long way. I want to know where it leads, and I shall, God damn it!"

"Be careful," Myrandhal replied. "You could easily go astray in this maze."

"I'm used to it," retorted the globetrotter. "It's not the first cave I've visited. And the danger isn't what you think—so let me go, and go back. I'll come back in my own time."

"You know very well that we won't go back without you."

"You'll have to—you don't have any more candles."

"So we'll wait for you at the entrance."

"That's all right—go and breathe. I won't be long. One last corridor to explore, and I'll rejoin you."

Serge ad his wife did as they were advised, and were soon outside.

"You see," said the American. "It's an obsession, a mania. My guardian doesn't dare talk about the Red Men any more, but he's thinking about them more than ever. It's them that he's searching for. What do you think of it all?"

The engineer made an evasive gesture. "What do you expect me to think? Your guardian was probably dreaming, but let's allow him to pursue his investigation. It's the best way of convincing him—him and us..."

A quarter of an hour went by. From time to time, Myrandhal or his wife called out to Pickman, who replied, from a distance "I'm coming—just a minute!" His voice, however, seemed to be drawing further away, going further underground—to such an extent that the young couple began to get seriously worried.

They still had a few magnesium filaments, which Pickman given to Anna in order that she could take photographs. They lit one, and went into the tunnel again.

They had gone through the first chambers and were about to venture further when a man appeared from a corridor, taking long strides. It was Pickman; his hair was standing on end, his cheeks were paler and his eyes were haggard.

The sight of his companions pulled him round. He blushed deeply, and in a surly voice, like a man furious to be caught running away, he complained: "What are you doing here? Where are you going?"

"We're looking for you," Serge replied.

"You're hurt!" the young woman cried. She had just noticed a trickle of blood running down her guardian's head.

The Eccentric shrugged his shoulders. "It's nothing," he said. "A graze, sustained when I fell."

"You fell?"

"Yes. I tripped. But my lantern went out, and I was suddenly frightened. Suggestion again...

"It seemed to me that someone was moving around me, whispering. I even felt something soft and sticky slide between my legs, but it was only mud. I saw that when I relit my lantern.

"Then, as I'd lost my matches in the tumble and my reflector wasn't working very well—it had got damaged when I fell—I came back...that's all." He forced a laugh. "Nothing serious, as you can see. What upsets me is that I became as nervous as an old woman. It's ridiculous...if you want to please me, you won't mention this ridiculous incident again—it's stupid, in truth."

The young people thought, rightly or wrongly, that Pickman was hiding something, but they feared offending him by probing, so they set off for home.

Throughout the journey, the Eccentric scarcely unclenched his teeth. He was furious about the frustration of his search, and especially a having been seen in a sorry state, seemingly running away, by those to whom he had boasted that he would go into the depths of Hell.

He remained taciturn all day, and busied himself preparing the dinghy and the fishing-tackle that he intended to try out the following morning.

A surprise awaited the castaways that day, however.

It was about ten o'clock. Serge and Pickman were smoking in the central compartment, while talking about the projected fishing trip.

"A little while longer," aid the engineer, "and as soon as the tide has gone out, we'll embark. You must have noticed that the tide, as I predicted, is getting higher every day. This morning the waves were less than two hundred meters from the submarine. A few more days and the *Annabella* will be refloated; we'll only have to raise anchor, and set off on a tour of Mars."

"With pleasure," murmured the Baronet. "This country pleases me less and less, to be sure.

At that moment, Madame Myrandhal, who was going past one of the portholes, uttered an exclamation of surprise, almost of fright.

She ran to the porthole, opened it briskly and pointed toward the retreating sea. "Oh!" she cried. "A monster! A shark!"

"Where?" demanded her companions, immediately rushing to join her.

"There...look! It's coming up again. There it is!"

"Yes!" Pickman howled. "I see it! It's a whale! It's going to run aground."

In the distance, a spindle-shaped mass, white with foam, was moving back and forth amid the waves. Suddenly, a hump appeared, with a hatch standing up like an open valve...

"A conning-tower!" cried Serge. "It's the *Velox*! The sea's returning her!"

Mad with joy, he launched himself toward the wreck.

VI. The Wreck

Anna and Pickman followed the engineer.

While they were crossing the distance separating them from the wreck, still running, the tide completed its retreat. When they arrived, the *Velox* was lying on her keel, buried about a foot deep in the wet sand.

Serge launched himself on to the walkway and tried to open the door.

"Blocked!" he shouted. "The submarine is full of water. We need to empty it first. That's the most urgent thing."

He got down, and the three of them discussed means of emptying the hull.

"I have a pump," the Eccentric began. "We can get it out..."

"It would take too long," Annabella interjected. "It would be much simpler to tip the *Velox* over, and let it empty by itself through the conning-tower..."

"Quite a task!" said Pickman. "Turning the *Velox* upside-down...we'd need fifty horses to haul her. There's a quicker way, and that's simply to bleed the *Velox*. I have the necessary tools; I'll drill a hole through the sheet metal, low down, and it'll run out of its own accord..."

"You've got it!" cried the engineer. "That's it!"

"You approve?"

"Entirely. Except that there's no need to inflict a new wound on my poor *Velox*. She has one already."

"I can't see it."

"That's because the boat's upright. The compressed sand is forming a plug and blocking the water's path. Hang on...can you see those trickles of water, there, toward the middle of the keel. That's the breach. I assume that it's the issue of the ballast-tank that gave way. A few blows of a pick-ax, and it will come flooding out..."

"All right!" cried Pickman. "I have the tools we need back home. Follow me!"

Then minutes later, the friends came back, each carrying a different implement. Serge was dragging a jack, and Pickman had a ditch-digger's complete outfit—picks, levers, spades etc. As for Anna, who fully intended to pitch in, she was pushing a small folding wheelbarrow made of sheet aluminum, in order to transport sand if the need arose.

"Before we do anything else," Serge said, "it's necessary to stabilize the boat. The *Velox* is leaning toward the sea, and the emptying will unbalance her. This isn't the time to let her fall over..."

The jack was set in place and the two men began digging the vessel out. Working in the loose ground, it only took ten minutes to expose a gash beneath the keel. Already, the water filtering through the sand was beginning to flow more abundantly. The stream was visibly increasing.

"Look out!" cried Serge, leaping out of the trench.

Pickman had followed his example. "What is it?" he asked. "The vessel hasn't budged. I thought..."

"No—but the *Velox* might empty in a sudden rush. I don't want to be underneath that shower."

"My dear Friday," the Englishman jeered, "I can see that you're afraid of getting wet."

"It's not a matter of getting wet. We have nearly fifty tons of water overhead. If that liquid mass came down on your head, it would be very inconvenient, Better to wait. The operation will proceed on its own. In the meantime, I'll go fetch a lantern; we'll need one to go into the hold."

Serge went back to the *Annabella*, but he was only twiddling his thumbs when the Eccentric leapt into the ditch and disappeared under the hull.

"Be careful!" shouted Anna. "Watch out for the shower!"

"You're a chicken," the Englishman replied, jovially. "A damp chicken, like that froggy." And he continued to dig.

The stream became a torrent. Suddenly, a cataract sprang from the breached hull, hollowing out the sand, at the Eccentric was swept away, dragged ten feet by the surge.

Frightened, Madame Myrandhal ran forward, shouting: "Help!"

Already, though, the flood was spreading out, and Pickman stood up in the middle of a pool, thoroughly soaked, yellow with mud and streaming like a triton.

"Shut up, little girl," he said. "It's nothing. A bath, that's all. A muddy bath, but bah! I've had many others."

His appearance was so piteous that he young woman burst out laughing; her guardian joined in with a good grace. "What a little fool you are!" he muttered.

Myrandhal was laughing too. "As you see, my dear Robinson," he said, "my advice was sound."

"That's true," the Eccentric admitted. "I'm a trout. But I was in a hurry. This way, we can go inside straight away."

"We'll go inside," said Serge, who was no less impatient. "But first let me examine the leak, I want to determine the gravity of the wound as soon as possible."

He disappeared beneath the hull in his turn. He soon reemerged, his face radiant.

"It's all right," she said. The wound isn't dangerous, and our dear *Velox* will recover from it. It's the bolt of the ballast tank that gave way. The seal is slightly damaged, but it will be easy to repair, so the disease is curable. I even have a portable forge in the *Velox*; unfortunately, it's combustible material—coal—that we lack."

"Coal," exclaimed the Eccentric. "We might find some, if we search..."

"I doubt it."

"We might be able to make some fuel," the American put in.

"How, little girl?"

"With wood."

"Where shall we find it? This satanic country is flat, and as bald as an egg."

"That's true. Anyway, my dear guardian, go and change. You might catch cold."

"No need. I'm used to it. Anyway, the sun's going down. I'll be dry in half an hour."

"No!" the young woman persisted. "Go and change." She pointed at the *Velox*. "Dou you think that I'm going to let you into my home, my drawing room, covered in mud as you are.

"Pooh!" murmured the Eccentric. "The *Velox* must be just as dirty." Nevertheless, he did as he was told.

While he went back to the *Annabella*, Serge and his wife went through the valve-door in to the *Velox*. The engineer's first concern was to move back the shutters protecting the portholes, and the light came flooding in.

"What luck!" he exclaimed. "The glass resisted. That would have been more difficult to replace.

They ran to the front, and then came back to the central compartment.

"It's bizarre," said Myrandhal, sounding the floor. "I can't find any crack. Something must have given way, though, in order for the water to rise up into the living quarters."

"Let's look under the furniture."

The advice was sound, and less than a minute later, they had found the fissure. It was under Serge's bed. He was content to replace the planks displaced by the pressure of the sea-water.

"That should suffice for the moment," he said.

They began a more careful inspection of the *Velox*, examining everything in detail and exchanging their increasingly favorable impressions.

"We're in luck," said Serge, delightedly. "The *Velox* could have been broken up, but apart from the luminous coating on the walls, which has gone, and the staircase, which it's necessary to consolidate, I can't see that she's suffered overmuch. That's lucky, especially after the fall from the summit of the geyser. The leak only occurred afterwards. The *Velox* was snagged by a reef; fortunately, we were in calm water at that moment, not far from a sand-bank—the same one that forms the shore—and the ship ran aground not far from the coast without too violent a shock."

"Hello! Good morning!" shouted Pickman, who came in at that moment. "Well, how's the *Velox?*"

"Not bad, as you can see. Well, her hull's solid—not even a dent—but it's the rest, the machines. As far as I can tell, they're in good condition. A few gears jammed by sand, no doubt."

"What about the food-supplies?"

"The food-supplies are my concern," Anna replied. "Everything in sealed vessels—tins, bottles and jars—is safe. The rest—biscuits, flour, dried vegetables, etc.—is lost, only good for throwing away or boiling broth for Stop."

"No!" the Baronet protested, sharply. "Don't throw anything away. You're a wastrel. We can dry it out, and I'll show you how. This isn't the first time I've been shipwrecked."

While laughing, Anna went in search of a bottle of old whisky. She uncorked it and held out a glass to the Baronet. "Your health, my dear sir!" she said, cheerfully. "Drink that. It'll finish off drying you out."

"Famous!" Pickman declared, clicking his tongue. "These three days at sea have aged me two years." He took another gulp. "Now it's a matter of getting down to work. I can see that my ward is in a hurry to take up residence. Where to begin? The first step, obviously, is to block the leak. If not, the incoming tide will invade her again. That's the danger..."

"Yes," said the engineer, but there's another matter more serious than that one, which is that when the sea retreats tomorrow, it will take the *Velox* with it."

"We could moor her solidly."

"That's difficult on this loose ground. Then again, a cable might break and the *Velox* might escape. On the other hand, blocking the leak isn't a sufficient guarantee. Better to carry out a complete repair. That operation, cleaning the machines, the furniture and everything else, the verification of the submarine from top to bottom, will take several days. Thus, we're going to move the *Velox* and put her in dry dock, so to speak, beside the *Annabella*. Once she's there, we can work at our ease."

"Move the *Velox!*" protested the Eccentric. "What Roman toil! We'd need rails, a locomotive..."

"We'll have to get by without. It'll be hard, but we'll get there in the end. Unfortunately, we only have one day to do it. At all costs, even if we have to work all night, the *Velox* has to be sheltered, out of reach of the waves, before the next high tide."

"And what if the tide gains ground, as it has already begun to do? We'd have done it all for nothing."

"We'll see about that tomorrow. I hope, however, that we'll have time to repair the ballast-tanks, at least, before the tide reaches us. I can only see one way to haul the ship out. I'll submit it to your competence; I believe you told me that you were once in the British Navy?"

"Yes, but it was a long time ago."

"Well, to begin with," Myrandhal continued, "We're going to unload the *Velox*, relieving her of all her contents: cargo, machinery, etc. The hull itself only weighs a few tons."

"Good! You don't imagine we can haul it manually, though. At the very least we'd need a capstan..."

"There's one in the *Velox*: a small version made of reinforced steel tubing, which, like everything else, can be dismantled. An apparatus I recommend to you, powerful but light. On the other hand, we have cables, pulleys, several gasoline engines and a solid fulcrum—the *Annabella*, which, full as she is, weighs twice as much as the empty *Velox*. With all that, I think we can bring the operation to a successful conclusion."

"Perhaps," murmured the Baronet.

"That said, the most urgent thing is the unloading. I'll take care of the machines, which I'll have to check and whose every component I'll have to grease. As everything can be dismantled, I'll be sufficient for that job, and will even be able to give you a hand with the rest, which I leave to you."

"All right," said Pickman. "On with the job, children!"

They set to work immediately."

In two hours the removal was complete, and the castaways had built up a formidable appetite by the time they sat down to lunch. What remained to be done was less difficult but more delicate.

It took more than four hours to extend the cables between the two ships, and then to fix the capstan solidly in the ground, along with the internal combustion engine that was to drive it. The sun had set some time before when the engine was started up, but the heavy work was done.

Less than three quarters of an hour later, the *Velox* was in place beside the *Annabella*, and our heroes uttered a cry of triumph.

"Hurrah!" proclaimed the Eccentric. "Tomorrow evening, it will all be finished. Everyone will have a cabin."

That night, again, they slept fully-dressed in the *Annabella*'s central cabin, and the following morning, at dawn, they were at work. The entire day was devoted to washing the *Velox* with clean water and re-equipping her. In order to do it more rapidly, part of the cargo—everything that could remain outdoors—was left on the sand, covered by a tarpaulin, forming one of those piles that are sometimes seen on the docks of ports.

When dusk fell, the installation was complete.

"Finally, it's done!" exclaimed Pickman. "Not without difficulty, by Jove! Everyone can be at home, in his own bed. How glad I'll be to slip in between the sheets. I suppose that you, too..." He suddenly interrupted himself, on seeing his ward blush deeply. "What a brute," he murmured. "I'm an old brute! It's true that so many things have happened since, that it seemed to me that they were already an old married couple, whereas..."

A few hours later, by the light of the two Martian moons, Deimos and Phobos, Serge and Anna were wandering along the beach.

The Eccentric, offering the excuse of a sudden headache, had gone to bed, and they were alone for the first time since they had been in the gardens of Almowrat, when the pastor had drawn away after having blessed them.

They were walking in silence, savoring the unique hour. Soon, Anna raised her eyes toward the firmament. On high, Jupiter, the monarch of the heavens, was advancing at the head of his brilliant cortege of stars.

"How he shines," she murmured, very quietly. "One might think that he's calling us, as he did back there in the convent garden—do you remember? And that star on the horizon is Earth, isn't it?"

The young woman had shivered as she pronounced that name, and Serge was already anxious. "Yes," he murmured. "Earth, to which we'll return, if..."

"Why say that?"

"I thought you were seized by regret."

"No," the American declared, distinctly. "Arrange for me to have news of my friends, and I'll follow you anywhere, everywhere, ever further and ever higher. *Excelsior!* That's our motto."

"How glad you make me!" Serge sighed, delightedly. "I was remorseful already—so it's really true? You have no regrets?"

"No," the young woman murmured, in a voice that sang delightfully in Serge's heart. "No, my dear friend, I have no regrets. I'm with you. I'm happy."

VII. A Departure...

The newlyweds' honeymoon did not last long. Circumstances scarcely lent themselves to the idle strolls and sentimental promenades that are fashionable in such cases. They set to work again the following day.

The necessity was imperious. Since he had recovered his vessel, Serge Myrandhal had only had one thought in his head: to conclude the repairs to the *Velox* as quickly as possible and to reach a more hospitable region than a coast that was simultaneously icy and volcanic.

The engineer, who carefully monitored the indications of the thermometer every day, observed that the temperature was gradually declining—slowly, to be sure, but regularly and continuously. He pointed it out to the young woman and the Eccentric.

"It's one more proof," he said, "of the theory I explained the other day. The heat that renders the atmosphere bearable is emanating from the ground. The birth of the volcano, which we witnessed, demonstrates that in this region, the geological crust of the Martian soil is very thin—a thinness that would scarcely be reassuring for us, if we were obliged to remain here for long..."

"In other words," said Pickman, "if it weren't for that subterranean pressure-cooker, that gigantic hot water bottle, this would be a true Siberia."

"Fortunately, "Annabella put in, "we're not going to stay her for long—at least I certainly hope so."

"Even if we wanted to," the engineer added, "it would be impossible. I anticipate a date in the not-too-distant future when the cold will triumph over this artificial heat. The season is moving on rapidly. In a few weeks, perhaps sooner, we'd be icebound. We'd share the fate of the first polar explorers."

"God damn it!" muttered the Eccentric. "After the obstacles we've already overcome, that would be a bad way to end up. It wouldn't have been worth deserting our old terrestrial planet."

The young couple smiled at that remark.

"Don't worry," said the engineer. "We won't arrive at such an extremity. We've solved more difficult problems." In a more serious tone, he added: "We don't have a minute to lose, however. It's absolutely necessary that, a week from now at the most, the *Velox* is repaired and ready to put to sea..."

Pickman started in surprise. "By Jove! Seven days isn't much. You don't like it at all here, then? Personally, I don't mind it. Although arid, I find the region very interesting. There are studies to carry out, research..."

The engineer, who had quite forgotten the Red Men, in whom he had almost believed momentarily, wondered what the Eccentric was getting at.

Anna smiled. "I can guess what's keeping you, my dear guardian. It's your kobolds, the spirits of the caves..."

Since his adventure, the word "caves" rang badly in the Englishman's ears.

"Let's leave the kobolds out of it," he said, in a surly tone. "If there are inhabitants here, as I persist in believing, they'll show themselves eventually, but that's not what I mean. I simply mean that the cold doesn't seem so..."

"It's not just a matter of the cold," Myrandhal put in. "I have more urgent reasons for diligence: among others, the fact that since we've been here the tides have been visibly increasing in intensity. The distance that originally separated the *Velox* from the waves at high tide has diminished by a good third. In addition, the high tides are getting earlier by about an hour a day."

"With the result," said Annabella, "that as well as being frozen, we're running the risk of being inundated."

"A danger that would become immediate if the tide were assisted by the wind. The waves, driven by aerial current blowing with gale force, could surpass their usual limit by several meters. We've had no reason to fear that thus far, but we can't rely on it. It would only require an abrupt change in the weather, and I'm too much of a novice in Martian meteorology to anticipate that in advance."

With a gesture, the engineer indicated the pale line of the slowly-ebbing waves.

"That's different," said the Eccentric. "It's a matter of preventing the sea from invading the *Velox*—of restoring her seaworthiness. We'll see after that whether there's a reason to leave right away. In that regard, I'm in complete agreement with you, and ready to set to work right away. I also think that we should start right away—which is to say, tomorrow."

"Or even sooner," said the engineer.

This conversation had taken place a few yards from the *Velox*, after a breakfast comprising tea and condensed milk taken from the ship's reserves.

It was decided that an excursion to the interior planned by Pickman should be pitilessly erased from the program and that they would get to work immediately improvising the forge necessary to repairing the *Velox*. The Eccentric yielded to the necessity, but was secretly discontented. Although he no longer talked about them, he had not given up on finding the fantastic Red Men. He dreamed about them every night. He told himself, not without reason, that the first thing to do, if they wanted a forge, was to set out in search of the indispensable fuel. Nevertheless, he set to work without complaining too much, and, once warmed up, did his best to assist the engineer.

They began by erecting a tent and placing the tools they needed inside it. Then they dug a trench under the *Velox*, unscrewed the heavy door of the ballast tank and carried it to the tent—not without difficulty.

When these preparations were complete, the Eccentric said, sarcastically: "That's all well and good; all that our factory lacks now is coal—black diamonds, as we say in England. We need to go in search of some—perhaps we should have started with that..."

"What's the point?" replied the engineer. "There's no coal here, I'm sure of that..."

"All right...but we can make fuel, as Anna proposed. We've only explored the immediate vicinity; further away, beyond the desert, there are certainly forests."

"Undoubtedly," said the engineer, slightly impatiently. "But we might have to travel hundred of kilometers to reach them. Between now and then, the *Velox* would have had time to be carried away by the waves. Given what I've observed since our arrival, I have every reason to believe that this desert region is no richer in vegetation than Spitzbergen or Iceland, to which it bears a considerable resemblance."

"Why not replace coal with the gasoline that we have in reserve for our engines?" asked Madame Myrandhal.

"I've thought of that, but I'd require special apparatus for that, which we don't have, and without which we'd squander a considerable quantity of precious liquid fuel without obtaining the high temperatures required to melt large pieces of metal."

"I've got another idea," said Pickman, gravely.

"Let's hear it," said the engineer, politely, but without any great confidence in the Eccentric's imagination.

"This is it: around the orifice of the volcano, I noticed some superb sulfur crystals. Nothing burns better. What prevents you from forging with sulfur instead of carbon?"

"A simply law of chemical affinity," the engineer replied, smiling. "My iron or steel would be transformed into iron sulfide. You must remember that the property in question was used on our old terrestrial world for sealing iron fittings in stone. That's another means we'll have to abandon."

"Too bad!" said Pickman, ill-temperedly. "Install your forge directly above or around the volcano itself, then. You won't be able to complain that the temperature isn't high enough. It would be very economical!"

That humorous sally had the response it merited—which is to say that it was welcomed with general laughter—and the discussion continued. Of all the methods proposed, however, none were veritably practical.

"There's only one means," the engineer concluded, finally. "I've been thinking about it for some time. We're going to install an electric forge."

"How are you going to do that?" Pickman asked, incredulously. "That seems scarcely more realizable than my volcanic forge."

"On the contrary, Mr. Pickman, it's quite simple. We have engines and gasoline, so we can produce electricity. With a sufficiently powerful current, nothing is easier than softening, or even melting, the metallic components in question. The only real inconvenience is the considerable diminution of our fuel reserves—but we don't have any choice."

This time, the stubborn Pickman gave in.

The rest of the day was employed in setting up engines, dynamos and accumulators; by the time dusk fell, the "factory," as Pickman called it, was ready to function. That evening, Monsieur and Madame Myrandhal retired early. They were exhausted by fatigue, and the next day promised to be just as laborious as the preceding one.

Pickman did not feel weary. When he went to his cabin he refrained from getting undressed. While whistling a vague tune between his teeth he waited until the darkness and silence were complete inside the hull of the *Velox*.

When he was quite certain that the young couple were asleep, he slipped a revolver into his pocket and went out, carefully closing the door behind him. A few moments later he set off on foot across the sand and plunged boldly into the darkness.

Still haunted by the obsession of finding the Red Men, the Eccentric was setting off on a mission of discovery. He had been careful not to let his companions suspect what he was planning. He feared their mockery, and wanted to have some conclusive evidence to invoke.

However, he came back three hours later, frozen, exhausted and covered from head to toe in red-tinted mud, without having glimpsed any of the mysterious Martian kobolds.

The next day was entirely taken up by charging the accumulators. Everything went well. Before the day's end, the engineer had the satisfaction of seeing a steel bar brought to red heat by the electric current.

That evening, the stubborn Pickman went out again—and came back as he had departed, without having discovered anything.

The following day, the repair of the *Velox* commenced, and was carried forward with great activity. The waves of the high tide were now beating the shore a few meters from the ship. They all understood that the minutes were precious, and worked with a veritable fever.

Finally, thanks to Myrandhal's ingenuity, the task was completed in time. The *Velox* was repaired, and ready to put to sea. It was just in time. The cold was still getting worse, and the tide was following the same progression. Every night, now, the waves came to beat the keels of the submarines. In another day or two, they would be afloat.

Serge resolved to profit from that interval to give satisfaction to his wife, who was pressing him to put the telepath in a state to communicate with the Earth.

"Remember," she repeated, "that my father is waiting for news of me. And there's the *Herald*..."

There, however, Myrandhal was less fortunate; all his attempts to improve the apparatus and enter into communication with the neighboring planet failed.

"Which is bizarre," he said. "Theoretically, the problem seemed to be solved, and that wasn't easy, given that there's a station—the one in New York—that I can't improve. I thought I'd overcome the difficulty by augmenting the force of the radiation emitted and the sensitivity of our receiver, but there's nothing! I've called in vain; the *Herald* continues to remain deaf. There must be another cause..."

"What cause?" Pickman asked.

"I can only think of one," Myrandhal replied. "According to certain observations, I have every reason to believe that we're very close to the Martian magnetic pole here. Its influence must be deflecting the waves."

"In that case," said Anna, "if we move away—if we go closer to the equator—we'll be able to enter into communication?"

"I hope so."

"What joy!" exclaimed the young woman, clapping her hands. "All the more reason for leaving as quickly as possible."

"You're in a great hurry," Pickman could not help saying.

Serge, however, had not yet despaired of attaining his objective. He had installed two posts on the coast some ten miles apart, with which he continued his experiments.

As often happens, he made a discovery quite different from the one of which he was in search. One morning, when he was corresponding with Pickman, who was at the other post, he was astounded to hear the Eccentric's customary oaths resounding in his ears.

The entirely fortuitous phenomenon ceased almost immediately, but the engineer soon succeeded in reproducing it in a constant fashion. It was an agreeable surprise for all of them, particularly for Pickman, who casually attributed a share in the invention to himself.

"We've found a wireless telephone!" he proclaimed, "and a long-distance telephone loudspeaker, if you please—which could be very useful to us, if ever we're separated."

"Are you thinking of leaving us, then?" asked Madame Myrandhal.

"Who said anything about that?" the Eccentric murmured, a trifle embarrassed. "What makes you think that, Miss Anna?" His attitude passed unnoticed in the midst of the work and preoccupations of the moment.

In fact, the departure was imminent. It was to take place the following evening, between ten and ten-thirty, to be precise.

That day—the penultimate one—was devoted to stowing aboard the submarines everything they had removed from them: items of furniture, scientific instruments, tools and machines of all kinds. It only remained to fit the vessels with the propellers and rudders that would enable them to navigate, an operation that did not present any difficulty. It was the same for the two inflatable rubber dinghies that were go back and forth between the two vessels.

When that was done, the two submarines were linked by a solid steel cable. It had been agreed, in fact—to Pickman's great displeasure—that in order to simplify the maneuvers and, more importantly, to save fluid, they would only employ one engine, that of the *Velox*, which as the more powerful and efficient of the two.

When all the preparations were terminated, it was nearly ten o'clock in the evening, and Serge uttered a sigh of relief. "Finally!" he exclaimed. "That's that! In twenty-four hours, we'll depart."

"Finally," his wife repeated, alluding to the promise made by the engineer, "we'll have news of the Earth. I can't wait to get to the equator and pick up the dispatches that are waiting for us there, at the post office!"

The Eccentric did not share in the general enthusiasm.

"What's the matter with you?" his ward demanded, as they sat down at table. "One would think that you'll miss this vile place..."

"Me—no, by Jove."

"Yes, yes, that's it. You'll miss your kobolds, the goblins of the mountain. You've been searching for them every night. Do you think we didn't see you coming back the other morning, covered in dirt?"

"You're a little pest," muttered Pickman.

"I saw you," the young woman continued, teasingly. "You might well look embarrassed. One could tell by your expression that you'd drawn a blank. No trace of Martians—vanished, melted away..."

"Hmm!" said the Englishman, sullenly. "Don't crow so loudly, my dear ward. It's not yet proven that I'm mistaken on that account. The Martians are hiding, it's true, but there's no proof that they'll let us depart in peace. I have a suspicion, myself, that we haven't heard the last of them..."

VIII. Footprints in the Sand

Serge and his wife had only smiled at that vague threat, in which they saw nothing but a further manifestation of the Baronet's obstinacy.

He's stubborn, they thought. *He'll never concede that he got it wrong, and that there are no Martians here.*

The following day modified their opinion on this point.

That morning, shortly after dawn, Serge was woken up by a handful of sand thrown at the porthole of his cabin. He immediately leapt out of bed and saw Pickman, armed from head to toe, who was gesticulating with his alpenstock, bidding him to get dressed as quickly as possible.

"I'm coming," he said, in a low voice, so as not to wake his wife, who was asleep in the next room. And he set about dressing in a hurry.

As on as he was ready he slipped a small revolver into his pocket and left the *Velox* without making any noise.

"Well?" he said as he joined the Baronet. "What's happened?"

"What's happened," replied the Englishman, swelling with pride "is that I was right. Remember what I said yesterday?"

"You've seen the Martians again?" exclaimed the engineer, incredulously. "The kobolds—the famous Red Men?"

"Yes," the Eccentric replied, arrogantly. "Or at least, something closely resembling them. But let's leave it at that, sir; we can chat later, if you please. But know this: what's happened is grave; it's no time for joking, by Jove!"

"I swear to you, my dear Baronet, that not for a moment have I..."

"Well, let's pass on. While we're arguing, they're taking action. A little longer and, they'd have been inside."

"Who the devil are *they*?"

"The Martians. Another minute, and I'd have been well and truly burgled."

The engineer's expression was so bewildered that the Englishman, content with his success, smiled self-importantly, fully confident in himself. "You still doubt me. Come and see the traces of their tools. They're burglars, as I said."

Pickman led the engineer to the rear of the Annabella and pointed at the hull. "Look!"

Serge frowned. "That's a bit much!" he muttered, between his teeth.

There was a groove in the metal fifteen centimeters long, which looked as if it had been made by a metal saw.

"Well!" said Pickman, triumphantly. "There's the proof. You know as well as I do that it would need a well-tempered implement to dig into that hull. You know better than anyone how hard it is."

"Yes, but how is it that you didn't hear anything. It must have grated?"

"Yes—except that I wasn't here. At least, I suppose so."

"What about the dog—Stop?"

333

"Him neither; we went out on patrol, and they chose exactly the right moment. They're cunning..."

"Indeed. But what surprises me is that neither you nor Stop heard or saw anything. You must have been a long way off."

"Fairly—more than half a mile."

"How long did this patrol last?"

"At least twenty minutes. I don't know exactly."

"That's not long. Are you sure that this attempt took place during your absence?"

"As I said, I assume so. I can't be certain. It might also have happened afterwards, while I was asleep, because I ought to mention that I went to sleep afterwards."

"But the dog?"

"That's true, I forget to say: the dog has disappeared."

"Why didn't you say so sooner. They've killed him, then?"

"I'm beginning to believe so. At first I thought he'd gone of his own accord. As you know, Stop has a habit, once his guard duty is over, of going to take a bath in the sea. That's why I wasn't worried when I didn't see him when I woke up..."

"You're admirable! But my dear Robinson, that was a clue—perhaps the most important..."

"Pardon me, Mr. Friday, but no—at that time, I hadn't yet seen this scratch. When I discovered it, my one thought was to come and tell you."

"I understand. In any case, we'd better go look for Stop right away."

"There's no point...at least, it's not urgent. I know my dog. If he hasn't come to bid me good morning, it's because he's a prisoner, or dead. It might also be that he's found a trail and let himself get carried away momentarily, but if that's the case, he won't be long. Let's wait..."

"If you wish," the engineer replied, distractedly. He had bent down and was examining the confused imprints left in the sand by the feet of their aggressors.

"You're trying to read the tracks," said the Eccentric. "I tried too, but they're too blurred. All one can say for sure is that they weren't very numerous—two, or three at the most."

"Let's follow them," Myrandhal replied. "Perhaps we'll find something further away. Look—as they get closer to the shore, the imprints become clearer."

Suddenly, Myrandhal stopped, his eyes widening.

In front of him, profoundly imprinted in the damp sand, he had just perceived the form of a foot of frightful proportions. That mold—a signature of sorts—left by the mysterious visitor, was very impressive. The enormous heel, and the large and separate big toe, were suggestive of a formidable bone-structure.

The engineer's intention had become intense. "That's precise," he murmured. "The man—or, rather, the anthropoid—who stopped here...for he must have stopped, and put his whole weight on one leg momentarily, for his foot to have made that characteristic print...is some kind of giant. Our cave-dwelling ancestor, the terrible hunter who confronted the mammoth and broke its skull with a blow of is club, must have left such large, forceful footprints. This certainly isn't a spoor that one could attribute to the homunculi you claim to have seen on the Norton Bennett."

"Why not?" said the Eccentric.

"You're sticking to your dwarfs, then?"

"Yes I am. That mark isn't contrary evidence. Dwarfs often have very big extremities—the hands and feet of giants."

"That might be one explanation, obviously—but there's another objection to your thesis. All these tracks, as you can see, are heading, not toward the volcano, but toward the sea. It's from the sea that our aggressors have come...from which they emerged, one could say."

"Hold on—we haven't seen the beginning. It's necessary to follow the tracks all the way. I'm ready to wager that..." The Englishman interrupted himself, extending his finger. "There! Blood! God damn it!"

He was pointing to a flat rock in which there was a large red pool, seemingly still fresh.

The two men went pale. For a long minute, they remained silent.

"I understand now," murmured the engineer, eventually. "The attempt on the submarine happened this morning, while you were asleep. Stop had detected the enemy. He went forward, and battle was engaged at this very spot. That deep mark might allow us to reconstruct the scene. The valiant animal leapt at the Martian's throat, but the latter's arms closed in a terrible grip. Stop was choked, crushed, before he was able to utter a howl. After that rapid drama, the unknown individual and his companions headed for the *Annabella*."

"Poor Stop!" said Pickman. "The brave beast..."

They were so absorbed that, when they suddenly heard the sand creak close at hand, they shivered and reached for their revolvers, as if they expected to see the terrible Martian surge forth.

"Good morning, my friends!" cried Madame Myrandhal, joyfully. "What are you doing here? You look as if you're acting a scene from Conan Doyle or Fenimore Cooper: the subtle hunter on the trail of the elk..."

"That's right," said Serge, "but this time it's serious—grave, even. I would have preferred not to tell you immediately, but it's probably better not to hide anything from you."

"Yes, speak. I'm not a little girl."

Once she had been brought up to date, she murmured: "All this is, indeed, grave. It's evidently a matter of human beings...gigantic human beings. But where did these giants come from? Did they emerge from the heavens, the earth or the water? And poor Stop—do you think they've killed him?"

"It's very probable," Myrandhal replied. "Let's go on. We might end up finding something more definite, if only the place where they disembarked."

"You're assuming they came by sea, then?" said the American.

"I can't see any other explanation."

Pickman muttered a few unintelligible words, while the young woman continued: "By boat or swimming?"

"They came on foot," muttered Pickman, increasingly furious. "They crossed the sea with dry feet, like the Hebrews." And so saying he turned on his heel and departed, taking long strides.

Ten paces away, he stopped and started gesticulating. "Hip, hip, hurrah!" he proclaimed, in a sudden fit of joy. "Come and see, sir!"

Serge ran to join him, and understood the cause of his sudden enthusiasm at a glance.

In front of them, the tracks abruptly changed direction, heading back inland.

"Well!" cried the Englishman. "Who's right? Do you still claim that the Martians came out of the sea? They came from the interior, by Jove! Probably from the volcano...we'll soon find out."

The castaways moved forward, crossed the beach at the double and reached the plain of lava that followed. There the tracks stopped, and they were forced to pause. The Eccentric, so full of ardor a few moments before, made a gesture of discouragement.

"Nothing more," he murmured. "That was to be expected."

His ardor soon returned, however. "In any case," he went on, "the Martians aren't far away. They passed this way less than an hour ago. We'll surely end up finding them. Forward ho!"

The engineer was thoughtful, his brow furrowed, but when he saw the Eccentric set off, revolver in hand, he grabbed him by the arm almost rudely. "Look out!" he said, curtly.

"What is it? What's the matter with you, sir?" the Englishman stammered, more surprised than irritated by that violent gesture on the part of a man as calm as Myrandhal.

"I'm trying to prevent you from doing something foolish."

There was such authority in Serge's voice that the Englishman, who had been on the brink of becoming angry, changed his attitude.

"Something foolish, you say? Explain yourself. I don't understand."

"You will, my dear Robinson, and unless you're determined to get us killed, you'll moderate that juvenile ardor. Until now, I believed, wrongly, that the Martians were far away, and that we could risk operating in the open. Now, the situation has changed suddenly, and we're obliged to change tactics. I agree with you that the Martians are nearby, on the prowl. In consequence, we have numerous and redoubtable enemies around us and before us. We can't see them yet, but they can undoubtedly see us. They're cunning individuals, as they've just proved. Undoubtedly, they're watching us at this moment, lying in wait for us, ready to surround us, only waiting for an opportunity to take us by surprise—and we're going to fall into the trap head first."

"You think that they're as malevolent and as terrible as that?" the Eccentric relied. "Why are they so quick to run away, then?"

"I've told you," said the engineer. "We intimidate them, and that's fortunate—otherwise we'd doubtless have been massacred a long time ago. They have force of numbers in their favor, we have the prestige of superior beings, demigods descended from the Empyrean—and it's that prestige, our best safeguard, that it's necessary to safeguard, without risking it lightly in certain encounters...

"I desire as much as you do to make the acquaintance of our mysterious neighbors, and if they continue to hide, we'll go in search of them and fight them...but before then, we ought to take measures to equalize the terms of the conflict."

"What do you mean, my dear Friday?"

"I'll explain shortly. Let's go back to the *Velox* first. There, we can confer..."

"All right," the Eccentric ended up saying. "You're talking sense—and there's Anna, whom we oughtn't to expose to danger. Go on ahead—I'll bring up the rear, making sure of the retreat. Forward ho!"

The little troop set forth immediately. The Eccentric, conscious and proud of his role as rearguard, turned round from time to time, but did not have to take action; the enemy did not put in an appearance.

"What did I say?" Pickman muttered between his teeth. "They're afraid, but it's us who are running away. That's utterly ridiculous."

In the meantime, Anna, increasingly intrigued, interrogated her husband, by whose side she was walking.

"Well, my dear Serge, what do you think of all this? Do you believe in the Red Men too?"

"No...and yet, I daren't deny it. One thing is certain: we have a mysterious, invisible enemy prowling around, spying on us, against whom we can't take too many precautions."

"Yes," the American murmured, in a low voice." Don't you think that this mystery surrounding us—gripping us, as it were—is disturbing, maddening? Do these Martians, like certain fabulous heroes, have the ability to make themselves invisible?"

"I don't think so," said Serge, smiling.

"Me neither—but then, where do they come from, and where are they hiding? The country is bare for ten leagues around..."

"How do they vanish without leaving any traces? One might think—it comes back to this—that they've descended from the clouds and departed by the same route. Without those enormous feet, which are scarcely those of flying creatures, I'd be inclined to admit the existence on Mars of winged monsters, flying sphinxes..."

Myrandhal shivered slightly. He had just remembered the fantastic apparition he had experienced on the morning of his arrival on Mars, but he hastened to chase the image away. "No," he said, with a smile, "Let's not let our imagination off the bridle. The truth, such as it appears, is already sufficient cause for anxiety. Anyway, we'll try to get ourselves out of trouble. We'll carry out a disciplined search, which will allow us to locate the Martians...unless they really can fly."

"You said a little while ago that they were there, in front of us."

"They might well have been. It was necessary to prevent your guardian from throwing himself head first into a possible ambush—probable, even."

They reached the vessels.

"Well," said the Eccentric, "you can see that we were wrong to be frightened. The Martians aren't as brave as us; they've stayed in their holes. I hope we can go after them soon. You have a plan, my dear Friday: tell us what it is. I'm eager to know whether these damnable devils, who are so handy with a file, have skins impermeable to bullets."

"Listen," said the engineer. "If the Martians are still out there, which isn't certain..."

"It's certain," Pickman protested. "I'm certain of it, personally. They're waiting for us, by Jove."

"So be it. It's a matter, as I told you, of equalizing the chances between us. We have just the war machine required for that, a rolling fortress that will permit us to approach the enemy without exposing ourselves. You can guess what I'm talking about..."

"Yes," said Annabella. "The automobile."

"Exactly. I'm reluctant, of course, to upset our packing, which is all ready for the departure this evening, but since it's necessary. Besides which, the damage will be quickly repaired. The auto can be set up in forty minutes, so we can be out on campaign in three quarters of an hour."

"All right!" roared Pickman, enthusiastically. "Excellent idea, my dear Friday. Why didn't we think of it sooner? As for me, aboard the *Annabella* I have a Maxim machine gun that fires twelve hundred bullets a minute. With that toy, one can scythe down a regiment at two thousand meters. I'll let you have it..."

"Thanks, but I have what I need: two machine guns improved and adapted by me for their future usage. You can judge for yourself; we'll start assembling the auto right away. The engine is ready, and greased. It's only a matter of getting out the various pieces of the chassis and fitting them together, which won't take long, the machine having been designed for it."

Indeed, half an hour later, the auto was full assembled and ready to roll. It was a sixteen horsepower, small but robust, equipped with solid pneumatic tires with metallic hubs. It had three seats-two in front and one behind—sheltered by a system of chromium steel shields that could be lowered over the wheels like mudguards. In case of danger, it was sufficient to lift up the plates and fix them in place by means of a bolt.

Two machine guns mounted on pivots, one forwards, on the hood, and one aft, on the trunk made the vehicle into a veritable mobile fortress, as the engineer had said.

Enthused by these bellicose preparations, the Eccentric congratulated the constructor warmly.

"It's admirable," he said. "Simple, light and solid, capable of going anywhere. With a machine like this one, one could make a tour of Mars in thirty days without a breakdown. Now, the Big-Feet can come; we're ready for them; they'll get a warm welcome."

The American was no less enthusiastic. "It's a marvel," she said. "A jewel of precision."

"Oh," said Serge, looking at his wife tenderly, "the jewel's a trifle primitive, and only reminds me distantly of the luxurious coupé that stopped one evening at the gate of Norton Cottage.

"Nevertheless, such as it is, our sixteen-horsepower will be very useful to us. I anticipate, for example, that you'll be jolted somewhat; I've only retained the indispensable components. It's a somewhat crude war machine. Anyway, you can judge for yourself. I'll start the engine. I'm eager to see what the Martians will do at the sight of this new monster racing toward them. I'm sure they'll turn on their heel at the first gunshot. If you'd care to get in..."

"Forward ho!" cried the American, leaping into the driver's seat. "I'll take the wheel to begin with."

"Bravo!" cried the Eccentric, taking the back seat. "That's mettlesome. You can step on the gas, you know—there aren't any policemen on Mars to tick you off, and you have the right to run over anyone who gets in your way..."

The three were full of confidence and impatience, and had almost forgotten the alarm they had experiences a short while before.

"Which way shall we go?" asked the American, pressing on the accelerator.

"As you please," replied the engineer. "Don't go too far to begin with, though. It's not probable that the Martians will come back to attack the ships, but we ought to be ready for anything."

The American looked at her guardian. "Suppose we head for Norton Bennett?"

The Eccentric made a gesture of indifference. "If you like. I can't see any reason for choosing that direction rather than another. Just try to run into the bandits—I'm avid to avenge my poor Stop."

"Let's start with the volcano," Madame Myrandhal decided.

In a matter of minutes, the distance was crossed. The excursionists made a circuit of the hill at high speed, and then headed back toward he submarines at the same pace. After having observed that nothing abnormal had occurred, they set out in another direction.

For three hours the auto wandered back and forth over the lava, enlarging its circle of investigation every time, but without success. Several times, the motorists, reassured by the solitude that reigned around them, got out in order to look for tracks on the ground, but found nothing suspicious. Every time the Eccentric got back aboard more disappointed and more furious. The check was all the more sensible because, thus far, events had seemed to have proved that he was right.

"God damn it!" he muttered, once or twice. "I thought we were going to confront these damned red devils, but now they've escaped, and everything's confused again. It will all clear up. We have to be patient—wait until the end. He who laughs last, laughs longest."

"If you wish," Myrandhal offered, "We can get out and climb Norton Bennett. Your kobolds will have to show themselves in the end. In my opinion, that further excursion doesn't present any great danger—but I'm hesitant, because of Anna."

The Englishman reflected momentarily, but ended up saying, with a discouraged expression: "No, it's pointless; we won't find anything today. The red devils have gone back to their underground holes. They only come out by night—but I'll be waiting for them. I'll have my revenge, God damn it!"

The Englishman was somber and preoccupied; he only replied in monosyllables to the questions that were put to him thereafter.

His companions thought that he was ruminating, and left him to his mutism.

As midday was approaching, however, Serge judged that the experiment had lasted long enough. "I think that we can go home for lunch," he said. "Our first impression was doubtless correct: the Martians arrived and departed by sea, and they're far away by now. Don't you think so, my dear Pickman?"

"Yes," replied the other, curtly.

"However," said Anna, rallying to her guardian's defense, desirous of shoring up his self-respect, "those tracks on the lava, the Martians' detour toward the volcano..."

"A ruse, quite simply. They wanted to put us off their track. Believe me, my dear friends, the more time passes, the more convinced I am that the Martians came by sea and left the same way. They're essentially maritime beings, and I doubt that they often go past the dunes where they land."

"What about those my guardian saw on Norton Bennett?" countered the American.

At that objection the eccentric uttered a grunt whose meaning it was impossible to determine.

Wanting to save their companion's pride himself, the engineer replied: "Oh, I'm talking about the mass, the majority of Martians. It's quite possible that some, the leaders, venture further on, even that they scaled the volcano."

"Why?"

"We can only make hypotheses: to examine our position, perhaps to make sure, before attacking us, that we really were alone."

"That puts your two theses in accord," said Anna. "I imagine, my dear guardian, that you approve..."

"Yes," growled the Eccentric, increasingly sullen—and from that moment on it was impossible to get another word out of him.

Serge and his wife had abandoned the Eccentric to his reflections, and started taking about the departure, still fixed for the next high tide, when—to their great surprise—the Baronet emerged from his obstinate mutism and exclaimed: "So you're leaving? You're going anyway?"

"Yes, my dear Robinson. Do you have any objection?"

"None," the Englishman replied, in a slightly sarcastic tone. "Go, if you want to, as quickly as you like. Everyone's free, God damn it. Personally, I'm staying."

IX. Port Burrett

"You're staying!" Annabella exclaimed, falling from the clouds.

"I'm staying," the Eccentric repeated, categorically. "I swore that I'd go in search of the Martians in the depths of their lair, and I'll go, God damn it. Otherwise, I'd no longer be Pickman..."

That was said in such a tone that Serge understood that there was no point in arguing for the time being, and that it was better to indulge the obstinate gentleman's new whim.

"So be it," he replied. "As we don't want to abandon you, we'll wait for you. We'll stay, even though the delay worries me. The cold is beginning to make itself felt, and I don't want to winter here."

"It's not a matter of wintering—just a few days."

"All right. It's a settled matter, to which we won't return. It's still necessary to make arrangements for those few days, and that presents a difficulty, which you must have envisaged. Soon, the submarines being afloat, it will be a matter of finding a haven for them, of sheltering the delicate machines from the hazards of the sea. Obviously, we could ride out big waves in the open sea, but our motive force is too strictly measured for us to waste it. We'll therefore be constrained to run aground again, unless we have the good fortune to find a bay of calm water, a kind of natural harbor..."

"The port is already found!" exclaimed the Eccentric, joyfully. "I've been looking for it for several days."

"You've been looking for it? So you knew that we'd need it?"

"I suspected as much. Your plan to raise anchor right away didn't meet with my full approval, and I promised myself that if there was anything new, if the Martians put in an appearance, to stay a few more days in order to see what they had under their skin. I would have let you leave."

"What!" cried Madame Myrandhal, indignantly. "You consented to be separated from us! You think that we're not sufficiently alone on this desert world?"

"Oh," the Baronet relied, "it would only have been for a few days. And we'd have stayed in communication, thanks to the telephone. So I looked around for a shelter for the *Annabella*, and the other evening I discovered not far from here, a kind of port that will suit our purpose very well. It's a very small haven, but marvelously sheltered by a line of breakers forming a dyke. The swell and the tide are scarcely sensible there. One might think that everything had been provided by nature with us in mind.

"Nothing is lacking there—not even the mooring-dock. A rock will serve that purpose very well; it's right on the coast, so that at low tide one can disembark with dry feet. At high tide we'd have a hundred meters to travel by dinghy. Our friend Burrett would say that Providence had hollowed out that basin expressly for us; that's why I gave it its name. And now, if you wish, we can go and visit Port Burrett!"

"Right away," replied Serge, getting to his feet. "I'm in haste to obtain information on this important point. Come on, Anna…is it far?"

"Two miles to the north. We could walk there."

"No, better take the automobile. It's more prudent…"

Half an hour later, the castaways arrived at Port Burrett, which conformed in every respect to the description given by its discoverer.

Serge congratulated Pickman. "It's a real find," he said. "Our submarines will be perfectly sheltered here, and I won't hide it from you that it was the matter that worried me most…"

"I know," the Eccentric replied. "I'm English, a former mariner. I thought of that too, right away."

"I only ask one thing, my dear Robinson, and that's that our sojourn here shouldn't be prolonged too long. Do you know why?"

"I know—but don't worry. Just give me time to get my hands on one of those damned Martians, who seem to be playing hide and seek, and I'll go with you. Agree, my dear chap, that it would have been ridiculous to come so far to see the inhabitants of Mars and then turn your back on them just at the moment…"

"But we aren't turning our back on them," said the engineer. "On the contrary, we're getting ready to chase them over the sea, their own element."

The Eccentric could not suppress a grimace of ill humor. "Listen, sir," he said. "Let's leave that. What point is there is starting that argument again. We'll never be able to convince one another. You think the Martians are far away, out at sea; I'm sure that there here, close by, gone to earth like field-mice. I've seen them with my own eyes, damn it, and I wasn't seeing things.

"Anyway, to reassure you, I promise that I'll leave with you in three days' time, come what may. As for the Red Devils, I'm so sure of my fact that I'll make you a proposition. In Paris, at the Dunkan & Co. Bank, I have a deposit of ten thousand pounds. If I'm mistaken, and I don't bring you the proof of what I'm saying within the next three days, that money belongs to you.

"And now, instead of arguing any longer, let's occupy ourselves with the departure—by which I mean the reflotation."

That was what they did. Having returned to the submarines, the castaways proceeded with the final preparations. The auto was dismantled and the pieces stowed in the hold again. An electric reflector was set on the prow of the *Velox*, which would serve as a searchlight.

These various operations and the dinner that followed went on rather late into the night.

It was ten o'clock when the high ride began to moisten the sand round the explorers.

Pickman made a final visit to the *Annabella*, carefully closed the hatch on her conning-tower, and came back to join his companions in the central compartment of the *Velox*.

Already the waves were beating he hull of the submarine, which oscillated occasionally. Installed at his captain's post with his head protruding from the conning tower, Serge checked the functioning of the machines one last time. "All's well," he announced. "A few more minutes and we'll be off."

As the mist increased, he switched on the electric beacon fixed to the prow. At that moment, the vessel suddenly tilted backwards, and that abrupt pitch sent Pickman sprawling at the far end of the compartment. He got to his feet, rather sheepishly.

"What was that?" he asked, feeling his sides. "We're not afloat yet?"

"No," said the captain. "It's our supportive bed of sand disintegrating, but it won't be long now; the *Annabella*'s already afloat."

There was a further shock, which righted the *Velox*.

"Pay attention!" cried Myrandhal. "This time, we're going. Forward ho!"

They heard the propeller start to spin, and the *Velox* moved off, towing the *Annabella*, which was dancing madly. The inshore waves were negotiated with ease, and not long afterwards, the two boats were moored in the bay so opportunely discovered by Pickman, who applauded himself once again for his find.

"The water's perfectly calm here, as you see. We're scarcely moving. Just enough to lull us to sleep. We'll never have slept better!"

He was still taking when a vague rumor became audible in the distance, on the coast; there were confused shouts and seemingly-stifled barking, in which Serge thought he recognized Stop's voice.

Intrigued, Serge and his wife pricked up their ears, and then looked at Pickman. To heir great surprise, the latter, either because he had not heard or for some other reason, remained perfectly calm.

"What's that?" Serge asked. "Can't you hear it?"

"Yes, vaguely," the Eccentric replied, quite phlegmatically. "What do you think it is? The noise of the sea—the tide, I mean."

"Yes, perhaps," Serge replied. "Personally, I thought about Martians."

"That's possible too." In a slightly sarcastic voice, the Baronet went on: "It is, in fact, their time. Deimos is rising, and it's time for the kobolds to dance in the moonlight..."

"I admire your phlegm. You're joking."

"No, by Jove! Why should I be astonished? The Martians are on the prowl, you say—personally, I never doubted it. So what? As for being anxious, there's no reason. The submarines, once on the water, in their element, have nothing to fear."

"I agree. That doesn't mean if I weren't fearful of a trap, I'd go as far as to hop over there, to watch, as you put it, the kobolds dancing in the moonlight..."

"It would be a waste of effort," the Englishman replied. "The devils are as cunning as you are, and it's necessary to play them at their own game, coolly. That's why I'm not getting excited. What's the point? I'm sure of what I'm doing, sure of winning the bet I mentioned a while ago.

"It's tomorrow that I intend to take possession of one of those goblins, which are permitting themselves to disturb our sleep. I've just discovered a means for which I've been searching for some time—oh, a very simple means, a sort of bait. We'll both lie in ambush on the beach with a lasso, like cowboys.

"That requires some preparation, however; that's why we're waiting until tomorrow. After a day of excitement and fatigue, we're all worn out. Personally, I'm falling asleep, so I'm going to take the dinghy and go home, back to the *Annabella*."

"To the *Annabella*!" said Anna, nonplussed. "I thought you were going to stay here. You'd be just as comfortable."

"Not on your life," said the Eccentric. "I'd embarrass you and you'd embarrass me. I'd rather be on my own at home. An old bachelor's habit..."

All insistence was futile. Pickman climbed out of the conning tower, took one of the dinghies moored there and headed for the *Annabella*.

As soon as they were alone, Serge turned to his wife. "What does that mean?" he asked. "Your guardian was in a hurry to leave. Evidently, he's got an idea in the back of his head."

"All the more so as he'd tacitly accepted that he was sleeping here. He's planning something. You noticed that he assured us that all danger was past and that we could sleep easy. He surely wants to profit from our sleep to go ashore and hunt for Martians."

"We've both had the same thought—and that's what we must prevent, at all costs. Trouble arrives quickly. I intended to stay on watch during this first evening—this is another reason..."

"Is that absolutely necessary?" Anna asked. "You're worn out too, and need sleep. Do you want us to take shifts mounting guard?"

"Not on your life. I feel perfectly fit. Go to your room, my dear Anna. I'll have a two-hour siesta tomorrow, and that will take care of it. As for your guardian, I'll keep an eye on him. Woe betide him if he tries of go out: he'll be punished like a conscript who goes absent without leave.

"There he is now, switching off the electric light. It's a feint. Just wait—we'll see who tires first. Now, my dear Anna, *bonsoir*—until tomorrow. Sleep tranquil: I'll keep watch."

Myrandhal escorted his wife to the door of her cabin; then he came back, picked up a book and started reading.

From time to time, in order to combat the drowsiness that was invading him, he took a few strides around the cabin.

At about five o'clock, it seemed to him that the mooring-rope was grating more loudly and that the *Velox* was dancing.

He went to the porthole, wondering whether the Eccentric was playing some prank.

He opened it, saw nothing, and was about to close it again when he perceived a bizarre noise close at hand, twice over: a kind of whistling similar to that of certain snakes. He tried to pierce the darkness, to discover the animal making the strange sounds, but could not do it.

"It must be some sort of fish," he murmured. "There are eels that whistle like that, I think..."

His watch concluded without any further incident.

As dawn began to break, Serge stretched himself out in an armchair. *Now,* he thought, *I can doze a little. Our man won't go out now. Anyway, I won't go to sleep—I'll be on my feet at the slightest noise.*

He had overestimated his strength. When he woke up an hour later, pale daylight was whitening the windows.

"What's happening?" he murmured. "I thought a heard the sound of oars. Is it Pickman?"

Serge ran to a porthole.

"Exactly!" he exclaimed. "His dinghy is no longer there. Our man has escaped, but he can't have got far. It was only a few minutes ago that I heard the oars—that's what woke me up. It's a matter over catching up with him."

During the monologue, Serge had taken his place in the second dinghy. He extended the oars, and rowed vigorously toward the coast, which he soon reached. As he landed he perceived Pickman's boat, which the latter had taken the precaution of mooring on land.

Close at hand, he heard the whistling sound that he had heard before rise up again, and could not help feeling a vague apprehension.

"There's my fish again," he murmured, trying to make a joke of it. "It's hissing to the left. Is that a bad omen on Mars too?"

Without hesitating for a second, however, he launched himself along the trail of footprints that Pickman had left in the sand.

He soon reached the lava plain. There the tracks ended. Serge looked round, and did not see anything hopeful.

Before continuing his search, he scanned the entire region with his eyes. He was on a vast rocky plain that rose up at a gentle slope to the horizon.

In front of him, less than fifty meters away, a line of rocks extended from left to right—blocks of all sizes, as if polished by the weather. One might have thought it the moraine of some vanished glacier.

Myrandhal continued searching for Pickman with his eyes. *Where the devil can he be?* He wondered. *A man can see for two leagues in this desert. He must be hiding behind those boulders over here, in order to lie in ambush, as he put it. I'll take a look.*

He was moving forward when a puff of white smoke rose up from among the rocks in question. At the same time, the sound of a gunshot drilled into his eardrums.

Serge set off like lightning. "It's him," he murmured, his heart gripped by anguish. "It's Pickman—he's been attacked."

He had covered the distance in a few bounds and ran through the rocks. Fifty meters further on, he stopped, his legs buckling, mute with horror.

Lying on the ground, which had been trampled by a violent struggle, were two objects: Pickman's helmet and his revolver, still smoking.

Of the Eccentric, there was no trace; he had disappeared, as if through a trap-door.

"That's fantastic," Serge murmured, his hair bristling fearfully. "One might think that the ground had opened up and swallowed him. What has happened here confounds the imagination. There's something here—some form of life— with an occult, mysterious power, which surpasses all our earthly conceptions."

Forgetful of the danger he was running himself, if the kidnappers were still there, he wandered around for some time, making a tour of the moraine.

In the end, he scaled one of the blocks of stone and looked into the distance, seeing nothing but the bleak and empty plain.

He turned round hen, and saw his dinghy dancing on the water. Suddenly, he shivered, and a cold sweat inundated his temples. He had just thought, not about his own danger, but that which an individual dear to him might be in.

"Anna!" he stammered. "I forgot about Anna, to whom I owe…what a horrible situation for her, if I were abducted in my turn, or if she were!"

His teeth chattering with horror, he leapt down and ran toward the beach like a madman.

X. *"Hello! Hello!"*

The days that followed were lugubrious for those who remained. Never had the desert world seemed so sinister to them.

All their searches had been fruitless. Having carried out their coup, the Martians had disappeared like enchanted beings. The lava kept its secret.

Anna was still hopeful, however, contrary to all appearances.

"No," she often repeated, "I can't believe that my dear guardian is dead. It seems to me that I would have known, that his soul would have come to bid me adieu. The incomprehensible beings that have abducted him, those mysterious spirits of some kind, can't be as ferocious as that. They spared Stop."

"Is that certain?" Serge objected.

"Yes, it was definitely his voice that we heard the other evening, a few hours before the misfortune. I recognized it, and poor Pickman did too, of course. Do you remember his strange attitude? And besides, remember, there was no trace of blood where the latest drama occurred. Everything suggests that the Martians had set an ambush to capture our friend alive. Why would they have killed him afterwards?"

"Let's hope so," Serge replied, not daring to voice the abominable thought that had been haunting him for some time: that it might perhaps be better if he were dead...

The days went by, and Madame Myrandhal also began to despair. At first she had imagined that the Eccentric would find the means to escape, that he would come back unexpectedly, at the moment when he was least expected. Then it was from the Martians themselves that she expected his liberation. She persisted in believing that the kidnapers would reappear sooner or later, that, having a hostage—which seemed to have been their objective—they would attempt to open negotiations; but nothing of that kind happened, and her last illusions flew away, one after another...

It was necessary to look reality in the face, to think about the salvation of the survivors, of their future on this baneful planet—all the more so because the abnormal temperature, from which they had benefited thus far, was lowering in an increasingly disquieting fashion. In ten days the thermometer had fallen fifteen degrees, to the vicinity of zero. Winter was approaching, with its cortege of frosts and privations.

One morning—it was the fourteenth day after Pickman's disappearance—when the young couple woke up, they saw that the coast was white with snow. Ice-floes were drifting on the sea, doubtless detached from some distant ice-sheet.

Anna was depressed by the sight of that polar landscape, and Serge took advantage of that impression to put the question of an immediate departure back on the table.

"This time," he said, "there's no more room for hesitation. Only pray to God that we haven't waited too long and that the heat and power we have at our disposal—our reserves of electricity and gasoline—are sufficient to take us to a more hospitable shore. We need to leave today. Who can tell whether, at the pace things are going, we might not be blocked in by ice tomorrow?"

"You're right," Anna replied, "and I won't resist any more. I can no longer hope to see my guardian again. We can leave whenever you wish. I only ask one thing, and that's to go over there to the moraine one last time, as one visits a grave. We'll build one of those monuments that polar explorers build, a cairn. We can even leave some food underneath it, and a letter for our guardian, indicating the direction we've taken. I doubt that he'll ever receive it..."

Madame Myrandhal could not finish. Tears were steaming from her eyes. Her husband, equally emotional, strode back and forth in the compartment, searching for words of consolation that he could not find.

They had been silent for a few moments when, before their startled eyes, the bell of the telephone vibrated, and a joyful voice resounded, bursting in their ears like the sound of thunder.

"Hello! Hello! Are you there, Anna? And you, my dear Friday? Good morning! Well, say something then, damn it!"

Serge and his wife looked at one another, mute with amazement, not daring to believe the evidence of their senses.

Finally, the American precipitated herself toward the apparatus and said, in a crazed voice: "Is that you, my guardian, is that you?"

"Not so loud!" howled a furious voice. "Not so loud, by Jove! You'll give the game away...I'm not alone, God damn it! Not alone, you understand..."

Madame Myrandhal only understood one thing, which was that the Eccentric was alive, really alive. Her joy and stupor were such that she felt her legs giving way underneath her. She tottered, and Serge came forward to support her.

She shoved him away, and in a lower voice, trembling with emotion, she said: "Hello! So, my dear guardian, it's you, it's you! I'm mad with joy, but how can it be? Explain yourself. Where are you? How can you talk? You have a telephone, then?"

"Of course—I've got mine: the one from the *Annabella*. I brought it with me in my knapsack. Didn't you notice that?"

"No, no, we'd lost our heads..."

"It's necessary to keep one's head—one's brain...I always keep mine. Where would I be without it? It's like my knapsack, you see. You mock when I fill it with all sorts of things...but I was right, God damn it! The other day, in particular, I stuffed it—three days' food supplies, ropes, crampons to explore the fissures, machines of every sort. But you were asking me where I am..."

"Yes—you're killing me. Speak! Where are you, then?"

"Where I am...where the Martians live, by Jove."

"Where the Martian live?"

"Yes, among the kobolds, the red devils—although they aren't as red as all that. Does that surprise you?"

"Oh! Yes..."

"I swore to get here; I did it. What I say, I always do. What do you think of this reportage, eh, Anna? This is an interview that that old buffalo Norton Bennett would pay dearly for, isn't it? Answer me..."

"Yes, undoubtedly, but I beg you, my dear guardian, don't joke any more...you're keeping us on tenterhooks. Talk about yourself, only yourself. We thought you were dead, and here you are, resuscitated all of a sudden. You seem joyful, quite well..."

"I've never been better. What next?"

"Next...but you haven't told us anything yet. Where are you? I mean, in what part, what region of Mars, in the air, under the sea or underground?"

"Underground, God damn it! What a thick head you have. Underground, by all the devils! I knew that there were inhabitants under the lava, that we had a subterranean world under our feet, a city—in a word, a Martian city. It only remained to discover it. That's done!"

"And is it far away, this city—far from us?"

"I can't measure it. Between twenty and fifty miles."

"And Stop!" exclaimed the young woman, seized by a sudden thought. "Poor Stop..."

"Stop's here, and says hello."

"Is he well too?"

"Very well—a trifle melancholy. Evidently, living like a mole doesn't suit him."

"And the Martians?" Madame Myrandhal went on. "You haven't said anything about the Martians. What kind of people...?"

"Good people," Pickman interjected. "A trifle coarse, but that would take too long—later..."

"One more word," said the American, breathlessly, her thoughts pressing in a crowd. "You're not unhappy? They're not maltreating you?"

"No—what a ridiculous idea!"

"Then why haven't you called before?"

"You're asking too much, damn it. I'd have liked to do so..."

"But you couldn't. You're a prisoner?"

"Not exactly—merely kept under surveillance. But the damnable rascals stole my bag, all my resources. I had to use cunning to get it back. Someone helped me: Tao."

"Tao? Who's that? A Martian?"

349

"Yes—my guard. I must admit that we didn't get on to begin with. He wanted to put one over on me, but I got the better of him. I'll tell you later. Now, he's my houseboy—he polishes my boots. He's the one who's watching me at the moment, while I chat He's just told me that the Martians are prowling around. That's enough for now, Anna. Pass the apparatus to that fellow Myrandhal, so I can hear his voice."

Serge did not make him repeat the request. "Hello!" he said, immediately. "Bonjour, my dear Robinson. Are you well?"

"Entirely," the Eccentric replied. "Bonjour." In a triumphant voice he added: "Well, what do you say, Monsieur Frenchman, Monsieur Scientist? You've lost the bet. I was right."

"I agree, humbly."

"Enough," said Pickman. "Time's pressing. Oh, you can boast of having exasperated me, you. I was enraged, God damn it! I wanted to crush you with my victory, but here are more important things to do. We'll chat soon. I've promised myself to get out of here, and I'll get out."

"You're planning to escape?"

"Yes. Tao's on board, so it'll go quickly, God willing."

"Can we help? Speak, command..."

"Look after yourselves. Don't budge—you'd spoil everything. Don't do anything until I tell you. Until then, play dead. I'll explain everything. Before then, have you anything important to ask?"

"Masses, but this isn't the time...I understand."

"No."

"There is one thing that troubles me more than the rest, though."

"What?"

"How did you disappear like that the other morning? I arrived almost immediately...and nothing! Are there trap-doors in the lava, then, and secret passages?"

"I think so, but it's impossible to say. I received a blow that knocked me out, and when I came to, I was far underground. Obviously, there are passages..."

"Good—that must indeed be the case. One more word about the Martians—what kind of beings are they?"

"I told you—dwarfs...a trifle baroque, of course. They're furry, like bears, and their fur has a reddish tint at times, although that gleam comes, not from them, but from the ambient atmosphere. Since I've been underground, I shoot off sparks from my own hair. There's a lot of electricity here.

"I should tell you that I haven't been able to investigate much. I'm not free, and I've used the time making myself comprehensible to my boy. Then again, they only talk about certain things. These people don't have brains conformed like ours, as regards ideas...as for words, their language, it's something unimaginable, that I don't expect ever to master. The Martians don't talk, they sing—or rather hum…"

"Don't they whistle?"

"Yes, when they're angry, or to call out. As for the words, they're cries, onomatopoeias. All vowels—I can scarcely recognize two or three consonants: a language fit for monkeys or parrots. And yet, these little monsters have a soul, or something similar. They know things, it seems to me, that still escape us no doubt…

"But I'm talking too much, and there are more urgent matters…let's talk about my escape. It will be soon…"

"We can't do anything to help you, you say?"

"No, nothing. Stay silent. I can do it alone."

The Eccentric's voice was suddenly cut off, and there was a sequence of little inarticulate squeaks, a kind of mewling modulated in three different tones.

Serge and his wife listened in anguish, fearful of some surprise. Unable to contain herself any longer, Madame Myrandhal leapt to the apparatus.

"Hello!" she called.

"Not so loud!" complained a furious voice. "Quietly, by Jove! What a piercing voice you have, Anna. God, damn it, you nearly…"

There was another interruption, during which the young couple could hear their own hearts pounding. Then the Eccentric called again: "Hello! Are you there, Myrandhal?"

"Yes, but what a panic! What's happening? Those shrill cries…"

"That was Tao, my boy. He was warning me that the Martians are coming. And here's one coming now… Shh! I'll call you soon…"

XI. The Anthropoid

It was almost midday when that conversation came to an end, and from that moment on the Eccentric gave no further sign of life.

As the hours went by, Ana felt the immense joy that had invaded her at first give way to a vague anxiety…

"What do you expect?" she replied to her husband, who tried to reason with her. "It's too much for me. I can't believe in so much happiness—and then, there are many things that are obscure. My guardian, although he didn't admit it, is purely and simply a prisoner. Who knows what might happen before his escape? To think that at this moment, while we're chatting tranquilly, a drama is unfolding down there. Don't you find the situation horrible…atrocious?"

"You're being unreasonable," the engineer replied. "Yesterday, we would have given half our blood just to know that Pickman is alive. Now we know much more than that. We've heard his voice; we're going to see him soon, I'm sure of it! You ought to be delighted—instead of which, you're tormenting yourself…"

351

"What do you expect? One isn't in control of these things. Until the last minute, until my guardian is here in our arms, I'll be in doubt!"

The evening passed in this state of apprehension. Darkness fell...

Even Serge could not help looking at the telephone bell continually.

Finally, the frail hammer began to vibrate. Anna stood up, breathless.

"Hello!" shouted the jovial voice of the Baronet. "Are you there? Good—I can only give you a minute. This is to tell you not to be impatient—there's a delay. The escape's been put off until tomorrow..."

"A delay?" said Anna, in an anguished tone. "What delay?"

"How do I know?" Pickman exclaimed. "I don't know everything, damn it! Tao tells me that there's a delay. I thought I ought to do the same, by Jove. That's women all over—curiosity! That's the way the Devil always gets hold of them. With that, good night—I'm sleepy. Good night, Milady...good night!"

Anna tried to call her guardian back, but he did not deign to respond.

As for the engineer, entirely reassured by that further communication, he smiled.

"You see," he said to his wife, "you were wrong to be anxious. The Baronet is still as cheerful and as jovial—that's a good sign. He's taking a malign pleasure in astonishing us. Who knows—perhaps he has a surprise in store for us?"

"The best surprise would be his unexpected arrival."

"That's more difficult. It's already a lot to know that soon—perhaps tomorrow—he'll be here, with us."

Myrandhal suddenly shivered. A whistling sound had just become audible in the darkness: the sinister whistling that he had heard before.

Water was splashing close by.

At the same time, violent blows struck the hull. Precipitate footsteps ran over the deck...

"Martians!" shouted the young man. He was launching himself toward the conning tower to close the hatch when a laughing face appeared in the opening.

"My guardian!" stammered the American.

"In person. What's astonishing about that? Hello, Anna; hello Mr. Friday."

The Eccentric had stepped into the conning-tower and was coming down the small spiral staircase, as calmly as if he were just coming back from smoking a cigar on the deck.

"What's astonishing," he said, "is that you're looking at me with such wide eyes. One would think that you'd never seen me before."

Already recovered from her stupefaction, however, Anna threw herself into her guardian's arms. Serge did likewise; and then there was a volley of questions, which overlapped chaotically.

The Eccentric, once his effect had been produced, emerged from his forced phlegmaticism. He gesticulated and uttered guttural exclamations.

"Hip, hip, hurrah!" he shouted. "What a joke! I didn't think it would succeed so well. So you didn't suspect?"

"Not at all, my dear Robinson. You saw our amazement..."

"Well, you had pale faces and utterly blank expressions..."

"But what's going on?" Anna demanded. "How did you get away? Have you been on your way for a long time?"

"Apparently. In brief, this is it: this morning, when I called the first time, I wanted to tell you about the projected escape, but I was disturbed."

"By whom?" Anna interjected. "The Martians?"

"Who do you think? Only, if you interrupt all the time, we won't accomplish anything. Let me talk first; you can question me later.

"So, I wanted to tell you about the projected escape, when there was a change of circumstances. Tao had just told me that the passage was free—a subterranean passage that we'd been keeping an eye on for some time—and we set of, Stop and I."

"Stop's here! Where?"

"On the shore, with Tao."

"Tao too!"

"Yes, he's keeping him quiet—had to be done, or the beast would have barked and it would have gone awry..."

"But that whistling?" asked Serge, in his turn. "Who was whistling?"

"Me, of course!" said the Eccentric, laughing. "I speak Martian...where was I? The escape...so, I was saying, all three of us decamped and went like rabbits in their burrow...eight miles at least, we covered at a trot. I scarcely thought of telephoning, as you can imagine."

"You were pursued?" asked the young woman.

"No, but we could have been. Then, when I thought of you, I said to myself: *I'll give them a surprise.* We'd just come out on to the lava. For three more hours we marched at the double, and then Stop started gamboling. He'd caught your scent..."

"Brave Stop!"

We approached the boats, and, as I feared that the dog might give the game away, I gave him to Tao to hold. As I still had my apparatus, that suggested the idea of doing better still, so I telephoned as if I were still back there, in a pickle—and there you go! As jokes go, it was a good one, by Jove!"

And the Eccentric laughed, slapping his thigh. His listeners were no less delighted to see him, so cheerful and looking so well, in all respects.

"You've never looked better," said Anna, ecstatically. "My word, you've put on weight...I imagine you were going to come back thin, dying of hunger, but you don't seem to have suffered at all You've been well cared for, then, and well nourished?"

"What did you eat, then?" Serge asked, his scientific curiosity resurfacing.

"Fish, uniquely—fresh or conserved. The Martians are ichthyophages. And mollusks. There are grottoes down there in which they're abundant."

While speaking, the eccentric was looking round.

"What are you looking for?" Myrandhal asked.

"The radiator. Turn it up, then. Brrr…it's not warm here."

"Not warm?" said Serge, astonished. "But it's over twelve degrees."

"Seriously, you're cold?" asked Anna, prompt to take alarm and running to the storage-locker. "I'll make you a hot toddy."

"No, don't make so much fuss. Just a glass of whisky. It's the reaction, and the change of environment. Oh, it's horribly hot down there, in their molehill. That's the only thing I suffered from—God damn it, it was hard, especially at the beginning. Except that the proof is made, and you've lost again, Mr. Frenchman. Oh, you made fun of my dwarfs, my Red Men. Well, I've brought one of them. That's proof, that is, by Jove!

"Oh, you claimed that in volcanic terrain there couldn't be inhabitants underground, that no one could live there…well, I've lived there, me, who wasn't used to it. Yes, I acclimatized—and that's one in the eye for you, eh?

"I was hot, of course. I was sweating like a sponge. Oh, I'll remember it, by Jove—my sojourn next to the Central Fire!"

Serge Myrandhal wondered whether the Eccentric was talking seriously. "Come on, my dear Baronet, don't abuse your advantage. There's no need to exaggerate. Your adventure is astonishing enough already. Was it really as hot as all that down there? What was the temperature, approximately?"

"I didn't have a thermometer, but believe me, it was forty or fifty centigrade at least. What's more, I'm talking about the place where I was, a kind of cool cave. Elsewhere, it was much worse."

"And the Red Men can live in that furnace!" Anna exclaimed. "What are these Martians, exactly?"

"Strange beings quite fantastic—some kind of subterranean spirits, kobolds, who live in fire, close to fire, as fish live in the water."

"Come on, my guardian," Ana murmured. "Enough joking. You're not going to make us believe in salamander-men…"

"I'm not joking—or only a little. What's astonishing about it, after all? Habit is second nature, and for them, undoubtedly, it's nature itself. After all, there are people of almost similar kinds on Earth—puddlers, glassworkers—who live naked in their furnaces."

"That's true," said the engineer. "All in all, there's nothing scientifically impossible about it. The human body has marvelous faculties of adaptation. Among others, one can cite the case of a baker who, for a bet, went through a hot oven where anyone else would have fallen down dead. There's also the classic example of the founder plunging his hand into a vast of boiling lead. Those phenomena of exceptional calefaction are the rule on Mars, that's all."

"Nothing simpler," said the Eccentric sarcastically, in his ward's ear. "Scientists can explain everything...afterwards! As for divining it, or going to see it, that's another matter. Now me, I've seen it. While you argue, I go in search of proofs, and bring them back...there! Are you convinced now?"

"Yes," said Madame Myrandhal.

Pickman swallowed a final gulp of whisky and clicked his tongue. "All the same," he said, "the goblins, the kobolds, extraordinary as they are, don't seem so to themselves... Now, let's go fetch Tao."

"That's true!" exclaimed Madame Myrandhal. "And Stop! In our joy, we'd quite forgotten them. Where are they?"

"Close by, in the dinghy."

"What dinghy?" asked the engineer. "You have a dinghy?"

"Yes—I didn't swim out here, by Jove! I had a dinghy—mine, which was still on the beach."

"That's true. The sight of it made Anna feel ill, and I left it over there...until further instructions."

A minute later, Stop, mad with joy, hurtled into the compartment.

"Here's Tao, now," Pickman announced—and Serge and his wife saw a grotesque dwarf appear, with an enormous head and feet: a kind of anthropoid covered in russet frizzy fur, wearing as a kind of fish-skin loincloth, still fresh and bloody.

The Martian looked around wildly and fearfully, uttering little plaintive squeals from time to time.

The Englishman had seized one of his hands and was encouraging him in low voice.

Extremely interested, Serge watched. One thing that struck him right away about the anthropoid was the eyes: cerulean, translucent eyes in which the fear agitating there cast violet shadows; child-like eyes, which contrasted strangely with the bestial face. One might have thought that all the intelligence, all the soul, of that bizarre being had take refuge therein, beneath the bushy eyelashes.

Gripped by an imprecise repugnance, Anna recoiled behind her husband. Her guardian called her to order.

"What are you doing?" he said. "Don't worry, Tao isn't malign. Are you scared?"

"No."

"Come forward, then," said the Englishman, as if he were introducing a clever ape. Tao will greet you first; he knows about gallantry. Come on, Tao, say hello..."

Tao was not listening. At the sight of Anna, suddenly moving forward, he had been immobilized, his eyes wide, ecstatic. Evidently, that brutal creature, that soul still wrapped in the swaddling-clothes of animality, had a sense and understanding of beauty.

Then his eyes moistened. He began to tremble, while a hoarse gasp was exhaled from his vast bosom.

Without knowing exactly why, the two men had launched themselves forward, but Tao's attitude had already changed. He recoiled, clicking his teeth, raising his hairy hands, as if to protect his dazzled eyes and beg for mercy. He was uttering moans, in the midst of which two inarticulate syllables recurred incessantly: *Zoa*.

He went to take refuge in a corner, near Stop, whom he took in his arms and began to caress, lamenting softly.

Gripped by a strange emotion, the castaways looked at one another, interrogating one another with their gaze.

"What does that signify?" asked the engineer, finally. "Do you know what it means, Pickman?"

"Hmm! Not really...and that annoys me, by Jove! You're forgetting that Tao and I only possess a hundred words in common, at the most, and that if we understand one another, it's mostly by means of sign language."

"But you must have some idea—a hypothesis. What does that word *Zoa* mean, which he's repeating incessantly? Where has that sudden terror come from?"

"I don't know. We're touching on a mystery there—the great mystery of Mars, the one whose knowledge would probably reveal to us the whole history of the planet, but which we don't yet have. Then again, remember what I said: the Martians don't talk, they sing. Every word changes its meaning according to the intonation, and the gesture that accompanies it."

"Yes, but in this case the gesture is particularly significant. Anna and I, who are seeing Tao for the first time, understood immediately."

"What have you understood? You speak first, Anna."

"I understood, or rather I supposed, that *Zoa* designated superior beings, spirits of some kind, of whom the dwarfs have a superstitious terror."

"That's right. I admire your perspicacity."

"It remains to be determined," Myrandhal added, "exactly what these *Zoa* are. Do you have any idea about that?"

"Yes," said Pickman, "but don't ask me for proof here. It's an impression I've derived from a heap of things, impossible to analyze. When you've been in Tao's company for a few weeks, and you've succeeded in exchanging a few impressions with him, I think you'll agree with me.

"Like you, the first time I heard the word *Zoa* I was struck by it, all the more so because I'd just had a nasty moment. By Jove, just thinking about it makes me hot under the collar..."

"What moment? Explain yourself, my guardian."

"Later. Let's not quarrel, by all the devils! So, that was how I began my investigation, and I suddenly saw things magnify, embrace the whole of the planet. That's how I formed an idea—a theory—about Mars and its inhabitants; a theory which, if it isn't true, isn't as far away from the truth as all that.

"That posited, I'll start with Mars, and say: Mars, as our astronomers have divined, is an empty, desert world—a dying world, as you declared right away, my dear Friday. The seas are gradually disappearing, filled in by the lava that's emerging all over, because although Mars is a moribund world, its central fire is by no means extinct.

"Nevertheless, the lava hasn't yet covered it entirely, fortunately for us. In the tropics, there are vast regions covered with splendid vegetation, immense oases of a sort. That's all that I was able to get out of Tao concerning his planet.

"Let's come to the inhabitants now, the Martians, who are getting rarer and rare, for the planet is becoming terribly depopulated. But it hasn't always been like that. Once—which is to say, a few thousand centuries ago—Mars possessed two kinds of inhabitants, two great rival races: the *Zoa* and the dwarfs, the *Houâ*, as they call themselves in their own language.

"If I've understood correctly, in the beginning, the superior race, the *Zoa*, were winged beings. That doesn't seem too absurd to you?"

"Not at all. It's entirely concordant with the feeble intensity of gravity here," the engineer approved. "Flying humans, if there ever were any, must have arisen naturally on Mars."

"Well," the Eccentric continued, "after terrible wars—Tao still shivers when he talks about them, either with rage or fear; one never knows with him— the dwarfs were vanquished, reduced to slavery, driven underground…they were sent into the Martian excavations as we send convicts to the mines. Once there, as the ground lent itself to it—Mars, from what I've seen, is hollow; by which I mean pierced, riddled with holes like a gruyere cheese—the dwarfs adapted to it and multiplied! Thus, with time, this bastard subterranean race was born, these mole-people, the *Houâ*…"

"What about the others?" asked Myrandhal. "The *Zoa*—where do they live? Will we have a chance of meeting them?"

"Too late—we've arrived too late. The *Zoa* have disappeared from the surface of the world. According to Tao, though, two *Zoa* still exist: a man and a woman, the last couple of the superior race. They're two very beautiful, very knowledgeable beings, but sterile, angels of a sort, like seraphim, in whom the spirit has worn away the matter, the envelope, the sheath. They know everything, they've conquered disease and old age, and have succeeded in prolonging their lives in a marvelous fashion. There's only one thing they haven't been able to conquer: Death! And at the present moment, they're dying, going out like a lamp running out of oil."

"Where are they?" exclaimed Madame Myrandhal. "Where do these strange beings live?"

The Eccentric made a vague gesture. "Somewhere far away, to the south. Doubtless in one of the oases I mentioned just now."

357

"We have to go there, as quickly as possible."

"That's my intention, but I doubt that we'll succeed in reaching them. The *Zoa*, who are all-powerful beings, don't allow themselves to be approached just like that. Besides which, their empire, like Armida's garden,[77] is guarded by monsters, dragons, flame-throwers..."

"You're exaggerating again."

"Not at all. At least, I'm only repeating what Tao has told me. You can interrogate him yourself. It's possible, though, that he exaggerates slightly. One thing that's certain is that the gnome has a holy terror of the *Zoa*. According to him, they're magicians of a sort, masters of water, earth and fire: the Great Fire that burns at the heart of the world, which they sometimes cause to spring forth through the burst crust. Their power isn't limited to that; it extends to the neighboring planets. It was them, still according to Tao, who made us come here, drawing us from the Earth—which singularly diminishes your glory and your invention, my dear Friday: the invention of which you were so proud..." The Eccentric concluded on a sarcastic note.

"Fortunately," Anna replied, "those are merely the dreams of a savage."

"But Tao didn't tell you the names of these seraphic beings?" said the engineer. "Their personal names...?"

"No. Tao thinks that if he pronounced their names, he'd be struck dead immediately."

Serge was pensive. "Are you sure that you've understood correctly?" he asked, eventually. "Perhaps Tao meant that the name meant 'thunderbolt'..."

"It's possible," said Pickman. "Yes, perhaps. Oh, the *Houâ* language is rather ambiguous...as for English, I've tried, but nothing doing. The palate, and the deformed vocal organ of one of these little monsters, will never be able to articulate a word of English, which is a superior language: the language of spirits and gods, by Jove!"

Having pronounced the final phrase in a resounding voice, the Eccentric stopped, as if to draw breath "Oof!" he said. "That's two hours I've been talking. I've never said as much, by Jove. So my throat's dry...another glass of whisky, my dear Anna...thank you! To your health, my dear Friday!"

"To yours, my dear Pickman, to your fortunate return, to the glory of the first man who penetrated the Martian realm. That's a record that no one can take

---

[77] Armida is a character in Torquato Tasso's epic poem *Gerusalemme liberate* (1581), whose French translation was long used as a standard text in French schools. She is a Saracen enchantress opposed to the invading crusaders, who becomes infatuated by the Christian knight Rinaldo and creates a magic garden where she holds him captive in a deluded state, but he is eventually recalled to his supposed Christian duties. The episode became a popular theme for operas, including examples by Handel, Vivaldi, Gluck, Haydn, Rossini and Dvořák.

away from you! So, I raise my glass and I drink to your health, my dear friend. To the glory of Sir Washington Pickman!"

"No!" cried the Eccentric, gripped by a sudden enthusiasm. "To the glory of England alone—all for old England! England forever! And now, let's eat. I'm devilishly hungry. I still have a couple of bottles of Cliquot in my own reserves. Now or never is the time to pop their corks, God damn it!"

XII. Southward Bound

Joyfully, they sat down at table, and the conversation continued while Tao and Stop shared the scraps of the feast fraternally.

"There's one thing that bothers me," said Myrandhal, "which is the sudden, inexplicable disappearance of the Martians after you were kidnapped. I arrived almost at the same moment...your revolver was still smoking, but I didn't see anything—nothing at all..."

"They must, as we were saying just now, have secret passages through the lava, known only to them."

"Evidently," said the Baronet, "but I wasn't able to take account of them. I was unconscious; I only know what the worthy Tao has told me, which is rather confused. If I've understood correctly, the passage is hidden under the moraine itself. That's why the dwarfs lured me in that direction. There must be a block that pivots..."

Serge slapped his forehead. "Of course!" he exclaimed. "I should have thought of that sooner. I remember that while I was searching for you, I felt one of the rocks oscillate under my hand. One push, and I could have come to your aid..."

"Thanks for the intention," the Eccentric replied, "but I'm glad, by Jove that you stayed here. You'd only have succeeded is getting yourself caught, and Anna would have been alone—a fine thing you'd have achieved!"

"That's true," Serge murmured. "It's better that I didn't find the issue."

The young people talked further about the dwarfs, the world they inhabit-ed, their civilization, their mores, asking many questions—but Pickman had re-counted almost everything he knew.

"What do you expect me to say?" he replied. "I emptied my knapsack in one go. You're forgetting that I wasn't free down there, and that I only saw what they wanted me or allowed me to see. My principal source of information—I could say the only one—is Tao, and you'll see, when you've had a little more practice, that the damnable fellow isn't easy to decipher at all. What a hard head, God damn it! It's more than patience that's needed, or stubbornness. You can't imagine..."

"Yes, my dear Robinson, I understand the difficulty perfectly—so well that I'm astonished that you've been able to take the deciphering so far in a matter of days. It's a veritable feat, which does as much honor to your sagacity as to your perseverance."

"It's necessary to say," replied Pickman, flattered, "that I had a capital interest; it was a matter of my head...well, of my liberty, at least. Then again, I had nothing else to do. I was like Pellisson with his spider[78]...and one always ends up reaching an understanding.

"That doesn't affect the fact that it was a great step forward. We've ended up getting our hands on a Martian, one of those mysterious goblins that were playing tricks on us. What a pity that we can't inform our friends in New York of that."

"Patience—that will come."

"And what a success when we go back," the Eccentric continued. "For we will go back..."

"I'm counting on it."

"Me too, if only to show Tao to the populations of the old world. I can already see myself strolling through the streets of London with my phenomenon on my arm—what a triumph!"

The three castaways burst out laughing.

"One more thing," the engineer resumed. "You told us just now, my dear Robinson, that the Martians were, in your opinion, semi-savage, only possessing a rudimentary industry. But they have weapons, and fishing tackle?"

"Well, they have weapons—axes, knives, clubs, harpoons—but crudely fashioned. For the rest—household utensils and so on—they seem to be more backward than negroes. No trace among them of any mechanical artistry whatsoever."

"Are you quite sure?" Myrandhal objected. "They must possess tools, and even quite well-tempered tools. Have you forgotten the groove made in the hull of the Annabella?"

"No."

"Then how do you explain it? You said yourself that only a file could have produced such a deep gash."

"I thought so then, but I've changed my mind. It wasn't a file that scored our hull but a stone, a kind of exceedingly hard agate, which the Martians have succeeded in working—I don't know how. They're still in the Age of Polished Stone, you see. However, I believe that the *Houâ* were once more civilized, and

---

[78] Paul Pellisson was a supporter of the French statesman Nicolas Fouquet; he was imprisoned in the Bastille when Fouquet fell from grace in 1661, during the reign of Louis XIV. The story was subsequently put around—popularized, but not originated by Alexandre Dumas—that while he was there he tamed a spider, teaching it to eat out of his hand when he summoned it by playing the flute. Allegedly, the skeptical governor of the prison, M. de Baisemeaux, demanded a demonstration of the feat, and promptly crushed the spider underfoot.

that some still exist, elsewhere on the plant, who are less backward than the ones I've had dealings with. The future will tell..."

After this brief digression, the Eccentric told the story of his captivity, which Anna was demanding clamorously.

"I can do so quickly, having not much more to add. As I've told you, when I recovered consciousness I was in an immense underworld—catacombs of a sort extending in all directions—being carried by four dwarfs, russet gnomes of some sort, who were holding me securely. Like gorillas, which they resemble, the *Houâ* are endowed with a prodigious strength.

"Anyway, I wasn't thinking about escaping. On the contrary, I was delighted with the adventure. Finally, I had found the Martians. I'd be able to study them, to interrogate them—and what a sensational interview that would be, as they say! Why the devil hadn't I thought of it sooner? I'd have got myself captured deliberately; it was the best means—the only one.

"The dwarfs weren't numerous: a dozen in all. Behind me came four individuals carrying my things. The first had my rifle, the second my alpenstock, the third my knapsack, and the fourth wasn't carrying anything, as in the song..."

"Pardon me," said Serge, smiling. "So there was light down there?"

"It wasn't bright, no, but it wasn't pitch dark either. Once the eyes got accustomed to it, one could make things out well enough. Imagine a very diffuse gray light. Where it comes from I don't know. In my opinion, it's the subsoil itself, the rock, that's luminous—radiant. Who knows? Perhaps I've discovered a radium mine. At ten thousand francs a centigram, the latest price in London, you can see what that represents. Anyway, rare metals and precious stones are abundant down there, particularly diamonds. Look, my dear ward, here are some I brought for you."

With a negligent gesture, the Englishman threw a handful of diamonds as large as pigeon's eggs on to the tablecloth.

"I found these stones on the ground. The *Houâ* make use of them to play knucklebones." Without taking any notice of his listeners' admiring exclamations, the Eccentric continued: "To think, my dear Anna, that back there, in the Far West, your father, old Allan, is breaking his back looking for nuggets, when we can get them here simply by bending down.

"With that, I'll continue my story. I mentioned the heat that reigns down there. It's something you really can't understand unless you've experienced it. As for me, I was melting, literally streaming. I even think, by Jove, that I fainted a time or two, like some little miss.

"The Martians, who didn't want me dead—I'd observed that right away, and this was one more proof of it—must have been worried that I might die in their hands. They carried me to the far end of the underworld, into a cooler grotto...less fiery, I mean, for I sweated there afterwards, but at first, I experienced a veritable wellbeing, an immense relief—that's the right word.

"There, the Martians set about examining me, feeling me all over. Evidently, I astonished them. It was my shoulders that intrigued them most, especially my shoulder-blades. I thought that, having seen us fall from the sky, they'd imagined that I was hiding wings under my jacket, and wanted to make sure of it. Perhaps, too—although the idea didn't occur to me until later—they took me for a cousin of one of the *Zoa* they fear so much.

"Then the other Houâ left and I remained alone with Tao, who was in charge of guarding me, I immediately started trying to enter into communication with my jailer, but he didn't want to hear anything. The understanding didn't make any progress that day.

"In the evening, Tao brought me a fish cooked under ashes, a sort of haddock, but much larger, and a gourd full of water. The gourd—made, so far as I could judge, from the swim-bladder of a fish—didn't seem appetizing, but the water was fresh and I was dying of thirst in that sweat-room. There was no cutlery either, but I scarcely gave that a thought. I was hungry and thirsty. I swallowed it all and became drowsy afterwards, like a boa digesting its meal.

"I was woken up some time later by Stop licking my face. Tao had gone to find him while I was asleep. That was a good sign. I thought that my jailer was softening, and I immediately began making signs to him, a host of gestures. A waste of effort; it was as if I were singing. The gnome remained as deaf and dumb as a corner-stone. I was seething with rage, God damn it.

"Finally, I lost patience, and headed for the exit as if I were going to leave. Then Tao, previously impassive, suddenly woke up. He threw himself in front of me and we stood there, looking at each other, ready to strike. It was a terrible moment. I could see everything going awry...

"Tao—who would believe it, to look at him now?—was bristling, hissing like an angry viper. Then, suddenly, he beat a retreat, as he did just now, before Anna. It was then that I heard the word *Zoa* for the first time. Tao was trembling, avoiding my gaze.

"Then I understood that there's something in our eyes—in the human gaze—that intimidates these brutes and tames them. From then on, the game was won. It was no longer a jailer that I had but a domestic, a houseboy.

"Immediately, I tried to strike up a conversation with him, but it still didn't work, in spite of Tao's willingness, and the days went by...

"Since my arrival down there I'd only had one idea: to get back, if not my weapons, my knapsack, and my telephone, which would permit me to reassure you. But Tao didn't understand, or perhaps didn't want to understand. He was afraid of the other Martians, and doubtless afraid of me too.

"He understood perfectly well that I wanted to escape, but the revolver shot I'd fired on the moraine had struck his imagination. He must have figured that if I had possession of my knapsack I'd open fire again, out of malice, killing him and the others, exterminating them all.

"It was necessary to put his mind at rest, to win him over with kind treatment and caresses. Finally, this morning, he gave in. Since then, everything has gone like clockwork. Tao, who was in fear of the consequences of his action, was even keener to get away than I was, and watched for an opportunity.

"Soon—it was exactly one-thirty by my watch—he came to me joyfully to say that the dwarfs, who had been prowling around when we were on the telephone, had just left. The way was free and we left at the double.

"After having run for a long time, I saw a red light in the distance, at the end of a sort of tunnel—it was the setting sun. I hadn't seen it for two weeks, and it had quite an effect on me, God damn it. I launched forward. Finally, as night was falling, we came out on to the lava through a natural fissure.

"Three hours later, I was here."

"Do you think that the Martians are pursuing you?" asked the engineer.

"No—but we'd do well not to wait for them. If you want my advice, we should lift anchor at daybreak."

"I'd like nothing better," said Myrandhal. "What surprises me is that you're in such a hurry. Is there a danger, perhaps? Do you think that the Martians might launch a direct attack?"

"I doubt it—but Tao seems much less confident. He's convinced that his brethren will try to get him back. Better not to run the risk, and to set sail for other climes. We have no more to do here, in any case. We know what we wanted to know; we have an interpreter and a guide who will be useful in going elsewhere. Don't you think so, Monsieur Myrandhal?"

"Yes, I always have. One thing astonishes me, though, and that's your haste to raise anchor. This might be the moment, it seems to me, to study these Martian a little—these *Houâ*, whom we've had so much difficulty discovering..."

"We'll find Martians elsewhere," the Eccentric interjected, "and more civilized ones. Those hereabouts are brutes, from which we won't get anything more. In sum, I'm in haste to go elsewhere to see what happens. Ever since Tao told me about these marvelous *Zoa*, I've been dreaming about them night and day. I've sworn to discover them, if any remain, to take one of those strange beings, who have wings on their backs such as one sees in paintings, back to London—and I've just proved that I keep my word! It's a matter of arriving in time; so, let's go, let's flee—the sooner the better, as you repeated yourself not long ago. Don't you agree, my dear Anna?"

"Entirely. I only want one thing: to get away from this place."

So, a few hours later, at dawn, the *Velox*, followed by the *Annabella*, emerged from Port Burrett and set a course southwards.

In the open sea the wind was blowing from the east, throwing the waves against the *Velox*'s flank and causing her to pitch and roll terribly.

The first hour of navigation in the small vessels were difficult, but towards evening the swell eased, and the passengers could get their breath back. The wind had dropped, and the voyage seemed to offer fortunate auspices.

XIII. Diving

From then on, the navigation continued without incident. The sea was as calm as a mirror.

While her husband and her guardian took turns on the captain's bridge, Madame Myrandhal, in order to occupy her leisure, tried to educate Tao, who still remained a trifle unsociable.

Renouncing any attempt to master the inextricable *Houâ* language, she set out to teach him English, by means of a new and eminently practical method invented by an American pedagogue, and, in spite of Pickman's contrary prognostication, the Martian made evident progress.

After a few days, Tao possessed a hundred words, and was beginning to make himself understood—although his brain, of course, remained refractory to certain abstract ideas.

Meanwhile, the temperature became rapidly milder. They sensed that they were arriving in a kinder climate, in a warm, animated region. As early as the second evening, the Eccentric claimed to have seen a seagull, or something very similar. At any rate, fish were beginning to show themselves, and were not very shy. They danced in the submarines' wakes. Tao caught several in his hands, which he ate raw.

Armed only with his cap, the Eccentric fished out a dozen of them, which were fried, but the dish was not a success. The flesh was tough, the odor nauseating, and Pickman was the only one who ate them.

Myrandhal had announced that at her average speed, the *Velox* would take five days to cover the distance of approximately three thousand kilometers separating the polar circle from the tropic of Aquarius, but he soon observed a significant acceleration.

"We must have encountered a current," he said. "At the moment we're making more than thirty kilometers and hour, which is half a Martian degree. You know that the Martian degree measures scarcely sixty kilometers."

In fact, on the evening of the fourth day, the engineer, having calculated their position, announced that they had crossed the tropic.

"All right!" said Pickman. "If we continue at this rate, we'll have passed the equator in a week and we'll be at the south pole by the end of the month. Except that there's no rush. First, I'd like to take a look at one of the lands of Cockayne that exist in these parts, according to Tao."

"Yes," said Serge, "but it's a matter of finding them, and our maps leave a great deal to be desired. Nevertheless, we have land to the east, which can't be anything except Copernicus, the largest continent on Mars. I'll take us closer to it."

From that moment on, the captain of the *Velox* redoubled his attention. Constant vigilance was necessary in those unknown seas, the reefs of which had never been identified by any geographer or pilot. However, the Eccentric lent Serge his devoted collaboration, and alternated shifts of that tedious sentry duty with him.

The engineer was carrying out a minor repair in the engine room when he heard Pickman's voice ring out from the central porthole, where he was on watch. The engineer ran to him.

"Land! Land!" cried the Eccentric, brandishing the marine telescope with which he was equipped in broad gestures.

Annabella had also come running, and even Tao, who remained timidly behind her.

The three explorers observed, with an indescribable emotion, the presence of a long somber strip above the horizon.

"It can only be the continent of Copernicus," said the engineer solemnly. We're finally going to see the habitable region of the planet. We've finished with the icy deserts of the polar region, and arrived at the magnificence of the tropics.

Their impatience was so great that Serge Myrandhal, ordinarily so economical with his motive force, could not resist the temptation to increase their speed.

Hour by hour, as they drew nearer, the details of the continent emerged more clearly. The marine telescope was passed from hand to hand, and already, thick masses of vegetation could be made out, which had to be forests of gigantic plants. They were ornamented, to the extent that the distance permitted assessment, by the richest colors of yellow, orange and red, as certain terrestrial forests are in autumn.

"It seems to me," said the Eccentric, "that I saw a flock of white birds rise up just now."

Serge Myrandhal and Annabella, looked in the same direction, but could not see anything. As usual, the eccentric's imagination was slightly in advance of events.

The aspect of the ocean had modified along with that of the horizon. The waters were encumbered by an inextricable tangle of marine plants analogous, or very nearly so, to *Fucus natans*, which sometimes grows to several hundred meters in length, to the "tropical grape" and other gigantic wracks of the terrestrial oceans.

All of these algae, some of which produced enormous corollas or fruits disposed in yellow or violet clusters, were iridescent with all the colors of the spectrum. Some of them were indented like acanthias, dark red in color with pink veins; others, similar to clumps of rhubarb or broad-leafed bananas, were bright yellow or pale green. Yet others, blue-black with silvery-white veins, displayed the complicated and fantastic indentations of certain German illuminated manuscripts of the Middle Ages.

Annabella never tired of admiring them. She would certainly have started a herbal, and regretted that the time was lacking to complete a collection of them.

That submarine forest had, in places, the emerald green color of spring forests, and little golden fish were wriggling there in millions. Nor was that the only manifestation of animal life. Crustaceans, blue or pink, were crawling under the foliage and using their pincers to crush small oval mollusks attached in clusters to the fucus stalks. There were other mollusks, and vast jellyfish with transparent gelatinous bodies, whose bells were dappled with the colors of the spectrum.

"In sum," the engineer explained, "this garden of enormous wracks offers many analogies with the Sargasso Sea, well known to all mariners who have crossed the Atlantic. In the same way, it's a dead area, a lake of tranquil water in the midst of currents. There, all the wrecks, all the alluvia and all the debris carried by the waves comes together and piles up, thus favoring this opulent submarine vegetation, which doubtless reserves for out descendants, when the oil wells have run dry, incalculable stocks of carbon, and also of soda, phosphate and iodine."

"Where does the name Sargasso Sea come from?" asked the Eccentric.

"It comes from a Spanish word meaning *floating seaweed*. It's the name that the companions of Christopher Columbus gave it, who spent three long weeks traversing those floating prairies. I can easily form an idea of the difficulties they must have encountered. Since we came into this marine marsh of sorts, I've been obliged to take a host of precautions In spite of the impatience that I'm in, as you are, to reach the shore, I'll certainly be obliged to reduce speed to a minimum..."

Annabella interrupted abruptly. "Look there!" she murmured, with a fearful gesture.

Serge Myrandhal and the Eccentric looked in the direction indicated, and perceived a hideous animal moving placidly, just under the surface, among the stems of wrack. Yellowish in color, it was almost entirely composed of an enormous mouth, which opened and closed continuously, in an almost automatic fashion. The body was non-existent, so to speak; the caudal fin commenced almost immediately after the jaw, which was surmounted by two white eyes, protruding and globular.

"What is that monster?" asked the young woman, trembling. "No creature as frightful exists on Earth."

"You're mistaken," said the engineer, smiling. "That fish, which is certain far from being beautiful, possesses certain structural details analogous to an Earthly relative, *Eurypharynx*, recently discovered—in the Sargasso Sea—by the scientific expedition of the *Talisman*.[79] It's inoffensive, however, feeding exclusively on mollusks."

"I'm reassured. What if we tried to catch it...?"

As if it understood the danger it was in, however, the eurypharynx had just dived down to the sea-bed.

They continued to advance at a prudent pace. The marine fauna revealed an extraordinary richness, offering species that only presented a distant analogy with Earthly species. Serge Myrandhal noticed, in passing, spiny fish furnished with fantastic fins, which left the inventions of Japanese artists, although fecund, far behind. There were fish reminiscent of blackfish, seahorses and moonfish, turtles with large fins and thin necks, like those of snakes. Thus far, however, apart from two bizarre varieties of sharks with red-striped black bodies, the travelers had not seen any animal capable of doing them serious harm.

It was only toward evening that Pickman, who was on watch, witnessed a submarine drama that gave him cause to reflect. He first perceived, lying on the giant wracks, a crustacean of considerable dimensions. With its spiny triangular carapace and its enormous legs, it was reminiscent of the sea-spider, but it measured at least one and a half meters over the broadest part of its carapace, and was a dark pink color. The animal, however redoubtable it appeared, seemed to be trembling, frightened and ill.

Pickman obtained an explanation of that attitude when he saw the debris of a mollusk shell floating some distance away. He was not unaware that the majority of crustaceans change their shell once a year, not unlike certain reptiles. The former armor is detached of its own accord, and until the new vestment has had the time to harden and become saturated with calcareous molecules, the animal is exhausted by fatigue, ill and at the mercy of its enemies. Such was certainly the state of the giant crab sprawled amid the wrack.

Suddenly, Pickman saw the animal shiver and attempt to flee. It did not have time. A kind of fleshy arm emerged from beneath the foliage and circled around the crab with the flexibility of a snake. A second, and then a third arm succeeded in immobilizing it. The animal was shaken by a convulsion of agony and disappeared, dragged away by the trunks that had enlaced it.

The Eccentric did not say anything about what he had seen to his ward, but he thought it as well to inform the engineer.

"The crustacean whose tragic end you have just witnessed," Serge explained, "was the victim of an animal of the cephalopod tribe, to which the squid and octopus belong. But if it has attained the dimensions that its suckers indicate, it must be a prodigious monster, a Martian realization of the kraken of the

---

[79] *Eurypharynx pelicanoides*, the "pelican eel", was discovered in 1882 by the zoologist Léon Vaillant, who undertook four scientific expeditions in the *Talisman* between 1880 and 1883.

367

Serge Myrandhal's voice was strangled by a profound emotion—not that he feared for himself, but the idea of the superhuman danger to which his beloved wife was exposed was unbearable.

It was not without difficulty that they were able to reach the compartment; the *Velox* was still being jolted by the somersaults performed by the monster as it dragged them away in a frenetic rage; they were obliged to crawl, supporting themselves on the furniture and the walls.

Serge succeeded in reaching the commutator. "Finally, we'll be able to see," he murmured.

There was a momentary silence.

"Well?" demanded the young woman, in anguish.

Serge Myrandhal made no reply.

"Light, in the name of Heaven!" shouted the Eccentric.

"The commutator is no longer working," the engineer finally replied, in a somber tone.

No one responded to that despairing statement. In the silence, heavy with anguish, they could distinctly hear the monster's tail thrashing the waves, and the friction of its scales against the metal of the hull, around which it was wound in a spiral and which it was continuing to drag at vertiginous speed.

The Eccentric struck a match.

For a few seconds, its light illuminated the pale and consternated faces of the three explorers. Suddenly, however, the flaming wax escaped Pickman's trembling fingers, and he uttered an exclamation of amazement.

Abruptly, without transition, the entire compartment had just lit up with a soft pale green phosphorescent glow. One might have thought that all the walls and all the furniture were coated with phosphorus, illuminated by thousands of glow-worms.

They all turned toward the crystal of the porthole, from which that fantastic illumination was coming.

A unanimous cry of surprise and fear emerged from their mouths.

It was the sea-serpent, the hideous face of which was stuck to the glass, that was emitting the macabre light. It was the globes of its eyes, twelve centimeters in diameter, like two balls of fire, that were radiating the luminous effluvia.

The profound holes of its nostrils gave it the appearance of a death's-head, and the gaping mouth, garnished with conical teeth, was hideously agape.

The monster stared at the three motionless friends, paralyzed by a supernatural terror.

At that moment, its jagged crest was swollen with blood, and a kind of uninterrupted whistle was escaping from its immeasurable throat.

Annabella looked away; she sensed that contemplating that horrible vision even for a few seconds might drive her insane and strike her dead with horror.

Serge Myrandhal wondered, with terror, whether the crystal of the porthole had the strength to resist that terrible pressure.

Crystal, it is true, is an exceedingly resistant substance; in recent experiments in fishing by means of electric light carried out in the North Sea, plates of that material only seven millimeters thick were seen to resist a pressure of more than fifteen atmospheres, although they allowed the passage of powerful calorific rays. Now, the portholes of the *Velox*, solidly embedded in their metallic armatures, were twenty times as thick. Serge Myrandhal knew that, but he was not unaware that crystal, so resistant to pressure, is also extremely brittle. An abrupt flick of the serpent's jaw, the impact of a single one of those conical teeth, might shatter the porthole to smithereens.

Fortunately, that mode of attack did not enter into the monster's plans—for the moment, at least. It stared.

It seemed to have been calmed temporarily by the expenditure of nervous fluid required by the emission of luminous rays from its pupils, from which two broad beams of that strange pale green light continued to emerge, as if projected by powerful reflectors.

Once he had overcome his initial and perfectly comprehensible terror, the Eccentric looked at the enemy with veritable admiration; he searched within himself for some means of attacking it, of becoming the chevalier Gozon relative to this other dragon.[80]

All these sentiments had succeeded one another in the souls of the three explorers with lightning rapidity. Meanwhile, the submarine's jolts had ceased. Still surrounded by the serpent, now calm, the vessel shot through the darkness like an arrow, drawn by a rapid current.

Suddenly, however, the fulgurant pupils were extinguished; the *Velox* oscillated momentarily, and then became motionless. The bellowing of the monster resounded, more terribly than ever and more sonorous, as if reverberated by an echo.

"One might think that it were fleeing..." stammered Serge Myrandhal, bewildered.

The engineer did not finish the thought; the electric light bulbs had lit up again, simultaneously, and everyone uttered a sigh of relief.

"I knew that my apparatus couldn't have failed like that—instantaneously, so to speak—without a reason," murmured the engineer. "How was it that the presence of the monster as sufficient to disturb the mechanism of the sources of electric energy so profoundly? That's a phenomenon I can't explain." He re-

---

[80] Dieudonné de Gozon was the Grand Master of the Knights of Rhodes in the mid-14th century. He was credited by legend (long after his death) with having killed a dragon that emerged repeatedly from a swamp to prey on the livestock of the island's farmers. The story was repopularized in the modern Romantic era by a ballad by Schiller.

Leaving the ruins of the lighthouse to the left, the *Velox*, once she had doubled the promontory, went into the bay, the profound concavity of which formed a near-perfect ellipse. For some time she moved parallel to a low-lying strand where clumps of ruddy thistles grew capriciously among heaps of azure seashells.

The shore was covered with majestic forests surpassing in sumptuousness the most beautiful terrestrial bays—Naples, Rio de Janeiro and various Oceanian bays. Trees of unknown species allowed their lower branches, heavy with flowers and fruits, to hang down all the way to the blue water. Others expanded in vast foliage that left far behind, in terms of dimension, than banana-trees, the talipot palms and the aquatic *Victoria regina* of Australia, whose leaves are several meters in breadth.[81]

Very few of the opulent vegetables, however, were green in color. Their leaves passed through the entire chromatic scale, from the crimson of autumnal cherries to straw and lemon-yellow. Annabella even noticed several clumps of a kind of poplar whose foliage, agitated by a perpetual tremor, was white with a reflective sheen like silk.

Flowering lianas extended between the branches made the forest into an inextricable thicket, which served as a retreat for thousands of radiant birds, like living gems, of all the colors of the rainbow. They showed no fear at the sight of the *Velox*. They watched the submarine pass by a few meters from the shore without quitting the flexible creepers that served them as perches, where they were swinging in hundreds.

Annabella watched this marvelous décor unfold delightedly. "But it's a true terrestrial paradise!" she exclaimed. "It's the Martian Eden. I've never breathed in perfumes sweeter and more intoxicating than those that the breeze is bringing us. And the birdsong! It's truly a divine music! Thus far, I have heard a single one of those disagreeable and unharmonious cries from which the most brilliant terrestrial birds, peacocks and parrots, are not exempt.

"I'm eager to land, in order to pick those flowers."

"A little patience," Serge murmured. "We'll have plenty of time to visit this country at our leisure, which is certainly admirable, but I want to reach the depths of this beautiful gulf, to kind a safe haven for the *Velox*. If we're going to find a port, it's there that Martian logic will have excavated it..."

The *Velox* navigated thus for two hours along the enchanted shore.

Serge Myrandhal was not mistaken in his conjectures. When they rounded a clump of large trees with heart-shaped leaves, constellated with a profusion of white lilies, the shore abruptly curved inwards. The mouth of a vast canal appeared, bordered with white marble quays. It was about thirty meters wide, and

---

[81] The *Victoria regina*, as it was then called, was actually native to South America, and is a species of water lily. It is now classified as *Victoria amazonica*.

it waters were covered with a carpet of aquatic flowers with blue corollas and fleshy leaves of a beautiful bright copper hue.

To the right and the left, tall pylons of the same white marble as the quays and the ruins of the lighthouse supported statues of animals made of an unknown metal, as pale as silver but with a slightly roseate tint.

In spite of the yellow and brown mosses that covered them, and the parasitic plants, it as easy to recognize that the statues in question represented the same leviathan or marine dragon that had attacked the *Velox* a few hours earlier.

"It has the same bizarrely jagged crest," observed Annabella, "the same globular eyes...and the gills displayed in the firm of ruffs, and the hideous mouth paved with conical teeth."

"Perhaps it's the Martians' god?" Pickman joked, laughing.

"I don't think so," said the engineer. "A god would be installed in a temple. These statues seem to me to have been placed there with a simple decorative intention."

"Perhaps," the young woman murmured, pensively, "the monster that almost devoured us is the dragon guarding this Eden, this Garden of the Hesperides?"

"One might think," Serge added, "that we were arriving in a country abandoned centuries ago. I feel a strange emotion in the presence of these majestic ruins. Are we going to encounter the debris of some Martian Palenque or Babylon? This canal obviously connected the sea to a powerful city; it's constructed in such a manner as to admit ships of the largest tonnage..."

"To judge by those lotuses and those splendid water-lilies," said the Eccentric, "it's a long time since anyone sailed along it."

"The *Velox* will sail along it!" proclaimed the engineer, proudly. "We shall find whatever Martian capital it leads to!"

Everyone's curiosity was excited to the highest degree. As they penetrated into the mysterious region, they felt a sort of terror: the kind of sacred apprehension that must have gripped the likes of Columbus and Vasco da Gama at the moment they arrived in new worlds.

For a moment, Serge thought he could make out, lost in the underwater lianas, the profiles of gigantic hulls with elevated prows, rotting there in oblivion, and his ardent imagination evoked the disasters of a Martian armada.

But the vision had already faded.

To the right and the left, the forest continued to deploy the sumptuousness of its rubescent foliage, undulating in a light breeze. At intervals, clearings opened, revealing new perspectives, magical horizons lost in a blue-tinted mist.

"It's a true realm of enchantment," observed the Eccentric. "It seems to me that we'll never arrive anywhere, that the enchanted voyage will continue perpetually between two banks of flowers, for days on end...

"In the meantime, I'm going to go down to eat a slice of corned beef and drink a whisky and soda..."

shoulder; she caressed it, smoothing the plumes of its wings with her finger, without the animal seeking to fly away.

Pickman gazed at that admirable tableau with ferocious eyes.

"Do you know," he said, "how long it is since I've eaten fresh meat?"

"What do you mean?" demanded the young woman, hugging the bird to her bosom as if to protect it against the redoubtable appetite of the Anglo-Saxon. "You wouldn't, I suppose, be so barbaric as to harm this innocent creature?"

The Eccentric sniggered. "I'm tired of eating out of tins," he said. "That pigeon would certainly be excellent, surrounded by a garnish of tinned peas. Give it to me! I can assure you that I'll put end to it quickly by wringing its neck."

"Mr. Pickman," said Anna, severely, "if you ever do any such thing, I'll never speak to you again as long as I live; I'll quarrel mortally with you. You can satisfy your taste for bloody flesh another time. This beautiful bird is under my protection, and I forbid you to trouble the confidence that these naïve creatures have in our peaceful instincts with your massacres..."

"Well," said Pickman, who would not really have wanted to disobey his dear ward for anything in the world, "we'll see about that..." And he added, in a tone of bravado that did not fool anyone: "Not today, then—I don't want to annoy you—but tomorrow, I'll organize a great hunt..."

The day was advancing, however; after casting that first rapid glance over the magnificent domain, they went back to the *Velox* and ate a rapid lunch. Then Serge Myrandhal, as he had planned for some time, resolved to enter into communication via the telepathic apparatus with his friends on Earth—but he was no more fortunate on this occasion than on previous ones. The transmitter emitted its waves in vain toward the old natal planet. To Annabella's great disappointment, the apparatus remained mute, the vibrator not emitting the slightest ring.

The young woman's beautiful face darkened. "So," she murmured, sadly, "they've already forgotten us back there—or perhaps the apparatus is no longer working. My God! As long as nothing bad has happened to my father!"

Serge Myrandhal did his best to reassure her. "I'm certain of the efficacy of my apparatus," he said, "but there's nothing surprising in the fact that our terrestrial friends are not at the appointed place to hear us. They must have corresponded several times and, seeing that we didn't reply, their patience has run out. Perhaps, too, their apparatus has been put out of order by some accident. It's up to us to put a little more perseverance into our attempts. I guarantee that we'll succeed; it's impossible for us not to succeed..."

Madame Myrandhal ended up yielding to his reasoning. An idea of the Eccentric's finished putting the smile back on her face.

"I'm tired of always sleeping in a narrow cabin where I don't even have room to turn over," Pickman declared. "Since there are palaces here—palaces that don't belong to anyone—I'm going to take advantage of the fact. No one will prevent me from setting up my camp this very evening in one of these magnificent halls. I'll be able to believe that I'm the gracious sovereign of the plant Mars, if the desire takes me."

And without waiting any longer, the Eccentric, aided by Tao, set about transporting the movable furniture from his cabin to a hall ornamented with fantastic unicorns that had struck him with wonder at first sight, doubtless because they reminded him of the arms of old England.

"Shall we do the same?" Serge Myrandhal proposed to his young wife. "After all, he's not wrong."

Annabella accepted the proposal enthusiastically. The two spouses chose a chamber paved with azure tiles and festooned with rose-bushes, jasmines and capricious lianas. Through the large bay window overlooking the grounds, a kind of citrus tree with enormous fruits was exhaling the sweet perfume of its flowers. The air was so warm, the azure of the sky so velvety, that they had no need to fear any chill.

While Serge and Annabella—to whom the Eccentric, delighted that they had adopted his idea, came to lend a hand—were busy with these preparations, night gradually fell.

Dew was pearling among the quivering herbage, the marvelous songs of the birds rose up from flowering bushes illuminated by soft nocturnal gleams, and millions of glow-worms lit up on the lawns. A breeze of infinite freshness and sweetness was blowing from the forest and the sea.

Serge and Annabella went to sleep to the caressant murmur of foliage gently agitated by the breeze, lulled by the distant melody of birds perched on lianas. They had never felt as happy, as confident in the future. It was the beginning of their veritable honeymoon...

XVI. A Martian Mausoleum

Exhausted by the emotions, of every sort, that had filled the previous day, the explorers slept late. It was Pickman who woke up first, tickled by a ray of morning sunlight that made the supposedly British heraldic unicorns on the tiles glitter magnificently.

To begin with, he summoned Tao, whom he had sent to sleep under an armful of foliage in an adjacent room, and instructed the Martian to brush his clothes carefully and wax his boots.

The Eccentric had a plan. While Tao was in the process of rendering him the services of an attentive houseboy, he inspected his carbine, cleaned out the barrel and made sure that the firing-pin was working properly. Having done that, he rubbed his hands together with a silent smile. The idea of opposing his ward by means of a hecatomb on Martian birds seemed particularly enjoyable.

Then he headed toward the young couple's room in order to wake them up.

He was surprised to find then already up.

Annabella suddenly frowned. She had just perceived Pickman's hunting apparatus, openly displayed on his bed. "So you're counting on giving free rein to your bloodthirsty fury?" she demanded, half smiling and half severe.

"Of course," said the Eccentric, in a determined tone. "I can't eat out of tins for the rest of my life. No, that's out of the question; I'm firmly resolved to eat fresh meat today, and I will."

"We shall see!"

"I refrained yesterday from wringing the neck of one of those magnificent birds purely to please you. Today, it's my turn to do what I want."

"A lively discussion, in which Serge abstained from taking part, was engaged between the ward and the guardian.

As usual, the Eccentric ended up giving in to one restriction. He would abandon himself to his cynegetic instincts as much as he wished outside the grounds of the palace, but he formally promised to respect all its inhabitants and not to fire a shot within its sacred boundary.

The debate having been terminated and the peace treaty signed, the morning meal was concluded with no further incident. It had been agreed that the day would be employed in a more complete exploration.

"We'll begin with the park," said Serge. "It seems to me, if it's possible, to be even more beautiful than yesterday..."

"I'm eager, at any rate," the Eccentric murmured, "to taste the beautiful fruits of which I only caught a glimpse yesterday. If they're as good as they look, I'm sure that people in London would pay half a crown apiece for them."

"Much dearer than that," the young woman joked. "There's certainly a royal fortune to be made with the idea of a Martian fruiterer's in the vicinity of Trafalgar Square. In the meantime, be careful. Nothing is more imprudent than eating fruits that one doesn't know..."

"Don't worry about that. We'll take Tao, whose instinct reliably causes him to avoid plants that might be toxic."

A few minutes later, they all set forth along the mossy pathways.

It was now in dozens that birds of every kind of plumage came to flutter around Annabella and settle on her shoulders and Serge's—but they kept away from the Eccentric with an instinctive mistrust. One might have thought that they were aware of his mores and carnivorous tastes.

Meanwhile, the explorers continued their excursion, without losing sight of the polychromatic towers of the palace in which they had made camp.

The Eccentric was so convinced that nothing in Eden Park—as he had authoritatively baptized it—was poisonous that he bit confidently into any fruit, without even taking the trouble to have Tao taste them first.

"Very good! Exquisite! Delicious!" he repeated.

Tao had drawn a long way ahead, attracted by some trees as slender as poplars but covered from top to bottom with small fruits about the size of a strawberry.

Further on, Serge, after a moment's indecision, headed toward a palace with majestic domes that he perceived at the extremity of a long avenue. The trees composing it were prodigiously tall and were linked together in their crowns by lianas thrown like flowery rigging from branch to branch. At intervals, on pedestals of porphyry, agate and onyx, statues of giant birds with human faces were posed in attitudes full of serenity and smiling.

The explorers had not yet covered half of the avenue, however, when they saw Tao running toward them at top speed, seemingly prey to a profound terror. He came to take refuge close to Anna.

"*Zoa! Zoa!*" he repeated, trembling in every limb.

"What's up with him?" murmured the Eccentric. "What did he say? I couldn't quite hear…"

Serge Myrandhal made a gesture of nervous impatience. "Don't you understand?" he exclaimed. "*Zoa*—that's the name of the mysterious and powerful beings, before which inferior beings of Tao's race bow down!" The engineer's voice was vibrant with contained emotion. "Tao," he continued, "must have perceived one of those elite beings. We're going to encounter the creators of the marvels that surround us; human intellect is about to confront Martian intellect…"

Then he tried to interrogate the Martian, in order to discover where he had come from.

He only replied with his eternal: "*Zoa!*"—but Anna had seen him come down the steps of the temple at the end of the avenue.

They hastened their pace, dragging the consternated Tao with them.

They went through a monumental portico in which columns of a metal with shifting reflections that Serge Myrandhal recognized as iridium were combined with precious minerals to obtain a grandiose collective effect. They found themselves in a gallery with elevated vaults.

Tao's footprints were distinctly visible in the dust on the floor.

The gallery could have competed, for calm beauty and simplicity, with the sphinx-lined causeways of ancient Egypt, but the sphinxes were replaced by the birds with smiling human faces, several specimens of which Serge and his friends had already admired.

The footprints ended at the place where the gallery gave access to a profound and high-ceilinged hall. The explorers went in.

There, they came to a stop, amazed and ecstatic.

The hall, which had the dimensions of the nave of a church, seemed to be constructed in alabaster and rock crystal. It was a dream of dazzling whiteness. In the central aisle, gigantic vases formed of nacre, jade, moonstone and opal were filled with bright flowers. But that was not the most extraordinary thing. The side-walls of the basilica of sorts were lined with steps along their entire length and each fitted with a row of niches.

The Mirror of Present Events: Ten scientific romances by Georges de La Fouchardière, Henri Lanos, E.M. Laumann, François-Félix Nogaret, Jean Rameau and Régis Vombal.

Nemoville: Twelve scientific romances by G. Bethuys, Alfred Bonnardot, Alphonse Brown, Emma-Adele Lacerte, Claude Manceau, René du Mesnil de Maricourt, Pierre Mille,José Mosellli, C. Paulon and Emerich de Vattel.

The New Moon: Four fantastic voyages by Henri Delmotte, Alexis-Jean Le Bret and Edmé Rousseau.

News from the Moon: Nine scientific romances by Georges Eekhoud, Stéphane Mallarmé, Guy de Maupassant, Louis-Sébastien Mercier, Eugène Mouton, Fernand Noat, Jean Richepin, Adrien Robert and Albert Robida.

The Nickel Man: Eleven scientific romances by Jacques Boucher de Perthes, Pierre Bremond, Léon Daudet, Georges Espitallier, Louis Gallet, Pierre de Nolhac and Ralph Schropp.

On the Brink of the World's End: Seven scientific romances by Raoul Bigot, Jacques-Antoine Dulaure, Charles Epheyre, Jules Hoche, Joseph Méry and Colonel Royet.

The Revolt of the Machines: Eight scientific romances by Michel Epuy, Emile Goudeau, X. Nagrien, Gaston de Pawlowski, Jules Perrin, Edouard Rod, Jules Sageret and Louis Valona.

The Supreme Progress: Eighteen scientific romances by Paul Adam, Charles Cros, Charles Epheyre, Eugène Mouton, Louis Mullem, X.B. Saintine and Victorien Sardou.

The World Above the World: Nine scientific romances by S. Henry Berthoud, Michel Corday, Alphonse Daudet, Camille Flammarion, Henri Lanos, André Mas, Jules Perrin, René de Pont-Jest and Charles Recolin.

www.ingramcontent.com/pod-product-compliance
Lightning Source LLC
Chambersburg PA
CBHW020256030726
47499CB00001B/215